CRIMINALLY INSANE

THE SERIES: BOOKS 1–3

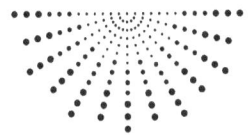

DOUGLAS CLEGG

ALKEMARA
PRESS

PRAISE FOR DOUGLAS CLEGG

"Clegg's stories can chill the spine so effectively that the reader should keep paramedics on standby."
—Dean Koontz, *New York Times* bestselling author.

"Douglas Clegg has become the new star in horror fiction."
—Peter Straub, *New York Times* bestselling author of *Ghost Story* and, with Stephen King, *The Talisman*

"Douglas Clegg is the best horror novelist of the post-Stephen King generation."
— Bentley Little, *USA Today* bestselling author of *The Haunted*.

"Clegg gets high marks on the terror scale…"
—*The Daily News (New York)*

GET DOUGLAS CLEGG'S NEWSLETTER

Get book updates, price drop news flashes, and exclusive offers—become a V.I.P. member of Douglas Clegg's long-running email newsletter:

http://DouglasClegg.com/newsletter

The Nightmare Chronicles

Wild Things

BOX SET BUNDLES

Bad Places (3 Novels)

Coming of Age (3 Dark Novellas)

Dark Rooms (3 Novels)

Criminally Insane: The Series (3 Novels)

Halloween Chillers

Harrow: Three Novels (Books 1-3)

Harrow: Four Novels (Books 1-4)

Haunts (8 Novel Box Set)

Lights Out (3 Collection Box Set)

Night Towns (3 Novels)

The Vampyricon Trilogy (3 Novels)

With more new novels, novellas and stories to come.

BAD KARMA

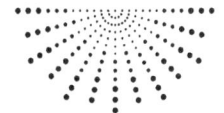

THE CRIMINALLY INSANE SERIES, BOOK 1

Created with Vellum

for Patsy Kensit

Escape me?
Never—
Beloved!
While I am I, and you are you.

— ROBERT BROWNING, LIFE IN A
LOVE

CHAPTER ONE

HE WAS ON THE BOAT WHEN IT HAPPENED. TREY CAMPBELL glanced up, thinking he'd heard something, perhaps the cry of a gull.

He saw the tall white cliffs to the west of the island, the natural wonder of Catalina. "The Kirk In The Rocks" as it was popularly known. Within those cliffs, a series of interconnecting caves and tunnels that he had once believed created a great labyrinth within the island.

As a boy, he'd scaled those rocks, and explored what seemed then like endless trails through the caverns. His father had taught him to shoot a gun from those cliffs, but not to kill anything. That was forbidden. To shoot bottles and skeet and even as a warning in the air, to a trespasser if the situation warranted it. But never at anything that breathed.

A gun firing in the dark morning.

He felt a cold sweat break out along his back and neck. Not from the heat, but from what seemed, momentarily, like a primal fear of creation itself: the sea, the rocks, the endless sky. He knew it was irrational, perhaps even a sign of a panic attack.

A second later, the world was normal again. Fear was gone.

The gun which had accidentally gone off in his remembered dream was silent.

A white flash in a dark room...

Later, he'd remember that sense as if he'd heard a warning shot, but at that moment he was more concerned with his fishing line. He had developed that capacity over the years, to forget painful memory and attend to what was directly in front of him.

During the three hours out to sea, all that he could possibly fear would come to pass, but from a distance.

For now, he could relax and try to enjoy the sea, the air, the boat.

The boat was a Bayrunner Westcoaster, a fourteen-footer, welded marine metal, made for rough weather, but not designed to traverse the twenty-six some miles between San Pedro, on the mainland, and Catalina Island. It was for harbor fishing, the man who rented the boats told him. It would be at anyone's risk to take it out further than two miles from the island.

He and his wife were barely out a mile in the boat. He wished he could take it out further, not just for the fishing, but for the peace and calm. The boat was rented for the week, and came with the requisite nicks and dents and a kind of pallor to the metal. The outboard motor was a two-cylinder with thirty-five horsepower, which he'd had a hard time starting. He had killed the motor an hour before, and cast his line down.

His wife, Carly, didn't enjoy fishing but loved being out at sea. She set her paperback down for a moment and scanned the island, as if she'd left something behind there and perhaps wanted to go back for it.

"Water's too warm," he said. "All the squid probably moved on to colder currents, and all the yellowtail followed, maybe even the white sea bass, too. I'll be damned lucky if I catch a halibut."

"Poor baby," Carly said, "We can have yellowtail up at the café without having to put a hook in some fish-mouth." His wife returned her attention to her paperback.

"Romance?" He asked.

"Hardly. It's the story of a guy who goes with his wife on vacation and manages to make the whole trip as stressful as possible until the wife has no choice but to run off with the cabana boy."

The sea was a sheet of brilliant cobalt, the sky was bone white, the boat was gently rocking. He did most of his fishing near the rocks, just beyond the breakwater. Carly had insisted on bringing a cooler full of sodas, and he knew that it would be a problem later. He watched her as she drank a Pepsi, her hair dark and shiny beneath his old San Diego Padres baseball cap, which was to keep the sun off her face—at thirty, she was becoming slightly worried about having spent her entire life at the beach down in San Diego, worried less out of vanity, more out of fear of the skin cancer that had weakened her father before his death.

But she was so far away from death—that's what he thought then. She still looked as she had at twenty, as far as he was concerned, although she claimed she was getting fat. Actually, truth be known, he was putting on a bit of a paunch which he was trying to fend off with an exercise routine, because he just couldn't give up the twice-weekly trips to the local ice cream place for banana splits. He was just thirty-six, jogged four miles three times a week, and swam a mile or two at the local gym whenever he thought of it. He had been an unathletic kid, but for some reason, in his late twenties, he'd started a regimen which allowed him a few beers and some ice cream. One thing he couldn't stand to do were sit-ups, and, thus, the paunch.

These were his thoughts as he sat in the small boat, clutching his Penn 850 SS rod, praying for a nice fat fish. There was the one thought which had plagued him for the past year, finally driving him to take this vacation, perhaps even quit his job. He kept that thought a secret, buried deep within him most of the time. He could forget about it for now. *Catalina. The Pacific. Sun.* So far removed from his nightmares. He soaked it in: the cool spray of mist as the boat rocked. The flatness of light across the water. The heat at the back of his neck from the sun. The feeling that one of his legs had fallen asleep. The first twenty-four hours on Catalina had been spent recovering from the stress of work; the next twenty-four in just wanting to get out of bed and do something.

And now, he wished things could always be the way they were, right at this moment.

Right now.

How beautiful his wife was to him. How much she had taught him in their fourteen years together, through the fights and the trials, how things had worked out as if they'd been meant to.

There was a loveliness in her he could not find when he looked at other women. It went further than flesh and bone. It was some spark within her. He grinned as he watched her. She was everything to him, sometimes. Before he'd met her, he had been stupid, a clod, someone who was destined to muddle through life uneventfully. After meeting her, well, to him at least, it had been like a magical transformation. Love itself had become the most powerful trans-former he had ever encountered. He knew of men who took their wives for granted, but he was not one of them.

"Trey," she said, calling him by his family nickname. "Trey?"

He leaned toward her, because apparently she was about to tell him a secret.

She whispered, "I got to go, sweetie. Right now."

"So lady-like."

"I thought so."

"I told you not to bring so many sodas," he sighed.

"I know. Why is this such a problem? You haven't exactly been reeling them in." She half-grinned. "Besides, you guys have it easy. You can just hang it off the side of the boat. I'd have to lean over the edge and probably capsize the whole thing." Then, she gripped his hand, and said, almost sternly, "I *really* have to go."

STARTING THE MOTOR WAS DIFFICULT. He had to put all his weight into it, pushing his feet against the transom as he pulled on the rope. The boat rocked less gently. Carly clung to the sides of it. Finally, he got it going, and steered towards shore.

It took half an hour to bring the boat back into the dock. It was early in the day, so the tourist boats were still circling around Avalon. He had to maneuver his small fishing boat around to the side of the docks, and then kill the motor and row in. As soon as they pulled beside one of the low docks, Carly practically leapt off the boat, leaving him rocking. She ran in her bathing suit, towel around her waist, carry-all slung over her shoulder, towards the restrooms.

He wiped his forehead—it was going to be a hot day—and grabbed a Dr. Pepper out of the cooler. He tried not to think about work, but every now and then it popped into his head. His work was a separate world—some of his co-workers didn't even know he was married. They didn't know that his nickname—from childhood—was Trey. They thought of him as Billy Campbell. William Campbell the Third. It was a world he hoped would never touch Carly or the kids—not in a big way. Not in the dangerous way he felt whenever he was among the patients. He wasn't even sure he could do anything else for a living—it wasn't like he was a doctor, or even a therapist—he was a psych tech, a supervisor, and even though it was a secure position, he had never expected to make it a career. He'd intended to go on and get a master's and maybe become a therapist, but then Teresa had been born, and then Mark, and Carly was actually able to go on and finish her master's. And then the money and security at Darden State became so good, how could he walk away from that? With kids and a life, how could he make a change without disrupting the entire flow of the world?

But now, he was considering quitting his job to start over because the stress had really gotten to him with recent events. Carly was making enough to cover for both of them, if they drew their belts in tight. He could maybe go back for that graduate degree...In these seven days on Catalina, he was going to figure out what the hell he was going to do with the rest of his life. His dream was to live in a Jimmy Buffet song and bum around on islands like this one to the end of his days. He knew this wasn't the most practical of plans, and would definitely not put Mark and Teresa through Stanford in the future. Neither would that plan entirely wash with Carly.

But, he thought looking over at the old casino and the hills beyond it as another magnificent day unfolded in Avalon, *wouldn't it be nice?*

No more Darden State, no more fears, no more stress, no more nightmares about the more extreme patients coming for me.

No more remembering Jo-Jo ripping his genitals off with his hands, or of Lorena Davis, naked and drenched in her own blood, using the broken off fluorescent rod as a weapon, jabbing at him.

These were the basics of Darden State, and that word that dare not speak its name in these politically correct times:

Insane.

And the shadow against the dark morning as it became visible with the white flash of gunshot.

As if the word "fear" could be written with light against darkness.

His beeper began vibrating in his shirt pocket.

"Damn it," he muttered, knowing it was some emergency from work that he probably didn't even need to know about. He couldn't leave Darden State for even three days before Jim Anderson messed up and gave the wrong meds to the wrong patient.

At least, he hoped it was something that simple.

Later, he would remember how innocent things were just a moment before he made that phone call.

Later, he would remember even the smell of the sea, wood-rotted and fishy, as part of a wonderful innocence that would never again exist for him.

CHAPTER TWO

THE DARDEN STATE HOSPITAL FOR CRIMINAL JUSTICE takes up twenty-three acres, and has its own post office.

Officially, it is located in Darden, California, although the town which encircles it is called Caldwell. It is in Riverside County, just north east of Moreno Valley, in a large canyon between two ridges.

Its chain link fences are twenty feet high, and, at the top, encircled with coiled razor wire.

Within the tall outer fence there is a shorter fence, less than ten feet high, which carries a thin electric current, enough to stun a human being for several minutes. Twenty years ago, it only had one high fence, but every once in a while a patient escaped. The town of Caldwell was none too appreciative of hearing the lone siren, a leftover from air raid days, after midnight, signaling that one of Darden's finest was on the run.

The history of Darden is the history of America's attitude towards both criminals and mental illness. The hospital was built in the 1890s, and originally was completely underground. In those days, a paranoid schizophrenic who had murdered or committed some anti-social crime was treated worse than an animal—chained to a wall, food pushed with a stick through the slot in the door. The underground chambers prohibited escapes, and the community at large did not have to be reminded of the hospital's existence. There were fewer than ten percent of the patients with a history of criminal activity; many of them were alcoholics and drug-addicts who were placed there by loving families.

Darden remained underground until just after World War Two, when it became a center for lobotomies and radical treatments, ice baths, shock treatments—one doctor used to walk room-to-room, and randomly shock patients whenever the mood took him. Sometimes, it was the best treatment available.

The patients who arrived at Darden began to come by way of the criminal justice system, a famous court in Los Angeles, 95-A, which was also known as the Zoo because of the outbursts from those suffering from psychotic rages during their hearings. With this new class of patient, Darden became known as the Crackup Palace, a joking reference to the comparative luxury with which some of its patient-inmates lived. There were escapes occasionally, reaching an all-time peak of three a year within two decades.

In the 1960s, with the availability and research with psychotropic drugs, pills became the favorite candies of Darden. The ten and fifteen foot high fences went up, and the nearly-constant escapes dropped dramatically with the constant sedation of the more dangerous patients, and with a more recreational approach to patient-care.

The Darden patient now wears an orange Darden T-shirt, and has calisthenics in the morning, recreational therapy in the afternoon, can call friends collect, can accept calls and money from outsiders. Occasionally, if they were sneaky enough, the patients can even make love, as the hospital is not only made up of both male and female patients, but they are allowed to intermingle freely at certain times of the day.

The belief is that the various meds which each patient ingests keeps them far enough away from his or her true feelings so as to be safe.

But even passion cannot easily be drugged or shocked from a patient's system.

CHAPTER THREE

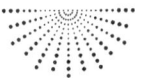

IT WAS AT FIVE A.M. THAT ROB FALLON GLANCED DOWN THE hallway to see if the night shift whore was still in the hallway.

His roommate slept on, snoring every now and then to punctuate the delicious silence of dawn. Rob loved that hour. That moment. It was as if the entire ward was drugged and groggy, and no one, not even the orderlies, could think clearly so early in the day.

It was two hours before the night shift personnel went home.

Ten minutes before the night shift whore walked down the hallway. Her shoes tapping the newly waxed floor. Her heavy orthopedic shoes.

Her wobbly ankles. Her smell. Her taste.

The corridors gleamed in the long stretch of fluorescent lights from above. It was a green glow, from the recent paint job, done, Rob knew, because the state inspector would be coming in a week. There was a grapevine among the patients, and someone at Patton State, over in San Bernardino, had come to Darden for some tests, and mentioned the inspector's visit there.

So, that's why the flowers were planted out on the edge of the base-ball field, and that's why the kitchen smelled of bleach and that's why Dr. Wijiwardene was conducting physical evaluations all month long.

The why of things was very important to Rob. He had been taught about the why of things early in life by his mother. Her why was to create him. That was her sole reason for existence. His mother taught him all the whys. She was a brilliant woman, but ultimately, she had outlived her why.

All women did.

He had a why: he was a child of God, and that was why he was on earth, to just be. He was a young man with a genius I.Q. Under different circumstances he knew he might have been a world leader or a brilliant poet.

Instead, he had murdered three of his girlfriends, keeping their heads in water in his kitchen sink.

The sink was large, the industrial kind. It could've fit a few more heads, but Rob had been arrested before he could collect another one. The heads still spoke to him when he was by himself, and they told him about all the secrets of the world. They told him about the whys.

He told the policeman who arrested him that just because he cut off their heads didn't mean they had stopped living. They were still there, hiding from him, talking to him, telling him that they loved him.

Rob tried to show remorse for his crimes, but he didn't really understand remorse, or guilt, or shame. Still, he was very good at convincing women that he wallowed in misery and pain.

And he was one of the most beautiful creatures in all of creation. He had been told so on countless occasions throughout his life. He was an Adonis from his earliest years, and women had always loved him. *Always.*

That was why the night shift whore was in love with him. That was her why—with women, he knew, the why usually had to do with love.

Donna Howe.

He thought of her as ugly. She had a nose like a potato, and skin scarred and mottled with pits and craters. She was on the small side but still had broad shoulders, no boobs, a rear end like two old sagging pumpkins left out too long after Halloween. She'd remained a virgin 'til she was forty-one, which is when Rob first did her. She was a beast on the outside, but a total romantic within. She was meant to be used. She was meant to be taken by him.

Six weeks ago.

She had been easy to seduce. She had never had a date, and Rob looked like a hunk, he knew it. He knew how to get a girl to like him, any girl. He could've written a book on it: *you just find out what they like in a guy, and then you become that thing, that guy, that dream.*

It was always so easy for him.

It was time, now, for her weekly dose of his lust, so Rob gave a whispery whistle, knowing that the night shift whore would be waiting, listening just for this sound. She had never had it so good, he knew, and she was just about at the point when she would do anything for him.

He didn't plan on killing her.

He didn't consider himself a killer. He had never killed anyone. He had cut off his girlfriends' heads, but it hadn't killed them. They had kept talking, telling him about the men their bodies were still humping, all the tens of thousands of men who were laying them, even now, humping them all over, every orifice they had, and then some. *Humping. Doing. Making.* He couldn't say the f word, just like he couldn't say the v word. He couldn't even think them. He had only used those words once in his life. Never again. He had learned not to use them from the scrubbing that his mother had given him. He had learned never ever to use the f or v words again. He had felt the wire brushes against his skin. *The Comet. The Clorox. The rubbing alcohol.*

His mother could not get him clean enough after he had said that f word. She spent half the night trying to, but she could not wipe it off his skin, his face, his tongue.

And the v word. His mother had told him to call it a purse. "It opens up like a purse," *she told him.* "It's where you put all the things you don't want anyone to see."

He was a nice boy. His mother had raised him to be a nice boy.

How could a boy like that kill anyone?

Rob Fallon did not plan on killing the night shift whore.

He could never do a thing like that.

But he did need her eyes.

CHAPTER FOUR

"Hey," Rob Fallon whispered. He leaned against the doorframe. He could be James Dean if he wanted. He was as cool as anyone could be. He flashed a grin.

The woman wearing the white and blue uniform was moving slowly. She held a chart in her hand, close to her small breasts. She wore too much make-up. Her eyes were blue smudges. Her lips were crimson.

Rob could tell just by the way she moved that she had begun getting frightened of him. She was like a rat standing before a snake. She stopped in the hallway, and leaned against the wall.

She stared at him.

In her eyes, that look of fear.

He would have to calm her.

He drew a folded piece of paper from his back pocket. He held it up. "I wrote this for you."

Her fear seemed to retreat. Her squinty eyes cleared. She was a girl in love. She was his.

She glanced up and down the hall. There was the distant echo of the cooks in the cafeteria as they clanged plate and tray and metal utensil.

No other sound.

Her heavy footsteps. Her fat ankles. Her uniform, so unbecoming on her unwieldy form.

The night shift whore stepped over to the doorway.

Rob Fallon handed her the note.

She unfolded the lined notebook paper. She read the poem. She half-grinned.

He watched her eyes. No fear there. They were bloodshot. They were small. Lurking within them, her *why*.

"It's beautiful," she whispered, looking over his shoulder at his roommate. "You wrote this?"

"Yeah," he said, and believed it himself, even though he'd copied it out of one of the books in the library. But Rob believed that he was the author of all.

He leaned forward and kissed her on the lips, slipping his tongue into her mouth. She accepted it, and he reached for her, holding her. When he withdrew from her lips, he whispered, "I've wanted you for so long. Just for a kiss. Nothing but a kiss. We don't have to do what we did before. I know it was wrong."

"I can't," she whispered, shrugging off his embrace, stepping back. "It's too risky. When you're released, we can be together. It's too dangerous now."

He sighed. "I know. I think about you all the time. I think about our life together. How I want to be with a woman like you, someone who loves and accepts love. I wish…I wish things could be different."

An expression of sadness etched across her face. "I wish life were easier."

Rob Fallon nodded. He leaned against her again, took her head in his hands, pressed her lips against his. He slid his lips across her face to her cheek, then her nose, then to her left eye.

He kissed her eyelid.

Something in him urged: *now.*

The why is in her eyes.

He tasted her eyelid. Salty. Bitter from the blue eye shadow.

She whispered, "Do you love me?"

He kissed from her eyelid to her forehead to the edge of her scalp down to her ear. He whispered, "Yes. God, yes."

He felt the rhythm of her body, something beyond her control, as it pressed against his. He knew that that place between her legs, her purse, was opening for him. He knew that her purse wanted him inside her.

He whispered, "Where can we go? I need you now. Right now."

CHAPTER FIVE

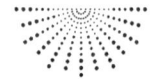

ANOTHER PATIENT, TWO DOORS DOWN FROM ROB FALLON'S room, on the other side of steel double doors, stirred in her sleep. The room was practically bare. A single chair in the corner, beneath the barred window, which was shuttered, also. The bed itself, a narrow hospital bed with crib-like bars along one side. The blankets were olive drab; the woman's skin, where her hand showed, was pale white. Her hand twitched slightly.

She was dreaming: *the gleaming metal in her hands, and looking into her lover's eyes as they shared this most secret of pleasures. The yellow flickering glow from the candles. The smell of animal fat as it cooked in a large pot set down in the hearth. The sounds of the street, beyond the cramped, stone basement—horses on cobblestones, a cry of a fishmonger, shouts as the copper from around the corner came upon some creature in an alleyway.*

But in their sanctuary, the man and woman, caressing each other.

The tastes between their lips, mingling.

She had a thin cloth over her face, almost like a pillowcase but lighter, like a thin gauze. Still, breathing was easy. She could see shadow, but only during the daytime, if they unshuttered the windows. She didn't mind the cloth too much. It was supposed to be removed at night, but sometimes they forgot. Sometimes they left it on because they didn't want to see the face beneath it. Sometimes, she wished she could scrape that face away, herself. She wished she could find her true face beneath this one, the one which was lurking. The face that had no skin.

Her arms were strapped to the sides of the bed. Her feet were similarly strapped. Her fingers were strapped, too, as if someone thought that if even one of those fingers were loose, it would be too dangerous.

That even a single finger might mean that this small, pale woman might tear her way out of her tether and claw her way through wall and flesh for release from this place. She was small—barely five foot one, and built proportionately, like a doll, perfect hands, perfect waist, perfect legs, perfect hips. Her hair was long and blond. It needed cutting, but sometimes they forgot to attend to this detail. Her skin had chafed some, and she had bedsores at times. They didn't even always have the decency to turn her over. They used to, but they were getting negligent. She longed to feel sunlight on her face again, to walk in the garden, to talk to the one she had lost; the one who was so close to her and far away at the same time.

A single shaft of light penetrated the room—it was the light from the hallway, as someone opened the double doors.

Opening the door to her room, too. The metallic scrape of the door as it slid open. The smell of the hallway—rubbing alcohol, a fresh coat of paint, the distant steam of food cooking in the cafeteria.

The woman in the bed began breathing more quietly.

She felt the light across her face.

It was warm.

She was sensitive to these things, now.

Time and space, all at once.

She smelled perfume, light, almost undetectable.

Backward and forward, one existence to the next.

She smelled something else. *Dirty clothes? Dirty underwear?*

The smells pleased her. She was too used to the stink of the putrid food, the odor of rubbing alcohol and the plastic taste of the red and green pills they shoved down her throat.

A woman had come into her room. The woman-smell was always the strongest, the most disgusting. This woman was just finishing her menstrual cycle. This woman entering her room had that last scent of dead blood there between her legs. Who else? There were other footsteps.

All right. And a man, too.

Good.

The man was very clean. He smelled like Ivory Soap. He smelled like— *baby shampoo? No, something else, something with spice in it,* she thought. He smelled too clean for someone at this time of the morning. He was someone who kept himself brilliantly clean. Someone who was terrified of filth on himself.

She knew this man. She didn't know him by name, but she knew him by smell. She remembered all, for all she had now were memories. She had a photographic mind, she memorized details and faces and smells and tastes. She had smelled the man once before, passing by her room. He was allowed free rein, she supposed. He was not like her. He was stupid. Men tended to be stupid, to underestimate others. To assume that women didn't have minds. Men thought women couldn't be doctors, could only be nurses, or orderlies, men thought women should stay home and care for their old people who vomit and urinate all over and stink the place up.

That was what men thought.

But she liked clean men, like this man in her room, with this woman. The woman was dirty—she had to wear an old Elizabeth Arden perfume, called Chlöe, the woman in her room did, to cover up the stink of her panties. Her hair smelled greasy, too. She only washed it once a week. She kept it in a net, probably, beneath one of those tacky white fake nurse caps.

When men were clean they didn't think, they just were.

But the woman who was walking near her bed, now, she smelled like she never douched. *Is the man putting his clean fingers up into the filthy woman's panties?*

The woman in bed held her breath so that she wouldn't have to smell what these intruders in her room were about to do.

They were going to do the most repulsive surgery right there. Right in my room, she thought. I am chained down like an animal. I can't do anything about these awful people, how that man is going to get his thing all disgusting with that woman's body.

The man moaned a little. He whispered, "She can't hear us, can she?"

The woman giggled. "Honey, she's got so many pills in her, even if she could, she'd never understand it. It'll be better doing it here than in the broom closet. And hell, even if she understands, who'd she tell? She never talks. She's just a thing."

The woman in bed almost giggled, too. She wanted to tell them that she could understand what the clean man was doing to the toad.

She wished the clean man would take this filthy woman into the shower—

Sprays of clear, pure water—
and clean her off, make her all shiny again.
A robe of red with roses sewn across it—

"Robby," the filthy woman said, "I want you inside me now. Please." By the voice, she recognized the woman.

Donna Howe. Just forty-one years' old. Single. Bad habits. Bad teeth. Born in Oxnard. Lives with two roommates in Moreno Valley, near the mall. Very needy. Large feet.

That was all the information she had on Donna. It was hard to find out about people in Darden, because once you asked someone a few questions, they became cautious.

The man was Robert Fallon. She knew all about him. He was a talker, and very nice, but since she'd only been unstrapped for a few months when she'd first arrived, she had not kept up with him.

Of course, he was insane, and not to be trusted, but he was a bit of a lapdog, so she didn't think he'd be too much trouble. He was a sociopath, she knew, by the standards of psychiatry.

She was not. She knew what she was, herself, what her life was all about. But she recognized sociopaths as brothers and sisters, people who had purpose to their lives, and an understanding of the god-like nature of man which was denied to the other animals.

When she had been free to roam, when she had been able to look the other patients in the eyes, she could see who was one of her kind. They were a different species from the rest of the world. They were the hunters and the gods of creation. In times past, she or this man Rob might've been the leaders of the animals.

Instead, they were cast into prisons and tortured for their superiority. But the woman restrained in bed knew that the true measure of civilization was in how a culture treated her species.

The hunters of men.

These thoughts didn't erase fear from her mind, however. She still knew that the animals like this woman could hurt her. She knew that this woman was the enemy.

And what if no one came in and saw what these two were doing near her bed?

What if they did something to her?

Oh, lord, the woman in bed thought, they are animals, lower than animals, trying to make me do it, too, I just know they are, they can't help themselves, oh, why doesn't someone help me, why doesn't someone come through that door and help me? These horrible animals are in my room!

The man was standing up and doing it to the filthy woman.

Like dogs, oh, someone come in and stop them!

They needed a shower, a warm, wet shower, with someone to scrub them down, to clean them, to sponge off the filth and muck.

The filthy woman was leaning forward. The woman in bed could smell her coffee-stained breath. The filthy woman set her hand down on the edge of the bed, near the straps.

Oh, please, someone help me. Take these obscenities away.

And then, a miracle seemed to happen for the woman in bed. She was able to draw her index finger and thumb out from the strap. The filthy woman's slapping hand had loosened it.

Two fingers.

The woman in bed twitched her fingers, restoring circulation, as the disgusting animals pounded against each other.

She touched the tip of her finger to the tip of her thumb.

Freedom.

It was all she needed.

It took the restrained woman ten minutes to get her hand loose, and slip it beneath the covers so the animals couldn't see that she was loosening her other hand from the strap. She would not be able to get her feet free, not right away, but she could grab Donna Howe and scrape her face clean before the toad woman would know what hit her.

She doubted that Rob Fallon would mind.

He might be scared of her, but fear was good.

Slowly, carefully, both hands free, the woman in the bed

reached up to pull the cloth from her face, the cloth that kept the others from looking at her, from seeing her as a woman.

They wanted to see everyone as animals.

But it was *them*.

They were the animals.

The woman in bed unveiled her face, and wanted to say, "Boo!" to Donna Howe, but when she saw Donna's face, she could only giggle.

Donna's face was covered with sweat. She was being taken like a dog from behind. Her eyes were glazed over from the barbaric act. Donna barely noticed her, as if she was just waking from a dream. Then, when she did notice her, Donna's eyes went wide, and her mouth began to open.

But the woman in the bed grabbed Donna's head by the ears, and yanked it down to the bed, next to her own face.

As the woman in bed went to work, the man behind Donna kept pounding his body against hers, his moans becoming louder.

CHAPTER SIX

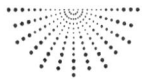

Memory:

The room off the alley, near the river, by the bridge. It smelled of rats, and only had a half-dozen candles for light. They flickered yellow and green against the peeling paint of the plaster wall. Water dripped slowly from the ceiling, some of it striking her on the head. But she didn't move, as much out of fear as of lack of will. She could hear the women on the street, hawking their wares to the men. She could hear the creak of wheels as the carts went by. Her skin felt cold. Her blood, warm.

He had set his hat down on the chair, and taken his cloak off, too. Beneath it, he wore a fresh white shirt, and the finest black trousers. He was a true gentlemen.

He said, "I saw it in you, girl. You liked what I did. You loved it, pet, didn't you?"

She nodded, still shivering. She could taste blood in the back of her throat.

"We are alike, you and I. We are of the same mettle. We've known each other before, isn't that true? Not in some wretched heaven or hell, but in eternity. We are soul-mates, child." His eyes were like diamonds—hard and sparkling all at once. "I brought you a gift."

He reached into his black bag and withdrew something covered in a monogrammed handkerchief. Blood had soaked through the silk. "It's something quite beautiful, if you have the talent for seeing beauty. Do you? Do you my raggedly little urchin?"

She leaned forward.

"Do you love what's on the inside, instead of what's on the surface? What is beneath the skin is the truth of our beings. Her is her truth," He said, squatting down beside her, taking her small hand, drawing her to her feet. She was shivering. He wrapped his arm around her, and held the thing in the handkerchief up to her face. "It was the part of her where she lived. It was her secret place. Isn't it beautiful?"

She looked on as he unfolded the corners of the handkerchief. When she saw what was within it, she looked away for a moment, because it was the part that she hated the most. She glanced about the room, trying to look at everything but what was in his hand.

She saw herself suddenly in the reflection of the mirror on the wall.

Her face scarred and hideous.

"You are beautiful to me," he said, kissing each one of the incisions on her face.

Someone was screaming out in the street.

She felt lightning burst through her.

Agnes Hatcher awoke in the bed in the last years of the twentieth century.

Her face was covered with blood.

CHAPTER SEVEN

Jim Anderson should've arrived at work between six and six-thirty, but because his Chevy truck was running poorly, his brakes about to give out, he decided to get there at quarter of and avoid traffic. It was still dark out, and he was sleepy. He'd been subbing for Campbell all week, who, the lucky stiff, was vacationing on Catalina for a week. But Jim wanted his three-to-midnight shift back. He wasn't a morning person. The mornings were a pain in the butt, all the patients getting wild when they first woke up, the meds having worn off. At night, at least after supper, they tended to watch T.V. or read or play board games. Only occasionally, when a television game show, like *Jeopardy!* got too exciting, did a riot break out. Even then, they weren't that hard to subdue—a little force and a few more pills.

When Jim Anderson got past security and had made it half-way down the hall in Building D, he knew something was different. Not in the usual way of some patient getting in bed with another, or some wild person trying to use one of the fluorescent bulbs as a weapon.

It was a stillness that he had not expected.

A quiet.

Sure, he was early.

Sure, he still wasn't all that familiar with the morning and its routines.

But Donna was not at her desk—and Rita Paulsen hadn't come in yet to relieve her.

Donna's desk was piled with papers and Twinkie wrappers. Although he knew that Donna was fairly disorganized, usually, by dawn, she would have cleaned her desk off for the next shift.

He looked into a couple of the rooms, but the inmates were still asleep.

The one he had never liked, never enjoyed being around—her room was just through the double doors.

He never looked there.

That woman scared him.

Agnes Hatcher. How she memorized faces and people, and anyone who had ever done her even the slightest harm. She was forty-two, but looked like she was twenty, small, petite, almost girl-ish. And yet, she was a tiger. She was the only patient in D that had to be restrained and covered except at mealtime. And even then, they spoon-fed her, with a very long spoon. She was in, as far as he could tell, for stalking and planning the killings of four cops, each of whom, she felt, had been rough with her when she'd been arrested for a double-murder. Jim didn't know everything about her —he had only seen her picture, and had never seen beneath the sack they put over her face—but he knew she was nothing but a destructive force in a human body.

And he stayed away from her.

Jim turned his back on the steel doors.

He shivered. He wasn't going to go through them and check on Agnes Hatcher at six in the morning with no one else around.

And then he noticed a door, slightly ajar.

Robby-Boy's room.

Rob was okay, a mild-mannered sociopath who had a thing for girls' heads, but was fairly easy to control. Like all good sociopaths, Rob aimed to please, at least to Jim's face—and that was all he cared about on the job.

Maybe Donna's there.

Rumor was that Donna had a thing for Rob. It was not unusual for psych techs and orderlies to start having feelings for some of the patients, but it could get out of hand and cross boundaries—and that's when it got dangerous. Jim shook his head: *Darden State is another world.* One of the patients, Crackers, had even told Jim that, now that they were friends, it was okay for Jim to screw his colostomy hole, and then Crackers had proceeded to poke at it with his own fingers.

Another world, all right.

Jim decided to go get a cup of coffee before checking on Rob Fallon. It was Campbell's shift anyway—*why should I put myself out this week?*

He went down to the vending machines in the staff room. One of the lazier employees, Sodherbergh, was napping on the couch. Jim poked at him with his finger. Sodherbergh snarfled away, and opened his eyes half-way as if he were undecided as to whether to fully wake up.

"Where's Donna?" Jim asked as he stepped up to the coffee machine. He dropped fifty cents in, and pressed the cream and sugar buttons. He looked back at Sodherbergh. "Get up, will you?"

Sodherbergh slowly sat up, shaking his head free of sleep. "Huh?"

"Donna. I didn't see her at her desk. She around?"

Sodherbergh shrugged. "I saw her a little while ago. What time's it?"

Jim Anderson glanced at his watch. "Six-ten." He reached into the machine and withdrew the small cup of coffee.

"I don't know how you drink that stuff, man," Sodherbergh said. "It'll kill you."

"What about Donna?"

"I told you, she's around. She was just in here a while ago. I was snoozing, but I saw her go by in the hall. She'd already changed out of her uniform."

Jim took a sip of coffee. "You don't think she's down there with Fallon again?"

Sodherbergh half-grinned. "Maybe. He's been sending her love notes."

Jim Anderson shook his head. "Jesus. I knew she was wrong for this ward. I knew it."

"Want me to go see if she's there?"

"No. I'll go. I just hope if she is there, she's giving him meds. I've seen him try this before. I was hoping Donna wouldn't fall for it. What a life, huh?" Jim finished his coffee, tossed the cup in the trash, and headed out of the room.

CHAPTER EIGHT

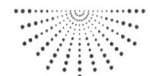

Walking down the corridor, back to Fallon's room, Jim Anderson checked the other rooms, briefly. There were fourteen inmates on D, all fairly docile, owing to the medications each received. But of them, five were considered sociopaths, and the rest had murdered enough people to fill a house.

Most of them were still sleeping. A few were sitting up in bed, either just staring out in space, or reading, or playing cards. They had that glassy look in their eyes, of Thorazine and Doltrynol.

He nodded to those who were up.

When he got to Fallon's room, the smell of Lysol was overpowering. That cold chill that Jim felt whenever he went into one of their rooms—he felt it, like ice. He never knew if it was him, or them. All he knew was that he felt it.

Sometimes, in the morning, Rob Fallon would be at his table, drawing cartoons on construction paper. Rob was quite a good cartoonist, actually. When he'd been on the outside, Rob had kept jobs drawing funny portraits at amusement parks, and made a decent living at it. Jim had one of his cartoons on his refrigerator at home—it was a caricature of Jim in profile, with a question mark over his head, and the word WHY written at the bottom.

But this morning, the table was bare. Through the bars at the window, the first feeble rays of sunlight speared across the darkness of the room.

Jim flicked on the light to see better.

He heard whimpering, and saw Rob there, hunkered down on the floor in the corner, shivering. He kept his hands clenched shut. He was naked except for a towel around his waist. Jim glanced towards the sink—it was full of dirty brown water. Rob, who liked to be squeaky clean, had been giving himself a bird bath.

"Rob? You okay?"

Rob didn't respond.

Other smells, beneath the Lysol layer: some kind of bleach.

Fallon cleaned himself and his surroundings incessantly. He could've gotten the brand-name cleaners from Donna herself.

Jim noticed that the floor had been scrubbed. There was a pasty white layer of soap across its shiny surface.

He glanced over at Rob's roommate, Petrie, who lay with his face to the wall. Asleep or awake, he was ignoring Jim.

"You been having nightmares again, old buddy?" Jim walked over to him, and crouched down. "Needing to clean up after yourself?"

Rob looked him in the eyes.

This was unusual for a sociopath, to be cowering like this, afraid of a world which only existed as a delusion. Unless something had threatened Rob's sense of himself as being real. Unless he had, for the first time in his existence, been made to feel small by someone.

But what or who could've done that?

Rob whispered, "Now I know why. It wasn't the eyes, Mr. Anderson, it wasn't the eyes at all. She showed me."

He unclenched his hands, something in them.

Something all smeared and red.

Curled hairs at its fringe.

Skeins of flesh, a loose tapestry unraveled in his hands.

"Damn," Jim said, standing, staggering backwards.

"It wasn't in her eyes, I thought it was, but it wasn't. It was in her purse," Rob said, holding the thing in his hands up, like a supplicant for Jim's inspection. "Just like my mother's purse. It's in it. That's where her why was. She showed me. She SHOWED me."

CHAPTER NINE

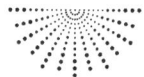

THREE HOURS LATER, AFTER DOCKING THE BOAT, TREY Campbell was dialing his work number from a payphone on Catalina. Carly was just coming out of the restroom several yards away. She had slipped into navy blue shorts and a turquoise T-shirt, and was stopping every few feet to get her sandals on.

Trey waved to her so she'd see him. She looked up, wrinkling her nose. She would know the call was about work. They hadn't had a decent vacation in six years, between her finishing her master's and starting with the county, handling adoptions, and his obsessive work habits (and he hated work, but could not keep from being a workaholic, as lazy as he dreamed of being).

And then, that thing. That incident. Accident.

With the gun.

It was always there, in the back of his head. He couldn't sleep some nights thinking about it. When he finally could sleep, he often dreamed about it, as if it was happening all over again.

"This is Campbell. I need to talk to Jim Anderson, Building D," Trey said into the mouthpiece, and the call was transferred.

Carly didn't even come over. She went to get her sun block from the boat. He watched her. She looked like she belonged there, a beautiful woman in a beautiful town.

He saw some children with their father walking past Carly on the dock. The children were all laughing. One held a large sea bass high in the air. Young couples in brightly colored clothes strolled along the promenade. An old man sat on a bench outside the drug store, clutching a cane, watching all the tourists with a look of disgust on his face. Carly got her sun-block, and walked back up to the promenade, ducking into a souvenir shop. The colors of the small seafront town were all pastel blues and yellows and greens. It was like an old painting to him, a town from another time, a resort of perfection and sleepy eyes.

The Catalina Express was docking a little ways up, with yet more tourists ready to disembark. Trey had hoped that not too many people would be on the island yet since it was mid-week. As it turned out, the place was packed. At least they had the boat. Later on, maybe he'd take Mark and Teresa out around one of the coves and let the babysitter have a break for a few hours. *That would be nice. Or maybe just lounge around at the rented cottage, read, watch television, relax.*

Finally, Jim's voice came on the line, "Hey. Glad you're around."

"I'm not really around. You beeped?"

"Had some trouble this morning. Just thought I'd report in. It's under control, but shook me up some." Jim had that deadpan way of speaking as if nothing was very important. But there was an edge to his voice.

"Someone bite his tongue off?" It was the joke at Darden, because between eye-poppings and tongue-bitings, there wasn't a lot else for the psych techs to joke about.

"A little worse," Jim said.

"Drop the other shoe," Trey sighed. He knew how bad things

could get. He had seen men and women do things to themselves and each other which were, to him, like coming upon a vision of Hell.

Some static on the phone line.

"Jim?" Trey said. "What was that? I didn't hear you."

Jim Anderson said, "I said, Robby-boy somehow got hold of a play toy. A real vagina. Only this one didn't have a woman attached."

CHAPTER TEN

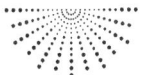

CHRIST. TREY CAMPBELL HELD HIS BREATH A FEW SECONDS.

It was more a prayer than a curse.

He brought the receiver down from his ear, and inhaled the clean salt air. Closed his eyes. Tried to block out the image that was forming in his head.

Then, back to the phone. "Fallon did that?"

"Other bad news. I think it's Donna Howe."

Trey remembered catching Rob Fallon flirting with Donna, and warning her about how Rob behaved. Trey felt tears coming to his eyes. *Poor Donna.* They hadn't had a murder on premises in thirteen years. "I *know* it was Donna. Damn it."

A pause on the line.

Then, Jim said, "we haven't found the body yet. Fallon isn't talking about why he did it or where he put the rest of her. Cops have been checking the lockers and the ceiling, but still no corpse. Since Fallon didn't run, the cops aren't putting us in lockdown, so at least it's not the hell we had when Kmetko ran in '91. Fallon's having his usual field day, but even he's acting weird. Fallon claims

Donna isn't dead. Had to give him some more meds..." Jim kept chattering nervously about Rob and poor Donna, but Trey barely heard him.

He was remembering something about genitals.

He interrupted, "Jimmy, it's not Rob. That's not his M.O., you know that. Eyes and heads are his thing. Go check on Hatcher."

Another pause.

"Jim?"

"Trey," Jim said, "are you nuts? She's bound and gagged—"

"Look, it's her M.O. Body parts. Surgery. Rob might've killed Donna, but the genitals are consistent with Hatcher. Check on her now. Right this minute. I'll stay on the line."

Trey watched as Carly finally came out of the souvenir shop, her hands full of postcards. She walked towards him, her sunglasses slipping down a little. As she got closer, he smelled the coconut oil. She smelled delicious. She managed a smile, and held up a postcard of a mermaid. "I'm going to send this to Mitch, he'll love it, and Rick and Kathe, I got one for them, too, wait, wait," she sorted through the cards.

She brought one out, but must've noticed how distracted he was.

"What's up?"

He sighed, reached over and put his arm around her. "A woman at work. Killed."

"Oh, my god," she gasped, and through clenched teeth said, "I hate your work. We did come here to think about you getting out of there with both eyes intact, right?"

He kissed her forehead, tasting coconut oil.

Jim came back on the line. "Guess what."

"She's not there, is she?"

"Rita says Hatcher's in her room. She's cuffed, still doped up from last night's meds, face cover still intact..."

"Well, thank god for that. Hope Rob talks."

"Me, too. If anything else happens, I'll beep."

"Okay. Thanks. And Tuesday, buddy," Trey said.

"Oh, yeah, Tuesday," Jim said.

Trey hung the phone up. Caught his breath. The fresh air was a relief. He realized that his breathing had been shallow ever since he thought of Agnes Hatcher. Sometimes he held his breath when he went into her room at Darden. Sometimes he held his breath when he heard her name. He inhaled deeply, shaking his head.

"What's all the stuff about Tuesday?" Carly asked.

"Well, besides being my first day back, he owes me fifty bucks. I told him something would screw up during my first vacation in years."

"He's an easy mark. Never bet against a sure thing."

Although he didn't completely believe it, Trey said, "Well, they can handle it on their end. They don't need me."

"Repeat after me: they don't need me, they don't need me, they can handle it," Carly said, mock-hypnotically. And then, softly, "I'm so sorry about that woman."

"Me, too." He shook his head, "She was having a fling with a patient. I saw it coming. I spoke with her about it. Next week, I was going to take her out of that building and put her in another one. I probably should've fired her for getting involved, but I wasn't completely positive that anything was going on. I should've acted sooner. I didn't think she'd really fall for his act. She must've trusted him."

Carly's eyes widened, "You're kidding. Why would someone do something that stupid?"

"If you're at all vulnerable, and inexperienced, it happens. The guy's a sociopath. He found her weakness, and he went for it. She probably had never been in love before, and here's this young good-looking guy who seems perfectly normal, and she's with him all night long, talking, laughing. Only she doesn't know that he's planning something for her. He's not like she is, he does things for effect, he does things only to get something for himself, because to him, she's not even real. To him, she's just an object, like a lamp or a doll."

"Sometimes," Carly began, "when I hear about those things at your work, it makes me not so sure that we live in a decent world."

"Yeah, I know."

"I sure hope nothing else happens this week."

"He'll beep me if anything does," Trey said, holding the beeper up, about to put it back in his shirt pocket.

Carly made a grab for it, got the beeper, dropped her postcards, and said, "oh, no he won't. No more beeps." She laughed, and he wasn't sure what she was going to do. She took it, and ran down to the boat, and by the time she threw the beeper in the water, he was running for her.

"No, Carly!" he said, but as soon as the infernal thing fell beneath the slight waves, he was somehow relieved. He had never been far from that beeper for the past ten years. Then, to his own surprise, he started laughing. He knew it was awful to be laughing after a co-worker had been murdered, probably sadistically. Nothing surprised or shocked him anymore, not after what he'd seen at Darden, the eyes smeared on the walls, the man who tore his own penis and testicles off with his bare hands, the woman who took a light bulb, broke it, and in front of him and Jim, sliced her nipples off. It wasn't just a hospital for the criminally insane, and it was more than just the archaic notion of a madhouse, it was humanity laid bare, with both its brilliance and its brutality.

Trey stood at the edge of the dock on Catalina Island and laughed, shocked that he could do so after the morning's tragedy. He could not stop for ten minutes.

He had trained Donna Howe in procedure.

He had tried to reach out to Rob Fallon, to try to make him understand how he had hurt people and how that was bad.

He had failed on all counts.

He could not stop them from doing what they were compelled to do.

Donna Howe needed love, and Rob Fallon needed scalps.

It almost occurred to him then.

CHAPTER ELEVEN

THEY ATE LUNCH AT ONE OF THE RESTAURANTS ALONG THE boardwalk. Trey ordered yellowtail and a salad, but didn't eat very much of it. Carly carefully avoided seafood, and opted for a hamburger. Neither spoke much during lunch. Trey's mind was on Darden State again, and he was fighting to put it out of his head.

At one point, she asked, "Are you going to be okay?"

He nodded.

"If you want to talk about this, we can," she said, and sipped her coffee.

After lunch, they strolled back up to the small cottage they were renting, set up against the hills just beyond the Zane Grey Hotel. As far as Trey was concerned, the place was costing them a small fortune, but it was beautiful, had a washer, dryer, a swimming pool, and a deck with a barbecue. In the mornings, he and Carly sat up in bed and watched deer cross the yard, heading for the stand of trees up against the hills. He joked that it seemed nicer than their house in Redlands. Once he saw the cottage, nestled as it was up in the hills above the sea, he knew it would be worth any expense. The sitter, too, was fairly expensive, but not much more so than Mrs. Quinlan, who watched the kids after school back home.

"And this is our summer vacation," Carly had reminded him. "What little there is of it."

Catalina's living area was small. The town of Avalon was no more than several streets that ended almost abruptly beyond these first hills. It reminded him of postcards he'd seen of the Mediterranean—blue and white and yellow buildings on a hillside over a blue expanse of sea. The town was packed in tight with shops and summer houses, as if these were exiled from the rest of the island. There were campgrounds and nature preserves beyond Avalon, but most of the tourists stayed in town and rode the golf carts around the hills for entertainment, or took horses up the trails, or the glass-bottom boat out into the harbor. He and Carly had come to the island years ago and stayed a few weekends, and then had forgotten its existence as a quick southern California get-away until they planned this trip. The choice had been either spend the cash and drive up the coast to do a little touring, or drop a bundle on a little sea-side place. Carly had won, as usual, because she wanted something relaxing, away from cars and especially work.

Now, with the beeper buried at sea, she got everything she wanted.

The screen door to the cottage was closed, but the inner door was wide open. Trey didn't like this. Although Catalina seemed a safe enough place, he wasn't sure that it was so far from the criminals and gangsters of the mainland. He opened the screen door, and went in ahead of his wife. Something about that morning's call to Jimmy Anderson made him nervous. Okay, so the Hatcher woman was still in her cuffs, still in bed…but the genitals in Fallon's hand just didn't add up for Fallon. Fallon would kill you as soon as look at you, but he wasn't a sadist, and his problems didn't seem to center around sexuality.

Carly said, "What is it? Something wrong?"

"Just my instinct," Trey said, turning around to look at the silhouette of his wife against the sun's reflection on the Pacific. "You want a beer?"

"I want you, big boy," she said, stepping into the house, letting the door slam behind her. "Actually, what I really want is to get back to my big fat murder mystery. I wonder when Jenny'll be back with the kids."

Then, they both heard a loud splash out back in the pool, and Trey went to get a beer from the fridge. "I guess Jenny's back. And I guess Mark's still trying to swim."

"Get me an iced tea and meet me out poolside," Carly said. "And bring the camera—I don't want to miss Marky's first swim."

JENNY REED, the local girl they'd hired for the week, was trying to teach Mark how to do the Australian crawl, but the eight-year-old would have none of it. Teresa, eleven, was an expert swimmer, and had never been afraid of the water. She sat on the edge of the small kidney-shaped pool and sneered at her brother's chicken-hearted-ness. They both seemed to have wisdom beyond their years, to Trey, who often felt that his children were smarter than their old man.

Carly had a book in one hand, and was pointing at Mark with the other. "Just pretend you're like Free Willy, Mark, you know, diving over the rocks." Then, she set the book on her lap and started reading, only looking up now and then to give Trey camera instructions.

Ever since they'd bought the video camera, when Mark had been a newborn, Trey had hated lugging it all over the place, but he had to admit that the memories it preserved were worth it. He got a nice shot of Carly shooing him away so she could read, and then, Teresa, making a neat dive off the edge of the pool. Mark just sat, his feet in the water, and refused to get in. When he turned the camera to Jenny, she blushed. She was sixteen, and blond, and had a kind of sparkling personality. She didn't talk a lot, but she seemed smart, and the kids loved her.

Trey turned the video camera back to Mark, who looked at the water, now less afraid for some reason.

Mark told the camera, "I can see me in the pool."

Trey laughed. "You can? Why don't you tell us what *me* looks like."

"Me doesn't look scared, I know that."

Teresa asked, "Oh, so you're not a fraidy-cat anymore?"

In the camera, with the sunlight filtering through the bougainvillea-shrouded trelliswork, Trey's daughter looked as if she was only half-there—the other half in shade, vanishing. She looked so much like her mother it was amazing. She would be just as beautiful, and she was smarter than her old man.

Back to Mark, who said, "I guess me isn't a fraidy-cat. Look," he said, touching his reflection. "Me is gone."

And then he stood on the edge of the pool, looked at his father and the camera and said, "Is it okay, Daddy, to get in?"

"Of course, Marky. Just jump. The water's not deep. Terry'll help if you have trouble."

"I don't want her to," his son said, "Will you help, Daddy, if something bad happens? Like if I can't get out? Like if something's down at the bottom?"

"Nothing to be afraid of."

His son shook his head. "Lots of things down at the bottom."

"It's just like the mirror at home, son. That's all."

Mark looked at the pool, at his father, into the video camera's eye. Just as he was about to jump in, Trey had an urge to stop him, grab him, and keep him from getting in, to keep him from anything that might hurt him.

Keep him safe.

But a second later, Mark was splashing around the pool, doing a modified dog paddle.

Carly looked up from her book, took her sunglasses off and cheered.

Trey kept shooting the video, because he knew it would be archival. One day when Mark was twenty-five and a father himself, Trey could show this to him, show him how scary it could be to watch your son take a step towards the unknown.

IT WASN'T until one thirty in the afternoon that his brain had pieced together what had happened back at Darden State that morning.

And what it might mean to him, if his hunch were correct.

Jenny took the kids down to go to the movies. Carly was taking a nap. He heard sea gulls overhead, crying out.

Trey made some coffee and picked the phone up. He dialed work. What he had thought of earlier in the day had grown into a theory.

Donna Howe needed love, and Rob Fallon needed scalps.

The phone rang six or seven times. He knew that when there was an attack or disappearance on the ward, that there was so much confusion that the phones were not always attended to. He had once been there during a riot, and he and his staff were so busy that they hadn't even bothered to buzz in the riot control police who would've ended the problem swiftly.

Run for the phone, Jim. Come on.

He felt certain of the outcome of the call before the line was even picked up on the other end.

CHAPTER TWELVE

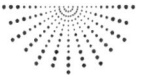

Trey said, "Jim? I want you to go check Agnes Hatcher's bed."

"I told you already, we checked it. Look, Fallon's in the bouncing room, and we've had the cops come through looking for the body—"

Trey cut him off. "I don't give a damn, Jimmy, now just do what I tell you. Anybody feed her yet? Hatcher have lunch?"

An almost petulant silence ensued. Then, "I don't know."

Trey sighed, exasperated. He took a couple of deep breaths, because his first instinct was to chew Jim Anderson out. But Anderson was good. He generally knew what he was doing. He just didn't know Agnes Hatcher all that well. "I'm willing to bet no one has fed her. I'm willing to bet she's lying in that bed, with her restraints loose, waiting for someone to come feed her."

"Hang on. I've got the log."

Trey could hear the papers being riffled through. He could almost hear the desperation in Jim's voice, as if Jim were beginning to fear that Trey's hunch might be correct. "It says—all right, it says she hasn't eaten yet. Says she was still knocked out at breakfast. Asleep. Her meds were heavy last night. She didn't fall asleep until four thirty a.m. Paulsen did the lunch log—she told me that she went into Hatcher's room today at one with the bedpan, only she was still asleep." Jim paused. He whispered into the phone, "They heard her snoring for god's sakes." Another pause.

Trey was sure that Jim was getting worried. It was like they all had a panic button related to some of the inmates. A panic button that was so easy to push, and when pushed: a bomb went off somewhere.

In a more normal tone, Jim continued, "You know what a live wire Hatcher can be. Paulsen decided not to wake her. I know it's negligent, but you know nobody likes dealing with Hatcher. They'll try feeding her in about twenty minutes."

Trey cursed under his breath. "No, Jim, here's what you're going to do. Get a couple of the big guys—maybe Howie and Dave—and get down to Hatcher's room right now, and if a cop's around, get him, too. My take is that Hatcher is lying there in that bed with blood on her face, and her hands are loose. She's tried this before. This is what she did on the outside."

Jim gasped. It occurred to Trey that Jim was not aware of the method of Hatcher's crimes.

"Look, Jim. Before D ward nicknamed her the Gorgon, she was called The Surgeon. She operated on people while they were still alive. She removed parts of their bodies based on what she felt was wrong with them. If Rob Fallon was having sex with Donna Howe, Agnes Hatcher would see her sex organs as what was wrong with Donna. What was causing her to be bad. I'm telling you, it's Hatcher's M.O." Trey waited for a response, but all he heard was Jim's breathing. "I'm telling you, she's lying in that bed waiting for someone to pull the covers back. She's waiting to attack again. When you go in, be ready for a fight. Get some more restraints.

Take a metal rod with you, something you can pry between her teeth if she tries to bite and lock her jaws on you." It took so long for Jim to respond again, Trey felt like slamming the phone down.

"She's drugged up," Jim said. "You'd think she was a pit bull. She's just a patient. She's got so much junk in her, I doubt she can lift a finger."

Trey chuckled at the younger man's naiveté. Graveyard humor was a staple of Ward D. "You've only seen her for the past four years, Jimmy. I knew her when. I know what she can do."

"Okay, boss, I'll do what you want. And if you're wrong, you owe me a hundred come Tuesday, deal?"

"Deal. Look, my beeper's not working. Just call me back," Trey said. He gave Jim the number to the cottage, and then hung up.

CHAPTER THIRTEEN

IN HIS OFFICE AT DARDEN, JIM ANDERSON SCRATCHED HIS head. The entire morning had been like a migraine about to descend upon him, and he had swallowed enough aspirin to kill a horse. Still, his head was pounding. The flickering overhead lights, all fluorescent bulbs needing replacement, compounded the headache.

It made him angry that he had to follow Campbell's orders again, given all the crap coming down that morning. He'd been hoping to prove himself to his superior. It seemed now that he was proving just how incompetent he could be at handling problems. He glanced at Rita Paulsen, who was pushing a rolling tray of meds and juice cups. Two psych techs were walking with the pretty recreational therapist down the hall towards the Game Room. A patient was screaming in South Wing, but that was for Lewis to handle.

Who would've thought that somewhere on this hall, a woman was murdered, her body hidden, her genitals cut off?

The police were still there, an invisible presence, for they were down in Ward A getting coffee. Jim didn't feel they were that necessary, except for incarcerating Rob Fallon yet again, this time in a less psychiatric-friendly prison—but that would come later, after Rob underwent yet another trial for murder and another psychiatric evaluation. Cops just got in the way, Jim thought. They tended to be brutish and nasty about the inmates; Jim felt a kind of paternal concern for the psychos on his shift. *Thank god the cops are out of my hair for now.*

But they'd be back soon, sniffing around for Donna's body. Jim had no doubt that she was stuffed into some locker or cupboard somewhere on the hall. It wasn't the first time a staff member had bitten it, but it was the first time, to Jim's knowledge, that it had been a woman murdered. And one as seemingly competent as Donna Howe. Only Rob Fallon would know where her body lay, and he wasn't going to start talking 'til his shrink showed up.

"Rita," Jim said. "You want to hear something funny?"

Rita Paulsen looked up from the tray. She was not very bright, nor was she particularly competent, but she was tough on the job. She had a face like an angel, but she could hold down a patient in the middle of a psychotic rage if the situation arose. She was definitely an asset to the ward. "What's up?" she asked.

"That was Campbell on the phone. He thinks that Hatcher killed Donna. Says she's in her bed waiting for us." He laughed thinking of how absurd the idea was. He had a laugh like a bull elephant. It echoed down the ward. "Ever since he shot that guy in his backyard, he's been completely paranoid."

Rita shook her head, "Can't blame him, given this place. But, let's face it, if Hatcher had wanted to get us, she would've done it earlier. I was in there. She was snoring like a baby, you know, same old same old." Rita looked at her watch. "Well, we can test out his theory. You want to come with me to go feed the Gorgon?"

Gorgon was Hatcher's nickname among some of the staff. They were all afraid of her eyes, because she seemed smarter and more watchful than the other patients. Although that was not the reason for the cloth over her face. The cloth was there because if the staff needed to feed her or be anywhere near her face, she had a mean overbite. Still, the face-cloth added to the myth of the Gorgon.

"Okay," Jim said. "Sure. Let's go feed the Gorgon. But I don't want to look at her. Last time I did, it was like she was studying me for something."

"For her next meal," Rita Paulsen grinned. "Ready?"

CHAPTER FOURTEEN

AGNES HATCHER'S ROOM HAD BEEN AN ENORMOUS WALK-IN refrigerator twenty years before. Then it was converted into a room for a patient named Emily Freund who had murdered her children and spent most of her life trying to tear the flesh off her own bones. The refrigerator walls were knocked out, and the room expanded, but it was again reinforced with steel doors. Most patients were able to come and go at certain times of the day, but Agnes, owing to her constant violent and aggressive tendencies, was restrained almost 'round the clock. In the afternoon, she was allowed to stand for four hours, restrained with her arms up in straps and her feet secured near the floor. She had one hour of exercise a day, in another room, almost a cell, by herself. A television monitor played an exercise tape, if she so chose to do calisthenics. But the majority of the rest of her life would be spent in that bed, strapped in, face covered. To outsiders, this often seemed horrifying.

But then, as the therapists, doctors, and psych techs and orderlies knew, this was Agnes Hatcher.

This was the Gorgon.

She had been a patient at Darden after being transferred from another hospital up the coast, because she had caused a riot among the patients. A very liberal-thinking doctor had given her a certain amount of freedom, believing that her psychosis arose from a childhood of abuse and deprivation. She rewarded her doctor by operating on him, as he was held down by the weight of concrete blocks, without the benefit of anesthesia. They said he lived for six more hours, but when he was found, he was begging for death—which came within minutes of the paramedics' arrival.

At Darden, she had bitten off three fingers of an orderly within two hours of her check-in. Within twenty-four hours, she was under constant restraint.

Outside Darden's walls, she had surgically removed a woman's liver on her coffee table, and played with it for awhile. She claimed that the woman was a recovering alcoholic who had lapsed one too many times. Her liver had been her problem. She had murdered a police officer, which was the crime that led to her arrest and the discovery of all her other murders. When the police arrested her, it took six men, and she had to be beaten into submission. On the walls of her house, they found dozens of notes with the addresses of all the policemen who had ever bothered her, and their children's schools; also, of doctors who had examined her, and their families, and of lawyers who had been unkind or threatening to her over bad debts. Others, too, names and addresses to which she had no apparent connection—all were slated for torture and death. On some of them, she intended to perform her perverse surgery.

She had been planning on slicing off parts of their bodies as souvenirs.

In her home, they found a collection of penises, bladders, livers, hearts, and lungs, and one jar of preserved brains. Some had come from animals, some from unidentified humans. She owned several surgical instruments, most of which had been stolen from hospitals over the years. She had created her own, using hybrids of fingernail scissors and metal nail files and other household items. She had turned the small den of her home in Pasadena into her surgery, and there was enough evidence of carnage there that one of the investigating officers had remarked, "Forensics is going to spend years trying to figure out what belongs to who."

She had been a high school teacher in Pasadena for several years.

She believed strongly in reincarnation, and that life was a continuum from one incarnation to the next; she attended All Saints Church, and considered herself an heretical Episcopalian.

She had graduated Phi Beta Kappa from the University of California at Berkeley. With a degree in forensic science.

At the time of her arrest, she was a teacher and lecturer at various police academies in the southern California area.

She was a member of the Junior League.

Her ancestors had come over on the Mayflower. She was a member of the Daughters of the American Revolution, but had not been to a meeting in several years.

She contributed heavily to the Children's Defense Fund and the World Wildlife Fund.

She voted Republican whenever she voted, but leaned towards a Libertarian philosophy.

She was a member in good standing of MENSA.

A neighbor, just before Agnes' arrest, had been trying to set her up with his cousin.

She had subscription tickets to the L.A. Philharmonic.

She was the Gorgon.

RITA OPENED the door to Agnes Hatcher's room. Flicked the light up. "Time to wake up, Miss Hatcher."

CHAPTER FIFTEEN

In the bed, the patient moaned.

Waking up.

"Jesus," Jim Anderson said, stepping around Rita Paulsen, "Has she been spitting up blood?"

A spackling of red was on the olive drab blanket.

In his mind, he knew that Campbell had been right. The Gorgon must've killed Donna Howe. She must've somehow gotten loose. She was playing a game with them. He held his breath for a second, wondering if he should call Howie and Dave into the room to help hold Hatcher down.

But he saw her hand; it was in the restraint. It was definitely in the restraint.

The cloth face cover was soaked red.

"It wasn't like that earlier," Rita said, sounding a bit defensive as well as confused.

Jim knew that Rita was occasionally negligent. He knew, considering all the black marks in her file, that she might be fired for not noticing something like this on her rounds. Maybe, he thought, with the lights out, maybe you wouldn't see the red. Maybe you wouldn't even look at where Hatcher's face was, because you thought of her as the Gorgon and didn't even like thinking of her as a human being.

His first impulse was to remove the face cover, but he remembered, for a second, what Campbell had told him.

Or warned him about.

No cops in the hall, and no metal rods on hand. He looked at Rita. "You ready to see her?"

Rita Paulsen shuddered a little. "Whenever."

"She may attack. Stand back a little, okay?"

Rita moved to the side, but did not seem very nervous.

At least, not as nervous as Jim Anderson felt inside. He figured if he pulled the face cover off swiftly, then maybe he could jump back. It was important to not lean into inmates like this. It was important to be ready to step backwards, so that if they lunged, you'd be safe.

Cautiously, he went over to the edge of the bed.

The hand in the restraint, what he could see of it, twitched slightly, then dropped as if Hatcher were asleep and dreaming.

Jim checked his own balance to ensure that, if she did make a grab for him, he could move back without falling.

He leaned over the inmate, and lifted the face cover.

Beneath it, a mass of blood.

A woman's eyes staring up at him, as if she were trying to scream but could not with her mouth, nor would her vocal cords muster much more than a reedy whine.

Only with her eyes, wide open, could she signal pain and suffering.

He knew those eyes.

His first thought:

Campbell was wrong.

CHAPTER SIXTEEN

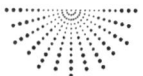

TREY CAMPBELL HAD GROWN EXPERIENCED AT BLOCKING BAD memories. This was one of the side effects of working at Darden. For those psych techs and orderlies who could not block out or deny the work environment reality, there were often breakdowns or burn outs. Several psychiatrists over the past three decades had left Darden never to practice their craft again because they no longer believed in the gods of Jung and Freud. Occasionally, there were suicide attempts.

But Trey could not block the memory that hit him full force as he sat back, after hanging up the phone with Anderson.

TREY WAS TWENTY TWO, a new hire at Darden. He was going for walks with Hatcher in the garden. He believed that Agnes Hatcher was somewhere inside the abused woman beside him. He believed her childhood had been taken away and her brain had been damaged through torture. She was smart, he thought. He believed then that if a person was smart enough, she could be rehabilitated in some form. He played chess with her often; he brought her books, mainly Charles Dickens novels, which she loved.

And then, one day, he slipped.

He told her something which he regretted as soon as the words were out of his mouth. "It's Ballantine. He has this theory about human behavior."

Agnes bent down to pick a flower. "Look at these roses," she said, glancing back at him. Her blond hair fell to one side of her neck. She was pretty, although the faintest scar tissue could still be seen just at the corners of her eyes, and along her neck. "The psychiatrist? I like him."

"I just don't think you need to be in those restraints all the time. That's all. You've proven to me that your illness is chemical and behavioral. Ballantine talks about my patients like they're..." He searched for the appropriate word.

"Monsters?" she asked. She stood up again. "You believe in me, don't you?"

"I believe that no human being should be shut away and hog-tied." That was when he knew he had said too much. She had a way about her, though. Something which inspired confidence. An almost hypnotic quality. For a moment, he felt like the patient, and she, the psych tech. "Let's go back. You're due for some meds."

"I don't like Ballantine," she said. He watched her face for signs of tension, but she seemed perfectly balanced, perfectly relaxed.

It wasn't until he came upon her two weeks later that he knew he had made a mistake of gargantuan proportion.

She had just gone in her room from one of her walks. The psychiatrist, Ballantine, had been there with his clipboard and drawings for her to examine. Agnes was already on every pill known to the medical community at that time. Every pill that would subdue the strongest man.

Trey could not forget: walking down the hallway, smiling at one of the nurses, who smiled back. The way his head was throbbing from a mid-afternoon headache. The smell of the laundry, for back then, it had been on his ward. That clean soap smell that seemed to cover all the other smells of Darden State. He was thinking of the fishing trip he and his buddies were going to take in a few days—deep-sea fishing off San Pedro, three hours out. He had thrown in his sixty bucks towards the boat rental. He was broke for the week from that, but he would catch enough fish to fill his freezer and then some.

He walked past Agnes Hatcher's room, glancing through the thick glass windows. Sometimes he nodded to her as he went.

He stopped, turned, and went back to her door.

Through the window, he saw Agnes leaning over the psychiatrist like a lioness over her prey.

She turned and saw him.

A faint oval of red around her mouth.

The psychiatrist's skin had been peeled back along his scalp.

She had been trying to open his skull up to find his brain. After hours of operations and grafts, Ballantine survived, but never practiced at Darden again.

Later, restrained, she told Trey, "He lived in his head. I wanted to set him free."

It was the last time that Trey Campbell had ever seen Agnes Hatcher without her face cover on.

It was the beginning of her obsession with him. An obsession which would last right up to the present summer day, July third, when he was thirty-six.

TREY TOOK THREE ASPIRIN, *and swallowed them dry. He stood in the kitchen of the rented house and kept trying to block those old memories.*

We're safe, he told himself. We're in a cottage on an island twenty-six miles off the coast, about one hundred and forty miles from Darden State. She's in her restraints. She can't do anything to us. To me.

Carly sauntered into the kitchen and said, "How about a little romance to take your mind off this?"

CHAPTER SEVENTEEN

"Now? I thought you were going to take a nap," Trey said, wiping his hands clean with a washcloth. He hadn't heard back from Jim Anderson just yet. He had gone to make some fresh orange juice, but spilled juice all over the counter instead. Carly stood in the doorway in his blue T-shirt that barely covered her thighs.

"Yes, now," she said. "I couldn't sleep. We have the place to ourselves for a few hours...why not now?"

Trey got a sponge and wiped the rest of the counter and cutting-board clean of juice. He dropped the sponge in the sink.

His mind was still on Agnes Hatcher. He found that the more he tried to block his fear about her from his mind, the more she seemed to be engraved in his thoughts. He glanced at Carly. Strange to think of both Carly and the Gorgon, as if one face was, briefly, superimposed over the other. Agnes Hatcher was not a bad looking woman, either; different, though, petite, blond, an elfish kind of face. Almost innocent. And then those eyes...When Agnes Hatcher flashed them at you, it was like a lightning bolt, it was like twin lasers cutting through your skin. She was only a human being, but Trey Campbell had seen those small blue eyes enough times to know that they contained the ferocity of a tiger.

Carly frowned. It must've been obvious to her that his mind was elsewhere.

"Trey, just you and me and Catalina," Carly walked right up to him and threw her arms around his waist. "The smell of the ocean, the clean air, the breeze…what are we waiting for, violins and roses? When we get back, it'll be nothing but work for months to come. No get-aways, no times to ourselves. Just enough time for kids and jobs. But, right now…" She brought a hand up to his collar and stroked the edge of his chin. She let her hand slide down to his chest. "Sometimes I forget how to even be romantic—where to put my arms, how to relax, how to be just like when we met, when it was you and me and chemistry. Remember?"

Trey nodded, grinning. "All that stuff at work," he said. "It's just got me so wound up." He felt incredibly warm with her, comfortable, as if they were not two people, but one person, complete, together. They'd had the roughest year of their marriage—not because they didn't love each other or care for each other, but because the kids and the job and school all seemed to conspire to keep them unconnected.

And that dark morning with the shadow and the white flash from gunshot.

The memory always threatened the horizon for him, like a coming storm. He shut his eyes, opened them, as if it would stop the memory from coming.

"No work talk," she rested her head against his chest.

"Jim's supposed to call back soon."

"Fine. Then he'll call back soon and you can deal with it. But if we have even a half hour to ourselves in this love nest, I say, let's take advantage of it." She looked up at him; he could tell that she was trying to see if interest was stirring. She kissed him, rather aggressively.

Her lips tasted like the sea. He closed his eyes. Her taste was always wonderful, sweet and sour at the same time. He brought his arms around her, his hands exploring her back, down to her thighs. The sensations he felt were both exciting and soothing.

She wiped her lips across his face, to his chin, his neck. He kissed the rim of her ear. As if by instinct, he lifted her up, his hands beneath her, her legs wrapping around him, and carried her over to the couch. The blinds were up, but there was nothing in view other than the pool and the hills. A hawk circled above the hills, against a blue and white sky.

She whispered, "I love you, I love you."

He, too, whispered the warmest things he knew, and felt burning and strong as he made love to his wife, the woman he had dreamed of loving since the moment he'd first seen her. She moved beneath him, and his body responded. In the last moment, he glanced out the porch doors, out to the hawk in the sky and watched it dive after some unseen prey, dive down until it was invisible among the trees.

CHAPTER EIGHTEEN

JIM ANDERSON, LEANING OVER HATCHER'S BED, FELT HIS heart freeze.

For a moment, he could not move.

For a moment, time stopped.

Hatcher's not about to attack anyone.

He knew the face of the woman in the bed.

He knew the woman.

Not Hatcher.

Not the Gorgon.

Jim Anderson felt nothing but stark terror when he saw the woman.

CHAPTER NINETEEN

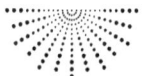

BENEATH THE FACE COVER, BENEATH THE BLANKETS:

Donna Howe.

She was still alive.

CHAPTER TWENTY

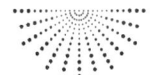

IT WAS STILL LIGHT OUT ON CATALINA ISLAND WHEN TREY Campbell awoke.

He checked the clock: not even four yet. Night would not come for another four hours or so. He would not sleep tonight, he knew. He would need to have a drink or two to stop the whirlwind in his head—thinking about Hatcher and what he had done once by letting her be free. Thinking about death, and the man he had shot in a dark morning. All swirling around his job, which was the most insane job anyone could have.

And yet, he had felt he had contributed some good to the system. He had to believe that.

During his nap, he'd been having a dream, not about Agnes Hatcher, or Carly, but about his mother and father and brother. And about the first time he knew about people. The first time he *really* knew. He was six, and his father and mother were taking him and his brother to New York to go sight-seeing. They walked along Sixth Avenue, at dusk, and he had lost sight of them. He didn't know where his mother was. His father had already gone off to some business dinner, but his mother and brother were supposed to be there. He looked at the people all walking, rushing, running, stomping, but he could not see his mother. Finally, he went up to a doorman who he thought was a policeman because of his uniform, and asked if he knew where his mother was.

The doorman looked at him, and the six-year-old Trey Campbell knew then that the doorman was insane, and would've been willing to do something awful to a little boy like Trey, except for the fact that Trey's mother, right at that moment, came up and grabbed him by the hand and hurried off down the avenue, scolding him for not keeping up. Trey looked back at the doorman, who was still watching him. It had been Trey's first run-in with what he came to know as the dangerous kind of person. All the psych techs knew them on sight, sometimes on smell, and Trey had developed his sense for them early in life. Trey sometimes wondered about the people whose lives were touched and ended by that doorman in New York.

TREY CAMPBELL, thirty-six, leaned back on the couch. Carly was asleep in the crevice of his arm and chest. She snored lightly. He was naked; she had managed to retain the blue T-shirt through their lovemaking. The house was dark; the sky outside, pink. It was late afternoon, maybe three-thirty, four at the latest. They had been asleep at least an hour. He wondered, for a second, about the kids, as he always did when he didn't know their whereabouts. But Jenny had taken them to the movie down at Monte Casino. Probably for ice cream cones and a walk, afterwards. Catalina was possibly the safest place to be in southern California. What was he worried about?

After a few minutes, he slid clumsily out from under Carly—

she snarfled before settling down again on the couch. He stretched, yawned, and walked outside to the swimming pool.

He stood at the edge, looking at his shadowy reflection. There was the "me" that Marky had been talking about, the self that looked brave and strong, the reflection; but the flesh itself, to Trey, felt weak and tired and ready to throw in the towel. *Another week of vacation*, he thought, *that's all I need.*

He dove into the pool carefully, his hands in front of his head even beneath the water to protect himself in case the pool proved too shallow. But it was fine and deep, as small as it was. He came up gasping clean pure air.

It felt good to swim naked. He splashed around, feeling a bit like a kid again. Carly came out with some iced tea, and kept her T-shirt on (no matter how much he begged).

"Well," she said, after he'd gotten out of the water and was sitting buck-naked on the pool recliner, "I guess you're feeling a little more frisky."

"A bit," he laughed, shaking his head in her direction to try to get her wet, "I guess I am not absolutely essential to the running of Darden State."

"Maybe not. But you're essential for the running of this family."

"Isn't it funny."

"What?"

"Oh, Carl, that we fight and get tense a lot at home, and then we come here and we're like two lovebirds on Spanish Fly."

"My my, Mr. Campbell, but you do flatter. And you know I hate being called Carl."

"Carly my baby," he puckered his lips in a mock-kiss.

"You better keep worshipping me if you want to stay happy, bubba," Carly lay back and pointed to the sky. "Look at that sky. Pink and blue and yellow. Yikes, it's like a Spielberg movie."

Trey watched the play of pink and gold light out to the other side of the western hills of Catalina. The sun wouldn't set for several more hours, but the heat of the day had abated, and the feeling was bucolic. "Like a movie," he whispered, feeling drunk although he was not. "You and me live happily ever after, Carly, and nobody needs to call me again because the whole complex of Darden State's running smooth."

He reached across to where she sat, took her hand in his, squeezed it.

She gave him a strange look.

"I've got to tell you something," she said.

He raised his eyebrows, expecting some further protestation of love or lust.

"Something you might not be too happy about."

"Okay. Shoot."

"I unplugged the phone before. Now, honey, you were just starting to relax. I wasn't about to have that Jim person calling every ten minutes with some screw-up that was going to keep us from enjoying ourselves. It's a hospital for the criminally insane, horrible things happen there. We don't need to bring them everywhere we go." And then, her head down, she said, "I'm sorry."

He felt himself tense up at first; but then, shook his head. "No biggie. You're right. I may be resigning soon, anyway, right? Who needs 'em?"

But, after a few minutes pretending to enjoy the view, he stood and excused himself to go take a shower.

On the way to the bathroom, he plugged the bedroom phone back into its wall-jack.

The phone rang immediately.

He picked it up. "Jim?"

The person on the other end of the line said nothing.

But he heard the breathing.

Her breathing.

The line went dead.

CHAPTER TWENTY-ONE

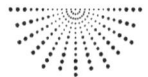

"What's going on?" Carly asked. She stood in the doorway.

Trey Campbell sat on the bed, staring at the phone.

"Trey?"

He looked up at her. "She's out," he said.

"Who?"

His mouth was dry. "The Gorgon."

CHAPTER TWENTY-TWO

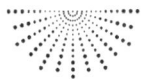

Agnes Hatcher stared at the phone.

She wanted to say something, but she was afraid of being over-heard. Someone had just walked back into the room. She couldn't trust the animals. She had spent most of the day squeezed into a crawlspace above the acoustic tile on D Ward. The rest of the time, she'd hidden in a room.

Someone stood over her, as she sat and thrummed her fingers on the desk's surface. One of the two who had come into the room, a man, was leaving. A man in a police uniform.

The woman who remained said, "I wish those cops would get out of our hair."

Agnes said nothing. Then, she looked up at the woman who had just spoken and said, "Thanks for letting me use your phone."

"No problem." The woman was preoccupied, scanning a chart on a clipboard. The woman had fine features, but her forehead was wrinkled from stress. Her badge read: *Kuehl*. Agnes had never seen her before. But then, Agnes had seen so few of their faces; likewise, few working on the ward had ever seen hers. The cloth face cover was usually on her face, except when the animals fed her. Only then did she see a face or two. Only then could she begin to understand how these animals operated.

The waiting room was large and square. It contained three small desks, six chairs, and two potted plants. There was a television set suspended from the ceiling in the northeast corner. An *I Love Lucy* rerun was showing. Beneath the television set, a long window. Outside, the dried, matted lawn of Darden State, and two other buildings. Double-doors led out to the sidewalk between the buildings. Agnes didn't know the layout of the other wards. She surmised that there was a diamond-pattern to them, for each one had a courtyard. Beyond these buildings, were the high fences, and beyond these, the canyon, and *freedom*.

Agnes Hatcher wore a dress that was loose and long for her frame. It was not the sort of fabric she would've chosen—these were Donna Howe's day clothes. Agnes had had to double-tuck the waist into the belt to keep from looking too clownish in the larger woman's clothes. The dress stank of barnyards, but Agnes tolerated it. She knew that a false move would land her back in the bed, back in the restraints. She'd had forty minutes after dealing with Donna Howe. She had washed in the sink in her room. She had shampooed her hair carelessly with yellow soap, and knew that it still contained some blood, matted at the nape of her neck. She had brushed it out with her fingers before leaving her room. Donna's street clothes had been in her locker, which was down the hall from her room. Because she knew that destiny was on her side, she was able to walk down the corridor undetected; changed in the hall bathroom; and then tried to go outside, but had seen the police arrive. She went to sit in an elderly patient's room, opened a bible, and began reading sections of it to the old man in the bed. When the police had come in to search the room, she had smiled at them and said, "Brothers, these poor souls, how desolate are their spirits." It was enough to make them leave her alone.

She watched the woman named Kuehl.

"Is something bad happening?" Agnes asked.

The woman didn't look up from her clipboard for a second. Then, she said, "Oh, just some trouble with the patients."

"But that policeman that was just here? Did he know anything?"

"Nothing new." This time the woman named Kuehl looked at her. "You said your friend is meeting you?"

Agnes nodded. "My boyfriend. Jack. He's a doctor here. We're supposed to have a very late lunch. Is it four yet?"

The woman named Kuehl glanced at her wristwatch.

Agnes stood up from the desk. She walked over to the woman as the woman looked up from her watch.

"It's just past."

"Well," Agnes sighed, "then it's too late."

The woman looked at her face strangely, and Agnes worried for a second. She normally was never worried, but the woman seemed to notice something around Agnes' eyes.

"I think you're bleeding," the woman named Kuehl said.

"Oh, that. It's an old wound. I think I'll just leave a note for my friend," she said. "Do you have a pen?"

The woman reached into her breast pocket and withdrew the weapon, the cutter, the slicer, the skinner, the Bic ballpoint pen.

CHAPTER TWENTY-THREE

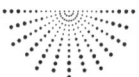

As Agnes performed the surgery on the woman named Kuehl, it came back to her like a scent from the past, a day from her childhood remembered in a few seconds:

Her father would go into her room and find her make-up every morning and then throw it out or hide it so she couldn't find it. She was eleven, and her father was a puritan from the old school who didn't believe that girls her age wore any make-up unless they were practicing to become whores. So, every day, on her way to school, she would walk up Laconia Boulevard, past the liquor store and the coffee shop, until she came to the gas station. She'd put coins in the machine to get a Coke, take a sip, and then ask the manager for the key to the rest room. She'd get it, unlock the room, and go in. It often smelled bad there, so she'd open her small purse and draw out a bottle of her mother's best perfume, usually Shalimar, which she had stolen from the dresser in her parents' bedroom. She'd spray some of it around the restroom, and apply a bit to the back of her neck. Then, she'd take lipstick from her purse, and mascara, and a small compact with powder. These she would've bought at the drug store and kept well concealed in a small music box in her room. Her father never opened the music box because it had once belonged to Agnes's grandmother. Her father hated her grand-mother so much that he had smiled when he had heard the news of the old woman's death two years before.

Agnes considered this her magic hour, when she would trans-form herself at the gas station restroom. From plain Agnes Hatcher to Francine, a young French goddess with dark eyelashes and rosy cheeks and cherry red lips, a woman of intrigue and seductive charm. Francine had shapelier calves than Agnes, and she had a great deal of poise and *joie de vivre*. She would brush her hair out again so that it sparkled, and spray it carefully so as to keep it looking full and fresh all day long. Then, she would finish her morning Coke, repack her supplies, pick her books up, and open the door to the rest room. School was two blocks further. If she walked slowly she would not sweat too much, and so the boys in homeroom would look at her a certain way, which made her happy. She had found that if she lifted her dress just a bit as she sat down, they would smile at the glimpse of panties.

Then, after school, she would walk back to the gas station, get into the rest room and wipe the makeup off with a Kleenex and some cold cream. She would wash her face and become, in her mind, plain Agnes again. Francine was there, still, in the mirror, left behind as Agnes trudged slowly home to a family which never fought or disagreed or said anything bad to each other.

It was on a Tuesday that this changed. Agnes walked up Laconia Boulevard by herself, but noticed someone watching her. She had just passed the liquor store, and looked at some of the champagnes advertised in the front window—she tried to see the reflection of the man who watched her in the glass, but all she saw was her own reflection and the sun's flat light. She turned to look at the man, shielding her eyes from the sunlight, thinking it was someone she knew. It was a man wearing chinos and boots, with a yellow shirt on. It looked like a cowboy shirt, because there were lassos and horses embroidered on it. The man had blond hair and looked cute to her, even though she knew he must be nearly twice her age. She realized that he wasn't watching her at all. Apparently, he was just watching the road. His thumb was out and he had a green canvas duffel bag at his feet. He was hitchhiking.

She continued on to the gas station, and waved to the two old men who sat out front. She tried to get a key to the rest room, but the attendant was busy, and the manager was nowhere to be seen. The manager was usually nice to her, and sometimes gave her a free Coke and patted her head. She missed him today; he was nicer than her father. Agnes bought a Coke and waited out by the garage bays, hoping to see the manager.

Then, she went to try the restroom door.

Someone was inside the restroom and seemed to be taking forever. She waited almost ten minutes, and realized that she'd be late for school if she waited much longer. The transom to the women's room was open, and she heard the fan from within, and the sound of water running. And still the woman inside didn't come out.

Agnes knocked on the door. She was already finished with her Coke. Her books felt heavy in her arms.

The door to the men's room was open just a crack. The transom up top was open, too, and there was no fan on, no sound at all. Agnes had never been in a men's restroom before, and had, frankly, been curious.

The men's room was shadowy. She pushed the door a bit further open, and it creaked. She glanced back to the attendant at the gas pump, but he was talking with a customer who had come for a fill-up. Quickly, Agnes stepped inside the men's room. No one was there. She heard the steady drip of water at the sink, and went to shut the water off. Once inside, she used the back of her heel to shut the door. She didn't want to touch anything, as it all looked extraordinarily filthy. She turned the lock on the doorknob. She sighed. She flicked the light switch, but no light came on. She tried it a few times, but the room remained dark. There was some light coming from the transom, and she had a pen light in her purse, so she set her purse on the sink and rummaged in it for the light. She brought it out and turned it on. Her reflection seemed spooky with the small intense light in her hand. She looked ugly in the light.

But I'll turn into Francine, she thought, *in a few minutes.*

She set the pen light down on the sink, and picked out the perfume from her purse. She sprayed it in the air, but the smell of the place remained bad. It was still fairly dark, so she had a difficult time putting the make-up on.

As she was carefully applying lipstick, someone tried the door. Because she hadn't used a key to get into the men's room—the door had been left open—she wondered if the man outside would go get the key from the attendant or the manager. She grew scared. She closed the lipstick up, and dropped all her make-up into her purse. She went back to the toilet stall and shut the door behind her. She would wait until the man outside went away, and then she would wait another five minutes. The toilet stank, so she had to hold her nose.

In less than a minute, someone opened the door.

She saw the light on the ceiling above her, as the door opened and closed. A breath of clean air whisked through the stink of the men's room.

The intruder tried the light switch. She heard the sound of water in the sink. She looked through the crack in the stall door. He was walking back. She hoped he was going to use the urinal, but instead he tried the stall door. He tried it twice. She wondered what he was thinking. Was he thinking: *Pretty strange that the door isn't opening, considering no one else is here?* Or was he thinking: *I better go to another rest room, this one's out of order.*

She stood there, back against the wall, holding her breath.

She heard his footsteps as he walked away.

She heard him peeing in the urinal. The flush. The door of the room opening and closing.

No sound.

He had left.

Water was still running in the sink.

She figured that she had better get out of there quickly, so she unlocked and opened the stall door and stepped out into the rest room.

He was there. He stood in front of her, blocking her way.

Agnes dropped her purse, gasping. She tried to move, but her limbs seemed to be made of stone.

She couldn't see his face because of shadow.

He said, "Knew I seen you come in here."

He reached down and grabbed her around her shoulders. She struggled against him, but he held her tight. He covered her mouth with his hand and took her over to the sink. She managed to work a hand free and slammed it back, hoping to hit him in the face. Instead, her hand went into the mirror, and she felt glass splinters. She grasped one of the glass shards and brought it up to his face and sliced across what she hoped was his ear, when she realized that she could not breathe at all, and that was the last thing Agnes Hatcher remembered until she woke up in the motel room in Las Cruces, her wrists tied together.

"Where am I?"

The man didn't look at her. He was watching TV. He said, "Las Cruces."

She began crying.

"I didn't rape you or nothin'."

After she finished crying, she said, "please let me go home, mister. Please."

She knew who he was. He was the manager from the gas station. Mr. Farquhar. She had known him since she was eight.

He said, "Can't do that."

She said nothing. Her throat was sore, and she was thirsty. She didn't want to ask him for a glass of water because she was afraid that he might do something terrible to her. She heard a fly buzzing at the window.

"It's not awful," he said. "What I'm gonna do. It's not awful."

She shut her eyes and pretended she was Francine and not stupid Agnes Hatcher.

"All I'm gonna do," he said, "is fulfill my destiny with you."

"You kidnapping me?" she asked.

"Naw. Can't call it that. But I know 'bout who you are…I seen it in your eyes. I know you go in the room to change so other kids'll think you're just like them. You and I, we know each other from ways back. Centuries." He turned to point across to the window, as if behind the curtains and venetian blinds was all of human time. She noticed that part of his ear had been sliced off. *I did it*, she thought, and her heart beat slightly fast, thinking that she could really hurt him if she wanted. If only her hands weren't bound. He said, "I been huntin' you a long time."

"I'm thirsty," she said.

He stood and went to the bathroom. She heard water. He returned with a plastic cup full of rusty brown water. He held it up to her lips.

After she took a drink, he said, "Do you remember me?"

She blinked. He seemed to get angry. She was afraid he would hit her.

"You don't believe me. I'll show you who you are," he said. He set the cup down on the night stand, and sat next to her. He put his arm around her shoulders. She could smell his sour breath. He squeezed her, and she felt a brief pain as he pinched her. "Look."

As if she'd been practicing for this all her young life, she said, "My name is Agnes Hatcher, I live in Empire, California. I get straight A's."

His eyes grew wide, and then he laughed. "Oh yes, sweet little one," he said. "You're hiding from me, I know you're in there."

He reached into his pocket and brought out a small, thin-bladed knife. He twisted her head so she was looking at the mirror that leaned against the low dresser.

(Remembering decades later, she thought she had seen a flicker of it, of that other face.)

He brought the blade up to the edge of her forehead. It was almost a tickling pain as he began skinning her face. He whispered, "Bridey."

She screamed, but he held her head tightly in place as he continued.

The screams echoed throughout the motel court, and the police were at the room within twenty minutes.

But by that time, the motel room was empty. Her abductor had already packed her into his car, and they were gone down a dirt road that led up into the mountains. It would be six years before she would see the light of day again.

Agnes Hatcher returned to consciousness, in the waiting room of Darden State, blood showering across her fingertips.

In her hands, cupped like a dark red bird.

A human heart.

CHAPTER TWENTY-FOUR

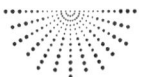

AGNES WAS FINISHED WITH THE WOMAN NAMED KUEHL IN less than two minutes. The woman had not had time to cry out, which was for the best. Unlike Donna Howe, the woman was dead, and very quickly.

Agnes Hatcher took the car keys from the woman's pocket, and her pocketbook. The woman had a Ford Mustang keychain, with a small beeper for an alarm system; forty dollars in cash; one MasterCard. Pictures of husband, children. Driver's license.

She glanced through the doors to the ward and saw the policeman speaking with one of the therapists.

She went to the double doors. She walked out through them as if she were just coming from a short visit to one of the mentally ill. She remembered a woman's walk she had once noticed, a sort of rhythm to the way she walked. She could imitate that. In her mind, she pretended she was the woman, and then the walk came easy. No one would notice Agnes Hatcher. They would think it was this other woman, someone who walked with less confidence, with less direction. It took her fewer than three minutes to get to the staff parking lot. She passed no one on her way. It was the afternoon, and even with the police milling around, it was slow, and people were sleepy and inattentive. She held the alarm beeper high up, and pressed it twice. Two high-pitched beeps came from the left of the parking lot. She followed the sound to a blue-gray '89 Mustang. She got in, buckled her seatbelt, and put the key in the ignition.

She felt the blood against her skin. It had seeped through Donna Howe's bulky dress.

It was warm like new milk.

She put the Mustang in reverse, and pulled out of the parking space.

A man in a suit, probably some kind of inspector, waved to her as if he knew her. He had a gray moustache, and very little hair. She thought she had seen him before once or twice.

She smiled and waved, wondering if he could see the blood on her chin. Not caring.

In her head, the one word that had fueled her in the loneliness of her captivity:

Destiny.

As she drove away, within the walls of D Ward at Darden State, she could not know that the second body was found.

She could not know that the police sealed the building within minutes.

Or that Rob Fallon had confessed that the woman named Agnes Hatcher was now hiding beneath the building, in the closed off underground chambers where once upon a time all the patients at Darden had been housed.

Agnes Hatcher knew none of this, but she was assured by her own feeling of her fate that she would reach the only man she had ever loved in time to prove to him that all she had ever done, she had done for him.

She had spent her life searching for him.

And now, they would be together.

Forever.

CHAPTER TWENTY-FIVE

"She can't get out, Trey," Carly said. "Not with all those people around at Darden. How could she get out?"

Trey shrugged. "Any number of ways. I know her. That was her on the phone just now. With cops searching the place, all the psych techs and doctors are going to be somewhat disoriented. Some of the patients will be acting-out right now because of the commotion. No one is necessarily looking for her, or they're assuming that she's somewhere within the gates. To be honest, nobody really knows what she looks like. We've got pictures of her when she came in, but her face gets covered most of the time, and she's been in ten years. She could have a disguise. Who knows with Hatcher? Instead of the Gorgon, she should've been called The Chameleon. I've seen her imitate people's voices and mannerisms almost perfectly. She can be anyone she wants."

"Call Jim. Find out what's going on."

"I just tried. The line's busy. It'll be busy for the next four hours. I might as well watch the news tonight, I'll get more information on it than I would over the phone. My assumption is that they know she's out now. The cops have probably shut down a few miles around Darden. If I were there, maybe I could do something. Maybe not. But I'm here. I'm on vacation. Damn it."

Carly put her hand on top of her husband's. She leaned against him. As if with some telepathy, he felt her warmth and love. He drew away from it. He felt cold inside.

Carly let go of him. She sighed. "She's four hours' away, surrounded by cops, and she's probably more than a little disoriented. This is probably the safest place we could be right now."

"Maybe you're right. It just has me in knots, what happened. And how the hell did she get this number? What—did she attack Jim? Did she get this from the weekly log? How did she know where to find me?"

Carly raised her eyebrows. "Well, there's not a lot we can do right now. I know. Let's go for a walk, okay? Down to the beach." She stood up and went over to the dresser. She opened the top drawer and withdrew a pair of sweatpants. She slipped into these, and tossed him a pair of khakis.

THE WORLD OUTSIDE, the path down the hillside, all of it was nearly silent against the sound of crashing waves out on the rocks. Because the fourth of July was coming up, banners had been unfurled throughout Avalon proclaiming the upcoming fireworks display on the water. Since it was still early in the week, day tourists were lined up along the docks, waiting to board the boats back to the mainland. The sun had gone beyond the far hills, but was still fairly high in the sky, casting a halo over the small town. Everything in it seemed peaceful and lazy. Carly walked ahead, wrapping her pouch around her waist, wearing flip-flops and sweatpants and that great T-shirt. The smell in the air was vaguely dusty, not as clean as the earlier part of the day, brought by a slight wind from the hills.

Trey took it all in at a breath: *vacation,* he told himself. *Vacation.* He slipped on his sandals, the Birkenstocks that Carly had given him for his birthday five weeks before, holding onto an old section of wooden fence for support.

"Wait up," he said.

She turned about, smiling. The sunlight created an aura around her. She drew the small camera from her pouch, and snapped his picture quickly, as if afraid he would lose his expression in the next second.

"Gotcha!" she cried out. She pivoted to the right, and took a picture of the harbor below.

Picture this: A beautiful happy woman, a wife and mother and social worker, caring, loving. With husband and kids. A family. Every-thing in the world at our feet. Life good for us. And I still can't enjoy any of this. Not completely. Trey feigned a smile, but it slipped when he caught up with his wife.

She didn't seem to notice. She took a deep, luxurious breath. "What is that? Hibiscus and—maybe gardenia? Let's just junk everything and move here."

She grabbed his arm, shaking it. "Wake up, wake up. I want the happy-go-lucky guy back who I married. I know he's in there somewhere."

Trey pulled away from her, and then gave her a sideways hug. His forehead furrowed with worry. "If only I'd been there. I could've done something. I know more about Hatcher than the others do."

Carly, sounding slightly exasperated, said, "That doesn't matter. They'll find her inside the gates somewhere. It'll take six men, but they'll get her tied down again."

Wearily, he said, "I don't know."

"This job is driving you nuts, Trey. Don't let it."

Something in the tone of her voice disturbed him.

"I'm not going to hold it in anymore," she said.

"Hold what in?"

"This is hard for me to say."

A minute passed, and it worried him, the way she was acting, the look on her face. They were almost all the way down the path, to the main road. Somehow, he knew what she was going to say.

He touched his fingers to his own lips. He pointed off to some scrub brush on the other side of one of the rows of small cottages.

A doe stood still, watching them also.

Then, it ran off into the underbrush.

"I'd like to wish the world away," he whispered, kissing her. When he drew back from Carly, it seemed as if his unhappy mood had been passed to her. Her face was etched with concern.

"You *have* to leave your job, Trey," she said.

It barely came as a shock to him, this previously unspoken demand. Yet, she looked guilty, as if keeping from saying these words was tantamount to cheating on him or abandoning him.

"Trey, I mean it. Not just think about quitting, but actually just do it. You have to leave your job because I don't want you like this ever again. And you're like this all the time. Almost relaxed, almost here with me and the kids, but not completely. You're always part there, and it consumes you. I can't manage with half a husband, and I won't let the kids have half a father. You need to get out." Carly had never been this direct about her anger over his work. It had always come out in little jokes, or a graveyard humor about the tragedies and near-misses at Darden. Now, she even looked cross. Sometimes, Trey had trouble keeping things in perspective, and it got the dog up in him to be told what to do—*to leave his job, not nudged, not asked, not manipulated into leaving it, but to be directly told to leave it.*

Then, he calmed down. He felt like a man defeated. She was right. He had to leave his work at Darden.

"It's funny," he began. "You get into a place like that when you're young and you think you can make a difference. You think you can actually save someone. But you can't. Not just at Darden, but anywhere. My dad was wrong. He always told me you could save someone if you kept yourself strong and prepared, but you can't. You can only save yourself."

"Oh, Trey," Carly said. "It's not that melodramatic. You can do all kinds of things. It's just I don't want our children to lose their father because he's too tied up in the lives of criminals. I don't want to lose you, either. We need our life. That place is too dangerous, and you're too sensitive. I know you're good at your work, but you need to get more out of life than just work."

They kept walking, and as Trey glanced down the hillside, he thought he saw the kids down below, near one of the ice cream parlors. Where was Jenny?

"Carly, is that Terry and Mark?"

She looked across the thin slice of the main drag that she could see clearly. "Maybe. It's hard to tell."

"Jenny's not with them," he said.

"I'm sure she's around there somewhere. Don't panic."

"We're paying her to stay right with them."

"Enough." Carly stopped in her tracks. "Nothing is going to happen to them here. See what that place has done to you? You think everywhere is like that ward. Well, it's not. Trey, you always go off like this, as if the worst thing's going to happen, as if every-thing has to be a life and death situation."

He could tell that she wished she hadn't said those words. Not exactly in that way. Not those words.

Life and death.

The white flash in the dark morning.

The gun.

The shadow against the dark.

"Sorry," she said. "I didn't mean it like that."

They didn't even have to talk about it directly.

It had happened, and then it was over.

A year ago, almost. The man had been released from Darden State because some loopy psychiatrist believed that he was "cured," but Trey had known better. The man was a sociopath named Wilson. And Wilson had told the others on his ward that if he ever got out, he'd hunt down anyone who had ever hurt him, including Trey. Trey had one nightmare after the next about Wilson, what he had seen Wilson do to people, from the autopsy photographs of the family in Long Beach. Trey bought a gun and then spent three months at a target range in San Bernardino learning how to shoot it.

And then, one morning.

When it was still dark.

The noise in the kitchen.

The fear, creeping up the back of Trey's neck.

Knowing that Teresa's room was near the kitchen.

Knowing that Wilson was loose and out to get revenge.

Trey went, shivering, with the gun, down the hall, through the living room.

In the dark.

Someone was at the backdoor. By the kitchen.

In the dark morning.

Trey stood in the doorway to the kitchen.

The morning light seemed purple.

The shadow against the dark was the exact shape of Wilson.

Trey could never be sure that he didn't rewrite his memory. Still, he felt even then that he knew that it wasn't Wilson, but he didn't care, because this was an intruder in his house.

He couldn't even remember actually drawing the trigger back.

All he remembered was the white flash in the dark.

And then, with the light on, seeing the man.

Where the bullet entered.

TREY BEGAN JOGGING down the path on the island, past the summer cottages, past the Zane Grey Hotel, not towards his children, but away from the memory. He had managed to stop thinking about it for four days straight and now it was back. It had him. He could hear Carly calling for him, but he had to run. He had to do something to get the memory out of his head.

He stopped at the bottom of the road, glancing back.

Carly was walking slowly down the hill.

He felt a gulf between them, as sure as if they'd just had a fight. And the blasted thing for him was that he knew it was not her fault. He knew that he was the one to blame for being panic stricken and paranoid and overly-protective and wary and...frightened. He sat down on the edge of the road, curbside, his head in his hands.

He waited for his wife.

The first words out of her mouth were: "It's been a year. The guy was breaking in. Nobody thought you did anything wrong."

He didn't look up at her. He knew it was a lie. He knew that he had been what one of the policemen had called "trigger-happy." He knew that he shouldn't have shot the gun. He knew he shouldn't have done anything other than perhaps call the police to come around and check out the noise at his kitchen sliding glass doors.

But he was afraid. Not just of some released lunatic who had sworn a vendetta out on him. But afraid of anything that might test his courage. Afraid of anyone who might suggest that he wasn't the strong man he pretended to be to the outside world.

"Trey," Carly said, as if from some great distance, as if she was on the opposite end of the world from him. "Are you all right?"

Luckily, she didn't mention the tears. He didn't want to acknowledge them himself.

She squatted down in front of him, touching his shoulder with her right hand. "It's about that man, isn't it?"

Trey nodded.

They didn't say anything.

After several minutes, he got up and dusted himself off.

"It's going to be hours 'til sunset," he said. "I wish I was at work right now. I think I could help. Let's go find the kids."

CHAPTER TWENTY-SIX

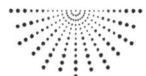

Mark whispered, "She's gonna get in trouble if Mom and Dad find out."

He stood in his sister's shadow while she bought a corn dog. She loved corn dogs, and Mark liked salt water taffy, which Teresa was also buying for him. When she had the corn dog in her fist, she passed him four wrapped up pieces of taffy.

"I don't care if she ever finds us again," Teresa said in what Mark thought of as her haughty princess voice. "She's a rhymes with rich."

"Witch?" Mark asked, not quite getting it. He opened a wrapper and popped a taffy into his mouth. "What do you think she's doing down there?" He pointed to the alley between shops. He didn't look down it, because it grossed him out to see Jenny and that boy together. What they were doing.

"Mom says it's called canoodling, and it's something that grown ups do. Only not on company time, and Daddy's paying her a lot to be with us. Even though I'm too old to need a sitter." Teresa took Mark by the hand and led him over to the arcade. "I've got six quarters left. I'll give you three and I keep three. I want to play Street Fighter."

Mark liked video games a lot, but the dark arcade scared him a little. It practically had no lights inside it, except for the game machines. He didn't like these types of games, either. They were all about attacking people or car races. He liked the Donkey Kong game they had at home, but he couldn't find it in the Island Arcadia World. He watched Teresa go over to the Street Fighter game. He wandered around between the machines. There were only a couple of kids hanging out there, and they seemed a lot older than him.

He decided that he didn't want to play anything. He put the quarters in his pocket and went back out into the sunlight.

Jenny was at the end of the block. He didn't want to attract her attention, so he tried to hide behind a dress display in front of a shop.

But it was too late. She saw him, and shouted for him. He stepped out into the slanting sunlight. Mark began walking slowly towards her, his head down, his hands in his pockets.

Jenny quickly stubbed out a cigarette. "Where the hell have you been?" She had a look in her eyes like a crocodile. Mark thought she was pretty, especially in the eyes, but not when she was in a mood like this.

"We were waiting for you."

"And where were you supposed to wait?" she said, grabbing him by the hand and jerking him forward.

"We just went to the arcade."

She dragged him back to the arcade, and got out of the sun. She stood inside, among the clanging and beeping machines. Jenny squatted down to be at eye-level with him. "I'm sorry, Marky. I just was worried."

"I know. We shoulda stayed near you."

"I was just saying goodbye to Tommy. He thinks you're both

real nice. Real well behaved. You won't tell your Daddy about this, will you?" The pretty look came back into her eyes.

He breathed a sigh of relief. For a minute, she had looked like a monster. Now all she looked like was the pretty girl who babysat him. "No."

"Promise?"

He nodded. He wiped his finger across his chest. "Cross my heart and hope to die, stick a needle in my eye."

Jenny Reed laughed. "That's so cute. Stick a needle in my eye. God, that's so cute. You are the cutest thing. That Terry over there?" Jenny let Mark lead the way to his sister.

WHEN THEY REACHED HER, Teresa half-turned and said coldly, "Oh, it's you."

"Listen, woman-to-woman," Jenny smiled. "You understand about boys, don't you?"

Teresa said nothing. On the game screen, one of the players kicked another in the head. Cartoon blood splashed out of the opponent's face.

"I only left you two for a second," Jenny said, defensively.

Teresa had run out of quarters. "I don't need a babysitter anyway. Just because my parents think I do and hired you doesn't mean I need one."

"That's right," Jenny agreed. "You're old enough. So if your folks ask, tell 'em I ran to the ladies' room or something."

Teresa stuck her nose up at this. "I don't lie. If my Mom and Dad ask anything, I'll tell them that Mark and I were fine all day long."

"Cross your heart, Terry," Mark poked at his sister's back, "and hope to die. Come on."

Jenny chuckled, and opened her purse, looking for something. "Hey, I'm not so bad. I'll give you some more quarters."

"Hush money," Teresa said, disdainfully. She held her hand out.

Mark knew this about his sister: she didn't lie, but she could be bribed. She liked money and what it could buy. Teresa took several coins from Jenny, and then crossed her heart to seal the bargain.

There were things about Jenny that Mark hated, and things he liked. Whenever her mood shifted to anger, she was a nightmare. But when she was like this, giving out quarters and giggling, he liked her.

"You know you have the prettiest eyes. They're like blue marbles," he told her. He felt himself blushing, because he sort of had a crush on her. He just wished she wouldn't smoke cigarettes or kiss that boy.

Jenny sighed. "You're an angel. And good for my ego. I'm sorry for taking off like that. I won't do it again. Cross my heart, hope to die, stick a needle in my eye. Friends?"

He nodded.

She hugged him tight.

The squeeze of her hug felt good. Even though his mother and father hugged him a lot at home, on this vacation they both seemed kind of wound up to him.

After two more games of Street Fighter, Mark saw his parents out on the street.

"Hey! We're over here!" He shouted as loud as he possibly could.

His mother grinned broadly when she looked over, startled, in the direction of the shout. His mother tugged at his dad's elbow, and pointed into the arcade.

Mark noticed that his dad seemed worried. His dad looked the way Mark had felt when he was afraid to dive into the swimming pool.

CHAPTER TWENTY-SEVEN

So much of life was unplanned, and yet it often seemed to work out the way it needed to. Agnes Hatcher pulled the car off the road, after she noticed the patrol car behind her. The patrol car followed her in to the Walmart parking lot.

She parked in one of the spaces, but was only slightly apprehensive.

It will work out, she thought. *It was meant to work out.*

It was her first time on the outside in years, and even the air was something of a shock to her.

But she had to behave as if she were the woman who owned the car. *Kuehl.* She had to behave as if she were just stopping off like anyone else might do on the way home from work.

The policeman parked his car behind hers.

Agnes opened the door, and got out. There was a jacket in the backseat. Although it was warm out, she drew the jacket over her shoulders in case there was any blood on her blouse.

The policeman was lanky and young. Possibly in his mid-twenties. He had blond hair and tanned skin. Blue eyes. He was very handsome. She wondered what it would be like to have him on a table. She wondered what she would need to remove from his body that would be his essence, his driving force.

He grinned. "You've got expired tags," he said, opening up a ticket book. "Can I see your registration?"

"You could," Agnes said, "only it's not my car."

His eyes widened a bit. "A friend's?"

She nodded. "A co-worker's. I borrowed it to run out and get her some new hose. She has an important meeting. She has a run in her hose." Agnes said each word as if a man could not possibly understand this problem.

"Well. Tell you what. Tell your friend that she's three months late. She needs to get down to DMV pronto. Okay?" The policeman nodded.

She could tell that he was flirting with her. It felt cold when people did that. It felt as if they were standing too close, and trying to peer inside her eyes. But she knew that it was what people liked. *It was the animal in them doing their mating dance, circling around, waiting for the moment to press their sweaty bodies against yours.*

She smiled. "You are just about the nicest cop I've ever met."

"You've met a few?"

Agnes nodded. "Uh-huh. I like cops."

"You ever go to dinner with them?"

She giggled. "Now you're embarrassing me. I feel like I'm trying to pick you up or something. And I'm not that kind of girl. And I'm far too old for you."

"I'm twenty-eight. You're in your thirties, right? Not much of an age difference there." He stepped closer, thrusting his hand out. "I'm Rick Hunt."

She shook his hand, delicately. She noticed the veins on his forearm. He was well-muscled. Muscles could be difficult, unless the cutting instrument had a sharp serrated edge. "Rick Hunt," she repeated. "I'm Kathy. You live around here?"

"Just the other side of the freeway."

For a moment, Agnes wondered if meeting this cop was part of her destiny. But something felt wrong about the moment. "Well, I have to shop and then get back to work. Can I call you? I don't really like to give out my number."

"I understand," the cop said. He scrawled his name and number across a ticket, and passed it over to her. "Give me a call soon, though, huh?"

She smiled. "Yes. I will."

She walked away from him, feeling more than a little nervous. He might report the car's tags to his dispatch, and Darden State might already have reported the Kuehl woman's death and the stolen vehicle.

Agnes didn't look back to see if the cop named Rick Hunt was writing anything down. She just knew that she would have to get away from this area of Riverside, California, quickly, if she was going to ever fulfill her destiny.

Inside the store, she found what she needed.

CHAPTER TWENTY-EIGHT

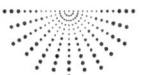

"WE COULD BE TWINS," A WOMAN SAID IN AISLE SIX.

Agnes had just picked up a box of hair coloring. She turned around.

A woman of approximately her height, with shorter blond hair was grinning at her. The woman was no more than twenty. She had brown eyes to Agnes' green. She had thinner lips. She had a mole at the lower left side of her chin. She was slightly heavier than Agnes. Southern accent. She was a talker. It was practically a disease with her.

"Don't you think? I know there are a million women in California with blond hair, but look how our faces are alike. I swear, we could be twins."

"Oh, my," Agnes laughed. Her voice melted slightly into a southern cadence. "We could, almost. Isn't that funny. And we're both from the South."

"I have a twin," the woman continued. "She lives in Memphis. We never see each other anymore. She don't look half as much like me as you."

"Oh, Lord," Agnes said. "And me from Chattanooga."

"No."

"Yes. I was only born there, though. We moved when I was three."

"Well, this is just too much…My Jerry's never gonna believe it." As the woman continued speaking in her friendly southern accent, Agnes noticed the basket in her arms. The woman was buying make-up.

"I wish I had your skin tone, though," Agnes said. "I'm old enough to be your mother."

"No," the woman said, making a gesture with her hand which seemed at first threatening to Agnes, but then she realized that it was a friendly, confidential sort of gesture. The woman was sweet, honest, sincere.

She would be easy to subdue.

"We buy the same make-up," Agnes said, nodding towards the Maybelline in the woman's hand-basket. "But I need to get a good pair of scissors. My son—he's got a school project. A lot of cutting and pasting. And I need, let's see, a map. I need one of the coast."

"Really? Taking a trip?"

Agnes nodded. "My husband and I are thinking of going to Catalina."

"*Twenty-six miles,*" the woman began singing and then lost the tune. "You never been there? Oh, you're gonna love it, honey. It's beautiful—and the history. That Cathedral Rock place with all the caves—my Jerry, he fishes sometimes with his buddies. He says you get the most fish early in the morning right out by those white cliffs."

Something in the way that the woman described the place made Agnes think it was the right place to go to.

Jack would be there, too, waiting.

Knowing.

"Let's go over the school supplies section, honey," the woman said. She grabbed Agnes by the arm, and they trotted off together. Agnes unconsciously picked up the cadence of this woman's movements: lively, syncopated, only slightly unsure. Agnes could clap out with her hands the rhythms to most people she had ever met. She could remember to the smallest detail tics and sweeps of limbs, the way a nose wrinkled at a laugh.

When they reached the appropriate shelf, the woman held up a small pair of rounded scissors. "Will these do?"

Agnes shook her head. "No. I need the sharp kind. When he's done, I can still use them for clipping coupons."

The woman laughed. "I swear we are twins. Here," she grabbed a pair of large scissors. She tore them from their cardboard backing. "This'll do you."

"Perfect, thanks." Agnes accepted the scissors, holding them with the box of hair coloring and the lip gloss.

"It is so nice to meet friendly folks in California. Everyone out here seems too rude."

"Ain't it the truth," Agnes shook her head.

Agnes made sure that she got behind the woman in the checkout line and kept talking with her about what a coincidence that both of them should be here, and both should be from Tennessee, and both should have husbands named Jerry.

Agnes told the woman that her car was parked behind the store, back by the dumpsters.

"I hate leaving my car in the sun, don't you? I practically melt in weather like this," Agnes said, practicing the woman's walk.

"Don't I know it," the woman said, slapping at the air as if fanning away mosquitoes. "But thank god there's no humidity out here. Couldn't you just about die when you think of how sweltering it was back East? Couldn't you?"

"Sure 'nough," Agnes said, slipping into a slight southern dialect.

As they rounded the dumpster area, the woman said, "You sure you parked back here, honey? Maybe you're 'round the other side."

Then, she looked back, perplexed, at Agnes.

What she saw made her gasp and she would've cried out had not her vocal cords been quickly severed with the dull edge of the scissors.

Agnes watched her hands do it, as if they needed no guidance from her.

As if what her hands were doing was natural.

Instinct.

AS THE AFTERNOON GREW LATE, Agnes parked the woman's Buick Skylark at the edge of an arroyo, out in Timoteo Canyon.

She took seventy-five dollars from the woman's purse, as well as two credit cards. She had noticed that a few miles down the road was a bus station, but she did not know where the bus might take her, or if one came through this time of day at all. Agnes might have to hitch-hike if she was to get to her destination in a timely manner. Everything was starting to work against her, she thought, after the Fates had to have brought her so far.

The woman she'd murdered had bought a Hershey's bar that day. Agnes, feeling hungry, tore into it and devoured it, feeling a little like one of the animals, herself. She would have to eat more later on.

She needed to keep her energy up.

Then, she opened the map she'd bought, folding it over until she found the island.

Santa Catalina.

She traced her finger from one side of it to the other.

She was looking for some sign from the Fates that this was the right place.

An omen that both his and her unconscious minds were working in unison.

As she traced a line from the town of Avalon south and then west, she found it.

The words: *Kirk-In-The-Rock Caverns.*

And, in parenthesis, beneath this phrase:

Capilla Blanca, 1607, Franciscan Brothers.

She didn't need to know more than rudimentary Spanish to understand what this meant.

It gladdened her heart.

The intersection of time and space.

Whitechapel.

CHAPTER TWENTY-NINE

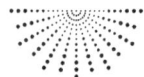

Trey Campbell kept trying to reach Darden State at the payphone down on the docks. Carly was pointing out fish near the rocks, while Mark leaned over the edge of the dock to try to see them better. Jenny sat with her legs crossed beside him. Teresa seemed a little despondent, and kept her gaze far out to sea as if nothing in her immediate surroundings was of interest.

Trey felt nothing but anxiety.

The phone line was busy for a few minutes before Trey had the operator cut in on the line.

"I need Jim Anderson," he said to the policeman on the Darden end of the phone.

After several minutes, Anderson's voice came on the line. "Who's this?"

"It's Campbell."

"We had another attack." Jim Anderson's voice was weary. He had taken some Valium, probably. The way these investigations went, all employees on the ward would be held within the institution for twenty-four hours while the police scoured every inch of the compound. "Debbie Kuehl. Hatcher did a number on her."

"Dead?"

"Yeah. She's luckier than Donna. Donna's so chopped up, even if she pulls through, she'll wish she were dead. The cops think Hatcher's in the underground."

"She's not," Trey said.

"Huh?"

"Listen, Jim. She called me. Just before four. How'd she get my number here?"

"You sure it was her?"

Trey said nothing.

"Trey, I'm the only one with your number here. She didn't get it off me, that's for sure."

"Check your pockets."

"What?"

"You have my number on you?"

A pause on the line.

"No."

"Did you leave it anywhere?"

Another pause. Jim said, "Aw, *hell.*"

Trey wanted to slam the phone against the booth. "What does that mean? She know where I am, Jim?"

"Yes."

"How in God's name did she get it?"

"Donna Howe. I gave her my number when she came on shift last night."

Trey closed his eyes. The words going through his mind were not the kind he liked to use with his wife and kids and their babysitter standing three feet away.

When he felt composed, he asked, "Why?"

"You told me to. You wanted to be on-call in case there were any emergencies. You told me that if something needed doing, you wanted to be contacted so you could get back in time and fix it."

"So you wrote the number down for Donna. At least Hatcher may not know where we are exactly."

Jim coughed.

"Please tell me you wrote the number down and handed it to Donna. Please tell me you didn't—" Trey erupted into a fit of cussing. He noticed, out of the corner of his eye, Jenny taking Mark and Teresa for a walk to the end of the dock.

Sounding as if he were about to bravely face a firing squad, Jim said, "We've just been passing it back and forth. It's not like I could've predicted that Hatcher would maul Donna and then take it."

Trey whispered into the phone, "Tell the cops she knows where I am and she's coming for me."

"Don't get all bent out of shape. She's not going to go catch the ferry to Catalina tonight."

"I know Hatcher, Jim. I know her. I'll contact the local police here. You tell the cops there that Hatcher has a vendetta with me. That she called me here. That she knows where I am."

"Don't get so bent out of shape. Rob Fallon says she's still here. Maybe she is."

"Rob Fallon is a sociopathic head-chopper. Trust me. I know Hatcher. She is going to come for me."

Jim Anderson hung the phone up on the other end.

Trey let his end dangle, as he walked over to Carly.

"I wish I smoked," he said. "I feel like doing something self-destructive."

"I guess that was bad news."

"What time does Jenny get off work?" Trey asked, waving to the babysitter and his kids.

"Another hour."

"All right. Let's not get Marky and Terry upset. You think we could pay Jenny some overtime tonight? Special circumstances."

"We can ask. Why?"

"This woman—this psychopath Agnes Hatcher—has our cottage address and phone number, and the last time I spoke with her at Darden, which is going on ten years, she told me that if she were free, she would get me. Simple as that. Now, one more question, love of my life. You mind going with me to the police station?"

CHAPTER THIRTY

THE POLICE STATION WAS SMALL. THERE WERE FOUR OFFICES, and two jail cells in back, primarily put to use over the past two decades as a drunk tank for locals who needed to sleep it off over the weekend. There was an IBM computer to each desk, and the woman who sat at the dispatch radio was not dressed in any kind of uniform. She had close-cropped red hair, and a good figure. Her name tag read: *Gloria*.

She was all business however as she logged Trey's complaint. "Okay. We've got four officers out, and two in."

She nodded to one of the glass-walled offices. A stout man with a crew-cut sat at the desk, also not in uniform. He wore a sweat-stained white short-sleeved shirt, and smoked a pipe.

"That's Oscar Arboles. You can talk to him. I'll contact the mainland and see what's up with this Hatcher woman there."

Trey turned to Carly. "If you want to hang out here, I'll talk to him alone."

"No way," she said. "I wouldn't miss this for the world."

She strode ahead of him with more confidence than he felt. He couldn't help but notice that his wife looked great, and always did in situations like this: pulled together, self-assured, a natural leader.

He tried to catch her confidence for himself as he followed her into the office.

After introductions, Oscar glanced at the blue computer screen, and then back to them. "So, you're a psych tech at Darden. My hat's off to you. And you think this woman might come here."

"Yes."

"I can't say if she's coming here or not, but she very definitely escaped. A police officer in Riverside actually spoke with her an hour ago. He radioed in a problem with this woman's car, and then when the license was traced, it was found to belong to another employee at your workplace. Deborah Kuehl."

Carly reached over and squeezed Trey's hand.

Oscar leaned across the desk, holding his pipe up. "Hope this doesn't bother either of you."

"A little," Carly said. "I seem to detect smoke at three paces."

Slightly disgruntled, Oscar tapped the pipe's smoking ashes into a wide glass ashtray beside the computer. "I just like the smell of it. So. Tell me how you play into this."

Trey took a breath, then began. "I've studied this woman for twelve years. I was her first and only friend at Darden. I thought I could rehabilitate her in a way that psychiatrists and drugs could not. I was wrong. We became close, briefly."

Oscar looked from man to wife and back. "Intimate?"

"Not like that. We just shared a lot. I felt there was a human being lurking behind the woman who, at that time, was called the Surgeon. But I was wrong. She's a machine. She fell in love with me, to some extent. And then, when I saw what she did to try to prove her love..." Trey closed his eyes, remembering. The attack on the other inmate. The old man who hit Trey hard in the face. Agnes Hatcher had known about that, and when she had the chance…"She operated on another patient," he said as matter-of-factly as he could. "Nothing fancy. Just a botched lobotomy. That was when she went back into the heavy restraints and heavy sedation. The orderlies covered her face most of the time, too. They called her the Gorgon, because of the way she looked at them. She looked at everyone as if they were bugs to be studied before they were squashed."

"Except for you," Oscar said.

Trey nodded. "With me, she felt we had a shared destiny. She couldn't understand my betrayal of her. She told me that she would find a way to wake me up to who I was inside."

"Mr. Campbell," Oscar said, leaning back in his chair. "That's not the most dangerous of threats."

Trey kept his cool, even though he wanted to explode. "I have worked with sociopaths and psychopaths and murderers and torturers since I got out of college. Agnes Hatcher isn't the same. She's a machine. She has no feelings, even for herself. All she has is a constant motion towards. Getting to me is one of her primary goals."

Oscar shrugged. "Let's assume she does come for you. There's an all points bulletin out for her arrest. Within the next hour, everyone in southern California will see her face on television. We already have an officer who saw her. We know what car she's driving. She's going to be caught. It would take her six hours at the earliest to get here. You and your family are probably safer here than anywhere else in this state. We don't have murders in Avalon. It costs too much to get here if you're just out to kill someone. This woman is already slipping up. She will be caught soon."

"Maybe I should talk with one of your colleagues instead," Trey said.

"He or she will say the same thing," Oscar said. "But don't get all twisted up about this. If you like, I can have another officer escort you home and stay with you at your cottage. Or, you might consider checking into one of our local guest-houses for the night. That way, if Agnes Hatcher manages to elude the police on the mainland and find a way out here after the last ferry has gone, and finds your rental, at least you won't be there."

"That's a terrific idea," Carly said, looking at Trey. "We can stay at the Breakers, there's a nice pool there for the kids. That way, you can get some rest tonight."

"I guess I'm over-reacting a little. That's a good idea, officer."

"Oscar. No Arboles, no officer. Oscar. So," he turned his attention to Carly, "How did you end up with a *gringo* like this?"

Carly half-smiled. "All the good ones were taken."

ON THE STREET AGAIN, Trey said, "I hate that word *gringo*."

"It's not the best one," Carly threw her arms around him. "My big baby."

Trey shrugged her off. "He was patronizing."

"And you are paranoid." Carly stopped in her tracks. "Maybe this woman is out and maybe she's dangerous, Trey, but you are on vacation. We can just check into a hotel for the night if you're that worried. I'm not. I think that crazy woman is probably out on the desert right now or up in Big Bear. Catalina is too hard to get to. Oscar's right. Maybe she could get over here tomorrow, but the chances are, they'll have caught her by tonight. Let's go pack up and get a room at the Breakers. And quit playing the victim." She stepped around him, and went out to the end of the dock.

When Trey got there, she was sitting with Teresa, braiding her hair and then unbraiding it. Mark sat at the edge of the dock, near the pylons, with Jenny, who was pointing out boats in the water.

When he saw his father, Mark leapt up and went running over to him. "We saw the funniest movie, Daddy. And I saw a shark."

Teresa corrected him. "It was a dolphin."

"It was big," Mark said.

Trey tousled his son's hair. "I'll bet it was."

"They come out of nowhere," Mark said enthusiastically, "It's really cool."

Jenny laughed, and swiveled about to face him. "They were a handful."

"We appreciate your staying the extra hour."

"Time and a half," she reminded him. She rose up, clumsily. "Mark's got a little cough. Not much of one. I don't think it means anything."

"*Hijito*," Carly said, reaching her arms out for her son. He trotted over to her. "Cough for me."

Mark smiled. He coughed twice.

"Oh, he's dying." Carly raised her eyebrows to Teresa. "Your brother's dying from too much fun."

Mark laughed, and Teresa smiled.

Trey grinned, too. It was okay. Nobody was coming after him. *Agnes Hatcher will be caught within a few hours. Or she'll hide out on the desert.*

This island is the safest place for us right now.

THIS WAS CONFIRMED after he'd walked Jenny home to her parents. Trey jogged back to the cottage, and Carly greeted him with, "Agnes Hatcher is dead."

CHAPTER THIRTY-ONE

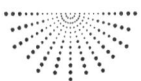

Carly had recorded one of the news broadcasts for him, as she sometimes did when he worked double shifts at home. It was habit. Oddly enough, the mayhem of the world often relaxed him.

A KCBS reporter was standing in front of an arroyo. "The body of serial killer Agnes Hatcher was found three hours after her escape from Darden State Hospital."

A photograph of Agnes Hatcher flashed on the screen.

It was an early one, from her first entry into Darden.

It was how Trey remembered her.

Then, the video switched back to the reporter. "Hatcher was found at the base of this arroyo." The video switched again to a lighted canyon, with a burning car. "She was dead on the scene. Local police told this reporter that the vehicle she was found in has not yet been traced to an owner, although it appears to be a Buick Skylark. Hatcher was notorious cop-killer of Pasadena, who, in 1981, known as The Surgeon by southern Californians…"

The reporter kept talking, and Carly said, "See? All that worry for nothing."

"She's not dead," Trey said. "Jesus. She's fooled them."

"She fooled the cops?" Carly said, somewhat bemused. "Trey, come on."

"She can't be dead. She's…"

"What," Carly said. "Smarter than that?"

"Well, damn straight."

"It almost sounds like you want her to be alive."

"Believe me, I don't. This just seems too easy."

"Or maybe it seems too real," Carly said. "Honey, you are too tied up with that place and with those patients. Watch it again. Hit rewind. Come on, just do it. Watch the news report."

TREY REPLAYED the news report three or four times before he could convince himself that Agnes Hatcher was indeed dead. "It looks like she really is dead."

"And you want to believe that she can't die," Carly whispered, slight tension in her voice.

"No, not that. She just seems human now. Now that she's dead. She didn't seem that way before. Christ. I feel terrible. And still I feel like getting plastered so I can get over terrible and get to relieved," Trey said. "My god, I can't believe I said that."

"I can. She sliced and diced, what, twelve, thirteen people in her career? You were like this when Jeffrey Dahmer died, too. Don't start feeling bad for people like that," Carly said. "I'll make the drinks."

"No, it's just that Agnes was different. She was a killer, sure. But she never really had a chance. Probably she was already something of a sociopath when she was tortured as a child. That's all it takes, though: some kind of torture. It's as if as kids they had this dark spot in their brains. Someone, usually an adult, takes the time to just step on the kid over and over until that darkness blossoms into a flower. Until it becomes the only thing they know. The only thing *she* knew. It's a mystery of life why it happens exactly like that. But it's no mystery as to where it came from."

"There are a lot of abused kids in the world who don't grow up to operate on unwilling victims," Carly said. "You had your own abuse at times when you were a kid. You haven't murdered anyone that I know of. You aren't awful to people. I don't think it's an excuse. There are a lot of kids who get stepped on, and they go on to run companies or become social workers or write novels. They don't all murder for fun."

"That's part of the mystery—why does one do that, and the other become a Gorgon? Where's the place where it happens? Maybe only reincarnation can account for that kind of personality, coming out of nowhere. Maybe it's not nature or nurture. But we know she was tortured for many years of her life. I think half of what she did was to try and make other people feel the way she felt on the inside. She just did it the wrong way."

"That's putting it mildly," Carly snorted. "Well, I'm jubilant that she's no longer of this earth, sweet psycho queen that she was. So, are we going to have wine or margaritas?"

"Maybe later," Trey said. "I have to watch this video again. To drive it into my skull that the Gorgon's destroyed."

CHAPTER THIRTY-TWO

AGNES HATCHER SAT BETWEEN THE OLD MAN AND HIS YOUNG grandson in the backseat of the station wagon. The younger man, only in his mid-thirties, who was the boy's father, drove. The wife, in the front seat, hadn't liked the idea of picking up a hitchhiker at all. But Agnes had given them gas money, and so she had proven honorable enough for the grandfather who sat beside her. It was the only car to pick her up in forty minutes. "All the way to Los Angeles?" The driver asked.

"Yes," she smiled. "My boyfriend Pete's meeting me. We're going to see *Miss Saigon*. I really appreciate the ride. If my stupid clunker of a Nissan hadn't broken down, I wouldn't've had to bother you. I hate the idea of hitchhiking. Haven't done it since I was nineteen."

"No bother," said the husband in the front seat. "The holy spirit told us it was okay to give you a ride. We're going to a revival downtown."

"Really?" She said.

The wife eyed her in the car mirror. "Have you met Jesus yet?"

"Oh, I think so," Agnes said. "Many times." She turned to the blond boy beside her. "What's your name?"

He looked up at her with weary eyes. "Timmy."

"You're a very well behaved young man," she said.

The grandfather tried to touch her knee, but she pulled away from him.

"Jesus is our savior," the husband said. "Let me tell you a little about him."

Agnes Hatcher closed her eyes and wished that they would go away. It would be a few hours until she got downtown, and then another hour to San Pedro. When she would arrive there, she'd finally dye her hair and change her look. She was exhausted. An hour or two of rest wouldn't hurt. Perhaps she could sleep while these animals in the station wagon droned on about their religion. She had a fantasy about slicing each one of their throats, but there were too many of them together. After all, she needed the ride. She had followed her inner voice, the one that led her hands to slice the nice Southern woman back by the dumpsters at Wal-Mart, the one that told her to use the nice Southern woman's body as her own decoy. The voice that guided her without words, just the vibrations of the universe. It had all been promised her from the past life, he had told her: *"With these lives, with this blood, we consecrate our own eternity together."*

The voice had led her to the arroyo, led her to stuff the oily rag into the Buick Skylark (the oily rags in the oven, surrounding her beloved memory threatened). Led her to burn the woman's body, the seats of the car, the slow smoldering fire that caught.

Then, using the natural leverage of the slight rise in the arroyo, she pushed the Buick, ever so gently, and it rolled, burning down further into the wasteland.

The voice within her let it be known that this would make the others leave her alone.

Let her follow the trail of instinct to her most beloved goal.

The voice had died down when she'd had to accept the ride. She had stood at the bus stop for fifteen minutes when the car had pulled up to her. It was Fate, she could tell. And with these Jesus sellers all around her, driving her to Los Angeles, she wished the voice and instinct would guide her hands to stop up their mouths permanently.

But it was silent in her head.

She had no choice but to play sweet and kind and compassionate.

Next time, she intended to take the bus.

CHAPTER THIRTY-THREE

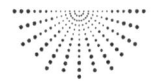

AT THE COTTAGE, MARK WAS DETERMINED TO OVERCOME HIS fear.

He slipped out of his flip-flops and went out to the patio. His mother was inside, teaching Teresa some guitar chords—Teresa played the piano a little, but was new to guitar. His mother had been taught classical guitar when she'd been a girl, but she was teaching Teresa some basic stuff like "Puff, The Magic Dragon." Mark considered that "girl's time" between the two of them. So now, he figured it was "boy's time" between him and his father. He stood a few feet back from the edge of the pool, and then turned around.

"Daddy?"

"Marky? What's up?" Trey was sitting in one of the lounge chairs nearby, watching the night.

The last gasp of day, almost an aura of pale lavender light, played about the edges of the undulate hills that rose behind the cottage. The scents of honeysuckle and jasmine wafted on a light breeze. Night was like a cloud, pushed from the east, towards the hills. It was so close to being dark, that it felt like it was past Mark's bedtime. Only his parents were letting him stay up later than usual because it was a vacation. His father seemed lost in thought. Mark felt his father worried too much about things.

Mark shifted his balance from one leg to another, nervously. "Will you help me?"

Trey sat up in his chair. He leaned forward. He was a tall man, so when he leaned like that, he seemed to stretch and almost reach where Mark was standing. "With what?"

"I want to dive."

"Now? It's getting late. How about tomorrow morning?"

"Well," Mark said, slipping his T-shirt over his head. "You always say 'Better late than never'."

Trey chuckled. "That's true."

"I've been thinking how I've been a fraidy cat. And it's dumb. It's dumb because Teresa can dive. I'm just scared when I look in the water and see me staring back. But with the lights out, I don't see me in the water. It's just water."

"You sound too logical for your age," Trey said, mussing up his son's thick, dark hair. "Okay. I'll get on the edge with you." Trey unbuttoned his shirt, tossing it on the chair as he rose. He unbuttoned and unzipped his pants, stepping out of them. He wore blue boxer shorts. Mark laughed out loud and pointed at them when he saw them.

"That's not your swim suit," Mark's eyes went wide. "It's your wonderwear."

"Them's my swimmin' trunks now. Okay, what you do is..." Trey went to the edge of the pool, leading Mark by the hand. He leaned forward, his arms all the way forward, too, palms flat. "Pretend you're like a dolphin. Push with your feet, press with your hands."

Mark imitated his father's position beside him. "I'll fall."

Trey said, "You won't. You'll dive. And you know how to swim, so once you're in, you just swim. Let's both go at the count of three. Okay?"

Mark nodded, but felt uncertain. He leaned forward and closed his eyes so he wouldn't have to see how far the water was from him.

Trey counted to three, and Mark pushed with his feet and pressed with his hands. He did a belly flop, and sank down into the water. His stomach burned, and it was so black around him, he didn't know which way to turn.

He swallowed water, and thrashed around, until finally his father grabbed him around the waist and brought him up.

"Marky, Marky, it's okay, it's me, are you all right?" Trey said, lifting him up to the side of the pool.

Mark coughed. He was crying, and felt like a baby. "I can't do it right," he said. "I get too scared."

Trey hefted himself up the side of the pool, and out of it. He went to get a towel. He brought a big striped one back and wrapped it around his son. "You did fine," he said, sitting down beside him on the concrete. "Let me tell you a little trick I do to get through difficult things."

Mark leaned his head into his father's chest. "What's that?"

"I use the 'As If' rule. The 'As If' rule states that if I don't know how to do something, I act as if I do, and then it works."

"Like pretending?"

"Kind of. But it works because it's not quite pretend. It's something that our minds have within us already. It's already in your body and brain to dive, Mark. You're half fish as it is. Look how well you swim."

"Yeah. But I can't dive."

"But act as if you can. Nobody can do anything until they work at it. But if you never try it, you'll never do it. Sometimes I do things I didn't think I could until I think of the 'As If' rule."

"So I'm supposed to act 'As If' I can dive? But what if I crack my head open?"

Trey grinned, rubbing his shoulders with the towel. "Then you act 'As If' you meant to do that. Want to try again?"

"Really?" Mark asked. "I'm almost dry. Won't Mom get mad?"

"I don't think so. Not if you're learning something new. Here," Trey pulled the towel off, and stood up, holding his hand out. "If we keep trying 'til you get it, you won't be afraid tomorrow and you can show off."

Mark took his father's hand. "I might still be afraid."

"Oh, yeah. I'm afraid sometimes when I dive, too. But fear is there to help protect you, so you'll think about how to do it safely. Let's give it one more try." He took his son over to the pool's edge.

" 'As If'," Mark said, leaning forward towards the dark water.

" 'As If'," his father repeated.

"Are you afraid of anything, Daddy?" Mark asked, solemnly.

"Everyone's afraid of something, Marky. We have to overcome fear to face whatever it is that we're running from. We have to live as if we're brave."

This time, Mark did a good dive, and came up, dog-paddling towards the pool ladder.

"Know what?" He asked his father.

"What?"

"I don't have to be afraid of nothing no more."

"That's right. Not grammatical, but still correct."

"Know what else?"

Trey shook his head.

Mark climbed up the ladder to the concrete. Then he leapt over the edge, cannonballing, making a huge splash when he landed. When he came up giggling and sputtering, he cried out gleefully, "That's what!"

CHAPTER THIRTY-FOUR

THE WOMAN WITH THE NEATLY TRIMMED REDDISH BROWN hair, wearing jeans and a light blue cotton sweater, glanced around the oyster bar. This was the sixth dive she'd entered along the waterfront that evening. It stank of fish and even urine, from the open men's room door.

It was only eight p.m., but already the place was packed, wall-to-wall with people drinking beer or devouring oysters and shrimp. The place was filthy, although the management had tried to cover this up with sawdust on the floor and dim lighting all around the bar and tables.

It reminded her so much of her past, of the very reason she was here.

In an ordinary saloon, or restaurant, no one would look twice at this woman. Her hair was an obvious over-the-counter dye job. Her eyes were pretty, but small. Her face was pale, as if she hadn't been in the sun in years. Her lips, thickened with glossy lipstick, were curved nicely. She would be considered moderately attractive in another setting.

But in the particular bar, near the harbor, she might be the most ravishingly beautiful woman in all creation.

There were seven men sitting at the bar itself, and when she entered the bar area, four of them turned to look at her. The others slowly turned, also, when they noticed their compadres doing so. She tried to read them, but it was difficult with the noise from the jukebox, and all the talking. She had been to three other such bars already, and was exhausted. It took a lot out of her to get a good reading of someone, particularly in this sort of environment.

One of the men winked at her. He was twenty two or three. Five o'clock shadow. Dark, thick hair. Brown eyes. Well built, but short. His eyes stayed on hers the longest. She counted the seconds until he looked away. Then, he glanced back again.

Boldly, she walked over to stand by him.

"Hi," he said. His breath was spit and beer. He was horny. That was enough.

"You'll do," she said.

"Huh?"

"You got a boat?"

He nodded. "Sure. Me and a hundred guys down here. Why? You into boats?"

She felt chilly, and was afraid for a moment that someone else was watching her. Someone who was threatening in some way. She felt that way whenever one of her own species was nearby. She could feel whoever was watching her just as if they were touching her face. She didn't particularly like that feeling. It passed, however, and she returned her attention to the man on the bar stool.

"Yeah," she said. "I really get into boats."

She turned slightly to the right, but could not tell where the threat was coming from.

When the dark-haired man ordered her a beer, she knew.

It was the bartender. *One of us.*

A former surfer boy. Blond, six foot, well-muscled, pre-melanoma. His hair was cut short and flat on top, long and stringy on the sides. He was not handsome at all, except for the athleticism of his body. He had pale blue eyes. Crow's feet about their edges. He was still, the way an animal being hunted was still. The bartender glanced at her, and she knew that he was one of her kind. He was reading her as much as she was reading him.

They didn't have to say anything.

When he went down to the far end of the bar, she followed him.

"Do you have a boat?" she asked.

He nodded. He kept his hands in the pockets of his yellow shorts. She assessed from his bad posture that he was weary. He had possibly been doing speed for a couple of days. He would need to wind down. He said, "I can get a sailboat. Do I know you from somewhere?" His voice was raspy, as if he'd spent years raking it with razors.

"I don't think so. I need a boat with a motor. It doesn't have to be very powerful. Can you help me?"

"Sure. They call me the Cobra." He thrust his hand out to shake hers.

She didn't return the gesture.

That was all it took. His shift was off by midnight.

Off-shift, he wore a Hawaiian shirt that was blue with blotchy yellow flowers over the black muscle shirt he'd worn at the bar. He kissed her as soon as she stepped up to him outside. His kiss was dry. He smelled like whiskey and *Old Spice* after-shave.

She stepped back, away from his kiss.

"I thought you liked me," Cobra said.

"I do. Not like that."

"Okay, whatever."

"The boat?"

Cobra cursed under his breath. He walked ahead of her, then stopped and half turned. A nearby streetlight cast a pale glow around his form, like a halo. "I swear we met before."

"Maybe," she said. "Do you believe in past lives?"

He answered her with a laugh. "My VW's around the corner. I can take you to my buddy's boat. Where you headed?"

"Catalina," she said. She stood beside him, and watched the darkness as if she expected something to attack her. Yet she did not seem afraid. Just wary.

"Tell me another one." He smiled good-naturedly as she caught up with him.

"All right," she said. "If you won't take me there, I'll find someone else. There's always someone else. But I can give you something you've never had in life before."

"Yeah? What's that?"

"Fulfillment."

Then she reached up to his face, holding it in the palm of her hand. She knew what the animals wanted. *I will train you, dog, and you will understand your place in life. I will lead you to where you need to go.*

She kissed him, and held him there for several moments.

"I thought you didn't want that," he whispered.

"Now I do," she said, feeling her eyes glazing over. Feeling her *mind* glazing over, too. "In this alley. Against this wall."

She pulled the sweater over her shoulders and head. She leaned back against the cold bricks. She moved out of her body, to a vantage point above them, as if she was not the woman below at all.

She watched the animals bite and kiss and explore each other's bodies.

Then, the lightning of time and space struck her, and its flash erased all memory of the present life.

OCTOBER WAS *a month of rain that year. A constant beating against the roof far above, and leaking down into the crawlspace where she slept.*

She slept too much, but she was too weary afterwards, after what she and her lover did, to do anything else. She awoke when a rat scurried across her leg.

She crawled down to the opening, into the coal storage room.

He was beating at the door again.

Beating so hard, she thought he would break it down, or call attention to their nest.

She couldn't let anyone else know about their nest or it would be all over.

She was sure that even her neighbors, if they knew what she did there with him, would set them both on fire inside it.

She glanced at the great oven, with its twin doors. Remembering a childhood fairy tale of a witch being thrust inside it by evil little children. Of being baked alive by evil children.

All children were evil.

She didn't like to think of the times she'd had to sleep in that oven with her lover, doors shut. Just to keep from being discovered, mashed in together, as if they were one person and not two. Hearing the hounds and the whistles as the coal basement was searched. Feeling his hands about her…Thinking of the children lighting the fire in the oven, laughing as the witch burned.

She hoped that he would take her away from here, as he'd promised.

She prayed that they could use the lifetimes they'd collected to fly away.

He was, after all, a gentleman. And she would be his lady

She stooped down, pushing open the small door. He was there. He grabbed her, dragging her into the night. His kisses were like poison, for she felt herself die with each one.

He cupped his hands against her breasts, squeezing gently, then more harshly. The gaslight was dimmed in the fog and drizzle, and she could hear the clatter of horses as the carriages went by on the street. She smelled garbage and sewer run-off. Rats squealed at the doorway to her left. She had never been so cold and so hot at the same time.

She felt her blood burning within her, and she wrapped her legs around his waist.

He had the most beautiful face she had ever seen. It was like a pagan god, wild and ravishing and golden.

"Do it," she moaned. "Do it."

He took the small scalpel and touched it against her breastbone.

She met the cold metal, and pressed herself against it.

The blood was warm, and he brought his face down to it, tasting it.

He kissed her lips, passing her blood back to her.

Rain began to fall, and she heard the others, in the alleys, among the tenements, their cries of lust, their tender moans.

Lightning cut across her vision.

"YOU A VAMPIRE OR SOMETHING?" Cobra asked. He touched the side of his neck, and examined the blood on his fingers. "I dig vampires. I tasted blood sometimes. That was some love bite you gave me."

Agnes Hatcher's eyes came back into focus.

She was in the wrong skin. It was the wrong place. She wanted to be back there, back with her beloved, back with the only man who truly understood her.

She wept for all she had lost over her lifetimes. Cobra held her tight.

His friend's boat was small, just a sloop with a nine-horsepower engine. It had a single cabin, with two narrow sleeping bunks, and a hot plate and bathroom. They kept the sail tied to the mast, and used the motor.

Agnes Hatcher fell asleep in the cabin. When she awoke, it was still not morning.

The boat was docking on the island.

She felt his power, his pull. *Jack. Beloved.*

Cobra wanted to fall asleep, but he was too keyed up. He told her how much he loved her. He confessed his crimes: the stolen things and the murdered people. He murdered like a child, from a quick temper. He loved like a child, too.

"Do you love me?" he asked.

"No," she said, truthfully. "But I knew all about you when I saw you. I knew what you had done."

"I saw it in you, too," he said, nodding off to sleep. Agnes knelt beside him and watched the dreams come to his closed eyes. Then, she went up on the small deck and waited in darkness.

The threat of memory enveloped her, not her beloved, but the man from her childhood:

The man tying her to the chair, carving into her skin with the wood-burning iron. Teaching her about the life they had been a part of. Teaching her about how he had been there, had witnessed what she and her lover had done in the previous existence, and he had taken her in order to punish her for what she had done.

After days of the torture, the memories of the past life had come so strong and vividly that she could not see the present world for the past one.

The past life exploded across her vision: She was nineteen, and living on the streets of London, occasionally sleeping in the great sweat-shop basements, which were warm at night, even though the machines clattered all through the dark hours. She had been forced into the life at twelve, by her mother, and did not enjoy any man's touch, no matter how much he paid.

Then, one night, she met the gentleman surgeon. He promised her more than money. He promised her immortality.

"Each life we take," he whispered into her ear as he made love to her, "we gain another. The ancients knew this. That was their reason for human sacrifice. I have taken several lives. If you will believe in me, I will never abandon you."

She had delighted when her lover scarred her, or drank a drop of blood from the tip of her finger. He had a hunger to consume life in every way. He taught her how to use the surgery tools, how to peel flesh back so as not to traumatize it.

They took the other girls, together. She held Mary Kelly's head down while her lover operated. She watched the terror of their victims' faces, and finally, the love, too, for in suffering these whores achieved a great beauty. She watched for the police, or she sat in the carriage, waiting for him to run out swiftly so they could drive off.

Her life was never the same afterwards. It was full of gorgeous moments, of the taste of blood, of the understanding that the immortal soul was in the body itself, in the part of the body which was most important to its owner. Sometimes, their victims lived in their hearts, and sometimes in their genitals and sometimes in their brains.

And always, afterwards, he brought the scalpel to her, to taste. He would combine their bloods: their victim's blood, and then hers, and then his.

Communion for eternity.

She took the scalpel from his hands. She pressed it lightly against the thick skin of his collar.

His eyes burned with excitement. She could tell that he was aroused in a way that he had never been before.

She brought her face to his and kissed him as a man kisses a woman, hard and deep and conquering.

"We are the gods," he said, after the kiss.

That was the day of the hounds.

That was the day of the Coppers with their shouts and fury.

That was the day of betrayal.

That was the day she opened the locket which was pinned inside his cloak.

AS THE SUN ROSE, slowly, from the east, behind her, she saw its first purple-pink rays slash the island.

There it was: the place of her dreams. Not the squalor of a district of an ancient city, but the reincarnation of that place in their new time, their new skins. It was sacred to her, now, this island.

This island was the place where time and space would meet.

The great spires of rock, ending in needle-like formation. The several mouths of caves, stacked on top of each other. The bottom, an opening into its depths. The magnificence of it in the early sunlight, where its white chalk seemed to glow against the rest of the island. It rose like the gothic cathedral of nature.

The sacred home of the Fates.

Capilla Blanca.

CHAPTER THIRTY-FIVE

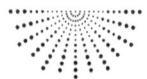

IT WAS ON THE MORNING NEWS, BUT TREY AND CARLY BOTH
slept late the next day, so they missed the news item.

The woman in the canyon was finally identified as Mary Beth
Clark, born in Tennessee, a resident of San Bernardino County for
the past eight years. Although much of her body was burned, it was
the eye color which caused the discrepancy with Agnes Hatcher.
Eventually Mary Beth's husband, Jerry, contacted the police about
his wife, and all of it was traced back to the Wal-Mart in Riverside.

Trey Campbell awoke at nine-thirty, innocent of this correction
in the news. He was feeling like he had the biggest hangover of his
life.

CHAPTER THIRTY-SIX

WHICH TREY DID, BECAUSE WHEN HE AND HIS FAMILY HAD gotten back home the previous evening, and after Marky's now-famous perfect dive in the pool—and after the kids stayed up to watch *The Little Mermaid* yet again—he'd made a couple of killer margaritas. Heavy on the Cuervo Gold. Light on the sweet and sour. Crushed ice. *Heaven.*

And had drunk them both because Carly wanted a glass of wine instead.

They'd stayed up until two watching bad late movies. Then he'd begun reading *The Three Musketeers*, which Carly had brought. He couldn't put it down until about three fifteen. He fell asleep on the couch, and when he awoke, it was because Mark was spritzing him with water.

"What the—" he gasped, wiping at his face with his hands.

Mark was giggling. Already in his swimsuit and wet, he held the plant spritzer up and sprayed a few more times. "It's only water!" Mark began dancing around, until he dropped to the carpet, exhausted.

Carly was out on the porch sipping coffee; Teresa was taking a shower.

"We already went swimming, Daddy. I dived six times. Just like a dolphin. Now get up," Mark said with some authority in his voice.

"Look, fish-boy, Daddy's feeling a little creaky today." Trey slowly rose, tasting the after-effects of the margaritas mixed with morning breath. He stumbled to the bathroom and shuddered when he saw what seemed to him an old man staring back at him. After his shower, he felt like going right back to sleep.

But Carly had an idea.

"Oh, no, nothing special today, please," he groaned.

"Just listen. We'll call Jenny and cancel today and take the kids horseback riding. Won't that be fun?"

Mark cried out, "Yeah!"

"I'm an old man, sweetheart. My ticker ain't so good," Trey faked a limp and hunchback.

"It'll be fun."

"Okay, okay, but let's not cancel on Jenny. Mark's too young to go on a horse."

"I am not!" He protested.

"Are, too. Nobody in their right mind is going to rent a horse to a kid your size, trust me."

"Discrimination," Mark said, and the word seemed too big for his mouth.

Trey looked at Carly. That would be a word that he'd heard her say. "It's because you can get hurt on a horse. Until you've had lessons…" The worst thing about telling his son this, was that Trey knew that he sounded just like his own father. He had always hoped he'd grow up to be a more liberal, easy-going dad, but it just never happened.

"Terry hasn't had lessons," Mark said.

Teresa appeared at the patio doorway. She dripped water from head-to-toe onto the stone walkway. "I don't want to ride horses. They're filthy."

"What?" Trey said. "Every girl likes horses."

"Not me. Why can't I stay here and swim?"

Carly sighed, clapping her hands together. "Okay, okay. Your father and I will go riding, and you guys hang out here. You're sure you want to do that?"

Teresa nodded, and padded back to the swimming pool. A loud splash in the water signified her approval of this plan.

Carly ran out to the pool, shouting, "But you are not to go swimming without Jenny watching you. Get out of there right now."

Mark looked cross. He eyed his father like he was the enemy. "I don't wanna."

"What can I do to make you happy?" Trey asked.

Mark furrowed his brow. "Take me riding."

"No can do. What else?"

"I don't care." Mark, who moments before had been in a good mood, got up off the floor and stomped off to his bedroom.

"You knew he couldn't go riding," Trey said after Carly came back inside.

Carly crossed her arms. "Don't jump on me just because you're tense. Why don't we just do separate things today? You go do what you want, which I'm assuming is 'get wound up,' and I'll go horseback riding."

"I'll go, I'll go," Trey rolled his eyes. "I didn't mean for this to become a production. I'm not jumping on you. Okay?"

"All right. And it'll be fun. You wait and see," she said.

The one piece of advice his father had given him that seemed to work in his marriage, the only decent piece of marital advice the old man had ever conferred upon him was: "Remember, son, the wife is always right. You remember that and you'll have many happy years ahead of you." It seemed like the code of the troglodyte to believe that, but Trey had found that it worked. When he and Carly got in a jam, he generally gave in and told her she was right. Things often worked out from there.

Jenny arrived at ten thirty, looking like she'd just come from working in a garage, which was not her normal look. "I forgot to wash my clothes," she said by way of explanation. "These were the only things even approaching clean in my dresser." She twirled around in the dungarees and bleach-spotted blue chambray work shirt.

"Like we care," Trey said, cavalierly.

Jenny's face lit up when she heard about the horseback riding. "Oh, god, it's so great. If you can get Elmer to let you off the trail with his old nags, you can ride out to the beach around the coast. It's so pretty. Just make sure you go to Elmer's. Tell him I sent you. God, I wish I was going."

"Thanks for the advice," Carly said, bringing Jenny's traditional morning cup of tea to her from the kitchen. "Sorry you can't. It's just that the kids…"

"I know, I know. Kids are always falling off horses around here. It's amazing to me that some parents let them ride at all. I've been riding since I was ten, but I took lessons the whole time," Jenny explained to Mark, who sat right next to her. Trey could tell that Mark had a crush on the babysitter, and would probably cry when he had to leave her at the end of the week. Jenny turned to face Mark and pinched his cheeks. "Hello you cutie pie. What do you want to get up to today?"

Mark's face went from fascination to disapproval. "I want to go riding."

"We can go hiking," Jenny said. "You like that?"

"Maybe. If I was on a horse."

"Well," Jenny winked at Carly, "we'll pretend."

OUTSIDE, Carly grabbed Trey's arm. "Jenny has a major crush on you."

"Naw."

"When you were outside with Terry, she told me she thought I was the luckiest woman on the face of the earth."

"You're kidding."

"No. Really." Carly leaned against his shoulder like a schoolgirl. " Of course, I set her straight."

OF ALL THE horses in the stables, Trey was given the one nicknamed "Assassin." And there was a good reason for it. It kicked several times just being brought out from the stables. He had a time just getting the saddle strapped on tight so it wouldn't slip off out on the trail.

"Why is it you get the horse named 'Dorothy,' and I get 'Assassin'?" He said, as he tried for the third time to get the saddle on the large dappled mare.

Carly grinned. "You can handle her."

"I haven't ridden for six years. She's tried to bite me twice already. My rear end is going to be burning soon from the friction, and she'll probably drag me in the dust for several miles. Come on," he groaned, finally getting the horse to breath in long enough to strap the saddle on sufficiently tight. He grabbed the horn, slipped his right foot into the stirrup and raised himself up to the saddle. "Just stay still for about a minute, okay?" Trey started giggling like a kid.

"What's so funny?" Carly asked, her back straight as she trotted her mare up to his.

"I was wondering what she's called for short: Ass?"

"Get your mind out of the gutter. Call her Sassy."

"That's cute. Sassy. Hey, Sass, ya wanna gallop?"

"Trey, no, no," Carly said.

But it was too late. Sassy was galloping across the sloping hill, and, in turn, Carly's horse started up, too, even though its rider kept calling out, "Whoa, whoa, slow down."

It became one of the best days that Trey could remember, between his horse trying to bite him even while he was astride, and the riding across the beach, at the water's edge. More than loving Carly, he liked her like he had never liked anyone before. He thought: *It's nice to be married to your best friend.*

Trey thought such warm, loving thoughts right up until the time Assassin threw him into the waves, and between the fear of breaking his back and the fear of drowning, he cursed his sorry fate.

Carly rescued him in due course, and he spat sea water out of the side of his mouth. "No bones broken," she said.

He sat in his wet clothes in the surf and watched the mare take off on its own down the beach. "Great," he said, "Now I'm going to have to chase down that damn horse."

CHAPTER THIRTY-SEVEN

JENNY WAS DOING SOMETHING VERY BAD, MARK WAS SURE.

He knew that even though she was a lot older than he was, she shouldn't be pouring the wine from the fridge into a glass for herself. But he said nothing.

He had just finished lunch, and Teresa was out by the pool, taking a nap in the sun. Mark was bored, and even though Jenny had told him to stay outside because she'd be right out, he had come back in.

"What's wrong?" Jenny asked as she sipped from the glass.

"Huh?"

"You're looking at me funny, Marky. What's up?" Jenny wore what Mark would call a phony grin. It was the smile he usually had when he lied to his parents (and was caught, as usual).

"I know what you're doing," Mark said, slowly. "And you're not supposed to."

"This?" She held up the glass full of wine as if it were a soda. "Oh, we grown ups are allowed. I already asked your Mom."

This threw him. If she had asked his mother's permission, than it must've been all right. He didn't pursue the subject further. She got sillier as she drank the wine, and picked up the phone and spent half the day yakking it up with her friends.

Between calls, he said to her, "I liked you."

"I like you, too." Her words slurred together.

"I mean I used to like you." He wrinkled his nose up, his eyes squinting. "I don't think you're very nice."

"Marky, Marky. I know you don't mean that." She leaned over to give him a hug, but he pulled away from her.

"I do too." He crossed his arms on his chest.

"You're still mad because you didn't get to go horseback riding."

"Am not. I don't care about dirty old horses. I'm telling my parents."

"You'd do that to me?" She took another sip of wine. The phony grin had disappeared. She looked like she was about to pout.

"Yeah. I would," he nodded. "You're being bad."

"Well," the tone of her voice changed dramatically into a nasty, low tone like a cat that was about to scratch. "How would you like it if I made up stories about you and told them? Who do you think they'd believe?"

"That's mean. To make up stories."

"You'd do it to me," she said.

"I'd tell the truth."

"Listen," Jenny said flipping her hair back behind her shoulders. "You're too young to understand these things. If you want, tell your parents. But that means they'll get a really nasty babysitter. Ugly and big and mean. There are only two of us on Catalina."

Mark considered this for a moment.

Jenny picked the phone up again and tapped in a number.

Mark got off the couch and wandered back outside. He stood over Teresa, who was sleeping on her stomach in her one-piece with ruffles at the edges.

After a minute, she woke up. "You're dripping on me," she said.

"I don't like Jenny."

"Me, neither. That's why I didn't want to go anywhere."

"Mom and Dad like her."

"That's because she fakes everything around them, like she's Miss Perfect. I can see right through her. If they knew why she wanted to take us to the movies…"

"Yeah," Mark said, remembering the boy that Jenny had met there, and how they had sucked face through all of *Pocahontas*. Although, it had been something of an education for him. He was curious as to why her boyfriend had kept sticking his tongue in her mouth. Mark had found it disgusting to watch. He squatted down on the concrete beside his sister. "We should run away."

"*Not*," she replied sarcastically. "Besides, where would we go?"

Mark shrugged. "I have five dollars."

"How'd you get five bucks?"

"I been saving," he said smugly. "Every week, fifty cents for cleaning out the cat box and feeding the fish."

"You save your allowance? Mine's gone before I get it. You've saved that money for ten weeks?"

Mark nodded.

"Five bucks can buy us ice cream," Teresa said, sitting up, doing a quick mental calculation. "And we can get some corn dogs. You wanna?"

"Huh?"

"Run away. Not very far. We can get some supplies with your money and then hide out in town. If we see her, we can just duck around the corner. Then, when Mom and Dad come back home, we can show up and tell them all the nasty stuff she does."

"I don't want to be a squealer."

"Okay, I'll do the squealing."

"But the only other babysitter's big and ugly."

"So what? You expect Mary Poppins? I just don't like Jenny. I thought you were in love with her, though, so I kept my mouth shut."

Mark sighed. "I was. I thought she was nice. But she's naughty."

Teresa got up. "Let's go. But we have to be sneaky about it. We don't want 'the witch' figuring it all out and stopping us."

As THEY SNUCK out the back gate, Mark heard Jenny on the phone.

"Tommy?" She said. "Sure. Yeah. No, really. I got the whole place to myself. Come on over. Hey, how often does a chance like this come around? No, no, they're real little. I'll pop *The Lion King* on the video player and shove some cookies in front of them. Really private. Yeah. Just you and me and a choice of bedrooms."

CHAPTER THIRTY-EIGHT

"LET'S EXPLORE," CARLY SAID, PULLING AT TREY'S HAND.

They had managed to catch the errant horse, and now both animals were tethered to some scraggly trees off the riding path. The road from Avalon was below them, but it was cut-off near the high rocks because of a mudslide that still had not been completely cleared from the unusually heavy rains of the late spring. Half the hillside there was difficult to navigate because of the way the rocks had fallen.

Trey glanced up the side of the hill. "All the way up there?" He turned and caught a glimpse of one edge of Avalon. They had come around the island far enough to barely see anything but the tip of the town.

"Sure," his wife said, letting go of him and running up the thin trail ahead. It lead to the caverns which tunneled back to the sea. He had hiked this area with his father when he'd been twelve and thirteen, on vacation then. Carly stopped half way up the hillside to read the sign. "The Kirk-In-The-Rocks," she said. " 'Where the Spanish monks lived in solitude from 1605-1620. It became known

Capilla Blanca, for the white chalk cliffs on the ocean side. Enter at own risk.' You want to risk it?"

Carly led the way, weaving between boulders and brush, until she came to the mouth of the cavern. A large chain-link fence had been erected there. "I guess there's no risk involved here. Wish we could get in. Smell that? It's bat *guano*."

He leaned against the fence. "My dad and I used to come up here. He knew all the trails through this. There's a carved out room where the monks slept. He used to take me there and tell me ghost stories."

"Nice nightmare material."

He laughed. "They were more funny than scary. He was a complex man. He drank. He could be a bully when it came to getting his own way." Trey's voice seemed to die down like a sudden gust of wind that was over. Quietly, he said, "But he was a good father in other ways." Then, he brightened, as if the good memories were coming back. He spread his hands out as if creating a canvas for his memories. "He could be amazing, too. He told great stories. He was cheap—really cheap. When I was in college, he sold all my old furniture from home. I came back the first summer, and I didn't even have a bed." He could smile at these memories now, from the distance of years. Suddenly, another memory hit him. One he didn't savor. He remembered the old man at the kitchen door of the San Bernardino house.

Trying to break in.

The gun firing.

The look on the man's face, the gray hair, the shabby clothes.

"I wish I had never killed that man." Trey went and glanced through the fence, down into the chasms and paths of the cavern.

Carly leaned against the chain-link fence. "It was an accident. Of course, you wished you didn't. He was trying to break in. We had three break ins in that house. I'm sorry he died, too. But it wasn't your fault. Get over it."

Trey shook his head. "I don't think I can. If only I hadn't bought that gun. I was just too paranoid."

"I know you were. With good reason. That inmate, what was his name? The one who had escaped. Watson?"

"Wilson," Trey sighed. "Just like Agnes Hatcher. I assumed he would come for me. I assumed I would be his target. I guess I was wrong on both counts."

"It's a moot point in Hatcher's case, now that she died in the crash." Carly went over, slipping her left hand across the back of his neck. It felt cool where she touched him. "It's okay, Trey. It'll all be okay."

He barely heard her voice. "Looking at that old man, lying there, dying. Dead. It was like watching my father die all over again, only I pulled the trigger."

A silent moment passed between them. He felt the cool of the shade from the nearby rocks and trees. He smelled the fresh salt of the sea below them. The soothing heat that rose, incongruously, from Carly's cooling hand at the back of his neck.

"When we get back, I want you to go to a counselor to deal with this," Carly said, gently. "I love you, I love our life together, but you have obsessed on this long enough. Between this and your job, part of you is numb. I don't want my children growing up with a father who's numb in that part."

"What part is that?"

Carly took a deep breath. "The part about forgiveness. Of even yourself. Now," she said, turning so that he couldn't see her tears, "Tell me the legends of the bat-cave."

He began to recount for her tales of the passages around the cavern, the stories which his father had told him, the lives of the order of monks which lived in silence among these chalk walls. He told her that he knew most of the trails, because his father had led him through each one, showed him the Great Room, where the monks had created their small chapel. "The statue of the Virgin Mary was in one of the recesses in the room, and it was long gone, but they'd painted the walls like a chapel, with the stages of the cross and angels and all kinds of things on white. It was really beautiful. It's too bad you can't go in there anymore. I guess graffiti taggers might ruin it."

Carly sighed. "I wish we could see it. Don't you think we could sort of break in somewhere? If you know all the trails, there must be another entrance."

"That might not be too smart," he said. "Some of those trails weren't even very sturdy when I was a kid. And there're these big drops, like wells, down hundreds of feet. Besides which, I don't think it would be a really good example to our kids if we were caught breaking in, do you?"

"Oh, it'll give them something to remember us by for years to come." She grabbed his hand, tugging. "Come on, we don't have to go in too far. Just a little ways."

CHAPTER THIRTY-NINE

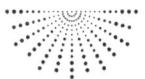

"Who are you?" Cobra asked.

"I'm you."

"Me? I don't get it."

"I know what you hunger for."

"You mean, what I done before? The killing?"

"More than that. The pleasure in it," she said.

Cobra and Agnes Hatcher had spent their morning washing up at the beach showers. Cobra sunned on the beach while she walked among the shops, hoping to catch a glimpse of a familiar face. She brought him a lunch of hamburgers and French fries. She ate nothing. Her hunger was not for food.

By the time Trey and Carly were riding, she was asking a local realtor about rental cottages. She was shown several photographs, and given directions if she wanted to walk around the town by herself and look at them.

About the time Agnes found the exact location of the cottage she was interested in, which would be available the following week, Trey was thrown from his horse two miles away.

When she and her newfound friend trudged up the road to the cottage, it was late afternoon.

CHAPTER FORTY

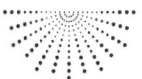

"IT'S NOT DARK AT ALL," CARLY SAID, LEANING AGAINST THE cavern wall. A shaft of afternoon sunlight cut from above and to the side. It lit most of the craggy rocks, and they could see all the way over to where the white chalk walls, which were smooth, began. They had climbed around part of the bent chain-link fence, obviously where local kids had been doing it for years. The cave was silent, except for the sound of waves crashing against its rocks, far below.

"I'm telling you, we shouldn't be doing this," Trey said. In spite of his own warnings, he was leading, every now and then reaching back to touch Carly's hand to make sure she was staying balanced. The trail was not particularly narrow at this point, but at its outer edge, there was a fifty foot drop into another cave.

"This is fun, Trey. This is like being kids." Carly tried to pass him, but when she did, he pressed her back. "Sneaking into a cave that's off-limits. It's like playing hooky."

"One at a time," Trey thrust his arm out so she couldn't go

around him. "I don't care if it seems like there's room to walk side by side. All it would take is for your foot to slip…"

Carly huffed. "We've hiked trails up at Big Bear more narrow than this. Give me a break."

"The difference is, if we fall here, no one can get here immediately to help us."

"You are such a stick in the mud," his wife said. "So, where's the room?"

"The Great Room? I'm not sure we can get there from this trail. Maybe we can look down on it."

"Well, let's go," she pushed lightly at him.

AFTER TAKING a few wider trails into dead ends, Trey finally got the right one. The light from above, where the caves opened up at the top of the hill, was growing weaker. The sun's light was shifting.

As he walked ahead of Carly, he almost stepped over the edge.

The trail ended abruptly.

Although he couldn't see them, he could smell the bats—this must be where many of them congregated. He glanced at the ceiling of rock. He could see their huddled, shadowy forms. He pointed at them to his wife. She gasped.

He whispered, "No loud noises, please. Nothing's worse than having a hundred bats swipe at you."

She nodded.

He brought her to the edge of the trail, where the rock dropped into a chasm.

The feeble sunlight descended where he pointed, and then seemed to grow brighter.

"There it is," he whispered.

.   .   .

BELOW THEM, a round chamber of pure, almost glowing white.

"It's not all chalk. Some of it's other minerals."

"It looks like baking soda," she whispered, mindful of the bats. "How do you get down there?"

"You don't get down, you get up. There's a trail that winds from the water level upward."

There were drawings of figures all along the white walls. It was hard to figure out what exactly they were from above, but Trey had seen them from the chamber's floor when he'd been twelve.

He said, "There're the stations of the cross. And see? In that recess? There's the Queen of Angels."

"I guess the paint faded over the years."

"It was probably really colorful when the monks were here. It's weird how I feel comfortable in here. Maybe it's all those hikes with dad. I've never been scared in this place. It's so…beautiful," he said, for lack of a better word.

"This should be some kind of national landmark," Carly said.

"I think they tried that. They just couldn't keep the kids from writing over it. Look." Trey pointed towards the far wall of the chamber.

Scrawled across a carved religious saint, the words *Cheryl and Robert 4-Ever.*

"It's still so beautiful." Carly hugged Trey. "It's like our secret garden."

He kissed her forehead. "Now, let's get the hell out of here before these bats wake up."

"Wait. What's that in the middle?" She pointed downward.

"It's just a drop. It's not a well or anything. But the monks used it to raise and lower supplies from boats. Back then, the Spanish could get little boats into the water-level caves. They'd raise food and fresh water up in animal skins tied to ropes."

"You mean those monks never left?"

"Not until they died."

Carly shook her head. "That's so weird. It's like they were the anchorites of the island." She shivered, and turned back on the path. She ducked to avoid an overhang, and then stubbed her toe and let out a brief but powerful cry.

Trey reached for her, and brought them both down against the floor of the trail.

The noise disturbed some of the bats, who flew as if stampeding the air over their heads, brushing Trey's back. He lay on top of her.

"Sorry," she whispered. "Stubbed my toe."

"The hazards of cave hunting," he said. "But now that I have you like this…" He kissed the back of her neck.

"Between you and the bats, I don't know if I'm ever safe," she pushed him off her, and he rolled back against the rock wall. "Let's get out. That whole monk thing has me feeling kind of creepy."

OUT IN THE OPEN AGAIN, Carly said, "I feel like I've just come out of some ancient tomb."

"You have," Trey said. "When the monks died, they buried themselves at different places in the caves. Like catacombs."

"And what about the last monk?"

Trey affected a bad Boris Karloff accent. "Maybe he's still in there, waiting."

CHAPTER FORTY-ONE

"No," Jenny said, pushing herself up to a sitting position. "I'm not going all the way." She combed her fingers through her hair. All the buttons of her blue shirt were undone. Still, she had kept her bra firmly fastened, despite her boyfriend's best efforts. She felt heat inside her, the kind that she would've liked to burn with, but she knew that boys like Tommy didn't respect girls that went all the way. No matter how blue his balls got, and no matter how much sex might clear up his acne. He had even told her that he thought masturbation was a sin, so if she gave in to him, then she could save him from sin.

Tommy lay on his back. His shirt was off, but so far he had kept his swimming trunks on. He was definitely cute, but she didn't intend to get a reputation in Avalon for him. The town was too small, and everyone would know in no time flat. She'd end up like her older sister, unmarried and pregnant at seventeen. Not in her plans. She was going to marry a guy like Mr. Campbell who would take her places. A guy who would treat her right. Not like the local townies. Jenny Reed was going to get off this island and go to Los

Angeles. She was going to maybe wait tables until she got some parts in movies. She was going to be famous...

"If I begged?" Tommy asked.

She laughed, buttoning her blouse up. "Not if you proposed marriage."

They were on the bed. They'd spent part of the day getting drunk, the other part making out and grinding against each other. She was winding down a bit from the wine, and figured she'd better fill the wine bottle up with some water so the Campbell's wouldn't notice that any of it was gone. Glancing at the clock, she cried out, "Damn—they may be back soon. It's almost three. Get up, get up."

"I'm up," he said, laughing. "That's the problem, I've been up for the last two hours."

"You are so crude," Jenny said. She leaned over and kissed him on the forehead. He tried to pull her down again, but she resisted. She pushed him away. Jenny slid to the edge of the bed, and stood up. "I'll get you one more beer, and after that, you have to leave. They never get back much before five, but you never know. Remember, if they surprise us, you're twenty-one."

"It's what my I.D. says." Tommy propped himself up on his elbows. "Where are those rug-rats? I ain't heard a squeak outta them for hours."

Standing in the doorway, trying to look sexy by balancing on one hip, Jenny said, "They ran away. But I think I saw Marky sneaking around the backyard a little while ago."

"Some babysitter you are."

"Hey, you get what you pay for. What's going to happen to them here? As long as I don't hear either one of them swimming, they'll be fine. I think they're just getting their revenge for you being here."

"Maybe they're watching us. Maybe they're learning all kinds of things," Tommy said, grinning.

"Like how to be drunk and stupid," Jenny arched her eyebrows, mocking him. She turned and padded barefoot out to the kitchen. She checked the road from the small kitchen window. A few tourists were bicycling by. There'd be a million of them come the Fourth. They'd come in droves on the morning of the Fourth and stay through the weekend. It was always like that when the holiday was mid-week. But no sign of the Campbells.

Jenny opened the fridge and grabbed a Rolling Rock bottle from the back.

A sound behind her startled her.

"Tommy," she said, turning. "Don't sneak up on me like that."

But it wasn't Tommy.

CHAPTER FORTY-TWO

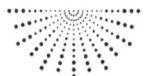

Teresa held tight to her little brother's hand. He knew to keep quiet because the man with the tattoos all over his arms and back looked scary. The man's shirt was in his hands, and he wiped it across his stomach and chest to get rid of all the sweat that was shining on his skin.

The tattooed man was stepping carefully through the French doors of the patio, into the cottage.

Teresa whispered in her brother's ear. "Maybe it's another boyfriend. She has a lot of them."

Mark wished his sister would keep quiet. He didn't want that man coming over and finding their hiding place. He was sure it wasn't a boyfriend of Jenny's, because Mark was positive he saw a small, slightly curved knife in the man's right hand.

Then, he saw the pretty woman in the jeans and sweater. She was already inside the house. He thought he saw Jenny, too, but he wasn't sure.

He heard glass break from somewhere inside.

Then, he thought he saw something that made a shower of red

water come out of Jenny's face, and it scared him so much he peed in his shorts. He couldn't help himself—he held tight to Teresa's hand, and jumped up, drawing her with him.

The woman in the house looked out across the patio.

She moved swiftly. Mark thought it was like the nature film he saw once where a lion went after a gazelle.

She was coming for him and his sister.

CHAPTER FORTY-THREE

Teresa screamed, "Run! Marky run!" She tugged at his hand, but his body was hard as stone. Mark couldn't move. Something about the pretty woman coming towards him had made him feel terribly cold. He felt like he wasn't even in his body, but was looking down at himself. At himself and the lady who moved so fast it was like she was running, only it was more like she was bounding towards him. He wondered why he couldn't make himself go. His feet felt like they were sunken into the concrete of the pool. He tried to scream at himself from inside his head to move, but nothing happened. Even his lips couldn't move.

Teresa pushed at him, and went running. There was a break in the hedge behind the cottage which led to another street. Mark couldn't even turn around to see if that's where his sister went.

Mark didn't feel he could budge an inch. He was frozen. He tried to tell his body to run, but nothing moved.

He wished his sister had stayed with him, but she was scared, too, and she would get help.

The woman came to him and leaned over. Her face was inches from his own. He could smell her sweet breath.

She put her hands on his shoulders.

She looked deep into his eyes, as if she were looking for something else inside him.

"You're his son," she said. Her voice was light. "You look like your father. You have his eyes. You have beautiful eyes."

There was blood on her teeth.

She brought her lips to his forehead.

CHAPTER FORTY-FOUR

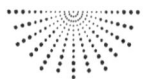

AGNES CLOSED HER EYES, STILL KISSING HIS SON. TASTING THE fear on the boy's face.

Lightning thrust a spear into her brain. She was pushed into the past body.

Her head throbbed with pain as she opened her eyes again.

She was there, in the nest she shared with Jack.

Looking at the locket that had been pinned to his cloak.

Seeing the picture inside it. The lock of hair.

The woman with the dark hair and pale skin.

She went to the corner of the room to gather more coal.

All she could think of was betrayal.

All she could think of was that he had betrayed her for all eternity.

Something wild and uncontrollable was released from deep within her.

It was as if a sleeping beast were awakened.

CHAPTER FORTY-FIVE

AT SIX P.M., TREY SAT ALONE ON A BENCH OUTSIDE AN ICE cream shop in town while Carly got a scoop of peppermint ice cream on a sugar cone. They'd wandered the hills and rocks, avoiding any humans they happened to spot. It had been their day to be completely alone together. He was happily bored with the early evening. Bored and still a little hungry even after they'd gotten a couple of burgers an hour before.

It seemed that the entire town was overrun with tourists at this point, and he attributed this to the fact of the Fourth of July celebration coming up the next day. His backside ached from riding, and the top of his forehead was bright red from sun. Carly got her cone, and walked down the block, window-shopping.

He could see the docks and beach from his seat, and was mildly surprised to see a medium sized powerboat with the letters: L.A.P.D. stenciled in white on its navy blue prow.

Several cops got off the boat, and walked up the docks.

Carly came over and sat down next to him. "I spy with my little eye a hat and some sandals that I want to buy."

Trey pointed to the dock. "Look what I spy."

"Oh. Cops on vacation?" she said, fanning the air. "God, it's hot."

"I wonder what's up."

"Well, it's not because the dreaded axe murderess is after you."

"Now I feel bad," he said. "She's dead. Poor thing. She never had a chance in life."

"Neither did her victims. Remember that next time you feel sympathy for a sadistic killer." Carly had a way of expressing herself which always seemed to override whatever mood he was feeling. He appreciated that about her.

"It's hard to understand that kind of mind, how it perceives things. She was kidnapped when she was barely Teresa's age. She was tortured by this insane person. For years. She was almost seventeen when she finally broke free, but it was too late. She had murdered the man who had abducted her. Who could blame her then? He had tortured her, skinned her in places, kept her in a basement, chained like a dog. Bled her with small, sharp knives. And he created a monster himself in her. He had turned her from a girl with some problems into a creature from nightmares. She had a fairly unique pathology, which her abductor had apparently tortured into her. She believed that she was reincarnated, living through the problems of another existence and that this drove her to be who she was."

"So, who was she?" Carly asked. He could tell she was trying to lighten things up a bit; her tone was facetious. "Cleopatra? Anastasia? The Iron Maiden of Nuremburg?"

But he couldn't even raise a grin. It all seemed so sad to him. He had always felt that none of the patients at Darden were really to blame for their situation. It was as if the ancients were right: some were born under unlucky stars. "She was a girl, also named Agnes, who lived in London around the turn of the century. A prostitute."

Carly seemed genuinely interested. "How much of her file did you see?"

"I didn't. Her psychiatrist kept that under lock and key. Agnes Hatcher told me all of it. She believed that everyone from the current life also played a part in past incarnations."

Carly's jaw dropped, in mock-drama. She touched his wrist, leaning towards him. She whispered, "You were one of her past life clients?"

Trey finally grinned. It did seem a little funny to him. *Quit taking yourself so seriously all the time.* "Not quite. She believed I was the reincarnation of her lover. He was quite a character. A man who tortured her and degraded her, but who understood her. A man who taught her about life."

Carly was silent. Then she said, "It sounds nuts but I'm actually slightly jealous. And I don't even buy the reincarnation thing. Do you?"

"Do I what?"

"Believe in reincarnation?"

Trey laughed. He glanced towards the beach, with its last stragglers still swimming or having evening picnics. "I really would hate to come back to earth and have to figure it all out all over again. But I do. A little."

"I married a heretic," Carly said. "A recovering Cathoholic like me."

He stood up, stretching. He looked back, above the shops, to the western sky above the hills, the rays of the sun still glowing. "I'm not talking about any orthodox reincarnation theory, just the one that goes, you know, you die and then grass grows from your grave and some animal eats the grass, and so on...you know, the 'no energy is lost' theory. Fragments of what we are remain." Trey felt a little exasperated trying to put this into words, since he was never sure of his exact belief system except in the most general terms.

Since Carly was a lapsed Catholic, religion only came up in their lives when the kids were baptized and when the in-laws visited.

Carly brought her legs up on the bench, crossing them in a pseudo-yoga position. "I'll be sure to remember to save on your funeral, then. Maybe I'll use you as fertilizer to plant some grass in the backyard. How did a nice Episcopalian boy from Riverside ever develop such independent thinking?"

"It's just a sense. It seems logical to me."

"So maybe you *were* Agnes' lover. We should go to one of those regression therapy hypnotists sometime and find out. Maybe I *should* be jealous," Carly said, knitting her eyebrows in mock-worry. "Maybe she's being reborn even as we speak, and in ten years some kid will come up to you and say, 'hey, I'm Agnes.' I'll be jealous through eternity."

"Well, you won't be jealous when you hear who her lover was."

"Queen Victoria?"

Trey laughed. "Not even close, except maybe by family ties. Apparently you are married to the reincarnation of a nice man named Jack who used to knife the odd hooker."

"Jack the Ripper?" Carly's eyes widened. "I wish I had never asked any of this. Yikes. She thought you were Jack the Ripper?"

"Her immortal beloved. I even had nightmares for awhile back then, she described it so vividly. She believed that I brought her into 'the life,' and then tried to destroy her. She told me that one day I would remember the Great Betrayal and then we would be united. One of those nice past lives."

"The Great Betrayal," Carly said. "Sounds like the Great Room those Spanish monks had." Then, she snapped her fingers. "*Capilla Blanca,*" Carly's eyes widened. "What a coincidence."

"Huh?"

"*Capilla Blanca*—the original name of that Kirk In The Rocks place. It means 'white chapel' in Spanish. Whitechapel was the area of London where Jack the Ripper did his dirty work. Isn't that weird?"

Trey caught his breath in mock-terror. "Yeah, it is. Very. But then again, Britain is an island, and we're on an island, and Jack the Ripper killed in Britain...so, oh my god, we've both been on islands. What's really weird is that you know where Jack the Ripper stalked his victims. Maybe you were there, too. Maybe *you're* Jack."

"Don't mock me, bucko," Carly said, "or you won't get any kisses. I just think it's weird that the day after she gets killed, we're walking around a place called white chapel. Maybe you *are* the Ripper reincarnate."

CHAPTER FORTY-SIX

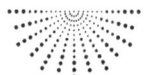

"It feels like it never gets dark here," Trey said.

They walked hand in hand along the promenade. The shops were all closed down, but a few of the restaurants were just serving dinner. "When is it going to get dark? I'm tired of daylight."

"Since you're calendar-impaired, I'll remind you that it's July, and we've only passed midsummer night by about a week. That's why it's not dark yet," Carly said. "Try back in a couple of hours."

"Oh. Right." He grinned.

"Hey!" Carly said as if she just got the greatest idea in the world. "Let's take the kids out tonight." She paused, dragging him with her, to examine a menu on the wall by a small bistro. "If Mark's gotten over his pout for the day, maybe he'll behave himself for some paella or…mmm…this looks good. Scampi. That's what I want." She sighed. "God, that was a fun day."

"Yep," was all Trey said. "I am a lucky son of a gun." He took her in his arms and kissed her. Closed his eyes. Blocked out poor dead Agnes Hatcher. Blocked out Darden State. Blocked out everything but the here and now.

For variety, they walked the narrow side streets up the hill, cutting over within several houses of their rental. The entire town of Avalon seemed silent, which matched the balmy weather. On the way back to the cottage, Trey noticed two policemen standing at the edge of the road. He and Carly exchanged glances.

"Don't get paranoid," she whispered, taking his hand. When they strolled near the two men, one of them held up his hand.

"I'm afraid I'm going to have to ask you to stop. We have an investigation in process," one of them said.

"Excuse me," Trey said. "Has there been some sort of accident? There seems to be a lot of police out tonight." Carly leaned against a fence post to tie the shoelaces of her tennis shoes. The sky was becoming overcast, which for most of southern California in July was unusual, but not among the coastal islands. The clouds didn't necessarily herald a storm, but perhaps there would be scattered showers that would come and go quickly. Noticing Carly, and the sky, and the policemen—these were his last moments of feeling safe in the universe.

The short cop said, "As a matter of fact there has been something of a mishap. Do you live up this road?"

"We're renting a cottage. Right at the end. Number 224."

He knew before they even said another word. It was in their eyes. He felt his heart rate accelerate suddenly, and he broke out in a cold sweat. He couldn't even bring himself to look at Carly. He was afraid she would feel it, too. The fear. As if it were a living, breathing thing that he only let out of its cage when there was nothing to stop it.

Trey knew.

He knew in a gut-wrenching way, and before they could stop him, before they could speak, he was running up the road, towards the house, only thinking:

Let them be safe.

Please, God, let them be safe.
Let our children remain unharmed.

CHAPTER FORTY-SEVEN

LATER, IT SEEMED LIKE A NIGHTMARE. IT SEEMED LIKE THE cottage was on the sea, adrift. Tables, chairs, walls, all seemed to rock slowly back and forth. His vision was limited, as if he were looking through a dark tunnel. Trey fought his way past the police. They were a blur of blue uniforms and gray suits. A woman in a black skirt and white blouse had a small baggie in her hand and was picking something off the floor with a pair of tweezers. A policeman made a grab for his arm as he stumbled across something on the floor—he couldn't bring himself to look at the thing which he was afraid might be a human body. He heard shouts as if from under-water. The living room seemed to rock back and forth as if it were being slapped with waves. His body moved faster than his mind, for he couldn't understand why there were so many policemen standing at the edges of the kitchen, using brushes and pen-flashlights on the counter.

He felt dizzy, and was afraid he would fall—but he held onto his consciousness, his sanity. He worked as hard as he could to be strong as he ran down the hall, calling their names as if he expecting each to be in the bedrooms of the cottage.

Trey felt somewhere deep inside himself that whatever was happening here, that God would keep his children safe. That children didn't deserve for anything bad to happen to them. Nothing like what he was afraid of.

He kept his mind racing, keeping the flame of hope alive.

Until he saw the spray of blood across Mark's bedroom wall.

CHAPTER FORTY-EIGHT

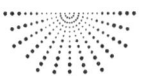

It wasn't Mark or Teresa in the bed. It was the body of an older boy. Even this was difficult to determine. Trey felt sweat break out all up and down his spine. He began shivering uncontrollably. It was as if he had stepped into another dimension of existence. As if he had stepped into Hell.

Trey's mind wiped clean, then, for the next several minutes. He took in the room with his eyes. He saw what was there to be seen. But his brain short-circuited, and he felt very cold. He felt for an instant as if he, himself, had the mind of the killer. As if he were stepping into the room, seeing the boy in the bed.

Seeing the terror in his eyes as the boy beheld the knife.

The curved knife held high and brought down in a slicing motion.

The ripping of skin.

The smell, from somewhere distant, of soot and mildew. The sound of clattering hooves on cobblestones. Beating of rain against shingles. The taste of blood in the back of his throat.

A human being lay on the bed, his skin sliced down the middle and peeled back, stuck with tacks to the bed. His face had been completely skinned. It was a mass of red pulp.

A cop turned around when he saw Trey and said, "Who are you?" He had something that looked like some bloody body part in a large plastic bag. The evening sunlight, through the long bedroom window cast a kind of rainbow across the blood-stained wall. The lampshade by the bed was spattered with something that had once been part of a human being.

Trey felt a stab in the back of his head, as if just seeing this hurt so much that he was about to lose consciousness.

On the wall, finger-painted in blood, the word:

BELOVED.

CHAPTER FORTY-NINE

Trey crumpled in a heap to the carpet. He closed his eyes. Please God don't let Marky or Terry be hurt. Please let this be a dream.

Down the hallway, he heard Carly cry out. He stood up on shaky legs, grasping the doorframe. He saw her, down the hall. She was calling for their children.

Trey marshaled what little strength he had, and went toward the sound of her voice like it was his own heart beat. He wanted to hold her until they were one being, together. Until there were no more tears, only warmth. Only comfort.

When he found her, among the cops, she was shivering. He wrapped his arms around her. He held her as close as he could get. Normally, he would feel her warmth. Now all he felt was ice.

"Trey," she wept against his shoulder. "My babies." Trey's mind couldn't focus on any one thing. Random and scattered images flashed through his mind: Mark when he took his first brave dive, Mark when he was a week old, lying in the old Beatrix Potter blanket in his bassinette, Teresa at her fourth birthday party, Teresa dancing on her grandfather's toes when she was six, the time when Carly miscarried...

Images of Dr. Ballantine, the psychiatrist, his scalp sliced open, the blood on Agnes Hatcher's face, the look in her eyes, at him, when she cried out, "Beloved! My only love!" The image of Agnes Hatcher, face covered, in her restraints, in the steel-doored room at Darden State... chess games, sitting across from her and trying to figure out how she would move her chess pieces...walking with her in the garden, and hearing her stories about her last incarnation with him...his babies, his little children, he couldn't block the images, torn as if a wild animal had dug its claws into them. His thoughts: it can't be Agnes Hatcher. She's dead. I watched the news. It's what was reported. She couldn't have done this.

A familiar voice, behind them, at the French doors to the patio, said, "My men have been looking all over for you two."

Trey glanced around. Through his own tears, he saw Oscar Arboles, pipe in mouth, shining with sweat. He was coming in from the pool area with a dark-haired woman. The woman had a camera in her hand. She would be the crime-scene photographer. She had a look on her face as if none of this blood spattering the room was anything out of the ordinary.

Oscar looked as if he himself was hoping this was all just a nightmare from which to be awakened.

CHAPTER FIFTY

"Your son is unharmed," Oscar Arboles said. He was wearing a very sweat-stained blue suit, the collar of his shirt undone, his tie askew. He was on the patio, walking Trey and Carly around the pool. "Your daughter ran down to get help. She's doing fine. A neighbor a few doors down called us. The murderer didn't hurt your son. It was that woman from the asylum."

"Agnes Hatcher?" Trey said, feeling confused. "But she's dead." He knew even as he said it that within him he'd known it was true already. He'd known as soon as he'd run up the road to the cottage.

He'd known as if he had some psychic link with Hatcher herself.

Oscar stopped pacing. "Mr. Campbell, she's very much alive." Looking at both of them, he drew a handkerchief from his breast pocket and handed it to Carly. "We received a report of a sighting of Hatcher at a harbor saloon in San Pedro. She was seen in several places, speaking with men at the bar. She found one, too. We've got him."

"We saw on the news that she died," Carly interjected. She blew her nose into the handkerchief.

Trey cussed a blue streak. "I should've known. It wasn't her, was it? It was some victim of hers."

Oscar nodded. "She's very clever."

"Clever? She's a genius." Trey cursed silently to himself. "How could I leave my kids alone like that?"

Carly asked, "Can we go to them now? I want my babies." Her eyes were filled with tears.

Oscar nodded. He went inside and spoke briefly with one of the investigating officers. When he returned, he said, "Let's go out the back gate. No use getting upset all over again walking through that…"

Carly clung to Trey the whole way back to the police station.

WHEN CARLY SAW the state that Mark was in, she began weeping loudly. She went to him, hugging both him and Teresa. "Thank God, thank God, oh thank you God." Teresa was doing fairly well. According to Oscar Arboles, their daughter had not witnessed too much. She had tried to get Mark to run, had pulled and pushed him, but he hadn't budged. So she had just taken off, assuming that if she got help quickly enough, nothing bad would happen to her brother.

Teresa hadn't known what was wrong with Mark.

"A mild catatonia," Oscar said. "It happens sometimes. An event is so traumatic, the individual freezes. He'll be fine in a day or so."

Trey picked his son up and held him. Mark's chin rested against his shoulder. Trey had never in his life seen a sadder looking boy. His eyes were all dark and seemed to have sunken into his face, becoming smaller. His lips were thin, and in a tight line. He said nothing. He reacted to nothing.

Teresa began crying, and Carly held her. Carly and Trey looked at each other. For a moment, he look stung. Trey didn't know if his interpreting her expression was just his own guilt for not being with the children, or if Carly was genuinely angry with him for having the kind of job which would bring with it this kind of monster.

"Although there's a good chance Hatcher's already off this island, I want to get all of you off-island tonight," Oscar said. "I'll have a couple of the mainlanders—cops—take you to Long Beach in a motor boat in half an hour. We can get your son to Long Beach Memorial for observation, but I'm certain he'll come through with flying colors by morning."

Too numb to speak, Carly nodded.

"What did Hatcher do up there?"

After a few seconds, Oscar said, "She lived up to her various nicknames. Not a tale to be told in front of children."

Trey set Mark down beside his mother. He held Teresa for awhile, smelling her breath, feeling her heartbeat. He wanted to stay with them. They were a unit, not to be separated. He felt like an animal protecting its young, for he wanted to guard them for the rest of their lives. Leaving Teresa with her mother, he put his arm around Mark. Trey just wanted the warmth to pass through all of them. He didn't want to ever leave their sides again.

"Why don't we go talk in my office, Mr. Campbell?" Oscar asked.

Carly nodded to Trey. "I'll stay here. Don't worry. We're fine."

A strange relief hung in the air between them. Almost an electrical charge. It was that monstrous human emotion of survival—self-survival.

Two teenagers had been murdered brutally in the rental cottage, but they were part of another world of tragedy. In this world of his own family and of happy endings, Trey felt as if he and his family were lucky. They had been spared that horrible tragedy. They had somehow skirted it. Days later he and Carly might be back at their home in Redlands, both working in the yard on a day off. They might laugh while they watched Marky run under the sprinklers then. Or Terry might show them a chord change on the guitar she'd just learned. An overdue notice from Visa might come in and ruin the weekend for him. That would be the next tragedy—light and easy to take care of. It was horrible what Trey was thinking just then, and he wished his mind didn't dredge up the thought:

Thank god it wasn't us. Thank god my children weren't inside that house.

Along with this, came the unspoken thought:

Just don't think about those other children, the older ones, Jenny and her friend, trapped by that monster, with no escape but death.

CHAPTER FIFTY-ONE

FIVE MINUTES LATER, IN HIS GLASSED-IN OFFICE, OSCAR pushed a Styrofoam cup of coffee across the desk. "No cream, but you'll live. You want doughnuts, we got cream-filled and glazed, no plain." He slapped a pink box on a side table near his chair. He reached in and grabbed a crumbly half-doughnut, and took a bite. Oscar spoke while he chewed, "I used to see things on a par with this back in my Hollywood days, but not since. Even then, it wasn't nearly so bloody. My local boys, they've never seen this before. Half my guys were losing their lunches. I suppose, working with these kinds of killers, you've been somewhat exposed to this."

"A bit," Trey nodded. "But when it's on the inside of Darden State, it doesn't seem as terrible. Usually, they do it more to themselves than to others."

Trey stared at the coffee.

Then, he picked up the cup and took a sip. It tasted sour. "She killed Jenny."

Oscar nodded his head, chewing the doughnut. "And a boy."

"I saw the body in the room. Who was it?"

"Jenny Reed's boyfriend, Tom Hyslop. They must've been surprised in the house. Jenny was in the kitchen. The boy was in the back bedroom." Oscar finished off his doughnut and reached into his breast pocket. He withdrew his pipe, thrusting it between his lips. "It's your wife with the asthma, am I right?"

Trey nodded. "Feel free to light up."

"*Gracias*," Oscar struck a match on the desk and cupped it in his hand around the pipe bowl.

"*De nada*," Trey replied.

"You fool around with this Reed girl?" Oscar asked.

"Excuse me?"

"Jenny Reed. She was pretty. A pretty babysitter. Many men might think about it. Maybe fantasize. She probably had a crush on you, no?"

"What in god's name are you driving at?"

"Agnes Hatcher. Maybe she was jealous of this girl."

Trey almost laughed if he weren't so insulted. "I guess character is something that nobody respects in southern California, but I've got some. I wouldn't cheat on my wife even if the opportunity arose."

"But if it did arise..."

"You don't know Agnes Hatcher, either. She killed Jenny Reed because Jenny Reed was in the cottage. She would've killed Carly or Teresa or Mark if they'd been there."

"She didn't touch your children. I take that back, she didn't hurt your children. And you didn't mention yourself. What do you think Hatcher would've done had you been there?"

Trey thought a moment. His mind was a blank, short-circuited by the recent events. He said the first thing that came into his head. "I think she didn't want me to be there, knowing her. Once she figured out where I was staying, she could've waited until I arrived. She could've hidden somewhere. But she didn't. Unfortunately, she wanted to kill anyone else she came across."

"Just for the thrill?"

Trey shook his head, setting the half-empty cup back on the desk. "No. She does get a thrill from it, but not for the reasons generally associated with psychopaths. She believes she's collecting time in eternity for herself with each murder. She told me once that that was why the ancients sacrificed humans: to ransom their own souls. She had a whole theory about it."

"Why do you think she spared your son?"

Without hesitation, Trey said, "He has my smell."

"Your smell?"

"Agnes Hatcher studies people. She studied me for years, even after she stopped seeing me. She knew more about me than anyone but my immediate family by then. She remembered smells. She remembered faces. She once told me that she could tell if a person had the heart of a killer or not. She could smell that, too."

A grin rose from Oscar's doughnut crumbed lips. "But, you knew she was insane."

Trey shrugged. "No. The courts called her that. She felt she was a different species from the rest of us. She may have been right."

"Does she think *you* have the heart of the killer?"

Trey didn't answer this.

"In any case," Oscar blew smoke from his pipe, "what she did to those teenagers was not just killing. It had the look of a ritual to it. We're not even sure that all the internal organs are there with either body…"

Trey wiped his face with his hand, remembering the skinned body in the bed. "God."

"I'm not going to go into detail about what was done to those kids. Suffice it to say, they didn't suffer long. And we caught her accomplice."

"She usually works alone."

Oscar nodded. "Or she kills whoever helps her. He's in the holding cell. He's a wild one. Named Nathaniel Coker, but known around the waterfront in San Pedro as Cobra. Not very bright. He was suspected of several murders of a group of Vietnamese fishermen several years back, but there was nothing solid to connect him to the crimes. The Hatcher woman tried to get him, too. But she failed. It's good to know she fails now and then, huh? She didn't have the time, but she was going for his balls. She heard the girl screaming for help, though, so she got out of there fast. Our friend Cobra only got gouged a bit, but we patched him up." Oscar winked, "Better than losing the ol' *cojones*, eh?"

"She's after me," Trey said after he finished the cup of coffee.

"I know," Oscar said. "She told your son that. She told him that she wanted his daddy. We found him standing on the patio, shivering. She had left a nice little lipstick mark on his forehead. Only it wasn't lipstick. It was blood. And it's all he would tell us. 'The lady wants my daddy.' You ask him, he'll probably tell you, too. It's all he seems able to say at the moment."

For a second, Trey felt defensive of his son. Not just with Agnes Hatcher, but even with the police. He didn't like the thought of Mark being questioned. Not after what he'd witnessed. He liked even less the idea of Mark being brought into court one day in the future to testify, while Agnes Hatcher sat there, watching the boy.

If Agnes would ever be caught.

"Can't you get a helicopter for my family? I want them back on the coast as quickly as possible."

"We could do an airlift," Oscar said, re-lighting his pipe as if it would help him to think better. He tilted his head side-to-side, weighing this option. "I don't think it's necessary. Your son is strong. He'll come out of this soon. There's just something inside of him that's keeping the door locked for awhile. Until he feels absolutely safe." Oscar glanced at his watch. "We can have a helicopter here in thirty minutes, forty, tops. But you and your family can get on a boat in ten minutes and have two armed guards as an escort right now. If she could still be around on this island, I think you should go for the boat. Why wait and chance anything?"

"I guess the boat's fine," Trey said. "But I'm staying."

"No you're not."

"If you want to catch Agnes Hatcher," Trey said. "You're going to need me. Once she knows I'm off this island, she's as good as slipped through your hands. I know her. I know what drives her."

"What drives her then?" Oscar leaned forward. The smoke from his pipe blew right into Trey's eyes. Oscar apologized, fanning the air.

Trey took five minutes and told Oscar about the Jack the Ripper reincarnation story. "She operates on the part of the body where she thinks the soul resides for each person. She claims that Jack taught her that when she finds this sacred place of the soul, that she gains another incarnation. That it's like a sacrifice to the fates. She thinks she's a different species. She believes I am, too. She believes that she and I have to come together again to resolve, I don't know, some kind of karmic debt. We're bound through eternity. Not to be too morbid, but I assume she cut out Jenny's eyes."

Oscar leaned forward, pipe thrust firmly in mouth. "Why do you say that?"

"Jenny had beautiful eyes. They were her best feature. Agnes probably intuited that from just seeing her once. So, she thought her soul resided in her eyes. I don't know this boy, Tom, but if he were in bed, waiting for Jenny, Agnes must've cut off his genitals."

"Right on the money," Oscar said, shaking his head. "With the Reed girl, it was more than just eyes." He thrummed his fingers on his desk. "I trained in L.A., Mr. Campbell, when I was younger. I've seen the worst a human being can do to another human being." He paused a beat. "This tops it. We know Hatcher took a quick shower to wash off the blood of her victims. We saw traces of her hair. It was red, and then, bits of it were blond. She used shampoo-in hair color. We also know she rummaged through your wife's closet. Probably changed clothes, although we didn't find Hatcher's clothes. She did this in just a few minutes. She's very fast as well as methodical. We assume, based on the time lag before we got the call for help from the neighbor, that she had about six minutes to get out of that house and avoid being seen by my men."

Trey covered his face with his hands. He remembered the kind of work that other killers in D Ward had done in the past. The images it brought up for him. Half of his job was repressing such memories. Carly was right; he was going to have to find another line of work. He didn't want his children to grow up in this atmosphere.

He didn't want to ever again see a look like the one on Mark's face that evening: the blank, empty gaze, the slight drool at the corner of his lips.

"Let's get your family on that boat," Oscar said, pushing himself up from his desk. He wiped his hand across the bald spot, swiping at several stray black hairs. "I have worked on this island for thirty years, Mr. Campbell. I never imagined anything like this monster would come here. What can I do to help catch her?"

Trey said the first thing that came into his mind. "Let me talk to the accomplice. Cobra."

CHAPTER FIFTY-TWO

CARLY DRIED HER TEARS, BUT COULD NOT BRING HERSELF TO let go of either of her children. She looked into Mark's eyes, and tried speaking to him, but he stared through her. She remembered when he was born, how they'd called him Tadpole for months before the formal name Mark took hold. How he still seemed like her little Tadpole now, a baby, so sweet and loving. She wished she had brought them with her and Trey for the afternoon…If only she'd insisted on bringing the children. They'd have been safer on a horse trail than in the cottage.

Teresa said, "I don't know why he couldn't run, Mommy." Her voice seemed now to be of a much younger girl, as if the experience she'd been through had taken away any maturity she'd developed. She began crying softly, and then stopped again. "I tried to make him run. Maybe I shoulda stayed with him." She nestled her head into her mother's shoulder.

"No, you did the right thing, Teresita," Carly whispered. "You got help, and if you hadn't've maybe things would've been worse."

"He saw it all," Teresa said, gazing at her little brother. "I only saw the woman and the man and Jenny. I didn't see what they did to her. Marky saw it."

"It was a horrible thing," Carly said.

"Poor Jenny," Teresa said. "She's dead. If we'd been in the house, we'd be dead, too." She began crying. Carly felt the wetness of tears seep into her blouse. "Mommy, I want to go home."

"We will," her mother cooed. "We will. Soon." She glanced around the walls of the waiting area, and felt like Agnes Hatcher was there, waiting for them.

The woman who had stolen her children's innocence.

If only Trey had never worked at that damn hospital, she thought. None of this would have ever happened.

At that very moment, Trey stepped back into the room.

CHAPTER FIFTY-THREE

"They've got a police escort for you and kids," Trey told his wife. He had to steel himself for this. His instinct was to go with them, to not let them out of his sight. He was afraid, too. Afraid that Agnes Hatcher would get him, finally. That she would do to him what she did to others. He was having trouble even touching his wife. He was afraid that if he did, it would be too much like a goodbye.

He was afraid it would mean that they were returning to life.

And that he would never return to that mainland, not if Agnes Hatcher ever found him.

"You're not staying here," she said. "No. Not with that monster running loose." She jutted her jaw out a bit to emphasize her determination on this point.

"Carly, I have to, " he said. "She's still here. I know her, Carly. I know what she wants."

Carly seemed like a fierce mother tiger defending her young. An anger sparked into flame behind her eyes. He could see the heat in her face. "You told me she's a machine. If they don't catch her, she'll just kill you, Trey. And then I'll be a widow and your children will be fatherless. No. I can't let you do that. Not for some psycho or some job. Get your priorities straight."

"I have to stay," he said, defeated. "I can help catch her."

Carly said nothing. She still held Mark in her arms; he was wrapped in a cotton blanket. She took Teresa's hand. Teresa looked up at her father with tear-filled eyes. Her lower lip was trembling.

Trey wanted more than anything to go with them.

But if he did, he might be leading Agnes Hatcher right to them.

He couldn't do that.

He had to trust his instincts on this.

Carly turned and left the police station. The whole way out, Teresa glanced back at her father, wide-eyed, as if wondering why he wasn't coming, too.

There were no buildings to block the view to the harbor. The town was to the left, the sea straight ahead. Pelicans were gliding and diving near shore. The place possessed an unearthly silence. Jenny's family and the family of the dead boy would be notified. Residents and tourists would be staying in, and locking up tonight. Catalina Island would be run by fear until the Gorgon was caught.

Trey went and stood in the doorway. He wanted to go with Carly, but he was afraid that if he did, no one would ever catch Agnes Hatcher. Or, if he stayed with his family, maybe Agnes would turn up and kill all of them. He knew how to handle Hatcher. He knew how her mind worked. If he had only known that she was alive that day, he would never have left his family. He sent a mental prayer to Carly: *Turn around. Look at me again. Tell me you love me.*

She didn't turn back.

"Wait!" he called. He ran out, through the street, catching up with her.

When he did, he said, "I love you. I love you."

"I love you, too," Carly said. Her eyes were dry. Her gaze was steady. The fire of anger was gone, replaced by resignation. "But do you love us enough to come with us? Do you love your children enough to stay with them?"

"That's not fair. If I can help in some way to catch her—"

Carly interrupted him. "I'm tired of watching our children get the worst part of you, while the inmates of Darden State get the best part. We'll be in Long Beach tonight. When you're ready to, join us. We're your family."

TREY WATCHED her walk with the children to a tall policeman. The policeman indicated one of the docks where an L.A.P.D. boat was moored.

Trey watched them get on the motor boat—the tall policeman, and a short policewoman, who was the pilot.

He stayed and watched until the boat was underway.

He knew that once the police had caught Agnes Hatcher, Carly would understand and forgive him.

He knew he was doing the right thing.

From behind him, Oscar Arboles called out, "Mr. Campbell! Let's go see the snake in his pit."

CHAPTER FIFTY-FOUR

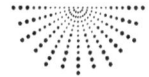

"Mommy?" Teresa asked as they got into the police motor boat.

"Sweetie?"

"Why isn't Daddy coming with us?"

"He has to help the police."

"Is that lady going to hurt Daddy?" Teresa asked.

"No," Carly said, not knowing whether or not she might be lying to her own daughter.

CHAPTER FIFTY-FIVE

A MAN WHO LOOKED LIKE A YOUNG SAILOR TURNED MIDDLE-aged fast sat on the cot in the other cell.

He had blond hair, in a buzz cut to the sides, longish from there. He looked like a poster-child for steroid abuse. His Hawaiian shirt was soaked with blood.

"Cobra, you have a visitor," Oscar said. He pointed to a chair for Trey to sit in. Then, to Trey, he said, "I'm going back to my computer to pull some things up. You need me, just yell. But yell loud."

CHAPTER FIFTY-SIX

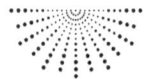

THE COP ON THE BOAT WAS NAMED ERSKINE. HE HAD A longish face—like a hound dog, Carly thought. He was sweetly goofy, trying to make jokes with the policewoman who was piloting the boat. He flirted innocently enough with Carly, but she was in no mood for such nonsense. She felt numb inside, and the only heat within her was anger at Trey for not coming with them. Mark, wrapped in the blanket, was tucked against Teresa's arm.

"Excuse me," she said, as the boat got underway. "How long will it take to get to Long Beach?"

Erskine smiled. "Well, the ocean's calm tonight, so it won't be bad. It might take as much as three hours. Four, if it gets choppy. You ever get sea-sick?"

"Sometimes," Carly said. She wrapped her arm around Teresa to help keep her warm.

The policewoman sitting in the pilot's chair was more business-like. She kept her face forward, and serenely guided the boat. Carly appreciated the fact that she hadn't tried to make small talk with them. She tried to watch the stars, but something of a fog was drifting in—the sky had been clear minutes before. This was what summer tended to be like near the coast. She hoped it wouldn't get any colder. The temperature could be seventy during the day, but then drop to a chilly sixty on the water at night. Carly closed her eyes, keeping her arm around her daughter and son.

Erskine made a few inane comments to the policewoman, which Carly couldn't hear. She was so furious with Trey for staying behind, the word *divorce* crossed her mind for a second. In her mind she smashed plates on the linoleum tile in their kitchen at home. In her mind, she was the most loving and understanding wife possible. Neither extreme was true.

And then she thought: *He's doing the best he can. He's doing what he believes in.*

The other thought, too:

Don't get hurt, Trey. Don't get hurt. Let the cops catch this woman, shoot her down, throw a net over her, whatever you need to do, but just don't get yourself in trouble.

ERSKINE SAID TO THE POLICEWOMAN, "So, what's it like working on an island? Not a lot of action." He was from San Pedro, brought out three hours earlier, only to turn around again. He glanced at her badge. "Stouffer. Like the frozen dinners."

"Paula," she said, shooting him a nasty look. Erskine was taken aback for a second. She had seemed like a looker to him until he noticed her mean little eyes. They were almost squinty, and he always thought women were somehow tainted if they had squinty little eyes. Then, the look vanished from her face. Her eyes widened, doe-like. She was a babe again. "What's it like on the mainland?" she asked.

"Oh, I don't know. I don't do much work in the harbor or anything. Mainly burglaries. Stolen cars. The usual."

The policewoman said nothing.

"I'm sure I saw you at the academy," Erskine said. "I never forget a face."

Paula Stouffer half-smiled. "I've lectured at various academies."

"On what? Island hopping?" He was trying to make a joke, but it died in his mouth. He knew how feeble it sounded. "That killer back there was some doozy. Did you see the blood on the walls?"

Paula Stouffer nodded. "Listen, can you steer for a minute? I want to get a smoke from my bag."

Erskine nodded. "Sure. I love piloting these babies." He kept his eyes straight forward. It was pitch black, the sun having set just a brief while ago, but there was always an incipient light along the horizon where the mainland began.

He felt the policewoman's hand on his shoulder, and he grinned, feeling like maybe he was going to get lucky tonight.

Her grip on his shoulder got stronger, sharper.

CARLY'S HEAD drooped to the side, until it was completely leaning on Teresa's. Teresa had fallen asleep, too.

Only Mark was awake.

Only Mark, wrapped in the blanket with his eyes wide, saw what happened to the policeman named Erskine. The dim green lights from the edges of the boat cast a shadow as the knife plunged into Erskine's neck. The policewoman cut so sharply into Erskine's throat, that his head fell almost completely backwards.

When the policewoman finished, she turned a key in the boat's ignition. She stepped around her seat. She walked calmly over and leaned close to Mark.

She had handcuffs in one hand.
In the other, a fishing knife.
Mark saw her shadow face.
Mark gasped, "The lady."

CHAPTER FIFTY-SEVEN

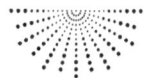

TREY CAMPBELL SAT DOWN IN THE FOLDING CHAIR. THE holding cell was gray. The bars were thick. Cobra had been finger-painting on the gray wall of his cell with his own feces. He'd painted a snake, complete with forked tongue.

And he'd painted a woman. Stick figure. Oval breasts. A halo around her head.

Cobra glanced over at him. Saw that he noticed his recent art. Seemed proud of it. He seemed so different than other human beings would be in the same situation. This man seemed as if he owned the world in which he existed.

Trey knew then. He could feel it the way he felt it about the psychos on his ward. The way he knew about the doorman when he'd been a little kid. Cobra was one of them. Trey felt that chill, and the slight confusion. The sense that there was something so different about Cobra that it verged on paranoia. Or a complete understanding at the subliminal level of another human being. Cobra was of the same species as Agnes—but not as smart.

"I like to draw," Cobra said.

"Did you draw the word 'beloved' on the wall at that cottage?"

Cobra shook his head. "That's a word. I don't do words. I draw pictures. You like?" He tapped the wall with the snake. "It's me and her. She's righteous. She's…" He seemed to burst with possible descriptions of her. Then, he said, "She's everything."

"Tell me about her," Trey said. Faking calm, he placed his hands carefully on his knees and didn't look Cobra directly in the eye, but just past his left ear. He didn't want to get into mind-games with this guy.

Cobra grinned. He had a wide gap between his front teeth. When he spoke, his voice was gravelly. "She's a goddess. She touched the face of the universe, man." Then, leaning forward. "You got a cigarette?"

Trey shook his head. "I don't smoke. Sorry."

As if this were enough grounds for dismissal, Cobra leaned back on the cot. He crossed his arms behind his head and shut his eyes.

"Tell me about her."

"Why should I? You can't even get me a cigarette. You some lowlife rag picker trying to get me to confess? You can sit on it and rotate."

Trey got up and walked out of the cell. As he did, Cobra called out, "I like Marlboro Lights 100 in a box!"

In the hall, he found a cigarette machine. He borrowed change from Oscar, and got the pack that Cobra wanted.

Trey brought the cigarettes into the holding cell area. He passed a cigarette and a book of matches in to Cobra. Cobra took them, touching Trey's slightly trembling hand.

"Don't be scared of me," Cobra said. "I'm only the tool. She's the operator, let me tell you. I could've sat out my days at the docks stealing from the till here and there. Nothing like this…" He lit the cigarette, and inhaled deeply. "This...magnificence...this brilliance."

"You mean Agnes?"

Cobra nodded. "Thank you for the cigarette. You are truly a compassionate man." He said this with mock-refinement.

"Do you know where she is?"

Cobra grinned. He had a grin like a sideshow barker: sleazy and compelling at the same time. "You're the one, ain't you?"

Trey said nothing.

Cobra laughed. "You're the one she's looking for. Those kids we took out. They wasn't. They was fun for her. She told me she was collecting lifetimes to give you. On a platter, buddy."

"What do you mean?" Trey sat down in the chair by the cell. He leaned forward.

"Before I say anything, can you get me a good lawyer?"

"What?"

"I'm an accomplice to murder. I know that. I'll be happy to turn evidence against her, but only if I got me a good lawyer. One who's gonna make sure she never gets out again. I know her now. It only took me a day, but I know her inside and out. She's that way. Can you pass me that pack?" He asked, his hand out in supplication. "I like to chain-smoke."

Trey passed the cigarette pack to Cobra. Again, Cobra's hand grazed the underside of his palm.

Cobra quickly lit one cigarette off the first. He stubbed out the last of the first cigarette, and began smoking the next. The room was filling with smoke.

"I can't do much with regards to lawyers," Trey said.

"Oh," Cobra puffed on the cigarette. "I guess I got nothing to say to you, in that case."

He swiveled around on the cot, and lay down.

"She's going to get you anyway," Trey said, standing from the chair. He walked towards the door.

As he touched the door knob, Cobra made a sputtering cough. "What?" He cried out. "Whatju say?"

Trey turned, leaning back against the door. "She's going to get you. Because you know her. She gets everyone who sees her in action. When she was caught last time, she had entire file cabinets with description of people who knew about her, and their families, and anyone who had ever come in contact with them. She was going to systematically operate on each of them. Even if it took several lifetimes. I may not be able to get you a lawyer, Cobra, but I can be a pretty decent witness. I know her. I know that she's the one who went for the girl's eyes and face. And I know why. I know that it was her, not you, who cut off the boy's penis and killed him. You were just the—what would you call it? —the tough guy who scared those kids. You played with them after they were dead. You were the one who didn't know how far she'd go."

"Hell," he said, his voice raspy with smoke. "I didn't even know she was gonna kill'em. I thought we was just gonna rough'em up and have some fun with 'em. I like blood and all, but not the way she did."

"So," Trey said. "Where is she?"

Cobra cursed and kicked the toilet. "She really screwed me."

"Yeah she did. Royally."

When the man in the cell had calmed down some, he said, "I thought we was just gonna, you know, have fun and scare those kids. She told me she was after you 'cause of that whole past life-time crap. I held that boy..." Cobra began bawling like a baby. While he cried, he still managed to smoke. Trey knew the tears were fake. Cobra was a sociopath. Cobra couldn't even understand that what he had just participated in, the murders of Jenny and her boyfriend, was wrong. He would think the mistake was in getting caught. If his tears were at all real, it was because he was caught, not because of remorse.

Trey went back to the folding chair and sat down. "Where is Agnes Hatcher?"

Cobra wiped his eyes, shuddering with tears. He took a long drag off a fresh cigarette. "Do you know about time and space? I mean, how she thinks about it? She sounds like friggin' Einstein, you ask me. She talks about some kind of continuing thing..."

"A time and space continuum," Trey said.

"Yeah. You do know her. The intersection, she said, of time and space. She collected all these things, you know, bits of hearts and lungs and livers, I thought she was some kind of cannibal, but she didn't want to eat them. She told me they were for the path. The crossroads of time and space. They were the fuel to the path. She talked like she'd been there. Like she knew where she was going. It was wild," he said this as if it were some wonderful trip. "You want to know where she is?" He asked, rhetorically. "I mean, you're never gonna find her. I tried to tell the other cops, but they weren't like you...they were morons. You want me to tell you? I can tell you, but you won't get it unless you know her. Unless you know her real well. She told me only one man was gonna understand it. Where she was going." He snorted and laughed, a big hyena laugh. "You're the one, ain't you? You're the love of her life, I can tell. She told me all about you. What you two did before. Seems like you should be inside here and me out there. How many women, mister? Ten, twelve? Slicing and dicing. Doin' things to them that no man oughta do. But you wanna know something? She let me do her, mister. She put out for me."

Trey listen dispassionately. "I understand she attacked you, too."

Instinctively, Cobra clutched his crotch.

Trey said, "It's because of what she let you do to her. If she remains free, Cobra, she's going to finish that job. I know her. She's a machine. She never starts something without finishing it. So tell me where she is."

Cobra, looking frightened for the first time, told everything he knew.

CHAPTER FIFTY-EIGHT

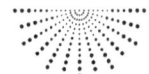

ON THE BOAT AT SEA, CARLY OPENED HER EYES WHEN SHE heard her son speak.

"The lady," Mark said, over and over.

Carly looked up at the policewoman. Carly kissed Mark on the forehead. *He's getting better. He'll be fine. This nightmare will be over soon.* "That's right, Marky. The police lady." The mist of fog, like a thin veil, drifted across the boat.

"The lady," Mark said again. Carly was about to say something to the policewoman, to ask why the boat had stopped, when she saw the large knife in the woman's hands.

The kind of knife that she herself had used a few times to help Trey gut and clean the fish they'd caught.

The policewoman held it against Mark's throat.

"You're Agnes Hatcher," Carly gasped. She didn't want to move, for fear of what this madwoman would do to her son.

"And you're the whore who stole my Jack from me," Agnes Hatcher said. "I can smell him all over you."

CHAPTER FIFTY-NINE

TREY FELT LIKE HE WAS MOVING THROUGH MOLASSES, FROM the cell area to the door. He heard Cobra's cynical laughter, and tasted the smoke in the air. He pushed through the door to the corridor which led to the offices of the police station. He passed a middle-aged man sitting at a desk, scribbling notes down from a phone call. He walked swiftly to Oscar's office, knocking on the door.

Through the glass, Oscar glanced up from his computer. He signaled for Trey to enter.

Trey opened the door and said, triumphantly, "I know where she is. She's at the caves. It's because of the connection to the word Whitechapel. It's a sign to her of where time and space will intersect. Where our karma will be resolved."

"*Capilla Blanca,*" Oscar said without hesitation. "Maybe that's it. Glad our Cobra talked to somebody. None of my boys could get through to him. Anything else?"

"He said she's keeping souvenirs."

"Body parts? Organs?"

Trey nodded.

It was 9 p.m.

CHAPTER SIXTY

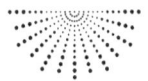

"You stay here," Oscar said, rising, grabbing his jacket from the coat rack. "Watch TV. or talk to Dinah out front. I'll get ten men and some motor boats over there. We'd go up to the other end of the cliffs, but I already have men out on the road setting up blocks. I doubt she'd have had time to go that way. For all I know, she knows her way around in a boat. And if she's there, I don't want her finding you. How'd you get our friend in the cell to tell you this?"

"I've worked with sociopaths for years," Trey said. "I understood him."

Oscar lip-farted at this, as if Trey were just some bleeding heart.

"You'll never find her without me," Trey said.

Oscar turned, and pointed at him. "You think too much of yourself. You need some rest. There's a couch out front. Use it."

Trey felt stunned by the authoritative command from him.

Several minutes later, he went to sit on the green couch in the front office. Dinah, the dispatch officer, listened to the police band, which she kept on low volume. She smiled occasionally when Trey looked her way, but kept her head down.

He watched the silent television. There was no news about the murders. He wondered how sensational a murder had to be to make the news.

He closed his eyes. He wished he'd gone with Carly. He wasn't needed here. Whether or not Agnes Hatcher was after him, he didn't need to be there for her. He should be there for his family.

He imagined Carly playing with Mark out at the swimming pool. Teresa, diving off the far edge.

Mark afraid of his own reflection which lurked at the bottom of the pool.

Without wanting to, Trey Campbell fell asleep.

HE DREAMED.

A chess game in hell, between him and Agnes Hatcher. All around them, fire.

She was picking her queen up and moving it towards his knight.

"You can't win like that," he said.

Agnes Hatcher grinned. Her teeth were blood-stained. "I don't have a strategy," she said. "Do you, Mr. Campbell? Mr. Campbell?" she asked, her voice melting into another voice, lighter and sweeter.

TREY AWOKE when he heard his name being called.

It was Dinah. "Mr. Campbell?"

His eyes fluttered open. He oriented himself to the room. The front office of the Catalina police station. He sat up. His back was all sweaty from lying against the leather couch. He wiped at his neck.

"Mr. Campbell?" Dinah repeated. She stood up from behind her desk.

He nodded. "Uh huh."

Dinah turned up the dispatch radio a bit, but it sounded like several voices speaking in monotones all at once. She turned it down again. "Oscar wants me to tell you they've caught her."

Trey glanced up at the clock on the wall.

It was almost ten p.m.

CHAPTER SIXTY-ONE

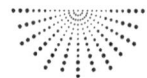

Half an hour later, Oscar stepped into the police station, soaked to the skin.

"The damn waves," he said, "I was either throwing up or getting soaked. We could barely see anything because the fog's coming in. I was sure we were going to crash into each other."

Trey had been pacing for almost a half hour. "So what's the story?"

Oscar glanced at him like he was the last person in the world he wanted to see. "The story is just about the way I'd've played it. We went out to those caves. My men and women are already coming down with colds, and the ones out of San Pedro think I'm a joke. We spend an hour and a half shining flashlights up and down the slimy walls of Capilla Blanca. Although I must admit, that central room, the round one with the well in the middle, is pretty interesting. I've lived here for fifteen years, and never went through there. It's amazing how those monks lived…" Realizing he was getting off the subject, he backtracked. "So we spend half the night looking there, and I get this call. Not on the general police band, but on my private band. Turns out the coast guard picked up a woman matching Hatcher's description, soaked in blood, on a sloop just up out to sea a bit. She was easy to subdue, and they're taking her to the mainland. So, we're all a little furious we ran off on a tip from a paranoiac. And I don't mean our friend Cobra." Oscar sneezed, and walked past Trey.

Trey stood there in the center of the office.

"I don't believe it," he said.

Oscar stopped at the door to his own office. He shook his head. "Believe it, Campbell. All I can say is, I hope they fry that woman. She deserves worse, but if there's a hell, she'll work out her damn karma from there."

"It's not her, Oscar," Trey said. "I know it."

"And how do you know that?"

"Instinct," Trey said.

DEFEATED, Trey walked out the door, out of the police station, into the cool night. He passed the closed up storefronts where Carly had window-shopped earlier that same evening. The ice cream stand, where he'd been sitting, thinking how good life could be. *It can all turn on a dime.* He remembered a biblical quote: *In the twinkling of an eye.* He wished he could step back through time, to that moment in the morning when he had forbidden Mark from coming horseback riding. If he'd followed through on Carly's plan, even Jenny and her boyfriend would still be alive, because the cottage would've been empty. Then, he might've been able to prevent those murders. And he would've prevented his son and daughter from having been exposed to that…creature. The thought gave him shivers: Agnes Hatcher kissing her son on his forehead. Like an animal cleaning another before the kill.

The Gorgon was in his life again. For all the good he tried to do her, none of it mattered. He had tried to understand her pathology when she'd been first admitted to Darden. He had been young and idealistic and essentially, stupid. He had given her information which fueled her fantasies.

Trey could not have felt worse.

He walked down the street to the docks. When he reached the pier, he sat down and gazed out at the night. The fog was light, and he could see the darkness of sea. He closed his eyes, sending a prayer out for Mark to get better.

And then, with sudden clarity, he remembered something that Agnes Hatcher had once told him.

He'd been sitting with her playing chess. She was a much better chess player than he'd ever be. It was in the recreation room at Darden State. Orderlies were standing guard at the doors. Agnes was rarely allowed around any other patients.

She wore the hospital gown, and green slippers. Her hair sparkled in the sunlight which cut through the barred windows.

He leaned back in the chair. It was his move, but he couldn't figure out for the life of him how to get around her queen.

She said, "It's a strategy."

He grinned, back then. He was only twenty-three, and he still believed that people could be saved from themselves. From their past, their psyches.

"What is?"

"This," she indicated the plastic chess pieces. "It's my strategy. You don't have one. You're just reacting to mine. That's not how anyone wins."

"How can I win? You're going to put me in check soon. You always do."

She looked quite seriously at him. "I would never do anything to hurt you. I don't want you to lose this game." She said it then as if what she were saying was of some great importance. "I want you to win."

"Why?"

"Because you understand."

"About chess?"

"About how all of it is one. Chess, life, death. You're not like the others. You have special knowledge. Only you need to open the door to it. You need the key. I am the key."

He let this go. There were some things the patients said which were indecipherable.

Then, she said, "Remember this. In this game, I moved my men around to this side, and so you followed. And then, to the other side, and then, you followed again. And back and forth. But if you watch the pattern of what I did, you'll see a thread through the middle. This is where I moved my queen. I wouldn't call this strategy."

"Right where you started. All your other moves were distractions from that main move," he nodded. "I wished I had noticed it. I'm dumb and you're smart."

"No," she said, leaning across the board to touch his hand. "My strategy is making you see that there is no strategy. All of it is chance. Fate. Fate is the guiding star. I believe Fate guides us to where we need to go. I may appear to win this game, and you may appear to lose it."

The warmth of her hand grew stronger until he wanted to draw back from her touch. It was too warm. Too inviting.

"But Fate is what draws my queen to her destination. The men may go to the left to fight, and to the right, but the players move where they are meant to, regardless. Your castle is mine, your kingdom, because it was meant to be mine."

With that, she moved her queen, and won the game.

He opened his eyes. The bay at Avalon was before him. He

stood up on the pier. He tried to look out to the bend of the island, but could not see any of the Kirk In The Rocks.

The men may go to the left to fight and to the right.

But the players move where they are meant to.

My strategy is no strategy.

Fate is the guiding star.

Your castle is mine.

Your kingdom.

CHAPTER SIXTY-TWO

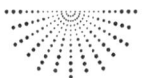

AGNES KNELT IN DARKNESS ON THE DECK. SHE WAITED UNTIL the last patrol boat had rounded the curve of the island. She had used the boat's police radio, and, from her years lecturing to police academies, she knew which band to use to make the frequency appear distant enough to fool the local police. She had spent most of her childhood and youth observing and studying the police. It always came in handy.

She was less exhausted than exhilarated from the day's kill. Operating on the boy and girl at the cottage had been refreshing, and she had showered in the spray from the teenaged girl. When she heard the other girl, the little one, go running and screaming, she knew she had to get out of the cottage fast. She did not intend to be caught before she attained fulfillment.

She would've taken his son, then.

The beautiful boy, so much like his father's smell.

But there had been no time that afternoon.

Instead, she had gone back inside the cottage, pulled some clothes from the woman's closet and changed into them. They were long for her, the shorts and T-shirt, but she had no time to worry about such things. She wrapped her jeans and sweater in a bundle with the soul-catchers. Then, she went out the front door of the cottage, leaving Cobra shivering in a corner of the kitchen, spineless man that he was.

Since the little girl was screaming at the road behind the cottage, no one seemed to notice the woman in shorts and T-shirt jogging down the side-path, as if she were just out for exercise.

The policewoman was easy to take care of. She was down at the docks, totally inexperienced, young, too—perhaps only twenty-one.

She was alone, because all the other cops had gone up to the cottage. Except Paula Stouffer had not wanted to. She's been scared. She'd never done more, probably, than catch a teenager shoplifting. She might have even known the girl and boy who had been slaughtered up the hill.

It was easy to approach her as a tourist and tell her that there was someone funny in the restrooms at the pier. Someone funny, not too scary. Just a weirdo.

"I'll go with you," Agnes had said. "I just think there's something wrong with the poor man."

Paula Stouffer was undoubtedly relieved that she didn't have to deal with murder and mayhem. Only someone funny, perhaps a homeless person, in the women's restroom.

When Agnes had her inside the filthy walls, she ripped the knife across Paula Stouffer's throat, using her own sweater to sop up the blood so that it didn't ruin the police uniform.

She stuffed the body into the last stall. Covered her with one of the dark plastic bags that was used to line the restroom garbage can. She closed the stall door, locking it from the inside. Then she climbed over the top of the stall.

But only after she scalped her, for Paula had beautiful auburn hair.

It had been that simple. She knew that there would be a boat to the mainland with his family on board. She'd been hoping he would come too. But it was enough that she had his family.

Their lives, their sacrifice, would be more crucial toward immortality than any others.

There was no moon that night. The fog came and went as if an unfelt wind moved it along. The boat was dark, too, for she'd shut off all the controls.

But even so, against the stars and mist and indigo sky, she saw the great Church of Fate rising, triumphant.

She glanced at the silhouettes of her prisoners:

The woman handcuffed to the girl, and the boy. The woman was gagged, and Agnes had draped a piece of cloth, torn from Officer Erskine's shirt, over her face. She would feel what Agnes had felt all those years. She would know what Agnes had been through.

And the boy. So like his father. He would not try and escape. She knew that.

She held tight to the fishing knife. It was so much like the knife they had used together in the fall of 1888. The taste of the blood that day had reminded her of all the lives they'd captured then.

Of all the lifetimes they had acquired.

He would come to her now.

He would come.

CHAPTER SIXTY-THREE

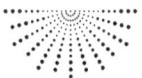

"She *is* there," Trey said.

Oscar glanced up. "Mr. Campbell." He didn't seem as furious as Trey had expected him to be.

The police chief looked sad, his eyes bloodshot.

"We were wrong," Oscar said. "There was no Coast Guard pick up. I located the frequency of the call—the one that claimed that Agnes Hatcher had been caught. I'm afraid I have some bad news for you."

Trey stood still.

"Your family hasn't been sighted near the mainland. They should've been close to docking by now." Oscar said, "She somehow managed to take the boat. Overcome the officers. We found one of them, dead, scalped. Paula Stouffer. In the beach restroom, in a locked stall, covered with a garbage bag. Hatcher's been out to sea almost four hours. She destroyed any equipment on board, so we can't track her. She has your family."

Trey Campbell said, "I know. That was her goal all along. Checkmate."

Oscar looked at him, perplexed.

"She's at Capilla Blanca."

"No," Oscar said. "We went over every inch of that place. I'm sorry. She's probably on the mainland by now, or near it. Maybe she's hiding up at San José Island. Maybe she's on the western side of our own island. We have helicopters coming from Los Angeles to check the local harbors. No more goose chases. I'm sorry. It's out of my jurisdiction now. The state boys will have her shortly, I'm sure."

Oscar said this as if even he didn't believe it.

CHAPTER SIXTY-FOUR

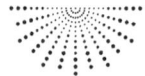

TREY RAN DOWN THE STREETS OF AVALON, HIS MIND RACING ahead of him. He had no one to turn to now. He was going to get no help from the police. They had their own agenda, their own strategy when it came to catching killers like Agnes. It often took days to track down such killers. By then, she might have added three more victims to her list. Usually, police were not that effective in the short term, for they didn't understand the nature of the beast they were hunting. Trey felt a cold sweat break out along his scalp and neck. He had to do something.

Time was running out. His family may already have been killed. But that wasn't what Agnes Hatcher would use them for. She would use them for drawing him out.

She wants you, not them.

CHAPTER SIXTY-FIVE

"Out," Agnes said.

She had the boy handcuffed to her left wrist.

She motioned with the fishing knife towards the small beach of pebbles at the sea entrance to Capilla Blanca. The waves crashed just beyond the larger boulders, but she'd been able to maneuver around them because the police boat was just small enough. But if they stayed in the boat much longer, a wave was likely to come over the rocks and do more than just spray them.

"I said 'out'." Agnes took the knife and held it against the boy's neck.

The little girl, handcuffed to the woman, moved. Agnes could tell she was afraid of stepping out of the rocking boat. The girl's mother, her face covered, her mouth gagged, made no sound whatsoever.

The girl gingerly stepped down into the ankle-deep water, shivering. Her mother followed; the girl helped guide her over the edge of the boat. The mother almost fell, but balanced herself against the girl.

The boy at Agnes' side said nothing, but when she walked, he stayed with her.

Agnes grabbed two of the flares. She popped one of them, and a fizzing red flame struck at its tip. She handed this to the girl. "Use this like a candle," she said. "If you try anything, I will kill your brother right in front of you. If you run off any path with your mother handcuffed to you, keep in mind, there are pits and chasms throughout these caves. You and your mother will both die if you don't follow me exactly. Do you understand?"

The little girl nodded slowly, tears in her eyes.

Agnes lit her flare, also, and held it in the hand that was cuffed to the boy. She said to him, "You will do exactly what I say, won't you?"

The boy looked up at her, staring blankly. He nodded.

"You saw what happened to your babysitter?"

Again, Mark nodded. He was not even shivering. It was as if he had adapted to this situation. As if some mechanism within his unconscious mind had kicked in, shunting fear aside for the time being. As if survival at any cost were enough to keep him functioning.

"She was very bad. She was vain. That means she thought the beauty of her face was more important than the gods. But I took that face from her. I bit it with my teeth." Agnes leaned closer to Mark's face. "I tasted her face. It was where she lived. Do you know where you live?"

Mark said nothing, but he didn't take his eyes off her.

"You live in your heart, little boy. And that's where I'll go if I need to find you." She stood up again. The girl's face was red in the glow from the flare. "Be careful," Agnes said, patiently. "Keep it away from your face. You might burn yourself."

She directed her captives to the cave's entrance.

CHAPTER SIXTY-SIX

THE BAYRUNNER WESTCOASTER WAS DOCKED AT THE SHORT pier. Trey Campbell had to climb over a low chicken wire fence to get to it; the rental boat dock was closed after dark, unless one had a key. He squatted down beside it, stepping, crab-like, into its stern. He slid across to one of the seats. He checked the motor for gas—there was still plenty. It took him several minutes to get it started, and when he did, he stayed down low in the boat, in case one of the local cops was still out, watching the docks. He loosed the boat from its mooring.

He drove the boat around the docks, going slowly so as not to bump any of the other resting boats. He steered it out into the bay, watching the shore to see if anyone followed him. The worst thing now would be if Oscar and his team of police followed him. Agnes would surely murder his family in that event. Only Trey knew that he held the key to stopping her.

The sea was calm.

Once he was out far enough from the town of Avalon, with its flickering lights, he noticed an incipient light across the sea, a greenish glow, as the waves crashed against rock and shoreline. He knew to keep the boat a good distance from the shore, because although part of the island was smooth with sand, there were outlaw rocks at sandbars just out in the bay, creating a fake reef. When the boat rounded the side of the island, to where Capilla Blanca rose up, he turned the motor off.

It was a silent night.

The night mist moved silently.

Trey took the oars beneath the slats of the boat, and began slowly rowing towards the cavern's mouth.

Agnes Hatcher's words echoed in his mind:

My strategy.

Then he thought: She thinks I'm Jack the Ripper. She believes we have to make things right together. That's what she's after. Not Mark or Terry or Carly. They're just in the way.

She has no strategy. It's more haphazard than planned. Even her escape, it was pure dumb luck. It was Donna Howe being foolish and Rob Fallon being his ever-lovin' sociopathic self. It wasn't fate. These were random events, which she has made to look like part of a pattern. I was caught up in it because I was afraid. I wasn't seeing it for what it was: the machine called the Gorgon just going where the wind took her, the easiest roads, the dumb luck of life. Her finding my vacation phone and address was coincidental to attacking Donna Howe. If Jim Anderson hadn't passed that piece of paper to Donna, Agnes would probably be at his residence in Redlands. Not here. It's all chance, and she's relying on it while the cops are looking for logic and pattern.

But her logic is nightmares.

The answer to stopping her is within her own pathology.

Becoming a nightmare.

Becoming what she wants.

An idea which seemed absurd and brilliant at the same time

suddenly occurred to him, something he'd never really considered. Something about telling Mark his 'As If' philosophy.

Trey Campbell was going to behave as if Agnes Hatcher's pathology was real.

He was going to become, for her, Jack The Ripper.

He was going to give her what she wanted.

He only hoped he wasn't too late for his family.

Rowing as fast as his heart and muscles would bear, he saw what he thought was the flash of a red flare just up at the shore, in the mouth of the cavern.

CHAPTER SIXTY-SEVEN

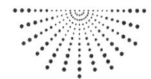

THE FLARE LIT THE CAVE A BRILLIANT RED, OUTLINING ITS recesses and sharply jutting rocks. Teresa walked carefully along the wet pebbles at the cave bottom. As she was about to step on what seemed a smoother surface, the psycho woman shouted at her, "Not that way!" Then, more calmly, "To the left, dear. See how it winds upwards. If you go straight ahead, we'll wind up in a lagoon. Look, do you see the spiral of the path? It represents the journey home. Spiraling, spiraling."

Teresa looked up at her mother's face. It was covered, but she could tell by the way her mother was walking that she wanted Teresa to obey the orders. Not seeing her mother's face was kind of scary for her; the handcuffs that bound them together hurt her wrists, too. But she knew her father would come, with the police, soon. She knew it would work out okay, just like it did on television shows like *Rescue 911*. Teresa had an opposing thought in her head, too. She thought that what happened to Jenny might happen to her. She tried not to let that thought control her.

Teresa went to the left. She kept the flare as far out in front of her as possible. It was warm at its base. Too warm, as far as she was concerned. She didn't like the way the fire sputtered at its tip, either. It wasn't like a Fourth of July sparkler. It felt too warm, like it was going to eventually get so hot that she'd have to drop it. She didn't want to be in the dark with the psycho woman.

She glanced back at Mark, cuffed to the woman.

Mark looked like he was somewhere else. His feet moved, and he stepped over rocks. But he didn't seem to be in his eyes like normal.

Teresa stepped up onto a rough, narrow path that quickly rose up from the wet pebbles. Before her, she saw the path rise and twist, like a staircase in a lighthouse. She hoped there were no wild animals living in it.

She didn't want to turn around and see the woman behind her. She didn't want to ever have to look at that face again.

She hoped everything would turn out all right.

Teresa tugged at the handcuff to keep her mother away from the edge of the path.

CHAPTER SIXTY-EIGHT

AGNES GAVE HER OWN FLARE TO THE BOY.

She whispered, "Hold onto this. It'll help us see. You can chase away all the shadows with it." She showed him how to hold it. He was a beautiful boy. Just like his father. She wanted to hug him tight, because he had a spark of her lover in him. But she knew this wasn't the time.

Then, as she followed the girl and her mother up the winding path, she opened the police knapsack at her side. Remembering when she first spoke with Jack in this new incarnation, the walks through the garden, the chess games, the way she looked at him and knew...

Agnes Hatcher left a trail for him. Each of the pieces was sacred, and he would follow them to their nest.

He would follow them, and remember.

THE LIGHTNING FLASHED in her brain, and she saw:

The oven was stuffed with rags. The oil jug, for the lamps

upstairs, rested in the corner. The coppers had left after searching the place. They had run back to the dead woman in the street. The one with her body sliced open. The one whose blood tasted like warm metal.

The locket was in her hands, open.

The lock of hair.

The picture.

She looked at the oil lamp. She could hear the whistles outside, and the endless rain. Would it never stop? She went to the casement window, looking through the grate. The street was enshrouded with fog. The rain was not as heavy as it sounded against the room. It sounded like drums beating; but it was only spitting rain outside.

She took the locket in her fist and crushed it, but it would not break. It only seemed to get warmer with her touch.

The time was drawing near. She knew that she must act fast, or she would never have the chance. How could he betray her?

A memory of being told a story as a little girl: of a witch pushed into a great oven and baked alive by merry children.

Agnes stepped over to the oil lamp, lifting it up. Its glow was warm. Warmth enveloped her, suddenly. The locket in her hand was like fire. The lamp's glow, so comforting.

In the corner, the great oven.

Lightning thrust its spear through her.

She was in the motel in Las Cruces. He was peeling away the layers of her face. He was showing her that she wore a mask.

"Do you see who you are?" he asked. "It takes several lifetimes for ordinary people to understand this. But I'm giving you a gift of sight. You see? Remember the past? Your life was different then, but it was your true self."

Red lightning cut across her vision like blood blinding her from her cut forehead.

She was in the cave, and the boy handcuffed to her stared up at her with the eyes of one who knows.

CHAPTER SIXTY-NINE

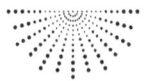

TREY WAS UP TO HIS SHOULDERS IN THE WATER, DRAWING HIS boat toward the shore. He had to stop the motor several yards from the ragged beach because the waves were getting slightly choppy. He was not a good enough seaman to ensure that he wouldn't crash the rented boat on the rocks. He gradually found sure footing, and was able to bring the boat up to the narrow strip of beach, just beyond the rocks. He secured it as best he could, and then went over to the police transport boat. He found Erskine's body, and a pool of blood in an aura around his neck and shoulders.

Without hesitation, he reached into the dead man's shoulder holster and withdrew a gun. It was a standard issue Smith & Wesson. From Trey's limited knowledge of cops, he assumed that the dead officer had rarely if ever used the gun. But it would be fully loaded.

Trey held it in his right hand. The idea of having to shoot it bothered him. Conflicting images rose in his mind:

Shooting the old man who had been trying to break in to his house.

Agnes Hatcher, bent over the psychiatrist at Darden, bits of his scalp between her teeth.

He checked around the boat, and found a small flashlight. He flicked it on. The police radio was destroyed. His first impulse was to take this boat, go get the police, and come back. But, what if there was no time? What if there were only minutes left to help his children?

I can't risk it. I can't sacrifice them to that madwoman.

From within the cavern, he saw a spray of red light. It moved, casting enormous shadows across the hanging rocks.

He waded through the tidal pool that would, within the next several minutes, be flooded.

When he stepped over the smaller rocks, and across what seemed a lagoon within the cavern, he waved the flashlight beam about the cave.

Then, he saw something which made him catch his breath.

He shined the light on the object that lay upon the slick path that led up from the water.

It was a human heart.

Beside it, one of Carly's sandals.

Trey Campbell felt a sudden sharp pain in the back of his head, and for a moment he thought he was falling.

Instead, he was leaning across a woman's body. Blood trickled from the edge of her neck. He looked up, and Agnes Hatcher was there—she looked different, but he knew her through the eyes. "The windows of the soul," she said.

He reached for her, and grasping her, brought her to him. Kissing her.

Trey opened his eyes. He was standing on the path that led to the Monk's Chamber. He felt dislocated, as if he'd briefly shared a vision with the Gorgon. *She's inside me now. I will find you, Agnes. I will keep you from hurting them.*

As he hiked the path that spiraled upwards, he came across other such finds. What might've been an eye, although it was all bloody. Several yards ahead on the path, a ragged patch of human skin, almost like sheer fabric. *Don't let this be my children. Don't let this be Carly. Please, be safe. Please, Agnes, don't hurt them.*

He wondered if he was too late. He moved as quickly as he could across the slick rock.

He shined his flashlight up the trail.

He knew where it led.

His father had taken him there many times when he'd been a boy.

The Monk's Chamber. The Monk's Well.

Capilla Blanca.

Whitechapel.

Trey shouted, "Agnes!"

The name echoed through the caverns, which to Trey now seemed like the spiraling chambers of a nautilus, all leading to the central place of destiny.

CHAPTER SEVENTY

THE ROOM WAS CIRCULAR, WITH NATURAL STONE BENCHES within its perimeter. A chasm was at its center, almost perfectly round, like a well without walls. However, there were several embedded rocks around its edges. The walls of the room were etched and shaded with pictures of Jesus and Mary. This made Teresa feel a little less scared. Graffiti, too, was sprayed and slashed across the white walls. Teresa began saying her prayers silently. She gripped her mother's hand.

Her mother gripped back, giving her a squeeze.

It felt like a signal from her mother that they would be safe.

Someone was yelling from below, almost like it was coming from the well that sat in the center of the room.

"Do you hear him?" Agnes said, turning to the children. The flares lit the room with a pink glow, and the psycho woman seemed to be bathed in blood on her face. She had eyes like fire.

The scream again, "Agnes!"

Teresa recognized the voice. *Daddy.* She glanced at Mark, but he still stared straight ahead, through her.

. . .

AGNES HATCHER GRINNED with blood-stained teeth. "It's the intersection," she said. "It's the sacrifice time."

She grabbed Mark and brought him close to her bosom.

She raised the fishing knife over his forehead.

Close to his eyes. "Life for life," she whispered.

Teresa screamed, "No!"

Her mother pulled Teresa behind her swiftly, and even with her hands confined, leapt forward.

CARLY COULD ONLY SEE blackness through the face cover. She had said her prayers, and held onto her daughter's wrist, even while the handcuffs had sawed against her own wrists. She had carefully followed her daughter up the trail, hoping that the police would come soon. Hoping that something would rescue them. Or something would help, some natural or supernatural agency. But no help had come.

When she heard Trey's voice, she thought he was near. But then, with Teresa's crying out, she knew that something was happening. Something bad.

Then, she heard a bleating sound from Mark.

Carly lunged in the direction of Agnes Hatcher's voice, keeping Teresa behind her. She had to make sure that nothing happened to her children.

What she felt when she lunged was a cold blade digging deep into her rib cage.

AGNES DREW THE KNIFE OUT, and began cursing her, but Carly barely heard anything, and felt as though she might be blacking out.

. . .

TERESA LAY BESIDE HER MOTHER. With her free hand, she tore off the face cover. She looked at her mother's eyes. They were closed.

Don't be dead, Mommy. Please, don't be dead.

Ignoring the psycho woman who knelt over her with the knife, Teresa used her hands and teeth to tear off the rag tied around her mother's mouth. "She has to breathe! You're killing her!" Teresa said, turning to look at the psycho woman.

AGNES HATCHER HELD ONTO MARK. She shivered when she saw the anger in the girl's eyes. "Dying is good," Agnes said, almost sweetly. "Hurting is good. It shows who you are on the inside."

Suddenly, Mark began crying. He tugged at the handcuff, but was held fast in Agnes' arms. She kissed the top of his head. "Don't worry, little one. I'll show you where your mother lived. Not in her heart. Not like you. She lived in the lower part of her body. She lived where she created you."

Agnes traced the knife down Carly's body, down her stomach. She raised the knife slightly.

"She lived where all whores live," Agnes said.

At that second, the sound of a gunshot rang through the caves.

Bats by the hundreds swept downwards upon them. Teresa started screaming. She kept her face low, near her mother's. The bats brushed across her hair, tangling it.

The monk's chamber became black with bats as they dived down among the children. Agnes flailed the knife in the air, as the bats slapped against her.

The knife dropped from her hand, to the hard-packed dirt.

When the bats had cleared, Agnes lay in a heap across Carly's body.

The shadow of a man stood at the entrance to the circular room.

"Beloved," the man said.

CHAPTER SEVENTY-ONE

"DADDY!" TERESA WEPT, CLUTCHING HER MOTHER. "DADDY!
Mommy's dead!"

But the man in the jagged doorway didn't look at her. He didn't
seem like her father at all, because the expression he wore was
different. He looked like someone else had crawled into his skin.

"It's taken me so long to come to you," he said, his arms
outstretched.

CHAPTER SEVENTY-TWO

AGNES FELT A DOORWAY OPEN WITHIN HERSELF. HE HAD found the key, finally.

He found the key!

It was as if they were back in their nest, beneath the street in Whitechapel. It was like that last day. She was transformed—no longer in the body of the Hatcher woman, she was Agnes Graile, nineteen. Her Jack was there for her.

She went to his arms. "I'm sorry for what I did," she whispered, pressing her face against his neck. "I brought you all these lives so we could be together forever."

She smelled again the mildew and the coal. She kissed his neck. The scent of his soap was there—the scent of the gentleman surgeon.

"Leave them," he whispered. "They're nothing to us."

She smiled, nodding, and reached into her pocket for the key to the handcuffs. She smelled wonderful, as if she'd just taken a scented bath. It was as if her entire body chemistry had changed. There was no sea to her, no blood. Just the scent of flowers after a rain. She handed the small key to him. Trey took it, and uncuffed the boy.

Then, he hooked the empty handcuff around his own wrist. If I can get her away from them. If I can just get her away from here.

"Bound for all eternity," he said.

And then she felt the metal against the flesh of her breast.

Instinctively, she drew back from him. She saw the gun in his hand. "It's karma," she said dreamily, "What I did to you, you now do to me."

She reached for the gun, her hand closing over his.

TERESA WRAPPED her arms around her mother, weeping. She didn't understand why her father was acting so crazy.

Then, she felt the breath on her cheek.

She drew back, looking at her mother.

CARLY OPENED HER EYES. She felt a pain below her chest. She tried to speak, but had some trouble. She tried to rise up, but had little energy.

AGNES SQUEEZED the trigger of the gun—

Trey pulled it back and up, not wanting to kill her—

The bullet grazed Hatcher's shoulder—

AGNES KNOCKED Trey backwards with all her weight. It was as if she had the strength of several strong men. He felt his knees buckle, and the wind was knocked out of him.

He fell to the floor, unconscious.

. . .

AGNES LEANED OVER HIM. "I didn't mean to," she said, "It was the locket. I didn't mean to…the oven…"

TREY, waking, hearing her babbling about "locket" and "oven," realized that his act as her beloved Jack had sent her mind back to her repressed memory. He drifted in and out of consciousness, for a few moments, had the hallucination that he was inside some dark cold metal closet and could hear rain outside.

AS THE RAIN spattered the streets and leaked into the basement, Agnes opened the small locket and saw the lock of dark hair and the woman's picture. It was some society woman. Jack had betrayed her.

He was there, hiding in the oven so that the police would not find him if they searched their nest. He was hiding behind rags and coal.

She felt the blood boil within her.

How could he betray her like that? They had sworn eternal devotion! They had mixed their blood with the blood of others—they were bound together for all time and eternity.

She soaked more rags in oil.

When she had several such rags, she opened the oven door slightly. She held the oil lamp up. In the light from the lamp, she saw his eyes. He looked at her with love. She knew it was not meant for her. She was just a whore. She was just the street-rag he had worn for a period of time. This other woman in the locket—she was the one he loved.

"Are they gone?" he whispered.

She answered him with fire.

. . .

CARLY WHISPERED TO TERESA, "THE KNIFE."

Teresa stretched as far as she could to reach the fishing knife which had fallen in the dirt.

She said to Mark, "Marky! Help...Mommy needs help..." She pointed towards the knife, which was just a few feet from him.

Mark took a step towards the fishing knife.

It lay in the dirt, its metal shining red in the unholy light from the flares.

The images of Jesus on the cross seemed to dance in the flickering glow.

TREY CAME TO FULL CONSCIOUSNESS. He reached for the gun, but it wasn't near him.

Agnes, cuffed to him, dragged him up to his feet.

"I HAD TO DO IT," she said, tears streaming down a face which still looked like a tigress ready to spring. She held the gun in her hand. "I had to. You were going to run off with her. You were going to forsake me. I couldn't let you. I knew it was the flesh that drew you. I knew that. I did it for us. So our love would not be tainted..."

She pointed the gun towards Carly. She drew Trey towards his wife and children. The handcuffs chafed his wrist. "When she dies, you'll understand."

"I do understand," Trey said. "And I love you."

A glimmer of hope sparkled in Agnes Hatcher's eyes.

For the first time since he'd been in his twenties, Trey thought she looked human. She was no longer the Gorgon or the Surgeon, but a much-abused girl who had not been allowed to fully develop. She looked like the most pitiable creature on the face of the earth. In a moment, he remembered her life: the torture as a young girl, the darkness that was forced to blossom within her mind.

"If you love me, you'll watch her die," Agnes said. She aimed the gun for Carly's face.

CARLY'S EYES grew wide with terror.

Trey brought his free hand to Agnes Hatcher's face. He turned it towards his own. He kissed her strongly, passionately. "It's me. It's Jack," he said. Then, he took the gun from her hand. "Let me murder the whore."

CARLY WHISPERED, "TREY?"

"Shut up!" He yelled at her. Then, softly, to Agnes, "We can always be together now."

"DO YOU FORGIVE ME?" Agnes asked.

"For what?"

Her mood suddenly changed. She wasn't buying the act. She went for the gun. "You'll know when I kill her. Your eyes'll be opened."

USING ALL the strength he could muster, Trey jerked the handcuff. The gun dropped without firing. He and Agnes fell to the floor of the chamber. He groaned as he felt her knee connect with his groin, hard. She ground her knee into him there. He retched, and jabbed his elbow into her stomach.

She scratched at him, blindly, as if fighting for her life. He punched her as hard as he could in the face. She bit down hard on his neck, drawing blood. They wrestled to the well—the rim of rocks at its edge keeping them from falling over. She managed to bring him down. She rolled on top of him, and put her face close to his.

She foamed at the mouth. It was like having a bobcat sitting on top of him, small but strong and mean. "I'll make it right," she spat at him. "It's not your fault." Through the wild look on her face, he saw into her eyes. She was a child there, they were swirls of colors, and she was lost within them. It was like watching someone where half their soul was at war with the other half. "It's not your fault. It's 'cause of me, what I did. That night."

And then a calm came over her. She half-smiled. "I know you love me. I know I was wrong."

Her strength seemed to mellow, and she was no longer a heavy weight bearing down upon him, but light. He felt he could push her off.

He was about to do just that.

AND THEN, as if fulfilling some destiny, she rolled over the edge of the chasm.

CHAPTER SEVENTY-THREE

TREY HELD ONTO ONE OF THE STONE MARKERS AT THE EDGE of the great well with his free arm.

The handcuff with Agnes' weight pulling on it, sliced into his wrist like a razor.

If he tried, he could pull her up.

He could save her.

All his training had been to save and help and understand.

But this woman was a monster.

This woman had stabbed his wife in her side.

This woman would've tortured and killed his family.

If he raised her up from the pit, even if he could, she would tear into him like a lion. But something within him still believed that she could be saved. That something in that monster soul could be salvaged.

CARLY CRAWLED SLOWLY, snake-like, to the edge of the precipice. Teresa crawled along with her, still handcuffed to her.

Carly gripped Trey's arm where the handcuff was cutting into his wrist.

AGNES, dangling, but holding on, too, to what she could of the walls of the natural well.

"Jack," she whispered, "please, help me. I love you."

Then, she tugged harder on the handcuff, kicking out from the wall. She didn't want help being brought up to safety.

She wanted to bring Trey over the edge with her.

CHAPTER SEVENTY-FOUR

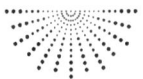

CARLY HELD THE FISHING KNIFE UP IN HER FREE HAND AND brought it down.

She hacked at Agnes Hatcher's wrist, cutting deep into her flesh.

Carly sawed with the knife until Agnes' small hand, bloody and torn, slipped loose from the cuff.

AGNES DROPPED into the darkness of the pit.

CHAPTER SEVENTY-FIVE

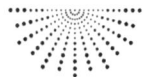

TREY HELD HIS WIFE AND CHILDREN AS CLOSE TO HIMSELF AS
he could get them. He tore his shirt off and wrapped it around
Carly's side to help stop the wound up. He wanted to drown in the
feeling of their skin, their smell, their sound, their taste as he kissed
Mark's forehead and Teresa's cheek. He held his wife the longest,
and they cried.

When he felt the strength, he helped Carly up. "Maybe you
should go get help," she said.

"No," he said. "We'll make it back to the boat. I'm not going to
leave you."

Carly was feeling weak, but she leaned against him as they
walked back down the winding path of the cavern. Teresa held
Mark's hand, but kept one hand on her father's back as he walked,
just to make sure he was there.

WHEN THEY CAME to the lower exit from the caverns, they saw

that the water had risen. The boats were gone, washed out with the tide.

"So, what now? An earthquake?" Carly asked, keeping her sense of humor intact.

Trey held up the flare. He set Carly down at the edge of the path. He instructed Mark and Teresa to stay with her.

Trey Campbell walked out into the dark sea, flare held high.

The water reached his chest, and he found a rock to climb onto.

He waved the flare back and forth, trusting that someone would see it and send help.

Within an hour, he saw the lights of another boat. As it got closer, he saw that it was an old fashioned fishing trawler. A man on board waved a lantern, and Trey shouted, waving the flare faster until it seemed like he'd painted the sky red with it.

CHAPTER SEVENTY-SIX

She heard him. The shout. Like a cry of joy.

Agnes Hatcher lay on a slanting rock shelf of the monk's well.
The smells all around her were of sea anemone and urchin, and
dead fish. The water was gently lapping at her back where it had
risen with the tide.

She would drown, or die from the fall. Or she would live and
starve, too weak to call out for help—and then die slowly in several
days. It didn't matter to her.

She stared up the sheer wall to the white chalk of the cavern,
which seemed to glow in the dark. A memory came to her, not of a
basement in Whitechapel, nor with the man who had taken her
from the gas station restroom.

*She was ten, and at her parents' house. It was her birthday, and her
father was taking her to the park to ride the ponies.*

The memory was brief but intense, like a birthday candle just
before it was blown out.

Her small hand within her father's larger hand.
Warmth.

She could not move, no matter how hard she tried. She felt the blood pulsing from her wrist.

It was like being in that room again at Darden.

Restrained.

But the cloth was off her face. She could see. At least, she could still see.

Sight was its own kind of freedom.

Her lungs hurt, and breathing was difficult. All her energy went into each breath.

Minutes later, she heard the rush of water as it flooded the well-like chamber.

The salt stung the stab wounds in her wrist. But pain was distant, like the crashing waves outside the caverns.

Death was like going home. It had to take you in when there was nowhere else to go.

And she was going home, finally. After all this time.

She awaited, patiently, the next incarnation.

IT CAME TO HER, not as the sea rushing over her face, nor as the blood drained from her body, but as *a cloak of fire in her mind.*

CHAPTER SEVENTY-SEVEN

AFTER THE OLD FISHERMAN HAD LOCATED THEM AND brought them back to town, and after Carly got patched up at a local clinic, they had spent the morning at the police station, giving their statements to Oscar Arboles.

They passed the afternoon sleeping at the Breakers Hotel. Trey slept in the bed, his body wrapped around his wife's; his children lay in cots in the same room.

He didn't know how long a time would pass until he would allow them out of his sight again.

TREY AWOKE to the explosions and whistles of firecrackers.

"Oh," he said, waking Carly. "I forgot it's July fourth."

She rubbed her eyes. He kissed her several times before he could bring himself to get out of bed.

"Would it be foolish to take the kids to see the fireworks?" Carly asked. She was feeling better. "I mean, after all we've been through?"

"We're on vacation," Trey answered. "Why not?"

IN THE BAY, a flat barge shot off the brilliant fireworks. Yachts and sloops of all sizes speckled the horizon. A band played John Phillip Sousa marches from the docks. The beach lit up with sparklers. Tourists had packed the place in twenty-four hours.

That night, Trey sat out in another rented boat holding Carly, while Mark and Teresa were amazed by the night fireworks.

The last rocket launched and sprayed a rainbow of color across the night.

For a second, Trey felt a strange tug within him. He shivered slightly.

"Something wrong?" Carly asked, noticing his change of expression.

He didn't want to say what he felt. He said, "Just happy we made it through."

"They'll find her body," Carly said. "No one could survive that fall. Not even her."

Trey Campbell returned his attention to the falling sparkles, and to the renewed joy in his children's faces.

But he felt it again.

Within him.

She's gone.

He thought he'd heard her voice whisper to him, *Beloved!*

Trey imagined *a stone alley, and a shivering young girl standing in its corner. She watched the basement of an adjoining tenement rage with fire. As the flames shot up through the night, the girl moved closer to the fire, as if looking for something.*

"Are you there?" she asked the fire. "Jack?"

Trey tried to warn her away, but the girl pulled her cloak closer around her shoulders. She moved towards the burning building.

She lifted a grate that was red from heat. The flesh of her fingers burned against it. As the tongues of fire shot up from below, the girl descended into the burning room.

Trey thought he saw them clutch at each other as if they were the only souls in the world. Clutch and claw and embrace as the flames engulfed them.

He watched the sky brighten with one last shattering spray of light.

For a moment, it illuminated the heavens.

And then, the sky was dark, a mystery.

Trey Campbell wondered if, somewhere safe, she would be reborn.

∾

Be sure and read Books 2 and 3 of The Criminally Insane series:

Red Angel

Night Cage

RED ANGEL

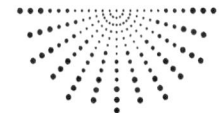

THE CRIMINALLY INSANE SERIES, BOOK 2

For Steve, with thanks.

Then I saw an angel coming down from Heaven, holding in his hand the key of the bottomless pit and a great chain.
    —From the book of Revelation

CHAPTER ONE

NIGHT. TWENTY-THREE TRIPLE-FENCED ACRES. BRIGHT lights create an unnatural daylight glow around the facility. The low, white, institutional outposts of a state hospital.

The Darden State Hospital for Criminal Justice on the engraved granite marker at the entry gate, flanked by a guardhouse and a parked police SUV.

Within, locked doors lead to the quiet of long green corridors. Patients asleep. Restrained. Drugged. Muffled sounds as some within the rooms talk or even touch. Rules are broken when authority is removed.

A nurse sets up meds for the late shift, counting pills, sorting them into cups.

The echoing rattle, squeak, slide of the wheels of a med cart as a psych tech and nurse move down the hall, their voices low and nearly inaudible.

A doctor passes them, clipboard in hand, flanked by two large men in white jackets and yellow shirts.

Sounds of someone jogging down another hallway—a *tap, tap, tap* of shoes.

Doors are shut; vending machine area is locked; the white light from the canteen cuts a rectangle of brightness into the dimly lit hall.

Ward D, at the end, is closed off from the rest.

Twin red lights set above the emergency box interrupt the white and green of the hallway.

Two correctional officers stand guard in front of steel doors, each with a porthole window.

Above the doors, a sign reads: "Program 28 | Specialized Treatment and Observation. Authorized Personnel | Access Limited."

Through the porthole windows, the hall has a metallic, futuristic look.

Rooms to the left, observation area to the right.

Three psych techs sit at desks but seem to ignore the rooms. Joking. Gossiping. Complaining. Voices kept low.

The rooms are dark, behind bars and glass.

Patients sleep.

One of the forensics patients within Program 28 begins to wail as if to wake the dead.

In seconds, a psychiatric technician unlocks the door and runs to the patient's bedside.

The lights come up in the room with the cot on which the patient sleeps.

Another psych tech stands in the doorway.

"What the hell?" the psych tech says.

"Jesus H," says the other.

The patient lies still, eyes closed as if he has been asleep the whole time. His prison-issue pajama top open, unbuttoned.

On his stomach are words, carved as if by sharp fingernails.

It is a long sentence and runs from just beneath his nipples to the small tufts of hair just below his waistline.

The psych tech near the cot scratches his head but doesn't for a moment stop watching the patient on the cot.

His name is Michael Scoleri, but he calls himself Abraxas, and he was known, in the outside world, before he was sentenced to life as an SVP and then reclassified as an SSPVS7, for carving his nickname on the bodies of the women he murdered.

Before he entered Darden State, he believed he was God.

Now, he's not so sure.

His restraints are torn at his wrists.

Blood all over his hands.

On his stomach, the words:

SUFFER THE CHILDREN TO COME UNTO ME.

In smaller cuts beneath this, along his thigh, when he is inspected, there are other names, including LUCAS.

CHAPTER TWO

THE STONE ANGEL STARES WITH SIGHTLESS EYES AT THE MAN.

In a stone room, miles from Darden State, steam rises from a pool of water.

The man holds a limp child in his arms, dipping the child's scalp back into the water.

CHAPTER THREE

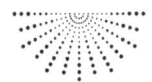

CHRISTMAS IS JUST A WEEK AND A HALF AWAY. THE SNOW-topped mountains above the Inland Empire of Southern California attest to winter, although, in the valley below, it is generally all palm trees and orange blossoms.

Two days earlier, in a ditch at the edge of an orange grove in Caldwell, California, a boy was found, dead, partially mutilated, with bird wings strung on a wire coat hanger wrapped around his neck.

Then another child, a girl this time, again with the torn wings at her neck, this time in San Pascal County.

"Another angel," one of the cops said, a young female investigator, who was on the scene soon after the second body's discovery.

The lead investigator, a broad-faced man of fifty, said, "Let's get some geography on this and the others."

"He puts them to sleep," she said. "Then he kills them. Then this. What do you make of these marks?"

"Bites," the other detective said. "They're his teeth."

CHAPTER FOUR

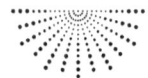

Suburban hillside, adobe ranch house, modest but lovely, lights on the front porch and in the narrow garden court-yard. Sunday night. The usual TV routine: flipping through forty or so cable channels to find a minute or two of some show or documentary. The TV screen alternating between a story about ancient Egypt on the History Channel, CNN, and the local news show. Settled on the local news, but now and then Trey Campbell flicked back to CNN.

Trey Campbell sat up after he and his wife had put the kids to sleep. She was doing the *LA Times* crossword, wearing her reading glasses, with the bright lamp turned up. Every now and then, she'd ask him for a word. "What's a seven-letter name of someone who starred in old MGM musicals?"

"The whole name?"

"Just the name."

"Well, I mean Astaire. Or Garland. I'm sure there's more than that."

"Mr. Trivia."

"It's my brain. It's like I have the most expensive computer chip in my head, and all it remembers are old pop songs and movies. Or what was the name of Henry the Eighth's fifth wife. Or which *Wallace and Grommet* episode involves sheep. Totally useless. If I could just apply it to solve the problems of the human condition … Hey, what about—" He was about to mention another name from the MGM musicals but had flicked to local news. He kept the sound slightly low, out of respect for his wife's crossword puzzle obsession.

"I don't think it's either of those. I think there has to be an *r* as the second letter."

He'd been hoping to catch the news before going to bed the same night that the third body was found. He'd heard from some buddies across town that there were some kids missing in over in San Pascal County, and when the news piece flashed onscreen he turned the volume back up.

"A killer that *The Inland Empire Daily* has dubbed the 'Red Angel.'" The news story ended. Trey had missed most of it.

"Red Angel?" his wife asked. "Weird name for a killer."

"Jesus," Trey said. "Somebody's killed kids in San Pascal. This must be the case Elise is being called in to consult on."

"Dr. Conroy?" Carly had a slight edge to her voice. Conroy was a beautiful woman on top of being an excellent forensic psychiatrist. Carly was rarely jealous of other women, but Conroy, more often than not, looked like a movie star.

Whenever Carly mentioned Elise's name, it was always with a hint of annoyance that Trey might have to work in close proximity to her. They even joked about it, but he knew not to push that button with his wife.

"We talked Saturday night. She wouldn't tell me the specifics of the crime, just that some of the detectives had been bringing her in to try and work up a psychological profile of the killer. I just didn't think it was right here. This fast. I thought it was an old case."

They watched the rest of the news broadcast in silence, but other than the name the local media had just given the kidnapper and killer, not a lot of information was being let out.

When it was over, he said, "They don't have anything. They wouldn't put this on the news if they did. Not yet. They're trying to get someone to come forward, I'd guess. Awful. Awful. I guess this guy has a strange MO for them to call him the Red Angel."

"Terrible," Carly said. "Makes me want to double-check the burglar alarm."

"What a nightmare for those parents. I can't even imagine," he said. He leaned over and kissed Carly on the forehead. "We're lucky."

She put the magazine section down and leaned into him.

"Sure are."

"I don't know what I'd do if something … well, not that it will."

"I'm sure they'll catch the guy. Soon."

"You never know. Back east with that sniper a while back, it took longer than anyone thought it would."

"You worry too much. They'll catch him," his wife said.

"I wish I knew what this guy was thinking. I wish there was a way the cops could stay a step ahead of him."

"Don't start that stuff," she said. Sweetly, but firmly.

It raised its ugly head between them. The conflict.

How he could sometimes start to think like the psychopaths he worked around at Darden State.

About getting inside their heads.

It was a talent he hated, but he had it and had tried to accept it.

"I just don't know," he said. "When you're a kid, you think the world is one way. And then you get older, and you grow up, and you get kids of your own. And you know it's never always a good place to be. The world. For those kids. For their parents."

"I know. It's like we're still living in the jungle, and there's always someone out there ready to attack," she said. "It's the world. What was it you told me? The predatory nature of human beings."

"Yeah, but not like that."

"I don't know. Seems pretty much like that. That's a human monster. You work with them. You know."

"I work with them where it's safe. But when they're out of their cages ..." He didn't finish the thought.

The weather came up on TV. "Lows in the twenties in the mountains. Good skiing up in Big Bear through the upcoming weekend. White Christmas up in Arrowhead. For those in the Valley, it looks like a mild sixty-five to a high of seventy on Monday, dropping slightly through the week. Chance of showers midmorning tomorrow, changing to clear skies by evening."

When he switched the TV off that night, Trey said a prayer for the dead kids, and then another one for his own two children. He went around and double-checked the locks on the door, his nightly ritual for the past several months. Also triple-checked that the burglar alarm was on and working, its small yellow light flashing in its white plastic case.

He tried not to run through the killers he'd worked with most of his adult life, as if sifting through them to understand the mind of this new murderer who went after children.

The Red Angel, he thought. *Why would they call you that?*

CHAPTER FIVE

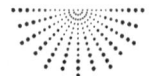

MOON LAKE, CALIFORNIA, ALONG THE SAN BERNARDINO Mountain range, eighteen degrees, three a.m.

Outside, cold as hell. Chance of snow likely. Ice along the edges of the roads. Ice hanging from trees beyond the stone walls of this sacred holy place.

The chapel of rock.

The Mad Place.

Steam and warmth within.

IN THE MAD PLACE, it moves frantically about its business.

The stench is unbearable. It is waking up what's inside it. The odor of fresh death in its nostrils makes it gasp with desire.

It doesn't want it to happen, but it's too late.

Bombs exploding in its head, the roar of the Other One obliterating his will, it presses its face to the arm and bites.

Tongue dry. Breathing hard. Heart pounding too fast.

Teeth press into skin.

Bites.

Savagely.

Tearing.

Repeatedly.

Until there is nothing left on the body to bite.

The angel whispers a prayer of hellfire and brimstone as the steam comes up against its face.

Then it cuts off the bird's wings.

AFTERWARD, inspired, it writes in the notebook that it has titled *Revelations*.

"AND SO I SAW THE GREAT BEAST ARISE AND TAKE WITH IT THE INNOCENT LAMB, TEARING ITS FLESH, BUT THE ANGEL OF THE LORD HAS COME AND SAVED THE INNOCENT ONE FROM THE FIRES OF PERDITION."

It tears out this page and crumples it up and sets it in the small hand.

It feels relief.

It feels Heaven shining on it.

It knows it's alive, because it is covered with sweat. It feels the warmth of a thousand suns upon its skin. It feels that all-encompassing love, that acceptance.

Transcendence itself.

It basks in the heat of the eternal as it senses its own breathing, stomping, maddening life with wonder.

Ah. That's what it expresses. *Ah.*

Then, seconds later, it feels the pounding in its head again.

The chill returns.

The lifeless, mutilated body of a child in its arms.

Sacrifice.

IT HASN'T SLEPT in four days because the voice of the Other One doesn't stop.

It comes home at three a.m. It is weary. It is tired of resisting. Tired of what it must do.

It has to go out again in a few minutes. It has to make its run and find another one.

But it's hungry, and it needs to get in from the cold.

It needs its mother.

Its old dog, Jojo, looks up from beside the fireplace, a slight wag of the worn old tail, and then head down again on the little wool rug, back to doggy dreamland. *The dog is better than people*, it thinks. *Dogs are better because they don't keep anything in cages. Dogs are better because they bite when they want. Dogs are better because they love.*

Music from the 1940s is playing on the old turntable. Glenn Miller. The place is all muted reds and browns and greens and yellows, between the fabric on the couch and chairs to the ceramic figurines over the mantel, above the glowing fire. The smells of stew coming in from the kitchen mingled with the faint but undeniable stink of urine, and the heavy brown stench of old cigarette smoke that never leaves the cabin. Years of smoking in the little house has left its marks in stains on the green curtains. There are four rooms, all of them small. This is the only home it has ever known.

It steps in and wanders first to the bathroom to relieve itself.

After this kind of night, it has to relieve the pressure of its bladder, which has been building up.

It looks at its face in the little square of mirror above the toilet, and sees the scratches and raised welts that cover it. Like wax melted over its skin.

The sound of the television in the living room. Like shouting. It hates that kind of noise, but she likes the TV and music on when she's alone. She doesn't like to think she's by herself, and it doesn't like her to feel that way.

No one should be alone, it thinks. *Devil comes out when you're alone.*

In the small living room, it tosses its coat over the back of the flower-print sofa, and is about to go to the fridge for a Coke or a beer, but its mother calls to it. It checks the windows for faces, but sees none. Piles of clothes in a corner.

It wants its supper, but it doesn't want her to feel bad, so it goes into her bedroom, where the piss smell is heavier, but cloaked with perfume that smells like orange blossoms. The bedroom has the dolls in the corner and her paperback books in piles near the window that has been covered over with plastic sheeting and duct tape to keep the wind out. The tubes are there, and the bed, and it has to check her levels so that she won't have pain. Her pills are all lined up, and it puts them in a small Dixie Cup and passes them to her. It gets a glass of water, one of many on a nearby table, and watches as she drinks it down.

It is weary from the previous night and keeping the Other One out of its head.

It sits beside its mother and strokes her hand, because she likes it to do that. She is a smart woman. It has known that all its life, and she cared for it when it was just a little boy, and it is grateful for that because it doesn't think it would have lived. But it had the thing inside it already, the Other One, and she couldn't know about that. She couldn't know what it had to deal with to keep the Other One, the Real One, in its cage. She had simply loved it for who it was, and it served her, and wanted her to sleep peacefully at night.

It completely loves her, and loves everyone, because it is a loving being, and it only wants what's best for those around it. It's the Other One that is the monster, and it doesn't even like thinking the name of the Other One for fear that the cage will start rattling again.

"Where you been all night?" she asks.

It doesn't want to tell her, just like it never told her when it was a child that it lived in the darkness and watched what happened when the birds started flying and when its other half felt the scraping and cleaning and purifying.

"I was callin' and callin'. That girl been callin' too; you need to go get her, she says, at four, or she's gonna just get a room down there, and I told her to get a room if she has to and never come back. I don't know how you put up with her. Don't give me that look. Yes, I know her name is Monica. Monica Monica Monica. I hear that name and it makes me want to spit. And I got a pain in my back." It tells her to turn over slightly, and it begins rubbing the middle of her back, because it's where she hurts the most, and when the pain gets to be the worst, it gives her a massage like this and she feels better.

"Read to me," she says, reaching near her waist, feeling for the book she's left there. "Read me from this one."

It picks up the small paperback book with the yellowed pages. On the cover, a muscular young man with blazingly brilliant blond hair that luxuriously falls down his back, as if he's meant to be the princess rather than the prince, embraces a scantily clad woman whose breasts burst forth from her tunic. She is wrapping her arms around his bare waist, her head tossed back lightly. It is called *Gladiator's Conquest.*

It opens the book to the dog-eared page.

It begins reading, its voice a ragged whisper.

"Louder," the old woman says. "I can't hear a god-blessed word."

It doesn't notice what it's reading to her. It hears what it thinks is a child mewling outside, and it panics a little, because the child can't run now.

The woman interrupts. "I think you need to rest up, baby. I think you've got to get out there in a few hours. You don't need to stay up like this. How about a little sleep? You're so good to me. But maybe you need a little sleep." Her voice is feeble and raspy, so he goes to get her a glass of water.

"Here you go," it says, bringing the water to her.

"What is it?"

"Water."

"Just water?"

"That's it," it says, and sits back down beside her, holding the glass for her while her twisted hands gather around its hands as it tips it up to her lips. After a sip or two, her throat clears and she sounds better. "I think you need some sleep," she says.

It nods. "I got too much to get done right now. I can sleep later. You might want to sleep."

"Read me some more. Please. Oh, please," she says, then takes another sip from the glass, a sound in her throat as if she is greedy for water.

"Nurse's gonna be here in an a couple hours," it tells her. "Sleep till then."

It feels the Other One, the one in the cage in its head, begin to snarl and snap like a mad dog, and it lets go of its mother's hand and checks the tubes to make sure they're clear. It reads the book as loud as it can, but even with it nearly shouting out the story of the woman in the book as she feels the man pressed into her, "his throbbing pressed against her femaleness, she wanted the heat of him more than life itself," it hears the child.

A little bird chirping in the woods.

Its mother says, "I bet it's gonna snow today. It'd be nice to have more snow. It makes the world all clean and ready for Jesus at Christmastime. That'd be nice, wouldn't it? Pure clean snow. Just like your daddy liked."

"If it snows," it says, "then Betty can't get here. You don't want that, do you? We love Betty."

"Well, you'll be here if she can't," its mother says. "You are such a good son. Such a good boy. I don't like that damn nurse that much anyway. Sticking me with her needles. Giving me those awful pills."

"They help with your pain." It couldn't bring itself to say the C-word. It could barely use the word "hospice" without starting to feel like it just wanted to go into the Mad Place and just let the Other One out for good.

"You help with my pain," she says.

Its mother smiles, feebly, and it can tell she is already drifting into sleep and peace, which is what she needs. It closes the paperback and sets it back down on the bed.

It stands and feels the throbbing in its skull as the mad dog in its head rattles the cage and begins howling.

It wonders if its mother can hear the howling, but it is working hard to keep its mask on, to keep the muzzle on, at least until it gets out the door, out into the snowy night.

It must stop the child from making noise. Little bird chirping.

The child keeps crying.

It can't keep the Other One in the cage any longer.

The Devil wants to come out and play.

CHAPTER SIX

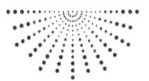

THE INLAND EMPIRE VALLEY, SIXTY-EIGHT DEGREES, FIVE thirty a.m.

THERE'S a vastness to the area of Southern California called the Inland Empire. It is a sea of land that stretches beneath snow-topped mountains, a valley that leads to the great desert beyond. Pockmarked and cratered by foothills and flatlands, endless tract houses near the freeway, beautiful homes and mansions up near the hills, it was once home to one of the biggest citrus-growing industries in the world. The old towns, like San Pascal and Redlands and Riverside, are beautiful and somehow untouched since rising out of the orange groves in the early twentieth century.

Redlands, California, can be found approximately two hours due east of Los Angeles, if the freeway traffic is bad. The town is atypical for the dry, near-desert area. Its climate in the winter is warm and stable, with generally clear blue skies, although the rains and wind sometimes descend between November and January for a week at a time without much warning. The smog from Los Angeles, more than sixty miles to the west, clears with the winds of autumn. The Santa Ana winds brush like invisible fire down from the desert, cleaning the skies.

In winter, the air seems crystal clear, and the snow-topped mountains of Big Bear and San Gorgonio rise above the temperate landscape below, palm trees and the tan-brown houses along the low hills and the flatlands of the orange groves among such towns as Mentone, Bannock, Yucaipa, San Pascal, Little Orange, and Redlands.

In his house in Redlands, Trey Campbell awoke in a cold sweat.

Unsure of where he was. Of who lay next to him. Another bad dream.

But it was only a dream.

A dream and a memory. He and his family had been attacked the previous summer by an escaped murderer named Agnes Hatcher. It was in the past now. He had been working through his fears. His family had been in many therapy sessions dealing with it.

It only was alive, still, in his dreams.

And in his work, to which he had to return after months of an enforced sabbatical of sorts.

Today was D-Day.

His work involved daily encounters with men and women who had committed the most unimaginable acts of violence and murder.

And he loved, and missed, his job.

But he dreaded it too.

He tried to wipe it from his eyes, the last of the previous night's dream.

Everything was out of focus in his room.

The blur of purple light from the window.

He reached across to the bedside table, feeling around the small stack of paperback books and the clock radio for his glasses. He had only started wearing them since summer. He had been told that his vision problem might be a result of the trauma from the experience. He wasn't sure. He didn't like to think of himself as so psychologically weak. All he knew was that one morning, he'd woken up and had not been able to see anything—it had all been a blur. Then he had seen some things in focus, but not everything. Then he could see better, but his vision was no longer twenty-twenty.

Then the psychiatric examination, and then the glasses.

That's how it had affected him.

His vision.

His kids, they'd had nightmares, and his wife woke up sometimes fighting him as if for her life.

With him, it was dreams and lack of good vision.

Within three months, he was used to the glasses, wire-framed, round. His glasses on, he felt better, more secure. The night, and its dream, was gone. Not just a dream.

A rerun of how I spent my summer vacation.

He was too old for this kind of silliness. Dreams. As if they were anything other than just the messed up innards of a guy who had spent most of his adult life working with the criminally insane.

Nearly thirty-seven, and he still had a fear of his own stupid nightmares. *Jesus,* he thought, *you can be rational all your waking life, but in dreams, that damn irrational superstitious side comes out again.*

You never feel safe again.

~

NOT AFTER HE'D watched his family be threatened by a killer. He knew he'd never feel the same about people. About people near his wife and kids. Once that had happened, it had changed everything.

Before the previous summer, Trey Campbell had not believed that evil had a human form. He had believed that the killers he encountered in his job were products of abuse. Many of them were, some of them were not. But whether they'd been abused or not, it didn't matter once they got power over someone.

All they needed was a feeling of power over someone.

He had learned that with Agnes Hatcher.

She's gone now. Put her out of your mind.

~

IT WAS the problem of his job: it put him in proximity to killers and sociopaths constantly. Where he worked, they had no power.

But if they were on the outside, they might.

Then they were truly evil.

Nothing mattered but protecting his family, when it came right down to it.

At a certain point in life, making the world safe for your own family, for your kids' futures, and for others, was the only thing worth doing.

He just wished, sometimes, that someone would tell him it would all be all right. The worries, the stress, the struggle and tests that life put you through.

Trey Campbell was never quite sure that life would be all right. Not anymore.

HE TURNED OVER, seeing the dark hair of his peacefully sleeping wife, Carly. He smelled her hair—it had an herbal scent to it from some new shampoo. He kissed the back of her neck, not out of ardor but from the need to feel connected, to be away from the world of his nightmares and of the recent past.

In sleep, lost in a dream herself, she pulled away, turning onto her back, her face so relaxed, her mouth open slightly to breathe in and then out. He wanted to wake her and hold her, but he knew that she wouldn't appreciate it.

This wasn't the first time in the past several months he'd had this nightmare.

This would not have been the first time he'd awoken to want to hold her and press his face beneath her chin to find some comfort.

But as with those other times, he would let her sleep.

His side of the big California king bed was soaked with sweat. His left arm ached from sleeping on that side. The smell of impending rain outside the half-opened window—that sweet, almost flowery smell, before the rain clouds would dust down across the hills. The fresh, cool air of December. He could hear the Steller's jays screeching in the garden. None of this was about insanity. None of this was about the people he'd worked with. Their faces.

Their eyes.

Eyes are the places where we live. That's what Agnes had told him once. Agnes Hatcher, of last summer, of his nightmares, of his children's nightmares.

That's over, he thought. *Over.*

Remember what the shrink said: You are enmeshed with the people you treat. Stop identifying with them.

FOUR AND A HALF months of three times weekly sessions with a psychiatrist had not erased the nightmares. One of those sessions per week included the whole family. Even the kids seemed to have put their nightmarish vacation in some perspective. *But not you. Maybe nothing could. Not that you have a great history of respect for psychiatrists ...*

The light had not completely come up outside the bedroom window. He could see hazy shadows of the oleander hedge that bordered their property.

HE SAT UP, sliding his feet to the edge of the bed. He wiped at his face, as if to iron out the last vestiges of the dream. He glanced over at Carly, who was snoring lightly. Her face had the slight crease of the pattern from the pillowcase from where she'd been sleeping on it. They had barely made love since summer. It had been his fault. He was almost afraid to touch her at times, as if anything he came in contact with might be threatened.

He wanted to not feel so alone, even surrounded by his family. Even next to his wife.

Alone. Like having a secret that you couldn't share with anyone, because it would affect them too much.

So as not to wake her, Trey rose slowly and gently from the bed. He padded over to the chair by the dresser, grabbing the underwear he'd left there. He slipped into these. Caught a glimpse of himself in the mirror above the dresser. Christ. He combed his hands through his greasy brown hair. His eyes were puffy, and his stomach seemed to be a little too paunchy. Four months of therapy, classes, studying, and housekeeping—and not much else. Oh, except dwelling on all the bad things. The Nasties, as he had described it to his son. Not just what happened to the four of them last summer. But what always happened at that place. Only Nasties.

For the first time in nearly six years, Trey thought of his father. It was the face. Trey was beginning to look more and more like his father.

Trey Campbell went out into the hallway. He shut the door lightly to the bedroom.

The sun was only just coming up.

He loved dawns. Loved them because they were peaceful. Nothing bad happened before the day started.

It was only the day itself that brought the Nasties with it.

Clouds gathered beyond the window.

Clouds gathered in his mind as well.

He dreaded going back to the job that had nearly cost his family their lives over the summer.

It was not going to be a good morning.

D-Day.

Dreaded Day.

Doomsday.

Ward-D Day.

CHAPTER SEVEN

Before the sun rises over the mountain, the blue truck stops abruptly, brakes squealing.

From within the truck, a girl cries out as if someone has just struck her.

December, Southern California, a side road off the main highway up the San Bernardino Mountains toward Big Bear and Lake Arrowhead and Bluejay and Moon Lake and Green Mountain. Trucks lumber up the main highway, groaning with gearshifts. Beams of purple light cut through the trees, burst from the cloud cover like an escaped convict. The sun lurks. A dark kind of light comes up. Melting snow along the rim of the road. Mud on boots as he walks away from the truck, the girl still inside it.

Male, Caucasian, mid-forties, five foot ten, stocky build, wearing chinos, a red flannel shirt, and a brown leather jacket, an unusual gait, as if he has a slight limp. Behind him, a woman. Female, late teens, dyed-blonde hair, five foot four, buxom, tanned. Breasts big and full, hips curved like a horseshoe.

She follows him, barely a woman, little more than a teenage

girl, her white-blonde hair pulled back and twisted, her brown-and-red-checked donut shop uniform still on from the night before, over which she wears a light-beige jacket. She smells of crullers and coffee and cigarettes. She pulls the earbuds from her ears as she goes, and the distant, nearly indistinct tinny sound of a pop teen princess's hit mingles with the noise of distant trucks on the lower highway. The earbuds dangle from the Walkman, clutched in her fist.

The air is cold and clean.

At the roadside, on the slight dirt shoulder, the truck, its engine idling, passenger door flung open.

"I said," she has the thick accent of a backwoods redneck even in Southern California, "get back in the truck, dammit! Do not do this to me. Don't run to your little hidey-hole and leave me to deal with you-know-who up there. Not that witch and her nastiness. You owe me. Big time. Now get back here right this minute. You don't take my car in the middle of my shift like that. You hear me? And that shitkicker truck, I hope I never see it again. You was gonna sell it. You told me we'd get the money for it. But you didn't. Didja? Nobody wants that goddamn truck. Nobody! Jesus! Jesus! Sometimes, I swear you are nuttier than a shit-house rat!"

He only slightly turns, grunts, and then continues on, slinging his backpack carelessly around as he goes. She is mad enough to spit.

"Duane? Are you listening to me? Get your ass back here. Jesus. All I can say is you better be inside for supper, or I'm not gonna wait for you, and you best not give me that look, or I ain't gonna wait on you no more. Don't you go treatin' me like some flophouse maid, you goddamn ... you don't talk trash to me like you did or you may not be eatin' your supper, you may be wearin' it, and that dog of yours may just wind up with a bullet in its head, that's all

I'm sayin'. I swear to God I will take down that huntin' rifle and put that poor dumb animal out of its misery!"

He stops when he hears this. Full turn to face her.

"You hear me, Duane?" She says the name "Duane" as if it has four syllables. *Dew-ay-enn-ee.* "That's right. I'm gonna take my daddy's gun and put that poor dumb animal out of its poor dumb misery; it can't even stand up to take a shit—you don't give me that look, Duane. You don't give me that look. That's your mama's look and I know just what it means." She talks fast and barely takes a breath until she stops. Then one final string of shrillness. "Look, you owe me an explanation, that's all I'm sayin', and hell yes I'm pissed off for waiting for three hours, you could at least tell me something or use the damn phone instead of running off to your little hidey-hole every time you go all fetal on me."

"Leave me alone. Just go home, Monica. Leave me alone." His voice is soft, barely audible. "And don't you touch my rifle. *My* rifle. It ain't yours."

He turns back around, shaking his head, and continues on into the woods.

The backpack around his shoulders, heavy.

Something squirms inside it.

"I did not move up to the backwoods to be treated the way I could've been treated if I stayed back in Palmdale!" she shouts, her voice becoming twangier as it grows louder. "Maybe I shoulda run back to Palmdale, and then where'd you be? You and the old witch."

THE SUN GLINTS off the edge of the mountain as the man she calls Duane enters the shadows of the woods on the side of the mountain.

THE GIRL STOMPS back to the truck, tosses the Walkman onto the seat, and shuts the passenger door. She lights up a cigarette and leans against the truck, shivering, puffing away for a minute, looking out over the valley below. She mutters something about families and men and love.

Then she tosses the cigarette and sashays to the other side of the truck and opens the door.

"I hate this goddamn truck!" she says as if he can hear her. "I hooked a loser!" Using the truck's door, she raises herself up slightly and slides into the seat. "You hear me, Duane?" Tears shine from the corners of her eyes. She swipes at them, as if trying to erase something she doesn't want to fully face. She glances out the window, up the mountain, to the turn in the road, the house that sits in the lightening darkness as the sun reveals itself through a thick mist to the east. The light is on at the front porch, and she thinks she even hears the damn dog barking.

Adjusting the rearview mirror, she notices that her lipstick is smeared.

She dabs at the edge of her lips with her thumb and glances at her reflection. Unhappy with the result—more of a lipstick smear than before—she reaches in the glove compartment. Feels around for some tissues. Pulls one out and wipes it across her lips.

Reaches down and presses her hand against her belly.

She can't feel the baby yet, but she knows it's there.

CHAPTER EIGHT

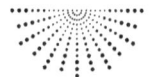

It doesn't like that whore Monica always yelling at it. It messed up its head and messed up its night, and had left her stranded down in the valley at her donut shop, but it had other things going on. It couldn't wait on that bitch hand and foot just because she was pregnant now.

Now, when it has important work to do.

Holy work.

It was heavy in its arms: its backpack, its bundle, its gift.

In the haze of steam, soaking its entire body with sweat, it could make out the edges and curves of the rock wall. It stepped carefully along the perimeter of the cavern so as to avoid the bubbling water. It moved as swiftly as it could. Even so, it was almost positive it heard their footsteps close behind, could hear the gang of them whispering, knowing that they were closing in on their prey.

It almost slipped when it came to the drop.

It set the bundle down and then squatted beside it. It felt the smoothness where the now-cooling waters flowed down the stones into the deeper chamber of the cavern.

The Chapel.

The Mad Place.

It sat down, grabbed the gift.

Something touched it, from behind.

The feeling of warm breath on its neck.

It felt its heart go cold.

Something bad inside it took over.

It pushed down through the drop, feeling water wash over it.

Not looking back to see what had scratched the back of its neck.

It lifted the door and went through into the stone room.

The lights were all on—twinkling outdoor garden lights strung around that always made the place look like a starry night.

Gave a sacred look to the Mad Place.

It was safe. That was all that mattered.

THE LITTLE BIRD WAKES UP. It got scared when that happened, because it wanted the bird to sleep right up until the time of the offering.

The bird cried out, a muffled scream.

NOW!

The Other One clawed at the cage.

The Other One would be out soon.

It unzipped the backpack to see the little bird's face.

Ripped off the duct tape.

It brought out the little pills and forced them into the little bird's mouth. Then it held the child's mouth shut, making it swallow.

"Good," it whispered.

CHAPTER NINE

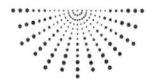

RAYS OF SUNLIGHT THROUGH A CLOUD HANGOVER. THE
foothills of Redlands, green-brown in winter. The vast valley
beyond. The snow-capped mountains. Palm trees between the valley
and the sky. Parrots, gone wild years ago, squawk as they fly in a
flock, tree to tree. Beyond the oleander hedge, a dog barking.

Trey Campbell fumbled through his morning routine.

Stepped outside to the flat pavement at the edge of the garden
to do twenty push-ups and twenty sit-ups.

The smell of impending rain in the air.

Back inside, feeling grumbly and not up to the day.

The house was an old adobe, one of only a handful in Redlands,
which was a town known for its beautiful array of homes. It was
laid out hacienda-style, so he had to pad across the cold stone floor
of the hallway, past the kids' rooms, through the living room
(careful not to stub his toes on unseen furniture), before he could
make it to the kitchen. Clear to the other side of the house. He
opened the fridge, grabbed a carton of orange juice. He went to
drink the last of it directly from the carton. Thought better of it and

went to get a glass. He checked the water cooler—half full. Two empty bottles beside the cooler on the red tile floor. His main drinking problem was water itself. He could not get enough. Poured out a glass or two of pure spring water "from the purest spring of California," so said the company's label. Drank it down.

Dehydrated. That's what you are. Scribbled out a reminder note for himself on the small chalkboard next to the fridge: CALL WATER GUY. GET MORE AGUA.

Beneath this, he left a note for his wife that she would probably not see until his workday had begun: "I already miss you. Let's take the kids for pizza tonight. Small celebration for Mark." His son had just lost another baby tooth, bravely, and the tooth fairy hadn't visited yet.

Then he sat down at the kitchen table, looking out at the dark garden. Slowly, the light came up. He sat and watched the sun's early light spray color across the bougainvillea that was still flowering pink and red across the garden wall. The clouds moved in swiftly from the west, dimming the sun's early brilliance.

He could not get his mind off the one thing he wished he didn't have to think about.

Work.

"You know?" he'd said to his wife a few nights back. "Since I've worked there, I've seen twelve murder cases. On premises. Eight suicides. Three eyes taken out. One case of genitals being ripped off. Other assorted mutilation. It's really the Welcome Wagon to Hell, isn't it?"

And she had looked at him. That look of hers that was part surrender and part fire. Then she said, "But you're still going back there. I know you. Even though you know I hate that you do it. And you know what danger it put the kids in—no matter if that was a fluke. There's potential danger. You're still going."

"Here's what I believe. I believe that my work there does some good. That if I keep learning, keep observing and interacting with these kinds of killers, I can build from it so that, in understanding them and how they operate, people can be protected. They're not monsters, even though they do monstrous things. I think they're throwbacks, at least the psychopaths. And they were okay at one point in their lives until a switch got turned on. Something went wrong. Maybe it was abuse. Maybe it was just hormones. But something turned on. And if I can help the psychiatrists and others, be part of that team, to try and see where the switch is, maybe there's a way to turn it off."

His wife had seemed less sure. "I think you see this as a mission. But it's not. There are other jobs you can do."

"That's why I'm going for my master's."

"Even with a master's degree, I know you," she said. "You're still going to work with them."

"This is my life's work, Carly. I'm nearly forty. This is what I was meant to do. I know it's going to lead to the right place. I know it in my heart."

"All right," she said. "I'll try and understand. But if there's an opportunity to get out of there, if another job presents itself that puts you out of the line of fire of those criminals, I want you to consider it."

"I will," he told her.

And this particular morning, he had to go back to that place. It wasn't like living in Redlands with a mortgage and kids in school and a flat tire on the way to the local supermarket.

It was a territory of madness.

WHEN THE PHONE RANG, he let the machine pick it up. It would be Anderson calling to make sure Trey was ready to get back to the job.

Psychiatric Technician, Supervisor of D Ward at the maximum-security hospital called Darden State.

CHAPTER TEN

It didn't like when the little birds, the angels, got out of the tape and rope.

The little bird had begun crawling through the space between the stone rooms. The little bird chirped a little, not even knowing that she chirped, and it wanted to cup the bird in his hands and make it all calm and quiet again.

It got down on its hands and knees. It sucked in its gut, drawing its shirt over its head, the sweat clinging to it even half-naked, like grease from an old fryer. The stink rose up from the solid dirt. On its elbows, crawling like a serpent, it went to where the little bird sat crouching, now, in a dark corner.

Flickering lights caught flashes of her face.

The little bird with the sad eyes and the dark hair.

It crawled toward the child, calling the little bird by name, keeping the hypodermic needle hidden in its left hand, the tip of the needle poking out between its fingers.

From the mattress in the corner, it heard the moans and whimpers but blocked it out. *Ruthie is dead,* it thought. *Dead. Gone to Hell. Ruthie was a whore. Ruthie was born of Satan. It's the voice of Hell coming up from the water.*

It calls to the little bird instead. "Don't be afraid, little bird. Don't be afraid."

CHAPTER ELEVEN

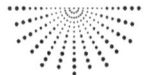

IN DECEMBER, THE WATER FLOWS HIGH ALONG THE NATURALLY
formed ditches, or washes, coming down from the San Bernardino
Mountains. The water, nearly ice cold, follows a trail of what had
once been dry riverbed down to the larger Santa Ana Wash. There it
creates a huge river in the winter from what had just been a shallow
summer trickle. In the unincorporated area of the Santa Ana River,
running between Riverside and an unincorporated area called
Bannock, the wash floods while stinging nettles and young
jacaranda trees are covered beneath it. This onslaught of water
continues west, until eventually it drains into the Pacific Ocean.

In the spring, by May, the rivers will begin drying again in the
near desert of the valley, until finally they will be nothing but a
memory come June.

But in December, the Christmas season, the water is high and
washes all kinds of debris with it along the banks, particularly after
a sudden and unexpected rainfall.

Victor Robles and his sister, Maria, stood on the bank just
above the rushing water. School would start in ten minutes, but

they had some time to do their daily treasure hunting. The wash sometimes produced beautiful garnets that they brought to their mother, and then sometimes she put them into jewelry she made for Maria. The rain battered at them, but Victor enjoyed it, moving out from under the umbrella his sister carried. Despite that fact that it was December, this was still Southern California, at the edge of the desert, and it was seventy-one degrees.

He had already found some pretty stones and one perfect garnet, and this was an exciting find for the first heavy rain since October.

Usually he just found old aluminum cans or an occasional lone shoe. He shouted for Maria to try and grab the branch that jutted up from the rushing brown water. She either couldn't hear him or didn't want to help. She stood up the bank, the large umbrella down around her eyes.

"Your loss!" he cried out. There was something out in the water, hanging from branches. A nest? Too far for him to reach without falling in the water. He stepped onto a large stone. He felt the icy water wash across his Nikes, but it put him closer to the branch. He tried to focus on it while the gray rain beat down. His glasses fogged; he heard his sister cry out. He looked up to her, and saw that she was pointing to the small island of ragged trees at the middle of the river.

There, among scraggly branches, was something that looked like brightly colored cloth.

Victor took off his glasses, rubbing the fog away. He put them back on and squinted.

He thought he was seeing an angel. It had wings tinged red around its neck. The tips of its feet seemed to be just barely touching water. But it was still a blur, and something in his young brain could not quite understand what he was seeing.

Its head seemed to hang down, and he thought it might be someone's idea of a joke: putting a dummy out there.

He almost fell into the river when he recognized what it was.

Later, he told the police that he thought the little girl was still alive because her legs seemed to move.

But that had probably been the water rushing over the victim's feet.

Victor Robles and his sister never saw the dead girl's face.

CHAPTER TWELVE

Five fifty-five a.m., town of San Pascal, San Pascal Valley, sixty-eight degrees

Jane Laymon awoke that morning with her boyfriend's head pressed down on her breasts.

She pushed him away. He rolled back on his side, his eyes lazily opening to the misty darkness. Then he drew back to her, kissing her shoulder. He was sort of cute, in a way that might normally arouse her, but not this early in the morning, and not when she had so much to get done. He had short dark hair and smelled like limes to her. It was the cologne he wore. It reminded her of islands and something of the beach. When she'd met him, his scent had been the first thing she noticed.

He rolled back toward her and murmured something about "horny."

"No way. And not with that kind of breath." She glanced at the clock. She'd had about six hours of sleep. She rolled onto her stomach, using her elbows to prop her up, and glanced out the window over the bed. Outside, it was still dark, but lightening. Noise and the smell of traffic out on the freeway, just down the hill. Her apartment faced the smog most of the year, but in the winter, the air was clear.

She felt his hands rubbing her lower back.

"I love you, baby," he said. Here was the thing about Danny. He was too good looking for his own good. Or her good. She kept wondering if she really cared for him, or if, after her last botched relationship with Rick Ramirez, that she was just looking for a safe harbor that would not put her through the ringer. Danny was the polar opposite of Rick. He was clean-cut, her age, athletic, loved *his* job, loved kids, loved getting out and coaching the local Boys' Club basketball team, loved dropping the whole police thing for a fun day riding horses up in Holcomb Valley, or getting out to the beach in LA to windsurf. And he loved his job. Just the kind of guy her mother wanted her to marry, or at least give her grandchildren by. Where Rick had come with his own baggage—a bitterness about women from his divorce, had been nearly thirty-eight, which meant they had very little in common other than mutual attraction— Danny had arrived with none of this. He had dated a few other women but did not have the long list that Rick had trailing him.

So everything about Danny should've made her fall in love with him.

But she hadn't fallen in love yet.

She had fallen in like. And that was good enough for now.

"Let's play," Danny murmured, kissing her gently on the lips. He was aroused, and she knew that if she stayed in bed another minute she might be also, but she had to remember that it was a workday. Not a play day.

"I'll see you tonight." She leaned back and looked at his sleepy face and half-lidded eyes. He had something between a snore and a smile on his face. "You can stay in bed for two more hours. I've got to get going."

Danny pressed his hands along her stomach and sides and whispered something that was meant to be sweet but just meant to her that he was tired of the sexual cooling they'd had for the past few days. The relationship had progressed from hot-and-heavy over the months they'd known each other to a regular routine.

It wasn't quite as romantic or spontaneous as it had been in its first flush.

Some days, he took second place to her work.

She liked Danny. A lot.

She even hoped they had more of a future together than just an on-again, off-again thing, like they'd had so far.

She liked nearly everything about him. Including the sex.

But she loved her work.

They were both cops. She was a newly minted detective, and he was busting his chops over in San Bernardino.

"I can't slack off yet," she whispered to him, kissing him too lightly on the mouth. "You sleep some more. I need to hit the road."

"It's okay," he murmured. "I'll get up in a sec and make the coffee."

But even after her shower, he was still in bed, facedown, catching the last of his sleep before the alarm on his watch would go off.

NAKED, still dripping water, she went to the kitchen and set the coffeemaker going. She heard the baby crying in the apartment next to hers.

She went to the walk-in closet, the one luxury that her small apartment afforded her, grabbed her running shorts, sports bra, and oversized T-shirt for her morning run. She dressed quickly, tying her hair back in a ponytail to keep it from flying all over the place during her run.

In the bedroom, she slipped into her Nikes. Danny, in bed, was just snarfling awake. "You don't have to leave so early," he murmured, rolling onto his back, stretching out like a cat with the canary in its mouth. "Just stay and ... cuddle."

"I've got twenty-four hours to requalify," she said. "Easy for you to sleep in. You don't have a jerk like Fasteau on you making comments about how girls can't shoot."

"You're a perfectly good shot," he said. "Jesus, this discussion gets old."

"Not to Fasteau. Not to the department. Maybe you'd take it less lightly if some woman sat around telling you how lousy a shot you were every time she looked at your balls."

"Keep talking dirty to me." He laughed.

"It's not funny. He's got this pissing contest going with me, and it's driving me nuts." Then, much against her intention, she started laughing too. "Why is this driving me up a wall? Why?"

"Riddle me this, Cat Woman, what's going on with you on the target range?"

"I don't know. I guess I just tense up. I guess I think about Dad and how he never really wanted me to hold a gun. And, well, even if I try not to think about it, I do."

"You just need to relax when you shoot," he said. "It's easier to hit the targets when you don't think about it."

"You sound like Fasteau."

"And you sound unsure of yourself. He's a moron. You'll requalify. Don't worry."

"Tomorrow, I have to. If I don't get past firearm requalification procedures, I'm screwed. So today, I need to get out and prepare. If I don't have this down by tomorrow, I'm screwed."

"Six months of getting up at some ungodly hour to go out and take shots at the range. You'd do better just to come back to bed and cuddle." He said it sweetly, but it was not what she wanted to hear.

Jane didn't want to say what she thought about this comment. She didn't want to explain to him that she had to be better than the rest of her team. That the men she worked with still, in the twenty-first century, didn't treat women coworkers as well as they treated other men. That she had to be smarter, faster, and even possess a better sense of humor than her bosses in order for to her move ahead in her investigative work.

Instead, she just told him, "It's not the cuddling I'm worried about." Then she went to him and kissed him on the lips. "I've just got to stay motivated. That's all. I'll see you tonight."

SHE WAS MOTIVATED AS HELL. She had to be; the San Pascal Special Investigations Unit was small, consisted of men (except for her, the trainee), and she knew she had to be better than any of the others in order to gain experience and get noticed. She was the lowest on the totem pole. But she intended to be the best.

At everything.

So far, it had worked, but not to the extent she'd wanted.

And the one thing she truly sucked at was handling her gun. Hitting targets.

Worse, her partner, Fasteau, rode her ass for it, and made her feel as if her qualification the year before was a fluke.

Worst of all, she was afraid that he was right.

Her morning began early, usually just before six a.m., with a three-mile run around the reservoir, followed by checking her e-mail for messages from Sykes, who was always one step ahead of her on the investigations, and who, along with Tryon over in Riverside, had taken her under their wing to try and get her more involved in ongoing investigations rather than the crib deaths she ended up having to spend time on. After her run and her e-mail check, she tried to put in at least an hour down at the firing range over in San Bernardino, and then, the real workday began.

The weapons training range had been built by US Marines just about the time that Jane had entered the police force, and it was primarily used for training San Bernardino County police in special tactical maneuvers. Jane loved the place. It had towers and barricades, and an amazing target range. It made practice fun, although it never helped if Fasteau came out and jeered from one of the towers. She had been given a special dispensation to use the firing range to practice, although there was a perfectly good shooting range in her own county. But the San Bernardino facility was top notch. It gave her a heightened sense of what her job was: to stop the bad guys.

That was how she saw it.

She was still a little unsteady with her 9-millimeter Glock 17.

But she was getting better.

JANE WAS A TALL WOMAN, muscular, imposing, from a race of giants—her father's side, Northern European, and from this she got height—although she was not quite six feet tall. Jet-black straight hair, dark eyes, courtesy of her Native American side, from the Cahuilla tribe, which was local to the San Bernardino area. She was not quite twenty-six years old. She looked like an Amazon, and she knew it helped her in her investigative work because her height was the first thing that intimidated the other detectives and the cops, and even the coroner at times. Second thing was her voice, a husky alto that her mother thought made her sound like a young Lauren Bacall, made huskier by a cigarette habit she'd had to kick by the age of eighteen because it slowed her down on the basketball court, but the voice remained husky and scratchy, and she used it when the men at the San Pascal County Sheriff's Office began to treat her the way they treated the girls in the office. But she had one problem that was more a badge of honor about the Good Old Boys than anything else, since she didn't think she'd ever have to use it in the field: she was a lousy shot, and she knew it, although she kept covering her ass by getting over to the shooting range just after rising at least five days a week.

Her motto was, *If you go, go big or just don't go at all.*

She'd been taught it by her mother, even after her father had tried to discourage her from getting into police work.

She intended to go big and make her mark in homicide investigations. She had wanted to do this ever since reading her first true-crime novel, ever since first studying forensics and criminal justice in college.

She had passed all the physical agility requirements of the San Pascal County Sheriff's Office and had advanced to working homicide, assisting mainly with cases as a liaison between Homicide and the Child Death Review Team—the CDRT—which generally had meant assessing, along with the coroner, Sudden Infant Death Syndrome cases and not much else. She had stepped up to this job because it was the only one available when she got into the department, but she soon discovered that it was halfway to social work and never quite as effective.

But the past week had become more active.

Someone was hunting.

Jane knew about hunters. Not the kind with a rifle, in the woods, in deer season.

But the kind who hunted people.

In this case, the hunter wanted children.

CHAPTER THIRTEEN

Jane blotted out other thoughts while firing at the outline of a man's form on the paper sheets at the practice range. For a fleeting second, she imagined it was Fasteau.

She was sick of the desk aspect to her work and wanted to get involved more with homicide rather than the mountains of paperwork required for working on cases with the coroner and his assistants. As far as she was concerned, she was a glorified administrative assistant who now and then got called in on investigations when nobody else was available to get coffee or call up potential witnesses.

She had been thrilled that Tryon and Sykes had called her in to do work with their team on a new manhunt that was just forming.

She would not be at her desk that day. She would not be checking fingerprints or brainstorming with detectives, who liked using her for her brain but didn't want her stepping on their toes in the field.

It had to do with the kidnapping and murders of the children.

So far, two girls and a boy.

She had been on the scene for the victim found in the orange

grove in Mentone, called in because of her work with the Child
Death Task Force. She was the bone that San Pascal threw to the
other counties whenever something happened that involved kids.

None of the other investigators liked the paperwork involved
with those cases. Or the fact that they'd have to work a lot of data-
bases with CASMIRC, the FBI's Child Abduction and Serial
Murder Investigative Resources Center.

Since she'd begun working on child death investigations, this
had rarely been an issue. Usually, it was a case of accidental death,
murder in a family or with a specific neighbor. *Not this time.*

The county sheriffs of the tri-county area (including San
Bernardino, Riverside, and San Pascal) liked their teams to catch
these killers fast. It made things easier, and it kept the communities
both safe and quiet.

Tryon, the sheriff's investigator from Riverside, had called her onto
this one. Normally, a San Pascal County detective trainee wouldn't be
called to cross county lines, but because of the body found in the San
Pascal Canyon two days earlier, this was a special case, and Jane headed
the task force on child death. She could be called in on cases of this
nature in Riverside and San Bernardino Counties, if need be. Although
she intended to move more into general homicide as her career
advanced, she was currently the one called in most for child-death cases.

Jane came off the firing range, her Glock holstered, her black T-
shirt blotched with sweat, her arm sore from the constant firing.

The call, relayed to her by another trainee, had come from
Tryon, and it had carried with it a note of "urgent." She jogged
through the lineup of trainees waiting their turn at the range and
saw Fasteau leaning against his dusty old black-and-white Caprice
Classic, a car that should've been retired several years before, out by
the road. Fasteau saw himself as an old-fashioned gunslinger of a
cop. She couldn't wait for a change in partner.

The sun was just coming up across the snow-capped mountains in the distance. That was the thing with Southern California winters: snow on San Gorgonio while it was seventy degrees in the valley of the Inland Empire. The breath of the dry desert to the east came up with the sun.

"Nice wheels," she said.

"Best I could do," Fasteau said with a look on his face that was indecipherable. "How was practice?"

"Enlightening." She passed him, going over to the passenger's side of the car. She opened the door and slid into the wide front seat.

"Hit the target this time?"

"Let's go," was all she said in response.

"Ready for this?"

"Well, if I can't shoot, maybe I can just look at dead bodies."

He shot her a dark glance. "What the fuck." It was his favorite phrase, and she was fairly sure he used it whenever his small reptilian brain reached an impasse.

"Fasteau. Let's just go."

"No. I'm like, what the fuck. *Bam. Bam. Bam.* We got kids falling out of the sky on us."

I'm stuck with a damn idiot cowboy instead of a cop.

When Fasteau pulled the car out the dusty drive, she asked, "Where'd he kill?"

"We don't know. The body was moved. Between Caldwell and Bannock."

"The Santa Ana River," she said. "Right on the line."

"Down in the wash. Our guy put him between counties. All the unincorporated areas. He's bright. Ice-cold water, to try and screw up evidence. Three counties. Riverside, San Bernardino, San Pascal. The one on the other side of Caldwell was in water too. An irrigation ditch. We need to get this guy," she said. "Do we have to draw straws to see who works this one?"

"It's a political nightmare," Fasteau said. "Kids getting killed. They've got some guys working on it, but it's stuck with Riverside and us. The boogeyman is loose. Once it hits the news, people start feeling like it's an epidemic."

"Hate to tell you, it hit the news last night."

"Can't Tryon keep them out of it? Ever?"

"Maybe he wants a little media. Maybe it'll flush out a witness. The bureau in on it yet?"

"Sure as the rain will fall."

"I know what Tryon wants. He wants to keep the bureau out of this. He wants to get the guy fast. I wish we could get some of LA's resources in on this."

"We got state coming in after three today to confer. All-out manhunt, that's what's on the agenda."

"Jesus," she said, glancing off in the distance as they merged onto the 10 freeway. "This is number three."

"One for each day," he said.

"Let's hope there's no number four," she said. "We're not getting this guy fast enough."

"I know. *What the fuck.* That's what I say."

"Clean up the language a little," Jane said.

"Can't help it. I was raised in a barn. Absolute evil. Killing kids, dumping them, but taking the time to tie little wings on them. 'Hark! The Herald Angels Sing.' Like it's a Christmas pageant."

"I know," she said. "Makes you wish you could change the world. Just get rid of the predators."

"The way you shoot," he said, "it'll never happen."

~

THIRTY-FIVE MINUTES LATER, she stood over the crime scene: a rift in the white gravel of the wash, the gray reeds and sprays of yellow grass rising up along the riverbank. In the middle of the river, a clump of gray trees. At the edge of the riverbank, an orange inflatable raft. They'd already removed the victim from the trees. She glanced at the others.

Hard as hell to keep a crime scene clean in the middle of a river.

Tryon's probably already pissed off.

A couple of detectives stood together, talking, smoking their cigarettes. Mills and Walker; they both were condescending assholes to her. They were from San Bernardino and Caldwell, out in Moreno Valley. Every county was pitching in on this one. The manhunt was gearing up fast.

The killer was gearing up too.

Sykes and Tryon were at the river's edge. Tryon glanced back, waved.

She was the rookie. They were the experienced ones.

They treated her the way she suspected they treated all young women.

She had to put up with it, to a point. Beyond that, she'd throw it back at them.

But she did her job, regardless.

It was what she had been born to do: investigate crimes. It had been her hobby, her interest, the way her brain was wired.

This case was a shot. It wouldn't be handed to her.

If she were going to crack it, it would be on her own.

The sun, nearly up in the sky. The grumbly sounds of traffic out toward Corona.

The day had begun.

Jane Laymon went over to where the victim lay on the sandy ground, alongside the banks of the river.

CHAPTER FOURTEEN

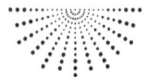

Jane leaned over the body.

Caucasian, female, age eight, brown, brown.

Gina Parsons.

They already knew the name.

When rich white kids got taken, things happened fast. It was the underbelly of criminal investigation. Nobody in the department talked about it much, but it was there. Black, Latino, Asian—it took longer to get those investigations going. She intended to change that. She intended to make things better. And it wasn't just because she was half-Native American, or "Indio," as Fasteau often reminded her, annoyingly, when he nastily suggested once that she try a bow and arrow instead of a Glock.

It was because kidnapping kids—rich, poor, white, brown— every single one of them deserved the same resources.

But it was true: the richer the kid, the whiter the kid, the more news got out and the more pressure came to bear on the investigation. Kids went missing all over, but it was when a white kid from an upper-middle-class background went missing and when the media was all over it that resources were marshaled to get that kid and get the kidnapper.

Gina Parson was not lucky.

But the next kid might be if the manhunt kicked into gear as rapidly as it seemed to be going. The FBI would be on it; three counties would be on it; and the hardest part was going to be blocking the media so that law enforcement could get the job done with minimum interference.

SHE CROUCHED DOWN, careful not to touch anything. Not until they started bagging evidence.

The victim had been lain out on the riverbank by the first cop on the scene. Mistake number one, she thought, but let it go. There had been no way to really secure the place where the killer had put the body.

She took a mental picture before too much got going: no blood on the corpse, but traces of red and pink around the white bird wings.

Red angel, white wings with a touch of red.

Some violence to the corpse.

Features partially obliterated.

If this one is anything like the others, she was dead before you hurt her.

You put her to sleep first. So she wouldn't feel anything. So that she was already gone. Dead.

Then you made her this angel.

She closed her eyes for a second, wishing the world was not such a terrible place.

Trying not to imagine the girl's last moments.

She heard the sound of an approaching vehicle. Shouts already came from the cops out on the road.

She glanced up to the edge of the highway.

A white news van with Los Angeles-based call letters had arrived.

"Damn it." She stood up, watching as Tryon barked at the cops to keep them out of the crime scene.

A cameraman got out of the back of the van, and some reporter came around from the other side of it.

"What a job they got," she said under her breath.

Fasteau, coming up beside her, chuckled. "I like that one reporter. The blonde. She's hot."

CHAPTER FIFTEEN

IST, NGI, MDO, SVP.

These are the main categories of patients at Darden State.

Incompetent to Stand Trial. Not Guilty by reason of Insanity. Mentally Disordered Offender. Sexually Violent Predator.

IST, NGI, MDO, SVP.

The Darden State Hospital is officially called the Darden State Hospital for Criminal Justice.

The unofficial title: The Darden State Hospital for the Criminally Insane.

Those who are incarcerated there are termed, by the state, "forensics patients."

DARDEN STATE IS SURROUNDED by razor-wire double fencing, and then a third electric sensor and electric shock fence in between those two. It further ensures its own security with redundant electronic detection systems, as well as an outside patrol from the

Department of Corrections, twenty-four seven. There has been at
least one catastrophic escape from Darden in the past twelve
months, and the hospital cannot afford another such error.

Within the fences, its twenty-three acres are neatly manicured.
A fruit-and-vegetable cooperative has been running successfully on
six acres of land since 1972, in order to provide a productive outlet
for inmates. The mild Southern California winters allow the crops
of apples, lettuce, oranges, tomatoes, and melon to flourish year
round. This is both a form of therapy for the patients and a source
of pride. But over the years, as patients' rights became stronger,
other activities and pastimes were added. The in-house newspaper
was begun, written and published by inmates.

Following this, briefly, a television production room was used
for the inmates to broadcast their concerns within the gates of
Darden. This was discontinued after three months when a riot
occurred as a result of a broadcast. During the riot, in the spring of
1997, six men were killed and three left in critical condition. No
staff was involved, as the rule on the wards is that once a riot breaks
out, the staff immediately leaves the ward and the doors are locked
down. When killing between inmates takes place on the state
hospital grounds, such as what happened with the deaths during
this particular riot, the investigation is minimal and charges are
generally not filed. Darden State is, after all, a hospital that incar-
cerates sociopathic murderers, serial killers, and those few sane
inmates unfortunate enough to have copped the insanity plea upon
the heels of their very sane and well-thought-out murders.

Darden is nearly a city unto itself. It holds upwards of eight
hundred inmates, as well as five hundred staff, on three daily shifts.
Staff includes psychiatrists, nurses, aides, orderlies, cafeteria and
laundry workers, recreational counselors, social workers, and a
distinct breed of workers called psychiatric technicians or psych
techs. These are generally well-educated staff, specifically trained to

work with the category of patient at Darden. The psych tech comes to understand the unpredictable nature of Darden State's criminally insane population in a way that the psychiatrist, who only sees the patient one hour a week, will never know.

There is occasionally a labile patient who requires more than one staff member at a time for supervision. A labile patient is one that is slow moving, apparently slow thinking also; then, all at once, he or she turns into a tornado and becomes the greatest threat to the individual standing nearest. A labile patient is rare; oddly enough, most patients seem fine. They seem normal. In fact, they seem extremely ordinary in this world of walls and fences and locked doors.

There is no one incarcerated at Darden State who has not murdered, or at the very least been accused of murdering, someone, but there are varying degrees of murders and murderers. The average term of incarceration is forty years, although several patients are released by their fifteenth year based on the court-decreed criterion of whether or not they are threats to the outside world. Occasionally, a psychiatrist will deem that a young recent arrival poses no threat to the outside world, in spite of a murder. Occasionally, such a patient spends less than two years in Darden State. That is, if a panel of psychiatrists, mental health officials, and a presiding judge clears them.

The size of an inmate's room is determined by both state and federal standards. There must be a locker, a bed, and a chair. The room is ten feet long by eight wide. There must be a two-inch fire door, with a small porthole window for outside observers. There are also three-, four-, and six-man bedrooms. Clothes are all khaki for the men and dark brown pants and khaki shirts for the women. Especially dangerous patients have wrist-to-waist restraints and one-to-one staff observation. Orange shirts and large ID tags are worn whenever the patients are working outside on the grounds, in a specially funded program called Living and Learning.

There is one new designation: a special dormitory with six rooms in it.

These are for the most violent of the human predators who enter Darden State.

These are the six forensics patients who have been labeled with a designation previously unused in the state of California. They have been transferred from each of the facilities in the state, specifically to Darden, which has received special funds for their care.

It is called Program 28, so-named because it is the twenty-eighth such program to handle specific psychologically labeled patients in a controlled environment since the programs were first implemented at Darden State in 1966, neatly coinciding with the era in which Darden went from a place of shock treatments and rumored lobotomies to drug treatment and sedation. All of the previous twenty-seven programs failed to some greater or lesser extent. Each of them was designed by a team of psychiatrists who brought in state and sometimes federal funding into the hospital. The positions at Darden State are as often political as they are medical and supervisory.

Program 28's patient designation is SSPVS7. Sexual Sadistic Predator Violent Sociopath, Level 7.

Each has been a high-profile case, involving the most heinous murders, even among the general inmate population of Darden.

Restraints through the night were the norm in Program 28. Each patient in Program 28 had at least two psychiatric technicians with them on each shift.

Michael Scoleri was in a room by himself, in Program 28.

Scoleri, good-looking young man, small eyes slightly wide apart. Blond hair, cut short.

The rain outside his window, like pebbles thrown on glass.

Restraints on his wrists and around his ankles.

Michael Scoleri nodded to the voice he heard.

"Yeah," Scoleri said. "Sure. You needed that one. The little girl."

AT DARDEN STATE, wake up in Program 28 was at six a.m. in the patient dormitories. This was to get the six patients through their routines a good forty minutes before the other patients were roused, so as to keep the Program 28 patients separate from the rest. The first meds of the day arrive at eight. Between those two hours, the Program 28 patients shower, clean up their rooms, make their beds, and then get breakfast in the cafeteria.

IN THE SHOWERS, twenty minutes later, a non-Program 28, Rob Fallon, counted the tiles as he washed, making sure to scrub the parts of his body his mother had labeled dirty twenty years earlier. Rob Fallon was an SVP, but often went with the Program 28s because of his recent attacks on staff. It was either that, or he'd have been transferred north, and north didn't want him. Neither did Patton State. He didn't live in the pods of Program 28, but just outside them.

Because Rob didn't have the harsher designation of Program 28, he had a bit of free rein on the ward and in the dormitories, although he still had a one-on-one psych tech at all times to make sure he didn't go off and begin his systematic seduction of other inmates or staff.

It had been his affair with a staff nurse, named Howe, the previous summer that had turned tragic. It was one of the problems of Darden State: if a sociopath was attractive and a staffer was messed up enough on the inside, bad things resulted. Staff members that had been at Darden more than a decade were now given routine psychological testing and subsequent counseling to ensure that they had not begun identifying too much with the patients.

THE WHITE BAR of soap smelled like others who had used it before him, and he didn't like thinking about their filth, their dirty parts. He had no name for them, other than the ones he'd found out about in biology class in high school, but even then he couldn't say them aloud. The soap lather felt like a foam pillow rubbing him. The more he rubbed, the more it began to smell like clean bleach, like a white bottle of clean bleach poured over a wound. So damn nice. He rubbed the soap against his skin so much that his skin turned a raw pink color, and the soap disappeared into milky fragments. He liked getting clean and had no respect for some of the patients who were depressed and remained filthy most days. He liked shedding his hospital clothes and getting under the hot jets of spray.

It was a lot like high school gym class, and he'd always enjoyed showering with others. He wished some of the guys would talk more, but they all went into their own little worlds in the shower. He watched the yellow tiles while he lathered up and rinsed off. Being spied on by the perv orderlies and psych techs just didn't do it for him anymore. He needed some entertainment. He hadn't had much entertainment in Darden State for a long time.

It was his sixth year in Darden State, for what the media had called the Adonis Murders. They were right on the Adonis part, he knew. Just not the word "murder." He had been merely asserting himself, taking his rightful place.

When Rob thought about how they bled, sometimes he smiled.

Someone watched him—they always did, he knew it, he kept watch of them as they watched him—along with the four other men from D Ward. The man watching them, named Jim, was big and stupid and was so used to nothing happening that he'd be unprepared for anything that could happen. It was the way things went at Darden. Unlike many others he knew in D Ward, he didn't fool himself into pretending they weren't in a prison, even though it looked a bit like a hospital at times, other times like an old junior high school.

He glanced at the others through the sprays of water.

Rob noticed how he stacked up against him. How much more masculine he was. How much more real. His chest and stomach had thin dark hairs, and his private parts (for he could not use the bad words for that area even when he tried) were not as ugly as other men's. His mother had always told him how beautiful he was because of his genes. Good genes were everything. Good genes and getting clean. His muscles, despite being in Darden, were still long and sinewy. He still had his youth inside him and knew that he would never ever grow old. He had been created that way.

Rob could tick off their names: Noodles, the guy who cut the heads off his girlfriends; Jake "the Whistler," a serial rapist and scalp collector; Arnie, the guy who tried to assassinate the president's wife but never made it further than a debutante ball in San Diego; and then Scoleri.

Michael Scoleri.

Scoleri was sometimes brought in. Sometimes the ward mixed them together. It was a Program 28 directive. Early morning only.

Rob Fallon didn't like it one bit.

It also meant more psych techs were around.

Not that Rob minded being watched in the showers. He looked damn good, and he liked the attention.

But Scoleri.

He still looked like a kid, even naked in the showers. Couldn't have been more than twenty-six. A scared kid in a den of wolves.

On his stomach, those words.

SUFFER THE CHILDREN TO COME UNTO ME.

On the inside of his thighs, names.

He was a damn sideshow freak, as far as Rob Fallon was concerned.

Like a fart, silent but deadly.

Rob grinned at Scoleri, holding his hands out. "Toss the soap."

Scoleri glanced at him. Scoleri picked up a bar of the yellow soap and handed it to Rob. Whether it was women or men, Rob knew that everyone loved him. He was beautiful, and smart, and irresistible. People told him their secrets.

That tended to coincide with the times that he'd cut their throats.

But not inside.

Inside he was a good boy because he was being watched.

He glanced at the orderly and the psych tech, who stood in the entryway to the showers.

"You still don't talk much, huh?" Fallon said. He arched his back as he scrubbed the soap beneath his underarms. "Well, I got some news down the wire today. I hear Campbell's coming back."

Scoleri barely glanced at him.

"I like Campbell. Always have. Last summer, one of the women here went after him. And his family. But Campbell got through it okay. I knew he would." Fallon turned around, showing that he didn't care if Scoleri watched him or not. He flexed his muscles. Rob liked to turn men on. To turn women on. It was a trait of some of the smarter sociopaths and thrill-kill junkies.

When he turned people on, he got things. He found out their whys. Their most intimate secrets. He was smarter than nearly everybody else, and once he figured out the whys of people, he could get what he wanted from them.

He knew that Scoleri had a why hidden somewhere inside him.

He rinsed off his back. The hot water was delicious on him. It washed away all the grit and nastiness of the night. Cleanliness was good. Dirty things annoyed him a great deal. Most of the patients were dirty. Practically crawling with vermin. Some of them didn't even know how to clean themselves well. Rob liked the ones who did. Like Scoleri. He got scrubbed good.

"I guess you didn't know Campbell. He's one of the good ones," Rob said this last part, nodding in the direction of the bulky psych tech standing guard by the entrance to the showers. "Not like him. He's what my mother would call a three-dollar bill."

Scoleri shrugged. "I don't know too many people here." He had a voice like a sparrow. Just a chirp. The water from the showerhead poured over his thin hair, matting it to the sides of his face. A halo of water. "I hear some things sometimes," he said, barely above the noise of the showers.

"Oh yeah? So what's on the radio this morning?" Rob meant it as an idle comment. Scoleri's nickname was Radio since he seemed to both be on another wavelength from the other sociopaths and psychopaths of Darden State, and because he claimed he got messages. Special messages. Scoleri would sometimes tell people things about themselves that he couldn't possibly know.

"He's out hunting, is all," Scoleri said in that little-boy voice that belied his six-foot frame and slightly receding hairline. "He wants more children."

"Who?" Rob Fallon asked.

Scoleri glanced at the guards at the shower exit, and then at the other inmates. For just a second, Rob Fallon felt fear, something he didn't always feel. It was refreshing to get a taste of it. It was a sexual fear. He suddenly had the feeling that Scoleri was going to touch him.

Scoleri stepped closer to Rob Fallon, pressing his lips almost to his ear.

Fallon thought he felt Scoleri's tongue on his earlobe as Scoleri whispered his answer.

Scoleri reached up, holding Rob's head close to him, so he could keep his mouth almost right inside his ear while he whispered all the secrets he knew.

When it was over, Rob Fallon drew back in disgust, furious that Scoleri had gotten so close to him. Invaded the space near his flesh. He was the one who did that to others. They didn't do it to him. He hated Scoleri. He hated him with a passion and wanted to hurt him. Nobody got that close unless Fallon himself was taking control. He didn't want men like that. He didn't want the touch of any man, not like that. He felt himself go all dark inside like when he'd been a kid and his mother had caught him doing dirty things to himself with pins and tape.

Rob made a fist and threw a hard punch into the side of Scoleri's mouth.

When the impact came, the *crunch* of knuckle to face was like a shotgun blast.

Scoleri slipped, falling against the tile floor.

Blood spurted from between his lips.

Rob watched the blood flow into the soapy water that ran pink down the drain in the floor.

Two of the other men stepped back, but Jake the Whistler leaped forward to grab Rob by the throat. The psych techs in the doorway were already running across the slippery tiles when Rob Fallon began to black out from Jake's expert strangulation techniques.

"Don't alarm!" one of the psych techs shouted to the other. "We can control this."

The other psych tech put his alarm pen back in his breast pocket. Then, when Noodles, out of nowhere, leaped upon him, he managed to reach in and press the panic button on the alarm pen, just before he fell to the slippery tile floor.

The strobe lights began going on and off, and the inter-ward alarm sounded.

A brief period of shutdown would follow. The doors to the ward would close and lock automatically, and no one would be able to get out. COs would show up momentarily, and with luck, the psych techs wouldn't be too banged up.

Now and then a ward-wide riot might erupt if controls and restraints weren't in place fast enough.

Or if staff members, including the psychiatric technicians and the nurses and the ward doctors and the corrections officers, didn't act in a timely and efficient manner.

MICHAEL SCOLERI STOOD over Fallon and the psych tech that wrestled around on the tiles. Water streamed off his pale skin.

Curious smile growing on his face as he watched the struggle at his feet.

The lights flashed on and off around him.

When a psych tech grabbed him from behind, Scoleri got violent.

He went for the eyes.

His fingernails went in the orbital ridge, and he felt that warm moisture around the eye itself.

MICHAEL SCOLERI, in his room, minutes later, bound, the restraints impossibly tight around his hands, nodded his head as if listening to someone who was not there.

CHAPTER SIXTEEN

ROB FALLON HAD BEEN SHUT OFF INTO HIS ROOM, STILL shivering from the shower, and with the taste of blood in his mouth from where he'd been thrown against the wall by a psych tech who was afraid of him.

He wrapped himself in his sheet, and when the staff nurse came around to give him some meds to help calm him a bit, he told her that he had an important message to deliver.

"Who to?" the nurse asked.

Two husky psych techs stood near the doorway, ready in case Fallon caused any trouble.

"My doctor," he said. "It's important. It's real important. I gotta tell her!"

But his psychiatrist wasn't in yet.

It was too early.

CHAPTER SEVENTEEN

MOST OF SAN PASCUAL COUNTY IS A SERIES OF HIGH PEAKS, low hills, and canyons off a corner of Riverside and San Bernardino Counties. Its mountains connect with the San Bernardino Mountains and National Forest, briefly, and sustain ski resorts at elevations exceeding eleven thousand feet. Far below lay the flatlands of the inhabited portion of San Pascal County. Now a bedroom community, it once was a flood area. Some say that if it rains hard enough, it'll be nothing but mudslides, like it was in the 1930s when a torrential downpour swept through the then-uninhabited area, taking out a chunk of a hillside with it.

EARLY MORNING, too early to get up, but the little boy always got up early. And this was an extra-special morning. A morning that would be remembered forever, he knew, because it was going to be Lucas Day. Officially. His mother had declared it, and he reminded her of it every single day until the day on his calendar came up: MONDAY.

Beneath this in red felt-tip marker, his mother had written:

"NATIONAL LUCAS DAY. NO SCHOOL. DAY OFF! CHRISTMAS VACATION STARTS!"

Lucas, who was just eight years old, scruffed his hair with his hands and yawned. He smelled the morning, the threat of rain outside his window, slightly cracked with one of his hundreds of toy soldiers. The smell, also, of the woman next door, beneath the condominium, who always put her laundry out in the mornings. Fresh, clean laundry smell mixed with that just-before-it-rains odor. He pictured Mrs. Randel running out as the rain came down, gathering up all her clothes from the line. It made him happy to think it.

When he got out of bed, he went over to the pile of toys in the corner of his room. He picked through them, tossing the little trucks to the side, stepping on some marbles and almost falling down. He picked through the toy lizards and bugs he collected. Finally, he found the large Mickey Mouse clock. He looked at the hands of the clock carefully. Then he picked up one of the big rubber spiders his dad had bought him when they'd spent the summer in Los Angeles with his dad's new wife. He stuffed the spider, named Charlotte, in the pocket of the shorts he intended to wear that day. Then he picked up a green toy soldier and stuffed it in the other pocket. He padded from his room, to the bathroom to brush his teeth and "go," then over to his mommy's room. She was still asleep. He got up on the covers and stared at her awhile.

Soon, she opened her eyes, almost startled to see him.

"It's today already," he said. He thought she was so pretty. A lot prettier than his daddy's new wife.

"Ten more minutes," she said, turning over into the comforter, covering her head with the pillow.

"No more minutes," he said, reaching over and tugging the pillow from her arms. When he had it, he gave her a scolding look. "Go get ready."

"You first," she said groggily. Her eyes looked like they were glued shut. Still, she managed a grin. "All excited about today, are you, kiddo?"

"You know who you look like right now?" he said. He didn't wait for her answer. "Like a movie star."

"I feel like a very sleepy mommy," she said.

Then her beeper went off on the bedside table. She reached for it, her hand fumbling across all the books and papers she always kept there. When she picked it up, she lifted it to her face, squinting. "It's too early for me to see," she said. Holding the beeper to Lucas's face, she asked, "What's the number?"

He read her the number and then frowned. "I know what that is. That's work."

"Coffee," was all she said in reply.

"Can I take Stuart with us?"

"Coffee," she repeated.

He scrambled off the bed and ran out to the kitchen to turn on the coffee machine. He went to the cooler and poured out exactly enough water to get to the halfway point of the coffee pot. Then he carefully poured it into the machine. It was always up to Lucas to flick it on so that it would start sputtering the coffee into the pot. As he watched it begin its steaming, he wondered if he'd be able to sneak a taste. Then he went and poured himself a bowl of cereal. He carried the bowl with him, munching on a spoonful as he went to feed his hamster. The hamster cage sat on a shelf in the small den, which was part playroom and part his mother's home office.

"Hey, Stuart," he said, having named his hamster for the book his mother had read him, called *Stuart Little*. He had had a guinea pig he named for Charlotte from *Charlotte's Web*. His mother insisted that the guinea pig shouldn't be named for a spider any more than a hamster should be named for a mouse. But he liked both names and both books. When Charlotte the guinea pig had died the previous summer, Lucas had transferred the name more logically to his rubber spider.

"Stuart, come on, it's breakfast time." Lucas picked up some food pellets, dropping them in the little bowl at the bottom of the cage. For good measure, he set a few pieces of cereal in the bowl too, and watched his pet eat. He picked up *Charlotte's Web* off the lower part of the bookcase by the wall and flipped through its pages. "See?" he showed the book to the hamster. "Charlotte is teaching Wilbur the pig things. She's spinning her web so people will see it. See?" He held up a picture from the middle of the book. Then he put the book down beside the cage. "Stuart, today is gonna be better than Christmas," Lucas whispered.

The hamster got onto the metal wheel in his cage and began running, spinning the wheel rapidly. Lucas went out into the hall, down toward his bathroom.

After he jumped in and out of the shower, he climbed into his shorts, and then put on his favorite T-shirt and his sandals. In the mirror, he scraped a comb through his thick hair and brushed his teeth with bubblegum-flavored toothpaste. In the mirror, while brushing, he thought he saw something move behind him, off near the door.

"Mom?" he said. He turned around. No one was there. Lucas shivered a little. He had been told at school all about the boogeyman. He'd been having nightmares since then about how the boogeyman waited for kids and then grabbed them. He didn't like to think about it, and he wished he hadn't seen that shadow movement in the mirror. It's all pretend. No such thing as the boogeyman.

He bravely looked all over the bathroom, behind the shower curtain, and inside the hamper. Empty.

"It's pretend," he said aloud, just in case the boogeyman was listening.

He went to check on the coffee, leaving wet footmarks down the white wall-to-wall carpet as he walked to the kitchen. Carefully, he lifted the glass pot. He poured the steamy dark liquid into his mother's favorite mug. On the mug, it said FOR THE BEST MOMMY IN THE WORLD. It had a big red heart right beside it. He'd given it to her for the previous Mother's Day. He'd saved his allowance of fifty cents a week for nine weeks running in order to buy it for her. His mommy loved her coffee.

He measured two teaspoons of sugar into it and stirred in a drop of whipping cream from the fridge. Then he walked down the hall to his mother's room. She was in the shower, so he set the coffee on the bathroom sink.

The phone rang. He went to pick it up. "Hello?" he said. "Hello?"

But no one said anything on the other end of the line.

His mother came out of the bathroom, wrapped up in a huge towel, her hair wet and sticking to the sides of her face in a kind of funny way. "Who was it?" she asked, sipping her coffee.

"They hung up," he said.

She held her small wristwatch up in her hand, and said, "Okay, well, slight change of plan, kiddo. We'll still go to the beach, but I have a quick errand to do for work. Okay?"

Lucas said nothing. He felt the pout beginning to thrust itself out from under his skin, right about where his lower lip stuck out. He put his hands in his pockets and looked down at the floor. He was not going to throw a tantrum, but he really wanted to do it. He wanted to fall on the floor and kick and cry, but it would be too much like a baby. And since his birthday, he was no longer a baby. His hand clutched the big rubber spider in his pocket. It felt good to squeeze it.

"Oh, stop with the face," his mother said. "It's only going to be for a little bit. I promise."

"I know," he lied. "It's okay."

His mother sighed. "No, it's not okay, Lucas." She crouched down next to him, putting her arms around his back. "We are going. I mean it. But you know how Mommy's work is sometimes …"

"Yeah, yeah," he said. He pressed his face against her neck. She smelled like lilacs. She always smelled like lilacs in the morning from the soap she used. It was purple soap. Just like he smelled like coconut from his favorite soap, she smelled like flowers from hers. He couldn't help himself. A tear or two came to his eyes. He felt himself melt into her a little bit. It felt good.

When he finally pulled back, he saw tears in her eyes too. "You okay?"

She nodded and kissed him twice on the forehead. "It won't be long. I'll run in and then run out. I promise. Then I'll race back here, and we go. And Nina's going to come over and be with you while I'm gone. But I promise to be back really fast." Then she brightened. "Knock knock."

"Who's there?" he asked, a half-smile creeping across his face.

"Boo."

"Boo what?" he asked, and then exploded in laughter, having spoiled her joke.

"Oh," his mother said, shaking a finger at him. "You've heard that one too many times. I need new material."

TWENTY MINUTES LATER, Lucas, wearing his Sponge Bob Squarepants T-shirt that stretched almost to his knees, sat in the front yard with his rows of small green plastic soldiers. They were in battle position.

Lucas knocked at a toy soldier with a twig. "Take that!" He was pretty bored with playing soldiers when his PlayStation was inside the house, but he had promised his mother that he wouldn't play any games on weekdays. Even if this was a special weekday—his first day of Christmas vacation and his official birthday celebration day all rolled into one.

But playing with plastic soldiers was for babies. He'd had the toys since he was little, since his daddy had given them to him. That had been the only reason he still had them at all—because they were from his father.

Lucas reached into his side pocket, where he had put Stuart Little, his hamster. The hamster was rolled up, sleeping. Stuart had already eaten the dry cereal Lucas had put in his pocket with him. Lucas always had to be careful to only put Stuart in his baggy shorts' pockets; otherwise, he tended to escape and run away. No matter how Lucas jostled him, Stuart was so used to going to sleep inside Lucas's pockets, nothing ever seemed to bother him.

His mother would be angry if she knew he'd brought the hamster for the trip, but Lucas did not trust Nina to feed Stuart while they were gone.

After patting Stuart's soft fur, he worked to bury a little toy soldier under a mound of dirt. Then he put a plastic pail upside down over it. "Here comes the tank down in the battle, tank tank tank," he said, picking up a rock that barely fit into his fist and pounded it along the grass, heading for its destination, the pail.

"It's gonna blow up now," he whispered, as he brought the rock up above the pail and was about to smash it down.

Lucas saw the man's shoes. It was as if the man had just suddenly appeared.

Lucas dropped the rock.

The shoes were black and shiny, but scuffed a little at the toes.

The pants were dark blue, almost black.

"Hi." The man's voice was almost squeaky, like a mouse.

CHAPTER EIGHTEEN

Lucas looked up from the grass.

"Oh, hi," Lucas said. "Want to hear a knock-knock joke?"

"Sure."

"Knock knock."

"Who's there?"

"Boo."

"Boo who?"

"Quit crying, you big baby."

"That's a good one. You're up early today."

"I got up with Mommy. We're going to the beach."

"Where's Mommy?"

"She had an errand. You want to talk to her?"

"I don't need to. Who's here with you?"

"Nina. She's inside. She's reading. Want me to get her?"

"A babysitter?"

"I'm not a baby. I'm almost nine. She does breakfast too. When Mommy's in a rush. Her name's Nina. Want me to get her?"

"Let's let her read, okay?"

"Okay." Lucas looked back down at his soldiers. "I'm bored with this stuff."

"Shouldn't you be in school?"

"Christmas vacation. It's my birthday." He didn't mind lying a little. It was, after all, the day that they were going to pretend it was his birthday and have fun.

"It is? Well, guess what? I have something for you. Back in my truck. It's pretty cool."

Lucas set his toy soldiers down, knocking a regiment over with his hand. He reached into his pocket, feeling Stuart's soft fur. Charlotte, his rubber spider, was in the other.

Just a hop, skip, and a jump to the truck. He ran down the driveway to where the truck was parked.

"You got a new truck," Lucas said.

Droplets of rain on the top of his head. His only thought was that it was going to turn out to be a bad day for the beach if it started raining. It made him a little sad to think of his mommy probably canceling the beach by the time she got back from work.

Of him not getting a special birthday with her.

Just as he stepped up to peer into the interior of the truck, Lucas felt a jolt, like a big shock, on his left shoulder.

CHAPTER NINETEEN

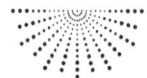

7:50 A.M.

It glances around after it shuts off the Taser and slips it back into its jacket pocket.

It rolls the little boy's body farther onto the seat of the truck.

It shuts the door.

It glances around the pretty neighborhood, as rain begins falling.

It looks at the house, with its big picture window in front and its lawn, and the way the foothills rise up behind the suburban property.

It goes around and slides into the seat and starts the truck up again.

It feels the Other One inside it.

It's got a growl in its throat as it pets the boy's head, messing up his hair.

"Don't be afraid," it says.

Then, it reaches in the glove compartment and pulls out the duct tape and the box cutter.

A hypodermic needle and a small vial of pills nearly roll out of the glove compartment, but it manages to catch them and push them back in.

For a second, it closes its eyes and is suddenly in the other place.

The place where its father roars like a lion and the sky is raining fire and brimstone down upon it.

Then, opening its eyes, it leans over the boy, raising the box cutter and tearing out a length of duct tape.

The boy's eyes have been closed, but they open suddenly.

It reaches into its jacket for the Taser, but fumbles.

The boy parts his lips as if to shout, and it claps its hand over the boy's mouth.

The boy bites the palm of its hand, and it drops the box cutter.

The cutter rolls back into the crack of the seat.

The duct tape rolls to the floor.

It cusses as the coffee cup spills over onto the mat that's lying beneath the glove compartment.

Slaps the boy's face.

Boy's hands grab around its forearms, pushing.

Presses its palm down.

Keeps its hand on the boy's mouth even though the boy is biting down hard.

And it hears the sound of the Other One, shaking the bars of its cage. Trying to get out.

To devour the boy.

Right here.

In the truck on the pretty suburban street.

Rain coming down.

Like blood.

It gets the Taser out of its jacket and presses it on the boy's chest at the same time it withdraws its hand from the boy's mouth.

The boy's body shakes when the Taser touches it.

The boy is still.

Breathing.

Eyes open.

But still.

Alive.

It glances out the windshield.

The houses all in a row, neat and clean with well-manicured lawns.

Somewhere nearby, a dog barks in a backyard.

It quickly duct tapes the boy's mouth and then wraps the duct tape around the boy's wrists and ankles, using the box cutter to slice the tape neatly.

From behind the seat, it grabs a blanket, the one its mother crocheted for it when it went out on cold days.

It tosses the blanket over the boy.

It turns the key in the ignition and starts up the truck and heads down the street, making a left when it reaches the bottom of the hill.

It turns on the windshield wipers and reaches over to the dashboard to turn up the radio.

It thinks about its workday coming up.

It thinks about how it needs to send a message to God.

CHAPTER TWENTY

EIGHT A.M.

After a jog in the cooling, light rain, Trey Campbell went into his home through the sliding glass doors off the kitchen. In the kitchen, something seemed different. There was some kind of smell that did not seem to fit with the usual house smell. He went to the fridge, opening the door. Smelled fine in there. He checked to make sure the stove and oven were off.

"Just your usual paranoia," he said aloud, feeling foolish.

Working around killers, breathing the same air with them, you get to thinking like this.

They get inside your head.

When he passed by his daughter's room, he stopped for a moment. He'd spent the past several months being a full-time dad. Paid leave. So different than going to work every day and seeing his children just before they fell asleep at night. He knew things about their daily lives now. He noticed that Teresa had got rid of all her dolls—exiled to boxes in the basement. The room was messy. On her dresser were a Nancy Drew book, a small statue of a horse, and her basketball trophy from school. At times a little demon, at times a perfect kid, he was damn happy that he had this life with her, and with Mark. He was damn happy that life was not all about criminals and work routines and mind games.

Her brother's door was wide open, and Mark had all his Harry Potter and Lemony Snicket books tossed in a corner; on the wall a big poster of the Tyrannosaurus rex from *Jurassic Park*. Trey couldn't see Mark's face because of the blanket thrown over him, but he heard his son's steady snores.

"You've had months of being house-husband," Carly said, coming up behind him. "Ready to give it all up and go back to nine-to-five?"

"No," Trey said. He felt her arm go around his waist. "Yeah, I guess I am."

He reached for her, pulling her back, turning toward her. Her nightgown smelled sweet, and she smelled like morning to him, always. He reached inside her robe to feel her skin against his arms, and although it aroused him, he let that feeling come and go.

"Maybe I'll call in sick," he said.

"Or you can call in well," she said, grinning.

He wondered how he had ever come to deserve such a wife. She had put up with him all these years. She had even sat out his sabbatical and now his return to work as if it were just another part of him she cared for. He brushed the hair from the sides of her face. Kissed her lightly. Hugged her. "Sorry about the argument last night."

"Well," she sighed, pulling away again. "Yeah. Me too."

"Thanks," Trey said. "Look, for better or worse, that job is important to me." He knew that on some level she meant it, but it was a constant sore spot for them. As long as he even mentioned that place, it always would be. He wasn't smart enough to know if this was how marriage went. There was the good and the bad, and you lived with both, learned to get along and just let some things slide. He wasn't sure if those things that you let slide would come up later and bite you in the ass. But for now, it was okay. They had a good marriage. They had a few rocky points. It was life.

He gave her a kiss on her forehead.

"Now, go take a shower," Carly said. "You stink." She turned and walked toward the kitchen.

"You are a vision, even before my first cup of coffee," he said.

As she padded into the kitchen, Carly replied, "And you look like a guy who's buttering up his wife so she'll forgive him for doing what he promised her he would never do again."

Damn it. It's what I want to do. It's what I need to do.

He knew there was some danger working where he did, but it was as if he felt more alive inside the doors of that place than he felt anywhere else in the world.

And yet, what kind of insane person would ever admit to that?

He watched her go and suddenly felt excited, if not entirely ecstatic, about going back to work at the maximum-security hospital.

When Trey stepped into the shower, he thought he heard the phone ring.

"Jim Anderson left a message for you on the machine. And Conroy's office called twice already," Carly said. She passed him a towel and set an extra cup of coffee for him on the edge of the bathroom sink. "Just her assistant. Wouldn't let me know what it was. Must be top secret." She said this last part a bit sarcastically. "I'm telling you, Elise Conroy's got her sights on you."

"Well, she's going to have to wait until you dump me then," he said.

He toweled off, got dressed fairly quickly while glancing at the clock, and then went to check the messages.

ON THE ANSWERING MACHINE, Jim's gruff Texas accent. "Hey, Bubba, looking forward to seeing you in the Crack Up Palace today. Listen, we got a live one on Program 28 I want you to meet first thing. Scoleri. Nearly took out Bobby Bronson's left eye this morning. A quarter inch from getting it. Dug right into his skin. Believes he's Lord of the World. Calls himself Abraxas. Has a whole mythology worked out about how he can hear the secrets. All that jazz. Brainard and Conroy are on him, and Conroy gave you a special pass to check him out. Can't wait for your assessment. I guess you're a big shot now. Conroy's been hunting you down too. It must have something to do with this profiling case she's working on. Some kidnappings over the weekend. I didn't get the details— you know Conroy—and then that dude Eric is in spaceville half the time. Well, Bubba, I wanted to be the first to welcome you back to Thrill Kill Row."

CHAPTER TWENTY-ONE

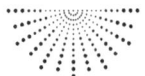

TREY ARRIVED to work a few minutes early.

Nearly soaked, despite his umbrella, he walked from his parking space into the main building. It was a large white-gray building. Were it not for the security fences, a person driving by might think this was some corporate headquarters, or perhaps a spa, rather than a hospital for criminals. He nodded to the two men at the desk, both in blue uniforms, crew cuts; one of them seemed to recognize him, even though Trey could not remember ever seeing him before.

He flashed his badge and walked down the main hall.

Ward A had low security clearance. A main central office area, off of which were three hallways, each with double doors. Always flowers on the sign-in desk, as if this were a happy place. The smell of institution. They might as well have bottled it and sold it to be sprayed around every state institution in the world: rubbing alcohol, air freshener, pine cleaner, and something not so breathtaking, something between ammonia and urine in the blend of odors.

The fluorescents still flickered along the ceiling as they had since he'd last been there. The corkboards along the wall carried staff photos and notices about apartments for rent, dogs that needed homes, old cars for sale. An open window office to the right, behind which was an entire open room of administrative staff, as well as some of the legal staff.

At the sign-in desk, three nurses were in line ahead of him, and one, Joe Houston, turned and slapped him a high-five. Trey was never sure of high-fives. He generally just put his hand up slightly, more used to shaking hands than slapping them.

"I thought you were outta this joint," Joe said, laughing. "Who drug ya back?"

"I live here," Trey said. "Didn't they tell you?"

He took a bit of a deep breath before he turned left to go down to what was called Level Two, which contained the Alphabet Wards A through G. He glanced toward the stairwell that went to the Rap Floor, as they called it. This was a bit easier as an area, because the older patients who had been around for forty or more years were up there. They were less bother than Trey's floor—the older the patients got, the less dangerous they were to each other and to staff. Additionally, the upstairs wards contained the least harmful young patients as well. The ones who had only committed one murder, or had not even completed a murder but had merely maimed. They were more sedated up there, happier, and with fewer attacks.

It would be like a promotion to move up to the Rap Floor, even if the salary and benefits didn't change.

But Trey was on the Alphabet Wards.

They were his territory.

· · ·

He flashed his ID badge to the overweight security guard who nodded him past the second checkpoint.

Hearing the heavy slam of the metal protective doors was enough to bring bad memories back.

Joe Houston smacked his gum as he walked alongside him. "I was on D for two emergencies last month. Man, I do not envy you in that place. I had to scrape up one guy off the linoleum."

Trey sighed. "Yeah, that's D."

"Man, I'd transfer out if I were you. Shit, you'd think they'd have got you off the floor after last summer."

Trey paused, adjusting his glasses slightly. "They did. They tried anyway."

"What happened?"

"I guess," Trey grinned, "nobody wanted my job."

An orderly he didn't recognize sat at the station at the entryway to B Ward. The guy looked a little wild, and Trey saw the telltale signs of speed—the bloodshot eyes, the peach skin, the slight jitter.

It was a problem with employees at Darden. Sometimes they turned to drugs to help get them through their shifts. Occasionally, a few of them ended up as inmates a few years down the road. Sometimes you couldn't tell an inmate from a psych tech or an orderly. If it weren't for the white jackets versus the khakis of the inmates, it would be hard to tell which was the crazy one.

The worst were not the Speedies, as the psych techs called staff who did meth on the weekends.

The worst were those staffers who were about one bad day away from becoming exactly like the patients they were handling.

"Campbell."

The orderly checked the badge. Then put an X on a chart. "William C. Campbell the Third. Trey. You're the guy from the Hatcher thing, right?" the orderly asked.

"Christ." Trey shook his head. "Yeah, I am."

"That's cool." The orderly nodded. "I just read all about it in the *Times*. You beat the shit out of her?"

"Christ," Trey said. "No. I was lucky to get away from her. With my heart and lungs intact. That's all."

"Hope you don't mind if I feel you up," the guy said, a grin on his face.

"Get your kicks any way you can here," Trey said, lifting his arm as the guard passed a handheld metal sensor over his body. Then he reached between Trey's legs, feeling for any hidden weapons.

It was a precaution that Trey appreciated. Not for the cheap thrill. Because they'd had problems with staff smuggling things in.

Staff who got too close to the patients.

Guards could be the worst, particularly if they were working Darden because they'd failed the psych exams for regular duty. If they'd worked the prisons out on the desert, as some had, they thought this was a cake position, but they always ended up complaining that they'd prefer the general maximum-security prison population to Darden State.

At least with sane prisoners, you had logic and reason and motive.

He waited for the guard on the other side to unlock the steel door.

～

ON B WARD, he passed the group rooms and the recreation center. One elderly man, tall and thin, propelled himself forward in his wheelchair.

As Trey passed by him, the old man said, "Goddamn motherfuckers. I'm gonna skin me the lot of you."

A nurse, holding a clipboard to her chest, flashed a smile at Trey. Lauren Childes—she'd been at Darden since before Trey's time. "Good to see you back, Trey," she said.

Her eye patch was new. Her left eye was covered.

One of the patients had got her, probably.

Trey didn't want to ask.

He didn't want to know.

Two COs at the double doors. Corrections officers had been brought in to beef up security even further.

The two cops frisked him as he stepped across the grate at the entrance to C. Their ID tags said Curzon and Bellows. Curzon, the younger of the two, held up a metal detector and waved it over his body.

"Glad to see Darden's met twentieth-century technology," Trey said.

The officers said nothing.

Trey knew their silence was from nervousness. He held up his ID badge. They scanned its bar code. Double checks and triple checks were the rule.

No cop liked being in C or D Ward.

"When they have you guys come in?" Trey asked.

"Nine weeks back. Extra protection," Bellows said. "Ever since Program 28 went into effect."

"What do you do when something happens?"

Curzon shot the other a look and half smiled. "We bolt for the doors and get the hell out of here. Let the crazies kill the crazies, that's my take."

Bellows shook his head. "You're on D, right?"

"Right," Trey said. "New assignment: Program 28."

"Oh man," he laughed. "Oh man. We lost a guy there last month."

"Dead?" Trey asked.

"No. Early retirement. Some lucky SOB banged his knees up something good. Somehow got a pair of pliers from some asshole working on the pipes and just busted his kneecaps. Went out on disability. They've transferred half of the SVPs from up in Napa down here, and they're ..."

"Different," Curzon finished. They chuckled. "Two nights back some guy on D tried to pull some chick's head off. It was bad. Real bad."

Bellows chuckled. "She grew two inches."

"Damn," Curzon laughed. "Why can't we send 'em to Patton State? Or send their asses back to Atascadero. We don't need the pileup here."

"Let me keep my cojones, that's all I'm sayin'," Bellows said.

THE FIRST CORRIDOR had bars on its entry door, but after that, the hallways all looked like a cross between hospital floors and elementary-school corridors, with fire doors at the end of each of them.

The artwork and creative-writing samples of many of the patients were taped up to long corkboards just above eye level along the walls. He passed the group rooms and the lounges. All the guards seemed to recognize him, even those he'd never seen before. He assumed this was because of the notoriety he'd received since the previous summer. Outside each porthole door, the clipboard hung with the various doctors' and nurses' names for the patients who occupied the rooms, as well as their daily schedules from morning showers to recreational therapy to who got cigarettes and who didn't.

For Trey, it was like walking down a long and lonely tunnel to the place that almost cost him and his family their life.

D Ward.

And an offshoot of D, the newly christened Program 28.

It looked, at first, like any other hall of the entire complex.

But it wasn't.

When he arrived at Ward D, he marveled at the beefed-up security. Cameras moved lazily back and forth along the ceiling. Reinforced steel doors were everywhere, it seemed—more than had been there when he'd last been at work.

"Somebody must be running for office somewhere," he told Mary Fulcher, who was doing soap and toilet paper counts near the guard station.

"Huh?" she asked. "Oh, Trey. Hey, old man. I didn't recognize you with those glasses." She threw her arms around him for a quick hug. When she pulled back, he noticed that she had aged ten years over the past few months. Her forehead was creased with worry lines—far too young to have them—and she had that overstressed look to her eyes.

"Good to be back, Mary. I meant all the security improvements. The cameras. The guards and stuff."

"Oh yeah. It was Hatcher that did that. Olsen got a call from the governor himself, and it was all donated by some security firm in Riverside. 'To make sure no one ever escapes from D Ward again.' Good PR for the neighborhood, huh?"

"Yep. Good PR," Trey replied.

"Think it'll work?"

He smiled.

"Me, neither," she said.

~

ON WARD D, the night shift nurse and psych techs were off on their duties, so he made a pot of coffee in the lounge and drank half a cup. The lounge was a mess—crushed Dixie Cups on one of the round tables, the microwave was filthy, and someone had spilled coffee creamer around the sink.

Same old, same old.

There would be three shift nurses making early rounds of meds on two different corridors. Six psych techs, most of them doing shower duty. Rise and shine wasn't for another ten minutes. Miraculously, another fifteen psych techs would arrive by seven thirty a.m. Then three or four would be late for their shifts. Other staff would come in, and the night staff would leave. The patients would wake up at different times, depending on how heavily they had been medicated, but most of them will have been up since six. Others would just be waking up. The showers would go in shifts, as would the cafeteria groups.

Trey finished his coffee, which tasted bitter but strong enough to energize him. He tossed the cup into the trash can by the lounge door, but missed it. He wondered if this was an omen for the rest of his day.

Because he'd been shift supervisor, he had one of three small offices at the opposite end of the corridor. He passed several patients' rooms, glancing at the charts as he went, noticing that Dr. Conroy now had six new patients, and Brainard had two. As usual, Brainard overdosed him with too much Doltrynol, but it was the man's methods: drug 'em and bury 'em. And before they die from lack of life, pretend that you actually care about their welfare.

Jim Anderson had been promoted to shift charge, and as Trey passed his office, he saw the desk covered in paperwork and the small lamp on. Tinny music from the small speakers on Anderson's desk—was it from *The Mikado*? Trey wasn't sure. Anderson was a big Gilbert & Sullivan fan, which seemed so incongruous with Anderson's demeanor and way of talking. But somewhere along the line, he'd gotten hooked on light opera and played it whenever he could. Trey smiled as he heard the lyrics, "I've got a little list of people we could do without who never would be missed," from the operetta.

They hadn't spoken since last summer.

It was as if what had happened had been too much to talk about.

Anderson was still on the ward somewhere. He'd be there till noon. He was the one guy Trey was looking forward to seeing.

Then, two doors down, Trey's office.

The door was still locked. Had anyone been in it during those four months? When he unlocked the door and went in, he saw the tracks of others. The papers out of place, the computer terminal turned slightly to the right, the file folders stacked on the cabinet.

Then he went about his morning duties.

TREY SIGNED for the alarm pens, to make sure they were accounted for. Next, he went down to the station and checked the razors, to make sure the correct number was there. After that he checked the sharps: scissors, razor knife, a special knife to cut restraints in case of fire, pliers, screwdrivers, a hammer, fingernail and toenail clippers. The others probably checked them too, but as supervisor it was his ultimate responsibility.

And since what had happened the previous summer, Trey Campbell did not want to leave anything to chance.

After he checked out the sharps, he walked up and down the corridor of D Ward. Several fire extinguishers lined the walls, and he checked each one of these. Then he moved on to check the defibrillators and oxygen bottles. As he passed it, he glanced at a crash cart—used for hospital emergencies, it was full of bandages, neck, back, and other braces, flashlights, special hospital material for people in sudden and acute respiratory or cardiac failure. The nurse on duty was in one of the patient rooms—he saw her through the porthole. She was in there with two psychiatric technicians, tending to one of six patients in the ward. It was Rita Paulsen. She smiled when she caught a glimpse of him through the round window. He nodded to her but was unable to smile. He both looked forward to his daily routine and wished he had not come back.

Trey flipped through the roll charts to see if there were any other female staff on D that morning. When female staff were on, he had to check with them every fifteen minutes. It wasn't that they were incompetent. It was that the patients often made their more gruesome attacks on the women. It was a dangerous job.

He checked the Site Incident Report at the nurse's station, but nothing out of the ordinary had occurred in the night. Walking the green halls, with the thick smell of rubbing alcohol and Clorox and then that all pervasive odor of mildew, it was as if he had not had time off at all. It was as if his life had begun and would one day end within these walls.

Within D Ward.

Any one of these patients was potentially dangerous in ways the community that surrounded Darden State could not possibly imagine.

Trey knew better than anyone that all it took was one.

He wondered if anyone was making the back-hall rounds and the long-hall rounds. Every fifteen minutes someone was supposed to check the ward and the patients' dorms. In a dangerous unit like D, no one wanted to miss those.

He did his own check of the ward, looking from room to room. Most of the patients were sleeping. Some had already risen and were with the orderlies down at the showers. All would be awake in a few minutes. Then the laundry detail and shower supervisors would miraculously appear from this silent ward, and the day would truly get underway as the med cart squeaked on its wheels down the bustling corridor.

After he'd gotten his phone messages and checked the computerized state forms, he went down to Conroy's on-site office, down through the corridors, on the opposite end of the building from the violent criminals' ward.

She wasn't there.

Her office, like all the psychiatrists' offices, was large and spacious—unlike the hole-in-the-wall he had as supervisor on D. She had a window to the inner courtyard and a side room for her secretary. It smelled of lilacs and cigarettes inside the office. Elise always broke the rules and smoked in her office. So far, no one had complained too bitterly about it.

He went in and looked over her messy desk. Half a dozen manila files, stacked one atop the other. A half-drunk cup of coffee —she was an early riser sometimes. A workaholic most times.

A framed picture of Elise and her kid. Trey had only worked with her sporadically and was often surprised that she had a life outside her work at all. She had offices at three different facilities, including the Riverside County evaluation site in Riverside. He had never known her not to work. Even after her husband walked out on her, she had been on the job the following day.

And she was a chain smoker.

Five cigarette butts in the ashtray. The staff had to go outside to the yard, or up through the locked area at the roof. Elise never left her desk if she wanted a smoke.

A notepad in the middle of her desk. A crazy doodle across it, as if she'd sat there less than an hour ago, drinking coffee, talking to someone on the phone, puffing on her cigarette ... forcing a pen down hard, making circles on the pad.

He found the file he needed fairly quickly.

MICHAEL SCOLERI.

From behind him, in the doorway, someone said, "Trey?"

He turned around. It was Conroy's assistant, Eric Lombard. He was short, blond, and too much of a surfer dude for Darden State. He belonged in LA at the beach. He seemed sorely out of his element in Conroy's office.

"Hey, Eric. Where's the boss?"

"Some bad shit's going on. Here's her cell," he said, and then passed him a number.

"Any idea what's up?"

"She's not even telling me," he said. "She's doing some profiling with the San Pascal and the Riverside Sheriff's Offices, working on some new forensics case. She got called in over the weekend. That's all I know. She was here for about ten minutes and then took off like a bat out of hell. She won't tell me anything. But she wants to talk to you ASAP."

Then, "You can use the office if you want." Eric left, shutting the door.

Trey reached for the phone and dialed up the cell phone number.

Elise picked up.

"Hello? Elise?" he said.

"Trey? Thank God."

"What's going on? You working on some case?"

"I'm in traffic. I ... can't talk like this. I'll be there later on. I've got ..." Silence on the line.

"Elise?"

"I'm driving over to San Pascal. I'll be back. Maybe an hour. Maybe more."

Another silent few seconds.

"Tell me what's going on," he said, expecting nothing more than a hectic schedule from her, as was her usual.

"Do something for me. Did Eric get you a file?"

"Yep."

"Okay. Okay. Read it. Just as an intro. And go see Scoleri. See if you can get him talking. About anything. Anything at all. Watch him. See if he's talking to anybody else. Staff. Anybody."

Trey grabbed the file on top of the pile of papers on Conroy's desk.

"Okay. Scoleri. Tell me who you are."

He opened the file.

CHAPTER TWENTY-TWO

INTERVIEW SUBJECT: MICHAEL SCOLERI
    INTAKE O/D : E. CONROY
    PROPERTY OF THE DARDEN STATE HOSPITAL, DARDEN, CA
    CONFIDENTIAL

NOTES: Found Guilty of the murders of six women, two men, rape, and mutilation. Postmortem sexual activity. Fascinated with the dead. Necrophilia. Goes for souvenirs. Collection included eyes, noses, breasts, and genitalia. Activity: labile.

    * * *

SCOLERI: Hi. You know my name, but I don't know yours.
CONROY: I'm Dr. Conroy. I'm a psychiatrist for the state of California. Do you understand that, Mr. Scoleri?
SCOLERI: Yes. It says E. Conroy on your tag …
CONROY: Elise. Dr. Elise Conroy.
SCOLERI: Okay, Doc. But call me by my real name.

CONROY: Might I call you Michael?

SCOLERI: No. I'm not Michael. I'm Abraxas. I am the true God.

CONROY: Let's talk about what you did.

SCOLERI: The pretty girls. Okay. I didn't kill them. What I did was date them, and that was about it. We partied. We had some fun. It was all pretty innocent. Yeah, they came on to me, and yeah, I just should've not spent time with them. But I didn't kill them. It got a little rough. But I only did what they told me to. What they asked. They asked for all kinds of things. They begged for some of them.

CONROY: And you killed them.

SCOLERI: Only when they begged. I didn't do it. They used me as a tool. That's why they called me the Handyman.

CONROY: Who?

SCOLERI: The newspapers. They called me the Handyman. Like the song. Do you know the song? I'm a handyman for a lot of things. It wasn't the hammers and nails that got me that name. It wasn't the pliers and the wrenches and the ropes. It was because I knew what to give their hearts. They spoke to me in prayers. They pleaded for me. And I gave them what they asked. There was one named Jenny, and she prayed the most. She prayed so much that I had to answer her prayers. See, she'd been beaten when she was a little girl. She couldn't get away from it in life. That's how life is. You don't get away from your problems. You don't, either, do you?

CONROY: Who had beaten her?

SCOLERI: Her parents. I think mainly her father. But her mother too. Her father was a sadist, but I think her mother was like, you know, one of those little yappy dogs. You know? The kind that just runs after and bites at you. So she sort of encouraged the father to be mean. She was probably the kind of mother who likes it when children suffer. And pretty Jenny suffered all the time she grew up. And her daddy did those things to her that daddies are only supposed to want to do with mommies. So when she was in my presence and crying, a big girl of twenty-four, bawling her eyes out, I showed her how to reach atonement. That means at-one-ment. That's where atonement comes from. She had to atone for her sins and her father's sin. I told her what it would cost. What was demanded. And she begged. And then she offered. It was just three of her fingers. She offered them because they were the part of her that still did bad things. That was her atonement. When it was done, she prayed that she would die. I was just the tool. The hand of Abraxas was upon her, and she thanked me when she left. She thanked me profusely. I stayed with her that night. All night long. I prayed with her. I knew how her life had gone to that point. Children really live in Hell. But I could offer her Heaven. And atonement.

CONROY: And how did you know that? About her childhood?

SCOLERI: I'm afraid if I told you, you wouldn't understand.

CONROY: And you believed her parents had beaten her and abused her as a child.

SCOLERI: Her body radiated it. She was small and weak from it. She had a little darkness in her head from where they'd hit her. She talked to me silently from the darkness. Do you know that's what we all have? All of us who are here? We were born with this small broken piece of glass—a darkness. In our brains. And then some of us were tortured. By nice people who thought they were doing good. I know what they did to her. They saw into her darkness and they hurt her so that her darkness would grow.

CONROY: Darkness?

SCOLERI: Yep. A small voice of darkness. Don't you ever hear them? You talk to enough of them. They grow up and do bad things later. Or they spend their lives being hurt. It's because of that voice in the dark. It grew in them. It didn't grow in someone like you.

You're attractive, well educated, smart. Not like the kind of people I'm talking about. They're lost, and they've been lost since that darkness grew inside them. I hear their voices as one voice. I do. All the time. They talk to me. The lost ones. The ones who get hurt. And the monsters talk to me too. The ones who hurt. I know them. They send me their prayers.

CONROY: Do you think that what you did to her was worse than what her parents had done to her?

SCOLERI: Of course not. What I did to her was the best thing for her. I wasn't going to let her go through the life they'd mapped out for her. How would she have turned out? She would've been just another messed up woman. She would've kept the species going, only her species. The messed up kind. The kind that raises children all wrong. The kind of woman who doesn't achieve any kind of balance in her life. The kind with darkness growing. Look around, Doctor. The streets are full of them. You may know some. They blot out the light. They're ... well, they're not like you. And none of you are like me.

CONROY: Do you believe that you are a different species?

SCOLERI: It must be hard to understand any of this, Dr. Conroy. You don't live in the world of direct experience. You're watching a movie screen and you think that's life. But you're not out there, in contact. Very few are anymore.

CONROY: Do you feel bad for what you did to her?

SCOLERI: How? She begged for death. But I messed it up.

CONROY: In what way?

SCOLERI: I did it too fast. The knife slipped. She was supposed to suffer for six minutes. It was too quick. She was gone before I could tell her.

CONROY: What did you need to tell her?

SCOLERI: About the gift.

CONROY: What is the gift?

SCOLERI: Suffering. She was so lucky to have it. But she should've had six minutes.

CONROY: Why is six minutes so important?

SCOLERI: Six minutes is enough time for me to take out what I need so that she could've seen it before she died. She could've watched it fly. All it ever takes is the power of six. She could've seen it.

CONROY: Seen what?

SCOLERI: The beauty of the world can only be experienced through terrible pain. Joy is in suffering. Even the saints knew that. All suffering is where God lives. I showed them God. And they found me there. I showed them my beauty. My true face. The doorway between life and death is always open. And it swings both ways, Dr. Conroy. They still talk to me. They tell me things. I can't keep the dead from speaking. What does it matter what I did to them? If I took their sight? They passed through suffering. They still exist. It's ridiculous to lock me up like this. I am Abraxas. I am all that there is. I hold life and death in my hands. Death is the true freedom in life. I hold their souls in my kingdom.

Scoleri transferred to Atascadero following conviction.

Scoleri transferred to Darden State/life threatened at Atascadero/sixth patient for experimental Program 28.

CHAPTER TWENTY-THREE

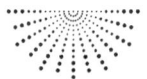

"Hey, Bubba," Jim Anderson said.

Trey glanced up from the page. He dropped it back into the manila folder, shutting it. Anderson stood in the doorway, taking up most of it. "Jimmy."

"My Trivia Dude is back in play."

"Absolutely."

"What's the name of the woman who wrote the poem that goes on the Statue of Liberty?"

"Easy. Emma Lazarus."

"Who was the first man in space?"

"Double easy. A Russian named Gagarin, 1961. We launched Alan Shepard up a few weeks after. You know I know the space race answers backward and forward."

"I need to check on that one. You may be wrong. Okay, one more. What was the name of Jayne Mansfield's dog?"

"You got me. No idea. She was in a 225 when she died, though. So was the dog. Does that get me trivia points?"

"No way, Bubba. No way."

Jim, a behemoth of a guy, larger than when Trey had last seen him several months before, grew wider the older he got. His blond buzz cut was still intact, giving him the giant-teddy-bear-crossed-with-a-Marine look. He had the telltale peanut-butter-and-jelly smudges of a slipshod breakfast all over his white coat.

Jim cracked a grin, his gold tooth shiny at the front of his mouth. "Back for the love of the job. Man, it's good to see you back."

Pointing to Jim's dirty jacket, Trey laughed. "Don't you think you ought to come to work in clean clothes?"

Jim glanced at the stains. He wiped at the peanut butter and then licked it off his fingers. "Ever since this new laundry service started up, I just throw it to them. Pretty soon, we'll have shoe shines here too. And massages. It's like paradise here, if it weren't for the patients."

Trey rose, offering his hand, but Jim slapped at it playfully.

"Hear you're going to work Program 28," Jim said. "Jesus, that's the shit end of the stick. I go in to help out, and I feel like I'm just waiting to get my head torn off. They're all labile in there. They move slowly; they get you all relaxed. Then when they see an opportunity, well, you know the routine."

"It's what I missed about this place."

Jim offered a smile. "Well, you worked with Hatcher pretty closely, didn't you?"

"Too closely. Jesus, Jimmy, they act like 28's a promotion."

"Sure, the docs think so. That's because they're all going to run off and write their books about the monstrosity of the human mind or some bullshit. Conroy herself was writing up some book and got a deal with a big New York publisher just to talk about her unusual way of dealing with the patients. You and me, we just have to watch out for the crazies. One thing I'll give Program 28: they're in restraints so much, there's not a lot to be afraid of. But hell yes, they creep the crap outta me."

"Agnes Hatcher was in restraints," Trey said.

"True. And she managed to get out of them. But 28 is Olsen's baby, and Conroy runs psych with it. So you know we're all safe," Jim said, winking. "It's super-duper freak show there. You think you've seen the worst? Twenty-eight is the scum in the toilet. Hey, you got a copy of *Sociopathic Times?*" Jim pointed to the file in Trey's hand.

Trey held it up. "Conroy wants me to consult. Not just work with him, but work with her. Christ, I had six messages from her when I walked in. I can't seem to reach her."

"Something bad's going on with her today. No idea what. She came in after seven but left real fast." Jim snorted. "I wish Conroy had never come down to D Ward. She's good, but it's 'cause she's pretty. Sexist as that sounds. It stirs some of these guys up. Christ, Rob Fallon was all jumping up and down this morning talking about her. Jillian thought he was gonna kill her. You gotta watch Fallon."

"He cool down?"

Jim nodded. "Yep. He clams up and is all smiles like the damn cat with the canary. We thought we were gonna have to tie him down, but you know Fallon. He's basically a good boy."

Trey half grinned at the intended irony of this comment. "Fallon greeted me in the lounge."

"Yeah, he's tasting his freedom. He's got some girl on the outside with big bucks who's trying to get early release for him." Jim Anderson paused, not having to add that everyone in Darden knew what Rob would do if released: just kill the girlfriend at some point. "She may just do it. She's an heiress to some fortune. Lives in Beverly Hills or something and drives in here for long visits with him."

"A lot has happened since I left," Trey laughed. "At least for Rob. Man, someone should counsel that girlfriend of his. Does she understand the definition of sociopath?"

"We tried, Bubba, we tried," Jim said. "So now that you're back, what's the first order of business, boss?"

"Tell me about Scoleri. The stuff I can't find out from a psych file."

Jim shrugged. For a big guy who had taken down some seriously dangerous killers in his time, having to wrestle them to the floor when they got hold of broken fluorescent light tubes to use as weapons, or when someone did a body slam at his kneecaps, he always seemed to have an air of innocence about him. "Okay, what I know. He talks about how he used to work in carnivals. You know, the kind that go town to town. I've seen him do some stuff. Real carny tricks, like he does this contortionist thing where it's like he can suck his own dick. Pardon my French. No, really. I mean he can get in these weird positions, like his legs all the way over his head. He also told me and Bobby that he used to stick needles all the way through his body. Long needles. A real sideshow freak as a kid, apparently. He had his first girl when he was sixteen. When he talked about it, I thought he meant sex, but what he meant was something different. I mean, he had her. He cut off her big toe as his first souvenir. When he was a little kid, he grew up in group homes all over the place—mainly between here and Chino. He said they were all Jesus freaks, and he claims he was battered into his whole God thing. He is Abraxas the Great or something. He reads comic books whenever he can. The basics: *Superman*, *Spider-Man*, and *Batman*. That and children's books. He's basically hooked on reading anything a ten year old might read. But he's sharp. He had one year at a work farm in Arizona because he'd committed some crime as a little kid that might've involved hurting another boy. I'm not sure. You gotta ask Conroy about that if you want. All I know's what he told me with his big fat mouth."

"He kill more than once?"

"I think so," Jim nodded. "Every time he talks about one of the people he killed, he acts like they're still alive. Still talking to him." Jim paused. Reached into his pocket and drew out a pack of Wrigley's. Offered a stick to Trey, and then unwrapped one for himself, popped it into his mouth, and began chewing. "You know something? On the outside, he was like Hatcher. He collected souvenirs. You know, the usual, jewelry, fingers, eyes. He liked having mementos. He looks like a kid sometimes. He's late twenties but looks like he's eighteen. But this one started early. He's labile, so you have to watch yourself around him. But he hasn't caused much in the way of problems. Until this morning."

"The thing with Fallon?"

"Yep. In the showers. Scoleri was there. Whatever happened, Scoleri ended up jumping on Dave Fenstler and Bobby Bronson. Nearly got Bobby's eyes."

"Why was he on Fallon?"

"Robbie says that Scoleri wants to do him, but Robbie thinks everyone wants that. Scoleri claims he had a message for Conroy, and that's as far as I know. He's definitely agitated. Maybe it's the weather. You know how it goes sometimes. If the barometric pressure goes all screwy and they start getting sinus headaches and then one of them gets all screwed up. Last night Scoleri started carving on himself."

"With what?"

Jim held up his fingers, displaying fingernails. "We cut his nails down this morning. He wrote on his tummy. 'Suffer the children to come unto me.' He spouts scriptural stuff a lot. He is the great god Abraxas." Jim laughed. "You'll like him. He reads minds and talks to dead people too."

Trey got out of his chair and went to the door. "I guess it's time to go to God."

"Sure," Jim said. "Room 3 on Program 28. Hey, you'll love it down there. It's like an isolation tank. Times six. Hey, got another one. What's the oldest written story?"

"'The Epic of Gilgamesh,'" Trey said. "Man, you'd think that my brain could remember complex mathematical equations instead of this stuff. You lead the way."

The two men began walking down the green corridor, toward Program 28.

Two COs stood at the entrance to Program 28.

Big, muscular guys who looked like they were hyped up on testosterone. That was good. They needed some scary guys to keep the really scary ones in line.

"This is Ash Freeman, and this is the infamous Pete Atkins," Anderson said by way of introduction.

Trey shook their hands, and the one named Atkins couldn't seem to make eye contact to save his life. Trey never liked that in people who worked on his ward. Even a CO. It might spell trouble down the line. It was a psychological checkpoint, and when a man in particular couldn't look him in the eye, particularly during an intro, it might mean that man was hiding something or, at best, was not all there.

It wasn't like Trey had never had problems with COs before. He had learned the primary rule of working with the forensics patients. There were three kinds of people who liked working with them: the ones who had a talent for the work, the ones who had the background for it and needed the job and could handle it. Then there were those who worked there who either actively hated the patients or liked to have positions of power of people they considered lesser.

Trey tried to engage Atkins in conversation briefly, but the CO exuded a bland disregard for him.

Trey had, once, years before, had to separate a CO from a patient when the CO had nearly beat the patient's brains out of him. It was a guy just like this one: young, smart, strong, and something was up. He had not been all there. Half the battle at Darden State was just making sure that the staff was saner than the patients.

It was the problem with life outside these walls too.

But inside, it could be deadly in a way that wasn't pleasant to contemplate.

Familiar patterns, back one day, he thought. *Put it aside. Deal with it later.*

For now, Scoleri.

They entered Program 28 via the standard reinforced double doors, but when Trey glanced through the porthole windows, he saw a different kind of hallway than the norm. This one looked as if it were for medical quarantine. It was completely metallic and gray instead of the usual light green of Ward D. It gave him an eerie feeling. It wasn't made for warmth or human habitation. Whoever designed and then built this special hallway knew the effect it would have on the patients.

They would feel especially trapped and separated.

It was like a twenty-first century science-fiction dog pound, with minor adjustments for human beings. Shiny and metallic and very cold.

It was a nightmare.

Trey felt as if this were more dehumanizing than necessary, but when he thought about the kinds of crimes these particular forensics patients had committed, he knew that Darden State was at a loss. None of the other state hospitals wanted the six patients in Darden's Program 28. It was a new experiment that the executive director was willing to try, mainly at the behest of Dr. Elise Conroy and a consortium of medical personnel from among the psychiatric community. They worked closely with the law enforcement agencies when the possible psychopath was out in the real world, to try and understand the inner workings of the kind of human being who had stepped into the territory of human monster.

And Trey, coming back, now would have Program 28 as his supervisory group. He would be spending the next several months working daily with each patient.

He both dreaded it and couldn't wait to find out more.

When he got through the doorway, with Anderson right behind him, they had to turn and lock the doors behind them. "Added security," Anderson said. "The sweet thing of it is, we have a lockdown, we're fucked. See that?" He pointed to the ceiling, toward what looked like a series of small round lights recessed into the ceiling itself. "Those are the strobes. But every third one is a camera. Every fourth one is for gas."

"Gas?"

"I told you it was unorthodox. They have a breach here, those doors," Anderson pointed back down to the doors they'd just locked, "can't be opened until the folks up there," he pointed up to the small recessed orbs, "see that whoever is in here—and that means you and me too—are down on the floor, either in sleepytime or overdose land."

"Jesus, it's like smoking bees."

Anderson arched an eyebrow. "Say what?"

"When you want to get the honey from a hive, you can use a bellows and get smoke on the bees. It makes them dormant. Like freezing them."

"I wish we'd just freeze these guys sometimes," Anderson said. "My love for humanity sort of goes south in here."

"Can't be true about gassing people. That sounds like Nazis."

"I don't know. It's what I heard," Anderson said, chuckling. "Maybe it's another Darden rumor, like the little pill that simulates death to try and get the worst patients to stop killing. I like those myths. Frankly, I'd rather pass out without knowing whether or not some loon had chewed my nuts off." They were several feet from the first room. The rooms were all on one side of the hall. "Patients don't look at each other here. They can hear each other sometimes, but it's basically isolation. Some outside stuff comes in. But it's very regulated, and three doctors have to sign off on it."

"That can be good or bad," Trey said. "They don't hear each other, they don't get in an excited state. But they spend too much time not interacting, they start to go kaboom."

Anderson grinned. "God, I'm glad you're back. Nobody knows about kaboom like you do. Here you go, first room."

CHAPTER TWENTY-FOUR

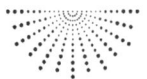

EACH OF THE SIX ROOMS HAD THE ILLUSION OF BEING OPEN to the hall, but with a thick transparent wall. Behind this, more bars. The door into each was barred also. Each room held a large cot, a washbasin, a toilet in the corner, and a table with two chairs. Trey was about to ask about the chairs—they could be used as weapons—but noticed the floor where the chairs were bolted down. The walls were bare. The ceiling of each room seemed fairly high, and at the top, there was a rectangular window that no doubt also had thick Plexiglas in it, as well as bars. The window was close enough to the ceiling that it would've been extremely difficult for even the most agile athlete to leap to them.

"They never hurt themselves?" Trey asked. "The Plexiglas? I'd think that might be worse than a little padding."

"It's not quite Plexiglas. It's a reinforced glass and plastic, bonded together. It's a bitch to keep clean. Especially when they scratch them up or put all kinds of crap all over them. But on the patients' side, it has some give to it. These guys never hurt themselves that way. They think they're little messiahs. They believe too much in themselves. Scoleri tried to kill himself, but using his fingernails. I don't know how he gets those suckers so sharp. We keep them as clipped down as possible, but he grows 'em fast."

"Is he on a suicide watch?"

"Scoleri? Naw. He just had a moment. He said he wanted to prove that he was God. Or something. You know the routine."

THE MAN in the first room was naked, and his body was covered with what could only be feces. He had been wiping his own shit across the walls, writing out long sentences that were unreadable.

"He's the artist," Anderson said. "Calls himself Ivory. Fingerpaints like this all the time. He's probably the only one I feel bad for here, just because he's alive. If I were like that, I'd want someone to put a bullet in my head."

"What was he on the outside?"

"Murdered his wife, his five kids, the dog, the works. Then started taking out the paperboy and the old man next door to him. He said he'd gotten word that it was time."

"Time?"

"Time to kill. Apparently the secret of all human life is something that was revealed to him by voices. Sort of like Joan of Arc. And the secret must've involved a pretty sadistic death too. I think it's on record that he didn't just shoot 'em. He played with them before they died. Look at him. He thinks he's doing the goddamn Sistine Chapel. Twice a day, at least, they have to hose this room down."

Trey was used to this, as was Jim Anderson. They had spent their adult lives working with people who were among society's most violent.

Yet, Trey felt an inward shiver. *A goose walking over my grave.*

They passed the next room, and the next. Each held a patient whose crimes seemed worse than the one before. It was like walking into the mouth of nightmares.

"Jesus, it's still a zoo in here."

"And we're the zookeepers," Anderson said. He pointed to the fifth room, fifth patient, who lay on his cot, facing the side wall. "That's Mandolar. He's in for beheadings. He's pretty depressed right now. Last night at one of his sessions, Brainard got him talking about his childhood, and it turns out Willy's family had weekend incest parties involving Dad, Mom, Grandma, the whole bit. He's been a little under the weather all day. And now …" They approached the last room on Program 28. "Your new boyfriend."

"ANYTHING I SHOULD KNOW before I go into the tiger's cage?" Trey asked.

"Want more Scoleri trivia? Absolutely," Jim Anderson said, keeping his voice low. "Michael Scoleri is the worst. His crimes on the outside are beyond the pale. He cuts them up, gets off on it. Some men too. Likes to collect souvenirs, you know that routine. Gets off on the memory of the kill. Went high profile when he killed that porn star, Fiona Raleigh. Her sugar daddy was pretty powerful in the governor's office, so when he got picked up, finally, they really went to town. Nobody was happy he ended up here. They wanted the death penalty. They got us. Scoleri used to do carney tricks like sticking long needles in his face and other stuff. Likes to carve into his skin. Claims he feels no pain whatsoever. Gets off on the pain of others. On fear. He told Bobby once that fear is a magical drug that you can inhale and get power from. He completely believes he's God and pisses off too many people to mention with his curses on them and his pronouncements of the end of the world. He'll be in here until the day he dies, I suspect."

Before entering the room, or "pod," as Trey would soon come to know these Program 28 rooms, he wanted to get a sense of the man within it.

He sat at the table, reading a book.

He looked too young to have committed the murders that landed him here.

He looked too young to have raped, mutilated, and killed other human beings.

He looked like an innocent.

Once inside the pod, Trey felt differently.

The familiar sense he had around sociopaths returned: a feeling of human cold. Of being in the same room as a lion. Only with less compassion. It was almost an aura around them. Scoleri's was strong—the feeling of not being all there. Of not quite being human. The sense, perhaps instinct, that some enormous gulf existed between the two of them.

A feeling of emptiness, of something being terribly wrong.

A preternatural sense.

"Campbell, William, thirty-six, Caucasian, brown, brown, not quite as tall as you look," the youngish blond man said, not bothering to glance up from his book. Trey didn't know books were allowed here. He was never sure, in these experimental programs, where the rules twisted. The young man's voice was sonorous and had an oddly hypnotic quality to it. He didn't seem like the killer that Trey had just read about. "Poor family from Yucaipa, or maybe Barstow, or San Pascal, or Yucca Valley—that kind of place that feels like nowhere when you're growing up in it. Brought yourself up pretty much on your own. Maybe some group homes. Jesus camp and bible school and memorizing the Book of Revelations like it was the Boy Scout Handbook. Lots of dreams of getting far away from your parents. Not your parents, though. Your foster parents. You were one of those unfortunate kids—at least you think that. I can smell it—that insecurity, that feeling that it might all be taken away. Sometimes you wonder who your parents were, your real parents. But you leave that door closed. Because you know one thing about them. You know your mother was put in a place kind of like the place you're in now. Only hers was for nice people who went crazy. Not like this place, where only bad people go crazy." His legs were crossed, and the book was spread open between his knees.

When the young man did glance up, sighing, he didn't look the way Trey expected. It was as if a man of twenty-three had dropped six years. He looked like a kid, not an adult. His face was peach, his jaw elfin, his youth startling. His eyes, pale blue, were the only distraction. They seemed to quiver, as if keeping his steely gaze on Trey's face were impossible. As if all the young man's nerves were in his eyes. Scoleri glanced down to the book again. "They call you Trey."

Trey Campbell shook his head. "Amazing. You're sharp, Michael."

"Thank you." Scoleri wore the tan fatigues and olive-drab T-shirt of the ward. Scoleri grinned, the sweet shit-eating grin of a farm boy. He didn't look up at Trey's face again, but stared at Trey's midsection.

"Like I told you," Michael said, "I created the world, so I know every secret in it. I was there that day, watching your foster father take the strap to your brother. And then, after he stopped moving, your father left him with you, in your room, for nearly a week and locked you in. Always in the dark. You had to be with your dead brother for seven days. And then he touched you. Even after he was dead."

Trey took it all in: Scoleri. Reading material, intuition, rapid eye movement, creative delusions, family construct, two brothers, one dead?

"Something about your eyes," Michael said, in a hushed tone. "You see a lot, don't you?"

"What are you reading?"

"*Beautiful Joe*," Scoleri said, rubbing his hands over the book. Trey knew it. He'd read it as a kid. A dog book. The kind of book that got kids crying. His daughter had read that book when she was in third grade and wept for a week.

"You like that story?"

Scoleri nodded. "It's wonderful. They chop off a dog's ears and tail. Another dog gets shot at."

Trey nodded slightly. He was not going to try to set Scoleri off. Sociopaths could be like lions if you tapped the wrong emotional key. It depended on who was watching. Since Trey had never before interacted with Michael Scoleri, he didn't want to chance anything. "Dr. Brainard tells me you've been doing okay. You've been talking up a storm today, I gather."

"No complaints. I really had nothing to say before. So Trey." Michael grinned. Eyes still down, unwilling to look him in the eye again. "I heard you had a run-in with one of my better creations."

"Really?" Trey returned the grin, unsure of where this would go.

"Miss Hatcher from D Ward. Catalina Island."

Trey glanced at Jim Anderson, who stood at the doorway. Anderson, big as a house, filled up the doorway. Jim suppressed a laugh.

"Word gets around," Trey said.

"Well, rest assured that it was not my intention to have her hurt you or your lovely family. Sometimes even these creations get out of hand." Michael set the book aside, bringing his knees up to his chest. The scars from his attempted suicide were clearly visible—striations along his wrists, still healing. "I was sure you wouldn't return to my domain so soon."

Trey shrugged. "Well, you know how it is."

"Have to earn a living, yes," Michael said. "You're already taking classes toward your master's."

Trey lost his good humor. Again, he glanced at Jim, who raised his eyebrows.

Trey squatted down beside Scoleri. He knew to keep his balance and push his face slightly forward. Sometimes they went for your eyes. It was the easiest thing they could go for in order to debilitate you. He had spent years making sure both his eyes stayed in his head. He wanted Michael to feel comfortable talking with him. "So you know all this because you're God, right?"

Michael threw back his head, laughing. He had a girlish laugh, high and sweet. He closed his eyes, opening them wide.

The pupils moved so rapidly back and forth they were a blur. It was almost too horrible to look at. The eyes moved independently of each other, seeming to spin and spin until all Trey saw was a viscous darkness.

How the hell does he do that? Trey thought.

Then Michael Scoleri whispered, "I'm Abraxas. I'm God. But there's a very bad Devil out in the world right now. He's making his little angels fly to me to give me messages. But I don't answer the Devil's prayers. Let me tell you, Trey, you're going to want to have God step in soon to stop the Beast before the world ends. Which might be in just a few hours, at least as far as Dr. Conroy is concerned. Do you know something?"

"What's that?"

"I hate the rain."

"It won't be that bad. It's pretty light."

"I like snow. But not rain. Have you ever made snow angels?"

"Sure. When I was a kid."

"I wonder if kids still make them," Scoleri said. He glanced up to the barred window that touched the ceiling.

"Would you mind showing me what you wrote on yourself last night?" Trey asked.

Scoleri closed his eyes. Opened them. They were normal again. Not moving rapidly in their sockets. "No. I'm tired," he said. "I don't want to talk anymore."

OUTSIDE THE ROOM, locking the door behind him, Jim Anderson turned to Trey.

"So I didn't know that about you and your family," Jim said, patting Trey on the back. "You had a brother who died?"

Trey said, "None of it was true. He wasn't talking about me."

TREY CONTINUED, "The physical stuff about my height and weight were pretty accurate. My family was pretty middle class, and my dad was a nut job, but other than that, it was an okay childhood. Not quite what he was saying. Most of the stuff he could learn from nurses, or heck, even you. But the other stuff—I wasn't raised in a foster family, I never was beaten, and I never had a brother get killed. But he has."

"What?"

"He was telling me his life story. That's how he does it. He makes himself 'you' and he tells his whole history," Trey said. His throat was dry. "I wouldn't mind that Wrigley's now."

"Spearmint pleasure coming right up," Anderson said, bringing out the pack of gum.

"Sometimes I just want to round up all these families and put them out of their misery. Or save them. But I don't know if they can be saved. I just don't know."

"Everybody can be saved."

"You think that?"

"I don't know. Maybe it's nuts," Jim said, "but I still have faith that things can work out. Even after everything I've seen here. No matter what." Then he brightened. "Man, he had me going. I was beginning to feel sorry for you."

"Well, he's good at it," Trey said, unwrapping the stick of gum and popping it into his mouth. "So he's mine now."

"Him and three others."

"What's with the book? I thought this was major psych isolation."

"Part of the program. They get some media, newspapers, books. A little radio. TV now and then. We even have Movie Fridays and Sunday Night Old Time Radio Shows."

"Meds?"

"Heavy."

"Sedation?"

Jim shrugged. "Pretty constant. It's Brainard. He's the zombie doc. Conroy's more anti-med and pro-one-on-one session. I think she wants to cut back on his meds so he can be more … lucid. Maybe."

"He seems pretty lucid. Sometimes I wish we had fewer meds and more techs." As he walked ahead of Jim, glancing at the charts outside the shut doors, noticing Dr. Brainard's marks in red felt-tip across all the graphs, he added, "And fewer zombie docs. What the hell does Brainard get out of all this?"

"I heard he's writing a book."

"Jesus, you and I should write a book. We'd have the real shit," Trey said.

"Yeah, mainly about how insane the psychologists are."

"Brainard is … a piece of work." Trey tapped his fist against the wall lightly. "Somebody ought to load him up with his own meds. Why is it some of the craziest people we know are psychiatrists?"

Jim laughed, catching up to him. "We've got Paulsen on the desk till four on D, and then Somers takes over."

As they walked toward Trey's office, Trey asked, "What was that thing about making little angels?"

"One of his fantasies," Jim said. "He keeps telling me how the Devil started sending him little angels two nights ago to tell him about the end of the world."

A HALF-HOUR LATER, in his own office, Trey picked up the phone. "Campbell, D Ward."

"It's me," Elise Conroy said.

CHAPTER TWENTY-FIVE

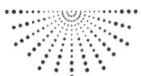

Trey went back down to the end of Ward D, past the security doors, to her office.

"Elise?" Trey said when he stepped through the doorway.

She sat behind her desk. Her hair was disheveled. Her eyes bloodshot. She looked like hell, a sharp contrast to her norm of looking beautiful and pulled together.

"All right. I'm really all right."

"I don't understand …" Trey said. "What's going on? Elise?"

"I couldn't say it on the phone. I couldn't. Trey. Just a few hours ago, just …" Nervously, she reached into a pack of cigarettes, then stopped herself and set the pack down. Before she spoke again, her eyes filled with tears, and she pressed the palms of her hands against her face as if she could blot them out.

Her voice sounded like a little girl's, not the sharp tone of Ward D's primary psychiatrist. "My baby. Got taken. My Lucas."

CHAPTER TWENTY-SIX

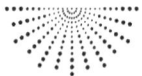

TREY WENT AROUND ELISE CONROY'S DESK AND WRAPPED HIS arms around her.

She leaned against him, her face pressed into his neck, and whatever she'd held tight within herself, she let go of it.

He held her for as long as she would let him, and felt as if she needed whatever warmth he could offer.

TREY SAID, "Do you want to talk? Do you need me to drive you home?"

She dried her tears, reaching for tissue after tissue. Her face, normally so lovely, had crumpled in on itself, a mass of lines and a kind of sorrow he'd only rarely witnessed. A private sorrow that most people never showed the world.

"No. What's the use of going home? What's the use? Trey, I was working with the police to help catch him. And he has my baby.

My Lucas. He's so helpless, Trey. He's so little. I can't let anything happen to him. I just can't."

The rain outside battered at the office window.

God, Trey closed his eyes. *God, please let this turn out good. Please let him be found. Safe. Alive.*

CHAPTER TWENTY-SEVEN

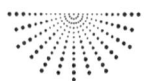

THE SAN PASCAL COUNTY CORONER'S OFFICE EMPLOYS TWO
pathologists, four part-time supervisors at the morgue, as well as
several part-time and full-time employees, from cleanup to bagging
to cutting.

San Pascal County Morgue is in the basement of the old Baseline building off Vineyard and Pepper Streets. Originally a small
teaching hospital in the 1930s until the 1970s, it has since become
primarily a research and development facility for the county, and
for the tri-county alliance interests, and the main housing for the
coroner's office. It is the subject of controversy, the Baseline building, because it is old, has ventilation problems, and is due for a
major renovation. But the county has not yet allocated funds for its
improvements.

It is part of a complex of buildings, including the sheriff's
department and other local law enforcement agencies, at the edge of
the Annex, an industrial park beyond the suburban sprawl off the
freeway. Once, the entire area was vineyards and orange groves.

Jane Laymon grew up wishing she could go into the morgue

with the county coroner, hoping to do forensics research (thus, her bachelor's degree in both criminal justice and forensics). But after spending two years, primarily on child deaths in the county, she was weary of the trip to the morgue and the unnatural camaraderie of those who worked there.

Seeing dead children, whether from natural or unnatural causes, always made her hate the world a little more each time.

ONCE INSIDE THE FACILITY, you take the stairs rather than the service elevator, unless you're bringing in a body. An increased caseload in the area, plus spillover from the Riverside County morgues, has made Baseline (as the place is known by those working in it) overcrowded. The elevators are for the dead. The stairs, the living. Even the refrigeration units, where the corpses are stored during examination and autopsy, are inadequate, and the corridor at the bottom of the stairs is often used as cold storage. Central air-conditioning, as well as swamp coolers, chill the halls below the building. Decomposition is the norm for those bodies that the coroner and his deputies can't get to immediately. The remains are covered or sealed in body bags on gurneys. The detectives and trainees joke about the place as Valhalla, the halls of the fallen.

Jane Laymon thinks it's the entrance to a slightly chilled version of Hell.

Whenever she goes into Valhalla, she takes a palm-sized face mask, slipping it over her nose and mouth. Additionally, she breathes primarily through her mouth when she pushes through the thick door from the stairs into the corridor. She generally slips on a pair of latex gloves, as extra precaution, annoyed by the talcum powder that ends up on her hands and wrists.

The stench is definitely something she had not gotten used to, despite visiting the morgue often.

There are four large rooms, the sizes of school cafeterias, subdivided into smaller spaces by drywall, freestanding dividers, or the refrigerators in the basement morgue. Two of the four are used for embalming and other services of the county related to the dead. The county embalms some of the bodies, subcontracting out to local mortuaries for the work, depending on its need for revenue. The two remaining rooms are the refrigeration units and the small rooms within them, known simply as the cutting rooms. The coroner's and the two deputy coroners' offices are off these rooms. The offices are glassed in. The floor drainage is inadequate so that Jane has, more than once, needed to wipe her shoes before leaving the cutting room. There are emergency decontamination showers—three units, two in the women's room at the end of the hall, and one in the men's. Jane showered only once here—the first time she had to view an autopsy performed on the body of a six-year-old boy.

She had felt, during that autopsy and what it revealed, a revulsion for the human race, and looking at him, it had reminded her of her little brother when they'd been kids. She'd had to turn the hot water up on the shower, nearly scalding her skin, to wash away the memory.

Jane walked in as if she owned the place. Turning to the chief deputy coroner, a middle-aged man who seemed more of a shopkeeper to her than a medical expert, she said, "I need to see all three of them."

She had gotten used to the mutilation done to the corpses. She barely took a breath when she saw all three laid out. Something in her turned off, like a switch she could manually toggle, so that she didn't think about the method of the killer.

Three bodies lay on three metal tables. They were so small that they made the tables seem large. The usual equipment—saws, bone cutters, scissors—lay on the table in their individual holders.

The children seemed haunting. She had already seen two of them. It was not easy to look at the face of a dead child.

Particularly not after what the killer had done to two of them—their faces, their arms.

The bites.

Jane had some small comfort in knowing that the killer did not mutilate them until after he had taken their lives.

But it didn't matter.

You violated them, even if you think you didn't. You could not leave them alone. You have to come after them, even in death.

You hurt them only after they're dead. Why? What does that do for you?

CHAPTER TWENTY-EIGHT

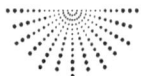

JANE LOOKED OVER THE VICTIMS ON THE METAL TABLES. IT was a double-check she did, in case her first impressions had been off. She'd spent an hour going over the details of evidence, mainly standing in the background while Sykes, Tryon, and Fasteau asked the questions of the pathologist. She was a keen listener and used a rather unorthodox approach that she felt might help add a fresh perspective that her colleagues might've missed.

SHE FELT as if she were alone with each victim as she looked over their bodies. She tried to clear her mind, empty her thoughts, hoping she'd approach the dead now as a blank slate.

Tryon had taught her this technique. It slowed down the process, he'd said. It opened your mind to possibilities other than the ones first presented.

Sometimes it was worse for her.

Sometimes, she felt as if she were going inside the mind of the killer when she looked at his handiwork.

THE LIGHT WAS bright in the room. It was chilly—the refrigeration units were behind her. She worked to keep her mind clear. Hoping. Waiting. Wanting something to come to her. She felt a strange desperation there. She wanted to make her mark with this case. It would have the profile. It would be important.

But she was fairly sure that despite Tryon's backing of her in the investigation, it would go to a team comprised mainly of veterans. If they didn't come up with something solid within a day, after two days of nothing, the FBI would be on it, and their manhunt would be so profoundly superior that the local cops would look bad.

The pathologist, the coroner, and Tryon and Fasteau were at the third corpse, talking quietly over the body. Tryon had a handheld voice recorder and repeated what the pathologist said into it.

THE FIRST CHILD, a girl, had no name yet. The missing child hadn't been reported, and they had not yet found an identifier for her. She was simply Victim One.

Jane wanted to give her a name. It felt inhuman to stand over her corpse and not think of her as Sally or Judy or Amy. It seemed wrong.

The second victim, a boy named Steven Latimer. He had been reported missing too late. The body had turned up in the orange groves at the same time that his mother and father had discovered that he'd never made it to his Cub Scout overnight campout. He had never even made it to the rented van that would take him there.

And finally, the third victim.

They had a name for her: Gina Parsons.

From San Pascal, like the Latimer boy.

Found in the Santa Ana River, near the town of Bannock.

Hanging from a group of trees in the middle of the river.

The coat hanger around her neck, with the wings, like a noose.

PRELIMINARY MATTERS WERE DISCUSSED, but none of them seemed interesting to her, until the coroner mentioned the soap.

"Camay," Tryon said.

"Little bits of pink soap. Under her fingernails," he said, indicating the dead girl. "Because the river hadn't washed it away completely, it may be that she was only in the water for an hour. At the most."

We just missed you, Jane thought. *You sack of shit. But someone could've seen you. It would've been daylight. You washed her hands. You wanted her clean. But not for us. For you. You wanted her pure. You killed her, and you wanted her scrubbed clean.* "What else?"

"The bites."

She looked more closely at the victim's arm. "But after death." She said this as much to confirm as to alleviate the tickle of dread she'd felt since viewing the body.

"Correct. It would appear that all mutilation occurs after the child is dead. He kills them. A little morphine to help them to sleep. Then he drowns them. That's the first two. It's probably the same with this one."

"Morphine?" Jane hadn't heard this before.

"We found traces in Victim One's bloodstream. And Two's."

"Jesus. He has access to a hospital?"

"Nurse, doctor, orderly. Maybe," Tryon said. Tryon had been hanging back, letting her look at the bodies. "We're running checks all over the place. He's going to trip up somewhere here."

"Or she," Jane said.

But, instinctively, she knew this was wrong. The killer was male. The murders had all the signs of a man doing the killing. Only the morphine seemed feminine. Putting them to sleep. *A gentle death.* The thought of it disturbed her more. If the murderer had just been a vicious killer, it was one thing. But he gave them morphine to sleep. He didn't want them conscious for the pain of death. He wanted them to go to sleep like … "Maybe he works for the pound. Maybe …"

"Sure," Tryon nodded his approval.

She noticed an imperceptible smirk on Fasteau's face.

She shot him an acid glance. "He's putting them down like kittens. He doesn't want them to know what's going to happen. Or hurt."

This is a test, Jane thought. *He wants to see how far I can go with this.* "If he only kills after they're asleep … well, he doesn't enjoy their pain," she said, thinking aloud. "Our guy doesn't torture. But something happens after that."

Fasteau shot her a glance. "Sure. He mutilates them." Then, more to Tryon than to her, "We'll get him from the bite marks. This guy has priors. I know it."

"No," Jane said. "He's stopping himself. He's resisting. Something is forcing him to attack them. Maybe. I don't know. Maybe he … well, it's probably whatever is inside him. Forensics get a good look at this?"

Fasteau nodded. "The odontologist took the impression. The bruises blurred it. This guy chews 'em up and spits 'em out."

Gallows humor, particularly around the child murder cases,

pissed her off. She ignored him, as she often did. As hard as it was, she kept her focus on the dead child who lay before her. "No semen, right?"

"None. Everything intact below the waist."

"He doesn't want them sexually. That's one for the books. I was sure this was a sexual predator." Then it occurred to her. *You care for them. You want them clean. You use Camay. They don't arouse you. You don't kidnap them because you have to. You kidnap them because …* But the thoughts led her nowhere. She hated where her mind wandered at times like this. She needed to focus on evidence and what it told. Not go off on her own mental gymnastics. It was one of her problems in life; in breaking down a problem, she sometimes found that she overcomplicated things. As Tryon had told her more times than not: *Let the evidence tell its story.* "Maybe the bite marks will lead to someone with a prior. But I doubt it." She brought the twisting lamp down near the face of the little girl found that morning.

It looked as if a scavenger had mauled the face.

She turned her back on the metal table, the small body, and the men.

Hold it together.

She managed to get out, "We'll just check dental records in San Pascal County," before she felt as if she was going to be sick.

Count to three.

One, two, three. Let it pass. They're dead. She's dead. Their pain is gone. They went to sleep, like a patient on an operating table. They didn't know. They didn't feel it.

She could tell herself all of this and believe it, but the one thing that she knew was a lie: *They were not afraid.*

Of course they were. You keep them for nearly a day. You take them and then you keep them somewhere. Where? Do they know you? Are you a friend of the family? What is your connection to them? And why do you want them for such a short period of time? What's erupting in you after ten or fifteen hours with them? You don't rape them. You don't torture them. What do you get from them that you need? What is it you want? What is compelling you for three days in a row, to expose yourself to suspicion and discovery and arrest and even death, to go to their front yards or to their neighborhoods and get them to go with you?

Why now? Why these days?

Is it Christmas? Did you do this before? If you did, we'd know. You're still young. Not too young. But you're not thirty yet. I can tell. You are frustrated. You look at these kids. They have something you want. You can only get it by taking them. And then you have to kill them. Without hurting them in any way that we can tell.

And, once they're dead, you have to attack them.

Once they're beyond life.

You make them angels.

Do you think you're protecting them? Is there something that you're stopping by killing them?

She took a deep breath, feeling it come over her again. The sense she had in those few murder cases she'd worked on. The sense that she understood the killer in some small way. "He's new to this. Something happened to him and he snapped. Some pressure built up, and our guy is going on pure instinct. He's trying to control it. He's trying to hold back. You use a knife if you want to obliterate someone's face. You don't use your teeth. You don't bite them all over after they're dead unless you get sadistic, sexual pleasure from it. But not our guy. He doesn't want to hurt them. He doesn't want them in pain. My guess is, either there are two killers, or ..."

Fasteau ignored her. He went to one of the other tables.

The coroner kept his gaze on her. "Jane?"

"Or," she continued, "one guy with two distinct personalities in his head. Both of them killers. One is just insane. The other is a sadistic monster." She glanced up from the body.

Thoughts came to her, but she didn't say them aloud.

You're a frustrated artist. Maybe. No. These are definitely angels. These are messages. Are you God? Do you believe in God? Are you doing this because Christmas is coming? Is that it? These are Christmas angels? Angels. Blood angels. Red angels. Bird wings. Flight. Found in or near rivers or streams. Cold streams. Water. Liquid. God. Angel. Devil. Fallen angel. You're religious. You have these conflicting thoughts. You want us to see them as angels. You want us to know that you are making angels. You're showing us—or someone—angels. Angels are a message. To us? To find you? You could bury these children somewhere. But you're putting them out for us each day. It's your game. Are you afraid? Do you not want to do this? Do you want us to find you? You want us to find you because part of you wants to stop this. You believe in God. Or you mock God. But you have this in you, this terrible thing.

You can't control it, and it's coming too fast.

Something is taking you over.

Then the one that made her feel cold.

Possessing you.

Something else is living inside you. You have a conflict. You kill these children. You cut off the wings of the birds. Waterfowl. Big wings. Angel wings. But you don't want to. You want to stop. But there's something inside you that keeps going. Maybe at night. Maybe at dawn, you put the bodies out for us. But at night, something else comes through. Something you can't control.

It annoyed her when her mind started spinning on its own like this. She knew the people who perpetrated this kind of crime were evil. She had no other word for them. They were not misunderstood. They were not passive victims of a larger world. There was genuine evil among humankind. She had seen it firsthand.

But something in her brain always tried to understand the killer.

To catch the perpetrator, you had to get inside the perp's head.

She stood over the metal table and glanced at the others around it.

For just a second, she imagined the moment when the killer strung the two torn bird's wings together with the wire coat hanger.

"Those are duck wings? Geese?" she asked.

The pathologist glanced at the evidence in the plastic bag that lay beside the victim's body. "Sure. A duck."

"So we're looking at parks. Bodies of water. Someone living nearby. Someone who sees these birds a lot and can get them easily."

"You're good," the coroner said, out of the blue, looking up from his work at the second metal table. "Water's in the lungs of numbers one and two. He drowned them. Strangely, there was a little burn in the throat."

"Burn?" Tryon asked.

"Not much. Like soup. Like they'd been given soup, but it was the water. I think hot water was used. No real scalding on the face, but the water was hot that they drowned in."

"He puts them to sleep, then drowns them," Tryon said, mostly to himself.

Jane appreciated Tryon, even when she didn't always like the assignments he passed to her. The entire team was somber. It was the difference between finding adult victims and child victims. In cases of adult murder, there was seriousness, but also the nervous laughter and chitchat—a way of removing oneself from the gruesomeness of the metal table. But in the case of a child death, generally, there was an aura of enormous tragedy. It was the human part of all of them, and Jane felt that those gathered around these corpses paid them respect, even in the examination of the minutiae of their deaths.

"He doesn't want them to suffer," she said, nearly a whisper.

"Jane?" Sykes asked, looking up from a small plastic evidence bag.

"He likes them," she said, speaking up. "He doesn't sexually touch them. He doesn't cut them. Doesn't shoot them. Doesn't seem to have tortured them in any way. He puts them to sleep. Then washes them in hot water. Maybe the drowning is accidental, but I doubt it. He washes them to get them clean, maybe. He's religious. I can feel it. He has a religious mania. That's why he makes them look like angels. He's sending them to Heaven. Pure. Washed. He's showing us that he's doing that. Or showing someone. Maybe God. I think he's going to crack and show himself to us soon. Tell me about the families. Do we know them yet?"

CHAPTER TWENTY-NINE

AFTER PUTTING THE LITTLE BIRD IN ITS CAGE, IT FEELS THE
rumbling of the Other One coming out of itself. It runs up the path
of the hill. The path is all muddy, and its shoes get suctioned, but it
keeps running until it gets to the house above the Mad Place.

It nearly breaks down the door, because the Other One is
getting loose, and the only way to control the Other One is energy
release. It hears all the angels singing, but it covers its ears.

It first checks in on its mother, who is sleeping. The visiting
nurse has come and gone but has left a new set of pills on the
dresser and has replenished the morphine in the drip.

It then goes into its bedroom, and there is Monica, lying facedown on the bed, wrapped up in the quilt, her skin pale and naked
beneath it.

It takes off its clothes, dropping its shirt and trousers as it steps
forward into the room, shutting the door behind it.

It can't control what the Other One wants.

The Other One is lusting.

The lust is evil.

But it can turn on the valve. Let the lust out. Let the sin out. Let the perversion out.

Monica is a whore.

Monica is a sinner.

Whore of Babylon.

It goes and lies down on the bed and presses its thing in between her thighs, and she groans, waking up from deep sleep. She has been asleep for less than six hours, and she doesn't like this.

But it doesn't care.

The Other One is out.

The Devil.

"What the hell are you doing, Duane? Not now."

"Now."

"No. Get off me."

"Now."

"I said—"

"Bitch."

"You—don't you touch me."

"Whore."

"You son of a bitch."

"Shut up. She'll hear you."

"Like I care—"

Three slaps.

"Now."

"You asshole. Don't you hit me ever again. I am carrying your baby. Your baby. Don't you ever hit me again."

"Now."

THE DEVIL PRESSES itself into her. She fights it, but the Devil won't let her go, and the friction she creates when she lashes against it only makes the Devil stronger as it bucks and moans and growls against her ear as it takes her there.

A white-hot feeling of moisture and anger all in that one spot, where it has her between her thighs.

WHORE!

SHE WILL GIVE BIRTH TO THE BEAST! SHE WILL BRING ABOUT THE END OF THE WORLD WITH THE BIRTH OF THE ANTICHRIST!

It feels the hammers in its head and the sound of its father's voice shouting from the stone angel in the Mad Place. Shouting about *THE DEVIL LIVES IN YOUR HEART AND YOU MUST SCOURGE THE BEAST FROM YOU! YOU MUST RAVAGE THE FLESH AND SAVAGE THE CREATURE THAT COMMANDS YOU TO EVIL!*

It wants her. Wants her stinky body. Her putrid flesh. It wants her sex. Her every fold. Her innards. Her privates. Her devil passage.

Wants to bite and tear her. To put his face into her womb and find where the baby is growing. It wants to rip it out of her and hold it in its teeth while her blood runs down its face.

It presses its devil member into her.

Ah, it thinks. *Ah.*

And then something within it explodes.

Like a bomb in its head.

And the release comes.

Too soon.

But the release makes the cage door close again.

It falls against her, and she swears at it. She shoves back, and it rolls off her. Her curses float off into the air, unheard. She takes up the quilt draws it to one side, wrapping herself in it, covering her face with pillows.

Inside her, its son.

The Beast.

It lies there, staring at the ceiling.

Bringing the end of the world into flesh.

Just like its daddy said it would.

Then it closes its eyes and journeys into the wet tissues of Hell.

CHAPTER THIRTY

Dr. Elise Conroy's office. Daylight shattered by rain, beyond the window.

Trey Campbell, across from her.

Silence.

Silence broken.

"I've consulted with these investigative teams before," she said. "On each case where I was called in to help profile the killer, they never caught the guys until after too many bodies had piled up. I've had seven years here, and during that time, two previous consults. In one case, they never caught the killer at all. They're not going to catch him in time. Not to save my son. He kills after sundown. Before morning. So far. That's the best they've figured out." Her voice, cold and distant, as if she were trying to move away from the problem in her mind.

Trey knew one thing about the psychiatrists at Darden State that was a key to their personalities: they knew, within themselves, how the human mind had too many doors inside it. That some locked. Some opened. Some never opened. Some were wedged open and should be closed. It probably was why they had studied psychiatry in the first place.

As he watched her, he wondered what door she was closing inside herself. If she was trying to keep the one closed that had hope in it. Or if she was trying desperately to open that door herself. By herself. Within herself.

But he was fairly sure she had closed a door. She looked as if she'd locked it and thrown away the key.

Her face was smooth, set.

She was a woman who had made up her mind, had locked a door, and had opened another.

It worried him.

It even scared him a little.

ELISE DREW a cigarette out from the pack on her desk. She shot him a look that he translated as: *Don't tell me it's illegal to smoke on premises. I break this rule all the time. Screw the rules.*

Trey reached across her desk to steady her hand as she finally lit her cigarette.

She took a drag. "They've already had police on this. The FBI is stepping in. I know they won't find him. At least not in time. They threw me off—told me to go home and get some rest. Goddamn it. My damn babysitter didn't even know it happened." She brought her hand over her eyes to hide the tears. She let out a string of curses as she pressed the palms of her hands against her eyes.

"Could he just be missing?"

At first she didn't respond. Then she looked up at him as if seeing him for the first time. "You know Scoleri."

Trey nodded.

"Fallon came to me this morning. He said it was urgent. He said that Scoleri had told him that something terrible would happen to me today. I asked him what. All he would tell me was that Scoleri told him something terrible and that it had to do with Lucas. That Fallon even knew my son's name was something. He may have seen his picture, but he wouldn't know his name. Maybe he overheard it. I don't know. I don't care. I went to see Scoleri, because I thought someone here must have mentioned it to him. Dr. Brainard, perhaps. Someone who had heard when I mentioned it. Scoleri told me, point-blank, something that I can't get out of my head."

"He knows the killer?"

"No. He told me that I should've just taken Lucas to the beach this morning."

"Why?"

"Trey," she said, her voice hard as if she had come to the most difficult decision of her life. "Because that is what I was supposed to do. I was supposed to take Lucas to the beach today. I came here to pick up some papers. Between the time I left home and the thirty minutes I was here, Lucas …" She paused. "I wanted to take a few days off at the start of Lucas's Christmas break. We hadn't spent enough time together. This damn job. Other things. I could consult on the Red Angel case just a few hours a day and then be home for the rest. And Scoleri knew. He told me that he gets messages from the man who took my son. And then he told me that the beach would have been awful today, anyway, what with the rain."

"Okay," Trey said, his mind crackling with ideas that came at him too quickly. "Scoleri has some contact. We don't know who. Let's find out."

Elise ordered sandwiches from the canteen to be delivered to her office. She spread out the files that she had on Scoleri. "I give you full access."

He glanced up at her. "You sure you want me to see this."

"The rules of this place are not going to save my son," she said.

CHAPTER THIRTY-ONE

In Tryon's office, in Riverside, Detective Jane Laymon picked up a Styrofoam cup and poured coffee into it from the small auto-drip machine on the corner table. Then, turning to Tryon, who sat at his desk, she said, "So when does CASMIRC get to work on this?"

CASMIRC was the Child Abduction and Serial Murder Investigative Resources Center that the FBI used in such cases.

"They already have. I heard from Tommy over at the bureau yesterday. They've been running priors, trying to see if this is in line with some kidnappings from three years ago down in San Diego."

"But it's not," she said. Then, "You need to get better coffee."

He ignored the comment. "You're not going lead on this one, Jane. I'm sorry to say."

"I suspected as much. Who is it?"

"Jenkins. And then Sykes, over in your area."

"Well," she said, tilting her head slightly to the side, "they're the best."

"They're mainly going to be working with Tommy and Bill

Murphy on most of the forensics."

"So what's my connection?"

"You'll work on your side of the line."

"Sure. But why call me in at all?"

"I think you're good. You've got the goods. You have intuition on your side. A knack for this. That's talent. And I need talent on a case like this. We're fucked here. We have a nut killing a kid daily, leaving them out in the open, and we don't have a thing yet." He paused, did a back-and-forth of his head as if weighing options. "Plus, you know the terrain. Every kid was taken from your backyard, not ours."

"But they get dumped in your sandbox. And San Bernardino's. And mine."

"Yeah," Tryon said. "It just screws with us when that happens."

"We'll get him."

"You should come to work for me."

"I thought I was. At least in this limited capacity." She urgently wanted to change the subject. "Look, we have a report of one kid missing already. So far. My guess is that our guy is going one after another. Grabbing the kids and offing them pretty fast."

"A sexual predator."

"Not quite. Nothing evidentiary to suggest sexual contact. This is a psychotic who just snapped."

"Just?"

"I think so. Sykes thinks otherwise. He thinks there'll be priors. I don't think so. Or if there are, it'll be juvy stuff. Maybe. Takes ten years or more to work up to this psychosis. Completely disordered mind. Has a focus, but has cracked. Something was always wrong but just got worse." She glanced over at him. Tryon watched her with fascination. "Hey, I was a double major: criminal justice and forensic psychology."

"I hope we don't lose you to the bureau someday."

"I like being a cop," she said. "My dad was a cop. My mom worked dispatch in San Bernardino for twenty-six years. I like this life."

"So what else? What do you figure?"

"Haven't gone over everything. I got the nudge from Morrison at the morgue and couldn't hang out long enough to ask the questions I really wanted answered. But I'm not sure they could even answer them yet. But our guy is not cunning. He's got dumb luck. He's got some way of accessing the houses near the country club in San Pascal—that's where the girl's family lived. Right behind the links. Maybe he's a golfer. But I doubt it. He's blue collar. He aspires, maybe. Maybe not."

"Age?"

"Maybe twenty-five, twenty-seven, twenty-eight. I'm guessing, but I don't think CASMIRC's going to come up with priors. I think it's his first week on the job of murder. He's learning as he goes. The second victim had two broken fingers. No marks on body at all. Suffocated. First victim, two broken fingers. He bit her cheek and her lip. By the third, the bites were all over the victim's body. Whatever is inside this guy is coming out now. Maybe he had episodes as a kid. But I'm guessing he's spent ten years trying to keep this down. Trying to live right. But he can't help himself. It's a compulsion."

"Why right now?"

"Something in his life is messing up, big time. He's under some pressure, but I don't know what type. Maybe he just lost his job. Or is about to. Or his wife left him. Or, let's see, maybe he's had some emotional trauma reenacted. The death of his own kid? I'm guessing. But something set him off, and he's going off fast."

"Tell me about the one today."

"Happened a couple hours ago. Scrub Jay Drive, nice hilltop community. Mother off to work for a couple of hours, planned on taking the kid off for his birthday late in the day. A sitter was in the house but not one that was with the kid every single minute. Claims she'd just looked out and saw the kid alone in front yard, playing with toys. Maybe ten minutes before she couldn't find him."

"No witnesses?"

"None that we've found. Nobody was looking out their front window during the minute or two it took to get the boy out of there."

"Checked neighbors?"

"Ongoing, but this is our guy. I know it. Something goes on where he's invisible in these neighborhoods."

"Delivery guy?"

"That's my guess. Or the gas guy. Or mailman. A gardener. Someone ordinarily in these neighborhoods. Someone nobody notices. Someone who's maybe in and around their lives every day. Maybe even inside their homes. Even the kid knew him. The kid must've just done whatever our guy said. No signs of struggle. Nothing but toy soldiers in the front yard and a plastic pail. The kid was playing, waiting for Mom. Just like the others did. He gets them in the early morning or right after school, but he gets them within one hundred feet of their front door."

"The Invisible Man," Tryon said. "Christ."

"We're checking everybody who drives those streets on a daily basis," she said. Glanced at her watch. "I better hit the road. I want to go take a statement from the mother before all hell breaks loose." She looked out the window behind Tryon's shiny bald head. "I wish this rain would let up. I wish I were up there." She pointed to the snow-capped San Bernardino mountain range. "Maybe Big Bear. I could be skiing. That's a nice thought for a day like this. We get the crappy rain, they get beautiful snow."

"You'd freeze your ass off. I like a little rain," Tryon said. "So what's the bug up your ass?"

She laughed. He was normally so dignified in his speech. "What do you think?"

"Johnny Fasteau."

"He's the flea on my dog."

"He's all I got for you."

"I could work with Sykes more. Or you."

"I want that to happen. I really do. But right now, this is too big a thing for me to break up the current team. And you know what? Part of me feels like he teaches you something."

"I already finished school."

"What's the worst thing about working with him?"

"He stares at my boobs. Too much."

"File a complaint. We have a department for that."

"You know I can't do that. You know if I do that, the rest of the old boys'll shun me. A little silent treatment."

"You might be surprised. You believe in taking his guff? That's all it is, just guff. Look, Jane, he's not my favorite either. But you two will work out whatever you need to, and then you'll move ahead and you'll see that guys like Fasteau pretty much stay where they are."

"If I believed in that fairy tale, I'd already be married to Prince Charming."

When Tryon's phone rang, she kept her back to him to afford him some small measure of privacy.

Tryon turned to her, still on the phone. "They found another one. In Little Orange. Look, Jane, we've got to get the bureau in here fast. This guy's crapping all over the place. I have a goddamn press conference to give with the sheriff in two hours. I don't know why we have to play with the damn media like this."

"You always look great on camera," she said.

THEY DIDN'T CALL it the Bull Pen, as she thought they would when she first began learning the inner workings of the homicide investigative unit. They called it, more simply, the Map Room, because of a large map on an erasable board that covered one entire wall of the conference room. The table was littered with coffee cups and memo pads that had been left behind from the earlier meeting.

Jane went to the board, took up a marker.

"San Pascal County. San Bernardino. Riverside."

Where the counties met, she circled in red marker.

They had sticky notes up where each of the victims had been found, and a blue check mark where each of the children had been taken.

Knowing that she'd have to erase it when she was done, Jane began connecting the lines together—from Caldwell to Bannock to Little Orange to San Pascal.

This is your territory.

This is your hunting ground.

You're coming from somewhere here.

She circled a spot where the foothills met the valley.

You're like a mountain lion, coming in.

Then she said it aloud. "The mountains."

She glanced up at the towns in the mountains, from the majestic Lake Arrowhead, to Big Bear, Blue Jay, Moon Lake, Windsock, and Slipping Springs.

"You think?" a voice behind her said.

She turned around. Fasteau. "My doppelganger," she said.

He stood in the doorway, bottle of water in his hand. Slurped some of it down. "You planning on snowboarding?"

"Maybe," she said. It annoyed the hell out of her that she was saddled with Fasteau, but she had to make the best of it. *One day, you'll be free of him.* "Just an idea. The victims are from the foothills." She pointed to the places on the map where they'd been taken. "The country club area, the hilltop houses, and over here, a little lower, but still near the foothills. Then, look, this is where they end up."

"Sure," Fasteau said. "Sykes already got on that. They end up in the valley."

"Flatlands," she corrected him. "The rivers and streams that feed into where they were found all follow a pattern from the foothills. See? These are the washes that flood this time of year and feed into the river." She tapped out areas on the map. "Where he dumps them is his farthest point away from where he's willing to go after he takes them. He must time it. He keeps the kids for about a day or less. Kills them. Then I'm guessing he only wants to go an hour to two hours from home. His home is ..." Here she took the marker and made a dotted line radius that went up to the mountain range, down past the 10 freeway, into Rubidoux and Moreno Valley, getting into the tip of the desert out at Banning but not quite to Palm Springs.

"So?"

"He's linear."

Fasteau gestured with the bottle. "Sure."

She could tell he didn't quite get what she was saying. He had that cowboy look in his eyes again, like everything was all about riding horses and roping dogies and riding off into the sunset on the way to a strip joint.

"Well, look, if this is point Z," she tapped Bannock, where they'd found Gina Parsons that morning, "and this is point, let's say, F," she tapped the foothills, "then point A, his origin, is somewhere here." She made five points along the map in four different regions of the three counties.

The valley. The flatlands. The mountains. The desert.

"He's not down here in the flatlands," she said. "And since he has to kill these ducks, he has to find them someplace. Now, he might raise them. But that sort of eliminates the desert, since it would be hard to raise or catch ducks out there. And that leaves the valley, the foothills, and the mountains. There are four man-made lakes in the valley, mostly at city and town parks, none that I know of in the foothills, except the reservoir, unless he's raising the ducks in his backyard pond. And then up here." She tapped the mountains. "Big Bear Lake, Lake Arrowhead, Moon Lake, Green Valley Lake. It's the damn land of lakes. Ducks aplenty."

"Hey," Fasteau said. "Wouldn't they fly away now? The ducks?"

"Maybe he has a way of keeping them."

"Maybe," he said.

She could tell by his tone that he was not interested.

"Those are interesting concepts," he added.

She could hear the condescension in his tone. What was most annoying about it is that she wasn't even sure if he understood what the word "concepts" meant.

"This guy has a route. A daily route. He grabs a kid, stashes the kid, murders the kid, and has his route set up. The kids are ones he knows. Somehow he knows them. Each victim's an only child. He knows that. A large family would scare him. He can't deal with more than one child. I'm guessing each of these kids were loners of sorts. Didn't play with a lot of kids in the neighborhood. As only children, they might've been good at talking to adults. I think he knew them in some way, even if the parents didn't know him. Each of the victims lived within fifteen miles of each other. Want to take a drive?"

"Up the mountain? It's probably snowing up there. We'd need an SUV. It's snowing up there today."

"No," she said. "Just here." She tapped the map at the designation for the foothills of San Pascal County. "To visit some of the families."

CHAPTER THIRTY-TWO

When Lucas awoke, he was surrounded by gray darkness that was only interrupted by twinkling white lights. He looked up to the ceiling. Not a ceiling at all, but rugged hanging rock. Christmas lights were strung along them. It freaked him out.

Bad dream.

At first, he thought he had been dreaming and was back in bed.

The fact that he'd peed in his pants made him remember where he was. He shivered from cold. His hands were duct-taped together, but he was able to reach down into his pocket. In one, Stuart, his hamster. Lucas was more worried about his pet than about himself for the moment, but as he smoothed the animal's fur, he felt the stirrings of a very sleepy hamster. Cushioned with a bit of napkin wrapped around it, Stuart had managed to survive the trip that Lucas wasn't quite sure along the way that he would. At one point, in the darkness, he'd been afraid Stuart had been smushed to death. But he was fine.

In the other pocket, two quarters and his favorite giant rubber spider, Charlotte. Lucas squeezed it, feeling its familiar contours.

He said the Lord's Prayer three times, at first fast, but by the third time so slowly, trying to imagine God hearing him.

Then, as his eyes adjusted, he saw shadows all around him.

He was in some kind of cellar, but maybe it was a cave. It was a strange place. Rock walls like a cave, and they had really scary drawings all over them, but they were only drawings. He knew not to be that afraid of them. The big statues nearby made him think of church, and that made him feel a little better. He liked church and always felt safe in church. But it reminded him a little of the kind of place where monsters lived. Ogres. Nightmares.

He kept hearing noises, like water trickling and like something moving, but not all the areas of the place had the Christmas lights hanging over them.

The flickering lights bothered him.

The room seemed like a giant box. Dark shapes in parts where he couldn't quite see. Piles of something. He couldn't tell. His head hurt so much, he thought it would split open. Where was his mommy? Where was Daddy? Why weren't they there to protect him? His confusion increased with each second. Maybe this was some game. Some strange game. Maybe he had done something really bad. Something he shouldn't have. He thought back to the morning, and the weekend. All he could remember doing that might be considered bad was stealing the picture from his father's drawer. The photograph that had his mother, father, and him as a baby in it. All of them smiling. He had stuck the picture in his pocket. When he'd got home from the weekend with his dad and his dad's new wife, he'd hidden the picture behind some books on the bookshelf. Maybe that was why he was being punished.

Maybe Duane was the punisher.

Why would Duane do this? Duane was his buddy.

He was Duane's helper whenever Duane came by, just like he helped the gardener, Mike, in back when he came over to check on the roses. Just like he helped Mrs. Portrero with carrying books to and from the public library. He didn't know Duane that well, he figured, but Duane had always been nice. Nice and friendly, and one time he gave him a dollar for helping him.

But maybe it wasn't Duane. Maybe it just was something wearing a Duane mask. Duane was always nice to him. Duane laughed at his jokes. His mommy even let Duane in whenever she was home. So did Nina. Why would Duane do this?

Duane even called him his "little helper" when he'd stand and watch Duane work.

But that thought again: maybe it wasn't Duane. Maybe it was just someone who looked like Duane.

Like nightmares where things came for you looking like your mommy or daddy, but they turned into something different.

Or maybe he was the boogeyman. Lucas had heard terrible stories from other kids in his first-grade class about the boogeyman. One of his classmates, Sandy Shapiro, told about how the boogeyman lived in dark of closets and under the bed. She told him how at night he came out and grabbed little kids and put them into the dark.

Just like this place.

Then he remembered one of his own nightmares, when the boogeyman came up behind him and grabbed him, and then slithered under the bed with him. In the dark under the bed, Lucas had screamed for his mommy, but she had never come.

He should've known.

He should've known that this was the day the boogeyman would come out of the shadows and grab him.

He wanted to wake up from this nightmare. He didn't want to be here. It hurt to think all this. And his shoulder hurt.

He closed his eyes as hard as he could and wished himself back in his bed, asleep. Wished himself to wake up. At the count of ten.

Ten, nine, eight, seven, six, five, four, three, two, one.

Lucas opened his eyes.

Water dripped in one corner of the room.

He heard a shooshing sound, like the sound the shower made when he took his bath.

When he had to pee, he struggled, but he was bound up too tight. He peed in his pants and felt ashamed. It hurt down around his thighs where he'd already peed.

His head felt like it was full of stones smashing against each other.

He felt Stuart crawl from his pocket, up his arm, and along the floor beside him. He wanted to tell Stuart not to run away, that he wouldn't ever be able to find him again. He watched his hamster skitter along the floor.

Come back, Stuart. Please.

He wished his mom would come and get him soon.

Then he heard a muffled noise—a human noise—from somewhere in the dark near him.

He saw a dark shape of movement, as if an inky blackness had just begun pouring from the shadows.

CHAPTER THIRTY-THREE

IT SPENDS A LITTLE TIME WITH ITS MOTHER, INSIDE, SITTING with her, talking to Nancy, the visiting nurse who was filling in, who checked the morphine levels and triple-checked the pills. "You sure this is all the Roxicet?"

It nods.

"There should be more."

She leans over its mother's bed.

Its mother seems to it like a jellyfish for a second. Tubes running in and out of her. Her skin crackly and pale. Her hair thin and white.

It feels nothing for her but doesn't like to think of her like this.

"She seems to be in more pain than usual," Nancy says. "But she seems to be dosing herself well." She leans closer to its mother. "You need to be careful, Mrs. Cobble. This is just for when you feel pain." She points to the intravenous tube and the button on its edge where the patient could self-dose.

"Maybe she needs more," it says. Hoping. *It* could use more.

"She seems fine as she is," Nancy says in a low voice as if she doesn't want its mother to hear her.

Nancy wears all white, like a nurse should. She is good to its mother, and although it doesn't like her that much, it appreciates when she comes around. The other nurse, Betsy, was better, it thinks, but Betsy is on vacation until after the holidays. It only sees the nurse once a week. It feels nervous about the nurse being there now, but the little bird below is silent, and since the Other One has control of all this, it is fairly sure that Nancy will not wonder too much about the morphine level being down, about the missing Roxicet or the Valiums that are gone. Its mother last saw a doctor six days earlier, at the office over in Big Bear when it drove her there. That's when its mother talked about dying. About not being around.

That's when the home care had begun, and the morphine had seemed to it to be a Godsend.

Morphine helped people not feel pain.

It doesn't like pain at all.

"Did you get a flu shot this year?" Nancy asks, interrupting its thoughts. She has her little dark bag full of all the wonders: needles and pills and plastic bags filled with liquid sleep. She reaches into it and withdraws a syringe. "I could give you the shot right now. Mr. Cobble?"

"Flu shot?"

"It's one of the services our visiting nurses association offers to family members of our patients. There's a nasty strain of flu going around. This'll help prevent it. It won't hurt much—I'll use a butterfly needle." She leans back over the bed, her face so close to its mother's that she must've gotten a good whiff of its mother's awful breath. "How about you, Genie? I'm going to give you a very little shot. A teensy one. It'll keep you from getting sick this winter."

The nurse draws out a small syringe from its plastic casing.

Its mother nods, closing her eyes. "I feel like a damn dartboard. I've had more needles in me than a pine forest."

The nurse laughs, but it did not. It knows that its mother is serious. She'd had blood tests and shots of things and intravenous tubes for weeks. Ever since she got worse. Ever since she called the hospice and the visiting nurse place.

Ever since she'd told him she was going to die before Christmas. "I know my body is going. I don't want to die," she had said to him. "But God is calling me."

Didn't even like thinking of it. Didn't even want to imagine what its life would be like without her. Lost Ruthie when she was a little girl. She didn't go to Heaven, not according to Daddy. She went to Hell. But his mother is going to Heaven. She is pure and holy. She is above all the filth of the world. Ruthie had been part of that filth. Daddy had told it about Ruthie and her sins and how she came into the world bloody with sin and how she was the whore who must never see the light of day, lest she unleash her disease and vermin upon all mankind.

Ruthie lives eternally in Hell.

But the idea of its mother leaving it is something that makes the hammers go off in its head. Pounding and thrashing inside it. Making the cage rattle. Making the Other One stronger.

Its mother is going to die.

Its dog, Jojo, is going to die.

It wants everything to just stop. To just keep everyone alive.

Its dog.

Its mother.

She is the only thing that had protected it.

She had saved it, in the last minute.

Saved. Not saved like the baptisms Daddy gave it all the time.

But saved from the place in the earth where its daddy tried to bury it alive.

It doesn't like to dream, but when it has been awake for so many hours—nearly four days, it reckons—it begins to dream with its eyes wide open, even sitting behind the wheel of its truck. It wonders about the child, the little dove, but it has to keep moving on its route or else nothing will go right.

It remembers how it and Ruthie would be down in the Mad Place with its daddy and how Daddy would read scripture and rock back and forth on his knees, raising his hand up to the dark above his head and cry out against the vileness of humankind. How Ruthie would begin speaking in tongues, and then it would follow her lead, although it felt fake. The Holy Spirit never came into its head, not like the Other One did. But Ruthie was holy and she got chosen young to be a blessed one of God. "Thou art a vessel!" its daddy would cry, his hands on Ruthie's scalp like he could feel the Jesus energy coming up from her. "You are chosen by the Lord! You are righteous and pure and your purity will be a light unto the world!"

It's not sure if that's exactly what its daddy would say, but in memory, that's what it seemed like. Its memories and dreams get all mixed up, and it has blocked out so much of what happened in the Mad Place that it isn't sure if it all happened exactly like it remembers.

Ruthie's face was truly pure. It remembers that much. It remembers how he loved her more than he could've if she were his flesh and blood. She came to them and stayed before the other children. The others were all bad, but Ruthie was sent by God. Its daddy had loved her too, like she was his own daughter, and it even got a little jealous when it saw the two of them together, singing hymns in the Mad Place or saying prayers so loud that their voices echoed.

Its mother had been there too, but its memories of her were weaker. It remembered her perfume, which was like juniper berries, and the way she never said much in front of its daddy. Sometimes its daddy hit its mother, and it got really mad, but then it was usually punished in the Mad Place and it knew that was right and godly. It never heard from God directly, but that was because it was born in sin. That was a problem it could never get away from.

It was born in the filth, that's what its daddy had said, and when its daddy had told it about how its mother had been a sinner and how she had given her soul to Satan until its daddy had SAVED HER. SAVED HER AND BROUGHT HER INTO THE HEALING LIGHT OF THE LORD!

"She was a whore, as all women are whores until they are saved by the hands of men who are of the Spirit! As your sister is a whore! Ruthie is cursed by God with her twisted spine and legs. She was born into sin, she remains in sin until a man shall bring her to light and redemption. And you, you children, the Lord saith, 'Suffer to bring the little children unto me.' And you must go to Him. You must feel the Spirit in you. You must let only God speak through you, for what is your flesh is the Devil. If thine right eye offend thee, cut it out. If they right hand offend thee, chop it off. If thy twisted legs offend thee, saw them and toss them into the fires of Hell! Do not mistake your flesh for life. Your flesh is death. Burn your flesh. Scourge it. Your weakness must become your strength!"

And then its daddy would bring out the cigarettes and press them into its back. "You are nothing. Your flesh is nothing. You are born of evil. You are an it. Say it. Say it. You are an it."

And it would say it, over and over again. "It! It! It! It! I am an it! I am! An! It!"

And Ruthie would say over and over again, "Whore! Whore! Whore! I am! A! Whore!"

And then, in the dark, she would hold it and tell it that one day Mommy would stop all of this.

And Daddy would get better.

But it never believed that.

It knew that the Other One lived inside it, just like Daddy had been telling it since the day it was born.

ITS WORKDAY DOESN'T BEGIN until nearly one. It works for six hours. It is a part-timer and can only take so much daylight and interaction. It is lucky to have the job since its daddy died.

It arrives at the gate. The guard, Pete, waves it in. It passes the dome and the main office and drives its truck right up to the back. Then it parks. Others are there, and it says a few words to them. They joke a bit about the crappy day. About the possibility of a storm brewing.

One of the guys says, "Man, that's the one pisser about Southern California. It won't just sprinkle. It's gonna end up pouring for two weeks straight if it starts."

Another says, "Naw, I bet this'll just be sprinkles. I predict sunny skies by Christmas. I bet it's snowin' up where Duane lives."

"How's your girl, Duane?" a guy asks it.

It looks up. It is good at mimicking them without them knowing. "She's great."

"You old dog," he says.

It smiles. Uncomfortable. It doesn't talk to many of them if it can help it. It wishes that Monica had never come around work that one day, wearing her skimpiest outfit, nearly flashing her tits for the guys. They all talked about her afterward. About how they wanted to get her panties wet. About how they wanted to stick themselves into her, all at once. It didn't like men when they talked like that. They couldn't help it, just like Daddy couldn't help it with Ruthie, because whores did that to men. Spirit was strong, but flesh is weak. The Devil made flesh to tempt man. These men were easily tempted.

But Monica had worked at it.

It didn't like Monica being so cheap. She was like a whore when she did that, and it had rescued her and taken care of her just so she'd never become a whore.

"How's your mom?" the one named Jeff asks. He's different than the others. He is saved and goes to church and talks about his bible study group. It likes Jeff.

But it has no reply for him.

"She's got my prayers," Jeff says, then passes on to his truck.

"Aw, dang, here comes Randy, now we're screwed. Well, have a good one, Duane. You too, Chad."

"Ditto," it says, and then goes to get its designated truck for the day's work.

IT DOESN'T EVEN NOTICE its routine anymore. It has been doing this for nearly six years, and it is used to the stopping and starting, the traffic on the 101, the side streets, the hills with their winding streets and the houses with their winding driveways.

It is dreaming, instead. It sees its daddy, gaunt and with a harsh expression on his face, one hand raised to Heaven, the other wrapped around a big, fat, worn bible.

When it dreams with its eyes open, it is always back in the big stone room with the pool of water and the angel.

And Ruthie is there too.

Ruthie, with her face so like a spoon, shiny and curved, and her hair all smoothed back because it would comb it with its fingers for her.

It had felt that Ruthie was its only happiness.

Ruthie with her little crippled legs and leg braces that didn't help her.

Ruthie with her smile that was like sunshine even in the shadows.

And in the dream, their daddy began shouting that they were possessed by demons.

"And the demons need to come out!" his daddy shouted, slapping the bible down hard on Ruthie's head. "OUT! OUT! OUT!"

Then Daddy went to get the barbed wire, and the first time Daddy did that was the first time it heard the Other One rattling the bars of the cage in its head.

CHAPTER THIRTY-FOUR

EATING A TURKEY-AND-SWISS ON RYE WHILE PORING OVER transcripts of tapes, Trey was beginning to get a picture of what had made Scoleri. Taken from his original mother soon after birth because she had been keeping the baby up at night with the same speed that she took herself, he bounced through Southern California group homes, some of which Trey knew of that were down in Chino, some in the outlying areas of San Bernardino. He followed the cadence of Scoleri's speech, his pontificating in this other personality that he called "Abraxas" of how he created the Earth, how the dinosaurs were his dragons, how he and the Devil knew each other too intimately, among other delusions and constructs. There was a history of hurting other children, particularly girls, and three admittances to hospitals before the age of thirteen, each time someone had beaten him up. Once, they'd used razors on him.

Despite this, Trey developed little sympathy for Scoleri. Trey was not a bleeding-heart, and he knew that there were other kids who were tortured the same or worse, whose psychological makeup allowed them to grow up into healthy, productive, contributing members of society. They got help. They worked at it. But in Scoleri's case, and in the case of other sadistic sexual predators Trey had seen and studied, he had the X Factor. That was the one mysterious thing—perhaps organic from birth, perhaps it had been the speed he'd been given as a baby, or perhaps, as Trey sometimes thought, human predators were a throwback in evolution. Every single human being exhibited a predatory nature of some sort, whether it came out in a competitive spirit that rejoiced while others failed, or in manipulating others to do one's will, or any number of mindless activities that involved one-upsmanship. It was not just getting ahead for some people. It was about destroying the competition.

But those were nothing compared to the predators Trey had come to know. These human beings are akin to lions on the hunt, seeing a herd of antelope, picking out the weaker, the sicker, the members less able to survive, and targeting them.

The only word that came to mind as he read Scoleri's file was evil. Not cosmic evil. Not spiritual evil. But ordinary human evil that was willing to break the social contract, to go outside normal behavior, that experienced great pleasure at the suffering and pain of others. It was that element of enjoying suffering that most disturbed Trey in nearly every single case file he had ever read.

Scoleri's was no different.

Then as he quickly scanned the last file, he said, "What about 1984?"

Elise looked up from her cup of coffee.

"He talks specifically about nearly every year of his childhood, except 1984. He would've been about eight years old then. We know he left the group home in Mentone that year. All it says is transferred. Then over here," Trey lifted a sheaf of transcript papers, "he talks about his God year, but he doesn't answer your questions about it."

"I don't have all the answers," she said. "He only tells me what he tells me."

"Well, maybe it means nothing. But I feel like I know the guy backward and forward from all this." He set the papers down, closing two of the file folders up. "I still think he's talking to somebody. To get this information. It's an inside job. He reaches the kidnapper somehow. Maybe one of these group homes or foster families that he kept bouncing around from. Maybe he's still in contact with one of those people."

Flipping through page after page, Trey came up with a list of people with whom Scoleri was in regular contact. None of them were anything other than trusted employees at Darden State. No outside family, no lawyer, no cop, even. Nobody but the ward staff.

"Someone here?" Elise asked.

"I wish I could say that. Maybe. Let me go talk to him about it."

"Look, Trey, I wouldn't ordinarily say this in any other circumstance, but I have been working with Scoleri for four months. Since his transfer from Napa. He believes he's psychic. He believes that he talks to others with his mind, and they talk to him. I am not leaving this up to the police. This is my *baby*. We know how these people think."

"How much time do you think we have?" he asked.

Through a haze of smoke, she said, "Eight hours. Maybe less. Between now and tomorrow morning. That's the longest he's gone. He doesn't want ransom. He doesn't want anything that he doesn't already have once he has one of the children. He kills the victims within several hours of taking them. The longest one was twenty-four hours. Maybe. I'm not sure." She took a deep breath, steeling herself. "He's dead. My baby's dead already."

Her hands trembled, and she stared at them as if she didn't know what to do with them anymore.

Another silence, brief.

Elise took a few deep breaths. Trying to control it. The thing inside her. The thing that wanted to explode. "It's been hell this morning. I want to believe he's fine, but I'm sure he's dead. The rational part of me knows he's dead. But the emotional part can't accept it."

"He's alive," Trey said. "You've got to believe that."

"It's the only thing I can believe right now. Look, I think Scoleri is a link to the Red Angel. He believes the Red Angel is the agent of the Devil. And he knows things."

Trey shrugged.

"Didn't Hatcher feel a connection to you?"

Trey laughed nervously. "You could say so. She thought we were past-life buddies."

"Were you?"

Trey was astonished. "You're a doctor. You don't believe in reincarnation, do you?"

"Do you?"

Trey was silent. "Okay, I concede the point. I'm not sure."

"And I'm not sure with Michael Scoleri either. I'm not sure, but if he's even ten percent right, call it perceptive, call it intuitive, I don't give a damn. Did you see what he wrote on himself? With his fingernails?"

Trey nodded. "I heard. Suffer the children."

"Not just that," Elise said. "He had names. There are seven of them, and the sixth one is Lucas. The fifth one is Mary. Trey, they haven't even found a fifth child yet. What if they do? What if her name's Mary? What if Lucas is the sixth, and then the seventh is named Billy? How would that happen, that a psychopathic personality in Darden State knew who the kidnapper would take next?"

Trey took a breath. Then, "Elise. You do not believe that he is telepathically linked to this killer. Tell me that."

"No. I don't. But there's something. I can't figure it out."

"When was the last time you had a session with Scoleri?"

"Friday. Normal day. We spent three hours together. He seemed especially troubled."

"In the pod?"

"There. And here. Bronson and Marcovich were here too."

"Restraints?"

"Not completely."

"Hands free?"

"Hands only. Leg cuffs."

"Not full shackles?"

She shook her head.

"Who else came in your office on Friday?"

"No one that I can think of."

"Any deliveries?"

"People come in and out of here all the time. But I'm here when they do that. I would've noticed someone. Or Eric would've."

"Did he have access to any writing material?"

"No. We cleared sharps before he came in."

"Did he do anything while he was here?"

"He stood most of the time. He said he was tired of sitting."

"Did he go to the window?"

"Maybe. I don't remember. Yes. He looked out on the grounds. He looked at—" she pointed to the pictures on the wall: calming images of waterfalls and countryside.

"I have to ask you a question that you probably already heard from the cops, Elise. But here goes: why do you think Lucas was targeted?"

"Targeted? Trey. This is a random kidnapping. The cops said the main link was the upper-middle-class neighborhoods and San Pascal itself."

"Okay. I guess I'm just doing scattershot here. But I just don't believe in telepathy. Or that he has some psychic link to the man who kidnapped your son. Those three hours you spent with him may be crucial."

She heaved a sigh of frustration. "I wish I could give you more. It was just a completely normal day, with him and with others. I didn't connect him with this at all. I only got pulled in on the Red Angel that night."

"You see any others who might have a link to the outside?"

"Program 28 only," she said. "With the other patients, I went to the pods."

"Why give Scoleri these little trips out of his pod?"

"He's not an animal, Trey. He may be a sociopath. A psychopath. But he was responding to some extent. I thought we were near a breakthrough." Her voice trailed off as she lost confidence in her own words.

"Okay," Trey said. "This is all we have to go on. Let's see what I can get out of Scoleri."

CHAPTER THIRTY-FIVE

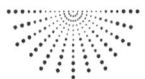

Twenty minutes later, Trey sat across from Scoleri.

Scoleri was spread out on his cot, arms crossed behind his head. Eyes closed. He grinned, as if knowing too much.

"You know what's great about this place?"

"What's that?" Trey asked.

"You kill someone in here, and all they do is transfer you. Either to another ward or to another institution. If I were to, say, kill you —not that I intend to—I'd get some extra meds and maybe a more comfy bed."

"Is that what you want to do?"

"No. I don't like hurting people. I only do it when they attack me. But I was just saying it as a for instance." Then, turning his head slightly, he said, "I knew you'd be back once you talked to Elise. I knew you'd be here. You want to know about the Red Angel now. But you don't believe in me, Trey. You must believe in me. I am the way."

"Sit up," Trey said, in as authoritative a voice as possible.

Scoleri's eyes blinked. Then he grinned. "You gonna be my daddy?" he asked in a little-boy voice.

"I mean it. Sit up. I want to ask you some questions."

Scoleri made a strange move with his body. Trey remembered what Jim Anderson had told him: *contortionist*. It was as if Scoleri were a snake, and his body *wriggled*. "Yes sir, Herr Doctor. But you're not a doctor, are you? You're just a cut above janitor. Psych tech. A nice title for somebody who wipes my ass. You meet Creep down the hall? He paints his shit all over like Picasso. Somebody should wipe his ass better."

"Sit up," Trey said.

After a minute, Scoleri decided to sit up. It probably helped that Trey had two COs from the end of the hall come in and pick up Scoleri and put him down in the chair at the table. "Very nice, Trey. Very nice. You got me where you want me."

Trey took the chair across the table from him.

"You're not at all afraid of me?" Scoleri asked. "Not the teensiest?"

"No."

"You should be. I'm God. I like hurting people."

"Tell me about the Red Angel."

"What do you want to know?"

"Who is he?"

Scoleri shook his head, grinning. "You don't get no pussy without some flowers and chardonnay."

"You don't know anything about him, do you?"

"Well, I know something about him. He's a very bad man."

"What else?"

"He has little Lucas Conroy in his secret hidey-hole. He calls it the Mad Place, and it's not because he's insane. It's because he's nuttier than a shit-house rat, and he thinks that it's where you're allowed to get very angry when you want, and nobody's around to hear you scream about it."

"Who's telling you all this?"

"Ah," Scoleri said, narrowing his eyes a bit. "You don't believe in me. That's right. Let's start with that. If you become my disciple, I'll let you in on my sacred secrets. There are six sacred secrets. In each of the six, there are another sixty. And within those six hundred. That's six hundred sixty-six, or 666. The mark of the Beast. And I am not the Beast. I am Abraxas. Believe in me or I will never tell you anything more."

"All right."

"Oh goody. A follower. First, only call me Abraxas. This Scoleri garbage has to go. Michael Scoleri was the flesh I had when I was a boy, but that got burned away when my Godhood came out. I was about eleven when—"

"I don't care. I'll believe in you. All right?"

Scoleri paused. "Believe in whom?"

"Abraxas."

"That's more like it. God likes to be called by His real name. The Red Angel was once one of my disciples. He was one of my most beloved. But he got a little too much Devil in him and now he's trying to bring about the end of the world. He's completely crazy. He thinks that by ..." But Scoleri stopped himself. "You know what, Mr. Trey Campbell? I want you to show me you believe in me."

"How?"

"Do something for me."

"Okay."

"A magic trick."

"You're God. I think you should do the magic tricks."

"I know, but I'm trapped in this." Scoleri pinched the skin on his face. "I can't quite cut my way out of it. What I'm thinking of is a vanishing act."

"You want me to leave?"

"Both of us. I want you to take me to Elise Conroy's office. We can all three talk there."

"I'm afraid that won't happen."

"Well, it was a test of faith. And you failed."

"How about you tell me a little bit more? Maybe with some more information, I can get around the house rules."

Scoleri closed his eyes. When he opened them again, he said, "I just heard from him. The Beast. Do you know one thing that the police don't know about him? He's been kept at bay. The part of him that's not Beast has been kind up to now. He put the little angels to sleep before he sent them off with their messages. But this one is going to be different. This one is number six, and number six is a magical number. It is the Beast's number. This one, sweet little Lucas Conroy, isn't going to go to sleep. The Beast is taking over fast now. The man who he was is burning away. He is losing the last of his soul. The others, he's only tasted. After they've gone off with their messages to me and then on to Heaven. This one, he is going to devour alive. He bites them. The Beast. The Red Angel. He bites them and he doesn't eat them. But he's going to eat this one. He's held back. He's fighting his nature. But he won't this time. This little angel is going to get eaten alive and may not make it to Heaven."

CHAPTER THIRTY-SIX

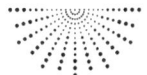

THREE P.M.

TREY HELD his breath in the last second while Scoleri spoke.

Then exhaled.

Then, "Where is he?"

"I had it on the tip of my tongue," Scoleri said.

"Where is he?"

Scoleri leaned forward, and Trey smelled his breath, which was foul.

Scoleri's face was less than an inch away from Trey's.

Briefly, and so quickly it was nearly imperceptible, Scoleri's tongue flickered out from between his lips and touched Trey's upper lip.

It was like being touched by a snake.

Trey recoiled, drawing backward fast.

Scoleri grinned.

From the doorway, one of the corrections officers stepped

toward the table where the two men sat. Trey recognized him. The guy named Atkins. The one that might have something not quite right within him. Trey didn't want a confrontation. He wanted information now. He didn't need a fight.

Particularly not with a CO who was ready to smash someone's head in.

Trey took a deep breath. *Fight the fear. Put it down. He's trying to knock you off guard. He won't attack you. He's under control here.*

Trey motioned to the COs to stay where they were.

"Tell me," Trey said, staring at Scoleri. *I will stare you down if I have to.*

"You can't stare me down," Scoleri said, as if reading his thoughts.

Trey felt a shock go through him.

He tried not to let it shake him up.

Damn. I know you can't read minds. Up yours, Scoleri. Abraxas. It's a trick. A trick based on the obviousness of the situation. It's a trick you learned in your carney days. You are smart. You have some enormous IQ and you have some nastiness inside you. You are a snake. A rattler. Waiting to strike. Somehow, some way, you are going to tell me how you know about the Red Angel and where he is.

"There's only one way in Heaven or Hell that I will tell you where he is," Scoleri said.

CHAPTER THIRTY-SEVEN

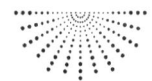

Trey had that feeling again: of feeling ice cold. Of being stunned.

The way a rat must feel just before a python opens its mouth.

Scoleri's face seemed to change. He seemed younger, as if he fed off the fear he was feeling from Trey Campbell.

His eyes began that rapid eye movement that seemed to blur so that his eyes fluctuated between all white and darkness.

Then Scoleri moved rapidly forward, grabbing Trey by the ears before Trey could lean back fast enough—

Trey heard the COs at the door shout, and other noise—

Scoleri pulled Trey's face close to his in a motion that was so fast that Trey felt as if the wind had been knocked out of him—

Scoleri's lips went to Trey's ear, and in that second or two before the officers pulled Scoleri back, lifting him up out of the chair and practically slamming him into his bed, quickly tying the restraints —in that second or two—

Scoleri whispered, "Get me out."

CHAPTER THIRTY-EIGHT

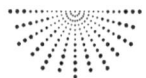

"THAT'S INSANE," ELISE CONROY SAID.

"Insane" was not a word she used lightly.

She stood in the corridor, outside Michael Scoleri's pod on Program 28.

Trey glanced back into the room. Michael Scoleri watched both of them from his cot. In full restraints, he could barely move a muscle.

"We could go to the police with this. Maybe there's a way ..." Elise began.

"Like you said, it's insane," Trey said. He drew her back from the pod, down the hall a bit farther. The COs watched them from a distance. "I don't want anyone else hearing this, Elise. But we could help the police catch him. They have no idea where he is, or something would've happened by now. Scoleri knows something. I don't know how. I don't know why. But he knows something. If we can get him to feel comfortable, he'll tell us. Look, we call the police in. Or the feds, if they're involved. Maybe they could interrogate him and get it out of him."

"Not if he goes catatonic."

"He's done that before?"

She nodded. "Sure. He did it for two weeks after he first got here. Nobody got a word out of him, and we had to feed him intravenously. I don't know how he hypnotized himself into that state, but he managed to do it. When he came out of it, he ripped the tubes out of his arm and started screaming that he was being buried alive. But during those two months, not a word or a movement. I'm not even sure if he blinked. His respiration was so low, that ... well, it was like a mild coma, if that were possible."

"He's a magician. A carney," Trey said. "In his late teens, he worked the carnival circuit. He probably learned tricks from others. He probably had a natural talent for it."

"Let me talk to my friend in Caldwell's police department. Maybe there's another way," Elise said. "Do you believe him when he says he's in communication telepathically?"

"I don't think so. I'm not a great believer in that kind of stuff. But he knows things he shouldn't know. And it doesn't seem, in a pod in Program 28, that he'd be able to get much information from the outside world. Unless a CO or a psych tech is delivering it. Now, realistically, it could be someone here. It could be someone who is as screwed up as any patient here and is passing messages on to Scoleri. But unless it's you or Fallon, it doesn't seem like anyone has been passing messages to this guy. I've checked the logs. How does he know? I have one guess. That is, he knows the Red Angel from when he was free. Or maybe even from Napa. He was told the Red Angel's plans years ago. Or else he knows, based on the Red Angel's psychosis, exactly what this pattern of killing means. Maybe Lucas and the other kids who were kidnapped have something in common. Maybe. It would probably take a few days of sitting down with the cops to figure this out. By that point, Lucas is dead. I'm sorry to put it that way, but it's the only way I see it."

Elise thought for a moment, lighting up a cigarette. "You're right. We're going to get him out. I'll arrange a day transfer to Patton for observation."

"Right. Nothing more than that. If we can just get him outside for an hour, maybe he'll do what he says he will. Maybe he'll give us more. Then we can pass that information on to the police. Look, I don't believe in telepathy. I don't believe he's God either. But I do believe Scoleri knows something and wants to tell you. I think he likes you, and I think he respects you."

"It's impossible for him to respect anyone."

"I don't know. He respects me. I don't know why. But he could've easily hurt me bad in there. He was showing that I could trust him. That even when he had an opportunity to do so, he didn't want to attack me. Scare me, yes. And besides," Trey said, "he'll be shackled and cuffed. We'll get a transport car so that there's a screen between the front and back seat. We'll have two COs sitting next to him. He just wants to get out for a while. He wants a drive. We'll give him a drive, and he may help us. If not, we'll get the feds in to talk to him. Look, Elise. We'll do this. It will work out. We will get Lucas back. Alive."

She touched him lightly on the shoulder. "Thank you. All right. I'll go make some calls and get this arranged. It'll probably take a couple of hours. I have to call the EC, and then Olsen will have to be in on it. Get some lunch."

"I can't believe you're holding up."

"It's a nightmare," she said. "But I'm going to get through it."

"So will Lucas. They'll get this guy."

"I guess I have to believe that. I have to," she said, as if trying to convince herself.

Trey found Jim Anderson in the employee canteen, sipping a Diet Pepsi and flipping through *Popular Science*. Anderson glanced up. "My man. Want half a bad ham sandwich?"

"No, thanks." Trey briefed Anderson on the situation. "Look, Scoleri is somehow getting messages from outside. Any idea how?"

"None," Anderson said. "He has minimal contact with staff."

"I didn't like that one CO. What about him?"

"Atkins? I know what you mean. He's the kind of guy who flies hard and fast. But unless his background check was screwy, he's not the kind of guy who would slip messages to Scoleri. He despises the patients in 28."

"How about cleaning staff? Or the midnight crew?"

"Again, minimal contact. And there are usually two to four people around whenever there's an interaction with Scoleri. Even when he's with one of the docs, he's got at least two people right behind him. They'd have to pass that message pretty quietly if they were going to do it." Taking a bite from his sandwich, Jim Anderson nodded as if answering a question in his head. "He's had a bad few days, though. Scoleri. Fallon punched his lights out this morning. Cut Scoleri's lip."

"Fallon's not passing messages," Trey said. "I wish I could think it was him, but he's the last one who would do that. He'd be more likely to hump Scoleri."

"What about the cafeteria?"

"He never goes in there. The most freedom he gets is in the a.m. for showers, and then at nine. Snack time."

"What happens at snack time?"

"We bring them in here. One at a time." Anderson pointed to the vending machines. "They get Twinkies or Ho-Hos or a soda. Four men supervising. Ten minutes each. It's their big treat."

"Who put that policy in effect?"

"Conroy and Brainard. It's for observation, I guess. They're pretty much shackled, though. It's just one way to give them a little something to look forward to before beddy-bye time. Only three on 28 are capable of doing it, though. The others are pretty much in another world."

Trey looked at the first vending machine. Fritos, Cheetos, the basics of snack foods. Then to the soda machine: Coke, root beer, Dr. Pepper, Pepsi. Then the Snapple machine. Then the bottled water machine. Then the sandwich and fruit machine. He came up blank.

"When do the vending guys come in?"

"Depends. But never when Program 28 is here."

"Okay. I guess I'm just hoping."

"Hoping for what?"

"That Scoleri's just like the rest of us. At least in terms of how he gets messages."

"Aw, Bubba, you *know* he's not like the rest of us. Well, at least not me."

TREY CHECKED out the showers next. It was eerie being there when they were silent and empty. Outside, a tiled room full of benches where the patients would disrobe. There were green metal lockers for them to store their clothes. Then the towel room— empty except for the laundry basket.

He stepped into the shower area. It seemed huge with only him standing in it.

How could a message be passed without one of the psych techs or the orderlies noticing?

Trey stood at the center of the showers, where the drain came out. He went so far as to get down and check the drain.

And then he knew one other way a patient in Program 28 might get a message.

One other time of day when he might speak with someone other than psych techs and COs.

BACK IN ELISE'S OFFICE, Trey sat down across from her desk. She was on the phone, but quickly hung up.

"You," Trey said. "You met with him on Friday."

"I meet with him every day."

"But in your office on Friday. What did you tell him last Friday?"

"Trey. There's nothing that was spoken of here that would have given him any information."

Trey reached for the picture of her son on her desk. He held it up to her. "He knows your son. Scoleri knows your son. He named him because he knows him."

"He wouldn't know his name," she said.

"That wouldn't be hard to find out. You've been treating him for months. Not just here, but at Patton too. You've spoken to him. You mentioned your son. Maybe in front of him. Maybe when you didn't think he was there—when he just was leaving your office. But he knew Lucas's name from you."

"What would that matter? Someone got a message to him."

"And it's not telepathy," Trey said.

And then Trey *knew*. He didn't know how, or who, or even where.

"No," Trey said, feeling as if his mind was processing information too fast. "He didn't get a message. He delivered one."

CHAPTER THIRTY-NINE

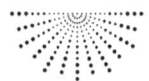

THE FIRST VICTIM'S HOUSE.

The living room. Simple, classic, and elegant.

Reminded Jane of a spread from a magazine like *House Beautiful.* This was the country club area of San Pascal. Nicer than where she'd grown up.

She sat across from the mother and father.

They'd been polite and haunted at the same time.

Fasteau sat out in the car at the street. He hadn't wanted to talk to them. He told Jane that she was wasting her time. *"Nothing new here," he'd said.*

Something about these two people across from Jane on the beige sofa reminded her of her own parents. These were wealthier people, but just like anyone else at home, grieving.

Their son had been killed four days earlier.

"We've spoken to officers twice now," the father said. "I'm not sure what else we can add."

"There might be some detail we've missed. I'd like to thank you for letting me see his room."

The mother sipped a cup of tea and looked as if she hadn't slept since they'd received the news and had to go identify their young son's body.

"That day," the mother said. "That day ..." She hesitated. The father gave her hand a squeeze, but she pulled her hand out from under his.

"Was there any delivery scheduled?"

The father shrugged. "I was at work. Nothing I knew of."

"Maybe something you ordered?"

The mother closed her eyes. Leaned back, sinking farther into the plush sofa. Opened her eyes. "Nothing. I mean, the mail came. The newspaper. No packages."

"How about workers? Do you have a gardener?"

"He's a fine man. They've already spoken to him," the mother said.

Then the father said, "I'm not sure, Officer, if we really can illuminate this further."

"He's got another one, doesn't he?" the mother asked. "You don't know anything. You can't know anything. That's why you're here. He's taken another child. I saw the news last night. He's taking one every day." She leaned forward and pulled a paper tissue from the box on the coffee table. She daubed the edges of her eyes. "I imagine the FBI are involved."

"Yes. But I wonder if there's something you might be forgetting. About that day. That morning."

"I was upstairs, doing some work on the computer," the mother said. "He was just outside for a few minutes. He goes out—" She stopped herself. "He was the friendliest little boy. The nicest little boy. He knew about not talking to strangers. I still can't believe it. I can't."

The father put his arm around the mother's shoulder. "I think we need to stop for now. We need to ask you to go."

"No," the mother said. "Maybe there's something. Maybe there is."

The father got up. "Can I get you anything? Tea? A Coke?"

Jane's throat felt dry. "Maybe some water?"

"Sure."

The mother began sobbing. The father looked at her, then sat down and embraced her. The mother pressed her face into the father's neck as her shoulders heaved.

"I'll get it." Jane stood and walked across the room, down the short hallway to the kitchen, which she'd seen when she'd first come in. She opened up the cupboards, grabbed a glass and turned to the sink. Noticed the water cooler by the kitchen door. Went over to it and pushed the blue button at the spigot and poured water into her glass.

She noticed the three big bottles of water by the cooler.

Back in the living room, she asked, "When does water get delivered here?"

"Water?"

"For the cooler."

"Oh," the father said. "I don't know."

When the mother glanced over, she said, "Maybe once a month. No, twice a month."

JANE DIDN'T NECESSARILY THINK a lot about this until she was back in the car with Fasteau, who told her he got a call from Tryon, who wasn't happy that Jane took it upon herself to re-interview these families.

"He'll live," Jane said. "Let's check on something else. You get water delivered at home?"

Fasteau let out a laugh. "Sure. Who the hell drinks the water out of the tap?"

"I do," Jane said.

"It ain't always good for you. There's a lot of stuff floating around in the water out here."

"What kind of water you get?"

He hesitated a second. "Usually Arrowhead. Since I was a kid."

"Ever heard of Moon Lake Spring Water?"

"Sure. It's that little outfit that's been trying to go national. I see their trucks all over the place."

"They get it," Jane said. "Delivered. I asked her if there was one particular delivery guy, and you know what she said? She had no idea. She said she never even noticed the guy who delivered it. It's like he had no face. She sees the uniform and that's it. She just lets him in her house, he goes in with the bottles, spends some time in the kitchen, and then leaves. She thinks of the guy as Green Shirt, because that's the uniform color. I wonder if the other families get Moon Lake Spring Water too."

Rain began coming down hard.

"What the hell," Fasteau said.

CHAPTER FORTY

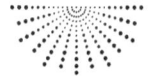

Conroy's office. Gray light from overhead from an overcast sky outside. The rain slashing.

"Elise, who does he know on the outside?" Trey asked. "Who came to see him at Patton? Or up north? Someone visited him. Someone on the outside knows him. And wants contact. Who is it? Because that someone is either the Red Angel or the person who knows the Red Angel well."

Elise leaned back in her chair, lighting up yet another cigarette. She took a few puffs.

"Who was at the trial? Who came to watch? Who knew him when? That's who this is. This is someone who has known Scoleri before."

"It could be anyone," she said. "Trey, this would take days to go through. We don't have days."

"Damn it," Trey said. He wanted to pound the desk and kick something. "I know that he has a way of getting messages out."

"Or in."

"I wish we had more time."

Elise glanced at her wristwatch. A pained expression on her face. She took another drag on the cigarette. "It'll be dark in a couple of hours, Trey. Look, I'm going to go talk to Olsen. I think I can get this arranged. We'll get an escort, get him in the back of one of the transport vans, and just take him out. Get him over to Patton, see if he'll talk."

"Okay. But I have this feeling. I just think … I think if I stay on top of him …"

Suddenly, Elise slammed her fist down on her desk. "Damn it!"

He leaned forward and touched the tips of her fingers with his. "This is a terrible thing, Elise. But we have got to put it in the hands of law enforcement. We can talk to Scoleri to see if there's any information he can give us at this point. But nothing else."

"Here's the thing. I want to give him something small like this. Something inconsequential. If it gets him to talk, that's all I care about."

"You're not talking about roughing him up," Trey said. "I wish you were. I wish you were talking about using sodium pentothal. Or sedating him further and then getting him to free associate before he blacks out. But you're not."

"I wish I thought that would work. I know him well enough, Trey. I know what his demons are. Whether he's getting messages through staff or whether he thinks it's all coming through the ether like a radio, I don't care. He knows things. I want to find my son. The man who took Lucas kills them after sundown. I need him talking. He won't talk this way. He may talk outside this place. He may just need to feel in control for five minutes. To me, that's worth whatever it takes to get information to the police. To save my son. How the hell are you going to feel if sometime before dawn they find Lucas in the Santa Ana River and that patient knows exactly where this killer is? Jesus," she said, "I would lay down my own life to make sure my baby gets back alive."

"Give me one more chance," Trey said.

Elise pointed out her window. The rain. "Look at that. That's how I feel on the inside."

"Just one more chance."

"Sometime between sundown and midnight, it happens. I'm guessing that it's an internal clock the killer's on. Lucas is somewhere out in that world and I am sitting here. He'll be dead. I don't care about procedure. I don't care about the law. I have a gun. I can …"

Trey drew back in the chair. "You what?"

"When I went home, I got it. I keep it locked up. I brought it with me. It's in my car now. A Sig Sauer."

Trey tried to quickly piece this together. This was irrational for Elise. *I need to get her home. She needs to get away from this. She's too entrenched. She's not thinking right.*

"What are you talking about, Elise? A gun? Come on. This is real life. Don't go off like this." He reached over and picked up the phone and held it in front of her. "Call your friends at the police department. Let them handle this."

She took the phone from him, setting it back down. "They don't want to hear from me again. At least not at this phase. Not till they know for sure. By then, it'll be too late."

"Do you even know for sure this is what happened to Lucas?"

"I don't want to go around on this again. Detectives in San Pascal called me in on Friday night. A body had been found two miles from here, over by some orange groves. It was the first one. A little girl. Then when I was working up, based on some evidence they'd shown me, they found a boy, same killer, in Little Orange. Bannock. Every day, another one. I am telling you, Scoleri is communicating with this killer. Somehow, some way. And the cops just aren't letting this information out. Not even to me. Who knows what they're doing while we stand around."

Trey glanced around trying to take in everything, hoping that something would catch his eye. *Desk. File cabinets. Telephone. Wastebasket. Water cooler. Bookshelves. Books. Magazines. Computer.* "The trash can. You threw something out. Notes? A phone message?"

Elise sighed. "Enough. I don't even care anymore. Here's what I do know. Here's what I care about. Lucas. Scoleri knows the Red Angel took him. Do you know what this killer does? He kills them. Drugs them, then drowns them. Then he takes a coat hanger and twists it around their neck. He cuts off bird wings and sticks them on the wire ends of the hangers so that they look like angels. That's why they call him the Red Angel—blood on the wings. He's making little angels out of them. When I spoke to the detectives today, they tried to keep me calm, but there's another detail. He's biting them. The last one found, this morning, her face was chewed up, her arms and torso bitten all over. I know what this is. He's been resisting doing it. But he's building up to it. The first one, nearly untouched. The most recent one, torn up like a dog got to her face. I've seen this before. So have you. With all the cases that come through. He's testing. He's trying out. He's getting more and more violent as he goes. Trey, his life is falling apart and he's taking it out on these children in monstrous ways. Jesus, I know this pattern of behavior. I've watched it before. I can't just sit and wait for these cops to find my son alive. It won't happen. He'll be dead. He'll have been tortured too. He'll have the worst kind of death. Not my baby, Trey. Not my beautiful little boy. Not *my* angel."

"CALL OLSEN, THEN," Trey said gently, after she'd composed herself again. "Get the transfer set up. Get at least two COs in the back of the van with him. I'll go in the front, and we'll make sure the driver is armed. I don't trust him. You can sit in the back with him, so long as there are shackles and cuffs. A neck brace if you really want to make sure he won't try anything. Don't ever forget he's labile."

"You've known him one day," she said. "I've known him longer. I know what to expect from him. I know what he's like."

"I'll back this all the way. I'll get to Brainard and get him signed off on this. Then we'll meet at the pod and get this going. It'll take about an hour. But if this is really what you think will help, we'll do it."

CHAPTER FORTY-ONE

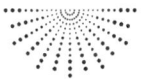

HANGING FROM THE WALL ON A HOOK, LARGE BIRD WINGS, blood dripping from them.

On the ground, a large dead duck.

Lucas was still crying because of what he'd just seen, but he fought to dry his tears. He felt stunned, but something in his brain was beginning to switch on. Something that was overcoming his fears.

It was a small gasp of a survival mechanism.

Duane had untied him, pulling off the tape. It had hurt, but it felt better than having it all over him so that he couldn't really move. He had to rescue Stuart, his hamster too. He had to somehow get out. Somebody would come for him. He was sure. His mom or dad would be there. Lucas knew it. He also prayed to God to send someone to help him. He knew that if he prayed hard enough, it would all work out. He just knew something would happen that would rescue him, just like on TV or in some of the books he read. Everything always worked out. He was sure of it.

But he shivered nonetheless and felt as if every moment made him more and more scared.

"You're in the Mad Place," Duane said to the boy. He seemed friendly again. It weirded Lucas out to see him like this. It frightened him too much. His head hurt from trying to understand it.

"Do you remember me?"

Lucas nodded. "You're Duane. The water guy?"

"No," the man said. "It *was* Duane. But it is the Beast now. It is the Devil. Do you understand? You are the angel I need to send to God. God needs to know. The War is about to begin. Are you aware, little bird? Between Heaven and Hell, on earth, it will begin. I am the Omega. I am the Last. You are my messenger."

Duane's look changed slightly. Duane's face scrunched up, not like he was mad, but like he was confused. He looked over at the bird wings hanging there. He stomped over to the small bed and touched the tip of one of the wings. There was blood on it. He wiped it on his fingers, and then wiped his fingers across his mouth.

Fear clutched at Lucas's heart, and he stepped backward, tripping on something on the stone floor.

Then he saw what he'd tripped over.

It looked like a rubber doll's head, larger than it should've been. Large, and distorted, with fine wisps of hair on its scalp.

Attached to a body.

It made a noise that sounded like a crow cawing.

"You boys have been bad again! It's time to find your salvation before the demons get you! You want the demons to find you? The Devil is inside you. The Devil won't leave. The Devil is coming out!" Duane shouted, only Lucas was no longer certain it was Duane because his face had turned all red, and the sweat shone across his forehead, and his eyes were large and wide. Suddenly, Duane clutched himself around the middle. His throat seemed to get larger—Lucas had never seen anything as horrifying in his life—it was as if his throat were twisting around on itself and growing. Then a deep voice boomed from within Duane's throat, shouting obscenities.

The voice grew soft.

Light.

Then the worst thing happened, as far as Lucas was concerned.

Duane fixed his awful gaze upon him and whispered, "Do you know that demons live inside my flesh?"

Duane began ripping at his own face with his bare hands, his fingernails slicing away at the skin beneath his eyes.

IN ITS MIND, it felt the presence of greatness, of the Beast rising in his blood, taking over the hands that tore, the teeth that bit, the very soul of the it known as Duane Cobble.

The past and the present mixed together in his memory:

Its foster brother, God, who had taught it about its inner nature the same way that its daddy had, about the Other One, the Beast, the Great Darkness known as 666, within its cage of flesh and bone. Its destiny marked by its little angels, sent to God to warn the Almighty of the coming fires of the world and the emergence of Hell.

Memories of Daddy holding it down, in the hot water of the spring in the Mad Place, praising Jesus while he tried to cast out its demons, praising Heaven while slamming and dunking his head beneath the too hot water. "You are an it! You are less than a worm! You are not worthy of the evil sinful serpent from which you came!

Your serpent is strong, but I will cast out the Devil from you! Do you hear me? Do you?" his daddy cried out.

And then, beaten so badly that he could only crawl, beaten with Ruthie lying there, her eyes blank and staring.

Locked in the Mad Place for weeks at a time, it lay and ate the scraps thrown down to it and drank the cold water along the ground, hearing its daddy reading the gospel to it from on high, hearing its daddy ranting in the dark about the demons its wicked mother had given birth to—given form. "From her cursed place, you crawled, you whore, and then the it followed, a child of darkness, a child who was not human, but was full of sin! The mark of the Devil upon you! Dear Sweet Lord, save these two sinners, save them from the foul creatures who inhabit their bodies! Save their eternal souls! Keep them from the fires of perdition!"

His two foster brothers with him, screaming as they watched his father break Ruthie's legs, but it knew that its daddy was right. Ruthie was the Whore of Babylon. She was the beginning of sin, and if Daddy did not subdue her—trod upon her as the serpent underfoot—then the last days would come.

Inside the Mad Place, bound for a thousand years, the world was safe from the Devil.

But when its foster brother left and Ruthie went to Hell, it was alone with its daddy.

And then, one day, Daddy died.

It was the man of the house.

It worked hard to hold the Beast in its cage so that it could take care of its mother, so that its girl, Monica, who had been a homeless whore down on its delivery route, could get cleaned up. But Monica's whoredom had tempted its flesh.

It had all fallen apart.

And then Jojo, its only friend for the past fifteen years, was dying.

And its mother was dying.

And it heard the voice of the Other One within it.

Louder.

Stronger.

Coming out.

It knew it was falling apart, and that the Devil was coming through more and more every day.

Christmas approaching.

God's birthday.

It had to send messages to Abraxas, the God of All.

Through the angels going to Heaven.

Through the signs and portents along its Moon Lake Pure Spring Water delivery route in the foothills and flatlands from San Pascal to San Bernardino, from Moreno Valley to Riverside.

It knew where God lived.

God spoke to it in omens.

It spoke to God with angels.

CHAPTER FORTY-TWO

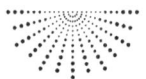

JANE CALLED TRYON, AS FASTEAU RAN THROUGH THE RAIN
into a McDonald's with too long a line at the drive-thru window.

"I've spoken with three of the families. All three get Moon Lake
Pure Spring Water. I think it's the delivery guy. The Latimers told
me that the Moon Lake guy talked to their son all the time. Funny
thing is, none of them remember one specific guy. I think he
grabbed the kids on his route. I think that's what he's been doing.
These kids happen to be the ones who give him the opportunity."

"You following through?"

"Sure. We dropped by the distribution plant and got the names
of three of the guys who work the area. They alternate routes. All
part-timers."

"Good going, Laymon," he said. "Names?"

"James Pratt, San Pascal. Lou Barron, Mentone, and Duane
Cobble, Moon Lake."

"What are the odds he lives in Moon Lake?"

"That's by the distribution center, but the guy at the plant told
me that Pratt lives on Sierra Ridge. That's within a stone's throw of

Dr. Conroy's and within two miles of the Latimers'." She read the addresses and telephone numbers for each one.

"Okay," Tryon said. "We'll get officers to each residence. Might as well cover our asses."

"You heard from Conroy yet?"

"Yes and no." Tryon failed to explain further. A pause on the line. "You and Fasteau are where?"

"Not far from the Latimers'."

"Okay, you two get up to Moon Lake. Check out Cobble. This may be one of many goose chases, but we need to nail the Red Angel, pronto. If one of these three pans out, you done damn good."

He hung up.

"You done damn good, he tells me." Jane closed her cell phone. *High praise from Tryon.*

CHAPTER FORTY-THREE

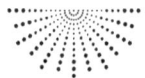

Trey Campbell spent forty-five minutes waiting for Dr. Brainard at his office, and then another twenty trying to convince him of something that Trey was sure he would sign off on. He and Elise needed both Olsen, the Executive Director of Darden State, and two psychiatrists to sign off on this kind of day transfer for a patient from Program 28.

When Campbell left Brainard's office, Jim Anderson, waiting in the hall, said, "So what's the verdict?"

Trey shook his head. "Maybe if Elise had luck with Olsen, we can do an end-run around Brainard."

But Elise's office was locked.

"Maybe she's talking to Olsen?"

"She'd phone it in," Trey said.

He reached into his pocket and brought out his cell phone. Punched in the numbers of the executive director's office. "Shelly? Trey. Hi. Listen, is Dr. Conroy over there?"

~

HE FELT a peculiar sense of panic as he walked swiftly down the corridor toward Program 28. ID badge flashed to the COs. Unlocked the double doors.

Down the metallic corridor, past the first several pods.

Scoleri's was empty.

Anderson, following behind him, said, "What the hell?"

Trey cussed a blue streak.

"Chill, boy," Anderson said.

"Jimmy, she got him out. She couldn't wait. She did it. I don't know how, but she did it."

HE DIDN'T WANT to expose her. She might not be in any trouble. She might be fine. She might have got him to her car. That would be it. Trey was sure. She would be out in the staff parking lot. He told Jim Anderson he'd call him within ten minutes and explain what all this was about.

Out in the staff parking lot, Elise Conroy's space was empty.

He checked the log at the front desk of the main entrance.

Elise Conroy had left with "Guest."

Trey stood at the front entrance to Darden and weighed his options.

Lucas Conroy will be dead by sundown.

There is no option.

IN HIS MUSTANG, out on the 10 freeway, he punched in Elise's cell phone number. Windshield wipers slicing against the heaving rain, increasing as the sun headed over into the western sky. Temperature, sixty-four in the flatlands and dropping.

She picked up.

"Where are you?"

"I'm sorry, Trey."

"No need. You got him out. Right?"

"Olsen said no. I'm sorry."

"He's with you?"

"Yes."

"Cuffed?"

"Very."

"How did you do it?"

"It was easier than you'd think. For the guards, I faked an ID. They don't know Scoleri from Adam on Wards B and C. They thought it was a Program 9 med transfer."

"But you kept him cuffed?"

"Yes."

"Shackled?"

"No. But he has leg cuffs on now."

"That's not enough."

She hung up the phone.

He turned off the freeway exit and up into the foothills of San Pascal.

In the rain, traffic slowed. No one in Southern California seemed to know how to drive in the rain. It was as if anything that smacked of weather scrambled brains as well.

Palm trees lined the fat sidewalks. Small bungalows blurred along as he drove up toward Baseline, then west on Date Palm Drive, zigzag back up to Baseline.

He pressed redial. Hated being on the cell while driving. Hated people who did it.

She picked up on her phone on the first ring.

"Don't hang up on me."

"Don't condescend to me."

"Where are you?"

"We're driving."

"What is he telling you?"

"He knows the killer, Trey. We should've done more of a background check. They were in the home together for a year. The Red Angel's family took him in. They got close."

"He may be lying."

"Enough, Trey."

"Don't hang up. Let me meet up with you. You need someone with you."

She paused.

He turned up a side street, north. Stucco beige suburban tract homes littered the slight incline heading toward the hills. "Are you near your house?"

"No."

Shit. He had just turned up into Sun Ridge, just on the other side of San Pascal, and Elise's neighborhood.

He wanted to ask her more questions but knew it would be pointless. Scoleri was right there next to her. He had no doubt that Scoleri intended to use her to get away. *You could have a medical degree from the best school in the country, you could work with serial killers for more than eight years, diagnosing, treating, studying, observing. And still, when your kid gets taken, you're just somebody desperate enough to risk your own life with someone who happily would rape, mutilate, torture, and then kill you.*

"Where are you headed?" he asked.

"Up the 16. Into the mountains."

She was taking the side road, the old highway, up toward Big Bear. He had hoped that if she took any roads, they'd be main ones. Big ones. Ones where the highway patrol might be.

He had an instinct to call the police in the mountains.

You're overreacting. We can bring this one in. Whether Scoleri has

information or not, we can control this. Get Scoleri back to Darden,
talk to Olsen. Clean it up. Anybody would understand Elise's actions in
the face of what she's going through. Given her record, this can be
smoothed over.

He knew there was a way to do it.

But he also feared something else. More than just what Scoleri
might *do*.

He had a fear that in working so intimately with Scoleri, Elise
had begun to identify too closely with him. She was a professional.
But then, he'd known other professionals, people who should've
known better, who got too close to that insane fire and burned
themselves.

"Have you reached the first rest stop?" he asked, carefully
maneuvering a twist in the road. "You know, the one near the falls?"

Pause.

"No."

"Pull over there. I'll meet you. It'll take me twenty minutes."

"You won't call the cops?"

He thought for just a second that he might lie to her. But
decided that this could be controlled. He could help take Scoleri
back to Darden State. There'd be a way to make it all work. He was
sure.

"I won't. But Elise, do not let him get inside your head. Not on
this. He knows your weak spot. He knows that you'll do anything
to get your son. He may not know this killer. He may ..."

She hung up the cell phone.

He pressed redial.

No answer.

She'd turned off her phone.

～

As HE DROVE, crossing into higher elevations, it was no longer rain coming down, but snow. He went up the 18, all the way to a small clutch of houses just where the mountains really began beyond the foothills. A dip in the slender highway indicated the turnoff to the old Route 9. He knew it well, from his make-out days as a teen, going up with girlfriends, going hiking with his buddies. It had mountain streams flowing down along the old road, and it had two rest areas off of it, usually used for picnicking or just parking.

It took him nearly half an hour of the windy road that was impossibly narrow to get to that first rest stop. The snow fluttered down, making the whole area seem magical and beautiful. It was piling up—he figured he must be at about three thousand feet above sea level.

Elise's Volvo was parked just inside the curve of it, near the picnic tables.

As he approached it, something seemed wrong. His mind began reeling, thinking of the possibilities, imagining from what he'd read of Scoleri as to what the man was capable of doing. *The mutilations, the torture, the souvenir gathering, the murders.*

The dreadful images came up to him, things he'd seen in forensics casebooks, pictures he'd seen when there'd been a trial of one of the patients and he had gone to the courtroom with the psychiatrists and COs: dead women, women like Elise Conroy, beautiful, torn, their faces staring at nothing.

His heart began pounding too hard, hammering in his chest.

Don't let anything have happened to her.

Don't let her be hurt.

CHAPTER FORTY-FOUR

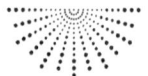

Trey parked his car and went over to Elise's.

Thank God.

She glanced over to him, but had an unreadable expression on her face.

Flakes of snow fluttered down.

He leaned into her rolled-down window.

Scoleri sat in the backseat, lying down, his head against the inside door handle. His arms were behind his back, cuffed. His legs, shackled.

Elise looked up at Trey.

"He knows where Lucas is," she said.

Her eyes, bloodshot. Her hair, a mess.

He noticed the revolver on the passenger seat beside her.

"All right," Trey said. "Let's take this slow."

"LET'S TALK ABOUT THIS," he said. "Outside." As an afterthought, he added, "Bring the gun."

HE KEPT watch on the car in case Scoleri made any move to get out of it.

He and Elise stood on the edge of the pavement and curb, close enough to run back to the car at a moment's notice and subdue Scoleri.

Far enough away that Scoleri wouldn't hear them.

"We have to turn around right now. Take Scoleri back. We can smooth it over. Right now. Every minute we delay it will be that much harder to fix this."

"No," she said. Her voice far too calm. "He knows where my son is. I'm going to go get him. And kill whoever did this."

"That's nuts, Elise. You're out of your league. You may be a smart person with degrees up the wazoo, but this is beyond what you or I can handle. You're going vigilante on somebody's ass? With your gun?"

"Yes."

"Elise, do I need to wrestle you to the ground and put restraints on you too?"

"If it were your son, Trey. If it were Mark. If you knew the man who had him intended to kill him within a few hours. If you knew how the police worked. When your family was attacked on Catalina. Hatcher. Did the police save you? Did they? Would they have got to your kids on time? Trey? Tell me truthfully. You tell me that I should take him back. My only hope. I've gone over and over this in my mind."

After a few seconds, he said, "Okay. One hour. We give him one hour to help."

HE WENT AROUND and got in the car. She passed him the revolver. He put it carefully into the glove compartment. Shut it.

Then he got out and opened the back door.

Looking up at him, Scoleri said, "I love rides in the country."

TREY SAT IN THE BACKSEAT, with Scoleri sitting to his left. Scoleri kept his eyes out the window.

Elise watched them both in the rearview mirror.

"All right. You have your fresh air, Scoleri."

"Call me Abraxas."

"Abraxas, then."

"You want me to just deliver everything on a silver platter," Scoleri said.

"Why not?"

"Doesn't work that way. You live in this realm of consciousness that's milky and clouded. You think that what you can see in your little bubble is all that there is. But there's more to existence than that," Scoleri said. He looked out at the snow falling. "I love snow. I created snow because it makes everything seem more beautiful than it is. The world is an ugly, grimy place. Filthy. Wallowing in it, people. People who are not really people, just pulsating amoebas, crashing into one another. The Earth is a woman and the parasites infest her scalp and her pussy. The Earth is a whore and she fucks the Devil. It gives her these lice and vermin called mankind. But I created snow to dress her. To blanket her. To freeze the lice. Isn't it beautiful?"

"Look," Trey said. "Tell us about the Red Angel."

"He once was a real angel, you know. Once, when the world was innocent and new. He was pure, but the Devil got inside him. The Devil came through into him, like the Holy Spirit comes into others when I inspire them. The Devil came into him and tore at his innards. He was strong, but not strong enough. I helped him build a prison for the Devil in his head. We spoke through the divine radio, and I struggled in the whorls of his brain-shit to build a strong enough cage for the Devil. But the Devil gets out now and then. The Devil knows his weaknesses. And something's happening to him now. The Devil is stronger."

"How do you know him?"

Scoleri turned to face Trey. Smiling. "Aren't we going for a drive? I want to see the mountains."

"I would think Abraxas would make the mountains come to him."

"Ha ha ha," Scoleri said, slowly and deliberately.

Trey's heart pounded. Felt heat in his face. *We are fucked if this doesn't go right.* "It's snowing. The roads might be bad."

"I think we should go for a ride," Scoleri said. "Up, up, up."

CHAPTER FORTY-FIVE

Moon Lake

Weather forecast for the San Bernardino Mountains: cloudy, chance of snow, twenty-eight degrees dropping to twenty by nightfall.

That was the forecast. At the higher elevations, it was already eighteen degrees by six p.m.

Snow covered the town of Big Bear and Moon Lake.

It was a peaceful snow. Winds, but no blasts. Made the whole world look like a snow globe. Santa's village. Christmas world.

Moon Lake is out of the way, a community rising from a recess in the mountainside, going flat along the lake itself, surrounded by trees, mainly incense cedars, sugar pine, white pine, and other conifers. The sheriff's station is a beige trailer down in the town

Moon Lake. "Town" is simply a bar, a coffee shop, and a sundries store. Six houses huddle nearby, occupied by those who work in the sheriff's station, bar, coffee shop, or sundries store.

In the forest beyond the lake, there are one hundred twenty-five cabins along the outcroppings and rises that can be reached via unpaved roads. These are used primarily in the summer, although some come up in the winter for skiing in the city of Big Bear twelve miles northeast. Few arrive after December, first without four-wheel-drives, although some of the flatlanders risk the windy road up to Moon Lake just to make fun of the locals, who are a bit country compared to those who live below the mountains, or to take in the quaintness of the small, tight-knit community. Most of the cabins are empty until ski season kicks into high gear in January, so even just before Christmas, the handful of winterized cabins are mostly empty.

The Moon Lake distribution plant is ten miles from the lake itself, but the town prides itself on being known for its spring water. "I go down and take a piss in that pure spring water every morning," is a favorite phrase that locals tell visitors over a few beers.

On one edge of the lake, the remnants of what looks like a small camp.

A semicircle of small cabins. One larger one, more of a house than simply a summer cabin.

An old, rotten arch of a sign in front of the gravel drive up to the house. It says, Cobble Christian Summer Camp for Saved Children. The lettering gray and faint.

Wind blows it back and forth. The lights on the porch of the house waver.

The snow coming down in the darkening wood around it.

A girl yells inside.

MONICA SCRUBB HAD BEEN sixteen when she'd first met Duane Cobble and had run away from her third group home up in Palmdale just to be with him. That was back when he did the route up through the mountains, instead of down into the flatlands below. She had been desperate to get out of the last place and had met Duane at a truck stop. He'd been eating creamed chipped beef, and she'd had a cup of watered-down coffee and a bear claw, which nabbed her last dime. Duane had not been cute, nor had he been particularly charismatic, but she knew when a guy was hot for her, and she needed to get the hell out of Dodge and find a new place to live.

He'd been good to her, at least better than the guy running the group home who'd pawed her up and down and the damn lesbos who had been on her like flies on shit every night when she went to bed. She was only just eighteen now and had thought that she and Duane would be okay together for a while.

But then that witch, his mother, had been taking him over, slowly but surely. Monica Scrubb hoped that the witch would die so that she and Duane could start their little family without the nastiness.

The witch and the dog. Death's coming for both of 'em.

Monica slept five hours a day. Pissed her off to no end. Got up in the middle of the day to relieve Duane or the visiting nurse to go sit with the damn witch and hear her complain about life and about how Jesus had forgotten her.

Then, at nine, she had to change back into her Donut Queen outfit and head back down the mountain to Bannock where the Donut Queen's Castle awaited her, full to the brim with the stink of grease and day-old coffee.

It wasn't the life she'd signed on for, and pissed was her normal state of mind.

And Duane had been getting worse. Duane had been spending more time down in that cave than with her.

And he'd been getting rougher with the sex. He didn't care about her feelings anymore.

But she'd show him.

"WE'RE HAVIN' a baby!" she shouted, throwing a spoon at him all the way from the kitchen.

The spoon barely missed his scalp and went clattering onto the floor by the TV. The old dog perked up and raised his head to start howling.

"Shut up, Jojo!" She cried out, "Goddamn it, Duane, you promised that when the baby comes we'd have our own place."

"We got the other cabins," Duane said, his voice small, like a little boy's.

"Rat traps," she said. "That's all they are. Leaky-roof, black widow-infested snake hotels is what they are. I should just burn those cabins down. Jesus, Duane. I mean, Jesus."

"She's usin' the Lord's name in vain again!" the old woman shouted from her bedroom.

"Shut the hell up!" Monica shouted, half turning to stare at the door. Then, in a quieter voice, "You tell that bitch to lay off talkin' about my family like we was white trash, Duane, or so help me God I'm gonna put her face in her own shit next time she starts in on me."

"Don't talk about her that way," Duane said. "She's a saint. She's a saint."

"She is a sick bitch," Monica spat. "And you are a sick fuck, and we are gonna have a baby, you goddamn Jesus freak. You and me. Whether you like it or not."

That's when Duane rushed over to her and slammed his fist as hard as he could against her jaw.

Before she blacked out, Monica heard a slight cracking sound.

SHE WOKE UP SECONDS LATER. He had already brought her to the couch, and he sat on the floor next to her.

"You okay?"

She hesitated before answering to draw out that worried look on his face. "I guess. You sorry for hittin' me?"

"Yes."

"Good. Get me a ciggie."

"Okay."

"Jesus, Duane, we got a baby coming in six months, and you ain't done none of the things you promised. You ain't done all the big-world things you said you was gonna do when I met you. You had plans then, baby. Plans. I shoulda stayed in Palmdale and let Granger play poke-Monica for all it matters. We got a baby. Thanks," she said, snatching the cigarette from his hands. She leaned forward as he flipped up the lighter and got the little flame up. She took a nice deep drag. "I gave up meth for this baby, honey. You need to keep up your end of the bargain. I'm killin' myself, I mean killin' myself at that place, donut crap in my hair, customers grabbing my ass when I pour coffee." Her voice went from a young woman's to a little girl's, a baby voice. "I just want you to be my daddy and take care of me and our baby, Duaney."

"I will."

"I know you need private time. I know all men do. But you been spending all that time down in that cave."

"I talk to God there."

"Sure you do. I understand. It's important to you. That's why I never go down there. Men got private things to take care of." She didn't want to tell him that she was happy when he spent time in that old bomb shelter. It kept him from bothering her if she was home. "But I need you to start makin' plans for our baby."

IT WATCHES her but doesn't want her to know. It has let the Other One take it over. Watching the Whore with her talk about babies, when it knew that the only baby that she'd pop out would be the Antichrist. It knew that the only seed it had was the Other One's seed. That's why it was chosen. That's why its daddy had tried to teach it to hurt itself, to drive the Other One out of its body.

It has only begun to think of how it will stop the Antichrist from being born.

But other things are on its mind.

Jojo, the only good dog who ever lived. He is dying.

And its mother. She is a saint. She is second only to the Virgin Mary. She is a Queen of Angels.

And she's going to Heaven soon too.

The Whore and her Devil Child will go to Hell.

It just has to figure out when it will send them to Hell.

Whenever it says Monica, looks at the Whore, it remembers its sister, Ruthie, and how beautiful Ruthie was before she got sent to Hell.

Monica is like Ruthie.

Ruthie and it and its brother playing together as children.

Playing together and finding out their badness.

Their hellish natures.

Its daddy with the boiling water, showing it how it didn't have any pain, because it had the Devil inside it.

~

Monica glanced at her watch. She shook her wrist slightly. "Damn, I just bought this two weeks ago and it already's slowin' down. I gotta go in at seven tonight, baby. Don't drive me this time. I can just take your truck."

"I need the truck," it said.

"Well, my car ain't making it down in the snow."

"I need it."

She sat up on the couch, touching the edge of her jaw and back to her lips. She was used to being hit. Even liked getting a slap sometimes, it knew. But it felt bad for hitting her so hard. "Okay. Take my truck. That's okay. You need to go into work."

Then its mother began calling out to it from the other room.

~

"Mama?"

"I don't wanna die," she says.

It shuts the door behind it, and goes to sit in the little metal chair by her bed. It moves the tubes that hang down around her so that it can see her better while it's talking to her.

"You won't die."

"I will, Duane. I will. I'll go to Heaven and see Daddy again."

"Don't talk like that."

"I guess I got to die. I guess that's the Lord's way."

It reaches across the covers and takes her hand in its own hand, feeling the rough warmth.

"'Member when Daddy used to talk about the sweet hereafter? The angels?"

It smiles. "Sure."

"I thought you were dead once," she says. "I dreamed it. After

Ruthie died. I was so sad, Duane. I slept for days. Do you remember? I slept and barely ate anything. Daddy kept telling me that it was the Lord's way. That the Lord was calling Ruthie and it was my pride that kept me from seeing that."

"Ruthie went to Hell," it says, and then wishes it hadn't said anything about Ruthie.

"I don't know," its mother says. "Sometimes I think Daddy was wrong. Ruthie was headstrong. She was a fighter. And yes, the Devil was upon her at times. There's no denying that. Remember the revivals? Remember the camp?"

"I was born after the camp closed."

"Oh, yes. Yes. Now I recollect, that's true. We used to run the most wonderful bible studies for the children. All children are little angels, Duane. Even Ruthie, as much as Daddy tried to get the demons out of her, even Ruthie was a little angel. Maybe I'll see her. Maybe if I go to Heaven, I can see her."

"Maybe," it says. But it knows that Ruthie is in Hell. In the darkness of Hell forever. Until the end of days. Ruthie was the Whore of Babylon the Great. Ruthie brought devils out when she spoke. That was what its daddy had preached.

"If I die soon," its mother says, "if I die soon … there's something I need to tell you. I can't feel good about dying if I don't let you know."

"Mama?"

"I promised your daddy I wouldn't tell you. But I should tell you. You should know." Its mother clears her throat.

It feels her hand clutch its hand tighter.

"Pain's comin' back."

"Want more?" it says, reaching to the small button on the side of the tube where the morphine comes down.

"Little more," she said. "More.

It presses the button slightly, and then releases it.

Then again.

"You know I always loved you the best. We took in those other children. I never understood Ruthie or why she was so troubled. You weren't like that. Not as much. You kids got up to no good sometimes, but I know children do that. But the other children we took in. Do you remember them?"

It nods. "My brother."

"Yes, there were three little boys at different times. Andy and Brian and Mikey."

"I talk to Mikey sometimes."

"Do you? How is he?"

"He's perfect," it says.

"I loved that little wild boy. I loved all my children. All of you troubled, but just in need of prayer and saving. Remember what it was like back then? I woke up every morning happy. Your daddy did too. He had his troubled times, but when we helped other Christian children, he was happy. He took you boys down to the shelter to pray every day. Every single day. And when you ran away …" She keeps talking, but it doesn't listen much. It presses the little button on the morphine so she'll have an easier time of it. Her pain can be fierce. It doesn't like her talking about those days, back when it was a kid, back when it was in the Mad Place too much.

It had not run away from home at all, but its daddy had put it down in the Mad Place for days on end. It had been a secret from its mother, and it knew it deserved to be there. But its mother had thought that it had simply run off to go camping in the woods in the way, its daddy had explained to her, that bad boys sometimes do.

Its mother had never known what they'd all been up to in the Mad Place. Or why its father spent so much time there, trying to save them.

Trying to save Ruthie from her destiny, preordained in perdition.

Its mother never even knew how Ruthie had gone straight to Hell. Its mother had been that sensitive, that gentle, that she had no idea how Daddy had sealed Ruthie up in the place between Heaven and Hell, buried alive in the bowels of the Earth.

"Duane?" its mother asks, her gnarled hand pressing against his fingers. "Duane? You thinking about that whore?"

"She's gonna be my wife. Don't talk like that."

"She's a whore if there ever was one, and you know it, and your daddy'd know it if he was here. Don't you let her ruin your life, Duane. She's trash and she knows it and she never even got baptized, she's that bad. After I die, I want you to find a good woman. A woman like me," its mother says. "Someone who ..." Her voice trails off.

"Mama?" it asks.

Then it looks at the hand that is not holding its mama's hand.

The other hand had been pressing on the morphine too much.

If thy left hand offend thee, cut it off.

It lets go of the intravenous tube and lets go of its mother's hand. She is off dreaming, sleeping without pain, and that's all that matters.

"You won't die tonight, Mama," it says softly. "I love you too much."

It always gives her a little more morphine at night, just in case one of the little birds in the Mad Place starts screaming.

She doesn't need to hear that kind of thing.

CHAPTER FORTY-SIX

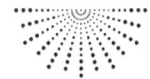

Fasteau took the curves of Route 18 too fast, and when they started hitting the accumulating gray slush as they reached higher elevations, Laymon put her hands on the dashboard, as if this would somehow save her in an accident. The road up the mountain was windy and gave her a lurch in her stomach now and then, particularly the way Fasteau hugged the outer curves, giving Jane a murky view of the canyons and valley below.

"We're not rushing."

"What the fuck," Fasteau said.

"Just slow down," she said, nearly under her breath.

It would normally take thirty minutes to get to Blue Jay, one of the first major communities up in the mountain range, but because of the snow, they clocked it at fifty minutes, and then, with the sun just going down, visibility "sucks big time," Fasteau said.

"Ever the poet," Jane said.

"I gotta pee," he said.

"Okay. Pull over at the next lookout area. See? Look, it's coming up," she said.

THEY PULLED OVER ONTO GRAVEL, and then onto the paved area that curved out a bit from the mountain road, overlooking the entire valley. It was misty gray with rain below, but that was nothing compared with the snow coming down.

She got out of the car, stretching.

He went over to the edge of the guardrail to relieve himself. "Tell me if you see anyone coming!" he shouted back.

"Are you kidding? I'm selling tickets."

When he'd zipped up and headed back to the car, he pointed at the wooden sign that had the words Scenic Overlook on it. "I bet you couldn't hit that sign."

"Don't get my competitive spirit up, I just might do it."

"You couldn't do it if you wanted to."

She actually had to bite her tongue—press down on it with her front teeth to keep from saying the nasty words she'd begun thinking.

Then she said, "Let's think about Lucas Conroy and a little less about who has the bigger dick."

The sun was far over to the west, somewhere, hidden from the gray-white view of cloud and storm.

The world began to darken as she got back into the car.

She didn't pray a lot, but she sent a little prayer out for Lucas, just because she didn't want to believe that God wouldn't somehow protect him. But God hadn't protected the other kids.

And that's when they got the call from the valley.

Another kid had been found.

CHAPTER FORTY-SEVEN

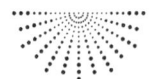

ELISE DROVE UP THE NARROW ROAD THAT WENT BESIDE THE main highway. The wind had picked up, and the snow came down at a slant. The sky darkened gradually.

Elise flicked on the interior light in the car.

Scoleri kept up his chatter. "I used to come up here when I was a boy."

"So the Red Angel is here?"

Scoleri shut down. Closed his eyes. No words.

Trey glanced at Elise's eyes in the rearview mirror.

"What's going to get you to tell us what we need to know?"

Suddenly, Scoleri opened his eyes. "You want to be inside my head? You want to come live here with me? Do you? If you do, you will not be the same. You will not live your happy little life of comfort, your suburban dreams of sweet birdsong. You want to crawl inside my mind? Because that's what you're going to do if you want to find the boy. Or should I call him 'the little bird'—that's what our dear Red Angel calls him. And you know what the Devil does to birds? He cuts off their wings. He slices them and he makes pretty little ornaments for angels out of them. Little bloody angels so he can have a choir in Hell. You want to see what I've seen? What I hear from the Devil? What I know? There are other children in the Devil's choir. Some of them never fly away. Some of them go missing, only no one has ever known it because they came from families who didn't care. They were easy for the Devil to take, but they aren't his angels. Do you know what an angel is, Trey? I mean, really, let's talk about it. Do you know?"

Trey nodded. "A messenger of God."

"And who is God?"

Trey hesitated. "According to you, you are God."

"Good boy," Scoleri said. "I am God. And the nature of God is what?"

"To create."

"Not just create. The nature of God is to forgive."

"Is he asking for your forgiveness?" Trey asked.

"He's the Devil. Of course he is."

"Are these children sent out as messages for you?"

"Does God send messages for Himself?"

"You lost me."

"That's because you're not inside my head yet. Once you are, you'll have the key. When you have the key," Scoleri said, turning his head to look out at the snow and the oncoming night, "then maybe you can open the door and get inside me. The way I know you want to be inside me. And then you and my dear Elise, will find that little angel before it gets all red with blood."

CHAPTER FORTY-EIGHT

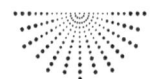

Jane Laymon was on the cell phone with Tryon.

"Is it Lucas Conroy?"

"It's a girl," Tryon said. "No idea of identity yet. The wings around her neck. Might've been dead just a few hours. Maybe more. We can't quite tell yet."

"Where?"

"In the foothills. Your town. Within four miles of the Elise Conroy's house and a mile from the Latimers'."

"He's moving fast," Jane said.

"Too fast. And too rough. This one is all torn up, Jane. This one looks like a mountain lion got to her."

"Should we head back?"

"No, go ahead and check out the guy up there, and also go by the Moon Lake offices. They've got night staff, and maybe someone there knows one of these guys well."

"Anything pan out on Pratt?"

"Well, he's nervous. He's got good reason. Today was his

delivery schedule to the Conroy place, only he says he didn't deliver because he knew they had plenty of bottles already. We'll keep him occupied. How far are you from Cobble?"

"Maybe another forty. It's slow going. The roads are getting bad up here."

CHAPTER FORTY-NINE

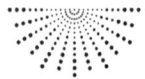

DUANE COBBLE HEARD IT CLEARLY, STARTING WITH A humming in its head.

Abraxas.

Coming.

CHAPTER FIFTY

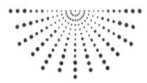

THE VOLVO CONTINUED ITS CLIMB UP THE NARROW ROAD. Elise was careful on the curves.

Have to get him to say something definite. Something that will tell me. Trey racked his brain trying to think fast. *Get him to talk, then call the cops and get the hell back to Darden.*

"Did I tell you about my wonderful childhood? I know I told Elise."

"You were raised all over Southern California," Elise said, nodding.

"You lived up here," Trey said. "Big Bear?"

"Let's not get ahead of ourselves. I lived in many places, all of them white trash, state fund-grubbing flytraps; Mentone, Barstow, Chino, Cucamonga. Other places. Sometimes for a few weeks, sometimes months, once or twice a year."

"The year you don't talk about," Trey said.

Scoleri leaned forward toward the back of Elise's neck.

Trey was ready to pull him back fast if he tried anything.

"I guess you shared my files with him, oh doctor my doctor."

"Back," Trey said.

Scoleri briefly flickered a glance at Trey, then leaned back in the seat. "I lived at one house that was more than just a house. It was a regular revival meeting. We were filthy little sinners all set to be saved. In the summer, we worked at the bible camp for children that this family ran. Servants to children even more fortunate than we. The papa of the house was a minister who had been thrown out of his own church somewhere farther up, maybe Victorville. He'd hightailed it to this place, bought a little land with what he could steal from the little old ladies whose souls needed saving. Ran a little weekend camp in the summers where Jesus freaks dumped their kids. But it wasn't doing so well, and Papa Bear thought maybe it was because of the little baby bears. Me being one of them. At one point, there had been a few other kids at this place, a regular group home without the home. Only those kids had run away or had been sent elsewhere. Who knows. But I was stuck there for a year. I found out what I liked, what I enjoyed, right in that little home. Papa Bear, he was good at keeping it secret from Mama Bear. He had this place, this secret little hiding place in the rocks. He called it the Mad Place. It was the part of Hell that leaked through into Heaven, he said, and made all of us children gather round in it. He told us that God wanted children to suffer. It was right there in the bible. But you see, I was smarter than my new brother and sister that spent time there with me. I knew I was Abraxas, the God of All, and that Papa Bear was just your average loony tuney. I knew, Trey, that Papa Bear had a kink, and it had something to do with the pain he inflicted on his own children. Sometimes me too. But his own kids, he was the worst with them. Little girl named Ruthie, she got it worse than all of us. Papa took a shine to her, I think. He didn't know I knew, but he watched her when she dressed. He didn't touch her. Not in that way. But he knew she had tempted him to terrible, sinful ways. He called her the Whore of Babylon in the Mad Place and scourged her flesh to drive the demons out of her. He loved doing that. He loved the barbed wire slashing at her pale little back. He loved watching her squirm when he pressed cigarettes against her bare shoulder blades. Truth is, I learned a few tricks from him. And then, my brother, we were bestest friends. We did everything together. We shared our secrets. Papa Bear liked to hit him too, liked to take little sharp knives from the kitchen and carve words into his back. I'm not even sure of his name right now, because we were supposed to call him 'it.'"

"Must've been awful," Elise said.

"Not in the least. I loved it there. They were my first real family. Some weeks, we'd spend the whole time in the Mad Place. It was dark. It was wonderful. Sometimes we'd be put to the task of writing bible verses over and over on the walls as punishment."

"For what?"

"Being who we were. Papa Bear didn't know I was God, and he didn't know God's name, but I did. And I knew that he was teaching me about Hell. That's what I needed to learn. Ruthie, she got taught that demons can't get driven out. And it—well, my brother—was unfortunate enough to become his father a little too well, I guess. But he always had the Devil in him. In a cage in his mind. I taught him where to put the Devil. How to treat it. How to make it go deep into his tissues. Into a dark part of him that he could lock up for a long time if he wanted."

"Are we headed there?" Trey asked, looking forward, up the road. A sign came up.

Moon Lake, 5 miles

Big Bear, 27 miles

"Moon Lake?" Elise said.

"I'm not telling. Not yet. Just keep driving. I love this old road. Look, see how there's a kind of embankment to the left, and to the right, just a little roll space into the woods and then down the mountainside? It's so beautiful here. It's not like the main highway. This is where old-timers used to go up. This is how I knew the route when I was little, because when the social worker finally took me out, noticing how I had cigarette burns on my stomach, this is the road she took. And I thought: this is just so beautiful. So secret. Why would anyone take 18 when they could take this lovely loopy road?"

"There was no investigation," Trey said. "A social worker got you out of there. But there was no investigation."

"Why should there be?" Scoleri said. "Papa Bear killed himself a few years later. I never talked. I never squealed on people who were good to me. You work at a state hospital for crazy killers. But if you had other jobs, you might understand. Not all social workers are the good kind. Some have problems of their own. This one, the one who really adored me and was worried about me, he was a good family man; he was a good upright man from San Pascal. Probably someone who lives not far from you, Elise. Maybe down the block for all I know. But he liked the unfortunate little boys who understood him. He got off on our sad little tales. But he didn't like to write them up. He didn't like to take action. Maybe because he had more to hide than anyone knew. I don't know. I never got to know him all that well. But do you know the saddest thing about this sad, sad story of Ruthie and my Devil brother?"

Trey hated to admit it, but Scoleri's story fascinated him. "What?"

"Ruthie got buried alive in the Mad Place. She never made it out of there. I used to hear her sometimes. Just screaming. Screaming. Then she got real quiet. So quiet it was as if she had never existed at all."

CHAPTER FIFTY-ONE

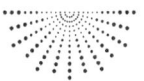

FASTEAU REMAINED SILENT THE REST OF THE WAY UP THE mountain. Snow slanted as it fell. Jane could feel the pressure of the wind on the car in a gentle tugging. She wondered who the child was who had just been found. She thought about Elise Conroy, about having met her briefly in a meeting that Tryon had with her on Friday, soon after the first victim had been found. About the coincidence of a consulting psychiatrist being someone whose child would be kidnapped. Wondered how Conroy might hook up to the Red Angel—why her son? Why that morning? Why just a few days after the first victim? Had someone seen her? Had the killer known that she was consulting? How was she connected to the other parents? She wasn't, really. She was just another unknown neighbor in the nicer parts of San Pascal. If the water delivery theory was right, she was just another unfortunate customer of the Moon Lake Pure Spring Water Company of Moon Lake, California.

How many were there in San Pascal? A thousand households that took Moon Lake Water? Some had to take Arrowhead or one of the other competitors. How many children were potential targets for this guy just because they got that particular brand of bottled water?

She closed her eyes for just a moment, the images of the children's faces going through her mind.

Speak to me.

Tell me what you know.

She felt ridiculous for thinking it. Something in her mind wanted to relax, wanted to listen to the dead children.

Tell me what you saw. Who he is. Where he is.

Is he a friend? Did he grab you? Did he force you? Did he take your hand? Does your mother know him? Were you frightened?

She almost didn't want to know the answers to the question.

LAYMON AND FASTEAU arrived in Moon Lake by dark, and the snow continued to fall. It was not a fierce storm, nor was it a blizzard by any measure, but the snow had begun piling up on the roadside, drifts rising along the fir-lined drive up to Moon Lake itself, and the police car slid now and then on patches of black ice on the pockmarked road up to the small town center.

"Some town," Fasteau said. "Reminds me of *Deliverance*. Squeal like a peeg."

"I think it's cute," she said. "Want a cup of coffee?"

CHAPTER FIFTY-TWO

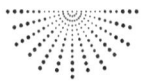

"Ruthie died," Trey said. "Were you sad?"

"You're not in my head yet, Trey," Scoleri said. He looked a Trey with a strangely sympathetic expression. If Trey didn't know his record, he would've thought that Scoleri was actually warm-blooded. *He really believes he's Abraxas. Some god of the universe. Some great omnipotent power. Like out of a comic book: the archvillain. Not the God of the Bible and the Koran and the Torah. Not the deities of other religions. He is some kind of amalgam of religious belief and comic books. He had made up his sense of who he was from childhood things: the religion he'd been tortured with, and a child's sense of power over others.*

"I'd like to get into your head more," Trey said.

"Cool, as they say."

"Help me do that."

Trey side-glanced at Elise. She was listening carefully, but having to be equally careful about the turns in the road. It zigzagged as it followed the mountain too closely, and the Volvo bounced as it went over one of several bumps in the old road.

"The easiest way to get in my head is for me to read your mind."

"Feel free."

"You don't believe I can do it. That I can hear what people are thinking. What they're about."

"I do believe," Trey said.

"Liar," Scoleri laughed. "That was a half-assed effort to get into my pants, Trey. How do you think I know what our Red Angel is up to?"

"I don't know. Maybe it's because you're Abraxas. God of All."

"Maybe," Scoleri smiled.

"What is he up to right now?"

"This minute?"

"Yes."

"He's trying to keep the Devil in him at bay. He's got him in a chapel of the damned, with an angel and a virgin and me, his God. But it's got bad stuff in it too. It's the heart of the Mad Place. It's a place in the earth where Papa Bear kept us. Down, down, down. When the world ends, it's the safest place to be. That's what Papa Bear thought. That's what he believed. Some nut had built it before Papa Bear ever owned it. It was a bomb shelter. Under the house, but you can't get there from the house anymore. You have to go down this little path to it. We lived down there almost all the time. When Papa Bear got his feeling about the end of the world. Just the kids. He thought we should stay there when the world ended. But it's a place between Heaven and Hell, and Lucas is there. Sweet, pure Lucas. The Devil wants to stop little Lucas's breath. But the human part of him wants to baptize the boy. To sanctify him so that the Devil can't get to him. You see, he hasn't been killing them because he is evil. That's the good in him. He wants to baptize them and then put them to sleep. A gentle sleep. He wants them to go to Heaven. Before the Devil in him can come out and devour them whole. The Devil is getting stronger in him. He can't control it anymore. But he wants to change, you see. That's why he's giving me his little angels. He wants me to know. He wants forgiveness."

Without wanting to, Trey let down his guard. He felt as if something was wrong. Something terrible within himself. As if, just staring at Scoleri, he'd begun thinking like him. Imagining some shadow man baptizing Lucas Conroy, wet fingers on the boy's forehead.

Scoleri looked out the window suddenly, as if in the darkness, which had deepened with each minute, he'd see something there. Something on the roadside.

Trey saw it too. A light in the woods on a rocky overhang.

So close to Moon Lake. *That's where he is. He lives in Moon Lake.*

Trey had been through it once or twice growing up. Didn't know it well, other than it was a redneck outpost of the San Bernardino Mountains. Friendly, quiet, but not particularly charming. He drank the Moon Lake Spring Water sometimes too.

When Scoleri turned to look at him again, Trey's mind flashed on the gun.

Scoleri's face had changed, somehow.

He's a chameleon.

It had gone from that boyish, innocent look to something that seemed, in the shadowy light of the car, like a vampire from a horror movie. He had a smile on his face, but it was too broad. Too knowing. His eyes did that trick—of blurred, rapid movement, as if he were not entirely human.

And then, faster than Trey realized, Scoleri's entire face became a blur as it moved too rapidly toward his own.

CHAPTER FIFTY-THREE

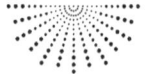

Scoleri slammed his head as hard as he could into Trey Campbell's forehead.

Campbell flailed backward, the back of his scalp hitting the window of the car door.

In the front seat, Elise Conroy cried out, and Scoleri moved so swiftly that it seemed to Elise that no human being could do that.

One thought shot through her mind: *What have I done?*

She felt his teeth tearing at the nape of her neck.

Twisted the steering wheel.

Reached for the glove compartment to the right, but had to get her hand back on the wheel.

The road seemed to shoot out in the opposite direction.

The car spun on the ice and slush.

From the road, if someone were watching, they'd see a Volvo spin on the narrow road, barely missing going to the right, downward along the mountainside. Instead, it spun to the left, into the embankment, and then slid down into the woods, along a stream that ran just beneath the next curve of the road.

The sound of airbags popping.

No sound at all for a very long time.

The snow was soft and deep along the embankment. It added a cushion of quiet to the night around it.

AFTER SEVERAL MINUTES, a man kicks the door open with his feet, which are cuffed. His forehead and scalp are bloody.

He bends his knees, arching his spine as he lies across the backseat. His legs seem to twist back on themselves like they're made of rubber. He moves his arms down, so far that they seem to dislocate from the shoulder. His spine continues to arch, and it is as if he will bend over backward from the lying down position.

And then, swiftly, his arms rise up in front of him. Cuffs remain on.

He slides forward. Gets out of the car.

He goes around to the driver's side door. Opens it with some difficulty.

A woman is frantically trying to undo her shoulder harness. Her legs are trapped.

The man with the cuffs on his feet and on his hands leans into her.

Over her face.

Whispers something.

For the barest second, there is a scream, a woman's, but it is muffled, just as the sounds of the forest and mountain are muffled with the heavy coat of snow.

The man appears to be going to work with his bare hands on the woman's face.

CHAPTER FIFTY-FOUR

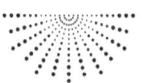

TREY CAMPBELL LIES LIKE A BROKEN DOLL IN THE BACKSEAT. An enormous bruise on his forehead, blood all along his scalp and running along his ears, down his neck.

His eyes are closed, but he is breathing.

In the front seat, Elise Conroy squirms as Michael Scoleri holds her down using his body weight, holding his hands over her nose and mouth until she is very, very still.

Rummaging through her purse, flung on the other side of the Volvo, he finds a small pair of fingernail scissors.

He returns to the dead woman in the driver's seat.

He wants something to remember her by.

CHAPTER FIFTY-FIVE

WHEN THEY CHECKED IN WITH THE LOCAL DEPUTY AT THE trailer just at the beginning of town, Jane let Fasteau ask all the questions about Duane Cobble because she knew Fasteau's masculinity and ego needed some stroking after her complaints about his driving on the way up the mountain. The cop on duty had nothing but nice things to say about Duane, although one comment stuck in Jane's mind after she and Fasteau went back to their car: "The Cobbles always kept to themselves since Duane's dad died." By itself, it was not a very damning comment, but given the nature of the visit, it planted a warning in Jane's head.

She and Fasteau drove around the rim of the lake, with the snow and ice increasing with each mile. The Cobble place was twelve miles around the lake.

When they arrived at the house, the only one with a front porch light on, Fasteau said, "Holy shit."

SHE GLANCED through the darkness and falling snow, to the small cabins that were off a bit in the woods.

A main house, hardly more than a cabin itself. Lights came from its windows. An old junk heap of a Monte Carlo that looked like it was at least twenty years old and had never been maintained sat in the driveway. Out in a clearing, an old truck up on cinderblocks, its doors completely taken off.

Six smaller one-room cabins in a semicircle in the woods.

Some kind of graying arched sign over the drive in, but the darkness obscured it.

"It's the Bates Motel."

"I doubt we can take a guy in just because he looks like he lives like a crazy person," Jane said.

"Yeah, true. Everyone I saw back in that town looks like a loon. Including the deputy."

The headlights cast a beautiful but disturbing brightness across the falling snow, through the pines that edged the property, and the thick woods beyond. They were at the edge of a hillock that went downward right behind the last cabin.

"This really is Bumfuck, Egypt," Fasteau said.

"Looks like this place has been going to the dogs for years."

A light on in the main house.

They parked on the side of the road and both got out. "We're going to be stuck here all night," Fasteau said. "We may have to rent one of these cabins. Just the two of us."

"Tell you what, you get a cabin. I'll go back and take my chances with the icy roads."

CHAPTER FIFTY-SIX

Trey opened his eyes, briefly.

Thought he heard a snipping sound.

Fought for consciousness. *Elise?*

We fucked up, he thought.

Then he felt himself drifting back into a cold sleep.

CHAPTER FIFTY-SEVEN

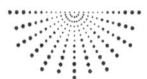

THE GUY WHO OPENED THE DOOR LOOKED TO JANE LIKE HE had just woken up from a nap.

"Can I help you?"

She got the preliminaries out of the way, just the basics of *show the badge, don't get his suspicions up, and see if he has anything to say,* or if she could notice anything in the house itself.

He made no move toward inviting her in, and she didn't have any legal way to get in unless he invited her. She wondered, briefly, how Sykes and Tryon were doing down in the valley.

"My mother's been sick," he said.

"I'm sorry to hear that, Mr. Cobble."

"Well, it's been a long time coming. She's in her room, but she's sleeping."

"Well, this won't take long."

Jane glanced around the modest home. It was a bit of a mess, and a dog, that was so old it practically was dragging its own hindquarters when it got up, came over to her. Fasteau remained behind her, standing by the door.

"We're just checking in with people from the Moon Lake Water Company."

"Is there a reason?"

"Routine. You've probably seen the news?"

His face betrayed nothing. He was a big man, a little weary looking and frayed about the edges, but looked like your basic big dumb guy. Nothing felt different around him, she got no sense of weirdness or hesitation in his part.

"I don't watch the news much. We don't got cable. Our reception sucks."

"Well, as you may know, there's a little boy who's missing. We're just talking to anyone who has come in contact with this boy to see if we can learn anything, or if there might be a witness to where he might've gone." She stumbled over her words, but had tried to be careful not to inform too much.

She watched his eyes. Either he was very good at this, or he was completely innocent.

"Geez, that's terrible. Do I know this kid?"

"He's on your Tuesday, Thursday route. His name is Lucas Conroy."

Fasteau drew the photo out of his coat. He passed it to Duane Cobble, who looked at it, nodding. "He's a nice little kid too. I know the Conroys," he nodded. "I didn't know his name, but that kid was really nice. What a terrible thing. I hope nothing's happened. Maybe it's … I mean, I hear a lot about divorced fathers kidnapping their own children."

Small alarm in her head: he mentioned the word "kidnapping" and she had not. She had just said "missing." This might mean nothing. But it might mean something. "Well, we didn't mean to bother you without calling first," she said, a minor-league lie. "But I was over at the distribution plant, and thought I might just drop by."

"Three other guys do my route," he said. "But they're all good guys. You think maybe one of them did this? No. No way. None of them could do that kind of thing. I don't think it was one of us."

"I don't think it was either, Mr. Cobble. We're trying to find out if anyone saw anything unusual recently in the Conroys' neighborhood. Any unusual activity. Or cars parked on the street. Anything you might've noticed or heard."

"Nope," he said after a moment. "I can't think of anything. I am sorry to hear about this. I had no idea. What a terrible world. I hope it turns out happy, like when they found that little girl in Utah a while back. I'll pray for his return."

He stood there, lingering, with his hand on the edge of the doorframe. He wanted to close it.

∾

JANE FELT something click in her head.

Something wasn't right. She wasn't sure what.

She glanced back at Fasteau, who stood behind and next to her.

Then looked back to Duane Cobble.

She wished she could tell Fasteau what she was thinking. She wasn't sure if she should say good-bye, make a retreat to the car, and then just phone this one in or not.

If you do, and it's nothing, you'll have wasted a lot of people's time.

If you want to go, go big.

Aim true.

She went with her instinct.

∾

"WOULD you mind if we came inside, Mr. Cobble? It's freezing out here, and we can probably speak more comfortably ... you might be able to provide us with some insight into your coworkers." *There,* she thought. *That sounded good.*

If he were innocent, he wouldn't really mind either way.

If he were guilty, he had to invite them in.

He had no choice.

CHAPTER FIFTY-EIGHT

IT HEARS SOMETHING IN ITS HEAD.

Not the Devil.

It sounds like Abraxas. Just for a second.

Like Abraxas trying to talk to it.

It watches the two cops. They don't look much like cops, but it knows cops well.

It watches the woman especially. She is a tall woman and looks like she could beat somebody up.

The man doesn't scare him that much.

It opens the door wider, letting them into its house.

The Devil starts to gnash its teeth inside its head, but it keeps control.

It will get through this. It is sure it can.

As the woman cop speaks, she's looking all over the room. Looking for things. *For stuff.*

Looking for something that will make her know that it holds the Beast inside it.

It speaks perfectly normal, like it does sometimes when it needs to mimic the way people talk. It tells them about the weather, and how bad the snow is for its mother's arthritis, how it always flares up when temperatures drop. It tells them about its girl, Monica, even though it calls her its wife just to seem more respectable.

It even makes a joke with the man about "women," and it can tell that it pisses off the woman cop too much, so it makes another little joke about how men think they're so smart when in reality women run the world. It mentions the baby that was coming. It is going to be a father, it says

But the woman's eyes bother it. She has sharp eyes, like little scalpels, and she slices away at the edge of things when she looks at them.

She's a whore. She's a whore, and you can't trust whores.

"Is your mother asleep?" she asks.

"Yes, ma'am. She's sleeping through the night. She has her supper and then pretty much is down for the count."

"I'm sorry to hear about her illness, Duane."

She calls it by its first name, and that makes it uncomfortable. What else does she know about it?

Does she know God too? Has she been to see Mikey? Has he talked about it to her?

No. Mikey is Abraxas the all-powerful. The secret name of God. He'd never talk to a whore about it.

Never.

Her eyes again. It watches where she looks. The mantel. The fireplace. Jojo. The sofa. The magazines piled on the floor.

It holds its breath for a moment, unsure what to say to get them out.

The Other One begins to snarl louder.

The Beast wants out of the cage in its brain.

The Devil wants to leap out at them.

Not yet. Not now. They'll leave. It'll be okay.

"My mother was sick for a while," the woman says. "It's rough when it's your mother. It's just very tough to get through."

"Did she die?"

"No. She survived. Breast cancer."

It doesn't like either of those words. The Devil likes them. But it hates them.

"She underwent chemo," she keeps talking as if pretending that she can't tell that the Other One is coming out inside him, taking him over bit by bit, rising up in his blood like a tea kettle about to whistle. She pretends not to notice, and so does the other cop. But it knows that they are pretending. "It was rough. But she pulled through, and she beat it."

Without meaning to, it says, "My mother's got the C-word too."

"Oh," she says. "Well, she'll be in my prayers."

It is getting that biting feeling inside it. Like it wants to attack. Like a lion.

Like the Devil.

"She's got nurses who come in and see her," it says, wishing it could stop, but something in the woman cop makes it feel almost like it has to talk about this. "But I don't think there's much hope."

"Hospice?"

"Sort of," it says.

"Well, I don't want to waste any more of your time," she says.

It feels relief at her words.

"Officer Fasteau?" she turns to the man.

"Thank you. We'll be in touch later on," the man cop says.

It returns to the door with them.

When it closes the door, locking it, the Other One takes over.

CHAPTER FIFTY-NINE

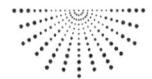

OUTSIDE, WALKING THROUGH THE SNOW, BACK TO THE ENTRY to the dirt driveway, the two police officers didn't say a word. Jane felt the excitement inside her, tempered with fear.

"I think we have him," she said as she reached for the passenger door.

"I know," Fasteau said, going around the front of the car, headlights still on, snowing coming down. "Once Tryon—"

And that's when Jane heard what seemed like an enormous *boom*, as if a bomb had been dropped down in the valley.

A rifle's blast.

Fasteau was blown back, first against the hood of the car, and then onto the road.

It happened so fast, she didn't even process it, but acted on instinct.

She reached for her Glock, but as she pulled it up, she felt nervous and scared in a way that she never had before.

She ran around the back of the car to use it as some kind of shield.

She shot into the darkness but could not see Duane Cobble—or anyone. She could only see along the line of the headlights, but beyond that, the house had gone dark.

The snow was affecting her vision, but her fear seemed to intensify—her heart raced; she worked to keep her breathing from becoming too rapid, kept telling herself to slow down, to look, to wait. Her mind went blank, and she wondered if she would get out of this alive. As quickly as she could, she glanced behind her, to the road and lake beyond. Many miles away, across the lake, she could barely see the lights of the small town of Moon Lake.

Someone might've heard the sound.

Surely they would've.

How long would it take for someone to come over here?

Could she get to the radio fast enough?

She ruled that out. She held her gun as steadily as she could.

She shouted, "Duane Cobble! Put down your weapon and put your hands over your head!"

She leaned to her left, putting her weight on her left knee.

Fasteau was still. Dead at the edge of the headlight's beam.

Blood on the snow.

"Shit," she whispered.

Visibility worsened as the snow picked up, and she felt as if she'd been crouching behind the car for several minutes, although she suspected only seconds had passed.

Where is he? Christ. Where the fuck are you, Duane?

She tried to focus on the darkness, but the bright headlights kept her eyes from adjusting to the dark.

Was that him? The darkness against darkness that moved?

"Put down your weapon right now!" she screamed as loud as she could.

It wasn't him. It was just the fir trees themselves, shaking off clumps of snow.

She could hear each of her own breaths, as if she had asthma in her lungs.

Her heartbeat seemed too loud.

She wanted to hold her breath but knew that would not make this go any easier for her.

She heard a whooshing sound, as if something were moving swiftly toward her

From the right? She looked to the right and saw a blurred shadow in the dark, and for the barest second thought she saw him—

And then something heavy hit her hard on the back right side of her scalp.

CHAPTER SIXTY

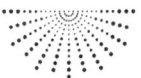

"Whore," it whispers.

It sets the hunting rifle on the trunk of the car.

Then it goes around to the driver's side of the car to turn off the headlights.

CHAPTER SIXTY-ONE

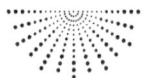

IN THE MAD PLACE, IT FINISHES TYING UP THE COP WOMAN, duct-taping her mouth, wrapping her up tight, checking ropes behind the chair to make sure she can't wriggle out of them.

Then over to Lucas, who was unconscious for a long time. Its mother's pills help them sleep. That's what they need, the little birds. *Sleep.* When the pills don't work, it uses the syringe. But Lucas didn't need the morphine. The pills work fine.

Lucas takes another little white pill from its hand like a good boy. The boy curls up almost in a ball on the dirty mattress near the statue of the virgin. Lucas no longer needs to be tied. No longer needs tape over his mouth. The Mad Place had sends him into another realm in his mind. He is halfway between Heaven and Hell.

As it wants him to be.

IT IS all going to be okay. It is going to work out fine for it.

Brother. It hears the voice in its head.

It turns around.

Someone is in the Mad Place with it.

Someone scratching around the entryway.

And then it sees Abraxas.

God of All.

Its brother.

"DUANE," Michael Scoleri said from the flickering shadows at the doorway into the Mad Place.

It is shocked, standing there, duct tape in one hand.

"Abraxas," it says.

"I heard your prayers. Your messages." Abraxas's beauty is extreme and frightening. Even though it knows not to fear, it can't help but be afraid. "In you, there is greatness. But you must set it free."

"Free?" it asks.

"The Beast. The Devil. The end of days is at hand," Abraxas says, and comes over to embrace him. "Within you, greatness."

"I wasn't sure if you heard me."

"I always will hear you," Abraxas says. "I know all. I see all."

"Why come here?"

Abraxas spreads his arms out wide.

It trembles slightly at the beauty of its brother.

"You have given me angels. And sacrifice," Abraxas says in the sweetest voice that it has ever heard. "I can't stay long. You know that. I must return to Heaven. But first, go home. Get your rifle. You will need it. Others are coming. You know they will. I have only a few moments here, then I must leave. But first, I want to spend those moments with this woman. This sacrifice."

It understands. It looks over at the cop woman tied to the chair.

She is still out. It hit her too hard. But it doesn't care. It should've killed her, but feels glad now it didn't.

She will be a sacrifice to God.

CHAPTER SIXTY-TWO

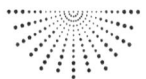

WHEN JANE WOKE UP, SHE DIDN'T KNOW HOW MUCH TIME
had passed. She was in the stone room, bound to a chair. Lights
flickered above her. She had to orient herself somehow. She barely
remembered what had happened at the Cobble house, but then it
came back to her suddenly.

Fasteau's dead.

Rope wrapped around her. Her hands cuffed behind her. Duct
tape over her mouth.

A man crouched down in front of her. His hands on her knees.

It wasn't Cobble.

This one had a boyish look to him but was in his late twenties.
Cobble had a helper?

He leaned into her, and she felt his coldness as he touched the
edge of her face.

He ripped the duct tape from her lips.

"I want to hear you when I take my memento," he said.

Then he kissed her on the lips. Before she had a chance to bite
him, he moved his lips up her cheek.

He whispered, "Your beautiful dark eyes."

He pressed himself against her.

It sickened her.

And then she felt his tongue across her eyelid.

And she knew.

"Beautiful darkness," he whispered.

She used her weight to pivot back, but his weight held her in place.

He liked the power.

She tried to go somewhere else in her mind.

Tried to prepare for what this madman was about to do to her.

And then she felt the suction of his lips against the eyelid of her left eye.

She could not help it.

She screamed.

And screamed.

The pain shot through her like a knife to the skull.

CHAPTER SIXTY-THREE

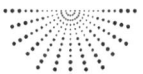

Jane's body went slack.

Scoleri undid her ropes. He lifted her up, holding her to him. She smelled so wonderful. She smelled like pain itself.

Her mind was free. The pain had driven it away for the moment.

Her suffering was fresh.

He kissed her lips and set her down on the mattress, beside the little boy who stared at him without moving.

"Madonna and child," Scoleri said.

Then he went back up to the house to see if he could borrow Duane's car.

It was time for Abraxas to get out into the world.

CHAPTER SIXTY-FOUR

Trey opened his eyes. Looked up. The interior ceiling of the car.

Then a rush of air filled his lungs along with a clutching fear.

He sat up, and as he did so felt a hammering pain in his head. Instinctively, he touched the top of his scalp.

Wet.

Blood.

He had been crammed into an uncomfortable position.

Mother of all migraines pounding at him.

He collected his thoughts.

Deep breath.

Remembered going off the road.

He saw Elise's hair falling over the back of the seat.

It took him minutes to find the strength to sit up.

Scoleri, gone.

Shit.

"Elise," he said, but his voice was like a croak.

No answer.

"Elise. Elise."

He felt strength in his arms again, despite the soreness. He could move his legs. Felt circulation come back into his extremities.

He rose up completely and slid along the car seat.

He looked over the edge of Elise's scalp.

Blood.

Shit.

Got out of the car on uncertain legs. Had to hold the car door for balance.

The driver's door was open wide.

The deflated airbag.

Elise, the steering column pressing down on her legs.

"Jesus," he gasped, and fell over into the snow on his hands and knees, retching.

He could not get it out of his head.

Her face.

What had been done to it.

What Scoleri had done.

His handiwork.

The Handyman, he'd been called before he'd been convicted and sent to Darden State.

Of course you didn't get me. Didn't kill me. You only go for women and kids. Only when they're vulnerable. Only when you know they can't fight back.

You wanted me to see this. That's half your fun. You wanted me to see what a monster you are.

You wanted me to get inside your mind.

Well, I'm there, you sick fuck.

Scoleri had taken both of Elise Conroy's eyes.

~

AFTER CLENCHED FISTS, tears that would not come, and a terrible feeling of helplessness had seized his gut, and then the feeling passed, Trey knew what he must do.

Checked his wristwatch: *ten p.m.*

Lost too much time.

Unconscious a couple of hours.

The cell phone, out. He checked the trunk of the Volvo. Flashlight. That was it.

Checked the glove compartment.

Elise's revolver, still there.

He took it, slipping it into his coat pocket.

Lucas, he thought. *Get help. Get cops. Get Lucas.*

With the flashlight, looked around the snow-covered woods.

Up the embankment.

Up the curve in the road ahead.

A light emanated from within the trees.

A clearing?

Apprehensive, Trey stumbled over the irregular ground, across rocks, up to the roadside.

Dark as all hell.

He went toward the light in the forest, feeling an urgency and a numbness in his mind that was not from the pain at the front of his forehead where Scoleri had slammed him, nor from the bitter cold of the high elevation of the mountain road where it turned up toward Moon Lake.

A numbness about life itself.

It took him nearly a half-hour to get up the road toward the light, and then just a few minutes as he trudged through the snow.

When he first saw it, he wasn't sure what to make of it.

Shining the light along the entrance.

What Scoleri had said. Scoleri hadn't lied at all. Scoleri knew.

It's a place in the earth where Papa Bear kept us. Down, down,

down. When the world ends, it's the safest place to be. That's what Papa Bear thought. That's what he believed. Some nut had built it before Papa Bear ever owned it. It was a bomb shelter. Under the house, but you couldn't get there from the house anymore. You had to go down this little path to it. We lived down there almost all the time. When Papa Bear got his feeling about the end of the world. Just the kids. He thought we should stay there when the world ended.

CHAPTER SIXTY-FIVE

IT SEEMED SURREAL, LIKE SOMETHING OUT OF A FAIRYTALE like "Hansel and Gretel."

Through the gap in the trees, a thin path, now simply an indentation of white upon white snow. It led to what seemed to be a rock overhang, a crevasse. Three large lights had been set up in trees to light up the rocky area. *He's not hiding. Not in the way you'd think. He's not afraid of anyone. Or else ... or else he wants to be caught. That's all it is. He wants to be caught.*

Trey had to calm his breathing. He felt as if he were close to Lucas.

Above the crevasse, a thick roof-rock, and above that, perched on the jutting mountainside, a small cabin. But in the indentation of granite was what appeared to be a small door—almost a trapdoor.

As he approached the door, he noticed that it was made of some kind of metal, and curved outward at the center, almost like a shield. Someone had made a bomb shelter out of the crevasse. This was somewhat unusual, but Trey had seen a bomb shelter built in the early 1960s during the Cuban Missile Crisis and the nuclear war fears of that time in a friend's backyard as a kid growing up in San Bernardino.

He had read, in magazines and online, about bomb shelters built into caves and caverns, but had never seen one before. He went to the door and pulled on it. It was latched, but not locked.

He's not afraid. He takes them down here. But he's not afraid. Of course not. He thinks he knows God. He thinks he has the Devil in him. He thinks he can make angels.

Trey stood over the entrance into the cavern, the metal door open.

For a moment, he felt the way he had when standing outside Program 28's corridor.

HE SHONE the flashlight through the doorway.

The entry area was not flat. It dipped down nearly immediately. It was dark, and he could hear water splashing from within.

As he positioned the light's beam around the entry, he saw a hanging work lamp—barely more than a bulb fitted within a protective cup of metal. He reached over to it, switching it on. Immediately, it lit up the first several feet of the shelter.

The floor was rough and covered with gravel. Water sluiced across the gravel.

An underground spring.

The ceiling was low and had what were not quite stalactites, but small teats of rock, as if water had been dripping from it over the years, although now it was dry.

A smell came up from within. Not unpleasant, but a kind of gust of humid air.

Some source of heat within the shelter.

He took a step in but turned and glanced back at the snow as it came down.

No one followed him.

Good.

Inside the entrance, he felt more alone that he ever had in his life.

He took another few steps in. The ground slanted downward, and he took care with his steps because of the thin layer of water that rushed along beneath his shoes.

Strangely, it wasn't as cold inside as he thought it should've been.

Warmth. Some source of warmth.

A gently heated breeze came up from within the shelter.

Instinctively, he reached for the rock wall and crouched down a bit, for the ceiling lowered as it went.

Two more steps, and he slipped, falling hard on the ground. He looked at the interior walls. Some kind of limestone along the walls.

Paintings of demons and angels against a yellow blur of what might've been chalk that was meant to imply fire.

Written on the walls, the words:

SUFFER THE CHILDREN TO COME UNTO ME.

TREY REMEMBERED those words on Scoleri's stomach.

What the hell are you doing here?

Can't call the police. Can't get out in the snow.

Lucas is here. I know he's here. I have to find him. I have to get him out.

Something within him that felt more instinctual, bypassing his brains and his fears, took over.

He had a gun, after all.

He had a gun.

The killer of these children was going to be easy to subdue. He was sure. He worked around these people. He knew that the ones who went after children were the weakest of all. Were the least powerful. Were scared of adults. Afraid of what a grown man could do to them.

And even if he was wrong … even if all his experience was in error … all his training … he had to get Lucas out. He had to save him.

He had to make it turn out all right.

As HE WENT FARTHER DOWN the wet floor, he glanced quickly from one wall to the next, recognizing biblical quotes.

End of the world quotes, scrawled across the limestone.

"Then I saw an angel coming down from Heaven, holding in his hand the key of the bottomless pit and a great chain."

"He was cast out into the earth, and his angels were cast out with him."

"But every man is tempted, when he is drawn away of his own lust and enticed."

"Then when lust hath conceived, it bringeth forth sin: and sin, when it is finished, bringeth forth death."

AT A CERTAIN POINT, far enough in that he could still see the light at the entryway behind him, the floor began rising again. Now, he knew what the warm humidity was—somewhere within the shelter there was a hot springs. He had been up to the Arrowhead Hot

Springs before and knew that the underground springs were often fed by this warm or near-boiling water.

Finally, as he went, flashlight in front of him, Trey had to nearly crawl.

This lasted for just a few feet.

Then, having gone upward with the sandy floor, he came into a room that was large enough for him to stand in.

This one was lit with white, blinking Christmas tree lights strung up from its ceiling. Somewhere there was a generator humming.

On the floor, in the corner, piles of cans of tuna and beans and spam and pineapple slices and peach halves and large twenty-gallon blue plastic jugs that were probably filled with water.

This was a survivalist's dream.

Or nightmare.

He saw a pile of something that at first looked like feather dusters, until he got closer. Two sets of white duck wings, freshly cut, with brownish blood at the joints where the cut had been made.

You were here not long ago. You've left. Maybe the snow will keep you out. Maybe you're stuck on the road.

On the wall was a crudely drawn image of Christ on the cross.

Someone has scrawled beneath it: "*And the ten horns which thou sawest upon the beast, these shall hate the whore, and shall make her desolate and naked, and shall eat her flesh, and burn her with fire.*"

He shone his flashlight in all the curves of the room and saw something move in one of the dark corners.

"Lucas?" he whispered. "Lucas?"

And as the beam of light hit what was there, he nearly dropped the flashlight from fright.

CHAPTER SIXTY-SIX

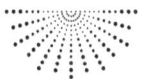

It was a woman of an indeterminate age, bone thin, her arms strapped to her sides with thick rope. Where her legs should've been, there were bandages around what could only be described as stumps. She was pale and looked as if she had spent her life in darkness, for when the light hit her eyes, her eyelids fluttered like moths, rapidly, as if the bright light were too sudden for her.

She made a noise, but it seemed like the bleating of a sheep.

Her mouth was blackened, and he didn't see teeth in it at all.

"Jesus," he gasped and moved toward her.

Her eyes were wide and sunken into their sockets, as if she had been kept moments away from death.

For months.

Or years.

You know enough about the patients to know what the predatory mind is capable of.

He knew from Scoleri's words.

He knew.

But he was afraid to say it aloud.

"Ruthie?"

Her mouth went wide as if she wanted to scream, but a rasping sound came out.

"Dear God," Trey said. *Sweet Jesus.*

He went and undid the ropes that kept her in the chair. Her arms fell at her side, as if they were already useless.

You kept her here all these years. Just like Scoleri said your father had kept her when you were kids. She's never seen the light of day since she was twelve. When your mother thought she had died from a beating. When it was all covered up. Closed up.

But it's still an open wound.

Dear God. Please, God, protect her. Please someone help.

Her scalp was nearly bald, with strands of hair hanging down across her face, which seemed crumpled and misshapen. Her body, what could be seen through the rags that were wrapped around her body like a funerary winding cloth, was covered with sores. Her arms seemed twisted, and because of her extreme emaciation, she seemed old, although he was fairly sure she was only in her twenties.

She began bleating again. A word seemed to form in his mind —what she was trying to say.

He knew in the next moment that it was too late.

She was trying to warn him about something.

Someone.

Her brother.

TREY HEARD the footstep echo in the stone chamber. He turned slightly, not wanting to startle the killer. But wanting to see him. To face him.

Trey felt for the gun in his coat, but even as he did, he thought that it might not be enough to have a gun.

He would have to use it, and use it correctly.

Something he had not done much of.

Always a first time.

CHAPTER SIXTY-SEVEN

It stands just outside the light of the Mad Place.

Ruthie is squealing. *She is a whore! She is the Whore of Babylon! Do not let her hurt you!*

It sees the man. Doesn't know him. Why is he here? Why is all this happening? All these intruders? All this now? Why now? Why just when the Other One is gaining the upper hand?

When the Beast is out and coursing through its bloodstream?

It hates the man as much as it hates itself, and when it sees the side of the man's face it knows that the man must die. Or the man must burn. *That's it. The man must burn for his sins. Burn in the eternal fires of the rivers of Hell.*

CHAPTER SIXTY-EIGHT

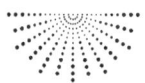

TREY TOUCHED THE GUN.

Began to draw it from his coat pocket.

A blur of movement behind him as the man rushed him.

Trey felt pressure in his side as the man knocked him down.

Got the revolver out.

Sig Sauer. Elise.

The gun went flying out of his hand.

He felt a *crack* of bone along his jaw.

Darkness.

A seeping pain.

Then, *nothing.*

CHAPTER SIXTY-NINE

IT STANDS OVER THE MAN WHO HAD INTRUDED ON THE MAD Place. It glances over at the Whore, and she is trying to lift up her arms, but cannot. She is weak. She moans as she watches it go over to her and crouch down.

It begins pulling the ropes up again, around her arms.

It says nothing to her, to Ruthie, but it knows that Ruthie is somewhere else in her mind. In Hell. Where all of them would be soon.

Once the Beast is out for good.

Then it goes over to tie up the intruder.

CHAPTER SEVENTY

TREY OPENED HIS EYES.

Consciousness came back. He felt like an enormous linebacker had tackled him. He was sore all over. Tasted blood in his mouth.

Saw a slightly overweight man in what looked like a green uniform. The man's back was to him. The jacket he wore had a logo of a lake and trees that read Moon Lake Pure Spring Water.

Duane. Scoleri's brother in foster care. When they were kids. Here, playing in the mountains. Getting punished in this shelter.

Duane refastened the ropes around the pathetic form of his sister.

Trey felt pains in his back and sides but managed to roll up to a sitting position.

He looked around for the gun, but he couldn't see it anywhere along the rock floor.

Have to use my body weight. He's a big guy. Maybe if I get him off-balance.

Duane turned, hearing the sound of his movement.

CHAPTER SEVENTY-ONE

IT FEELS THE OTHER ONE IN THE CAGE. IT OPENS THE CAGE to let the Other One out.

The Beast is coming.

It is coming inside his head.

It is burning through its brain to get out and use its flesh to tear the intruder.

It only feels the Beast inside it now.

Its hands seem like the claws of a lion.

Its feet seem to move in a blur of motion, as if it is flying to the intruder.

CHAPTER SEVENTY-TWO

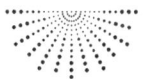

TREY STAYED DOWN AS DUANE CAME RUNNING AT HIM. *WITH the patients, you lean forward so they come for your face in front of you. When they're close enough, you pull back quickly. They're off guard. The way Scoleri did it in the car. The way he got you.*

Duane did what Trey expected—went for the face. Having some delusionary idea that many of the patients at Darden State had—that all power was in the face, in the eyes, in the brain. When Duane did this, his hands outstretched to attack, Trey rocked back, maintaining his balance. Duane's eyes widened as he realized that he was going to tip over Trey instead of hitting him. Trey slid to the left. Duane tumbled to the ground. Trey swiftly moved on top of him, a knee to Duane's back.

From Duane's mouth, growling like a dog.

Using extreme force, Trey pressed Duane's face against the rock floor, focusing all his own weight into Duane's back, but staying clear of his legs. Duane would probably, in another moment, use his hands and a push from his knees to throw Trey off, but Trey reached and got his flashlight fast and slammed it down as hard as he could on Duane's head.

Duane was out.

For the moment.

Trey breathed too fast. He tried to calm himself from within, with a brief mantra that was little more than, *Easy, easy.* He dragged the unconscious Duane over toward Ruth. Then he swiftly undid the ropes again around Ruth's arms. She had already begun screaming, and it echoed through the chamber like a high-pitched shriek.

Duane was just coming around. He looked up at Trey.

CHAPTER SEVENTY-THREE

IT WILL KILL HIM AND DRINK HIS BLOOD! IT WILL SACRIFICE HIM like it did the little angels!

It summons its Devil strength, and it pushes up, feeling nothing but a redness within its body, a firepower that comes from Hell, and it knows that its daddy was right, that it would be the end of the world, that it and Ruthie would one day be set out on their paths to destroying the world.

It swings its elbow into the intruder's ribs.

CHAPTER SEVENTY-FOUR

THE FORCE OF THE BLOW KNOCKED TREY BACK. THE ROPE
went flying.

Duane was up, and Trey had to dodge him quickly.

Jesus, he's strong.

Trey quickly glanced around for the gun, hoping to see it in the
twinkling white glow of Christmas lights.

He felt a swift kick to his groin. Trey doubled over, feeling
nausea and pain.

Then a kick to his head.

Duane stood over him.

Something in his hand.

What? Trey could not quite make it out because Duane's hands
were shaking so much. It looked as if Duane were about to explode,
if that were humanly possible, as if something were boiling in his
blood.

Trey realized it, and then his first thought was, *Lucas, I'm sorry.*

"Cocksucker!" Duane shouted. "You don't mess with the Devil.
I am going to send your soul to my homeland! You think you

know what Hell is! You don't know what Hell is! Fucking worm, you are going to burn for eternity! And when you feel the fires inside you and the worms in your eyes and the cold darkness around you, you will know that you are an it! You are an it, and an it means shit and you live in shit and you will die in shit and you will burn in shit!"

His hands clutched a gun. Not the Sig Sauer. This looked like a Glock.

He doesn't know how to use it. He doesn't quite know.

Then Duane began lowing like a cow, alternating with bellowing and a sound like a child crying from deep within his body. He became racked with coughs, but he kept the gun, unsteady as his hands were, on Trey.

Ruth made a noise, a keening sound. Trey looked over, and she rocked back and forth. Falling forward with a clattering racket.

Distracted for a moment, Duane glanced at her.

As he did so, a shot rang out.

Trey saw, in a second, a brief flare of light burst from Duane's gun as it fired. He saw Ruth crawling on her hands, dragging her torso along as if it were dead weight.

Duane's jacket sprayed blood.

TREY FELT numb all over his body, but found that he could stand. He wasn't shot.

Duane had missed him.

From behind him, from the narrow corridor of stone, a woman in a police uniform emerged, a gun in her hand. She held it in front of her.

Elise Conroy's gun.

The policewoman clutched the gun. Her left eye was bloodied

and the eyelid swollen shut. Blood covered half her face. She shivered nearly as much as Duane had been.

Then she collapsed to the floor.

Trey heard sounds like mewling coming from Ruthie, who went to her brother, laying her body across his.

But Duane was not dead.

He might be able to get up again.

Before even checking on the collapsed police officer, Trey grabbed the ropes and crawled over to where Ruthie hugged her brother. As gently as he could, Trey drew Ruthie back. She fought against him, feebly, but moved away from Duane.

Not a lot of blood was coming out of Duane's wound, so he assumed that was good. Duane would be caught. He'd go to jail.

Probably end up in Darden State.

Michael Scoleri, already driving into the valley in Duane Cobble's crappy car, pulled over, feeling an intense headache.

Pounding at him.

He put the truck in park and left the engine idling. He leaned against the wall of a liquor store at the edge of a strip mall.

Something in his head seemed to be triggering a massive headache.

He felt he heard Duane Cobble's voice in his head again.

Just a brief flicker of a voice.

Then it was out.

The words he heard in his mind:

Help me, Abraxas. Mikey. God.

CHAPTER SEVENTY-FIVE

In the bomb shelter, with Duane safely tied up and Ruthie lying nearby—hardly a threat—Trey returned to check on female police officer.

"Thank God," Jane whispered, her voice raspy. "Thank God. I thought I'd die here." Although she seemed to have been beaten up, and he soon discovered that her eye had been pulled out, there was an unusual optimism in her voice.

"You're going to be fine."

"They're monsters. Those men. Monsters."

Trey couldn't respond. It was too soon.

He was afraid to ask about Lucas. He was afraid to hear from this woman that all of this had been a waste.

"The boy," she said. She pointed back to the narrow space between the walls.

"Alive?"

"Scared. Alive. Maybe drugged."

"It's all right. You don't have to talk anymore. It's all right."

"Go. Go. Tell him. Tell him it's all right. Go." She pushed him weakly. "Up. Up above. On the hillside, a house. Car. Phone. Police radio. We're beneath it. The house."

Just above. The Mad Place was between Heaven and Hell.

"Go. I'm fine. Fine," she repeated.

She was not fine, but because he wanted to make sure Lucas was okay, he leaned her against the wall.

Then he retrieved his flashlight and went into the narrow, dark stone corridor.

He had to press himself against the rock.

When he arrived on the other side, it was, again, dimly lit with the strung lights. This was more like a room, and even had a metal ladder at its center going up into what looked like a gap in rocks just a few feet above his head.

But the layout of the room made him gasp.

Stone statues, as if for either a chapel or a graveyard, were laid out in three of the roughly sliced corners of the room. The one that drew his eye immediately was of a stone angel; another of the Virgin Mother; and finally, one of Christ, his hands spread out in front of him.

He remembered Scoleri's words: *a chapel of the damned, with an angel and a virgin and a statue of me, his God. But it's got bad stuff in it too. It's the heart of the Mad Place.*

They had been defaced with some dark substance. He could guess what it might be.

He hoped it wasn't blood.

The room's floor was rougher than the outer room and covered with pebbles. At its center, a small bubbling pool of steamy water. A hot springs. There must be several in the caverns.

The waters come up from Hell, Scoleri had said.

And there, gone fetal in a corner, his knees tucked up against his face, his arms wrapped around his knees, Lucas Conroy.

"It's all right now," Trey said, softly but firmly. "Lucas. We're going to get help."

The boy stirred and looked over at him. His eyes reddened and surrounded with dark circles. His look, blank. He was in another world.

Been drugged. Trey wasn't sure what it might be, but he'd seen drugged people before. *Darden State patients.*

"Your mother sent me," Trey said and went to lift Lucas up in his arms.

As Trey did so, he took in the scrawls on the walls of the chamber: devil faces and drawings of little children with angel's wings around their necks.

CHAPTER SEVENTY-SIX

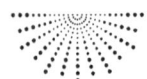

FEELING RAGGED, TREY CRADLED THE BOY IN HIS ARMS AS IF he were his own son. He walked the hundred or so yards to the roadside. The crunch of fresh snow under his shoes felt good and pure.

He'd been feeling the filth of the life that the Red Angel had at his core. He intuited too much of the killer.

It made him feel dirty.

But the fresh cold air, the snow, the beautiful trees, and the dawn as it came on, it was like a new beginning.

It gave him a sense of the spiritual. There was more to life than just the here and now. He was meant to find Lucas. He was meant to do something to stop the man who had killed children.

His thoughts did not center on how he'd probably lose his job now for helping break out Scoleri.

For setting Scoleri free.

He could not give a damn at the moment.

Elise Conroy was dead.

Children were dead.

But Lucas was safe.

It was all that mattered at the moment. Making sure that little boy got out of Hell.

Somewhere, over the chilly mountains, the sun was coming up from the desert.

The valley below, already warm, its lower elevations probably just reaching seventy degrees, while the mountains were in the high twenties.

From the cave behind him, steam from the hot springs.

Trey kissed Lucas on the forehead.

"It's okay," he said. "It's okay."

He took the boy up in his arms.

He trudged through the snow, following the stone path, and then saw the house in the near distance.

He went into the house to call the police.

CHAPTER SEVENTY-SEVEN

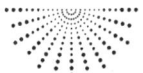

Six a.m.

AFTER THE AMBULANCES, and the plow to help get the ambulances through, after darkness bled into the purple beginnings of dawn, after too much questioning, both in the small trailer in Moon Lake and then more of the same down the mountain at the San Pascal Police Department, after a trip the emergency room to make sure he was okay, an officer drove Trey back to Redlands. The cop told him that Trey's wife Carly had been up most of the night, once the county police were on the horn about Laymon and Fasteau going missing, as well as the disappearance of two staff members and a patient of Darden State.

Trey felt numb and had nothing more to say.

Nothing to feel.

All he thought about:

Home.

T<small>REY WALKED</small> into the dark house.

He flicked on the hall light.

Looked at the living room—the knickknacks in cubbyholes, the Spanish-style fireplace jutting toward the center of the room, the old sofas, the grandfather clock Carly's father had made. He looked out on the garden, the lights near the small reflecting pool hitting the shadows of birds-of-paradise and trumpet vines ... He heard them.

Breathing.

His children.

He went into his son's room. Messy as it was. Stepping over a basketball left in the middle of the floor, around some plastic track he was building for his Hot Wheels. He sat down gently on the edge of Mark's bed. Mark snored a lot for a kid. Trey put his hand at the back of Mark's scalp and just held it there lightly.

Then to his daughter's room, where he kissed her gently on the cheek. She turned slightly, her eyes still closed. In a dream.

After nearly an hour, he padded as quietly as he could down the hallway.

As he unbuttoned his shirt, Carly said, "You've been hurt."

He went to her and grabbed her, holding her as tightly as he could.

He kissed her, and then smelled the faint scent of baby powder and felt a tremendous burden lift.

Home.

"You okay?" she asked.

"Completely. Go back to sleep."

"They catch him?" she asked, but he could tell she was already back on the path of sleep.

"They did. I'll tell you the rest when I get up," he said. "Good night. I love you."

Even saying the words made him feel safe.

He slipped into bed beside her. They slept together, his arms around her. He felt her warmth and didn't fall asleep for several minutes while he just listened to her gentle breathing.

It was the most beautiful sound on Earth.

Exhaustion finally took him into dreams.

LATER THAT DAY—AFTER he hugged his kids, after he checked the bandage on his scalp—he went to see two people in the hospital, getting treatment.

First, Lucas Conroy, whose father had spent the night with him in his hospital room.

Then Trey went to see Jane Laymon.

THAT MORNING, earlier, when it was still dark out, Monica Scrubb got off her night shift at the Donut Queen and dropped by the doctor's office to pick up a prescription for the witch before she headed back up the mountain to the house on Moon Lake.

It took her longer than usual to get up there. When she pulled off the road to park the truck, she knew something was wrong because the local deputy, Hank Dollard, was out front with a few folks from town. Yellow police tape wound around the house.

Instinctively, she touched her stomach. "You're gonna be all right, Matthew or Greta, don't worry. The witch probably died."

But she wasn't sure why there'd be the sheriff of all people out there if old Mrs. Cobble had finally kicked off in her sleep, which

Monica had been hoping would happen, along with that damn old dog of Duane's.

AT THE CRITICAL-CARE section of ICU at San Pascal Valley Hospital, Ruthie Cobble lay in a bed, a ventilator to keep her breathing, with monitors all around her bed.

She looked out through the half-opened blinds at the clear morning as it came up.

It was the first dawn she had seen in nearly fourteen years.

Ruthie Cobble continued sleeping, waking up now and then and believing that the hospital room was a dream. Although no one predicted that a woman who had been kept for years in a bomb shelter would still be alive, she seemed to show every sign of getting a little better as each minute passed.

IN A JAIL CELL at the San Pascal County Sheriff's Office, it looks up at the ceiling and begins praying that God will release it from its torment. After all, God had put the Other One in Hell and had made it live in the same body as it, the guy named Duane Cobble —a sniveling little freak.

No match for the Devil.

Abraxas. Abraxas. I need you. I need you.

Shackles on its ankles, it leans back against the cold wall.

It closes its eyes and wishes it were a little boy again, in the dark of the Mad Place, its father scourging its body with the barbed wire while Ruthie prayed as loud as she could to drown out its cries for help.

To stop the Beast from bringing about the end of the world.

The Other One begins fighting for supremacy within its body, and the "it" called Duane recedes again, going into the cage in its head to sleep.

CHAPTER SEVENTY-EIGHT

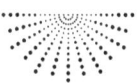

DAY. SUNNY. CLEAR BLUE SKIES FROM THE MOUNTAINS TO THE sea. The mountains, snow-capped; the valleys, like a vision of Heaven with palm trees.

A beautiful Southern California Christmas coming up.

Michael Scoleri rode a bus to downtown Los Angeles, all the while listening to a grandmother in her sixties, who had been a science teacher when she was younger but now was just a grandma, talk about her beautiful grandchildren and her wonderful daughter-in-law and brilliant son. He liked listening to her, and he found it refreshing to have so much noise around him. Wonderful human noise. When he got downtown, he stepped off at Rose Street, then walked over to Santa Monica where he caught a bus going toward Hollywood.

At Cahuenga, he got off.

He decided he needed to find someone to take him in, at least for the night.

He'd work out what came next when he had the chance.

First things first.

Have to get a good meal and find a pretty girl to have some fun with, he thought.

He began walking through the city, taking the wide boulevards, thinking of how beautiful and radiant it all was.

No snow here, he thought. *No rain.* Just sun and shining buildings that reminded him of holy places.

The shrines of worship. The cathedrals of mankind.

He needed a different kind of girl this time. The kind who understood him. The kind who would take care of him and help make everything all right this time.

He was sure he'd know the right girl when he saw her.

There were lots of pretty women in Los Angeles, nearly on every street corner.

To him, it was just like taking a stroll through paradise.

Pretty girls as far as the eye could see.

AFTER A FEW DAYS had gone by, the Moon Lake Pure Spring Water Company sent a new guy to deliver a hundred more bottles to the Darden State Hospital for Criminal Justice. He loaded up jugs onto the water coolers in offices, including the one in Dr. Elise Conroy's now-unoccupied office. The delivery guy was named Josh Schwartz, and he found a slip of paper under the empty plastic jug in Conroy's office.

On the paper, a slim note, addressed to "Red Angel" and from "Michael."

The note eventually made it into Jane Laymon's hands.

It read:

Thank you for the beautiful angels, my brother. Love to Ruthie.

NIGHT CAGE

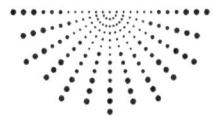

THE CRIMINALLY INSANE SERIES, BOOK 3

For Raul

CHAPTER ONE

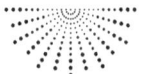

October was hell.

The Santa Ana winds blew like the roar of a lion along the arroyos and canyons of the desert, across the mountain passes into the bowl of the valley, across three counties all sharing the dry October of Southern California.

The mountain pass beneath Big Bear was blocked off by wildfires that had spread along the ridge, and beneath the fireline,foothill communities rose and beyond them, the flatlands of freeway and neighborhood grids covered the landscape.

Heat and dust coughed through the air. The young man who felt them most, choked by a chilling terror at the shadows that flew by night, stared up at the window, listening to it rattle with the wind.

Those burning winds brought the shadows to him.

Blew them all back from the edge of hell or heaven.

Night fears.

Fingers coming toward him, scraping at his throat.

The fears grew with darkness. They were shadows he saw sometimes, moving toward him, reaching for him.

He could barely breathe when they touched his skin, and he lay awake all night waiting for dawn through the window.

Then, first light slowly came up from outside.

He heard the woman get out of bed in the next room and run the shower in the bathroom.

He called himself Doc, although he hadn't yet cured himself of the night fears that came on unexpectedly.

Still, he knew how to heal, and set limbs, and make infections go away.

But the night fears were always after him, and he had slept badly yet again.

Sometimes, he didn't fall asleep until the rest of the world awoke.

In all his nineteen years, he could not remember a good night of sleep. The night fears came in the dark, and they crawled all over his skin and kept him from drifting into the dream world he wanted to find. But by the time of the first light out the window, he knew he was safe, after all.

The purple light outside the window relaxed him the most. The white-hot light of midday hurt him. The dark of night brought the crawling fears.

He curled up into as much of a ball as he could make of himself. His arms hurt, as they often did, but he felt that warmth of happiness in this position.

His special bed.

The cage.

The crate was just large enough for him to scrunch himself into, and just tall enough that he didn't press against the top of it.

He felt good in the cage, and more important than that, he felt safe, at least until she returned each day to take him out of it.

The night fears couldn't get in there with him.

It was just big enough for him and no one else.

His early memories of the cage, from the time he'd been four, were calming and sweet and allowed him to sleep at night without fear. Sometimes, she brought fear with her, like a smell that clung to her. She didn't always shake it off at the door, as she promised. She sometimes brought rage with her too, and then he didn't mind being locked in the cage.

Sometimes, after she'd let him out, she would tell him about his father and where he'd been conceived, and how it was like an enormous cage itself. He liked her best when this happened.

He liked to hear her memories of that place with its special rooms and all the people she talked about, and how she described his father to him.

"He was a good man then," she said, "but he made promises. And he broke some of them. He made some things terrible for me. And for you. But everyone who breaks a promise pays a penalty in life. You know that, don't you? Someday, you'll get to meet him. Someday, he'll find you or you'll find him. Someday, he'll pay the penalty for what he's done. Punishment always comes to people, whether in this life or the next. And the punishment always fits the crime."

In the cage, curled up in a ball, he fell asleep just as the sun was coming up beyond the room.

He dreamed of the place where his mother and father had met, as if it were a promised land to which he'd one day return.

It was a hospital.

He felt he knew the place by memory—just from what his mother had told him.

About the high fences with the wires made out of razor.

About the police everywhere.

About all the doctors, all of them smart as he himself was, smart as his mother.

The long corridors of rooms with windows in the doors so patients could look out.

In his dreams, he felt he floated down the corridor and saw the people staring through their door-windows, watching him as he went, ghostlike, to find the cage where his mother had lived when his father had made love to her.

Even in the dreams, he saw the words emblazoned on the sign as he passed along the outside wall of one of the buildings:

The Darden State Hospital for Criminal Justice.

CHAPTER TWO

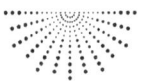

THE PAST:

DISCHARGE PAPERS for Mary Chilmark
  The Darden State Hospital for Criminal Justice

THE PATIENT EXPRESSED, on more than one occasion, remorse for the torture and murder of the three patients under her care while she was a registered nurse. Although she still maintains that the ward fire was an accident (therefore two of these deaths were accidents) she admits that at that time she did not have full mental capacity to understand how her actions might have led to this tragedy.

She understands that the fire began because of her own actions. She just expressed great remorse and evinced anguish over what she had done.

In the current interview, the patient was fully oriented. The patient was calm and expressed remorse for her past crimes. She understood the full importance of what the word "murder" meant and expressed a moral view and judgment of her own actions in the past.

She stated that she had suffered depression and anxiety, exacerbated at the time by drug and alcohol use, precipitated at the death of her parents (in 1974). "I got to the groups, including the PARTNER meetings and the MOVE group sessions. My individual sessions have proved more than satisfactory with Dr. Brainard."

When asked about the Offense, she stated, "I know that I committed those murders, but I could not see this for several years. I suppose the part of me that had no mental control believed I was doing them good. But I know now how tragically wrong that was."

She has internalized blame, as has been noted since October 1983. She does not view others as causing her maladaptive behavior, and she appears in every respect willing to take responsibility for her behavior.

Remission Status:

Is the patient's severe mental disorder treatable by medication and psychological as well as social support avenues?

RB:

Extreme progress with this patient. Her functioning level is high and has been instrumental in the "Patient In-Care" Reach in Wards B and C. The treatment team assessed her as in the top functioning category, and she has family support beyond the walls of Darden State. Her hallucinations from intake until spring 1984 were frequent and delusional. These might have been aftereffect flashbacks to her prescription drug addiction and seem to have cleared up completely.

The patient's severe disorder is completely in remission and has seemed so for more than eighteen months.

Level of Danger:

Does the patient represent a substantial or implicit physical harm to others based on disorder or past history?

RB:

In my opinion, and the opinion of the treatment group, Mary Chilmark is ready to transition back into the community.

Outpatient Treatment:

What is recommended to continue the patient's treatment?

RB:

Psychiatric treatment should be continual, and the state's supervision of this treatment is implicit. However, the patient is ready for the challenges and rigors of the outside world. She has the support of her fiancé and his family, as well. Additionally, her pregnancy seems to be a mitigating factor, and I strongly recommend Mary Chilmark be given a second chance at this point in time. With outside supervision, continuing treatment by a state-appointed psychiatrist, continuing medical supervision, parenting classes, and ongoing medications as listed in the previous report, she should be out of the hospital and will not pose a threat, significant or otherwise, to the world at large.

Control Factor:

What is the nature of the patient's past crime, and the original diagnosis?

RB:

The murders of two women, one man, and an unborn child. Her depression and anxiety have been successfully managed for eighteen months with medication therapy.

CHAPTER THREE

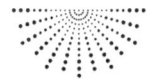

Now: October

Mary had a face like love itself.

That's what he thought whenever he looked at her.

Late forties, but could pass for thirty-two on a sunny day. Maybe even twenty-eight. She was prettier than any girl he had ever known. Her eyes were warm and brown, and her forehead was low, hidden by sweeps of raven-dark hair. Mary had been a nurse all her life, with the exception of the handful of years lost to a hospital where she'd stayed after her breakdown. But in her face, anyone could see that her conscience was clear, her mind her own, and she moved and spoke as if each step she took were methodical and controlled. She was a gift to life.

And she kept the fears away.

Doc trusted her completely.

She shifted the curtain slightly, and bright sunlight entered the room.

"Look at it out there," she said, so softly that he barely heard her. "It's beautiful."

He set down the instrument he'd been testing and stepped over to the window. Mary stepped away and left him gazing outside as if it might relieve some of the anxiety he was feeling.

"Just an ordinary day," she said, stepping over to where the instruments were kept, all in a neat row on a napkin-covered plate.

Outside, the pure flat light of Southern California September, dappled by the palm trees and the two enormous avocado trees at the edge of the back lawn, by the guesthouse, beyond the swimming pool that was blue and lovely.

"Too much light," he said. "Too bright."

"But it's good in here, isn't it?" she said.

"The dog's barking," he said. "I wish it would just stop."

"Block it out," she said. "Doc, you need to concentrate."

"It's distracting."

"You're letting it do that. Come away from there. Ignore it. Focus."

He let the shades drop—the curtains were thick and too dark for such a room. His hand felt greasy; he had begun to sweat, which sometimes happened. He had to calm himself.

You can do this. You can do it.

His heart seemed to pound in his chest. His mouth, dry. His mind focused, yet aware of the sensations that had begun.

The excitement.

The examination room: not sterile enough. He would have to deal with less-than-optimal conditions. His hands, washed with antibacterial soap, still he felt dirty. He looked to her face for a sense of calm. She had it. Her skin was lightly tanned, and even though he saw the creases of age in her face—around her eyes and at the edge of her lips—he couldn't help but feel just a little better from seeing those deep brown eyes of hers.

"Don't worry," she said. "It's all right. When this is over, you'll be fine. We'll clean up, and you'll see. You'll see. She'll be better too."

"I don't like this," he kept saying.

His left hand trembled. He looked at it, hoping to calm it just by taking deep breaths.

"It can't be helped." She stood by, her hands cupping the small metal basin to catch the blood. Surgery of this type was never a perfect option. But when a need arose, and the question became life and death for the mother and child, a good doctor had to be prepared to work even under the most rudimentary conditions.

In this case, that meant the master bedroom of a suburban house, while the woman on the bed stared at them, her eyes wide. Noises came from her mouth.

He could turn her off in his mind. Good doctors could do that. There was no time for anesthetic, and his assistant—who was nearly a doctor herself—tied the woman's arms so that when he brought the blade down to her belly to help with the removal of the child, the path would not be obstructed.

The woman's mouth had been taped, but only for her own good. She would pass out from the pain, or her body would take over, knowing this was for the good of the child inside her.

Nature was like that—it was both healer and caretaker. Her own body would begin to divert the signals of pain to her brain so as to release the body's own natural painkiller.

As the doctor prepared the woman's belly and cut and opened, he felt inside her for the tumor.

He glanced up at his assistant. "I can't find it."

His assistant—who was also his own mother—raised her eyebrows. Her face had been spattered with blood.

"The baby," he said. "It's not here."

"Of course it's there, Doc."

"No," he said, feeling around within the cut.

"We need to get her to the hospital right away, Doc," his mother said.

"I think it's too late for that," he replied. "Let's close her up."

"No," his mother said. "See? She's just sleeping. She'll pull through. Here. I can feel her pulse. She'll be fine. She's still there. I can feel her. She hasn't passed yet."

His mother put her hand on the woman's sweat-soaked forehead and then reached down to tear the duct tape from her mouth.

That's when Doc thought he saw a shadow pass across the room, and he whispered something about how souls moved at death. He didn't mention the dark spiders he saw crawling off the woman's hand—the tiny little spiders of fear that stayed behind.

He didn't have to mention them.

He hoped he could leave the room without coming too close to them.

LATER, in the dark of their own home:

"I saw her pass," he said.

"Did she say anything, Doc?"

"She told me that it was all right. She thanked me. You too."

"Ah. I thought she might. She understands."

"She had her baby with her too. She was going toward a light."

"They do that. Were there others with her? Beings of light?"

"She smiled at me," he said, and his mother's hand stroked his hair softly.

"Were there others?" she asked.

"I think so. I'm not sure. I saw shadows."

"They're shadows if they can't pass to the other side. They stay here. Did you see the fears?"

He nodded. "But I didn't go near them."

"I'll always keep them away from you. I promise."

"There were some light shadows and some that were darker than dark," he said. "And then, once she left, the light faded. I think she wanted to go."

"You're a good doctor," his mother said. "All those books on surgery really taught you a lot. It's amazing what you can do, Doc."

She drew him out of his cage.

"Don't ever leave me," he whispered to her, and then his mother pressed her lips against his slightly parted mouth.

CHAPTER FOUR

THE SAN PASCAL MURDER LOTTERY, AS THE HOMICIDE division's staffers liked to call it, usually hovered at under twenty per year, but the one that happened that afternoon put them just over, and if you counted the baby, it was twenty-three, even though they hadn't found the baby yet.

In the soft-focus neighborhoods of the foothills, with the beautiful homes, expansive lawns, and long pale blue swimming pools, murder of this type could usually be kept at bay by extensive alarm systems and the patrolling cars of off-duty policemen who were hired to notice unwelcome and uninvited visitors.

At least, that was the myth.

While there had been three suicide attempts in the area within the past six years, seven arrests regarding domestic violence, and one very suspicious crib death, murder had not walked these particular streets for at least thirty years.

Homeowners often owned at least one firearm, and the Neighborhood Watch program was in full effect, run by a man named Mr. Moulton, who walked his Corgi three times daily along four of the streets. Mr. Moulton made stained glass, which was popular with the neighbors, out of the home studio, which had once been a guesthouse at the back of his property.

Alanna Rogers, whose passion was gardening ever since her early retirement from Jet Propulsion Laboratories, also was often in her front yard, tending to the maze of color and blossom. She had noticed when a small blue truck had come through, loaded with yard workers, none of whom were legal. She took down license plates of cars, at times, from her picture window, particularly when they didn't belong to any of the neighbors.

Others in the neighborhood felt they were well aware of the comings and goings of nearly everyone, from the young man who regularly bicycled through the neighborhood wearing very little other than Speedos and sneakers, to the three goth-looking teen girls who seemed to sweep through on autumn afternoons, smoking and snickering and picking flowers at will from perfectly nice gardens of homes that were not theirs.

But no one had seen the murderers that late September day.

THE FLOCK HOUSE had its two cars in its driveway.

Mr. Flock—rarely called Dan by the neighbors because he and his wife had never really mingled since they'd moved in two years earlier, buying the enormous house at earthquake-sale prices—worked for one of the studios in Los Angeles, although no one in the neighborhood was sure if it was Disney or Universal. He worked in the finance department and had done well for himself in a short period of time.

Diane Flock was better known because she walked the golden retriever in the early evening. Sometimes, when she was up by the golf course several blocks away, she ran into others out on their jogs or walks, and talked about the water problems or the earthquake damage from too many years back that still affected the houses, or about how someone had lost their beloved cat to a coyote.

She worked at a law firm downtown but had been going part-time since she'd become pregnant, and was looking to leave the firm to "become just like my mother—someone who gets to be home all day. I'll go insane, I know it," she had told Paula Sherman when picking up dog poop in a baggie near the entrance to the canyon-park area, just beyond the neighborhood.

The doors to the house had all been locked from the inside, although Diane Flock sometimes left the sun porch door open when she was home. The pool had been emptied because of some damage found. She had, that day, apparently stepped down into it and looked along the crack that ran from the bottom middle all the way up to the diving board.

Because she'd left Molly, their golden retriever, in the dog run that was out by the three olive trees at the back fence of the property, the dog had been spared her master's fate.

"We heard her barking," Mr. Moulton told the police later. "But she barked all the time. That was the one complaint everyone had about the Flocks. That dog."

"They had exquisite taste," Alanna Rogers said. "They bought their furniture at the big shows at the Pacific Design Center. They had antique dealers come to them. It must have been inherited, some of that wealth. They were such a beautiful couple. So blessed."

Within the house, tiny pencil writing on the wall, above the gold paisley sofa:

Diseased.

A hypodermic needle on the Stickley table, near the front door.

On the Mission bench, in the enclosed, shaded room called the sun porch, a scalpel with the brown of dried blood and the smallest of hairs upon it.

A stained glass window set into the kitchen door, a smudge of blood against amber.

In the kitchen, the phone, dropped on the Mexican tile floor. Beside it, a broken vase. Three purple iris that had been picked from the garden the morning before.

In the upstairs hall, a bit of a cotton shirt, torn, with microscopic skin fragments in it where someone had used their fingers to tear the shirt from one of the victims.

In the second-floor bathroom, the shaving kit on the back of the toilet, open. The small window slanted to allow air. The medicine cabinet's mirrored sliding doors pushed to one side. In it, Crest toothpaste, Shower-to-Shower deodorant powder, a small vial of liquid foundation, a plastic bottle of Neutrogena facial moisturizer.

Razor blades on the light blue fuzzy rug beside the sink.

A deodorant bar on the floor.

A surgical mask, just to the left of the toilet, almost behind the small wicker trash basket.

In the trash basket, latex gloves.

Down the hall, along the expensive Persian runners bought on a trip to Morocco in 1998, a sliver of fingernail caught in the fabric.

In the master bedroom, the victims.

In pencil, tiny writing, just above the headboard on the wall:
Tumor, malignant, removed.

THE HOUSE WAS in a small web of neighborhoods off Hill, a long street that went up into the gently rounded slope of hills in San Bernardino, California. Beyond the foothills, there was a fire up on the mountains, just beneath Big Bear and Arrowhead. The Santa Ana winds shifted hourly, but so far, the fire had not spread down into the foothill communities, which seemed unaffected by the smoke thousands of feet above their streets and swimming pools.

A brief street turned off Hill, and then another came down, called Minuet.

Detective Jane Laymon glanced along the ivied lawns and richly textured gardens of the area.

Jane was in her mid-twenties but had jumped in rank since the previous winter, qualified for her firearms, and had begun working on more murder cases, much to the chagrin of her mother, who told Jane she needed to "stay away from all that killing."

But Jane had begun to love the puzzles that built up around her work and particularly had become fascinated with the work of the forensics experts in San Pascal.

JANE FOUND the house number and pulled into the driveway of one of the craftsman houses. Rosemary hedges in front. Twin palm trees, thick and looming, on either side of the driveway. Jade plants, the height of a small child, untended, growing wild. A low apple tree in the front yard, as well as what looked like two pomegranates; their fruit, long past, lay in clumps along the spotty overgrown grass.

The forensics team had arrived there three hours before. Two SUVs were in the driveway. The police tape was up. Two cruisers parked just down the block.

She parked her car at the edge of the long driveway and walked slowly up to the house.

"LAYMON. Glad you came out for this." Marty Davis, looked worn and tattered from lack of sleep, his hair a bit wild, and his eyes circled with dark smudges.

One of the other detectives, named March, glanced over at her. He was short and stout and wore a starched white shirt stained at the armpits. Didn't say anything, but she felt some kind of criticism in the way he looked at her. Maybe it was her eye patch. The legend of her missing eye had gone far afield, because the investigation of the Red Angel killer had become a big one in California. She went over to March, and he seemed a bit startled by this.

"Look, I lost my eye chasing a killer. Want to know what he did to get it? You want a good look at it?" She reached up to lift the patch, but March turned away.

"Laymon," Davis said, "we didn't bring you out here for your eye."

"What kind of consult are we talking about?" she asked, turning her attention back to him.

"It's a team effort. Come on," he said. He led her along the route that had been understood to be the blocking of the murders. "She's out here. Maybe there." He pointed to the empty pool. The sunlight out back seemed blinding. Jane shielded her eye. She squinted, trying to imagine a woman in that pool. "They had some damage. Already there when they bought the house, apparently. A crack at the bottom of the pool. They had tried repairing it since they moved in, but nothing had worked. They bought the place in an earthquake sale. It should've gone for over a half a million, but it went for three hundred. The neighbors all felt it was scandalous to get this place that cheap."

"There's a guest house," Jane said, looking at the small blue house beyond the pool.

"Yep. A one bedroom. No occupants. Looks like they used it for storage."

"It's been checked?"

Davis nodded. "The pooch was in the dog run," he pointed to the chain link rectangular area back among some trees.

"What time of day was it?"

"Not sure. Maybe midafternoon. I guess three. He gets home from work early on Fridays."

"So he came in while it was going on."

"Maybe," Davis said. "Come on, let's go."

THREE COPS WERE in the kitchen, just standing around.

"The techs already come through?"

One of the cops nodded, grinning. "Hey, Jane."

"Hey, Pete. You might want to clear this place a little," Laymon said.

"It's because it's unincorporated land up here," Davis said. "It's county, not city."

Jane knew. Red tape. Too many departments to call.

Davis walked her around the broken glass on the floor. The flowers, drying out. Iris, a pink rose, a daffodil. "She was at the pool, looking around it, who knows. She comes back in the house. She cuts some flowers on the way. Those, right by the back steps to the sun porch. She gets this vase from there," he pointed to the sink. "And just as she puts the flowers in, someone grabs her. Or scares her. Or she hears a noise."

"Maybe," Jane said. "Was she messy?"

Davis glanced at her, a question forming.

"Some people drop things. And they think, 'I'll let someone else clean that up.' What if she just dropped it and left it?" Jane asked. "It might have nothing to do with her murder. Did she have a maid? A cleaning service? A gardener?"

"This is why I want you here," Davis said, beaming a little. He escorted her along the narrow hallway with its dark, elegant table. A grandfather clock near the front door. A portrait of a teenage girl on the other side of the door. "Nearest we know, that's one of the victims. When she was young."

The girl in the portrait had long, dark hair, cut in a way that reminded Jane of the 1970s. She smiled, and had a peaches-and-cream complexion. The artist had been a good one. It looked expensive, and nearly museum quality.

"How old was she?"

"Late thirties."

"I thought she was younger."

"They were a young couple—meaning new. Married four years. First pregnancy."

"She was pretty," Jane said, feeling a bitter sadness when she looked at the painting. It reminded her yet again that the victims of murder had once been someone's beloved children. That while the murderer often perceived the victim as an object, a toy, a means to an end, the victim had a history, a life, a richness of experience, and dreams of the future as well as memories of the past. That was probably the worst thing about any murder. Thinking about the victim's life. Seeing all life within that dead body. All chances ended. All hopes gone.

"And here," Davis said, as they came upon the low Stickley table, "is where we found the needle. And over there," he pointed to what looked like a blackened portion of the rug, "they tried to set a fire, I'm guessing. Didn't stay long enough to complete it. Maybe it was to try and cover up the crime. Either way, it just died down— nothing caught. Maybe it was an accident. Who knows? I guess 'til we find 'em, we won't know."

∾

JANE FOLLOWED DAVIS, room by room, looking at everything, taking mental snapshots as they went. The worst thing to see was the nursery. Diane Flock had already begun stenciling scenes from Winnie the Pooh and Peter Rabbit along the pale blue walls. A crib, barely out of the box, was in the corner. On the walls, pictures of Grandma and Grandpa, and friends, and Mommy and Daddy. A stroller, still in the box, up against the walk-in closet's door. Two or three baby shower gifts on the windowsill, still wrapped up. It made her want to weep when she saw this. Knowing what she would find next.

In the master bedroom, she found it.

"I told you to be prepared," Davis said.

"I am," Laymon lied.

AFTER EXAMINING the scene of the murders carefully, she left the room and went and sat outside in the sun by the pool.

Davis followed her out and sat by the empty pool, his feet dangling over the edge. "I guess when you're middle-aged like me, you see enough of these that it doesn't hit you the same way."

"It's not that," Jane said. "I just felt a bad vibe up there. I felt as if the killers were still in the house. I know they're not. But it felt like it."

"You're about what, twenty-five?"

"Twenty-six."

"You've been through a hell of a lot for twenty-six."

"I took the job to handle all this. Don't worry, I'm not cracking."

"Tryon thinks the world of you."

"That's good to know."

"I wish somebody had said this to me when I was about your

age and getting into this line of work. Don't worry about it when it gets to you. It gets to all of us. You never quite get numb," he said.

"Thanks," she said. Then, her mood changing, "We got Dahl coming in on this?"

"He'll lead, and you and I and maybe Jack March'll be on this."

"The one fascinated by my eye patch."

"You're a legend. You have to accept it. Nobody here has that. They respect you. Believe me. They do."

"I hope we catch the people who did this," she said.

"We will," Davis said. "They're sloppy. And we got a great team working on it."

LESS THAN TWENTY MINUTES LATER, the call came in that they'd caught one of the killers down at a pharmacy in town, trying to get the victim's prescriptions refilled.

That evening, Jane Laymon called Trey Campbell.

"A consult?" he asked.

"They're going to put him in Darden until the trial. We can get Hannifin and Brainard on it, but I want you on it too. We're not getting much from this guy. He's really a Darden case. Just out there. Talks about spiders coming to get him. His mother's Mary Chilmark. She's part of it. We just haven't gotten her."

"Oh," Trey said. "I haven't thought about her in years. I came in after she'd already left. She was sort of a legend here. I knew patients who talked about her. She was a beauty who walked in, used the system, and walked right out again."

"I guess she never quite got the cure," Laymon said.

"I really like to think that when someone gets released from Darden, it's for a good reason."

"Well, if the rumors of the kid's father are true, then maybe that's the good reason."

Trey didn't respond to this. "Was it a rough takedown?"

"Six men, two women. All holding a nineteen-year-old on the floor near the vitamin display. He really spun out of control."

"What was the prescription for?"

"That's yet another weird part of all this. Sleeping meds, basically. He risked getting caught just for sleeping pills."

"Maybe he has trouble sleeping."

"Given what he did in that house, I hope he does."

"Anyone hurt?"

"A few bruised egos, but no real damage."

"That's good."

"He calmed down right away, once they had him pinned."

"When does the guy come in?"

"Tonight."

"I'll see him when I get in tomorrow, I guess."

"We're leaving it to Hannifin to sort out. But she knows that you're the one for intake. She squawked about that, but there's not much she can do. Brainard probably shut her up."

"What's his first name?"

"He goes by 'Doc.'"

"What's his real name?"

CHAPTER FIVE

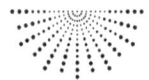

AT HIS HOME IN REDLANDS, ACROSS THE FLATLAND OF VALLEY, Trey closed his cell phone.

Trey Campbell, late thirties, hadn't yet noticed age creeping up on him in any defining way. He felt as good as he had since as far back as he could remember. But he felt the years in one way: he now had basic fears about life that he hadn't had up to his mid-thirties. While he had been working with psychopathic killers at the Darden State Hospital for Criminal Justice since he was in his twenties, fresh from his studies in psychology, the effect of the terror that a man or woman in a psychotic state of mind could inflict upon others had begun to dig into him as it never had before. He had witnessed deaths and mutilations at the hands of a few of the worst killers that Darden State kept within its gates. He had seen the sorrow of victims—even of a boy whose mother had been brutally murdered trying to save him.

And though he loved the work, and felt it presented a multitude of challenges that kept him on his toes and thinking and growing in some way—he had begun to feel genuine fear about life.

And yet, cell phone in hand, looking out the back kitchen window, it was an idyllic moment—twilight approached, the cries of the wild parrots among the palm trees in the field beyond their property. The late smell of orange blossoms that never seemed to leave the area, whether winter, fall, or spring. They had chosen Redlands as home because it seemed so separate from the rest of the area—avocado trees along its hillsides and city orange groves throughout its park system. In the summers, there was local theater and shows at the Redlands Bowl that the kids loved as they grew up. The house itself, an old adobe that had been one of the original ranch houses of what had once been miles of orange orchards. It was a one-story L-shaped adobe with a beautiful Spanish-style courtyard filled with birds-of-paradise, bougainvillea, and even a plum tree by its far, low wall.

And yet, the few times his job intruded—a call home, a vacation interrupted, a midnight emergency—he felt less safe. Less safe for his wife Carly and their two children, Mark and Teresa.

He felt that the world itself was unstable, and that something—or someone—lurked in shadows.

He felt as if the bad guys who were out there—the ones who made him sometimes wonder if there were a God at all, given the way the human mind could create its own monsters—had stepped into the kitchen with him, at the glass table, right there, looking out on the backyard. Thinking now about murder, instead of the steak he had just finished marinating for the barbeque.

He glanced across the room to his wife, chopping onions near the sink. Her hands were a blur of movement; the smell of sweet onions in the air. From the open window, he heard the bickering of scrub jays and mockingbirds at the bird feeder in the yard. It was an ordinary day. He knew from experience that it was the ordinary days that bit you in the ass and held on.

Carly grinned. "What's up?"

"The son of one of Darden's former patients. Back at Darden."

"Second generation sociopath," Carly said, a bitter edge to her voice. And then, "Come on, I'm joking. Who's the father?"

"Mother. Mary Chilmark. Bloody Mary. That's what they called her in the press. You remember the murders?"

"Was she one of the Manson girls or something?"

"Nothing that infamous. She was a nurse who murdered a couple of patients. I can't remember the particulars. I just remember hearing some things about her. She left before I got there."

"So Jane's bringing you back into something," Carly said, and it struck Trey that she said this almost as if she meant something illicit between the two of them. "I'm glad you've got this work, but I just wish sometimes you could do the nine to five and that'd be it."

"I'm being asked to consult. That's all."

"How's that different?"

"It's with the police. And apparently against Hannifin's wishes. But, in this case, they're going around her. They want me to handle the intake interview."

WHAT HAD HAPPENED to Trey over the past months had shocked him. He had been sure after the incident with the Red Angel killer that he'd be demoted, fired, or worse, hidden.

But the opposite had occurred.

Officer Jane Laymon and the San Pascal County Sheriff's Office lobbied the state on his behalf, and a promotion had booted him up the ranks. He had already consulted on a case in Riverside, in the spring, and though there were administrators at Darden State who would've liked to get rid of him because of the ensuing scandal and lawsuit after the murder of a psychiatrist, he was exonerated of all blame, and wonder of wonders—at least to Trey—had actually been asked to give monthly talks to the psychiatric community on the criminally insane mind. New title: *Psychiatric Special Project Director*. The title had come with only a slight bump in salary, an annoyance from some of the psychiatrists on staff, and the added bonus of being called into the field when a former patient of the Darden State Hospital for Criminal Justice escaped or when a potential future patient had been caught and needed what was called a "special circumstance intake" at the forensics hospital pending trial.

In the intervening months, he'd been prepping for further study by going nights to the University of Riverside, hoping to complete a master's degree in psychology within four or five years. Even Carly had conceded that the changes that came about from his few encounters with the livelier patient-inmates at Darden State had ended up being good for him and for the future life they envisioned. "You're passionate about this," she said. "I know. I have to step back sometimes. Sometimes, what goes on there is too much for me. But I know this is your path. I've seen you change these past few years, for the better. I know it's been rough. You've gone through things that I don't think I'd be able to handle more than once in a lifetime."

Then, she kissed him softly on the nose and whispered. "I married a guy who likes working with psychotic killers."

"It's not that," he said. But he could not say why he loved his work so much. He couldn't express why the human mind in all its aberrations fascinated him. Why he sought to understand the sociopath, or the sexual sadist, or the one who killed simply for pleasure. It was the predator of humankind that drew him to his work, time and again. There had been—for the first fifteen years— the simple routine of the job. The lack of knowledge of opportunity elsewhere. The interest in working within the State of California, in mental health, and a complete admiration for the psychiatric profession.

But after his experiences of the past few years, he was more involved than he ever thought he'd be. He cared about the victims of the crimes, but he also cared about the rehabilitation of those who committed some of the most heinous crimes.

And yet, something about his work scared him too. If he thought too much about it, it nearly paralyzed him.

That same fear led him to want the know more, want to study more, want to keep returning to the triple-fenced, guarded buildings of the forensics hospital known as the Darden State Hospital for Criminal Justice that had once been simply known as the Darden State Hospital for the Criminally Insane.

In bed that night, he and his wife snuggled and talked about things other than either of their jobs. They made love when the snuggling turned to a passion. Made him feel less weary of things and reminded him of when he and Carly had been younger and probably more passionate about each other than they were about work and the kids. When they were done, she whispered in his ear. "I have some news, sweetheart."

But he had begun drifting off to sleep—by then it was after midnight and he had a big day of meetings and talks and intake with Bloody Mary Chilmark's nineteen-year-old son—so he missed what she said.

But as soon as he woke up, it was in his head. He knew exactly what she'd said as he had gone off into dreams.

Five fifteen a.m., time for his morning jog, but instead, he put his arms around her and said, "We're having another kid?"

"Takes you a good eight hours of sleep to get it?"

"I think I was half-asleep when you said it. I thought it was a dream."

"Well, it's real. I thought maybe it wasn't. But it is."

"Wow."

"You're a little more enthused than I am," she said, drawing away, crossing her arms in front of her, and looking up at the ceiling. "I'm almost forty. I didn't really want this to happen."

"Surprise," he whispered, and moved over to kiss her on the forehead.

EARLY MORNING in the courtyard in back, Trey and Carly, sitting in the wood-slat chairs, looked down on the bowl of the valley with the great San Bernardino Mountains in the distance and the pitch-black of roiling smoke somewhere along the range of foothills. A dazzling sunrise, between the yellow and pink of sky and the darkness of the hills. Peaceful. Calm. All harm was at a distance; Trey liked it that way.

Six a.m. was for Trey Campbell and his family. Before work. Before the all-consuming time spent at Darden State on Ward D. Quiet moment for him and his wife, out on the patio, looking out on the beautiful valley below.

Even with some fire up in the mountains blackening their view.

"The Santa Anas," Trey said. "Like clockwork."

"They're a little early," his wife said. "I thought they contained the fires."

"I think that means they let them run out of control."

He and Carly sat out along the brick walk of the small courtyard of their adobe house that had a near-perfect view of the distant fire. At the beginning of October, it was slightly early for the fires, but the Santa Ana winds had their own season.

"I hope it doesn't make it over here."

"It won't."

"It almost did. Last year."

"Didn't jump the freeway." He took a sip of coffee, then reached over to pick up the soy creamer. Poured in a bit more. Another sip, and it was perfect. He closed his eyes, forgetting the distant fires, which were the bane of the dry California summer and fall. Images of Mark as a baby, rolling around on the floor, making his "dit-do" noise and blowing spit bubbles. Teresa, with her pout and the way she grasped his finger with all her might. *Babies*. Opened his eyes to gaze at her. "I can't believe it."

"I know. I'm too old."

"You are not. Aunt Kelly had her first one at thirty-nine. My cousin had her fifth kid older than you."

"Not much older. Aren't you scared?"

"No way. I'm thrilled," he said. "I definitely think we should name the kid 'Surprise.'"

"Let's not tell the kids yet," Carly said.

He nodded. "Sure."

"We can always change our minds. If we want."

He let the comment sit. Everything was too new, even to Carly. He had to let it go for now. With each child they'd had, she had been skittish at first about having them. She weighed all the pros and cons, and she eventually would come out on the side of "pro." She always did. She had told him when Mark was a baby that she wished she could always keep him a baby because she loved looking at babies all the time, and he had told her that when Mark grew up and went to college, she better not still be babying him.

But even then, the pregnancy with Mark had been rough, and that was nearly thirteen years ago. He also remembered the birth, and how labor had to be induced, and how he spent thirty-seven hours convinced that the worst would happen. He didn't want to go through that again.

AFTER THEY GOT the kids up and the showers began going and Trey went to put cereal in the bowls, he began thinking about the future, about the new baby that would enter their lives, about the disruptions it would cause, maternity leave, paternity leave, and remembering all of what they'd gone through with Mark and Teresa, so many years ago—that seemed like the day before yesterday.

When his son came out of the bathroom near the den, a big towel wrapped around him, dripping all over the floor, having left the shower running and possibly overflowing on the tile of the bathroom floor, the last thing on Trey's mind was the nineteen-year-old killer he'd be interviewing within two and a half hours.

CHAPTER SIX

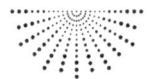

SOMEWHERE, A CAR ALARM WENT OFF, AND THAT WAS ENOUGH to wrench Jane Laymon right out of her soon-forgotten dream.

Jane woke up late—she'd been up until two a.m. going over the Flock murder case with her colleagues—and Danny, her boyfriend, had just come back into the bedroom after showering.

"You always look better naked than dressed," she said, grinning. She shot a glance over at the clock radio by the bed. *Nearly nine.* She normally leaped out of bed around five for an hour of running before she headed off for work.

As a joke, Danny began posing, flexing his muscles, and she had to admit that his regular workouts were paying off.

"Dance for me," she said.

"I could put on my uniform and strip, but I draw the line at dancing," he laughed, and nearly leaped on the bed. He crawled up to her, drawing the sheet back. "You slept in your clothes?"

"Gross, I know," she said. "I was too tired to take 'em off. I got my pants off, though."

"Poor overworked baby," he said, kissing her hand. Then, he sat up, straddling her waist. He leaned over and began unbuttoning her shirt. "I'll help you get ready for the day."

"You are always way too much into morning sex," she said.

"Morning, afternoon, evening, late night," he grinned. "But since somebody was out working hard all night, I think that somebody deserves a little special attention."

"Okay," she sighed, and then grinned right back at him. She lay back while he undressed her. His hand was cool against her warm skin. He kissed her nose, and then her neck, and as he drew her shirt open, he kissed her throat, and then her breasts as he cupped them in his hands.

"Let's take the day off," he whispered. "Just you and me and maybe a trip to the Laguna."

"I wish," she murmured.

"You've been under a lot of stress," he said.

"You're a dirty boy."

"I know. And you like dirty boys," he said, looking up at her from her stomach where he had begun kissing all around her navel.

As he slipped her panties off, she let the pleasure take her over. *Not a bad way to wake up on a lousy day,* she thought.

Later, after her own shower where he got in the stall with her and shampooed her hair, which always drove her nuts in just the right way, she dressed in fresh clothes and switched on the TV. "No five mile run today?"

"I told you, stress, stress, and more stress."

"A jog might help. I'll go with you."

"I can't face it. Plus, I mean, I don't want to take another shower."

"Want to talk about it?"

"No."

"Aw, come on. I love hearing about all the murders."

"It'll drive you nuts."

"No it won't."

"It always does."

"I promise."

"Okay. Okay. A nineteen-year-old is in custody. We're keeping him at Darden for now. He hasn't yet been formally accused, but we're keeping him there for a couple of days."

"He's insane?"

"Seems to be. And his mother is also one of the killers. She's still on the loose."

"Who'd they kill?"

Feeling overwhelmed by the question itself, he shook his head in response.

"You gonna be okay?"

Leaned into the cradle of his arm. "Yeah. I think so."

"Promise me something. Promise me you won't do what you did last time. You won't go into anything unprepared."

"I was as prepared as anyone could be."

"It scares me sometimes. This world you deal with. Murderers."

"Most of them aren't dangerous to anyone but their intended victims."

"If this guy's at Darden, he's like the Red Angel. Or that other creep. The one that …" He didn't finish the thought, but she had to block out the memory of how she'd lost one of her eyes.

"Well, at least we know who he is. We know who his mother is. They may be monstrous, but they don't have magic abilities."

"I know. But I want you to promise me. You'll be okay. You'll be prepared."

"Scout's honor," she said, and gave him a kiss while they watched a morning talk show where the subject of murder wasn't mentioned at all.

❧

AT THE SAN Pascal Sheriff's Office that day, getting her third cup of stale coffee, Tryon, who ran the department, came out of his office. "I've been looking for you all morning."

"Sorry. Slept in. Need those eight hours sometimes."

"There's another body," he said. "I want you to run over to the morgue and meet up with Dahl. He's there now. And there's some trailer park to get out to. And don't be late like this. Throws everything off. Davis and March already have the techs out at the trailer, so at least it'll be kept clean."

"Will do," she said. "Where's the trailer park?"

"Over in Caldwell, up on Sunset Ridge," Tryon said, and then shook his head. "We've got to catch that woman today, damn it. It's already on the news, and we're getting crank calls about seeing Bloody Mary everywhere. I don't have enough officers as it is to track 'em all down."

CHAPTER SEVEN

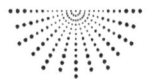

THE GUY WAS DRUNK AND IT WASN'T YET EIGHT IN THE morning. The bars out on Main Street didn't close sometimes until three, even though legally they had to be shut down sooner. But the one called the Silver Coyote usually had an after-hours poker game going, and he came stumbling out the back door around six a.m., the winner for the night with a good three hundred bucks in his pocket and the need to pee, real bad. His name was Nick Spitzer, he was forty-four, and Mary Chilmark had met him once or twice in her work. She was sure he'd remember her.

Sure that he'd help her.

She hadn't slept well that night, not without her son. She knew his car—a 1984 Cadillac that had all but gone to hell in the years Spitzer had been driving it—and it had bumper stickers plastering the back bumper that said, "Sometimes I Wake Up Grumpy, Other Times I Let Her Sleep" and "There's Too Much Blood in My Alcohol System," as well as the classic "I Got A Gun for My Wife, Best Trade I Ever Did."

It was unlocked when she found it, so she crawled inside and slept much of the morning in the backseat. She only awoke when she heard Spitzer's drunken calls to his friends as they left the bar, and then his fumbling with his keys before realizing the doors were unlocked.

When he slid into the front seat, he saw her in the rearview mirror and said, "Well, looks like somebody's lucky day. Hello, baby, long time no see."

CHAPTER EIGHT

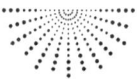

CALDWELL, CALIFORNIA: SMALL, A DUST BOWL OF A TOWN, A landscape full of ridges and foothills and canyons and the kinds of houses that looked as if they were meant to fall apart twenty years after they'd been built. The most noticeable landmark—one that had been there for more than a century—was the hospital.

The triple fence with razor wire, the small sensor detectors at key points along the fences, and the guard booths at every entrance and exit—all of it made the series of buildings look as if they were prison. Yet the grounds looked well-tended, no guard towers were in evidence, and cars drove fairly freely in and out of the main driveway. A few palm trees were planted around the buildings, and brief streets connected the long main building to the administration offices. It had the look of a corporate park built in a style that had all but vanished thirty years before.

Darden State Hospital for Criminal Justice was nearly a town unto itself, and recently had known prosperous times as its criminal population blossomed. Those patients who earned, bought, or otherwise obtained the insanity defense in their murder trials had worked its vegetable gardens and the great greenhouse where beautiful orchids had been grown. They had put together a Crafts and Decorative Arts workshop that produced hanging baskets and wrought ironwork for the home that had sold well in shops in Southern California; and they had created job skills within the hospital itself, bringing a sense of pride to the patients.

However, a group called Rights Advocacy of the Penal Institutions of San Pascal County had determined that this work was enforced labor and had lobbied to have it stopped. This particular advocacy group seemed to have a good motive on the surface, but, in fact, digging down through its layers, the group was funded by a handful of multimillionaire land developers who wanted state money diverted from the hospitals toward their own interests. Still, their lobbying efforts had a chilling effect on the Darden State Hospital for Criminal Justice. The work was stopped. The gardens left untended, the crafts workshops, the job skills—all of it stopped because the inmates of Darden State were hospital patients, after all, and putting them to work in some capacity was evil.

The results of this fine humanitarian effort on the part of the developers group was that within six months of the pressure on Darden to change their approach to patient care, the medications had to be increased for all patients, who then became more lethargic and well aware of their status as liabilities of the state. Because the hospital itself could not increase its own funding by sales of the works of its inmates, half the guards had to be let go, despite an increase in violent attacks on hospital staff.

This was the Darden State Hospital for Criminal Justice, also called the Darden State Hospital for the Criminally Insane. Once, in the nineteenth century, it was simply one of the many state asylums "for the insane and inebriate," and had looked like a Gothic castle. In that castle, the administrative offices, and beneath it, a true dungeon that held the many so-called "night cages" that housed the insane, the sociopaths, the tubercular, the alcoholic, the addicted, and now and then, the menopausal. If a child were irrationally violent, he might end up in the underground children's ward. If a family's daughter did not exhibit traditional feminine traits, she might be institutionalized and given what was called, in the early twentieth century, "bath therapy."

In the 1950s, the castle had been torn down and a new row of boxes had been erected, and by 1982, the current look of Darden State had emerged, looking more like a military base than a hospital, with guard booths along its avenues that connected the wards to the administration's offices to the row of bungalows where some staff chose to live rent free, within the fenced acreage.

There were other hospitals like Darden State in California, including nearby Patton State, but none carried the level of criminal that Darden did, since it took in the killers that the other state hospitals did not handle well.

But no matter how orderly and clean the aboveground area of the hospital seemed, beneath it, the night cages still existed, and though they had not been in use for more than seventy years, it was as if, buried beneath the new, the dark ages of psychiatric treatment still waited patiently for someone to creep down and switch on the light.

There were three things that caused some disturbance at the Darden State Hospital for Criminal Justice the previous summer and fall:

The high-voltage system that ran through the wards, generally above the ceilings, was taken down into the underground—the warren of corridors and tunnels that were no longer used, beneath the hospital itself. It became a two-million-dollar project that had caused patients to have a disruptive season, which was no help to the staff who cared for them. The ceilings had been ripped open; work crews came through, which required more lockdown time than normal; and the sounds of the work below—scraping, hammering, and the general thumps and metal clanks below the patients' rooms on the first floor—led to the widespread belief that ghosts were beneath the hospital.

This was not helped when news that a graveyard was found in one of these underground tunnels, and the bones—from the patients of the late 1800s to the early 1900s—were relocated to a cemetery eight miles away in Caldwell, California.

Somewhere in all this, a news reporter with a name that seemed as fake as his hair color—Lance Victor—had decided to do a three-part documentary on the scandals, the terrors, and the takedowns of what he called "the world of the criminally insane psychopath at the murderers' hotel—Darden State, in Caldwell, California."

~

Memo from James Willard, Executive Director, Darden State
  TO ALL DARDEN STAFF:
As many of you know, a television station out of Los Angeles has been working on a four-part documentary about the Darden State Hospital, specifically recalling last year's escape of Michael Scoleri and the murder of one of our psychiatrists, as well as other issues we have had with unfortunate incidents that have gained some unwanted publicity in local media, as well as national, in the past decade or so. The recent relocation of the graves has obviously focused interest here. We must come to expect that some of our community will be maligned, misrepresented, and shown in a less-than-favorable light, and realistically, none of us will be able to respond per Article 99.8 of the Media Contact Handbook.

Given that the cameras continue to come into our workplace, my best suggestion is for each employee to simply do his or her finest job, speak only with a supervisor present, or defer to your ward supervisor. The State of California has given the television crew an open window into our day-to-day operations, and we need to accommodate this change in routine as we would any other.

I ask you to join me, your new director, in resolving to continue with the excellence and diligence and care that Darden State is known for. One last note that I wish was unnecessary: when referring to Darden on-camera, please do so as the Darden State Forensics Hospital or the Darden State Hospital for Criminal Justice. We have not referred to our hospital as "for the criminally insane" since the early 1980s, and we feel it casts an unfortunate light on our work here.

We have nothing to hide here, and there is no need to cover up anything in the past. There may be disciplinary measures taken should any junior staff members take it upon themselves to speak directly with the reporter or his crew.

LANCE VICTOR, the television reporter, held the microphone up to Trey Campbell, just as he entered the security checkpoint in the main entrance at Darden State. "Mr. Campbell, what do you think of the murder of the Flock family by Bloody Mary and her son?"

CHAPTER NINE

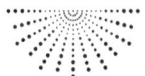

TREY HELD BACK HIS FIRST REACTION AS HE LOOKED FIRST TO the reporter and then to the cameraman. He glanced over at one of the nurses, and then to the guard who stood next to him. "I'm being ambushed again?"

In front of him, Lance Victor, who was six foot, blond, broad-shouldered, and as plastic as a pretty boy of thirty could be. Lance had won Emmys for his news coverage, had been named one of the sexiest bachelors in *Los Angeles Magazine* ten years earlier and still tried to cling to the title, and he had a look in his eyes that always reminded Trey of one of the new patients when they arrived at Darden, before the meds kicked in.

The cameraman behind him had kept the lens on Trey, and someone nearby had a blinding light that seemed to have laser-perfect accuracy for just Trey's face.

Trey squinted into the light. "Look, we can talk about procedure and technique, like we did last week, but you're not going to help anybody—least of all the victims' families—by dredging this one up today. Not this one. Go bother the police."

"The people want to know the truth," the reporter said in an incredible imitation of a sincere tone. "We know he's here. We saw the transport. This is an important aspect of this series we're filming. Why, without an arraignment, are they putting a killer in Darden State?"

"Listen to yourself," Trey said. "You believe your own bullshit?"

A guard nearby chuckled, "Get that clown outta here."

The camera came off the cameraman's shoulders; the light shut off. The cameraman said, "Come on, Lance, let's give it a rest."

The reporter gave a sharp glance to his colleague. "I just wanted a reaction," Lance Victor said, returning his attention to Trey. "It's a story. A good one."

"You want an interview with me, you schedule. No more ambushes. Understood?" Trey said. The reporter had caught him—and at least a half dozen psych techs—off guard to try and get a so-called "candid" moment too many times over the past few weeks. Often such moments took place right when a patient was going for someone's eyes, or when a violent fight had broken out and three techs had to go in and calm the patients involved, subdue them so they would not hurt themselves, get them in restraints, and still make sure they didn't get their balls ripped out in the process. The cameraman and the reporter were there to expose any little crack in the hospital, and Trey knew too well that most of the big cracks were in the administration, not among the staff of Wards A through D.

"I want in on Program 28," Lance said.

"No way in hell."

"If you care so much about these people, Trey, you'll get me in there."

"I can't risk your life and mine just for your show," Trey said. "If you had seen what some of these guys in 28 did, you wouldn't want to do it. You're going to have to make a special arrangement with the governor if you want to get in there."

"I have people working on it," Lance said. "I believe in Program 28, Trey. I've read up on it. I know they're the most violent, sadistic patients here. I know their crimes. I can list their names for you. If you can help me get inside there, I'll have my story, and I'll make you and your coworkers look like gold. I promise."

Trey calmed down a little. "Look, for some reason, Lance, you just get my hackles up. I apologize for the reaction. I know that what you want to do is a good thing. The more the public knows about Darden, the better off everyone is. But my understanding is there's already a stack of patient refusal and authorization papers in administration that have to be processed simply because you haven't done your follow-through. We're here for the patients, for the state, and so that people like you on the outside don't have to worry about these patients on the inside. We're dealing with daily stressful situations here that are not meant for anyone's entertainment."

"Why can't I bring the camera to Program 28?"

"You know why. It's for the most far-gone sadistic of the socio-pathic psychopaths," Trey said. "That's not the psych term you want or the state wants me to say. But there you have it. And above all that, they're human beings who deserve their privacy, even here. They deserve to get treatment within their hospitalization period."

"You mean 'incarceration,'" Lance said. "I think those people are animals. Monsters. I know what they've done to innocent victims on the outside. I've read the files. Do you think it's right that they get to hide inside here? That they get millions from the state thrown at them to keep them safe and alive?"

Trey hated the reporter for putting it that way, but something within him understood it. Sometimes, no matter how he cared for the patients, there were a handful of them that he wasn't sure deserved to live. And he hated having those thoughts. He felt that to be good at his work, he had to put that kind of mindset aside and focus on the good that could be created at Darden. He had to believe that if the psychiatric community kept studying and seeking to understand how the human mind went to the extremes that it did, that something good and powerful for the betterment of life would emerge.

But many days—and nights—Trey felt exactly like the reporter.

Some people didn't deserve to live.

And he knew that very thinking was not far distant from the minds of those extreme killers themselves.

"You have got to understand that you wanting a story does not supersede privacy issues and psychiatric considerations. Only the highest clearance would get you in there, and as far as I can tell, that's the one place you're not allowed."

"Campbell, look, man to man," Lance said. "I just ... I want to show the world what you do here. How you and the psych techs and psychologists are ... well, heroes of sorts. The truth of all this."

Trey wasn't sure whether to laugh or cry. *What bullshit.* "Show them whatever truth you decide on. But don't expect me to spoon-feed it to you. If you want to get clearances and permission, you know where Willard's office is, and you know where Sacramento is if you need more than that. Now, I've got work to do."

Lance Victor sighed, and for just a split second Trey felt a twinge of sympathy for the guy. *Just doing his job.* Trey had even watched Lance's reportage on the big earthquake a few years' back and had felt the guy was pretty good. He just hadn't known how in-your-face he got until the camera came into Darden.

"I just want something exciting to happen here," Lance said.

"I know, it's pretty boring," Trey said. "It's not like the snake pit you wanted."

"Hey, you got a takedown last week," a guard at the desk said. "How much more excitement you want? You want a riot, stick around. Maybe it'll be your lucky day."

"Yeah," Lance Victor said, grinning with perfectly capped, brilliantly white teeth. "I want a riot."

CHAPTER TEN

TREY NODDED TO THE GUARDS AT THE ENTRANCE TO WARD A; ID badge out, he passed through. The halls of A were decorated with drawings and paintings done by the patients. These were the least dangerous of Darden; some of them had attempted suicide and perhaps hurt someone else on the way out, but often it had been unintentional. Still, the state put them here rather than in a regular psych hospital, and there was good reason for some of them. A few psychopaths had open-door policies here, as well, for they weren't dangerous to any but their original victims; some were in their seventies and eighties and had been at Darden State for more than thirty years. Ward A was low-security, and the patients mingled with the staff, had small birthday celebrations. During visiting days, family and friends might come through and spend time with them, and all in all, it fairly closely resembled a hospital ward at nearly any other hospital, but in this one, the residents tended to be long-term.

He passed through the checkpoint at Ward C and nodded to Rita Paulsen, who was standing with two psych techs. When she saw him, she stepped over and mentioned the TV reporter gunning for him. "I already got gunned," he chuckled, and then he stopped by the refreshment lounge and popped a dollar in a machine to get a can of apple juice.

When he reached Ward D, Pete Atkins, a Correctional Officer whose post usually was at the entryway to Program 28, stood there, waiting for him.

ATKINS WAS A BEEFY, muscular guy and looked the way Trey figured most people on the outside thought of the guards: commanding, imposing, and even a little threatening. He looked like he could crush skulls in his hands and still feel good about himself.

"We're keeping Chilmark in 28," Atkins told Trey when he'd gotten past security at Ward D. "We had a minor incident earlier."

They both walked swiftly down the hallway. Now and then Trey glanced in the windows of the therapy rooms, seeing what groups were already in session.

"How's Victor know about the Chilmark kid being here?"

"He's in the news biz. They know," Atkins said, walking slightly ahead of Trey.

"I was sick of seeing that guy a month and a half ago," Trey said. "He's like the boogeyman, popping up when you least expect him. I don't want him to even know where Chilmark is. I wish Lance Victor would just go back to LA."

"Hannifin keeps him close," Atkins said, and then smirked. "She probably wants a new book deal, so she keeps the publicity going around her."

"Where is she anyway? She should be here."

"Running late. Start without her. That's what she said."

Trey walked swiftly down the corridor, stopping by his office briefly just to pick up the clipboard that had the material from Hannifin and from the police. "Was he given meds?"

"As per Dr. Hannifin, no."

"Good. Was he hurt in the takedown?"

"Not visibly. But it took six of us. I want you to know that, Trey. He's like a mountain lion when he's not in restraints."

"Did he get anybody?"

"Minor knee injury to Feldman. Other than that, once we had him on the floor, he calmed down. He took the restraints fine. In fact, he practically started purring when the jacket went on."

"I want the restraints off, if possible."

"Not yet, Trey," Atkins said. "He has another hour in them. Then, he can get out. That's per Hannifin herself. She wants a two-hour minimum restraint period, if a patient doesn't yet have meds, until all intake and assessment is complete. It's purely a safety measure. For the patient."

At the entryway to what the staff called the "silver wing" of Darden State, Trey showed his security badge, a formality that had to be observed in order to get through the double doors into Program 28. He didn't bother glancing in the other rooms that he passed, but kept moving down to the very last room where the temporary patient had been housed.

Program 28 was still a relatively new program, and funds for it had begun wavering already. It had cost a fortune to equip and had been set up to take on all the Sexually Violent Offenders divided into a few classes of human predator. They tended to be the patients no other hospital wanted, and they required additional expense to house. But the staff psychiatrists nearly begged the Board to okay the funds for the program, and it was their little golden egg—both prestige and money flowed to the department with Program 28. It was considered the worst of the worst, in terms of killers, and Trey wasn't even sure that Doc Chilmark belonged down in it.

The new patient was not sexually violent, but because the rooms were nearly their own isolation tanks for the patients, it served the purpose of keeping Chilmark out of the general population of Ward D.

The corridor had a blue-green metal cast to it and shone as the overhead lights bounced off the steel of doors. Thick panes of observation glass separated the patient from the staff. The rooms themselves were spare. The cot and table were secured to the floor. A sink and toilet were in one corner of the room, and a window that was narrow and barred, far above the reach of any patient.

At the locked door to the patient's quarters, Trey waited for the others to arrive before unlocking and entering the room.

CHAPTER ELEVEN

THE ROOM WAS WELL LIT, BUT TREY WISHED THERE WAS A dimmer switch. In the white light, the killer looked like a little abused boy who had just happened to grow up and begin to look like a man. Trey had already spent most of the morning going over the killer's mother's past records at Darden State, and had, briefly, seen some photos from the recent crime scene at the house in the foothills, faxes sent in as soon as Jane Laymon knew he'd be showing up for the intake evaluation.

In the photos: a woman on a bed. Dark blotches all over the mattress.

A man on a staircase, his bloodied handprints all along the walls.

And this man—this boy who had just recently become a man—had done it.

With his mother.

Instruments used include a scalpel, a bone saw, a bone file, bandage scissors, large metal forceps, several hypodermic needles, and what looked like a medium-sized hammer with a coin-sized circular saw attached to it and a sharp point at its tip. The note by the picture: "A trephine for trepan."

Sitting behind Trey, a psychologist named Whitfield, a young man himself, just out of his master's program, in this room to observe. Whitfield had thin wisps of prematurely thinning blond hair and a wide face that seemed to be cherubic, except he rarely smiled. He was one of the most serious of the younger group of psychologists and had made it known to Trey in past encounters that he did not intend to be anything other than cold and professional.

Trey leaned back in his chair and whispered, "Thanks for coming."

Whitfield remained silent.

In the doorway, a Correctional Officer with a big gut and a stern look.

Trey glanced up from his clipboard to the patient.

He marked in his notes: Patient has ankle hobbles. In strait-jacket. Appears calm.

The patient was approximately five foot four, brown hair that had not been cut in a while, narrow shoulders, narrow hips. Not exactly a slight build, but something about him was elfin. The snapshot taken upon his arrest did not resemble him much with the exception of the faint scars on his face. He had looked angry in the photo. The scars were somewhat visible as streaks of lines along his face. Here, in person, he seemed calm. He was relaxed, even in restraints. He looked like a nice guy who had run a red light and somehow ended up here, but was good humored about it.

The scars, though faint, had been from being burned and possibly sliced, but so many years before that they'd healed over several times. The scars were likely along his arms and legs as well. Trey easily guessed the reason: Mommy. She had been torturing the kid since birth. She had probably burned him with cigarettes and matches, and possibly taken a knife to his face more than once. It amazed Trey how sometimes a child could survive and grow up in such an environment at all. It surprised him whenever they turned out to be sane.

Chilmark was no surprise. His mother had raised him to be a psychopath, probably. She had done her damnedest to make him into her own image, and had apparently succeeded.

Trey swallowed the feelings of compassion he had, for the moment. The guy had just murdered a woman, a man, and an unborn child.

Tortured or no. Abused for years, perhaps, but it was hard for Trey to get around the images of the dead he'd seen.

Plus, Chilmark was smiling at him.

His smile, amiable. In fact, he seemed too comfortable.

In the fluorescent light, his skin was pallid. He had spent a lot of time avoiding the Southern California sun. Streaks of scars, pale, and somehow far too happy.

From where he sat, Trey wasn't sure if there was a birthmark of some kind on his neck, or if it was a tattoo. Some discoloration, just to the left of his neck where it slipped down beneath the collar of the straitjacket.

Trey had a photo of the patient's mother from the 1980s. The patient resembled her quite a bit, and also resembled—in his nose and lips and something even in his eyes—the psychiatrist who might, in fact, be the patient's father.

Trey wondered if Dr. Brainard would show up for any of the intake or evaluations related to the young man who might be his son.

"I WANT TO SEE A PRIEST," the patient said.

"We can arrange that. Catholic or Episcopalian?"

"Catholic."

"Mr. Chilmark," Trey began. "Do you understand why you're here?"

"Doc."

"Excuse me?"

"I've been called Doc since I was a little kid." His voice was soft, but deep, and sounded as if he'd practiced speaking in order to come up with such a smooth delivery.

Trey kept his eye on Jane Laymon's notes. Then, he looked up.

Handsome, troubled, muscled, looking far too innocent for someone who had just committed the atrocities that Trey had seen in those photos of the victims.

He looked like an ordinary healthy American youth, basically. Not completely clean-cut, and not terribly experienced. But that was a mask sometimes. A mask for deeper, hidden secrets.

Certainly for this young man, the secrets were just about coming out into the light of day.

"But your name is Quentin. Quentin Chilmark."

"Everyone calls me Doc."

"Why 'Doc'?"

"Doctor Quentin Chilmark. But please. I've been Doc since I was a kid."

"Tell me about medical school."

The edges of the patient's lips curled slightly. Chuckling to himself. "Do you know about talent? Some people are born with it. Some have it thrust upon them. Some have to earn a degree to pretend they have it. Before doctors, there were healers. And those healers didn't need to go to college. They had talent. When you have it, you don't need to be taught the craft of medicine. You know it."

"You're a healer?"

"I understand the nervous system of living things. I know how to set it right. I see death sometimes. Not the way people think. It's in shadows. Shadows of those who've already passed."

"Ghosts?" Trey asked. "Are you psychic?"

"I see people who have died, yes. Sometimes. They've taught me the secrets. The healing arts. The meanings of things. They brought it out in me, this talent. Some people are born with beautiful voices. Training only ruins them. My talent is healing, and my art is medicine for the body and soul. I have my father's hands and my mother's heart."

"Do you understand why you're here?"

"Sometimes, when a doctor does something for a patient's well-being, he ends up blamed for something he didn't do."

Trey leaned back in his chair. "You're here until a trial date is set. At that point, you'll be transferred to a facility in Los Angeles County. I imagine you'll just be here a few weeks."

"I'm here because my mother once spent time here."

"Yes, your mother was here."

"She was pregnant with me then."

"Ah."

"My father was a psychiatrist. He had troubles early on. I never knew him."

Trey refrained from telling all he knew. The rumors that Dr. Brainard was Bloody Mary Chilmark's lover before she was discharged into the arms of another psychiatrist, who married her, briefly, before taking his own life.

Dr. Brainard had denied it in a formal inquiry, and it remained rumor. Brainard now ran the Psychiatric Board of Darden, and although he was a difficult man, Trey had never believed he'd stoop to enter an intimate relationship with a patient. It was a popular delusion among some of the patients—that their doctor was also their lover.

Trey checked off the intake questions one by one, knowing that they'd get passed on up to the psychiatrist who would handle the patient's therapy for the time he was in Darden State. He became self-conscious of Whitfield behind him, probably wondering why he wasn't asking more pointed questions at this stage. Provoking the patient was sometimes as important as gathering specific information. Sometimes the patient said exactly what needed to be said.

In this case, Trey's directive from Jane Laymon was to try and get him to tell where his mother might be hiding.

"I'll bet you're writing fun stuff on that little clipboard of yours," Chilmark said. "I'll bet you're mentioning that I show no remorse. That I am in a state of delusional thinking."

"I'm not qualified to assess you in that way," Trey Campbell said. "This is called the preliminary intake. We do it with new patients or with those—like you—awaiting trial and recommended to this facility. Do you know why you've been recommended here?"

"They want to catch her."

Trey kept his poker face. It was important not to show the slightest surprise at one of the patient's answers. "It's because of the nature of the crime committed."

"Alleged crime."

"I have photos from the crime scene. Would you like to see them?"

"No."

"Why not?"

"They're fake."

"Why not look at them to see for yourself?"

"I don't need to. I was there. We were working to help that woman."

"She was nearly five months pregnant. But she's dead now. And her child within her. And her husband."

"Sometimes when you attempt healing, the spirit leaves the body. If you could see spirits, you'd know."

"Do you see spirits here? With us?"

The patient broke eye contact with Trey and looked around the room at the others. "Not right here. Not right now. They make themselves known to me as shadows."

"At this house, where you say you healed, what shadows were there?"

"The dead are everywhere around us," he said. "Most people are too caught up in the illusion of movement to recognize them. But some people see them."

"Healers?"

The patient nodded.

"You look uncomfortable. Would you like the restraints taken off?"

"No. I heart my straitjacket," he said.

"You like it?"

"I love it. When I was little, I had one of these. It kept me calm. More kids should be put in them," Chilmark said. "It was like warmth all around me. I loved it. I love it now. It's a blanket of love. Sometimes, if I was just tied down right, I felt completely at peace. Like I do now."

Trey scribbled a few notes. Behind him, Whitfield cleared his throat as if about to ask something, but no question came.

"You can sit down if you like. That might be more comfortable." Trey had the Correctional Officer get a chair and bring it in for the patient. When Chilmark sat down, he closed his eyes and whispered something.

"I'm sorry. Would you mind repeating that?"

"Yes, I mind."

"Are you thirsty?"

"No."

"I'd like to ask you more about these shadows you see."

"If you look, you'll see them too."

"Did you see them when you tried to heal the woman?"

The patient shot a harsh look at Trey. Trey felt an unpleasant intensity in the young man's expression. "Their shadows left them. It was the healing. Their bodies were already decaying. They needed to move to the light."

"The light of heaven?"

"I can't say. I've never gone to it. My mother thinks it's heaven. I just know it's where they go."

"Does your mother see them too?"

"No. But she knows I do."

"Where is she right now?"

"Everywhere. She is love. She is the most beautiful being on this planet. She is light itself. Light in the darkness. She is in everything. She's always watching."

"Even now?"

"Right now. She's watching. When I was a boy, she could go through these doors in my mind and see what I was thinking. She still can. That's her talent. Mine is for healing."

"Is she nearby? Watching you now?"

He grinned, shaking his head. "She told me wonderful things about this place. She told me that there were shadows of death along the corridors. She told me that no one who had entered this place ever really left. It seems fitting that I'm here."

"How so?"

"I was conceived here. It's my womb," he said. "Inside my mother, I felt the howl of Darden State."

"You were born after your mother's release."

"I was here, inside her, for four months. It's like coming home," he said. "I belong here. It called to me. Home at last. She told me about it. She told me that it wasn't as bad as you'd think.

She's right. It's not. I like it here. I could stay here a long, long time."

Trey cleared his throat. "Tell me about her," he said.

"She's pure love," Doc Chilmark said. "She's like fire. She's that pure."

CHAPTER TWELVE

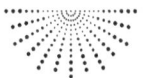

DR. SUSAN HANNIFIN WAITED FOR HIM IN THE HALLWAY outside. She was dressed smartly in a tailored suit with a skirt that showed off her legs. She wore the white jacket required of all psychiatrists when on the ward, but even with that on, she looked better than she had a right to look. She had no trouble confirming her status as the resident celebrity psychiatrist—between her makeup, the neatly trimmed bangs of her hair, and her clothes, she was nearly always camera-ready. She was also the only black female psychiatrist in residence at Darden, and that had added something to her celebrity as well, besides the book she'd written. Truth was, Trey felt a little intimidated by her, and a bit dazzled by her presence.

"How'd it go?" she asked.

"Good. So far. Want my notes?" Trey said, passing them to her.

She glanced at them briefly and put the clipboard back in his hands. "Let's get those typed up. I'm going to spend part of today and then I hope most of the morning tomorrow with Chilmark. I don't want him to be alone too much. I think there's some good work to be done with him—even if he only ends up staying her a month or two before the county starts up the case."

"He might be here longer."

"That's assumed," she said. "We can't keep him in 28 too long, but maybe we can find a place for him in D. What's your arrangement with the investigation?"

"Basic consult. No spying, don't worry." He said this last bit as a slight joke, but he could tell that it didn't go over well by the rather blank expression on Hannifin's face.

"The patient's rights are a bit void at this point," she said, and then when Whitfield came out from the room, she drew him over and they began what Trey often characterized as a "whisper-conference," made to make him remember his position at Darden as being still-lower than a staff psychologist. After a few moments of whispering, Hannifin came back over to Trey, put her arm on his elbow and said, "You've done great. We'll take over from here. If one of the detectives needs to talk to him, let's suggest either an early evening or early morning meeting."

"Dr. Hannifin," he said, "look. I know you aren't happy, having me assigned to this. I'll do my best to serve your needs here. And I promise to stay out of your way the rest of the time."

Hannifin glanced at Whitfield, then back to Trey. "I'm not unhappy that you're working on this with me, Trey. What gave you that idea?"

"Well, I know that you prefer to keep this—"

She interrupted him. "You're good at what you do. I'm not thrilled that your consult is with a homicide investigation, but I understand how the needs of Darden and the needs of the community-at-large are sometimes at variance. I have no problems with this arrangement. I have seven patients to see today, and if you can work up your evaluation, get it on my desk this afternoon, believe me, my job just got easier. I appreciate it. I'm glad you're on this, frankly."

And then, she took off down the corridor again before he could say anything more. Whitfield shot him an odd glance as if to say, *Don't you feel stupid?*

"Call Father Joe for Chilmark," Trey told Jim Anderson after the intake, once he'd gotten back to his office. Jim Anderson was not only one of his best friends—at Darden just about as long as Trey had been—he was the only one who got his jokes, his asides, understood the inside and out of irony, and had been with Trey in more takedowns of patients-gone-wild than anyone else in the hospital. Jim was a big linebacker of a guy, but still had the face of a kid with his fingers in the cookie jar. If Anderson had stayed at the job, working now directly with Trey on Ward D and Program 28, Trey felt he probably would've ended up in restraints himself.

"You think we'll get a confession?" Jim asked. He took the chair opposite Trey's desk, leaning back in it, checking his pager.

"I don't give a damn. That'll be Laymon's issue. He wants to talk to a priest, so let's get a priest in to him. I feel bad for this guy."

"A guy who just ripped a baby out of a woman's body?" Jim asked, even while he clicked through his pager messages.

"That kid was abused. In ways you and I probably have trouble imagining. Darden State made a mistake twenty years ago by releasing his mother. Someone made a mistake by impregnating her. That boy is paying for the mistake, and I'm guessing he's been paying his whole life. He thinks a straitjacket is comforting. Like a teddy bear."

"I don't buy it," Anderson said. "A lot of kids get abused who don't do what he did."

"Maybe they didn't get abused in quite that way."

"What way?"

"He was raised to be the perfect lover to his mother. Who knows how long that's gone on? Who knows what toll it's taken on him?"

Anderson winced. "Ew, incest. Yeesh. Can't imagine. You think that's it?"

"Yep. And somewhere in there, he was physically abused to the breaking point. He thinks he's a doctor because she made him fix himself. Did you see his arm? It was slightly askew at the elbow. I didn't notice 'til the jacket came off. She's broken his bones. Maybe years ago. I'm guessing he had to set them himself. I'm guessing he had to heal his own body when he was a little boy. He had to be his own doctor."

"Did you see Whitfield? Hear no evil, see no evil," Jim said, putting his hands over his ears. "He sat there like a bump on a log, and you know he's going to somehow make the intake all about him. He always does."

"He's definitely got issues with me working with Hannifin. But she surprised me. I thought she wanted me completely off this case, but she seemed great about it."

"Yeah, I can never tell with her," Jim said. "Sometimes she's a ball buster and sometimes she's just reasonable. I like strong women like that. It's kind of cool."

Trey drew out the notebook computer from the side table at his desk and opened it up.

"Want me to leave?"

"No. Just gonna type up some of my impressions. You on break?"

"Taking a breather. I have to get down to 28 and check on Ivory and Mandolar. Atkins and Freeman told me something's up down there, and Paulsen doesn't want to deliver any meals if she can help it unless at least three of us are there to help out." He glanced at his watch. "I figure I have ten minutes to kill. I call it my coffee break."

They sat around, Trey typing in his evaluation, and Jim just shooting the breeze about stuff he was up to out in the world—what was up at home, how he wanted to go deep sea fishing in a couple of weeks out at Point Mugu.

Paula Stewart, a psych tech on Ward D, came by the office and told him that someone had escaped into the underground.

"Who?" Trey asked.

"Fallon," she said. "Somehow, he got through the canteen."

"Rob Fallon? Christ. Can anyone else handle this?"

"Hannifin requested you for it."

"And I shall hop to it," Trey said. "This is what—the third time?"

"Fourth. You forgot Candler. She got in there too. Back in July," Paula said. "Didn't get beyond the fifth step down, though."

"Oh yeah. Do those guys hauling the wires ever lock the door behind them? Do they not understand where they're working?" Trey asked, shaking his head as if already knowing the answer. "Okay, well, thanks, Paula. I don't get this place sometime. Tight as hell security at the gate, but inside …"

"It's a free-for-all, sure," she said. "You want me to help?" But even as she asked this, he could tell by her tone that she had other things to get back to on Ward D. She was one of the best, and often had been run ragged by the psychologists who liked to assign everything to her because of her volunteerism.

"No, it's okay. I'll go down there with Jim," Trey said, glancing over at Jim, who had a big smile plastered on his face. "I appreciate the offer. Thanks."

"Robby'll be easy enough to nab," Jim said. "Like stealing candy from a baby."

"Reminds me," Trey said. "All morning I forgot to tell you—we're having another rug rat in the Campbell household."

CHAPTER THIRTEEN

Trey and Jim walked down the institutional-green hallway, recently painted and still smelling of turpentine; the groans and chattering of patients and staff somewhere nearby was at a low hum as they passed by nurses with their squeaky med carts and the open-door therapy sessions.

They passed by the inmate-patients of Program 6 on Ward D—some of the inmates looked out through the rounded double-glass windows. It always gave Trey a strange feeling whenever he saw them like this, as if they were observing details about the staff.

"I can't believe you're having another kid," Jim said.

"Yeah, weird, huh? Two kids nearly in their teens, and now we start again."

"How pregnant?"

"Six weeks."

"Hey, you should tell Mark that this one's a replacement model and he needs to scoot."

"Very funny, wise guy. We're holding off on telling the kids. Just for a bit."

"Carly?"

"She's still in shock. Here she was, thinking she couldn't really have any more after all that trying about six years ago. She told me she thought she was past her expiration date."

"Aw, you guys are still a little young for that," Jim laughed. "Hell, you could probably have four more kids."

"I suspect this'll be the last one." Trey sighed. "I guess I just knew my home office would get turned into another kid's bedroom someday."

"That's what they're for," Jim said, slipping his hand across Trey's shoulder. "Three kids are perfect. You can't get good sibling rivalries going with just two kids. Plus, you know, hand-me-downs. And the blue skies take of all this is that Teresa and Mark can actually babysit so you won't be stuck at home every Friday night."

"I love being with the kids on Friday night, Jim. I really do. My dad had all these hobbies and problems and other things. I just like being there with the kids. I like the idea of a big family. I'm good with this. Carly's a little overwhelmed. But I can't wait. But you know, I'm going to be old. I mean really old, when the kid's heading to college."

"You'd be old with or without another kid," Jim said. "Man, I am so happy for you both. You're lucky. And that kid's going to be damn lucky to have a daddy like you."

"Yeah," Trey said. "If I keep both my eyes intact."

"You and me both."

They walked around the workers who had to repair damage to the upper grillwork, along the fluorescent lights. A group session was going on in the Merritt Room—Trey saw Hannifin conducting. For just a second she glanced out the open door, and then said something to the attending psych tech, who got up from his chair outside the circle and went to close the door.

"I think you should name him after me," Jim said, a twinkle in his eye. "I mean, after all, Jim's a good name. If it's a girl, name her Hulga."

"Hulga?"

"Well, or Jim. Jim can be a girl or a boy. Jim's the best name there is."

"That's true," Trey grinned. "Many good Jims. Like Jimmy Dean."

"Jimmy Cagney."

"Jimmy Cricket."

"That's Jiminy."

"Same thing. Jim Beam."

"Jimmy Durante."

"Jimmy Smits."

"Jim Thorpe," Jim said, and by the time they got to the back of the canteen, they'd gone through a good fifteen well-known Jims and had started in on famous Hulgas, which made Jim crack up because he realized there were none.

By then, they'd made it through two locked doors, which Trey kept unlocking and then relocking behind him. They'd gone from the sterile halls of Darden State to the stainless steel kitchen of Ward D's canteen. The cleanup crew scrubbed down pans and washed out the grease pits and griddles from breakfast, with the big industrial dishwashers steaming up Trey's glasses to the point that he had to take them off and brush them against his breast pocket every now and then.

"Fallon get in here through the pipes?" Trey looked up at the grillwork above and the heating pipes that ran along the industrial green of ceiling.

Jim shot him a look. "Easier than that. One of these state guys left the door open. We locked it up afterward so he couldn't get out again."

The small room they entered after the third locking and unlocking, unlike the others, was made of cinder blocks. Trey tapped at the wall. "Under these are the old stones. Quarried from the foothills."

"Jesus, stinks down here," Jim said.

"Can't believe he even knows about this place."

"When one of our boys wants a hidey-hole, you can't really stop 'em."

"You'd think the cameras would." Trey pointed up to the top corner of the room, just behind the door. A slim beige camera mounted there—little more than a lens and a rounded hump of camera. The techs all called it the Watcher, and Trey had no better name for it. They'd installed them within the past two years. Some Watchers were larger than others because they wanted the inmates to know that someone supervised them at all times. It helped with the sociopaths, who tended to obey the rules so long as they thought someone watched them.

Some Watchers, like this one, were smaller, almost like the kind of internet cams Trey had seen in computer stores—barely noticeable until you gave a room the once-over. These were generally installed where fewer had access, and if someone breached the area —either staff or inmate—someone higher up the food chain would notice via security.

Trey reached up for the Watcher but couldn't quite reach it. He glanced at Jim, who, much taller, had no problem grasping the camera and giving it a gentle tug.

Just as Trey had thought, the camera came out of its mount too easily.

Wires had been cut.

Then, he pointed to the narrow low doorway, with the slightly open, thick wood door that seemed to him almost something out of Hansel and Gretel.

"Do you think he's down there alone?" Jim asked.

"Sure."

"How the hell would he even know about this place?"

"Staff talks. He's pretty good at being unobtrusive. With all the rewiring going on, he probably just listened to the workers over the summer."

"He's a little weasel."

"Rob Fallon's a genius," Trey said, glancing at the door. "What tools you got?"

"Basics. Taser if necessary."

"Not necessary."

"I don't trust the little lying son of a bitch."

"Trust isn't the issue. Anyone else down there? Guys working on the voltage system?"

"All of 'em got called up once they heard a patient was down there."

"Good."

Jim pulled out his walkie-talkie. Before he pushed the button to speak, he glanced at Trey. "Just calling some COs over. We might need firepower. I don't like taking chances with Fallon."

"In all the years you've known Fallon, when was the last time he hurt anyone on staff?"

"He did a number on Donna Howe."

Trey grimaced. He hated thinking about it; Howe had been killed because she had been seduced by Rob Fallon's charm. It was a problem for a good-looking sociopath—there were men and women out there who might as well have had the word "victim" emblazoned on their foreheads. And Rob, the Adonis Murderer, had been all too willing to charm his victims into giving up their lives—or limbs—when he'd been on the outside of Darden.

"That was Hatcher, not Fallon. Fallon may have set it up, but

Hatcher did the slicing," Trey said. "Christ, maybe we should call one of the guards. Who you recommend?"

"That new guy. Floyd. He's always talking about how he wants to see what's down here," Jim said. "Now's his chance."

FLOYD NELSON WAS A FIFTH-GENERATION CALIFORNIAN, and it had been his dream to be a cop in San Bernardino, but when it hadn't worked out, he'd gone into the field of corrections, first working, fresh-faced and upbeat, at Chuckawalla State Prison, maximum security. He had loved it so much that he'd had to undergo a series of psychological tests after he was caught beating an inmate within an inch of his life, and instead of getting dumped out of the system, he'd been transferred to the Darden State Hospital for Criminal Justice, and, at twenty-five, had decided to stop beating up inmates and start learning to handle them. He was tall and lanky and a little bit scrawny. His legs were too long for his body, and his uniform always looked like it didn't quite fit him. He had a happy look about him, and was quick to hum a tune while at his post over at the checkpoint between C and D. They'd cut back on correctional officers to the point that some at Darden were getting a little nervous about supervision, but Floyd had enough energy to do the job of two guards.

Trey had watched Floyd handle takedowns well enough to know that his story about getting a bad rap from his fellow prison guards might've been the main reason for his problems at Chuckawalla. Sometimes, the guards themselves could be the problem. Sometimes, the guards were heroes. It was like anything else in life —you never knew with some of them. There was good and bad in the staff; good and bad in the patients. You couldn't always separate it out, and sometimes, Trey had come to learn after all the years at the hospital, you just had to deal with it all.

Trey had a lot of respect for any officer who worked with criminals in the system and had met more good ones than bad ones. He was pretty sure Floyd Nelson was one of the good ones, despite what was in his file.

Trey knew enough about personnel files to know that sometimes they didn't tell the whole truth.

Only two things annoyed the hell out of people on the floor about Floyd. First, he was always smacking gum in his mouth, and it never seemed to faze him when people complained about the noise. And second, he had a voice that came out somewhere between his nose and his eyeballs, and people assumed he couldn't help it, but the shrill sound of him sometimes even upset the prisoners.

He was an odd duck.

FLOYD ARRIVED on the scene within minutes of the call, and although he had his club with him, and his gun holstered, he said, "Eh, if it's Fallon, I'll just sweet-talk him."

"You been down there before?" Trey asked.

Nelson, looking like a boy scout of twenty-five who would volunteer for wrestling a mountain lion, shook his head. Smacked his gum around his mouth, acting cocky. "Barely. Just looked down. It's all this stuff going on. Rewiring and shit. Didn't go far, but far enough to not like it down there."

"I've been all over it," Jim said. "Once. Back in the olden days, about nine years ago. They used to take us down here. Just to show us."

"It's like one big dungeon, that's what one of the guys told me,"

Floyd said, his grin spreading ear-to-ear, his hand lightly touching the edge of his holster. "Or a rat maze, I guess."

"Floyd, can I ask that you just don't chew gum when we're working together?" Jim asked. "It's like hearing a clock ticking real loud."

"I need gum. It keeps my mouth from dryin' out."

"Come on, dude. Spit it out. You can get some more when we get Fallon out of there. Please. Oh please. If I get another migraine, I'm gonna go postal," Jim said.

Floyd glanced over at Trey, who said nothing. Then, he spit the gum into his hand, and then put it up behind his ear, which made Jim wince a little to see. "Please tell me you're not gonna chew that later on."

"My ear's clean," Floyd said.

"IT'S A SERIES OF CELLS, operating rooms, administrative offices," Trey said. "Not much different from what's above. Just think of it like that. He may have squirreled himself down in one of the tunnels, and then we'll be a little screwed. But it's just a big basement if you think about it."

"Big frickin' basement." Jim grinned. "Back when lobotomies and shock treatment were the norm. And drunks got put away."

Trey nodded, grimly. "The dark ages of psychiatry."

"They still do shock treatments in Mercato," Floyd Nelson said. "At least, that's what I heard."

"They may want to, but they don't," Trey said.

I hate going down here, he thought. No matter what anyone said, nobody who worked in the aboveground hospital liked going below. Most of them forgot about it. Most tried not to think about what was below their feet as they walked the corridors of Darden.

And then, he went and drew back the door.

"I once had to go down there with two others because the pipes had some problems," Jim Anderson said. "There are tunnels heading all over the place. Rooms so small it makes you want to run out of there fast. And I did, believe me. I found a place where there was an incinerator."

"A furnace?" Trey asked.

"An incinerator. Back in the day, when someone with tuberculosis died, they had to burn the body on the premises, by law. I hated even seeing that thing. Big old ugly metal furnace that looks like it could fit six people comfortably, and twelve if you stacked 'em. Creepy, creepy. I wish they'd just fill it with concrete and brick the whole thing over."

"How far does it go? A mile?" Floyd asked. "When I was down there it looked like it went on forever."

"The whole length and breadth of the grounds above us, pretty much. If Fallon's down there right now, he's staying put, though. Some of the wings of the underground got caved in. Like back where they found the burial area. But I don't think anyone's gone exploring down here for at least a decade. Who knows?"

"I heard somebody tried to escape under the street coming up from down here," Jim Anderson said. "But that was before my time."

He toggled a couple of switches just inside the doorway. A green-yellow light came on, and then a red one, just inside the narrow corridor that awaited them.

"Gentlemen," Trey said. "Start your engines."

"Sort of exciting in a weird way," Jim said, turning back to look at the Corrections Officer. "Hey, Floyd, you ready for a takedown?"

And that's when they heard someone coming up behind them. Well, smelled him first. It was as if Calvin Klein himself wafted in the air—the strong cologne was smothering as it moved ahead of the man who wore it, the man who walked rapidly toward them.

Trey glanced behind his back—Lance Victor and his cameraman in the doorway, camera's red light on, Lance looking like he had just won the lottery.

CHAPTER FOURTEEN

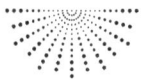

"No, no, and no," Trey said. "Floyd, escort Mr. Victor and his camera guy—what's your name?"

"Alex," the cameraman said.

"Okay, Floyd, let's get Alex and Mr. Victor back to the canteen, please."

"I just want to get a shot or two down there," Lance Victor said. His face was shiny with sweat, and his hair had matted against his scalp. "We can do it on low-light, so you won't even notice us."

"I'm sorry, sir," Floyd Nelson said. "I've got to ask you, for your own safety, to step back into the other room until we've come out of here."

"I've been in riots before," Lance said. "I've had a murderer point a gun at me when the camera was on. It's all right. I know you will handle this guy. This just would really make the series click."

"I'm sorry," Trey said.

"Look, this guy could rip your face off," Jim said, his face turning grim. "I've seen him tear a man limb from limb."

"I've met this inmate," Lance said. "Robert Fallon. I doubt he could tear anyone up."

"Then you've never seen him at his best. He's in here for slicing a woman up. Well, several people, actually. Sometimes he scalps them. Nobody's here just because they committed a nice neat murder," Jim said. "You ever see a staffer with one eye? Or the ones who limp a little? Attacks are the norm."

"No matter what," Trey said, "we have a responsibility to the patients to protect them from this kind of exploitation. Even if we took you down there, Mr. Victor, your network would never be able to run that segment. You know that. Without our explicit permission, and the permission of the state, you can't expose a patient like this. Now. Go back into the canteen. Or go find one of the administrators to take you on a tour of Ward D. You can probably sit in on a group. All right?"

Lance Victor drew his cell phone out of his pocket, flicked it up, and tapped in a number. He spoke into the phone and then passed it to Trey.

Trey put it to his ear and heard the voice of the Executive Director of Darden State, James Willard. "Trey, we've given him access. The state has approved this."

After he closed the phone up, he tossed it back to Lance. "Stay close. Do not start interviewing anyone. Do not talk to the patient if you see him. If he comes for you, scream as loud as you can so that we hear you. If you and your camera guy decide to go off on your own, we can't guarantee your safety. Also, and listen up, there are some high-voltage wires down there, not all of them secure. My advice is, don't touch one if you see it hanging from the ceiling. Do not talk to me. Do not ask me questions. Do not stand directly behind me at any time once we're down there. Stay back at least three feet. This is for your own safety. Understood?"

Both Lance Victor and his cameraman, Alex, nodded.

"What's it like down there?" Alex asked.

Floyd Nelson grinned, glancing at the others. "I've been down twice already since July. It's not all that bad. Just some old administration offices, some corridors that don't really lead anywhere anymore. Rooms, basically. Crumbling a little. Messy. But it's just like you'd expect old offices to look that haven't been used in a long time."

"It's not precisely a dungeon," Trey said. "At least not where we're going."

THE CORRIDOR within the doorway to the underground led to the stairway. It was metal, and had been built in 1994 when the old staircase had given way after nearly a century of neglect. The steps and banister were almost ornate in structure and shivered slightly with so many people on it. "Maintenance guys come down here more than anybody," Trey said, turning on his flashlight as he descended the staircase. The light below grew feeble as they went down, and Trey felt as if he sensed something bad.

"Jesus," Jim said. "I wish we didn't have five people going down. It's gonna make Fallon panic."

"It'll be okay," Trey said. "We'll handle it. I'm betting that Rob wishes he hadn't run down here at all at this point."

"I heard a few other patients got down here," Lance said, his voice hushed as if he were entering a cathedral.

"Nobody got out if that's what you're hoping," Floyd said. "The guys have been working for a few months on the big rewiring project. Lifting grates, ripping out ceilings, and then repurposing and adding abatements. We got some high-voltage wiring down here, though, so don't stand around touching pipes or nothing."

Something not as right as he had hoped it would be. He had

anticipated that Rob Fallon would just be here hiding, maybe playing with himself or even hurting himself, which he'd sometimes done.

"Why'd this guy come down here anyway?" Cameraman Alex asked, shining his light in the dimly lit room far below, which took on a greenish cast from the lights above. Water dripped from heavy pipes that ran along the walls and ceiling.

"He wants to escape," Lance whispered.

"*What?*" Jim Anderson asked, as if this were the most lame-brained thing he'd ever heard.

"I always do my research," Lance said. "I know a patient got out through here about ten–twelve years ago."

"That ain't true," Jim said. "There's no way."

Trey put his hand on Jim's shoulder. "Yeah, someone tried to. Didn't get far. But somehow made it out to the middle of Jackman Boulevard."

"Pipes," Lance said, pointing to the wide green pipes of the ceiling. "The wiring guys told me some of those tunnels caved in over the past thirty years. You follow the big green pipes and eventually you're somewhere just outside the fence. It's impossible to get through there now, though. It's all clogged up."

"I know Fallon too well," Trey said. "He's not interested in escape, believe me. It's more likely he's just down here playing with himself."

"I don't feel great about this," Alex said, lowering his camera. "Lance, look, let's just stay up top here."

"We're getting the stories of Darden," Lance said. "Now, switch it to low-light and keep it on your shoulder."

"I don't want chatter down there, unless it's me, Jim, or Floyd. Got it?"

"Yes, sir," Lance said without much humor in his voice.

Trey looked over at Floyd, who remained back a ways, as if he didn't want to look down into the underground area known by most staffers as "the Pit."

Floyd leaned against the wall, his sight wandering from door to door and then back again. *Floyd must hate this part of his job.* Trey didn't even like to admit to himself how creeped out he was about going down these stairs into the underground tunnels and warrens.

"Robby's smart," Jim said. "Holy crap, look at that." He shined his flashlight over in a corner.

A pile of dead rats, their stomachs ripped open.

"I guess the rat poison worked," Floyd said.

"Poor little guys," Jim said. "I know it's soft of me, but I hate seeing dead animals. Even rats. I like rats."

"But not in the food," Floyd Nelson said, and Trey was sure he heard the familiar smack of gum again coming from the guard's mouth.

BY THE TIME they reached the bottom step, Nelson's hand had begun trembling enough for Trey to notice. "It's okay, Floyd. It's Fallon. He's doesn't bite like some of the others."

"Not unless you get cozy with him," Jim added.

When Trey stepped down onto the floor, the planks creaked. The floors were made of slats of wood raised over a stone and concrete surface. Not the original wood, but a more recent addition, mainly raised up because of flooding that occurred now and then when the rains came through Southern California.

At the floor level, Trey noticed the smell more than anything. It was an awful mix of mustiness and mildew and even the rotting rats, as well as something that reminded him of a swamp. He never liked thinking about the underground when he was above it. He felt it was part of the shame of Darden's past—back when, instead of medication, they used what now seemed like medieval torture on the patients. He didn't like thinking about the kind of asylum Darden was in the late nineteenth and early twentieth century. Whenever people bemoaned the use of medication or the compassion of modern-day criminally insane hospitals, he wished they had seen the evidence he had of the past: of the operating rooms, the treatment facilities, and the cells that were known as "night cages" by the patients themselves because they were kept in isolation and darkness.

TREY WALKED AHEAD of the others, shining his light into the dimmer areas. The overhead lights were unstable, flickering in the main entry foyer, which was nothing more than a big empty room with a cracking wood-slat floor and exposed wiring and pipes all along its walls. Straight ahead, the first corridor down and to the left, a large room-length square hole where a window had once been. Inside, old file cabinets, a pile of rubble and another pile of tools left by the construction and repair crews that came down occasionally. He didn't like to anticipate fear. Not in his work, not in his life. His wife had told him, "Don't die twice," and it was a huge lesson for him about dealing with fearful situations. He knew she had meant, "Don't suffer before you have to," and he tried to apply that whenever faced with situations that raised the hackles of his old fears.

But since the Red Angel killer—a man who was now a heavily medicated patient in Ward D—Trey had begun having nightmares about work and life that had not subsided. What bothered him the most was that sometimes, when he woke from the nightmares, he wondered if patients at Darden State didn't experience the same sense of dislocation and anxiety that he felt. This manifested itself as a certain confusion of the mind when working so close with the criminally insane population, sociopaths, especially.

"They get inside you," Dr. Brainard had told him years before. "And you have to do what you can in life to leave this place behind every day you walk out that door. Because once you stop leaving it behind, once you take Darden State with you, it's too late. You are no longer helping the patients. You're becoming one of them. And you'll start self-medicating. You'll begin to hallucinate in the same way the patient does. It's the close working quarters that does it, and I can't advise anyone to stay on the psychiatric technician staff for more than fifteen years. I think it's a mistake to make this your life's calling."

It had been bad for Trey before. When Agnes Hatcher had escaped a while back, he'd gotten caught up in her delusions to some extent. And with the Red Angel killer, he'd had images in his mind he'd never be able to erase: the memories of the most horrifying thing he'd yet experienced in life. He could name patient after patient that had no effect on him—terrible murderers, sociopaths, and psychopaths. But something of his feeling of safety had eroded in the past year, despite his new position at Darden and his consulting work with Jane Laymon.

His mind had begun to believe too much in the nightmare and not enough in the positives of life.

Being in the underground did little to brush away these fears.

But with a reporter and cameraman nearby, he wasn't about to mention it. He just took a few deep breaths and toggled a light switch near the entrance to the corridor as they all stood before its darkness.

"Let there be light," Jim said, like a voice of comfort beside him, as the fluorescents above them flickered to life.

CHAPTER FIFTEEN

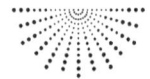

"This is the back way. The main entrance is at the opposite side. It's completely sealed off from the grounds above," Jim said. "Twenty rooms on this level, twenty-five below."

Lance looked down at his feet, then back at the others. "Below? There's another floor underneath this?"

Trey nodded. "They used to call it the Bunker. But before that, they were the cages."

"Night Cages. That's what they called 'em. They kept them all there," Jim added.

"Loonies," Floyd said. Floyd still hadn't quite gotten the hang of calling the patients by their more politically correct designations.

"People who were ill," Trey corrected him. "Back then, it wasn't a forensics hospital. They weren't all murderers. Patients with tuberculosis were housed in the same area as those who were violent schizophrenics, and beside them were sociopathic killers, and in the next bunk might be a woman who had been put there by her husband, just because she was menopausal."

"Gay men and women too," Jim said. "Just because they were

gay and somebody with power over them put them here. Shock treatments. Insulin-induced shock. Thoracic surgery. And all of them having to live together. Before meds. Well, before really effective meds."

"Sounds like a torture chamber," Lance said.

Trey glanced back at him. Lance kept back a ways, and the cameraman moved around to take in the sights of the hallway.

"It's got some kind of night vision?" Trey asked. "That camera?"

"Yeah. It can get a reasonably decent image with almost no light at all."

"With luck, the lights'll come up as we go. But if they don't, I may have to ask you to use it to look around in the dark."

"Sure," Alex said, his voice utterly serious.

"The few times I've been down here, I always get the heebie-jeebies," Trey said.

"Makes me want to just go back upstairs and wait for this guy to come up on his own," Jim said.

"Knowing Rob," Trey said, "he's terrified right now. Poor guy."

They followed the old corridor down past the empty administrative offices, past where any light reached, and they found Rob Fallon nearly shivering under one of the old operating tables.

Trey stood at the entrance to the room. It was a medical theater, and although not particularly large, it had seating for about ten on a raised platform that overlooked the room and its three metal tables.

"Rob, it's okay. You can come out," Trey said, shining his flashlight near Rob's hand, which stuck out from beneath the table.

"I can't," Rob said, his whisper echoing in the chamber.

"It's okay. We'll just go back up and get settled."

"She brought me down here," Rob said.

"Who?" A shock went through Trey; had someone else come

down here with Fallon? Had Fallon managed to seduce another female employee?

"The girl," Rob said.

"Where is she?"

"By the door."

Trey shone the light in the doorway below them.

"There's no one there."

"That's what she wants you to believe."

"Let's go back up," Trey said. "Maybe she'll come with us." He motioned to Jim and Floyd to step back quietly. Then, Trey leaned over the railing and turned about, hanging over the edge of it, his flashlight between his teeth. He jumped the few feet down, landing in a crouching position.

Rob Fallon scooted back under the operating table.

Trey walked to the doorway and found the light switch. He flicked it. *Thank God it works.*

The white glow of the light came up, accompanied by a buzzing sound. It began flickering overhead almost immediately.

On the platform above, both Floyd and Jim stood still, watching. Behind them, obeying all the rules set out for them, were Lance and Alex.

Trey crouched down again, looking at Fallon.

Beneath the table, Fallon looked like a young bird tossed too early out of the nest. Weak, hungry, frightened. Not the murderer who had torn the face off a woman and had chopped her up, back in his early twenties. Not the same one who had raped and murdered his own mother.

His face was pale white and shiny with sweat.

"Who is she?" Trey asked.

"She's here," Rob said, glancing around, his voice a whisper. "I can feel her."

"Is she from Darden?"

He nodded.

"Is she a nurse?" Trey felt dread as he asked the question, fearing that Rob had lured someone here and had killed her.

He shook his head. "She's a little girl. A little girl. And she told me terrible things about this place."

Trey crawled closer to Fallon, putting his hand out. "Come on, Rob, it's all right. Just take my hand and come out. We can go upstairs. You can watch TV or get some rest."

Fallon looked at Trey's hand, and then looked over Trey's shoulder as if looking for someone. Trey resisted the urge to turn around. He had to keep his eye contact square with Fallon's, although it was best not to look Fallon directly in the eye. Better to look a little off to the side so that Fallon would not begin to see Trey as the enemy.

"I think she's lived down here a long, long time," Fallon said.

"Give me your hand, Rob." Trey extended his arm as far as it would reach. He needed to be close enough for Rob to take his hand, but far enough away should Rob suddenly attack, which was not unusual for the patients in Ward D.

If Rob went into hyper speed, Jim and Floyd would have about twenty seconds to get down in that pit with him and wrestle Fallon off him. For all of Fallon's slight build, he was like a mountain lion when he attacked.

Trey's fingers brushed the tips of Rob's fingers.

Trey felt his mouth go dry. *Come on, Robbie. Give it up. Let's not have any trouble.*

Rob's eyes went wide suddenly, as if there really were someone standing behind Trey, and when Trey felt a gentle whisper of air on the back of his neck, he twisted around for just a second—nothing behind him, just the suggestion had given him that feeling—but it was too late. Rob had already grabbed his hand, and pulled him fast beneath the table. Trey began trying to hold Rob's arms back, but

Rob, using teeth and hands and legs and even his head—banging it against Trey's—became relentless in his attack.

Trey felt claws rake across his face as he tried everything he could to gain the advantage, but it wasn't until Jim and Nelson got down into the operating pit with him that they were able to pull Rob Fallon back and hold him in a four-point star—a man on the legs, another on the arms and shoulders, and another to hold his chin back so that he couldn't use the strength in his spine to get free.

"Hey, buddy, good going," Jim said, panting as he looked down at Trey, who had Rob's legs and pelvis pressed against the floor. "You've still got your eyes."

AFTER THEY CALLED for a nurse to come down with a dose of Cambex, and after Rob got a nice shot in the butt of the fastest sleep-aid known to Darden, they carried Rob back up into Ward D. "Jesus, it's like we're croc hunters. I'm Steve Irwin today," Jim said. "We'll be on TV. Crikey!"

"My kid loves that show," Trey said. "I have to keep him from grabbing snakes when we go hiking."

After they got Rob settled nice and snug in some restraints in his cot, and Rob began muttering something about wanting to kick some serious psych tech ass as he drifted off into med-induced oblivion, Floyd Nelson stood in the doorway to the room and said, "That was one creepy place down there."

Trey glanced back at him. "You lock it back up?"

"YOU KNOW WHAT, CHIEF?" Jim asked, after they'd left Rob

Fallon's room and made sure that Lance Victor and Alex had gone off in search of another docudrama treasure for his series, and they were headed back down the hall to the door to the underground.

"What?"

"You're an anal son of a bitch."

"You say that so happily," Trey said.

"Of course the guy locked it up."

"I think Floyd was freaked by all the stuff down there."

"Floyd and Lance Victor both," Jim said. "Alex seemed to be cool as a cucumber, though. I guess they expected it to be more like a basement of horrors."

"I get freaked down there too. But I need to make sure."

When they reached the entry to the underground, Trey pulled at the door, checking the lock.

"See? Floyd's on top of this stuff."

Trey withdrew the keys from his pocket and unlocked the door. He opened it.

The green and red of the stairway lights were still on. Trey gave Jim a knowing look, reached around to the switch, and shut them off.

He looked down into the darkness.

Then, he stepped back and shut the door again.

Locked it. Locked the bolt.

It didn't make Trey feel any better, knowing that some workmen would be going down there again before evening. Couldn't have a guard put on the door every second of the day, not with the reduction in the number of correctional officers.

IN HIS OFFICE, going through Mary Chilmark's files, Trey heard a slight tap at the door, which was open. He glanced up.

Floyd Nelson stood there, leaning against the door, as if he'd been watching Trey for a while.

"Come on in," Trey said. "What's up?"

"Just a question. About that place."

"Sure. Some of the old-timers can probably tell you more about it. Marshall was part of the relocation crew in fifty-three."

"Why do they keep it like that? I asked some of the guys, but nobody seems to know. I mean, beyond using it for storage and maybe for the rewiring job."

"Oh," Trey said, grinning slightly. "You mean the tables and the offices and stuff?"

"It looks like ... well, it looks bizarre."

"Some wiseass administrator found out it was cheaper just to let it all rot down there than to do anything about it. I think it's called 'administrative atrophy.'"

"Yeah, but in some of those rooms ... hell, I saw a supply room that looked like it still had ... all kinds of shit in it. Medical stuff."

"Old useless medical crap, probably. You might not want to dwell on it too much," Trey said. "We live above it in the sunshiny world of our hospital, and below us is that pit. Well, separated, I'm told, by a ton of pipes and insulation and all kinds of grids that keep us from sinking. I'm sure Willard or some Board member is eventually gonna clear it out, or they'll fill it in like they did with the north wing. Yeah, they bulldozed in a lot of dirt and rocks and then concreted over part of it to the north—right over the field out by the fence. I bet Alice in B has got the files on the whole thing if you want to look it up. Floyd? You okay? Look, here," Trey went to his side desk that held the files and drew them out. "I have a cool centennial book on Darden." He brought out a thin magazine-sized paperback. On the cover was what looked like a Gothic castle. "See, this is the aboveground part, circa 1906. They tore it down for a newer building in 1963, but this one went all the way down to the cells."

"You ever get freaked out by being here?" Floyd asked.

"Unofficially? Sure," Trey said. "All the time. You got to develop some gallows humor about this place to get through it. What about you? You were at Chuckawalla."

"It was rough," Floyd said, a shadow crossing his face. "But this is a different kind of rough. There, you knew who the mean ones were. You expected them. Here, you just can't tell. Sometimes ... sometimes when I do my rounds, I think they all just seem like nice people."

"Until they try to bite your tongue out," Trey said, trying to get the guard to laugh. When Trey's phone rang, Floyd waved good-bye and went back out the door. Trey picked up. "Campbell, D."

"You called me earlier. I'm calling you back," Dr. Brainard said.

CHAPTER SIXTEEN

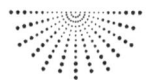

BRAINARD'S OFFICE WAS UPSTAIRS AT THE END OF THE EAST wing. You entered it first through safety doors—those double-thick steel doors that shut like a trap if even one alarm sounded in the building. It was a suite of offices used by the on-staff psychiatrists who did not keep outside offices. Outside each office was a cubicle for the psychiatrists' main assistant. The floor had a beautiful Persian carpet runner, and the smell in the air was of coffee and roses. Behind a long impressive desk in the reception area, a woman named Lara worked phones and a general assignment board when staff supervisors arrived to check on any med changes authorized.

Lara hadn't been at Darden long, but she had managed to get to know everybody by first name within her first three months. "Hey, Trey, how ya doin'?"

"I'm here to see Dr. Brainard."

Lara smirked. She didn't have to say what she was thinking—it was telepathed to Trey—*He's in a mood. Be careful.* She readjusted her headset, pressed a button on the phone. "Diego? Is he in? Trey Campbell's here for him. All right. Thanks." She drew her headset off, setting it next to her coffee mug. "He's making you wait. You know that."

"I expected it. What's the word up here?"

"Well, that TV guy was with Hannifin early, right when she came in. I think she's milking the whole thing. I think I caught a little whiff of jealousy up here about it."

"Naw, they're behind her one hundred percent. She can do no wrong," Trey said. "Besides, I heard her book was pretty good."

Lara reached under her desk and drew up a copy of the hardcover. *The Killer Instinct: Inside the Minds of Seven Psychopathic Murderers.* She opened it to show him how far she'd gotten. "It's weird to think the guys she's describing are just one floor down and to the left. I practically feel like I've been reading their diaries."

"She doesn't name them, right?"

"No, but you don't need a name tag to figure out who they are. She has your pretty boy in here."

"Rob?"

Lara nodded. "Oh yeah. She calls him the Movie Star, like he's on *Gilligan's Island.* I heard you had an adventure with him today. Down under."

Trey grinned. "Word gets around."

"Well, I'm the one they all come running to with their secrets," she said. Then, a buzzer went off on her phone. "Okay, well, it looks like it's time for you and Dr. B. Have fun."

Trey picked up the book, hefting it from one hand to the other. He turned it over and looked at the picture of Hannifin. "Look at her. She's a star."

"Don't say anything bad about her. I love the book."

"Can I borrow it?"

"Get your own copy," she laughed. "I'm only on the third psycho."

DIEGO, Dr. Brainard's personal assistant, was at the closed door to Brainard's office at the very end of the hall. "He's in a mood," Diego said.

"So I gathered."

"I'm guessing you know why," the assistant said, and then opened the door into Brainard's office.

THE OFFICE WAS the largest one Trey had seen inside the ward. Sprays from green plants were at either side of the doorway, and the white carpeting had Persian rugs thrown over it, just in front of his desk, and farther back near a sitting area at the far end of the office. The filing cabinets were made of cherry, and the desk itself was enormous and curved around to provide an area for Brainard's assistant to come in and take dictation. On either end of the desk were two crystal vases with roses and lilies in them. On the wall, the requisite certificates and degrees and pictures of Dr. Brainard through various decades with the famous and politically connected of California. On the bookshelf next to Brainard's desk, a handful of his own books, published over the past twenty-six years, on the nature of the human mind and its psychiatric deviancies. On his desk, Dr. Hannifin's book, closed, looking as if it had never been opened.

Two green overstuffed leather chairs sat on the opposite side of the desk from Brainard himself.

Brainard, at his desk, glanced up from a stack of papers, as if surprised to see Trey Campbell at all.

Dr. Robert Brainard was a hard-ass of a psychiatrist, but Trey had developed some respect for him over the years. He had silver-gray hair, very thick and neatly trimmed. A longish face, and a slight indentation from some old scar just below his lip. Other than that, he was of the "handsome doctor" school: well groomed, stayed trim by morning trips to the gym, and was always dressed in a suit that looked like it cost a thousand bucks or more. He had an edge of class and the kind of condescending attitude that annoyed many, but not Trey. He knew it was a defense for some little dark corner of insecurity.

He also had steely blue eyes that seemed piercing at times.

Trey stepped into the psychiatrist's office, shutting the door behind him. It was shadowy in the office; the blinds were drawn; the overhead lights were off, but an imitation Tiffany lamp on a corner table gave off a reasonable amount of light. Still, it was as if it were nearly dusk in the office.

"I can give you ten minutes," Brainard said.

CHAPTER SEVENTEEN

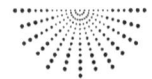

"It's about Mary Chilmark's son," Trey said.

Brainard leaned back in his chair, folding his hands over his chest. "Sure."

"Quentin Chilmark. In Program 28."

"I know. I signed the papers."

"I want to know about Mary Chilmark. His mother."

"It's all in the files. Surely, Dr. Hannifin…"

"With respect, sir, I've been assigned to do all intake and eval with the supervision of Dr. Hannifin. I have been going over some of Mary Chilmark's files. Given that you were the psychiatrist who worked with her and signed her release evaluation, I thought you might be able to give me some insight that's not on paper."

"You know," he paused slightly, a bit of bitterness creeping into his voice, "as involved as you are these days in matters of police and legal interest relating to our patients, you must never forget that they're patients. Quentin Chilmark is not in Program 28 today because we're going to spend time catching his mother for a homicide investigation."

"Sir, if I may," Trey opened up the envelope in his hands and brought out a sheaf of papers, "in your exit evaluation, you said this about Mary Chilmark. 'The murders of two women, one man, and an unborn child. Each seemed to have an element of irony to the murder, for they were people who, in her original state, the patient felt had done some moral or spiritual wrong that needed to be brought back to them, ten-fold.' I'd like to know what that meant."

"Mr. Campbell, it was a long time ago. I do not always recall the inflection of a patient's voice when reiterating psychosis. Particularly after twenty years and thousands of other patients who have become residents here."

"I know she murdered her victims in the hospital where she worked. San Pascal. I have pictures here—"

Dr. Brainard raised one hand slightly, his voice a little weary. "All right. I don't need to see them. I remember those pictures well enough."

Trey nodded and went to sit down in one of the chairs that faced Brainard's desk.

Brainard leaned forward, brushing his hand over some papers, and flicked on a small halogen desk lamp. An intense square of light hit the desk. Brainard reached up to rub his eyes and the bridge of his nose. "I'm not unaware of the connections that have been drawn between Mary Chilmark and myself. She was pregnant by some tech who worked with her at the time, but for some reason that wasn't glamorous enough for the staff. Because I spent a quarter of a year working with her—primarily because she was showing extraordinary progress—the rumors flew that I had fucked her."

Trey leaned forward in his chair, his hands nearly touching Brainard's desk. "That's not why I'm here. I want to know about her."

"I'm clearing the air, Campbell. I knew her well enough to know that she had become attached to me in a way I didn't think was healthy for her. I am willing to bet she's even convinced her son that I'm his father. When Dr. Massey married her—once she had been released—I felt that she had moved on successfully. It wasn't until his suicide that it crossed my mind that she might have had a reversion of psychotic behavior. It was the death of her father that led her to murder those people in the hospital."

"That, and revenge."

"Revenge. Or not. It was trauma and repressed memory that triggered the event then. And if she has now—with her adult son—murdered, while it's not pleasant, it doesn't surprise me. I suspect Massey failed her."

"By killing himself?"

"Exactly. And don't raise those eyebrows; he did kill himself."

"Yes, sir. But the coincidence of both her father and her husband killing themselves ..."

"I'm not saying that Mary herself may not have abused them both in some way. But their lives were taken by their own hands," Brainard said. "I should've seen the signs with Massey. He was a troubled soul if there ever was one. But I thought he had gotten on the right track. He resigned, you know, after she left. He made a break and got into private practice."

"And then he killed himself."

"People do that now and then," Brainard said. "He was complex. She was too. I have no doubt he loved her very much."

"How does it happen?"

"What—suicide?"

"No. How does a woman who kills three people—and at least with one of them, does something pretty nasty before the victim dies—get her time in Darden State completely cut?"

"You know how it works. She met the criteria."

"But she'd only been here two years."

Brainard shook his head. "You think this is quantifiable. It's not.

We did our best by her. And it's not as if she went on a rampage after she got out of here. These current murders—which, I'll remind you, she's allegedly connected to at this point—are nearly twenty years separate from her time spent here. I have no idea what set her off, if indeed she was set off at all. We have her son here. He's the one we can talk to. But for all you know, Mary Chilmark is dead too. Has anyone thought of that? Has anyone considered that her son may have killed her?"

Trey brightened a bit. "He says she's still alive."

"And he may be operating under delusional thinking right now. Are you playing detective here?"

"No, sir. I'm doing my job."

"Your job is made up," Brainard said. "The State of California wants you here. Even the Board members want you here. But I don't. I'm not happy about the way you handle the patients. A psychiatrist is murdered in the foothills because of her own stupidity, and you, along for the ride, get a promotion. My best advice to you is to find a more administrative position and get away from the hands-on approach until you have full medical training."

Trey felt his hackles rise a bit at this remark but tried to focus on the Chilmark case. "Sir, I don't care about rumors. I don't care about what you think of me or what you think of my promotion here. I respect your authority and your work. I just would like you to tell me about the murders she committed in the late 1970s."

"It's all in the files. But I guess with your new position here, I need to follow through or someone on the Board will slap my hand. Mary came here when she was young and troubled. She was in her early twenties. Just out of nursing school. She was smart. She had graduated early from her program, top of her class. She worked on the terminal ward at St. Anne's. As I recall, she murdered a man who was seventy-four, a woman of twenty, and a pregnant woman. In my work with her—after she came to Darden, which was soon after her trial—she exhibited signs of molestation, trauma, and intense stress at the death of her father. She had precipitating incidents, including possibly the threat of rape, and sometimes, Campbell, we all have a button. When that button gets pushed, it sends someone over the edge. Her button was pushed, and there was no fail-safe for her. Additionally, she had attempted suicide a few years earlier, although this was not known until we found the scars on her body. As we worked with her, she became a model patient and began showing remorse for the murders," Brainard said. "She told me that the old man had reminded her of her father. When she took him his medication one night, he had begun fondling her. This triggered the event which led to his murder. And unfortunately, she also went out of control that night. The others also were killed, although in some respects, they were bystanders in the hospital to the main killing. Certainly, it was with the old man that she got her most ... well, creative is a word I hate to use."

"Not so creative," Trey said. "She cut off his testicles and penis and put them in his mouth. He bled to death."

Brainard wore a grim look. "She was in the height of her psychosis. She had been raped, repeatedly, as a girl. She had been tormented and tortured by her father. A repeat victim of incest of the worst type. Her degradation was constant as a girl, and her father was responsible. And yet his death triggered feelings of guilt and fury. Trey, you know by now how this often goes. Psychosis meets abuse meets trauma meets opportunity to act out. It's not always in such a neat package, but this one was practically textbook."

"I understand. So, she took revenge on the man in the hospital for his sexual advances by castrating him. But why in the mouth? What's that about?"

Brainard stood up and went over to the windows. He raised the blinds. Outside, a haze of light. "She liked for the punishment to fit the crime. That was part of her behavioral deviance. But she got beyond it. Through therapy and work, she responded, Trey. At least … at least it appeared that way at the time." Then, Brainard wiped his face with his hands, as if he could somehow take the mood away. "I will say this. She was an extraordinarily sexual creature. Her appetite was enormous, which made us wonder if the traumatic episodes had not awakened a part of her brain. She could not seem to shut it off. Thus, her advances to the staff—and to me, yes— were constant. It could not simply be explained by acting out. She was seductive to the extreme. She knew that she was a beauty, and she did everything but unzip flies. I always brought two female nurses in whenever I met with her. Even so, she knew how to give subtle sexual hints of her availability."

"I doubt that poor old guy in the hospital ever touched her," Trey said.

"There was evidence to the contrary, of course," Dr. Brainard said, a slightly disappointed tone in his voice. "Look, Campbell. Her past history is there. It's in the files. You're welcome to them. We don't know who the father of that boy is, and I've always assumed it was Dr. Massey's."

"That one still baffles me," Trey said. "He married her after he got her out."

"Yes."

"Until he took his own life. And yet this seemed to trigger nothing in her. No incidents reported. She lay low and was quiet. How well did you know Massey?"

"Not well enough. He was a troubled man. Sometimes those who enter the psychiatric field do so primarily because they are deeply troubled," Dr. Brainard said. "Some of us are here out of genuine curiosity of the mind, other are here because it was their training, and still, now and then, a man like Dr. Massey will show up who has spent his life studying the mind and its psychoses because he does not have a handle on himself. When he told me he wanted to ... well, take care of her on the outside, I assumed that baby was his. But it might not have been. Maybe it was another patient here. A tech, or an orderly. Anybody. We may never know. But despite her sexual proclivities, she met all the criteria for release. And, per the law, we could not keep her if the Board felt she would benefit from release. You weren't around then, but some very progressive judges were looking over cases like Mary's, and she met every one of their criteria as a good candidate for continuing therapy and reintegration into the outside world."

Trey remained silent. Seconds ticked by on the wall clock—it was nearly noon.

Dr. Brainard half-grinned, like a man who remembered his youth much better than it ever could be. "I was fresh out of my first internship and came here to really help these people. I hope I have. I hope I continue to do so. She was different. She didn't even look like the other patients. She seemed healthy and vibrant, and sometimes ... sometimes when I spent time with her, I felt as if she were a psychologist sitting there talking to me. Intelligent. Curious. Not at all like a patient or a prisoner." Brainard shook his head. "I just can't believe she's regressed to this point. I mean, she hasn't had a history since leaving here. Not 'til today. Are they sure her son didn't act alone?"

Trey nodded. "Yes. Even Doc Chilmark puts himself there with her."

"Doc?"

"Her son. His name's Quentin, but he goes by Doc. He thinks he's a natural healer. He claims she acted as his nurse for the operation."

"He may be lying."

"I don't think he is. I don't think he cares. He believes he did the right thing by the woman and her baby."

Something changed in Brainard's demeanor. He suddenly looked as if he had some insight that hadn't occurred to him before. "With that man in the hospital. Back then. She cut off his penis and testicles and stuffed them in his mouth and stitched his lips together. She said she did it so he'd know what it felt like too. What she'd felt like having him want to put it in her mouth. Is there something about this murder like this? Some kind of warped poetic justice?"

CHAPTER EIGHTEEN

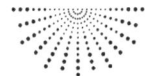

As soon as he'd left Brainard's office, Trey went out to the grounds and opened his cell phone. Jane Laymon picked up after two rings. "The Flocks knew the Chilmarks somehow. They had some relationship with them."

"Nobody seems to be able to put them together. I wonder how they interacted."

"I don't know. But they had to. Tell me exactly what was done to the bodies."

Jane cataloged the murder scene for him: the way the woman was cut open. The blood. The man was first attacked on the stairs, but likely was not meant to be the victim. He had simply surprised them. If he'd come home an hour later, he'd be alive.

The woman was the intended victim.

She had done something to Bloody Mary and Doc.

They had extracted their revenge in some way.

IN THE ROOM, with Doc Chilmark. Straitjacket, hobbles. Doc looked too comfortable in them.

"How did you know Mrs. Flock?" Trey asked.

"I don't know nobody with that name."

"Your mother. How did she know her?"

"My mother is a nurse. She knows when people are sick."

"But you're a doctor," Trey said. "Don't you know?"

"Not always. Sometimes a nurse knows more than a doctor. Everybody knows that's true. Sometimes doctors can be very, very blind to things."

Trey kept his eyes on the young man. In restraints, sitting up in his cot. Then, Trey got up and left the room.

IN THE HALL outside Chilmark's room in Program 28, the guard, Atkins, stood by.

"Why's he still in a jacket?" Trey asked.

"Every time we take it off, he goes for the balls."

"His or yours?"

Atkins chuckled. "I don't care if he goes for his. It's mine I'm thinking about."

"I want the restraints off."

"With respect, I think that's unwise, Trey."

"We can bring in some more officers if you feel the need for protection. There's no reason for him to have that straitjacket and the hobbles on in there. The only reason for it would be if he hurt himself in some way."

"Can I ask why?"

"He's too comfortable in that straitjacket. He likes being bound up. I want him a little uncomfortable for a while."

Atkins' expression soured. "Okay. Well, we're gonna need some heavy hitters. Let's get Anderson, Jarrett, and Schwartz down here. If this gets into takedown territory, I assume you'll accept responsibility."

"Completely," Trey said. "Let's do it."

TWENTY MINUTES LATER, three more beefy guys showed up, including Jim Anderson, with a big smile.

"Five guys with a nineteen-year-old. I think we should be able to keep this together," Trey said.

He unlocked the door to Chilmark's room.

Inside, Chilmark had already taken off the straitjacket.

"IT'S AN OLD TRICK," Chilmark said, once Trey had entered the room again. "When I was little, I loved Houdini. He was into ghosts and séances, just like me. He could escape from anything. Straitjackets are easy. I have a jacket like this at home. When I was little—when I was bad—my mother would put me in it. She told me it was so I wouldn't hurt myself." The cadence of his voice had a chilling effect on Trey, and he felt that the other guards with him must've felt it too. Chilmark was too relaxed. It was nearly as if another personality had come out from him. Nothing threatening. Nothing worrisome, but a completely different aura to his tone and the slight grin he wore. It was as if he were playing a part for them.

"Okay. Okay, so you can do the amazing escape trick too. So, why didn't you do it before?"

"I wanted to impress you," Chilmark said. Then he grinned. "Well, plus I don't mind the jacket."

"I know, Doc. You feel good in it."

"I like this place," Chilmark said. "It feels like a calm place. Not like that other place."

"What other place? The Flocks' house?"

"That was awful," Chilmark lost his smile. "Awful. I couldn't stand the light outside. The shadows. It all came crawling at me."

"What crawled at you?"

"They're like spiders sometimes. Crawling, crawling. From shadows outward. They like to bite when they touch you."

"Spiders?"

"Not spiders. Like spiders. The fears. The fears come at you. They crawl and they hiss and they come from a very bad place. Very bad." As Chilmark spoke, Trey felt the level of tension in the room rise.

"It's all right now," he said. "It's okay, Doc. You're here. Right here. No fears around. No shadows."

Chilmark took a deep breath, and when he breathed out, he groaned. "If you take a breath and count to four before you exhale, you can make them go away. Sometimes."

"Why do they come?"

"The fears are there after healing. The ghosts move on, but the fears they leave behind start wanting to find someone else to get inside. You know about night fears?"

Trey nodded.

"No, you don't," Chilmark chuckled nervously, clapping his hands together. "You don't even know how many you have. But I know how many I have around me. In the dark."

"How many do you have?"

"Oh. Thousands. Thousands and thousands, but they can't get in me. No, no, no. They want to, though. All the healing releases them. And they're waiting for me at night. They want me to close my eyes, but when it's dark out, I always keep my eyes open. Always. When that lady got healed and I saw her shadow go off to heaven, I knew that she left behind fears. Nothing you can do about that. Fears always stay back, and they want to make a nest under your skin. That's what they do. They dig under your skin with their sharp little claws—teeny-tiny so you can feel them but you can't see them at all—and they want to get inside you so they can do all kinds of things to you and eat you up from the inside out. That's what they do. They eat at everything under your skin. But I don't let them in me. No fears have gotten into me. They all wait to try and get under my skin. But they haven't gotten in yet. Well, once. But my mother destroyed them for me. You see how she did it? She did it right," he said, pointing to the streaks of scars along his face. "They got under my skin, nearly a hundred of them, but she went in with her cutters and she got them all out, and if I don't sleep at night, they can't get back in me."

Trey let him calm down before returning the conversation to the murder. "Let's talk about the Flock family."

"Who?"

"You operated on a woman who had a baby inside her."

"It was a malignant tumor," Doc said. "She would've died with it in her."

"She's dead now."

"So you say. But I've seen her. Since. And she looked fine to me."

"How well did you know her?"

"I didn't know her," Doc said. He had a mischievous look on his face, as if he were playing some kind of prank.

"Your mother knew her then."

"You could say that," Doc grinned.

WHEN TREY HAD GOTTEN Atkins to unlock the door again, he

brushed past him toward the double doors that separated Program 28 from the rest of Ward D. He walked swiftly down the hallway and opened his cell phone, tapping in a number and waiting. Jane Laymon picked up.

"Okay," she said. "Look, meet me at the morgue. It might help to see the handiwork. If you're ready. You sure you're up for this?"

"I'm not. But she's out there somewhere. And she might be ready to kill someone else again," he said, trying not think of Carly at work or at home or going to the post office, pregnant, the way Diane Flock had been pregnant. Just having an ordinary day at the very moment someone decided to torture her—and her unborn child—to death.

CHAPTER NINETEEN

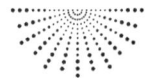

THE MORGUE IN SAN PASCAL WAS ACROSS TOWN, BUT THERE was no traffic on the freeway, and he managed to avoid the red lights on the streets up to it. He parked, and Jane was already there, at the automatic doors in front of the sheriff's building, looking grim but still managing to smile when she saw him. Once inside the building, a slender man of fifty or so came up to the two of them, and Jane introduced them. "Trey, this is Howard Dahl. He's our lead investigator."

"Good to finally meet you, Mr. Campbell," Dahl said, shaking his hand vigorously, continuing to walk with them toward the stairs down to the morgue. "Laymon's told me she prepped you on the murders already."

"Yes," Trey said, noticing the smell of alcohol and bleach that wafted up from the staircase below.

"What she probably hasn't mentioned yet," Dahl said, "is that there was another murder. Only nobody thought it was a murder until we found some evidence linking it to the Flocks."

TREY HAD PUT on a breathing mask, both because of the chemicals in the vicinity and the stink of the corpses. The smells were unavoidable at the morgue, no matter how the ventilation system worked and no matter how low the temperature of the rooms. The lights overhead were nearly blinding if Trey looked up from the table, and they afforded the corpse on the table a glistening white sheen, almost as if it were an alabaster sculpture rather than human flesh.

And it was not one of the Flocks. They were on separate tables toward the far end of the room.

This was a victim that had not been thought of as a victim.

Until now.

"HIS NAME'S COOPER FENN, and he lived in a trailer park. The body was found a day before the Flocks' murder. He was a well-known drunk in three counties, causing brawls, and he had warrants out for his arrest for everything from traffic violations to bounced checks to petty theft. Nobody was surprised when he was found dead," Dahl said. Then, he looked at Trey and grinned. "You doing okay?"

"What? Sure." But even as he said this, Trey realized that he was sweating up a storm. His throat had gone dry.

"You look a little clammy," Dahl said.

Jane touched Trey's shoulder. "Maybe this was a mistake."

"No," Trey said. "It's okay."

"Sometimes the smells are a bit much. You open a body, and there's a lot of nastiness in it," Dahl said.

Get hold of yourself, Trey thought. *It's okay.*

But it was like the nightmares he'd had. The bright light. The pale skin of the dead. The dead man, himself, looking nothing like anyone Trey had ever seen. Yet, he had nightmares where he was in this morgue. In this room. It was the downside of his new position: he had to get used to death. He had to see things as these investigators did. But something within him resisted, and he longed for his home and his kids and his wife and all the things that reminded him of a happier world.

"It's okay," Trey repeated. "So what ties this guy in with the Chilmarks and the Flocks?"

Dahl glanced first at Jane, and then at Trey. Then, down to the corpse. "Here's the thing with Mr. Fenn here. He died apparently of natural causes, at least for him. Blood alcohol level was through the roof—.50, basically. So, sure, that's death. Only problem was, he's two hundred seventy-seven pounds at five foot four, and he'd survived alcohol poisoning in the past. Not to say he couldn't have died from it, anyway. That's certainly what everybody thought. But here, the coroner's assistant found this." Dahl reached to the dead man's lips with his latex-gloved hands. Using two fingers, he drew the man's mouth open. "You'll have to move a little closer to see this," Dahl said.

Trey leaned down farther. He breathed through his mouth and felt queasiness in his stomach. Inches from the corpse's face, Trey saw the inside of the mouth.

The gums were swollen toward the back of the mouth.

"He's got eight teeth missing—someone pulled them. Now, sure, maybe he was drunk and went crazy and pulled them himself," Dahl said, drawing his fingers out. "But we found the teeth. We didn't really know whose they were at the time."

"At the Flocks' house," Jane said.

"Perfect matches," Dahl continued. "So then, we come back to Fenn here, and we feel like we didn't study him enough."

"Let's not show it," Jane said. "I think Trey's just hanging in here."

"I'm fine. Let's do this. What else?"

Dahl stepped over to Cooper Fenn's thighs and drew his legs apart. "Twelve eight-inch needles here. Maybe more. Once we get the X-rays done, we'll know. Thrust up beneath his scrotum."

AFTERWARD, sitting in Jane's car, Trey leaned back in the seat and took a sip of Starbucks coffee Jane had nabbed for him.

"Near as we can tell," she said, "they got him so drunk that he died of alcohol poisoning. But someone—one of the Chilmarks—spent a lot of time carefully pushing those needles up inside him. It was after that that some of our guys searched Fenn's trailer. Because he had died out on the street, everybody assumed it was whiskey or meth, and nobody bothered to do a thorough search of his place. They did, just about an hour ago. And they found that Doc Chilmark had lived with Fenn for four years. Everybody in the trailer court thought they were father and son. Nobody who has been interviewed so far knew what happened to Doc after the age of twelve, but someone did say they thought his mother came and got him then. And that's when we figured out how Mary knew the Flocks."

"Was it about Chilmark?" he asked.

"No. But in his past life, before the drinking got too heavy, Fenn had been an unlicensed acupuncturist. He ran a somewhat legit massage parlor down on Harland Avenue for years. It's gone now, but the people in the trailer park talked about how good he was at massage therapy. Acupressure, Swedish, deep tissue massage. He apparently did pretty good."

"Legit massage?"

"No idea. But Fenn brought out the acupuncture needles now and then when he thought somebody needed them. The business was a little off-the-books. I think she was working for him in that massage parlor. I think she went to Diane Flock's house because she got called in to do a massage. Diane let her in. Maybe she expected the son too. Or maybe Mary worked on her own and let her son in once she had Diane Flock subdued. We're doing some checks at area medical offices to see if she left her business card around."

"Nobody on that street saw those two?"

"Sometimes," Jane said, "in the light of day, people just aren't looking for murderers. How's Doc doing?"

"He's practically in heaven at Darden," Trey said. "He feels a connection to the place. I've never seen a patient adapt so well that quickly."

"Fenn's trailer park is in Caldwell, just over the ridge from Darden State. Mary Chilmark and her son might just have been living within a ten-minute drive of the hospital."

THE CALL CAME IN LATER, and Jane heard it replayed for her over the phone by Tryon, from a "Mrs. Kilpatrick," who lived in "Caldwell. I'm a property owner and taxpayer and I think the woman they're calling Mary on the TV news is one of my renters. The picture on TV ain't exactly what she looks like, but that boyfriend of hers—no mistaking his mug."

Jane found the rental house where Bloody Mary Chilmark and her son, Doc, had lived for at least five years, on Third, right off Main Street with its strip of shop fronts that made up the nearly nonexistent town of Caldwell, California.

Less than a mile from Darden State.

CHAPTER TWENTY

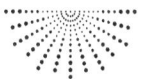

It was a scraggly little house, white shingles, an arched roof that nearly went flat over the box of house; it was set one dusty block behind Main Street and its bike shop, bank, markets, the animal shelter, three bars—one with boarded-up windows—a Pep Boys, and the railroad tracks that crossed the road right in the heart of town. There were six houses down the side street on each side of the road, and then it dead-ended in a cul-de-sac. The driveway was mainly dirt with a thin veneer of crumbly pavement. Jane Laymon, who drove out alone to the place, parked in the street.

A thickset woman of seventy with owl glasses and a white frizz of hair stood in the driveway, looking as if she expected unwelcome relatives to show up. She wore a chambray work shirt and blue jeans. When Jane got out of her car, the woman took the magazine in her hand and held it over her eyes to block out the sun that had turned to red and black on the distant burning mountainside. "You the cops?"

"Detective Jane Laymon," Jane said, walking casually over to the woman. She drew her badge out for identification, and then put her hand out. "You're Mrs. Kilpatrick."

"Mary-Louise," the woman said with the desert rat accent that was nearly southern redneck, prevalent out along the dusty ridges of inland Southern California. Her face was that strange orange-brown of too much sun and too much age, and lines crossed and looped her skin like crop circles, making her look much older than the age she stated on the phone when Jane had been put in touch with her. "You should get yourself one of them glass eyes. Those eye patches draw attention."

Jane nodded. "I prefer a patch."

"I'm just sayin'. You're a pretty girl and all. What are you, six foot? They grow 'em tall where you come from, I guess."

"Yes, they do."

"All I'm sayin's I know a guy with a glass eye where you can't even tell he's got it until he pop it out and shows ya. His name's Ricky and he's sixty-three years old and he pops it out and laughs at ya and it looks just like a real eye. I mean, a real eye with color and everything. Nobody'd know the difference, you ask me."

"Is this the house?" Jane asked.

"Yeah. I can't say nothin' too bad about her except she's a little long in the tooth to keep lookin' like she's twenty or something. She likes her men, I guess. Bad men, but she picked 'em, all's I'm sayin'. Best renter I got in other ways. Does all her own maint'nance. When the driveway had cracks and holes all over it, she hired the guys to do it. Never once called me. She never complained. When the roof got a leak, she got up there and fixed it herself. She was that way."

"When was the last time you saw her?"

"She's been gone about a week. I come over every day," Mary-Louise Kilpatrick said. "I take in the mail. The papers. Check the lights. Make sure nothing's up. It ain't a bad neighborhood, but all's

I'm sayin' is there's bad and there's good, and sometimes we got worse on this block. It all comes outta LA. They chase the gangs out this way—what, ten, fifteen years back. And now we got problems. She didn't like that. No riffraff except that boyfriend. But when I went in today, somebody had got all the mail I had stacked up by the door. Maybe day before yesterday was when I saw it last. I take care of what I got. I own three of these houses." She pointed across the street and then to the house next door. "I don't never rent to no people without runnin' a credit check. I do a TRW and sometimes that other kind. If they get late on their rent, they gotta go to Western Union down next to the Wienershnitzel and get a money order. I don't play no games. They owe, they owe. All's I'm sayin', I didn't have no trouble here. I had one of them Mexican families tossed out, well, they just never were up to no good." Even as she said this, she glanced at Jane's face as if studying it. "You one of them?"

"One of what?"

"Mexicans? You look Mexican. Not that there ain't good ones. They just don't live up here. We got Mexican cops now?"

Jane tried to forget the stink of beer in the air, a halo around Mary-Louise Kilpatrick.

"She's not here anymore," Jane said, confirming what Mary-Louise had said in her phone call to the police.

"Sometimes I seen her boyfriend around. That's why I made the call. But you people got him, so I knew it was safe to go over."

"You went inside?"

"Well, I don't normally do it, but I just let myself in the back. And the place is a wreck. I cleaned up a little, knowin' you was comin'. I don't keep no pig sty."

"Her name is Patty?"

"Patty's the renter, but it's her sister been livin' here for a while. Patty took off, but ya know, I don't care if it's one or th'other, I just care that they keep the place up and pay up. Payin' up is hard as hell for some of these folks. I had queer folks down the block, but they're pretty good with money, just bad with sin, if you know what I mean. I mean, I'm a good Christian woman. We got the meth people near the end, by that house that got burned out. We got some bad people. Patty, the sister, now she was good folk. And Patty went to church over in Moreno Valley, but I told her that the Church of the Desert was a better place. But that sister of hers, she never went to any church I ever heard of."

"Mind if we go inside?" Jane asked.

"Don't see why not. Nobody home, and she's three weeks behind on rent," Mary-Louise said. "I been worried sick about her since I saw the news."

THREE EVICTION NOTICES were taped to the front door. Mary-Louise snorted as she turned the knob and opened the door, a step ahead of Jane. "She ignores them. Always late. I guess if Patty were here it would be easier, but that sister of hers. All's I'm sayin' is she don't like payin' rent. But she usually ends up comin' in just before I file with the court, and I get a sob story about money bein' tight and then she pays me cash and we're good for another go 'round."

"What's her sister's name?"

Mary-Louise did a half-turn, and took off the glasses as if doing so would help her think better. "It's on the tip of my tongue. Can't quite get a hold around it."

"Did she ever write you a check?"

"I'd say yes, but I'd be lyin'. She was cash only."

"But she's the woman in the picture."

"Yeah, the one on the news. I knew that boyfriend of hers was up to no good."

"Boyfriend?"

Mary-Louise nodded her head, crossing one arm under the other with her free hand touching the edge of her chin, as if it helped her think. "He was a no goodnik. He was way too young for her, but women who stay single too long like she did, they invite that kinda trouble sometimes. Ya gotta marry young and stay married and then it all goes fine. But wait and wait and wait, and you end up with a guy half your age who'd as soon slit your throat as look at ya."

INSIDE THE HOUSE, Jane first noticed the massage table, open, in the middle of the small living room. The shades were drawn. The room was furnished with things from the Salvation Army, or perhaps garage sales. Nothing matched, everything had a dinginess to it, and the lampshades—as Mary-Louise went around turning them on—had blotchy stains on them. "I didn't know nothin' about her clients coming in here at all hours of the day and night. She said she was a nurse and a licensed masseur," pronouncing the word "masser," "and peoples' business ain't none of my own, but she was okay most times I saw her. But that man of hers. She was robbin' the cradle, and then some, and he was into drugs or some-thin' because he always looked shifty. Shifty eyes." She pointed to each of her eyes as she said it. "Shifty. Shady. He was never around, and then he was suddenly there. If you ask me, she's the innocent one. Maybe she's a sinner, but he's the shifty one."

Jane went room to room, and it was in the tiny bedroom that was not much bigger than a closet that she saw the dog crate. It was the size one might get for a German shepherd or a Great Dane. "She had a dog?" she asked the landlady, who stayed back in the hallway.

"No, no critters. She was at least good about that. She couldn't stand animals. I swear I once saw her try to run down a cat that was just racing across the street."

Jane went over to the crate, crouching down beside it. The metal grid of the door was open.

A smell came from it, and she immediately thought of an animal.

But inside, there was a pillow and a man's soiled underwear,, and pushed to the very back, a pair of handcuffs.

AFTER SHE'D RADIOED for two of her guys to show up and start a real inspection of the place, Jane went with the landlady out to the backyard. The back was concrete from the kitchen door out to the end of the property at a chain link fence; beyond it, another house, nearly identical to this one. There was a plastic table out under the roof overhang, and a couple of lawn chairs. On the table, an ashtray and a small bucket with a citronella candle in it. Jane walked out to the chain link, and then looked between the houses in back—an alleyway ran between them, and there were two little girls playing with naked Barbie dolls, with the clothes for the dolls lying in a small pile.

Somewhere distant, a dog barked.

Jane glanced into the backyard of the house next door: a swing set, a children's playpen of some design that included a bright orange slide and a netted area for climbing. A barbeque grill, its top up.

She went back to the white plastic table by the kitchen door, where Mary-Louise sat. She'd already lit the citronella candle.

"When was the last time you saw her?" Jane asked.

"Well, she comes and goes. But I sit up waiting for her," Mary-

Louise said. Then, she pointed to Jane as if she were the tenant. "I say, 'You better pay me what you owe, Missy, or I'm gonna call the sheriff and get you into court, you hear me?' And she's pretty good when that happens, and I get rent. But she's never this late, and when I saw her picture on TV, and that boyfriend's picture, I got a little afraid for her."

"Afraid her boyfriend had killed her?"

Mary-Louise nodded. "Mind if I light up?" She drew a pack of cigarettes from her jeans.

"Sure, go ahead."

"That boyfriend. I mean, he had that face. He had that look. It was like a pit bull, that guy was. I mean, not strong or anything. But he looked like he could go off on you any second. Luckily, I never saw him around here much. He killed those nice people over in San Pascal, didn't he?"

"He's been arrested."

"He's a kookooberry."

Jane raised her eyebrows.

"You know, cuckoo. Like you can feel it when he's around."

"Does she have friends in the neighborhood?"

Mary-Louise seemed a little taken aback that Jane didn't ask more about Doc Chilmark. She took a long drag off her cigarette and blew a perfect smoke ring from between her lips. "Not friends as in friends. People seen her now and then. I guess you gotta ask around. I been on this block too long. I don't get to know nobody unless they get me my rent money. But I doubt nobody knew her. She was all quiet, and I think a little ashamed of her business, having men in to give, well, what women *like that* give to men."

"You think she was a prostitute?"

"I never woulda had her here if I thought that!" Mary-Louise said, raising her cigarette up to eye level. "She wasn't bad like that. But she had *bad men*." She made this last point with a midair jab of the cigarette. "That kookooberry boyfriend and some others. Any girl who rubs men down for a living ain't gonna get the guys you take home to mother, if you hear me. She was surrounded by badness. But she was a nice girl. I know she was. Patty woulda never let her stay there that long if she wadn't."

"Where's Patty now?"

"Eh, no idea," Mary-Louise sucked at the cigarette and set it down in the ashtray. "Her mother got sick in Barstow and she took off to help with that stuff. Why that sister of hers wasn't back there helping, I don't got a clue. They was both nurses, so you'd a figured they'd trade off on that stuff. But Patty took off, and the sister— what's her name?"

"Mary."

"No, that's not it, no. I'd never forget Mary, believe me. I know they called her that on the TV, and I guess that's what confused me. I kept seeing her picture and thinking, 'That's no Mary.' But it's one of those names that you don't forget, but look at me," Mary-Louise chuckled. "I'm too old to remember, too young to forget." She started snapping her fingers as if it would jog her memory. "It's like a movie star name. Not movie stars now, but back when I was a girl. Jean. That's it—Jean something. Different last name than Patty, 'cause her husband left her. I got that much outta her before she started hidin' from me. Jean Kearney. Reminded me of Gene Tierney. Both the name and the way she looked. Like in that movie, *Laura*. Ever see that one? It was good. That's who she looked like, a little. She had the teeth and the hair and that kind of glamorous look without even putting on too much makeup. Hard to believe that she and Patty were sisters, 'cause Patty was so plain, but you know, my older sister was the plain one and got the bad teeth and an inch too much nose that twisted a little to the left. So it happens. Patty was plain and bottle blonde and musta had a harelip when she was little 'cause there was always this scar and the way she talked. Thometimeth thee talk like thith," Mary-Louise said, chuckling to herself as if she had done a perfect imitation of Patty. Jane was fairly sure now that Patty was probably buried somewhere, not far from here, while Mary Chilmark was still on the loose.

Mary-Louise lit up another cigarette, took a swift puff off of it, and said, "Well, seeing her and then seeing Jean, it was like night and day. That's why I didn't mind Jean being here. When she kept up with the rent. But that boyfriend of hers—he was bad news like you never heard bad news before in your life."

"What was Patty's last name?"

"Mullen. Patty Mullen. I used to think of her as Patty Sullen because she moped a lot. But she thought the world of that sister of hers."

THREE COPS SHOWED UP, and Dahl stood there in a gray suit as if he'd been pulled from an early dinner date.

Jane met them out front, warned them about Mary-Louise, and said, "Kilpatrick's touched things in there, but I don't think it matters much. It's definitely Bloody Mary. Let's go over the place carefully, and maybe we can find out what her plans are."

"My guess is she's on the road," Dahl said.

"She loves her son too much," Jane said, shaking her head slightly. Then, she looked out across the hills and the valley. The heat from the Santa Ana winds was blasting up a notch, and she had a taste of bitterness in her mouth. "I think she's nearby. I want officers to patrol the area here. The trailer where Fenn lived is two miles up the road, and Darden is just over that ridge. She's watching out for him now. She knows where he is. I think if we work fast, we can find her sooner than later."

Then, she mentioned Patty Mullen and asked for a follow-up on her, her family in Barstow, to see if there might not be another murder on Bloody Mary's hands. "Chilmark went by the name Jean Kearney. Claimed to be Patty Mullen's sister. She ran the massage business out of her house but probably mainly did out-calls. All her business was cash only. Let's find out if she had her business card in the local shops or if anybody got to know her at all. We probably can't dig up her past clients on short notice, but maybe if we get the word out, they'll come forward."

CHAPTER TWENTY-ONE

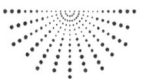

JANE WALKED TO HER CAR AND WAS ABOUT TO GET IN, BUT decided she needed a walk instead. She went up the street to the end, by the cul-de-sac. The yards were unkempt, with splotchy yellow grass surrounded by dirt. Behind some of the chain link fences, she saw a pit bull or a Rottweiler or two. A child's tricycle had been left out at the end of one driveway, and the house at the end of the cul-de-sac looked like it had been burned at one point, perhaps years before. Its windows were boarded up. It obviously had been abandoned, so she stepped into the yard and went to the back gate. She opened it and went out into a yard that looked like it was more desert than lawn. Local gang members and kids had spray-painted their symbols all over the back of the house. The sliding-glass doors were broken, and trash of various kinds lay in piles under the shade of the roof. She went toward the back, where the chain link fence had been cut, and pushed her way through it.

On the other side, a slight rise in a plateau barren of everything but tumbleweed and dried grasses. She went out into it, and when she came to the edge, not more than eight yards from the back of the house, she saw the valley beyond.

The hillside curved downward, and there, beneath where she stood: Darden State.

You watched it. Why? You and your son were here for years. Just watching the hospital. Waiting for what? For now? For the inevitable? Did you know he'd end up there? Or was that luck? You left the hospital, you got away with a new husband. You had your baby. You were fine for a time. And then, things started to happen. What you'd kept away from your life began to come back. What happened? What was it that brought you back here six years ago to rent this house? Did you sit up on this hillside and look down at it like this? Were you here before you went to kill the Flocks? Before you killed Cooper Fenn? Were you here last night—thinking about your son—hoping he'd find his way back?

Jane stood there a long time, feeling the hot winds against her back, asking question after question in her mind. Having no answers.

And then different questions came to her. *What were you doing up here all those years? Between your first murders in your twenties, to the Flocks in San Pascal, and then Fenn? Did you not have the desire to kill? Did someone cross you at some point, and you didn't hurt them? What were you doing up here in this neighborhood? Giving massages to strangers. Letting men touch you. What triggered you now that didn't trigger you three years ago or even six months ago?*

When she thought of possible answers, one struck her as utterly ridiculous.

But she couldn't ignore it.

You were killing then too. Maybe not often. Now and then. When the madness got hold of you. When something awful happened. When you couldn't take it out on your little boy. When your husband had killed himself just to avoid you and the world he'd gotten involved in.

Your deranged world where you lashed out at people like a rattlesnake when you felt they'd somehow intruded on your territory.

But if you were killing, why weren't there bodies before? You left the Flocks in their house. You left Fenn in his trailer. Where are the others, if there are others?

And then something came to her lightning fast, and the hot wind seemed to make her feel as if she was going to jump out of her skin if she didn't go see if it was a possibility.

Without even realizing she was moving so fast, Jane began jogging back to the abandoned house, back down the street, back to the house that Mary Chilmark had been renting for several years.

Dahl was still there, and when she reached him, she said, "If there are bodies, they might be under the concrete in back. It's new. Kilpatrick said she didn't have to do any maintenance while Mary lived there. She told me that Mary even repaired the roof and hired workmen to redo the pavement in the driveway. I think she did the backyard too. Men came here all the time for massages. Whatever triggered Mary to murder Diane Flock and her husband, that trigger may have been with her for years. Mary's husband killed himself exactly six years ago. If that event triggered this, then my guess is she's been killing people since she moved up here. She just didn't hide the Flocks. Maybe she intended to and got interrupted by something. Maybe she didn't care."

"Maybe she wanted her son to get caught," Dahl said.

CHAPTER TWENTY-TWO

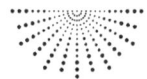

MARY CHILMARK HAD SPENT THE DAY SLEEPING IN THE ARMS of a very drunken Nick Spitzer, who wrapped his flabby arms all over her. But she felt safe with him, and she needed rest. Spitzer lived in a modest home near Belleview Park, in the nicest part of Caldwell, and the country club—which was not quite as green as it should've been for that time of year—was just over the fence in his backyard. His wife had left him two years earlier and had cleared out the kids and the dog and the bank account. He'd been running on the last of a small trust fund left to him and had been hemorrhaging money through drink and sloth from nearly the moment his wife left until that day when he won at poker and found a pretty woman who used to give him excellent deep tissue massage.

Mary gradually woke up just as twilight came in, and the stink of the man disgusted her, but as she moved away from him, his arm grasped her more tightly. "Gimme kiss," he said. "Come on, baby. Just a little one."

She pressed her lips to his and felt his hand going to her breasts. She let him continue, and soon he had unbuttoned her blouse and was rubbing through her bra before she reached back to undo it for him. In her mind, she was younger and feeling the heat of fire within her as it rose up. She knew she had power over men like this, and she wanted more from him than he'd be willing to give her if she resisted.

Soon, his sweaty fingers teased her nipples as he began to grind himself against her. His tongue was all over her neck as if he could lick up all the sweat on her body, and she felt his hardness down there.

"I knew you wanted me," he whispered, his breath like warmth and bitterness together. "I knew you wanted me. All those times I was lyin' on your table. Practically naked. Just that little white towel you had. You ever see how it rose up sometimes, when you worked on me? Ever notice? I bet you did. I told the guys that Jeannie wanted me like she wanted nobody else. You're that kind of girl, Jeannie. I knew it when I first saw you. You're so beautiful, baby. You are so beautiful. You may be almost my age, honey, but you look like a girl. That kind of girl. My kind of girl."

"I am," she murmured as his face moved from her breasts to her tight belly. "I am that kind of girl."

She no longer felt as if she were in her forties, but felt as if she truly were a girl again and her stepfather was doing those things to her that brought out the wild animal inside her.

The thing that turned her on, in a way that no other woman had ever been turned on.

He looked up at her, a sloppy grin on his face. "You like Daddy, don't you, baby? You like what Daddy does to baby?"

"Oh," she gasped. "Yes. Yes." She pressed both hands against his scalp, pushing him farther down. She closed her eyes and felt the shame course through her blood. She didn't hate him the way she hated them sometimes. She wanted him to feel how bad she was feeling. She wanted the pleasure of his understanding.

Then, she let go of his scalp. She wrapped her legs around his face, and she leaned over just a bit, just enough to get her right hand on the small can opener she'd grabbed from the kitchen that morning, when they'd come in the house. When she told him she wanted another beer, and he'd grabbed a bottle for her, and she had popped it open and taken a sip. He had been fumbling all over her, trying to make love then, only he was too wasted to even get his own fly down. And she had taken the can opener and put it there. Thinking she might use it. Thinking of its little sharp point.

Thinking of what kind of girl she was, and what things girls like her liked to do.

How she wanted to make sure he knew what it felt like to have someone jabbing you between the legs.

Mary took a shower in the enormous tub he had in a bathroom that was nearly as big as her own house. It felt good to wash the blood off, to be free of that awful feeling. As she passed the bedroom again, she went in, passing the body that lay sprawled on the bed, and reached into Nick's pants pocket for the key to his Cadillac.

Once in the car itself, she started it up and noticed that the gas gage was almost on empty, nearly at the same time the car's radio blared about the fires in the mountains, and that's when the idea came to her.

Two hours later, out on the ridge beyond the Belle-View Park where Nick Spitzer's house was, Mary Chilmark felt the dry gusts of wind at her back. The sweat on her body had evaporated, and she felt clean again.

It was a burning hot afternoon, and she smelled the distant fires across the freeway that had already jumped the San Bernardino Wash and had begun to head toward the railroad tracks off Baseline. The sky to the north was blackened from the smoke.

She knew the fire would never come this far. Caldwell was protected by too many natural fire breaks—unlike the San Bernardino foothills that just connected community after community right down to the 10 freeway.

She set the gas can down and then went to gather dried sticks and tumbleweed. At the edge of an arroyo, she glanced over and saw the high razor-wire fences that surrounded Darden State.

She closed her eyes, sending a prayer to her son. Knowing that this would help him. Hoping that by her actions, she could free him again. Free him and find the one who had broken all promises to her. The one that reminded her of every man she had ever been with.

The man who needed an even greater healing than her father had.

She blocked the bad memories of that place and tried instead to remember where the entryways were, how the nurses looked when they walked into the building. Nobody would have a recent photo of her. The one in the newspapers made her look nearly blonde, and although she had retained her youth in a way most women approaching fifty had not, and her figure now was better than at twenty-two with the first few months of pregnancy upon her. Nobody at Darden State would even know who she was if she managed to get past the gate.

Well, maybe you, she thought. *Maybe you will know me. But if I see you, it'll be the last thing you see.*

Only one person still worked there after all those years.

They would think she was just another nurse coming in, checking in to her shift. She was a nurse, after all, and people could tell that about her when they saw her. She had that air of authority and compassion. She knew the words to speak that made people understand her position.

The Santa Ana winds had picked up. The sky from the north blackened.

And then, she found the perfect property. It was surrounded by two acres of dry scrub brush and high yellow grass and a few dead orange trees at the center of this field.

She could taste the heat on the wind.

She poured two gallons of gasoline over the dry underbrush.

Then, she set the fire.

By her calculation, it would spread, house to house in Caldwell, and travel the fairly direct route right down the canyon. Might take the whole night to reach the flatlands, if the wind kept up. Might only take a few hours. It all depended on how the wind went and how dry the grasses were. She had seen on the news how the fires in the hills leaped acres, like a burning angel flying over rooftops. She had seen a car on the news where a couple had gotten trapped inside it while trying to drive away from it.

And that wind was hot and moving exactly where she wanted it to move.

The wind would carry it down the ridge, across the suburban community, and if luck was with her—as it always had been—it would bring the tongues of fire to Darden State.

She would find her child.

And his father.

CHAPTER TWENTY-THREE

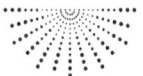

PATIENTS WHO HAD NOT HAD RECENT VIOLENT OUTBURSTS
were allowed to mingle during certain activities—even the sexual
psychopaths, so long as there was adequate supervision. In this
respect, Darden State most resembled a maximum-security prison.
During the day, there might be classes and group therapy, and even
time in the game room playing video games or board games. In the
library, patients were allowed to talk quietly, although if there was
even the hint of someone getting out of control, the library would
be shut for days at a time. Although budget cuts had helped layoff
many of the guards and correctional officers, the canteen, during
lunch and supper hours, always had at least six guards on hand in
case of an outburst.

At six p.m., Doc Chilmark, still in leg restraints that kept him
hobbling as he walked, was escorted by two guards to the canteen in
Ward D.

His supper consisted of spaghetti with meatballs, a small salad,
and a Kaiser roll. There were no knives with dinner, but plastic
spoons and forks sufficed for most of the patients.

Because he had remained docile, and because several correctional officers supervised the shifts of the canteen in the evening, upper body restraints had been removed from Doc as he sat at one of the long tables. A few other patients sat nearby, but few looked up at him, and no one seemed to want to sit near him, perhaps because one of the COs sat next to Chilmark.

But Rob Fallon had noticed the new guy and had gone over with his tray and sat down in front of him. "Rob," he said, nodding.

Doc Chilmark looked up at him, then back down to his plate. He dragged his fork through the spaghetti, rolling it up a bit before bringing it to his lips.

"I like welcoming new patients," Rob said. The CO next to Chilmark shot Rob a look, but said nothing. Rob ignored him.

"I don't like eating here after what I saw downstairs," Rob said.

Chilmark kept his eyes down. Reached for his small carton of milk, taking a sip from it.

Rob leaned forward. "You got scars all over you."

Doc Chilmark finally looked at Rob Fallon. Said nothing. Kept chewing his food.

"I saw a ghost downstairs," Rob said. "Right under where we are."

AFTER HE WAS FINISHED with supper, Doc Chilmark rose, with some assistance, and carried his tray over to the garbage can near the window into the canteen's kitchen. Rob Fallon walked with him. As he scraped the last of his food into the trash, Doc said, "I see ghosts all the time. There are a lot of people who died here. They're like shadows."

"I know," Rob said. "The one I saw downstairs was a girl."

"Where's downstairs?" Chilmark asked, his voice so quiet that Rob barely heard him.

"Underneath here. There's a door. It leads underground," Rob said.

"I heard about it," Doc said, nodding. "My mother told me. She was here once. She was down there when my soul came into her body. She told me the dead were everywhere there."

CHAPTER TWENTY-FOUR

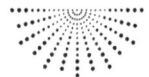

HRD—Human Remains Detection—was a special police canine department out of Riverside. Dahl and Laymon wasted no time calling them in — with the help of the Medical Examiner — to Mary Chilmark's house.

The detectives arrived with two dogs—one a black Labrador retriever, and the other a mutt that looked as if he were part border collie, part Lab. Jane had expected the usual German shepherds. "Cadaver dogs," the HRD guy said. "These guys are trained for this."

"I'm worried they might ruin evidence," Jane said, leaning down to give the mutt a scratch on the head.

"This one's named Scroungy," the officer said, grinning. "Best dog in the world. Training them's a weird experience, since you're burying body parts just for the puppies to go sniff out. But these two are the best. If there are bodies here, we'll find 'em."

"Let's check the backyard first," Jane said. "It's concrete."

"Ah," the officer said. "The classic burial."

IN THE BACKYARD, the dogs sniffed around, and the one called Scroungy stayed close to the back door with his sniffs. The back lights were up bright, and Jane shone her flashlight around until she saw a series of discolorations—a slightly darker, more smooth concrete area when compared to the rest of the yard.

And Scroungy had begun scratching at the area not far from it.

"Let's get the jackhammers!" she shouted to Dahl, who was inside the house with the techs, carefully gathering anything that might be evidence.

AFTER NEARLY AN HOUR of two of the guys cracking the surface with the jackhammers, Jane held up her hand in a "stop" gesture. She crouched down along the crumbled concrete and brushed some of the debris away.

Embedded in it, not far beneath the surface:

A human foot.

CHAPTER TWENTY-FIVE

IN HIS OFFICE, TREY OPENED MARY CHILMARK'S FILES. THEY were made up of several pages of the usual state paperwork, the trial transcripts, the listings of the murders she'd committed. But those told him nothing. It was Brainard's notes he wanted. But the first set of notes he found—scribbled as if by an eleven-year-old on torn spiral notebook sheets—were those of Dr. Phillip Massey.

The man who helped get Mary's early release, and who married her a few months after her release.

The man who had killed himself about five years before Mary and Doc Chilmark murdered the Flocks in their home.

THE NOTES:

She is calm. She talks about her childhood. She talks about how she was kept hungry when she was a little girl. She talks about how she got so thin by the age of eleven that her father began force-feeding her by putting his hands on either side of her jaw to open her mouth. How he made her milkshakes made out of beef and tomato juice and made her drink them or she would receive punishment.

Her mind seems clear at this point. The time spent here has done her good. I think she was living in a cloud of abuse as a child. Darden, and her therapy here, as well as the medications, have helped her examine these problems. She has begun to acknowledge the murders, but she still feels that someone else did them. Someone who was near her all the time. I don't think this is a multiple personality problem. I think she clearly knows that she is responsible for those actions. She told me that she became aware of what she had done when she had tried to set fire to the beds. She felt as if she were a little girl again, trying to destroy evidence of some bad act she'd committed before her father had come in to punish her for it. When we go for walks on the grounds here and talk about how she handles pain, she said that she used to burn herself sometimes just to feel something. Or cut herself with scissors when she was a young girl. She expressed regret and horror at her own actions with regards to the murders, but she still feels disconnected from them at this stage.

Yet I cannot help thinking that Darden State may end up not being the right place for her. A halfway house, perhaps, with medication and ongoing therapy, might be better for her. She definitely has a moral sense of right or wrong and talks about blackouts she had around the time of the murders.

There is one thing that still concerns me, though, and that is her interest in the occult. Not in some Judeo-Christian definition of it, but she believes that she has seen ghosts, particularly of those who she killed. I suspect this is a manifestation of her conscience, and I hope that through our daily sessions I can bring her to a clearer understanding of her acts and her responsibilities with them.

She doesn't seem prone to depression at this point. Neither is she over-medicated or lethargic. She has been developing a healthy attitude toward the world at large and has been more than helpful with the other patients.

The patient is generally better adjusted than most of the other patients here, and given the overcrowding that has occurred with the shutdown of the A and B Wards while construction is ongoing, and the transitional state of the residence halls as well as D Ward, I recommend a course of therapy as well as an early release program.

TREY TURNED the notebook page over and saw Dr. Robert Brainard's neat handwriting on two pieces of memo paper:

Dr. Massey,

I can't encourage you on this current course of action. We had an issue with Mary Chilmark with regards to her pregnancy. She will not tell me who the father of her child is, but she's aware that her pregnancy may help her gain early release into the general population. I know you've worked with her, and I understand your eagerness to see this patient back functioning in the world, but our responsibility to the community-at-large comes first. While she may be capable of living in the world, I recommend the low-security units, perhaps even in the residency housing outside the ward, but still on Darden's grounds.

Yes, I agree that her progress has been both remarkable, and her remorse convincing and authentic. We have all gotten to know Mary Chilmark well here, and she has many supporters among the staff.

I understand your professional commitment to her, and if you are willing to provide additional support and supervisory care for the duration of her pregnancy while she undergoes continued therapy and daily visits to Darden, I can sign off on this to some extent, but with caution. However, I do not think it advisable for you to take such a risk with a patient, no matter how that patient has recovered from past trauma and delusional behavior.

I want you to remember a patient named Shattuck in 1979, and how an early release impacted his life and the lives of the community to which he was released. Sometimes, a patient manages to fool us all. While I certainly feel that the years we've known Mary Chilmark mitigates against a reprisal of this kind of behavior, I can't help but feel that she should be in residency at least for another year of observation.

Sincerely,

R.B.

WHEN TREY HAD FINISHED GOING through the letters and notes in the file, he flipped through the pictures inside them.

There was one of Mary Chilmark, then in her twenties, sitting on a chair in a lounge. It was an old scene, and her legs were crossed, her head thrown back slightly as if she owned the place. She had a cigarette in her right hand.

She was beautiful. She looked like the most glamorous young woman who had ever walked through Darden's doors. She reminded Trey of another patient who also had a great deal of beauty.

Beauty could be a weapon, particularly of the criminally insane. It could be used to seduce and then destroy what it had power over.

Strikingly, she looked like a feminine version of Doc Chilmark. The same waiflike face with large dark eyes. The dark hair. The slender arms.

But what Trey noticed most about this photograph was that it was not just another file photo taken of a patient. Whoever took this must have loved her. Whoever took this had caught her relaxing, and in her face—in those eyes—he saw the gleam of power.

She knew she owned whoever took the picture.

She knew she would be free of Darden State.

Where was the lounge? Things had changed so much a few years after Mary Chilmark had been a patient there that Trey had no idea. He couldn't identify the wall behind her, or the cigarette machines—which they no longer had at Darden and had never had in Trey's memory.

Had Massey taken the photo? Had he brought her into an employee lounge for the cigarette and snapped the picture? If so, why keep it in the files?

With Massey dead, there would be no answers to the questions.

Idly, Trey turned the photo over. Written on it: *Mary Chilmark, Darden State.*

Didn't seem particularly odd, but he was unsure why such a casual picture had been taken of her. It made her look like she was an employee on a cigarette break. There were a few other photos in there of her, more official shots, but none quite like this one.

The file on Chilmark was fairly thick and had the usual lists of her therapies, her meds, and the letters from victims' families that always went to the Board whenever the decision of early release was upon them.

Somewhere in there he saw a small scrap of paper that nearly fell out from between the rest of them.

He looked at it. Could barely read it.

Brought it right up to his face. Like a chicken scratch across some printed words.

It had been torn from something else. Some kind of paperwork. He rifled through the nearby papers, checking them, but none had been torn.

Trey closed the file, trying to forget that curious smile on Mary Chilmark's face in the photo of her in the lounge.

A smile that might've meant nothing at all.

Or might've meant everything.

He went through the papers again, the transcripts from her trial that were briefly excerpted, and paused when he saw a page with a word crossed out in black magic marker. He flipped through the transcript: the name of the hospital—where Mary Chilmark had murdered three patients—was blacked out.

LESS THAN FIFTEEN MINUTES LATER, he stood outside Dr. Brainard's office. Diego, Brainard's assistant, had tried to dissuade him from standing vigil, but Trey kept Mary Chilmark's bulky file under his arm and just waited outside the door.

After a minute, the door opened.

Brainard stood there. "I'm leaving in twenty minutes."

"Where did she commit those murders?" Trey asked.

He was sure he already had an answer.

CHAPTER TWENTY-SIX

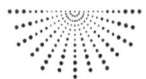

IN BRAINARD'S OFFICE. LIGHTS DIMMED, BLINDS DRAWN, AN end-of-the-day neatness to it. Empty wastebasket. The top of his desk was in perfect order, and his computer had been shut down. The smell of a cinnamon-and-vanilla sachet in the air.

"You write in a note to Massey, in Mary's file, about having known her for years. Not the two years she was here in Ward D. But years. She was twenty-five years old when she committed the murders. You said she came to Darden fresh from nursing school. She was in Darden for just under two years, which was remarkable in and of itself," Trey said, following Dr. Brainard in. "I saw a picture of her. A photo someone left in there. It looked like a nurse on a break, and not a patient."

Brainard went to the file cabinet, withdrew a key from his suit jacket pocket, and unlocked the cabinet. He opened it wide, thumbed through some files, and pulled a thick one out that had a rubber band around it.

When he turned around to face Trey again, Brainard wore an expression on his face that Trey could only think of as bemused.

"It's sealed information," Dr. Brainard said. "But I'll let you see it. The State of California would crucify me professionally, Trey. If this got out, particularly with that news guy all over us, well, it would not be a pretty moment of Darden's past."

Trey took the files that Brainard had stacked on his desk. He opened the first one.

It was an employee file of the Darden State Hospital for Criminal Justice.

There was an old identification card with its clip still on it.

The photograph was of Mary Chilmark.

"In the 1980s, we were still transitioning," Brainard said, going to sit on the edge of his desk. His voice was low and almost soft, as if he didn't like telling secrets. "Most of the wards were still the mentally ill. Ward C dealt with the mentally retarded, and only D had been used for the criminally insane verdicts. But state funding got cut, and eventually, we had to release a lot of patients, and it was about '84 when the funding came in to develop Darden as more for criminal justice than mental illness. She came to us as a nursing intern. In fact, I think she was in her last term—going to school during the day and working the night shift here. She was here two years before the incidents."

"The murders of three patients," Trey said, glancing up from Mary Chilmark's employee records.

"Yes."

"The state wanted her employment records sealed?"

"Sure. What are you, a boy scout? Scandals happen in hospitals. Particularly ones like this. Not often. Maybe every thirty years. Somebody bungles. Hospitals don't just run on purity and light. Something happens," Brainard said. "It was a sensitive point, you've got to understand that. Funding was coming in. It was simply to keep trouble from happening. When a hospital like Darden transitions, nobody wants trouble. You think this information would help the police in their investigation?"

Trey thought for a moment. "I don't know. Maybe it would. Maybe it wouldn't."

"It wouldn't. She was a good nurse. Very young. Even gifted. I suppose that's why we were all protective of her. The patients loved her. But the PST she sustained, and her father's abuse all those years, and then, if she was at all to be believed, when the male patient raped her ..."

"He raped her? Do we know this for a fact?"

"No. There's no way to know it. It was simply her word at the time after she murdered him. But he had been a sexual deviant, per the state code at the time."

Trey closed the folder. "Is there anything else that needs to be known about Chilmark?"

"She saved another nurse's life. We all were witness to it. A patient was coming after the other girl, and Mary put herself in harm's way, getting stabbed twice in the shoulder. But the other girl —another young nurse—would've been killed."

"The way Mary Chilmark kills," Trey said, "she probably killed the patient who attacked."

Dr. Brainard said nothing in reply. He stood up again and went to his office door. "If we're finished here," he said, opening the door.

The light from the hallway seemed too bright as Trey rose and set the file back on Brainard's desk.

As Trey went out into the hall, Dr. Hannifin's assistant, Lara, called out to him. "Hannifin wants to grab you, if she can."

"Why not?" Trey asked, and leaned against the reception counter. "Day I'm having, I'm never getting home."

❧

"You wanted to see me?" Trey asked after tapping lightly on the door. When he tapped, the door slid open slightly. As soon as Hannifin saw him, she swiveled around her chair and got up and came toward him as if she were in a rush. "He's been acting out some more. I want you to come with me."

She brushed past him out the door, and he stared at her a second before he began following her as she went out into the corridor.

In the elevator down to the first floor of Ward D, he said, "I'm probably breaking a confidence, but his mother was a nurse here."

Hannifin glanced up at him. She'd been staring at her feet waiting for the elevator to move between floors. "Mary Chilmark was here?"

"Darden was transitioning between being a hospital with both the mentally ill and the criminally insane, to being what it is now. She murdered patients here."

She shook her head slightly. "Nothing surprises me anymore. Well, that doesn't really help us with the son right now. Look. He wants you there when I talk to him. For some reason, he's attached to you," she said. "I can't tell if this is good or bad—his feeling too comfortable with you."

"Probably bad," Trey said. "Maybe I shouldn't go."

"No, it's good for the most part. There's something about you that makes him relax." She looked straight ahead as she said this, at the closed elevator doors.

"Maybe it's the straitjacket," Trey said.

She ignored his comment. "Do you know where this rumor about ghosts came from?"

"Ghosts?"

"He started to get violent and screamed about the shadows of the dead crawling on him," she said. "Right after he ate. Nobody knows what brought it on."

"He started screaming? Wow. He was calm when I saw him earlier. Maybe it was Fallon."

"Why him?"

"When we found him in the underground, he said he saw ghosts. Maybe he's been talking this up on the ward. That's the only thing I can guess."

"Ugh," she said. "That underground. I don't know why they don't just seal it up."

The elevator doors opened, and they stepped out, went through the security check, and on down to Program 28.

"He let them out," Doc Chilmark said. In the comfort of his straitjacket, he leaned back on his cot and looked up at the ceiling rather than at Trey, Hannifin, or Atkins, who stood near the door to Chilmark's room.

"Doc, there really are no ghosts down there," Susan Hannifin said. "Let's talk about the anxiety you're experiencing. Are you managing to rest at all?"

"No. I can't remember sleeping. I feel like I've been up for a week."

Then, Doc twisted his head around to look over at Trey. "I'm glad you're here."

"Why's that?"

"You keep them away."

"Who?"

"The shadows," Doc said. "They live underground here. And

they come out now because people have been opening the door for them. There must be a lot of them down there."

Susan shot a glance at Trey that seemed to suggest, *Just let him talk.*

"I heard one of them when I was eating tonight. If you call that food. I heard this little girl."

Trey remembered Rob Fallon claiming there was a ghost girl, and filed this away to mention it to Hannifin later on.

"I heard her. She's trapped down there. Others are trapped there too. But they're leaking out now. At night they come out and change shapes and get through doorways," Doc said, fairly matter-of-factly. "The world changes at night in the dark. That's why they become night fears. They move through keyholes. They take people over. I'm not safe here." He had never once let his gaze wander from Trey's face. It was as if the only thing in the room he could look at was Trey.

Afterward, in the hallway, walking swiftly back down the ward, Susan Hannifin said, "He trusts you at this point. That's good. I don't want you to do the police's bidding too much with this. He's at a very delicate point. Even though he's a prisoner here, we can't ever forget his mental state and his health needs, Trey. Let's leave the lights on for him tonight. No point in him staying up all night after lights out. His prescription should start kicking in tonight too. When the nurse's do the ten o'clock meds, he'll get some Cambex to help him sleep through the night, but we'll keep the lights on in his room anyway. If the Cambex doesn't work immediately, I want him to feel safe above all else."

"Sounds good," Trey said. "Let's hope Fallon hasn't infected everybody on Ward D with the ghost story."

≈

Rob Fallon had already been telling others about the ghost he'd seen beneath Darden State, and the word got around further. Even when Trey took off for the night, Rita Paulsen, who was working double-shifts that week, stopped to tell him, "This is going to be one of those nights—a full moon, ghost stories, and one of the psych techs already has been pretending he heard a ghost too."

It was the way of the wards at Darden. Once a rumor started among the patient population, it became like a contagion. Trey figured that by the next morning, every single patient on the first floor, particularly of Ward D, would be complaining that a ghost had come into their rooms through the vents.

Once he reached the parking lot, sitting in his car, he took a deep breath and let it all out. He knew he'd have to do a good two-to-three mile jog that evening, once the kids were in bed, just to blow off the steam of the day.

On his way home, he stopped in a bookstore in the State Street Mall in Redlands and picked up a copy of Dr. Susan Hannifin's book.

CHAPTER TWENTY-SEVEN

In his room, wrapped in the warmth of his straitjacket after having it taken off when he needed to use the toilet, Doc Chilmark curled up in a ball, not on top of his cot, but just beneath it. He tried to pretend that it was his cage. He tried to pretend, squeezing his eyes shut as hard as he could make them, that he was just back at home with Mary. Feeling her kisses on the back of his neck before she went to her own bedroom.

But, instead, he remembered things that frightened him.

He remembered the men who regularly came into the house, the ones who took off all their clothes and lay down on the table.

All the filthy men who touched her. She was too pure for them. But they touched her anyway.

All of them needed healing, and after they had left, each one leaving money on the table, Mary had come to him and held him and told him that it was all right. That time was not the enemy. "All men are like that, except you," she murmured to him, holding him tight, drawing him from his cage and out onto the floor. His head against her breasts, his arms about her waist. "They all need healing.

Women too. Everybody has the disease in them. But you have the cure for it. You and I both, Doc."

Doc lay in the room in Program 28 and began crying, because he missed her touch too much. He didn't know why she hadn't come for him yet. She always had come for him in the past, even after she'd left him, as a boy, with Cooper Fenn. Even after Dr. Massey had died. She'd come for him, no matter what was keeping her back.

He didn't think he could live without her.

He fought the feelings of sleep, though he was exhausted.

Something made a noise in his room. He opened his eyes, looking out from under the bed.

Something was there.

Even with the lights on.

The shadows were coming.

Crawling.

Night fears on their way.

Maybe just outside the door.

Out in the dark of the hallway.

He glanced over at the grate just on the other side of cot.

What if they were down there, trying to come up?

For just a second, he was sure he heard the voice of a little girl say something.

He closed his eyes and tried to blot out any sound he heard.

Please come soon. Please, Mary. Don't leave me here. You promised you'd never leave.

CHAPTER TWENTY-EIGHT

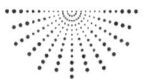

THE FIRST CALL CAME FOR TREY AT ELEVEN O'CLOCK THAT night. It was Jane Laymon. He'd tried to reach her earlier but had to leave message after message for her. He hadn't expected to hear from her again until morning.

Trey had been reading Dr. Susan Hannifin's book *The Killer Instinct: Inside the Minds of Seven Psychopathic Murderers*, lying in bed with the covers half on and half off while Carly did her yoga over near the French doors that led to the courtyard. He'd just read beyond the introduction when his cell phone light began blinking —he barely noticed it at first, and then wanted to ignore it.

He took off his glasses, picked up the phone, and popped it open. "Hello?"

"Trey. Got a minute?"

Trey sat up, setting the book down. He got out of bed and slipped his briefs on, and made an understood hand signal to Carly, who got out of her stretching position and stood up, watching him. He covered the phone for a second. "It's Jane," he said.

"I figured," Carly said.

Trey walked past her to the bedroom door, went out into the hallway, and then took the phone with him out the front door. He sat on the low step. It was a peaceful night, although the vague scent of smoke from distant fires was in the air. "Jane? All right."

"We found more bodies."

"In her house?"

"Beneath it. I should've noticed it the first time I went out back. The whole backyard is concrete, but there's a little color difference near the back door. That's where she must've repaired the concrete and then reset it—after burying her victims. Two of the victims were buried shallow. I'd guess about eight inches down, under just about two inches of concrete."

Trey swore under his breath.

"Yeah, we got cadaver dogs out, and when they seemed to locate a spot near the back door, we got some jackhammers and went to it. First time I've ever seen this kind of work. Bloody Mary was quite the handywoman. Her landlady told me she fixed things all the time. But there's one other thing, Trey. She lived within spitting distance of Darden."

"You're kidding."

"Nope. And get this: she had him sleeping in a dog crate. Her son. Handcuffs, ropes, all kinds of restraints."

"Straitjacket?"

"Yep. She had lots of stuff right out of a medical catalog. Looked really S&M to me. I'm assuming you figured out the nature of their relationship?"

"Incest. Abuse. I wish none of this surprised me," he said. "She's in Caldwell?"

"Yep. If I walk to the end of her block and go to the back of the houses there, I can practically wave to the guards at Darden. You know how the town grows out into the foothills? Her neighborhood's up there. And I bet she spent a lot of time looking at Darden. Why would she do that?"

"Because she worked as a nurse at Darden. The three patients she killed as a nurse were patients at Darden."

Jane remained silent for a few seconds. "What?"

"I saw the state records of her employment earlier today. I just didn't think it would matter. I didn't think she'd be living up on some hillside watching the place. Jane, I think she's obsessed with Darden State."

"She was a fucking nurse at Darden?" Jane said as if she hadn't heard it right. "Does that happen much?"

Trey chuckled. "Okay, it's not funny. I'm just tired. It happens now and then. Sometimes the person who gets hired to work at Darden comes with a full set of serious psych issues themselves. I've certainly seen it happen. Usually, it's the psychologists." He chuckled again, and then apologized for being a little punchy. "In fact, her obsession with Darden might be entirely normal, given everything else. She works there, she murders patients, she's put in Ward D, she gets pregnant by someone there, and she gets out. Makes some sense that if the major events of her adult life—being that dramatic—it becomes her little pond to watch."

"Who's the candidate for Daddy?"

"You mean to Doc? No idea. Rumors fly. Most likely it was Massey."

"And he's dead now."

"That definitely was suicide?"

"Yep," Jane said. "No question. Here's what we have so far," Jane said. "She befriended a woman named Patty Mullen. Patty was having money troubles, so she needed a roommate, and Bloody Mary stepped right in, but she left her son with Cooper Fenn for a bit. Then, Mary killed Patty—possibly. We can't quite track down who Patty Mullen was. We haven't found a body yet, but I suspect we will."

"Jane, I know that name. Patty Mullen," Trey said. "Christ, I think she used to work at Darden too. I don't know everybody, particularly in the other wards. But that name is too familiar."

"Can you check on that for me?"

"Tomorrow, sure," he said. "But I may be wrong. Maybe it just sounds familiar. God, maybe I'm just getting paranoid about Bloody Mary."

"It would certainly fit if she worked at Darden. And it would make sense for her to live so close to work," Jane said. "My guess is that Mary, who called herself Jean, murdered Mullen right away. Set up the massage practice to pay bills and now and then felt she had to kill a client or two. There's more stuff in the house—indications that Doc Chilmark had a hellish life with his mother. I still can't quite figure out the timing on this."

Trey said the first thing that came to his mind. "Poetic justice."

"Trey?"

"It's the thing Brainard said. It's why Mary was in Darden State in the '80s. She cuts off a guy's balls and stuffs them in his mouth because she claimed he tried to force himself on her that way. She and Doc kill Diane Flock and her husband—and their unborn baby —for some reason we haven't figured out yet. And now Doc is in the house where he was conceived."

"His father's house," Jane said.

"Right. Right. I know there's something in this that we're not noticing."

Then, Jane's voice changed when she spoke next. It seemed to come out as almost a cough. "The baby," she said.

"What baby?"

"We never found the unborn baby at the Flocks'. Diane Flock was four or five months along. Definitely dead. They cut Diane

Flock open, kill the baby in the process, and take it. For what? She's kept it, Trey. Maybe she hid it someplace."

"Why in God's name would she do that?"

"We can safely assume she's operating on a different set of rules than most of us," Jane said. "At this point, I think she's getting creative."

AFTER THE CALL, Trey had trouble going to sleep, so he kissed Carly good-night and took his book out to the living room. Switched on the lamp by the couch, plopped down in it, and began flipping pages. But he couldn't focus on Dr. Hannifin's tales of Ward D, or her past work at Camarillo. He stared out the windows into the courtyard and kept thinking of Doc Chilmark. Not as a nineteen-year-old, but as a little boy in a crate. Tied up. Treated, at best, like a dog.

He tried to imagine what Doc's mother must've been like. A woman who, through her own psychosis, had nurtured her son to the point where he could not distinguish between reality and fantasy. Where he had become his mother's perfect lover. Perfect confidante. It was almost as if she had bred him in order to have a second set of hands to do her dirty work. She'd raised and trained a psychopath—in her image.

To the point where he did not feel pain at the suffering of others.

Did not feel remorse at the torture and murder of a pregnant woman and her unborn child.

Trey closed his eyes, remembering the thin scars on Doc's face.

Bloody Mary had burned him. She had abused him. She had

...

Trey opened his eyes. He didn't like to think about it.

Jane had told him previously that the crime scene in the Flocks' house had been set up almost as a makeshift operating room.

Doc had performed the surgery. He was a healer. He was a doctor, at least in his mind. Doc had been raised to believe he had this power, and for some reason he had decided to use it on the Flocks.

Mary had been there. She was a trained nurse. She probably even told him exactly how to cut Diane Flock open. How to kill the unborn child. And then, how to tear open Diane's husband when he intruded on the scene.

How could a woman trained to help the sick do what she did?

Finally, as these thoughts roiled around Trey's mind, he fell asleep on the couch dreaming of psychopaths and too much bloodshed, only to be awakened several hours later by another call on his cell phone.

CHAPTER TWENTY-NINE

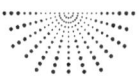

THE FIRE THAT MARY CHILMARK HAD SET EARLIER IN THE evening had begun slowly. The underbrush burned gradually, steadily, along the overgrown side yard of the house she'd chosen, and she had gone some distance away from it to watch. After several hours, it had finally picked up speed as the hot wind began shifting again. By that time, she'd gone back to the house by the golf course, where the body of Nick Spitzer lay in the bedroom on the second floor. She needed a few hours' rest before she went down to Darden State to find her son.

She had left a small bag in the Cadillac and had checked for it before entering the house.

She opened the bag and gazed down at what was in it.

For a moment, she remembered the first time she'd felt her son growing inside her.

FIRE BEGAN to rise up sometime after midnight, climbing the

house that burned quickly. Inside, a family had to get out fast, for the smoke alarms hadn't worked, and if it hadn't been for the pet German shepherd barking, there was a chance that no one inside would have been saved. The owner of the house turned on the sprinkler system and began spraying the roof of the house to try and protect it, but it was far too late, and if he were to describe how the fire moved, he would say that it was like a demon from hell, leaping from his rooftop to the house next door, while all around his backyard became a wall of fire.

It moved quickly through the community, with palm trees bursting into flame along the roadway. Because new growth had come up after a fire in the wash several years before, the flames found new fuel, and the fire department was called, but firefighters were already up on a mountain on the opposite side of the valley, many miles away, so it took more time than usual for the trucks to come out. Helicopters were the first to get there, but they were few and far between because of the fires in the distant mountains that had been raging for several days.

From not more than four miles away from where Mary Chilmark had spent the past five years in a rental house, under which she'd buried Patty Mullen, a man named Wilcox, and another man named Harrison, the fires raced along the canyon, palm trees like giant torches lighting up the night sky in Caldwell, California.

The dry winds met the flames, causing them to flare up to the sky.

Trey Campbell, who lived more than twenty miles away in Redlands, received his second call at 4:30 a.m.

This time, it was from Jim Anderson.

CHAPTER THIRTY

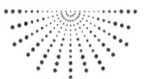

TREY LEFT HIS HOUSE AT FIVE A.M. AFTER A QUICK SHOWER and some cold coffee that had been left over from the previous day. He felt a little bleary-eyed, but something about the emergency got his adrenaline pumping.

On the cell phone as he drove along the streets of Redlands, heading out to the freeway, he asked Jim, "What's the scoop from Willard?"

Jim said, "Somebody was supposed to call for a lineup of buses. We're anticipating six hours of loading and cleanup."

"What's the guesstimate for the fire?"

"Might be as long as fourteen hours if it doesn't jump the wash. If it jumps the wash and the drainage ditch out at the boulevard, we're looking at eight. You almost here?"

"Almost," Trey said.

"You as sleepy as me?"

"Sleepier."

"Marcus Weirdo is here," Jim said, giving the nickname to one of the Clinical Directors, who had a more-than-slight problem with cocaine addiction. His real name was Mark Weir, and whenever any major emergency happened—a near-riot, a lockdown, or even misplaced files that the state needed fast—the guy went into coke-head overdrive. Although Weir had spent time in rehab, it obviously had not yet kicked in on his destructive habit, and Trey could just imagine how things were going with trying to keep the patients calm and in some semblance of order while Weir and others were cracking up in the face of an emergency.

"I don't get it; did the fire jump over the freeway?" Trey asked as he came around the curve off Oleander and turned onto the aptly named Brown Industrial Road, a shortcut over to Caldwell and the hospital.

"Not that fire from San Berdoo," Jim said. "This is a new one. Started up in the hills in Caldwell. Some streets are toast now. It's skipping houses now and then. You know. It's like the hammer of hell coming down up there. Once you get on the boulevard, you'll see it."

Just as Trey closed the cell phone and made a few zigzag turns, he saw the wall of flame up in the canyon. It was both magnificent and terrifying. "Holy shit," he said.

He pulled the car over for a second and just looked at it.

It was as if the canyon would be gone soon. Up beyond it, the town of Caldwell. On the other hillside, about two miles away from where Trey had stopped, Darden State.

THE SKY HAD GROWN darker than night, and billowing clouds of black and gray smoke covered the sky. The air definitely was warmer as he drove up the side streets to the main boulevard to Darden.

He thought he heard the shouts of people nearby, and then he saw pedestrians out on the street, pointing to the hills. Trey looked up quickly, in time to see a fireball explode in the darkness. Then, another, up on the burning hill.

Traffic on Jackman Boulevard, the main road that passed by Darden, was heavy as people were getting out of Caldwell and its surrounding areas. Lines of cars blocked the road, all of them with belongings tied to the roof of the car or bulging from overstuffed trunks that had been tied up with ropes. There was no sound of sirens at all. Trey assumed that was because it was unnecessary. The firefighters were probably up in the hills, doing what they could to contain the conflagration.

Trey imagined most of the houses, on three of the hills and the nearby arroyo, were just gone.

Parking in the Darden lot, he glanced back at the fire up on the hillside.

"Shit," one of the nurses said to another woman, as she passed him on her way in to work. "I can't fucking believe I have to come in here four hours after I just signed off shift."

One of the Senior Psych Techs from Ward C passed by, a man in his fifties named Dave Sledd, and when Trey asked him about his house up in the canyon, Sledd said, "We barely had twenty minutes to get out of there. We grabbed the kids, the wedding pictures, and the cat, and just ran out. My wife had cinder burns on her shirt."

"God," Trey said. "I'm sorry."

"Hey, if I think about it too much, I'm gonna start crying," the psych tech said, a crooked grin on his face that looked more grim than jovial. He sighed. "We got insurance. It'll just be a problem for a while. My wife and girls are down at her sister's in Corona at this point. I can't believe that somebody started that thing. With all the fires over on the mountains, you'd think these firebugs would just get a clue. Sons of bitches. Almost six hundred thousand acres up in the mountains have gone. Now this, over here. There must be at least seventy or eighty homes gone already, minimum. Including mine. And now look at us, Trey. We're gonna somehow get more than a thousand psychos and sociopaths out of these buildings in the next five hours? You think? What a day we're heading into."

"WHERE ARE THE BUSES?" Trey asked the security guards at the front.

"Somebody fucked up," one of them said. "They were supposed to get them from Riverside, but Riverside already had sent some over to San Bernardino and Pomona because of the fires over there. A lot of hospitals are in evacuation mode right now. We're just the newest one. This is happening all over—four fires off the freeway. We're just number five."

"When do we get ours?"

The other guard chuckled. "I suggested they try the schools. Get school buses. Get our guys in restraints and just move 'em out."

The hallways were a madhouse—and none of the patients were out of their rooms. It was all administrators and nurses and psych techs. Some of the psychologists had come in to help calm patients, but Trey began to feel that they'd be better off working with the administration. Nobody wanted to do what had to be done here. Trey had seen this kind of mess more than once, each time with a different administration. Nobody really planned for the big emergencies, and Trey wondered how they were going to get all the patients out, and even when they did, where to?

He pressed his way between staff—several of them people he'd never seen before in all his years at the job—and as he passed the patients' rooms, he saw most of them up and getting ready to move out. Just standing at their doors, staring out through the small windows into the hallway.

He met up with Jim Anderson on Ward D, and Anderson took

him through the checklist that Marcus Weirdo had set up. They went room to room. Susan Hannifin was already in, also going into each room to speak with the patients. "It's ballsy of her," Jim said. "She's operating on caffeine, as far as I can tell. But she's doing the job none of the other doctors seem to want to do."

"She's good," Trey said. "Okay, let's go through this bogus checklist and make sure our ward's all set. How's Program 28?"

"So far in its own lockdown for now. That was Brainard's call."

"He's here already?"

"Yeah, somewhere. But he called early and told Hannifin and all the directors to close down four of the programs off the wards because they could wait until the Wards had gotten their all-clears. Everybody's in a rush to get this show on the road. I say burn the place down." Jim guffawed. "Okay, I'm just going nuts 'cause of lack of sleep. I think I got about four good hours in at the most."

"I don't think I even got three," Trey said.

"So, we got our marching orders, and most of the wards are in good shape, patient-wise, but not so good with staff. Surprise, surprise. We get D all hooked up, roll 'em out like a cattle drive, and then maybe we're home free."

"Makes sense," Trey said. "Okay, well, where do we start?"

"I guess we use the emergency drill procedures and hope for the best." Jim grinned, slapping Trey's arm lightly with the clipboard.

"More coffee first," Trey said.

CHAPTER THIRTY-ONE

Outside, the fire burned along the canyons and arroyos. The morning sky, black with smoke, the smell of burning mesquite and sage and rubber and fresh wood and dried grass and gasoline from cars that had been blasted with flames. The fire department had helicopters flying overhead to bring water to part of the canyon that could not be reached, but these only arrived once every hour or so because they were being used with the fires up in the San Bernardino Mountains to the north.

The buses rolled in and out to the Darden State grounds. Boxes of files were being transferred into SUVs that were lined up along the residency halls; the psychiatrist and psychologist parking lots were full, as the professionals got in to save their computers and work and take out the family pictures in their offices. The psych techs had been recruited to stand alongside the patients, many of them in leg hobbles and wrist restraints, waiting to board one of the buses that had yet to be filled with patients. Nurses worked alongside some of the patients in wheelchairs or those needing special assistance, and with the exception of the lockdown in Ward D, things on the outside of the hospital looked as if they were moving well toward evacuation of the buildings. Every single employee of Darden State—from the janitors to the work crew to the techs and orderlies and guards—were called in to assist in the evacuation.

No one with an official identification card was refused admittance, although the security guard who checked at the front gate did not always notice the expiration date of the card itself, nor were most of them scanned into the system as would be the normal procedure.

Mary Chilmark walked up the sidewalk to the guard who sat in his black and white SUV at the gate, near the now-closed sentry area. She showed her ID, and though it was the identification badge of a woman named Patty Mullen who had not worked at Darden State in nearly five years, the guard waved her through, along with several other staff members from various departments—from the night shift, from the three a.m. swing shift, from the day shifts, many of whom had never seen each other before, who had parked out on the street and walked up to the entry to the grounds.

In Mary Chilmark's hand, a small grocery bag. If anyone asked her, she would tell them it had her uniform in it. As nonsensical as that might seem for a woman coming to the grounds of a hospital threatened by fire, she felt that it would have to do, because if she told them what she had in the bag, they would most likely stop her.

But she'd been waiting a long time for this.

She had spent years planning how she'd return to Darden State.

How she'd perform the operation that would be her and her son's greatest work.

And it moved the way she had dreamed it would. It moved with a rush of excitement within her, as she began to see the world again as one that had a clear and urgent purpose. Her mind felt revived by the smoke in the air and the hushed yet excited talk among those who were headed into the facility.

She floated above all of them—she was the wind itself, driven to this place, this present moment, and her son, waiting for her, probably watching for her to come and protect him from the fears that crawled in the dark.

And her boy's father there too.

The one who had made her a promise so many years ago, broken, but not discarded.

The promise lived in her heart.

He would feel what she had felt.

He would come to understand it.

THERE WAS an old bungalow-style building behind the residency hall, and within it a gardener's toolshed. It was kept locked at all times because of the potential for patients to find weapons—known in the hospital parlance as "sharps"—and Mary Chilmark had a set of keys that her late husband, Dr. Massey, had in his possession at his death. In fact, she had keys to nearly every building in Darden State, because her late husband had gathered them for her one by one over the years they were together—and whenever he wanted to touch her, he had to bring her a key. It was a game they played, and it made their love life exciting. They played so many games together, and she missed him. He had played games with their son too, not the naughty kind, but the ones that involved the cage. He had been the only man who had ever understood what went on in her mind, and she had loved him for it. She had loved him and had been truly bereft after he had the accident in which he died.

After he had taken a scalpel to his own wrists one night in a warm bathtub.

One night when she was with her son, holding him to chase away the fears.

She had kept the keys, labeling each one with a code so she would know where it fit. Where the secret places were at the hospital. Where she would find what she needed.

It had been to this very tool shed—really just a small room of the bungalow that had been used for storage for years—that she and her various lovers might go when she was young and in love with a handful of doctors at the hospital.

INSIDE THE TOOLSHED, she bypassed the shears and the pitchforks in favor of a large metal cabinet full of spades and trowels and small pots for plants. The cabinet was not one she had ever seen before, but it didn't surprise her that it was there.

She slipped her fingers behind it and drew the cabinet back from the wall. Slowly, she pulled the cabinet and then shoved it a bit to the left and outward.

Behind it, a short wide doorway, shut tight and padlocked.

But she had more keys, and after she tried several of them, one fit. The padlock clicked and opened.

She drew the door back; it was no more than four feet high.

A warm gust of mildewed air came back to her.

She crouched down, feeling with her hand along the wall within the room. When she found a switch, she flicked it up.

A pale blue light flickered on and then went out. When she toggled the switch again, it came up, and she saw the slender stairs downward into the uppermost level of the hospital's underground.

It had been the place where she had made love to her son's father for the first time. Down in the secret spaces where only certain personnel had access.

Down among the night cages, where he had lain her back on

the table, and she had wrapped her legs around him and given herself to him in a way she never had for any man before.

Risen to meet his thrusts, all the while feeling the shadows of the dead around them, and knowing that above them in the world of light, the hospital continued.

Knowing that the promise he made to her was real and would last forever.

MARY CHILMARK STEPPED down into the blue-lit stairwell at six a.m.

CHAPTER THIRTY-TWO

By seven a.m., prison buses from Chino had come out, and then the lining up and loading of the wards began. The best that anyone could do was house the patients down in Riverside, at the Parkside Community Hospital in a new wing that hadn't yet been filled. Ward D—the maximum-security ward—would have to be shipped out to LA County and their prison hospital that was new and not yet filled up. So Ward D would go last, and probably wouldn't get the final patients out until about eleven.

Lance Victor got through with his cameraman Alex and was in the administration director's face, having hauled ass out of the hotel over in San Bernardino to get an "on-the-scene report as the Darden State Hospital for the Criminally Insane attempts to evacuate its patients within three hours before a raging fire descends from the hills." When Trey passed by him, Lance sidled up to him and said, "I just want some footage of the wards."

"They're nearly empty," Trey said. "What good's that gonna do you?"

"Please," Lance said. "You won't notice Alex or me."

"Just you," the security guard behind them said. "Not both of you. If you want to go get some pictures for your show, only one of you goes through."

"Yikes," Jim laughed. "Don't let either of them in. This place is circus enough."

After nearly all the wards were clear, with only Program 28 left to escort out, the worst thing happened.

Somewhere between the nurses running around with hypodermic needles full of tranquilizers, psych techs having to hold back patients who had started getting the idea that this could turn into a free-for-all, and the administration's complete lack of understanding that they had a city full of psychopaths who, if their meds weren't quite kicking in, would be happy to tear out some eyeballs and rip some throats just because they got excited by doing it, Trey, as he had begun talking to the other techs and guards in Ward D about a calm and peaceful procedure, heard an alarm pen sound from one end of the nearly empty ward. Every staff member on Ward D had one, and once the button at the top of the pen was punched, a brief clanging alarm sounded for a duration of about three seconds, followed by strobe lights along the corridor, leading right to the person who set off the alarm.

And this meant, in a matter of five minutes, a lockdown, unless it could be determined that none was necessary.

"Jeez Louise," Jim said. "Lance Victor's gonna love this."

"At least the ward's pretty clear," Trey said.

The strobe lights came up on the ceiling, moving like lightning along the corridor. Trey, Jim, and two of the guards began walking swiftly, past the thick of nurses and other staffers going the opposite direction. As they went farther down the corridor, the ward seemed empty of all but a few stragglers from among the staff.

CHAPTER THIRTY-THREE

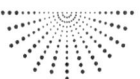

Jane Laymon tried to call Trey on his cell phone. When that didn't work, she attempted to reach him through the main switchboard at Darden, but she could not get through.

When she'd been called back up to the rented house on Third Street in Caldwell—forensics felt they had to make sure that the place had a last going-over, in case the fire spread up toward that end of the hillside—she had sifted through the evidence and found a detailed layout of Darden State.

And worse, a layout of the basement level of the hospital, with rooms marked: Night Cage. Several of them.

Another area—an upper floor of Ward D—was marked with just the words: *His Office.*

With traffic backed up on the hillside and plumes of darkness coughing from the burning canyon, Jane drove alone down toward Darden State, determined to find out if Bloody Mary might be traced right back to the place where she had worked, where she had met her husband, and where her son was being held.

CHAPTER THIRTY-FOUR

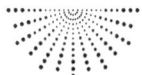

When Trey rounded the first hallway in Ward D, he saw something near the elevators. The strobes continued to flash on and off, and what he found inside the elevator, its doors open wide, nearly made him drop to his knees and scream.

Dr. Hannifin's assistant, Lara, lay face down on the floor in a pool of blood.

In her hand, the alarm pen that she'd punched to set off the warning.

Trey crouched down and reached over to feel her pulse.

She was gone. He touched the back of her neck. Right at the base of her skull, someone had jabbed a knife of some kind into her.

"Jim! Hurry up!" he called out. Jim Anderson came up behind him, cursing under his breath as he saw the dead woman.

Down several hundred feet and to the right, at the entrance to

Program 28, Mary Chilmark, still clutching her grocery bag in one hand, had the other pressed into Dr. Robert Brainard's spine.

Brainard waved them both past the guards and said, "We're going to escort Chilmark to a special transport. I'll send someone else down for the others."

Floyd Nelson grinned. "You're gonna need a guard with you, Dr. Brainard. You see those strobes?" He pointed back down the hallway. "I think we're gonna be in lockdown any minute, and the ward's not even clear yet. Hope nothing too awful's going on."

"It's nothing," Brainard said rather stiffly. "Someone accidently pulled it."

"Accidents happen," Mary Chilmark smiled slightly.

"Well, at least let me escort the two of you," Floyd said.

"Yes," she said. "That's a good idea." Then, as if it needed to be added, "I'm a nurse from San Pascal General. We'll have a special place for him over there."

"Lucky him," Floyd said, and then accompanied the two of them down the corridor to Doc Chilmark's room. He unlocked the door and stepped inside before the others.

Doc got up out of bed, standing before the guard.

"Okay, Mr. Chilmark," Floyd said. "It's time to move on."

But at the door on the way out, Mary Chilmark took the long ice pick she had in her hand and swiftly jabbed it into Floyd Nelson's ribs, holding it there before cutting upward, using all her strength.

Brainard grabbed her arm, but she pulled the pick out and pressed it against the hand that held her, piercing the skin until Brainard let go.

Doc Chilmark was already on Dr. Brainard, using all his force to push the man down to the floor, ramming the doctor's head twice against the wall as he did so.

After he'd subdued Brainard, Doc went to get the gun and the Taser from Floyd Nelson's body.

TREY AND JIM took the walkie-talkies off two of the guards, who went running back down the hall to get some reinforcements. The strobe lights kept flashing, and Trey decided for the safety of others it would be better to not shut them down. "You go check out 28," Trey said. "Get Floyd and Atkins, and maybe anyone else you can find. I'm going upstairs."

He took the stairs two at a time, as he ran up to the second floor to check the psychiatrist offices. Had someone gotten her on D? Didn't seem likely, given that the ward at floor level was in pretty good shape.

When he came out of the stairwell into the series of offices, he saw Dr. Hannifin standing at the elevator, trying to get her cell phone to work. Beside her were several boxes full of files.

She glanced over at him. "What the hell happened to you?"

He looked at his hands—covered in blood. "How long you been up here?"

"What?"

"The strobe's going off downstairs," he said. "Someone killed Lara. Someone got on the elevator and went down from here, with her in it. "

"Dead?" Hannifin gave him a puzzled look. "What the hell is going on? Are you bleeding?"

"A patient's loose. Someone. Running amok. Has a knife, maybe."

"Christ," Hannifin said. "I saw Lara not even ten minutes ago. She and Robert got on the elevator."

"Dr. Brainard? Just them? Anyone else?"

Dr. Hannifin squinted at Trey as if trying to remember something. "Somebody else. A woman."

"A patient?"

"No," Hannifin said. "I don't know who. She looked like she was staff. I thought ... I thought she was helping." Then, "Jesus, Lara's *dead*?"

Trey heard a crackle along the walkie-talkie. He lifted it up and pressed the button. "Jim?"

"In the canteen," Jim said, his voice a whisper. "Brainard. He's got some people with him. God, Lance Victor's there with his camera. But one of them ... one looks like Chilmark. What the hell does Brainard have him in the canteen for? Hang on ... hang on ..."

"Jim, is there a woman with them? Jim?" Trey asked. No answer. Just the crackle of static on the line. "Jim, Brainard went down on the elevator with Lara. And that woman," Trey said. "Jim?"

He clicked the button several more times. It didn't work. He tried not to think of the worst that could happen. He tried to think that maybe Brainard and a nurse had gone to get Chilmark for the escort out of Darden. That maybe Lara had gone back to the elevator to go back up for some files. That whoever had murdered the secretary had come after Brainard had gone to the canteen. He tried to think of all the things that made the scenario work in Jim's favor.

But he couldn't help but think of Doc Chilmark and remember the photographs of the Flocks, torn apart as if by a lion.

And now, was the woman with Brainard ... *Bloody Mary*?

Trey stared at Hannifin. "Dr. Hannifin, I want you to take the stairs with me. I'd like to ask that you leave those boxes here."

"Trey," she said. "Why is Robert with her? What ..." Hannifin seemed to be trying to puzzle something out. "What ... he usually

... when he left, I thought ... this morning ..." Then, she pulled herself together. "Okay. Let's get down there."

"Whoever killed Lara's still in the building," Trey said. "The lockdown of the exits ensures it. I want to get you down to the security checkpoint. There'll be other guards down there. The building'ss nearly empty. I can even send someone up here for these boxes. I just will feel better if I get you out of here. But we have to go now. Understood?"

"Oh my God," Dr. Hannifin said. "Robert. She has *Robert*."

Trey had a strange thought, one that seemed absurd in this situation. He had never heard Dr. Brainard called "Robert" by anyone on staff.

AT THE CHECKPOINT at the entrance to Ward D, Jane Laymon had just come in from the outside. As soon as Trey told her about Brainard and Chilmark, Laymon said, "Trey, she's here. You know she's here. It's got to be her. And I think I can guess why she's in the canteen."

CHAPTER THIRTY-FIVE

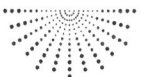

"His mother's here? Chilmark's mother?" Dr. Hannifin asked. "Holy shit, you're kidding me?" Susan Hannifin looked as if she were losing it. Watching the psych techs lose it was one thing—they were expected to go a little nuts given the daily interactions with the worst of the patients. But seeing a psychiatrist of about thirty-six, who had always seemed so together and even on top of everything, start to meltdown was unnerving. Trey wasn't sure whether to put his arms around her to keep her feeling safe or to tell her to snap out of it.

"Doctor," Trey said. "We're going to gather up some guards and get down there and get them."

"Down where? Where'd they take him?"

Even as she said this, Trey began to put two and two together.

Dr. Robert Brainard was a career seducer. She was in love with him. She acted as if she were afraid for her colleague in a way that only lovers felt.

And then he remembered little snippets of thoughts he'd had when he'd seen them walking out to their cars at the end of a work day. They walked a little too close. Brainard had grinned whenever he saw Susan Hannifin. Even Hannifin and Brainard both working on Doc Chilmark was unusual—the psychiatrists were territorial and didn't often share patients.

He began to feel more sympathy for Hannifin—and Brainard—than he had previously. They had a secret life together, one that they couldn't expose at Darden or one of them would have to leave and find work elsewhere.

It all came to Trey in an instant, and he filed it away in his mind, but it made him see Dr. Hannifin differently than he had just seconds previously. The man she loved was in serious danger.

Trey glanced at Jane. "The underground. The lockdown on the ward is in effect. Nobody can get in or out a door, except here. There's one exception. There are three exits from the underground. We don't know if Brainard knows of them, but if he does, he is likely going to help them get out."

"He doesn't need to know," Jane said. "She knows, Trey. She had maps. She may even have keys. I'm not even sure she wants escape. I think she wants Brainard. I think she's wanted him for a long time. What's a Night Cage?"

Trey was about to say something, when Hannifin interrupted. "They're cells. Special cells. Outfitted with operating equipment. They were used back in the '40s mainly. Some earlier, some later."

"They're down below, correct?" Laymon asked.

Hannifin nodded. "I took a tour back when I started here. Darden was famous for them. More lobectomies, thoracic surgeries, and lobotomies were performed here immediately following the Second World War than any other hospital in California."

"Do you know where they are?"

Hannifin nodded. "Been there. Second level down. A couple on the first level, but most at the bottom."

"All right, she comes too," Jane said.

Trey lip-farted. "No, she doesn't. This may end up being a violent takedown. I don't want anybody else's life at risk here."

"I'm going," Hannifin said, shooting a stern look at Trey.

"We have COs here. She'll be fine," Jane said.

Keeping her eyes on Trey, Hannifin said, "Doc Chilmark is under my supervision, and if you believe his mother is also there, I intend to be on hand. Surely, the guards—with guns—will prevent any mishap."

"No," Trey said. "No way in hell. Dr. Hannifin, you may have been involved in takedowns, but this is not the same thing at all."

"Two people who are sick are exactly my business," Dr. Hannifin said. "And you still report to me on Chilmark," she added. It felt like a slap in the face to Trey, but he didn't give a damn. All he thought about was Jim, and he hoped the reason that the walkie-talkie didn't work was simply because of a malfunction. He imagined that all Hannifin was thinking about was Dr. Robert Brainard.

When he led them back down the corridor toward the canteen of Ward D, he had a sick feeling in his stomach before he reached it.

CHAPTER THIRTY-SIX

THE CANTEEN WAS EMPTY. THE TABLES WERE STACKED UP IN A corner as they always were when meals had not been served. Chairs piled up by the doors to the kitchen.

Jane and three correctional officers went through the kitchen, followed by Trey and Hannifin.

The entry to the underground was open wide.

The light on the stairs was turned on.

Inside the staircase, Jim Anderson, his legs over the edge of the stairs, his head back on the landing.

His throat was slit so far open that only a thin layer of skin connected it to his body.

CHAPTER THIRTY-SEVEN

WHEN TREY SAW HIS FRIEND'S BODY, HE SAID TO JANE, "I think we need more than three guards to stop these guys." He had to work hard to keep his emotions back. They threatened to take him over at any moment. But he was good in an extreme crises. That was why had had his job. That's why he could do it. He could momentarily put aside those feelings; the adrenaline pumped through him; he could put it in a compartment somewhere in his mind. He'd always been able to do this, at least for the length of time it took to handle what needed to be handled. He was an endurance guy. He could take it in and hold it and keep it safe until the crisis was past.

But this was different. This felt as if it threatened every atom of his being.

He had loved Jim like no other friend. He had wanted Jim to always be in the world with him.

Always be there. Had taken for granted that Jim would be there. That he and Jim, at Darden, could laugh off any situation that rose up to meet them.

They'd worked side by side for more than a decade.

But Trey swallowed his feelings. For now. Later, he would let them take him over and crush him.

Jane turned back toward him, touching him on the shoulder. "I'm sorry, Trey. I'm sorry."

Dr. Hannifin backed up slightly, pressing her hands against her eyes as if willing herself to blot it out.

Trey crouched beside his buddy's body and put his hand on his forehead. He closed his eyes and wished he were thousands of miles away. Wished that Darden State had never held criminal psychopaths.

Wished that he had never passed the walkie-talkie to Jim at all.

Please God, let Jim be in heaven. Let him be someplace better. Please. Please.

After a few seconds, he rose up, wiping at his eyes. He said to Jane, "Let's get them. Now."

"Trey, I want you two to stay up here. We'll be fine. We will. But I can't risk your lives next. We may have to do any number of things to stop the two of them. Do you understand?"

Trey nodded.

Jane glanced over at Dr. Hannifin, who had sunk to the floor, her face in her hands. "She needs you up here. This is no longer a takedown situation. We have to assume that they're going to kill Brainard and anyone else they have."

"Who else could they have?" he asked.

Then, he saw the large video camera, set behind the door back into Darden's canteen. "Fuck," he said. "Jim mentioned who else. They have Lance Victor. The reporter. They have at least two people with them. Brainard and Victor."

"Okay," Jane said. "Well, we've got guns. We'll stop them any way we have to. They're delusional. It can be handled, if we're careful. If we take it slow and easy. We'll get the two guys back. They've had it easy so far, Trey. Don't worry. They're using knives right now. We'll get them." Then, to the guards that flanked her on the stairs. "Okay, boys, let's go."

CHAPTER THIRTY-EIGHT

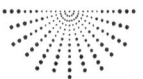

Doc Chilmark held the gun he'd taken from Floyd Nelson's holster against the small of Lance Victor's back. "Keep going."

"Please," Lance whimpered. "Please."

"You making a movie?" Doc asked. "You better be making a movie. Make a movie with your eyes. Everything you see, just put it in the movie."

Lance glanced about the corridor which was poorly lit. In various rooms, he saw a shadowy darkness. "Where are you taking me?"

"Not you. You're just along for the ride," Mary Chilmark said. "Just shut up. If you shut up, we'll all be fine."

Mary Chilmark had already blindfolded Dr. Brainard using a strip of his jacket. She pushed him along, having him carry her large paper bag in his hands, which they'd bound up using wrist restraints she'd brought with her. His left hand, which had been jabbed with the sharp pick she carried, had stopped bleeding.

"Mary, I want you to listen to me before this goes any further," Dr. Brainard said, his voice well-modulated, belying the sweat that poured from him and the slight tremble of his chin.

"Just shut up," she said, pushing him along. "Just keep walking and keep it shut."

CHAPTER THIRTY-NINE

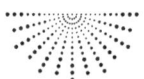

T REY STOOD AT THE TOP OF THE LONG STAIRWAY DOWN INTO the uppermost level of the underground, watching Jane and the guards go first through the main hall. The lights were fairly bright —a blessing for a hunt like this—and he could see them all the way until they'd passed down the end of the first corridor.

Hannifin, behind him, asked, "There are so many tunnels down there. They could hide anywhere if they wanted to."

"Jane'll get 'em. She's good. I've seen her in action."

"I'm sorry about your friend."

Trey turned around and leaned against the railing. "Thanks."

"It's awful to lose someone you care about," she said, and then covered her mouth slightly, as if catching herself.

"I'm sorry about your friend too," Trey said.

Hannifin looked at him as if startled. She didn't say anything for a few seconds. Then, "Oh."

"Don't worry," Trey said, as warmly as he could. "They'll get them. They'll bring them back up."

The doctor's face looked as if a cloud had passed over it, and she closed her eyes. Trey guessed that she was fighting back tears. "We just couldn't talk about it. Not to anyone here."

"Sure. I understand," Trey said. "I've seen office romances before."

"It's not like that."

"I'm sorry. I didn't mean it the way it sounded." He reached over to her and rested his hand lightly on her shoulder. "It'll be okay, though."

She glanced down over the railing. "Could you do me a favor?"

"Sure."

"When they bring them back up. If Robert's okay. Could we still keep it a secret?"

"Of course," he said.

"I don't talk about my love life," she said. "I guess now's not the time to start."

Trey sat on the first step and looked out over the hall below, glancing up and down the first of many corridors to see what he could see. Old notes posted decades before still remained behind glass frames. Debris lay in the corners. Desks were piled up, and old gray carpeting lay in rolls of mildew near the entrance to what was once an administrator's office.

"It's funny."

"What?" she asked.

"I don't even hear footsteps."

"It's the way sound goes. It's all … muffled down there. You've been through the whole thing?"

"Some of it," he said. "Just a bit. I've never liked going down there."

"It's not so bad," she said. "It's like an archaeological dig of psychiatry's sedimentary layers. This level is mainly '40s and '50s. It's the second level down that gives me the creeps. It's hard to believe what doctors used to do to people down there. I felt like I had found the ancient city of ... Troy ... or something the first time I went down. I felt I could practically see the people who worked there. And the ones who lived there."

"I know you're scared," he said. "Me too. But they'll come through this."

"I know they'll be all right," Hannifin said, as if it was a prayer. "I know it."

They remained there, looking down, and after nearly ten minutes, the lights below them went out completely.

CHAPTER FORTY

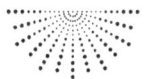

Jane felt nervous as hell as she led the guards down the corridor. She glanced in the rooms—each well lit, and each containing what seemed to her to be fully stocked medical supplies. Now and then she glanced over her shoulder slightly to make sure the officers were with her. She didn't know them, and she sure as hell wasn't sure how good they were with their guns or Tasers. She just hoped it would go easy, and they'd get a good jump on Bloody Mary and Doc.

Thick wires hung down from the pipes overhead, and there were stepladders and ceiling debris in some of the larger rooms. She assumed it was recent work being done. When she glanced up at the ceiling of one of the rooms that looked nearly like an operating theater, she thought she saw a running grate up top. Then, to the left, she saw a long room with several metal beds all stacked up against each other. If it hadn't been for the peeling paint on the wall and the bits of plaster that had dropped over time, she would've thought this was a fully functioning ward.

It was like a storage closet time machine.

She looked back. The guys with her looked scared shitless. For COs working with the criminally insane, they didn't exhibit any sense that this was going to be a routine takedown.

Her depth perception was off too. It was the problem of her eye —the eye a psychopath had taken the year before. She didn't intend to have another one drawn out by a whole new set of psychos.

When they got to the end of the corridor, where it shifted to the left, she pressed her back against the wall. Gave her guys a quick glance of, *Be ready for anything, boys*, and then, holding her Glock up, she swiftly turned the corner.

She swore under her breath.

Another long hallway loomed, and it looked as if at the end of it, it branched off in two directions.

The lights here were old hanging bulbs with metal back-shades above them. *Must've been fancy in the '50s*, she thought.

A series of rooms lined the new corridors, and each doorway was empty of even a door. As Jane went along, she had to check each doorway in case the Chilmarks were hiding in them.

She turned back to the other officers, waving for them to keep up.

When she looked in one of the rooms, she saw at least a dozen large traps, and each had one dead rat in them. Another room was filled with wheelchairs. Still another had broken glass all along the floor.

She moved faster. She could see their footsteps in the dust on the floor. Not clearly, but enough of a swipe in the grime that had built up that the killers had continued down at least to the end of the corridor.

Just as she got to the end, she saw a man kneeling down just to the left of the wall's edge, and she drew up her gun. He had blond hair, tamped down with sweat and what she assumed was blood. His face dripped with blood, and his hands were behind his back. A strip of cloth had been wrapped tight around his mouth, and there was blood coming from his lips. He was breathing through his nose such that his nostrils flared and then closed as if he were gasping for breath. His eyes widened as he stared at her.

A hostage, she thought, and immediately pulled back against the wall and turned about to tell the guards behind her.

The lights flickered—just once.

She saw a blur of movement as a woman leaped from one of the doorways they'd passed, some large metal instrument in her hands, coming for the guard who was farthest back.

The lights overhead began flickering again—this time almost as the strobe lights had upstairs. She noticed it all at once—the hostage, then the woman leaping almost as if she were a lion going after its prey. The two guards directly behind her saw her expression and began to turn to look back.

And then, they were plunged into darkness.

CHAPTER FORTY-ONE

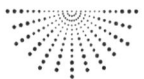

"Someone's shut off the switch," Trey said.

"The guards wouldn't do it," Hannifin said. "They wouldn't."

Trey strained to listen, as if he'd hear their voices.

"I hate waiting here," she said. "Just waiting. God knows what's happening."

"It's just the lights. Maybe Jane shut them off for a reason."

"I know where it is," Hannifin said. "The switch. It's in that wheelchair graveyard area."

"The what?"

"The main switch. There's a bunch of old wheelchairs just collecting dust. If you wait, if it works right, the emergency lights will come on in a few minutes."

The only light that entered the stairwell was from the door behind them.

"It's strange in the dark," she said. "My main studies have been about seeing what we do exposed to daylight. The secrets. The dark places. But if you sit in the dark sometimes, you remember things. Things you might want to forget sometimes."

"It'll be okay," he said, sensing the weight of her words—she was thinking too deeply, too seriously. He wanted to try and offer her some comfort.

"Other doctors here knew we'd been a couple," she said. "But we've been doing our best to hide it."

"Sure. I never guessed. Well, I mean, 'til now."

"Everybody keeps secrets from somebody."

As she spoke, he felt the darkness below them, and the unanswered questions it posed were not worth dwelling on. He sat there, wishing he could lighten her mood. Wishing whatever darkness she now felt within her mind could be allowed to escape into the light of day. He remembered what Brainard had told him about psychiatrists. How they sometimes were in the profession for the very reason that they themselves needed to untangle their minds.

"Trey," Hannifin said. "I'm worried about him. All of them down there. Even Doc Chilmark."

"They have flashlights," Trey said. "Just like this one. Don't worry." He drew a long slender flashlight up and flicked it on. He shined it down into the dark. The light bounced off peeling walls and the open cabinets and storage closets.

"The emergency lights should be up by now."

"Jane knows what she's doing," Trey said.

A sound like a distant pop. Then another.

And another.

Gunfire.

CHAPTER FORTY-TWO

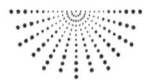

JANE FELT HEAT RISE BENEATH HER SKIN AS SHE TURNED around. She couldn't shoot. She couldn't even see. There was the sound of a scuffle behind her; one of the men shouted; another shot —a brief brightness. For the barest moment, she thought she felt a hand on her neck; she wrenched away from it, pivoting around to bring her gun to eye level, ready to shoot. Her hands trembled. *You've been through worse. Hang on. Hang on. You can do it. You can get through it.*

Then, silence.

She crouched down, figuring she was less of a target closer to the floor. Then, she lay down on her stomach, keeping her elbows bent and holding the gun upward in case she detected movement near her.

A terrible sound began somewhere not far from her in the dark.

It was a slicing and ripping, and then a wet slurp of a body as it was being cut open.

A groan, but so faint it was as if it were far away.

CHAPTER FORTY-THREE

TREY HELD HIS BREATH AS LONG AS HE COULD. HOPING THAT it had gone the right way below them. In the dark. Beyond the first corridor of the underground.

Susan Hannifin said, "We've got to get down there, Trey. If they've shot anybody. The patients, or … well, if anyone's hurt, I've got to."

"Dr. Hannifin, no," Trey said.

But Hannifin stepped around him and began running down the stairs to the floor below. He kept the flashlight on her as she went. He didn't know what had come over her, and part of him wanted to race back down to the checkpoint at Ward D, but he didn't like the odds of any of this.

"Damn it," Trey said.

He thought of Jim Anderson, just beyond the doorway behind him. Thought of what he would've done to save him if he'd only gone to the canteen with him.

What two people could do that one could not.

He thought of Jane, and even of Dr. Brainard and Lance Victor.

Their faces in his mind. He imagined them dead, throats slit like Jim's had been. Nothing but meat in the end. Nothing but a plaything for the human monsters who couldn't even understand what they were doing when they killed.

He thought of the good and bad of life and wanted the good to come out this time.

He followed Hannifin into the underground, calling out to her to wait for him. "I got the flashlight, damn it. Hang on," he said.

CHAPTER FORTY-FOUR

LIGHTS FLICKERED UP FROM THE EDGES OF THE HALLWAYS. They bathed the peeling walls in a hazy blue. For Jane, it flattened out the vision in her eye further. She could no longer tell the distance of objects and people. She scooted behind a doorway, rising to a crouching position, keeping her Glock at the ready.

Down the hallway, the patches of blue light did not permeate every square foot of the hall—the emergency lights were only at the ends of the corridor and in every other room along it.

Behind her, she saw two bodies on the floor. One of the guards lay on his back and continued to shiver as blood poured from his throat; his gut, also, had been ripped open. Another, several feet behind him, was so covered with blood she couldn't even see his face or scalp.

She felt a panic seize her as she glanced back and forth, trying to make out who else was there.

Then, from down at the nearest end of the hall, one of the guards stepped forward. He looked at his feet as he came. She had not gotten a good look at him when he'd joined up with her to explore this area. He was young—too young to be facing what he now had to face.

Behind him, the woman.

Bloody Mary.

Focus. Come on, focus, Jane kept telling herself. But there was something about the blue lights and the shadows between them that weren't helping with her vision.

Bloody Mary must have something in his back. A gun. Something, Jane thought. *Okay, you'll get through this. You will. If you aim, you'll miss him. You'll wing her. But that may be enough for her to drop him, and then you'll get a clear shot.*

"We're going to perform surgery today," Mary said, her voice calm and smooth as if none of this had any effect on her. "Today. My son. He's a doctor. He's a healer. There are too many to be healed in this world."

"Let him go," Jane whispered, then repeated herself in a normal tone. Or as normal as she could get it. She held her gun steady. She began to look for ways of distracting Bloody Mary so that she'd let the guard go for a split second.

She heard a noise behind her. Quickly, she turned her head to the side.

The hostage that she'd seen in the hall on his knees was far back in the shadows of the room she'd chosen. She could just make him out. Her eye began tearing up. Or else the sweat on her forehead had dripped down into it. She swiped at it with her hand.

The man with the gag over his mouth had begun crawling toward her. She had no time to signal him to stay where he was. She had to turn around and keep watching Bloody Mary.

When she glanced out into the hall, Bloody Mary had stepped closer with the guard in front of her, a shield.

Suddenly, the young guard began trembling, and his eyes went wide. His legs seemed to be buckling; Jane saw the strength in the structure of his body collapse, as if he had just lost all muscle coordination.

The guard's mouth opened wide in a scream, but no sound came out.

He dropped to the ground.

Bloody Mary stood there, her dress soaked with blood, her hair wild, and a long cutting saw of some kind that had scissorlike attachments.

Jane knew she had a split second to act. She took fast aim but heard someone running toward her from behind.

She had to turn—she had no choice. As she did, she saw that she and the hostage had not been the only ones in the room.

Doc came running for her as if he were about to throw a shot put—and at the very last second, she saw the Taser, and before she could react fast enough, her gun went off in her hand, and she felt the bite of electric shock when the probes of the Taser connected with her left hip.

CHAPTER FORTY-FIVE

Doc got down on all fours beside the woman who'd just dropped. "A cop," he said. "Cool."

Behind him, Lance Victor began to make bleating noises under his gag. Doc turned around. He pointed his finger at him, "You just keep still from now on. You hear?"

As he looked at Lance, Doc was sure he saw a shadow behind him. Not like the other shadows when people got healed. These were shadows that lived down here.

The ghosts that the other patient had told him about.

From the doorway, his mother reached down and stroked his scalp. He felt good when she touched him. Safe. He looked up at her. "I see shadows all around us."

"Good ones?" she asked.

"I think so. I don't feel the fears. Not like I did in the dark. I felt them when the lights went out. I felt them crawling from all the cracks in the walls."

"I'm sorry about the dark," she said. "But we had to shut it down. They might've hurt you."

"I know," he said. "You kept me safe. Where'd you put my father?"

"Back there," Mary said, cocking her head to the side to indicate any number of rooms behind her. Beyond the bodies of the guards. "Come on, sweetheart. Let's go."

"I have your bag still," Doc said, pointing toward a stack of magazines in a corner. Just visible over the tops of them, a grocery bag.

"Good. Get it. I'll go get your father. We'll heal him soon."

"What about this one?" Doc swiveled around to look at Lance Victor, who had slipped to the floor and could not get back up with his hands tied behind him.

"Yes," she said.

"And this one?" He looked down at Jane who lay there, her eyes closed.

"She'll be up soon. Let's get her bound. Check the supply closet up the hall. I bet there's some restraints still in it," his mother said.

CHAPTER FORTY-SIX

TREY SWITCHED THE FLASHLIGHT OFF WHEN THE BLUE emergency lights came up. Dr. Hannifin walked ahead of him.

"Slow down," he said.

"They're down there. You heard the shots. That they haven't come back ...." She stopped and glanced back at him.

"Dr. Hannifin," he said. "Susan. Let's go back up. The lights are up. Jane and the other guards know what they're doing. I'll take you back upstairs. We'll see if the ward doors are open yet. There'll be someone to help them if anything happened."

"I know where they're taking him," Dr. Hannifin said. She no longer seemed like a superior, a psychiatrist. For the first time, in that pale blue light of the corridor, he saw her as a frightened person. A woman who had held something back. "He told me about her. He told me about what she does. What they did. He never lied to me, Trey. He loved her. Too many years ago to bother me. He loved her. A patient. He brought her here, and they ... they did things. Nothing sick. Not like what was in her head, I'm sure. She fucked with him then. She's fucking with him now. She's going to gut him, Trey. She told him that years ago. She told him after she'd been released. After he worked hard to get her released. Believing she had been badly treated. Believing her lies that the patients she'd killed had provoked her attack and had keyed into the triggers of her psychosis. He believed she was a victim, Trey. Oh God." Susan slid down to the floor, her face in her hands.

Trey went and sat beside her, putting his arm around her. "It's all right. It'll be all right."

Susan began weeping. "Please forgive me, I can't believe I'm doing this," she said. She pushed her tears away with her fingers. "I'm not weak. I'm not. I hate doing this. But ever since they brought him in, I knew."

"That Doc is his son."

Susan nodded. "I knew it was all there. I knew she was out there again. I thought we were both safe."

Trey felt a chill spread over him. "You felt unsafe before?"

Susan Hannifin didn't reply.

"Dr. Hannifin," he said.

"She came to his house once," Hannifin said, and then cleared her throat. "She came to his house. I was there. I didn't know who she was. I was just staying for the weekend. She said she was an old girlfriend. Robert has had many girlfriends. Lovers. I'm not blind to that. I've been around the block too. You know, you can have a medical degree, be top of your class, and research the human mind into its darkest corner. And still, still … you just don't fathom what you yourself are willing to go through when you love someone. You reach a point when you say to yourself, 'I forgive him.' I can move beyond this. His past is nothing. He was younger then, and foolish. It's none of my business. But she told me about their games."

Trey drew her close to him. "Susan. Let's go back up. We don't need to be here."

"They played games, she told me. Games where he'd tie her up.

Games where he and another doctor—the one she married, Massey —tied her up on a table here. They took turns. Well," she wiped at her face again, "well, I knew it was a lie. It was a lie. I know Robert well enough. We've been seeing each other for almost six years. I know his … his ins and outs. He's not like that. But the worst thing that she told me was that he had asked me to play games with him too. She knew it. She said we were alike. We both loved him. We both would do anything for him." She paused, and then heaved a sigh. "I knew that much was true."

Trey leaned back against the wall. He didn't want to hear anymore. None of it surprised him, and he passed no judgment on anyone else's private lives. He didn't like hearing about them. He didn't like hearing this story either. He wished she had never begun talking about it.

He just felt an overwhelming sadness for her as they sat there. She loved Robert Brainard too much. And Brainard was basically a jerk and possibly a creep. Maybe he was the smartest man alive. Maybe he made love like Don Juan. But he wasn't worth what this woman had put into him. She loved him above all else. Trey could tell by the way she said his name. Some women did that. They loved their men beyond their own sense of happiness.

Trey felt he loved Carly like that too. He understood. He would put her first every single time that he could. He'd failed her some- times, but as he thought of his wife in that twisted corridor, he sent a little prayer to her and to the kids. *Dad'll be safe. Dad loves you. Honey, I love you. I'll be home again. Promise.*

"I never mentioned to him that she came by. I never mentioned what she said to me. Until Chilmark came in, I didn't really have to think about it. She was elsewhere. Even when Dr. Massey died, well, Robert had cut himself off from that lunatic years before I met him. But when I saw her picture in the files yesterday, Trey, when I saw that face again, I remembered her well from her visit to his house. I remembered how she told me that we had a lot in common. And when I asked her what she meant, she didn't have to tell me. It wasn't just him. It was that other thing. That thing women don't talk about with men. Or in their jobs. It was that thing where despite all our training, all our education and disposing of the nonsense of thinking the man is everything and the woman is nothing … sometimes, certain women give it all for a man. Sometimes, the things a man shares with a woman, in the dark, in the places of secrets, becomes a place of surrender of all the civilized ideas of what is right and wrong."

Then, she fell silent, and Trey was glad she did. He didn't want to hear about her inner life. He preferred to think of her as a ward psychiatrist, not as a woman. Not as Susan, but as Dr. Hannifin, who kept her distance most of the time. Professional. Above reproach. Perhaps nobody was that professional or that untouchable in life.

She had acquired a soul here with Trey. Beneath the hospital. She had opened up under the stress of the moment. She had shown him a little of the private woman he never would have otherwise known. He almost grinned, thinking of what Jim Anderson would've said. *Hannifin's a friggin' lunatic. Can't always tell the doctors from the patients in here.* That's what he would've said. Trey held back a breath, trying not to let the grief of Jim's murder overwhelm him. *Christ, this is a sorry place to be. Under a building. Beyond us, a fire that might be sweeping over us soon. Within here, two very psychopathic killers with delusions of medical expertise and an entire world for their madness.*

Trey felt as if the two of them were alone in an underworld, a city of the dead—of psychiatry's past folly and vanity and monstrosity. He remembered Fallon with his talk of ghosts down here, and it would not have surprised him if they did, indeed, wander these halls. The tubercular who had died here, the mentally retarded who had once been hidden away and forgotten, the mentally ill who had the unfortunate circumstance to be alive before the prescription drug revolution, and others who matched society's definition of outcasts who needed hospitalization deep in the ground just to hide them from the rest of the community.

Finally, he said, softly, "Everyone has secret places. I understand. Let's go back. All right? We'll get help."

She wiped her eyes again and took his hand as he rose up.

From somewhere off in an unknown place ahead of them, the bloodcurdling scream of a man echoed along the walls.

CHAPTER FORTY-SEVEN

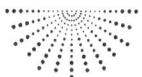

"You do anything—run, hide, anything," Mary said, her arm raised up, her fist around what looked like a long slender ice pick pointed to Lance Victor's head, "I will be on you. I will slice you open and trepan your brain and draw it out for you to look at while you're dying. Do you understand?"

Lance Victor nodded vigorously.

Mary lowered the pick, and with her free hand reached up and adjusted Lance's gag, which had slipped down from the lips she had only recently sliced with her scalpel. From one of the supply closets, Doc had brought out an array of old moth-worn straitjackets and ankle hobbles that were heavier than the modern ones he had been used to wearing in his home cage.

He secured the jacket on Lance and then hobbled his ankles together. Then, he went to restrain the policewoman who had begun showing signs of reviving from the second Taser shot he'd done to her.

"Your father took me to the night cages," Mary said. "When I was young. They're downstairs. It may be dark. Do you understand?"

Doc, who had begun tying restraints at Jane's wrists, nodded.

"We'll heal him. All of them," she said.

"I know. I can feel a healing coming to me," he said.

"I will never leave you in the dark," his mother said.

Then, stepping over one of the dead guards, she went back to the room full of wheelchairs to get the man she had loved her whole life, the father of her child, from the room where she'd secured him.

ONCE DOC HAD the policewoman all wrapped up tight with restraints and a gag, she opened her eyes and watched him. He still had the Taser and pressed it point-blank into the same hip where he'd shot her before. He squeezed the trigger, and the prongs went into her.

Her eyes fluttered for a moment or two, and her body convulsed.

He glanced back at the room. There were little metal cabinet-like doors on the wall.

As he dragged her toward them, he was nearly positive that her eyes—which remained open—watched him.

"It's okay," Doc said to her. "It's okay. We'll come back for you. We will. I'll heal you too. Don't worry. We just have too much to take with us here."

Then, he opened one of the cabinets and drew out a long tray. Inside, it looked almost like a metal oven. He stretched his arm all the way in.

It was the perfect size.

ONCE HE'D PUT the woman on the flat surface, he pushed it in, and shut the drawer.

"It's a morgue," he said aloud. "It's perfect."

He went and grabbed an open lock from the pile on the floor. Although it was rusted, it still closed. He put it through the loop of metal at the morgue cabinet door.

"Don't be afraid," he said to the door. "You're safe there."

CHAPTER FORTY-EIGHT

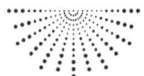

Trey ran with Susan Hannifin down the hallway, toward the scream they'd heard. As they reached the end of one corridor, they turned onto another.

Susan shrieked when she saw the bodies on the ground.

Trey came up behind her.

Three of the guards were accounted for, but there was no sign of Jane. Trey held out a hope.

He grabbed a gun from beside each of the bodies. "You ever use one of these?"

"Never," she said.

"First time for everything," he said. "Let's go. Let's go. We may not have any time at all now."

He ran ahead, quickly ducking in and out of rooms, hoping to see a sign, something that might indicate that Jane was alive. That she had survived. He saw rooms full of chairs, and one that had strips of newspaper clippings all over the floor; still another seemed to be the morgue of the underground—a wall that was made out of cheap metal, showing signs of rust along its drawers; another room had all kinds of bottles, large and small, set in rows throughout, as if they'd been collected from all over the hospital and stored here.

Finally, following the trail of blood, they reached what seemed to be the dead end of the ward.

"There's a door, off there," Susan pointed toward one of the utility rooms. "To the next level down."

"They're taking them to the night cages," Trey said.

THROUGH THE DOORWAY into the lower section, Trey saw that it was completely dark. He switched on his flashlight and kept the gun in his right hand as he stepped down onto the metal stairs.

Susan followed after him. They went carefully down into the dark hole of a room below.

About three steps from the bottom, Trey missed a step, stumbling. His flashlight flew out of his hand.

Then, he fell down to the bottom step, hitting his head hard against the floor; as he did so, his gun rolled across the floor.

"YOU OKAY?" Susan asked. She felt her way down the last few steps and got down on all fours, reaching for the flashlight. When she had it, she pointed it along the floor until she found Trey. "Trey?"

"It's okay," he said. "Get the gun. It's … it's over there." He pointed somewhere off to the right.

After she'd helped him up, and after he had the gun again and the flashlight, she said, "There are six tunnels down here. Not all of them are functioning."

"What's that mean?" he asked.

"Some go out under the grounds, beyond the buildings. Some have caved in over the years, so they're nothing but rubble at one end."

"We can't get lost down here, can we?" he asked.

THERE WERE rows of metal beds along the corridor of the second level. Trey shined his flashlight along the wall.

"The night cages," she said. "There are nine of them. Three here. Six at the end of the hallway that goes to the tunnels."

"It's like the catacombs," he said, directing the flashlight's beam all along the various avenues that shot off from the main hallway. The other pathways were narrow and must have made the patients who had been virtually imprisoned down there feel as if they were buried alive at times.

There were three closed doors in a row along one side of the wall. Along the other, the therapy rooms that had been used for hydrotherapy and minor operations.

"Lobectomies. Thoracic surgery. Lobotomies," Trey pointed the flashlight farther down the long corridor. What looked almost like dried human feces was smeared along the crack-filled walls. At the end of the hallway, the entrance to where the pipes and the tunnels intersected. "The major one—shock treatment—was upstairs. It's hard to think of all this as minor surgery."

"What was that?" she asked.

"What?"

"Over there. By the door."

"Which door?" he whispered, feeling a chill within him. *Think of Jane. Think of Brainard. Hell, think of Lance Victor. Don't be afraid. Don't let the darkness win.*

She took the flashlight from him and shined it to the second Night Cage door. It was open slightly, and it might've even been moving. It was as if a light wind pushed at the door from the inside, a draft that kept it opening and closing, almost imperceptibly.

Trey stepped forward but kept the gun held up, ready to point it toward anybody. He crossed the large room, keeping the light on the door.

When he got to the Night Cage, he reached for the door handle. It was slick and wet. He drew it outward, shining the light inside.

The Night Cage was small, with a low ceiling that had a grate in it. Above the grate, a metal fan for ventilation. In one corner a hole that had once been the toilet. In another, a shelf that must've served for a bed, although there was no mattress or blanket on it.

Written on the wall in a dark smear: TUMORS MALIGNANT.

Trey took one step into the room.

And that's when he felt something on his foot. Something grasp at his ankles.

He looked down. A shadow there. He shined the light on it.

He didn't identify the man right away. And then, he knew. It was Lance Victor, the television reporter. But it took the longest time for Trey to realize this, because there was so much blood along the man's back, which had been split open to expose his spinal cord.

They had ripped his skin from his back and had dug into him while he had been alive.

CHAPTER FORTY-NINE

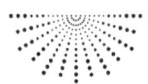

BECAUSE LANCE'S FINGERS STILL MOVED, TREY KNELT DOWN beside him, setting the flashlight on the floor to cast light across the dying man's body.

"It's Lance, come on," he called to Susan, but in the few seconds it took for her to get there, the man died.

Susan stood in the open doorway. She crouched down beside Trey and put her hand on his back. "Let's go," she said. "Trey. We have to go find them."

"I know," he said. But he could not leave the dead man yet. He felt an ache within him. And an anger that had grown since finding Jim dead upstairs.

A fury. *Please be alive, Jane. Please. I will find you. I promise. I will stop this. Somehow.*

"I wonder about the fire," Susan said suddenly. "I wonder if it's reached the grounds above us."

"Maybe we're safer down here," Trey said. Then, he felt the slight madness in having said that. He began to feel a little lightheaded. Something within him was changing down in this place.

Some sense of human decency had begun to vanish. He wanted to tell her about it, but he was sure she wouldn't understand. He wanted to tell her what he felt rising up in his craw—in that primitive place inside him.

He had faced psychopaths before.

He sometimes even pretended to understand their delusions.

But not this time. These people were worse than predatory animals.

Bloody Mary was like an alien species. If she could do this. If she could twist her son's soul into doing this. Doing it quickly. Doing it without remorse. Without a sense of empathy for the suffering of the ones beneath her knives and saws … she wasn't even human anymore.

Not in his eyes.

Years of training just exploded for him.

"Let's check every Night Cage," he said.

Susan began making a strange sound.

He stood up, grasping her elbow. "Susan?"

"I want them dead," she said.

"I know. Me too."

"I want to kill them," Susan said, her voice nearly a growl. "I'm not supposed to think that. But it's what I want to do."

"Yeah, I know," he said. "Let's go."

CHAPTER FIFTY

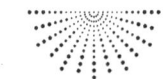

Doc had warned his mother that others would follow, but she told him that it all would be taken care of. "We're healers," she said. "What we bring to them is good. They understand."

Doc had spent the better part of the past half hour gathering up more of the surgical tools they'd need. The place was full of all kinds of little hammers and picks and long saws that cut just like scissors. He was fairly sure they had been used as bone saws. He'd spent most of his childhood and all of his adolescence studying medical practices and had a good feel for the tools of the trade, large and small. But as he went down one particular tunnel, he thought he saw someone standing nearby. He didn't exactly see the person at first. He felt it the way he always felt the shadows. In the area where they had decided to perform the major surgery, the red lights were on, and these comforted him. But he could not see the shadow, even in the glow of the light.

"Who's there?" he asked.

He tried to ignore the feeling that he was being watched. He didn't think it was one of the night fears. His mother had told him they couldn't find him this far down. But when he opened the door of what had once been an office, he was sure it was a little girl. Hadn't the patient above talked about seeing her? A little girl who was dead. A little girl who had not passed over into the light.

He opened the cabinets, looking for just the right tools for the surgery, and at one point caught a glimpse of her in a broken mirror that hung on the back of one of the cabinet doors.

She had a yellow-blue aura about her. He just saw her face. A little bit of her face. He turned around quickly.

She didn't try to hide.

In the light that she gave off, he saw the shadows of others who had lived here and had died here without moving on toward the light of heaven.

"Hello," Doc Chilmark said to her.

"THERE'S a little girl down the tunnel a little ways," he told his mother when he'd brought the rolled up towel full of instruments back to the Night Cage where they had his father tied down to the table. "She's dead. But she's like a bright shadow."

CHAPTER FIFTY-ONE

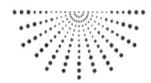

DR. BRAINARD LOOKED UP AT MARY CHILMARK'S FACE, bathed in red light. The gag was still tight over his mouth, and he had pains all over his arms and legs. He was sure a rib had been broken as they'd pushed him and thrown him around on his journey down to this room.

He tried to rein in the fear he had. He resolved to remain calm. He felt a sense of peace. If he could just get the gag off. If he could speak to her.

She operated off of delusion and pleasure. She did not desire pain for herself. He knew that.

If he could just speak to her. Reassure her. Talk to her about what had happened.

He knew that, given her personality type, she would respond.

But the gag stayed on, and so nothing was said.

When Doc returned, Mary began to open Brainard's already torn shirt. "I'll prep the patient, Doc."

CHAPTER FIFTY-TWO

"HERE'S HOW IT GOES," BLOODY MARY SAID AS SHE TORE THE shirt and then undid his pants, slipping them down as far as she could before the restraints that held him to the operating table got in the way. "Robert, your son has grown into an excellent healer. A real doctor. Not one made by some school. But a natural-born doctor."

She leaned over Brainard's body and rested her hand on Doc's face. Doc felt warmth flood him. She hadn't touched him like that since the last time he'd lain in her arms. She was purity. Purity and love in the flesh.

On the table, Brainard tried to mumble through the gag.

"The way I see it," Doc said, grinning to his nurse, "there's a lot of work to be done here."

"Yes. Let's get started," she said. "Do you remember how this goes, Doc?"

Doc nodded. "Like the Flock woman. With the malignancy."

"That's right," his mother said. Then, she went to get what she'd brought all this way in her grocery bag.

Doc heard a voice behind him and turned, afraid that someone would stop his healing.

But it was the dead girl he had seen before. She smiled at him, and he nodded back. With her were others, although he couldn't see them as clearly. He said to his mother, "They're with us."

"Who?" Mary asked.

"The ones who never left here. When he gets healed," he said, nodding toward his father, "will he stay here?"

"I don't know," his mother said. She brought something from the bag—it was wrapped in newspaper. "He might go to the light."

"I'm not scared down here," Doc said.

"You shouldn't be," Bloody Mary said. "It's where I brought you into me."

CHAPTER FIFTY-THREE

Trey heard the noise first. It wasn't quite a shout, and it wasn't a scream. But it was as if someone had called out in the red-lit pathways between the night cages. He followed it, running ahead of Susan. When he reached the door that was slightly ajar, he let his adrenaline take over and held the gun up, figuring he'd have to aim for Bloody Mary first, since Doc could be subdued. He thought about this within seconds, and then pushed the door open.

The operating table at the center of the room.

The restraints at the uppermost and lowermost parts of the table had been torn open. A streak of blood absorbed against towels that had been stacked as if underneath a patient's body.

But no one.

Whoever had been operated on no longer was in the room. When Susan caught up to him, he had her turn the flashlight on into the dark corners of the room. They both heard a slight noise that sounded like a little child blowing milk bubbles.

There, beneath the operating table and back against the wall, was Dr. Brainard.

Naked.

Clutching what seemed to be his belly that had been greatly distended.

Trey quickly moved to him, getting down on his knees. "Doctor. Dr. Brainard?"

Dr. Brainard looked into the flashlight's glare and looked as if he were eighty years old rather than in his late fifties. Bubbles of blood came from between his lips, and the whites of his eyes showed as he blinked in the light.

Trey tried to keep the feeling of nausea within him.

He could not help but look at the man's purplish, blood-smeared distended belly.

It had a row of sutures or stitches—but made with material that seemed more like twine—holding his stomach together.

They had cut into his stomach.

"Dear God," Trey said. "Dear God."

HE STAYED with Dr. Brainard until the man died in his arms.

They had put something inside Brainard's stomach. They had opened him up and put something inside him that had caused swelling, and then they'd brutally sewn him up again.

Trey hoped it wasn't the dead fetus that had been killed two days previous at the Flocks'. But something in his mind went there. He wished he hadn't worked around psychopathic killers for so long right at that moment because his intuition rarely was off when it came to the most monstrous possibilities.

He hoped that Bloody Mary's insane sense of poetic justice—of taking the man who had impregnated her, the man who had abandoned her to someone else, had not fulfilled his promise—hadn't spent nearly twenty years waiting for a moment when she had a dead fetus in her possession.

But she's insane. She isn't like you. She belonged in Darden State all along. She didn't belong out in the world. She didn't belong where other people lived. She belonged on meds, in a hospital for the criminally insane.

Trey hoped he was wrong. But it didn't matter to Brainard. The psychiatrist was dead now.

From behind him, he heard Susan's voice cry out in alarm. As he spun about quickly, he felt something sharp go into his ribs, and for just a moment he saw Bloody Mary's face above him. The red glow of light all around her.

The face of madness.

Then, he passed out hearing Susan Hannifin screaming in a way he'd never heard another human being scream in his life.

CHAPTER FIFTY-FOUR

DOC HAD TO SLAM HANNIFIN'S HEAD INTO THE WALL THREE times before she was knocked out. "This the bitch?" he asked his mother who was across the room with Trey Campbell.

His mother nodded.

"I should heal her now," Doc said. "Right now."

"Get her safe," Bloody Mary said to her son. "Baby, get her safe. We have lots of time. It's a busy day at the hospital. One operation after another."

SUSAN HANNIFIN AWOKE SITTING up on the operating table in one of the night cages. She was alone. Her head ached like hell. She had been put in leg restraints, and her arms were strapped behind her, attached to a small lead that was hooked to the wall. She looked up—a cage-like ceiling, and above it, the red emergency light.

She felt as if a truck had hit her. She called out for Trey, but there was no answer.

She spent the better part of an hour struggling to get free of the restraints.

JANE LAYMON REGAINED CONSCIOUSNESS. She felt as though she were buried alive but soon came to terms with the space she'd been put into. Some narrow morgue-like drawer, perhaps. She wasn't sure. She tried to move, but realized that the numbness in her arms had something to do with the straitjacket they'd put her in. Her ankles, too, were tied together.

She felt weak; her mouth was dry; her throat was sore; and her left hip was still a little tender from the Taser burn.

The space she was in felt warm—probably the air. Probably not enough fresh air coming in.

Her heels pressed against wall. If she pushed herself up slightly, her head was pressed against wall also.

They put me in here somehow.

She assumed that her last sight that she had remembered was what looked like a series of drawers along a wall. A small morgue of some kind. A storage for bodies back in the day.

"All right. You didn't kill me. That's good for me. Bad for you," she whispered.

Then, she began bending her knees. She could bend them halfway to her stomach. She stretched them back down to touch what she hoped was the drawer opening. Not a wall, but something that could move outward.

If she could move it.

She bent her knees as far as they'd go, toward her stomach, then kicked them down to the other side.

Her shoes slapped against the base of the drawer.

It gave slightly.

Okay, she thought. *A thousand more of these, and maybe I get out of here.*

CHAPTER FIFTY-FIVE

TREY AWOKE ON THE TABLE. THEY HAD BROUGHT HIM INTO his own Night Cage.

He saw the red light above the cage.

He looked first to the left, then the right. He felt a soreness along his jaw. They'd tied a gag over his mouth.

Restraints at his wrists. His ankles.

His lower right side hurt.

She stabbed me. Great.

He heard footsteps coming into the room. He strained his neck looking up from the table and had to lay his head back down.

He looked to the left—there was a small kidney-shaped tray.

On it were several instruments. He recognized the little hammer and the pick, as well as the Hay saw—a special saw for cutting the skull and brainpan open.

He knew enough about Bloody Mary's MO to know what he was up for. *Lobotomy or just simple brain surgery. Christ.*

He wondered how much time he had. He knew he had to work

his way out of this. He doubted there was anyone left to come to the rescue.

Please, God. Please. Help me. He thought of Carly again—her face. The news of bringing a new baby into the world. The shock of it. The surprise. The last look she'd given him the night before. That look of love that he hoped he'd given back to her.

Use what you know, he thought. He remembered enough about at least one escape from restraints to know that there was always a way to do it if you really wanted to. Doc had talked about Houdini and how he had read up on how to get out of restraints. How to get out of a straitjacket. There was a way.

Give me five minutes, he thought. *God, just five minutes. I don't expect you to come out of the wall with a full-blown miracle. Just five minutes and I can do it myself.*

As it turns out, he got less than a minute and a half before Bloody Mary came in and leaned over him. Her breath was foul, but at least she'd cleaned the blood from her face. Her dark hair had turned stringy and hung down in his face. "You're vexed," she said. "I can tell." Then she drew back and turned to someone at the door. "Doc? Are you ready for this one? It may be an emergency."

"Hello again," Doc Chilmark said. He had a boyish grin on his face as he peered down at Trey. "You should've stayed upstairs. You know that."

Trey nodded. He tried to keep the movement around his hands minimized. He was hoping to draw his hands through the wrist restraints, but it didn't seem to be working. But as Doc spoke to him, Trey focused on the edge of the table. He was able to get his hands flopped over it just a bit, on the side with the surgery tray. He felt along the table underside, and when he found the metal edge, he rubbed the strap of the restraint against it. *Nice. Keep talking, Doc. Just keep talking.*

Trey ignored the bad stuff he saw: the words said to him about the operation to come, about how the brain could be modified with just the boring of a hole or two. Tried to ignore anything but that one little restraint strap at his wrist, and the slow but steady sawing movement he got going. *Old restraints*, Trey thought. *They're bound to give it up. Bound to tear a little here and there. How many years ago were they used? Forty? Thirty? So long ago, and in between time, a lot of possibilities for falling apart.*

He felt that surge of madness again. He looked up at Doc and Bloody Mary. *I can be as crazy as you if I want to be. You had no problem slicing my best friend's throat. No problem with poor Lance. Or Brainard. In fact, you haven't seen crazy until you can see what I can do. I'm gonna go temporary insanity on both your asses.*

Bloody Mary had a long pick in her left hand and a small rounded hammer in her right.

Great. I get a lobotomy. No thanks.

He felt the fabric of the restraint that held his right hand give. The sharp metal edge of the table had cut through it.

TREY DREW his right arm out from behind him, the restraint flopping to the side, and grabbed Mary Chilmark's hand midair as she brought the pick toward his eye. He tugged hard with his left hand, and it hurt like hell, but he tore the restraint out completely as he swung around. He felt her strength, which seemed greater than a woman her size should have. He pushed at her arm to get the instrument away from his face. At the same time, Doc Chilmark tried to pull him back down onto the table. Doc punched him hard in the jaw, and Trey fell backward, sliding halfway off the table, his ankle restraints keeping him from rolling off it.

Doc reached over to the surgery tray and drew up the trepan and the small hammer that would be used to break a hole in his scalp. Trey mustered all his strength and kicked out, tearing at the ankle restraints and hitting Mary in the gut as she came back at him, but Doc had descended upon him, wrapping his arm around Trey's neck. With his free hand, Doc pressed the Hay saw against Trey's scalp.

Trey felt the slightest feather of pain there, and knew that Doc had begun to cut. Blood poured down over Trey's eyes, but he fought back as best he could, knocking Doc backward. Trey managed to drop from the table to the floor, feeling a sickening pain in his head from the cutting Doc had done. He could barely see for the blood that covered his eyes. *You'll get through this. You just have to. You have to stop them. You have to. Nobody brought you here. You came here. You weren't meant to die today. Not today, you son of a bitch. You got a kid on the way.*

He rose up again, using every ounce of strength he had. He grabbed the pick from the table and made a half-turn toward Doc.

Mary came up behind Trey, leaping onto his back, knocking him to the floor again, on all fours. She had her weight on him, and she began screaming as if she were a wildcat, her arms around his throat, obscenities flying from her mouth.

Trey crouched on his knees and took the pick and with both hands and swung it as hard as he could above and behind his head.

He felt it go into Mary's neck.

He didn't stop. He stabbed her again and again and again, his own voice hoarse from shouting through the gag, "Get off me, you bitch! Get off me! Get the fuck off me!"

Finally, her hands loosened at his throat, and he shrugged her off. She landed beside him on the floor.

He rolled over onto his back, too weak to stand, gasping for breath.

He held up the pick to defend himself if Doc came at him.

Doc stood , watching him.

Doc no longer looked like a young man.

He looked like a little boy. A frightened little boy.

In his hands, the saw and small hammer.

His lips were trembling, and his eyes crinkled up as he began weeping.

I'm safe. He's weak without her. He has nothing without her, Trey thought.

Doc Chilmark crouched down beside his mother's body. He took it up, embracing her and kissing her lips and cheeks and eyelids.

"You promised you wouldn't leave me," Doc wept, pressing his face against his mother's bloodied throat. "You promised. Don't leave me. Put me in my cage. Put me in my cage."

CHAPTER FIFTY-SIX

Doc couldn't see for his tears and felt an awful ripping of something inside his body, as if his heart were breaking. He looked up to see if her shadow was there. If her spirit was nearby.

He was sure he saw it—it left her mouth as he kissed her—floating up like steam in the room.

She was there, her spirit, in the room with him.

And then he felt them coming.

He knew that they would once she was gone.

She was the only one who kept the night fears back. And in this place, it was always night. She had protected him from them all his life, but now she was a shadow herself.

He could hear them making their smacking noises just beyond the door.

Doc glanced at Campbell and whispered, "Can you keep them out?"

But Trey Campbell had passed out, blood all around him where Doc had begun cutting at his scalp.

Nobody's gonna save you, the fears whispered within Doc's mind *We've been waiting a long, long time to find you. We knew she would go away someday. We knew you would be ours.*

"Please," he whispered, crawling over to Trey's body. He shook the man's arm and slapped his face lightly. "Please wake up. Please stop them from getting me. I can't stand it. Please! Please stop them! They're crawling all over me! Stop them! Stop them!"

CHAPTER FIFTY-SEVEN

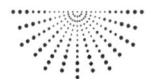

Trey opened his eyes. He looked straight up at the ceiling of the Night Cage, and beyond its mesh ceiling to the red light above.

He heard a noise—someone whispering near him.

He thought of Susan Hannifin. He needed to find her. He felt as if he was about to pass out again, and he took several deep breaths to fight it.

It took some effort, but he turned over onto his side and then onto his stomach.

He couldn't quite stand, but he began putting one elbow in front of him and sliding forward. Then, the other.

Doc lay shivering in a corner, clutching his dead mother's body to him like a rag doll. Scared out of his wits. "Please," he whispered. "They're crawling. I can feel them. They're gonna get inside me."

Trey reached for the pick, which lay a few feet from him. He crawled on his elbows for it. Got it. Then, he began crawling slowly, almost snakelike, toward the open door of the Night Cage.

He glanced back at Doc. "You tell me where she is. Where

you put her. I'll make sure the night fears don't get you. But you better tell me. Or I'll cut you open and put them right in your skin."

So, Doc told him where Susan Hannifin was, and then he told him where Jane Laymon had been put. "The others are shadows now," Doc said, his eyes still wide with fear. "They're here now. Or they're headed for the light."

TREY TRIED to crawl forward but had no more energy. He wondered if he was dying. He had wounds in his legs, his wrists had been slashed, and his side ached from another wound he could not remember getting. His scalp burned from the cut along it. He rolled over onto his back to breathe better. *Got to help Susan. Have to help her get out. Jane and Susan both. Gotta.*

"Susan? Susan!" he called out, but his voice was weak. He thought he heard a noise coming from the corridor that veered off to the left—the arm of the "crossroads" of the hallways where they began moving more and more into the territory of tunnels. He glanced over to where he heard the tapping of footsteps and down into the dimly lit corridor, with its peeling paint and broken wheel-chairs propped beside the walls.

And then he thought he saw an angel. A woman outlined by a halo of light from the dim yellow glow of the distant tunnels.

Coming toward him.

Moving swiftly, as if she had wings.

JANE LAYMON HAD FINALLY BROKEN through the old morgue's rotted walls using the kick technique,.

"I knocked my way out," Jane said to him. "Christ, Trey, you're really hurt bad."

"I thought you were dead," he said.

"I thought we all were," Jane said. "Thank God you stuck around. Where's Bloody Mary?"

"Dead," Trey said, exhausted, full of an indescribable sorrow, unsure of his own sanity. "I killed her. With this."

He let the long pick drop from his fingers.

"What about the other one?" Jane asked, reaching to lift Trey up.

"Down there," Trey murmured so softly that Jane had to put her ear near his mouth to hear him. "Down there." He tried to move his head so that it indicated the Night Cage. "He's scared to death that night fears are coming for him now. She was the only thing that protected him from them. That's what he thinks. Look, go get him. He'll tell us where Susan is. Brainard's dead. Lance is dead too."

"Trey, I have never been so happy to see anyone in my life," Jane whispered, tears in her eyes.

"Me too." Then, he whispered something but didn't quite get it out.

"What?" she asked.

"The goodness of life itself. I knew it had to be here. Even down here," he said, but his voice was growing weaker. Trey felt himself blacking out.

As he drifted into unconsciousness, he thought he heard Susan Hannifin crying out for help from within one of the cages.

CHAPTER FIFTY-EIGHT

JANE CHECKED TREY'S PULSE. IT WAS WEAK, BUT THERE. HE was alive. He'd get through it. She was certain.

She stood up and went back to the three doors to the night cages. "Dr. Hannifin? Susan?"

"Help me! Dear God, somebody help me!" came the scream that was not as loud on Jane's side as it was on Susan's. But Jane found the door, and using some of the tools that Mary Chilmark had left, she managed to pull the door open a quarter inch, and then Susan pushed it on the other side.

Jane held Hannifin close while the psychiatrist wept against her shirt. "Look, we've got to get out. I'm going to need your help. It's a long way back upstairs."

"There's another way out," Susan said. "From down here, there's an exit that goes out into the residency halls. But … what if the fire …"

"I know you're feeling some form of shock. But it's important. I need your help to get Trey out of here. We have to find one of the other ways."

Finally, Susan Hannifin said, "Please. Please. I don't know."

"Get a grip," Jane said. "No one knows we're way down here. We might as well be buried alive if we can't find the other exit."

"I know." A voice that sounded like a little terrified boy's came from one of the doorways. Doc Chilmark sat there, his knees drawn to his chest. "I know everything about this hospital. Since I was little. I know where every secret room is. I know where every doorway is."

"That guy gives me the creeps," Jane said under her breath. Then, she stood up and went over to make sure Doc Chilmark wasn't going to try anything. When she reached him, he had already bound up his hands in restraints, and he'd locked hobbles on his ankles. "He said he'd protect me from them," Doc said, pointing with both wrists extended toward Trey. "I know how to get out. I'll take you out. There's nothing but shadows here."

THE TWO WOMEN lifted Trey up between them, each bearing half his weight on a shoulder. Trey drifted in and out of consciousness, and as they went down one of the tunnels, Trey murmured, "It's all right. It's all right."

Doc Chilmark walked slowly in front of them. Jane retrieved the gun that Bloody Mary had and kept it pointed at Doc in case he was trying to trick them.

They passed other dark cells and rooms. Jane could not help but glance down them as they went—various cages and cells, and one long room off a tunnel full of metal beds. On the ceiling above, pipes of all shapes and sizes running the length of the tunnel.

When they came near the end of the tunnel, where it veered off to the right and left, Doc kept them moving to the left, back toward the buildings of Darden State rather than away from them.

Finally, they came to a utility room, and within it, metal stairs up a towering stairwell.

A blue light wavered, as if it were unstable, near the ceiling above. And at the top step, another door, this one short and wide and slightly ajar.

JANE LAYMON, with all her strength, drew Trey up the steps, slowly, painstakingly, until they'd reached the low doorway at the top. She pushed through it and drew him out into the gardener's shed within the residency building. Then, out onto the lawn of Darden State.

The sky, dark with clouds—but rain came from them, rather than more black smoke.

Beautiful rain, Jane thought, as she drew Trey into it.

His eyes opened slightly as he looked up from her lap to the sky.

"It didn't reach us," Jane said. "The fire. It didn't reach us at all."

Trees along the edge of the grounds had been turned gray with ash, but the fire had not crossed the boulevard. The firemen and rescue workers had held it back—and something more, Jane considered, as she looked skyward.

Fate. Or God. Or luck. Or chance.

And then she remembered Trey's own phrase: *the goodness of life itself.*

Behind her, Susan emerged from the doorway, limping slightly,

It was a moment out of time—an uplift from the horrors of the day that they'd experienced. Each of them felt, within that moment, a sense of overcoming the worst that anyone could throw at them. In the next few seconds, that might be gone, without any of them realizing why it had touched them and then passed.

But in its touch—of rising up from the darkness into ordinary daylight, ordinary rain—there was a spark of something that would never leave them even in the worst hours of their existence.

Except for Doc Chilmark.

The night fears always came back.

CHAPTER FIFTY-NINE

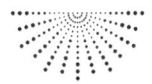

His first night home after his release from the hospital, Trey lay in bed with his wife and held her so much that she nearly had to push him away just to breathe.

"I'm sorry," he said.

"It's okay. After what you went through …"

"I want the baby."

"Oh."

"Do you?" he asked.

She nodded. "I guess it was such a shock to find out. But I do. I'm just scared to have a baby this late. All the things we have to go through, what's going to happen with my work. What'll happen with the other kids, and how old we'll be when the baby's eighteen, and well, all the stuff you think about."

Trey reached to her and drew her back to him. "I want the baby because I want to know that something good can come into the world," he said. "I want us to be the kinds of parents who raise kids who have purpose. Who get help when they need it. Who allow their kids to be productive and happy. Who protect them when we can."

She kissed him on the neck. "That's why I married you. Because you're a good man."

"There are plenty of good men out there," he whispered.

"None like you," she said.

"There's so much bad in the world," he said. "I don't even like thinking about it. Or our kids—how they'll be affected by it."

"You see too much bad," Carly said.

"I do. Now and then, I do. This family keeps me sane," he said, trying to block out the memory of what he'd seen beneath Darden State. "You make me think about what's good." He began kissing her, and he never wanted to stop.

QUENTIN "DOC" CHILMARK was given a new cage as part of his therapy in Darden State. It was not quite a dog crate, but simply a large box. He slept in it at night, but with all the lights on in his room, which had gotten smaller and had no views at all.

He lay in his straitjacket at night, his eyes open wide, listening to the shadows that came and went, talking of death and of heaven. And sometimes the dead girl came to him too, and sat with him in the cage and told him that she was happy to have made a friend, because she had been so lonely when she'd been alive.

But sometimes, she didn't come.

Sometimes he felt the crawling fears moving toward him, coming for him just as he fought off sleep.

Sometimes they spoke with his mother's voice.

WITHIN THREE WEEKS, much of the underground to Darden State was sealed up. The entrances in various underground buildings were closed off with concrete, and the doorway in the canteen of Ward D was refitted with a reinforced steel door that only opened with specific identification cards in a barcode-like device. An administrative memo circulated about the need for a cleaning crew to go two levels beneath Darden State, clear out any material, as well as to seal rooms individually, particularly the old night cages on the lowest level.

At Darden, a budget was drawn up after six months of meetings between several directors and the Board itself, and so it was put to the state to provide three million dollars for the project to clear out the underground once and for all.

Nothing came of this, and the hospital ran as it always did, and always would.

Above ground, several new patients were admitted; there were staff reassignments; Trey Campbell returned to work once he'd recuperated from his injuries completely; Dr. Susan Hannifin sold a second book about her time at Darden State, called *Inside the Night Cage: The American Asylum and the Mind's Secret Places*, although she resigned from her position and went into private practice in San Diego.

And when Trey and Carly Campbell's son was born, his wife suggested they name the boy Jim.

Trey felt that was a damn good name if you asked him.

=

ABOUT THE AUTHOR

Douglas Clegg is the *New York Times* bestselling and award-winning author of *Neverland, The Priest of Blood, Afterlife,* and *The Hour Before Dark,* among many other novels, novellas and stories. His first collection, *The Nightmare Chronicles,* won both the Bram Stoker Award and the International Horror Guild Award. His work has been published by Simon & Schuster, Penguin/Berkley, Signet, Dorchester, Bantam Dell Doubleday, Cemetery Dance Publications, Subterranean Press, Alkemara Press and others.

A pioneer in the ebook world, his novel *Naomi* made international news when it was launched as the world's first ebook serial in early 1999 and was called "the first major work of fiction to originate in cyberspace" by *Publisher's Weekly,* covered in *Time* magazine, *Business Week, Business 2.0, BBC Radio, NPR, USA Today* and more. His book *Purity* was the first to be published via mobile phone in the U.S. in early 2001.

He is married, and lives and writes along the coast of New England.

Find the Author Online:
www.DouglasClegg.com